MOONRISE

Praise for Ben Bova's novels

'Bova has let his imagination soar; in doing so he sets ours free as well.' *Locus (Mars)*

'The prophetic vision of one of the world's great masters of the genre.' *Books (Death Dream)*

'A book that puts Ben Bova not only at the forefront of hard SF writers but also establishes him as one who can write a novel of character with the best of them.' *Orson Scott Card (Mars)*

'By far the best of the Mars novels.' *Sunday Telegraph (Mars)*

'An exciting thriller . . . high technology in the characters' everyday routines provides a diverting twist.' *(Kirkus Reviews (Death Dream)*

'The science fiction author who will have the greatest effect on the world is Ben Bova'. *Ray Bradbury*

About the author

Ben Bova holds degrees from the State University of New York and Temple University, Philadelphia, and most recently received his recently completed doctor of education degree from California Coast University. He has taught writing at Harvard University and at the Hayden Planetarium in New York, and lectures regularly on topics dealing with high technology and the future.

An award-winning editor, president emeritus of the National Space Society and a Fellow of the British Interplanetary Society, Ben Bova is also the author of more than eighty futuristic novels and non-fiction books. He and his wife live in Florida.

Moonrise

BEN BOVA

NEW ENGLISH LIBRARY

First published in Great Britain in 1996 by Hodder and Stoughton
A division of Hodder Headline PLC
First published in paperback in 1997 by Hodder and Stoughton
A New English Library Paperback

10 9 8 7 6 5 4 3 2 1

A CIP catalogue record for this title is available
from the British Library

ISBN 0 340 68249 3

Printed and bound in Great Britain by
Caledonian International Book Manufacturing Ltd, Glasgow

Hodder and Stoughton
A division of Hodder Headline PLC
338 Euston Road
London NW1 3BH

To Barbara, as ever . . .

To the men and women of the Lunar Underground, may they
soon emerge into the light . . .

And especially to Jean and Bill Pogue.

CONTENTS

We have power, you and I,
But what good is that now?
We would build a new world
If we only knew how

Jacques Brel

ACKNOWLEDGMENTS

The concept of glassteel, together with many other ideas concerning lunar manufacturing, was originated by Neil P. Ruzic, founder and publisher of *Industrial Research* magazine and author of *Where the Winds Sleep* (Doubleday, 1970).

The concept of nanotechnology was pioneered by K. Eric Drexler, founder and chairman of the Foresight Institute, in his books, *Engines of Creation* (Doubleday 1986) and *Nanosystems: Molecular Machinery, Manufacturing, and Computation* (Wiley/Interscience, 1992).

PART I:

Destiny

MARE NUBIUM

'Magnificent desolation.'

Paul Stavenger always spoke those words whenever he stepped out onto the bare dusty surface of the Moon. But this time it was more than a quotation: it was a supplication, a prayer.

Standing at the open hatch of the airlock, he looked through his tinted visor at the bare expanse of emptiness stretching in every direction. Normally the sight calmed him, brought him some measure of peace, but now he tried to fight down the churning ache in his gut. Fear. He had seen men die before, but not like Tinker and Wojo. Killed. Murdered. And he was trying to get me. The poor bastards just happened to be in his way.

Paul stepped out onto the sandy regolith, his boots kicking up little clouds of dust that floated lazily in the light lunar gravity and slowly settled back to the ground.

Got to get away, Paul said to himself. Got to get away from here before the damned bugs get me, too.

Twenty miles separated this underground shelter from the next one. He had to make it on foot. The little rocket hopper was already a shambles and he couldn't trust the tractor; the nanobugs had already infected it. For all he knew, they were in his suit, too, chewing away at the insulation and the plastic that kept the suit airtight.

Well, he told himself, you'll find out soon enough. One foot in front of the other. I'll make it on foot if I make it at all.

Twenty miles. On foot. And the Sun was coming up.

'Okay,' he said, his voice shaky. 'If it is to be, it's up to me.'

The sky was absolutely black, but only a few stars showed through the heavy tint of his helmet's visor. They stared steadily down at Paul, unblinking, solemn as the eyes of God.

Turning slightly as he walked, Paul looked up to see a fat gibbous Earth, blue and gleaming white, hanging in the dark sky. So close. So far. Joanna was waiting for him there. Was Greg trying to kill her, too? The thought sent a fresh pang of fear and anger through him.

'Get your butt in gear,' he muttered to himself. He headed out across the empty plain, fleeing death one plodding step at a time. With all the self-control he still possessed he kept himself from running. You've got to cover twenty miles. Pace yourself for the long haul.

His surface suit held the sweaty smell of fear. He had seen two men die out here; it had been sheer luck that the berserk nanomachines hadn't killed him, too. How do you know they haven't infested the suit? he asked himself again. Grimly he answered, What difference does it make? If they have, you're already dead.

But the suit seemed to be functioning okay. The real test would come when he stepped across the terminator, out of the night and into the blazing fury of daylight. Twenty miles in that heat, and if you stop you're dead.

He had calculated it all out in his head as soon as he realized what had happened in the shelter. Twenty miles. The suit's backpack tank held twelve hours of oxygen. No recycling. You've got to cover one and two-thirds miles per hour. Make it two miles an hour, give yourself a safety margin.

Two miles an hour. For ten hours. You can make that. Sure you can.

But now as he trudged across the bleak wilderness of Mare Nubium, he began to wonder. You haven't walked ten hours straight in . . . Christ, not since the first time you came up here to the Moon. That was twenty years ago, almost. Twenty pissing years. You were a kid then.

Well, you'll have to do it now. Or die. Then Greg wins. He'll have murdered his way to the top.

Even though it was still night, the rugged landscape was not truly dark. Earthglow bathed the rolling, pockmarked ground. Paul could see the rocks strewn across the bare regolith, the rims of craters deep enough to swallow him, the dents of smaller ones that could make him stumble and fall if he wasn't careful.

Nothing but rocks and craters, and the sharp uncompromising slash of the horizon out there, like the edge of the world, the beginning of infinity. Not a blade of grass or a drop of water. Harsh, bare rock stretching as far as the eye could see in every direction.

Yet Paul had always loved it. Even encased in a bulky, cumbersome surface suit he had always felt free up here on the surface of the Moon, on his own, alone in a universe where he had no problems at all except survival. That's what the Moon gives us, he told himself. Brings it all down to the real question, the only question. Are you going to live or die? Everything else is bullshit. Am I going to live or die?

But then he thought of Joanna again, and he knew that there was more to it. Would she live or die? Was Greg crazy enough to kill her, too? It's more than just me, Paul realized. Even here, a quarter-million miles from Earth and its complications, he was not alone. Even though there was not another living human being – not another living thing of any kind – this side of the mountains that marked the Alphonsus ringwall, Paul knew that other lives depended on him.

Joanna. Mustn't let Greg get to Joanna. Got to stop him.

He stopped, puffing hard. The visor of his helmet was fogging. A flash of panic surged through him. Have the nanobugs gotten to this suit? He held up his left arm to check the display panel on the suit's forearm, trembling so badly that he had to grasp his wrist with his right hand to steady himself enough to read the display. Everything in the green. He tapped the control for the air-circulating fan in his helmet and heard the comforting whine of its speeding up.

Okay, it's still working. The suit's functioning okay. Settle down. Keep moving.

Turning to see how far he'd come from the underground shelter that Greg had turned into a death trap, Paul was pleased to see that its gray hump of rubble was just about on the horizon. Covered a couple of miles already, he told himself.

His boot prints looked bright, almost phosphorescent, against the dark surface of the regolith. In a couple thousand years they'll turn dark, too; solar ultraviolet tans everything. He almost laughed. Good thing I'm already tanned.

Paul started out again, checking his direction with the global positioning system receiver built into the suit's displays. He hadn't had the luxury of timing his exit from the shelter to coincide with one of the GPS satellites' passing directly overhead. The only positioning satellite signal his suit could receive was low on the horizon, its signal weak and breaking up every few minutes. But it would have to do. There were no other navigational aids, and certainly no road markers on Mare Nubium's broad expanse.

The other shelters had directional beacons planted in the ground every mile between them. And they were no more than ten miles apart, all the way to the ringwall. Greg had planned it well; turned the newest of the temporary shelters into his killing place.

He plodded on, wishing the suit radio had enough juice to reach the tempo he was heading for, knowing that it didn't. There's nobody there, anyway, he thought. It's just a relay shelter. But it ought to be stocked with oxygen and water. And its radio should be working.

Suddenly, with an abruptness that startled him, Paul saw the horizon flare into brilliance. The Sun.

He checked his watch and, yes, his rough calculations were pretty close to the actualities. In a few minutes the Sun would overtake him and he'd have to make the rest of the trek in daylight.

Christ, he thought, if the visor fogged up when it was two hundred below zero outside the suit, what's going to happen when it goes over two-fifty *above*, and the damned suit can't radiate my body heat away?

A sardonic voice in his head answered, You'll find out real soon now.

The sunrise line inched forward to meet him, undulating slowly over the uneven ground, moving toward him at the pace of a walking man.

Despite the fear gnawing inside him, Paul thought back to his first days on the Moon. The excitement of planting boot prints where no one had ever stepped before; the breathtaking grandeur of the rugged landscape, the silence and the dramatic vistas.

That was then, he told himself. Now you've got to make it to the next shelter before you run out of oxy. Or before the Sun broils you. Or the damned bugs eat up your suit.

He forced himself forward, dreading the moment when he stepped from the night's shadow into the unfiltered ferocity of the Sun.

Yet, even as he walked toward the growing brightness, his mind turned back to the day when all this had started, back to the time when he had married Joanna so that he could take control of Masterson Aerospace. Back to the moment when Greg Masterson had begun to hate him.

It had all been to save Moonbase, even then. Paul realized that he had given most of his life to Moonbase.

'Most of it?' he asked aloud. 'Hell, there's a pissin' great chance I'm going to give *all* of it to Moonbase.'

SAVANNAH

They had spent the afternoon in bed, making love, secure in the knowledge that Joanna's husband would be at the executive committee meeting.

At first Paul thought it was only a fling. Joanna was married to the head of Masterson Aerospace and she had no intention of leaving her husband. She had explained that to him very carefully the first time they had made it, in one of the plush fold-back chairs of Paul's executive jet while it stood in the hangar at the corporation's private airport.

Paul had been surprised at her eagerness. For a while he thought that maybe she just wanted to make it with a black man, for kicks. But it was more than that. Much more.

She was a handsome woman, Joanna Masterson, tall and lithe, with the polished grace that comes with old money. Yet there was a subtle aura of tragedy about her that Paul found irresistible. Something in her sad gray-green eyes that needed consolation, comforting, love.

Beneath her veneer of gentility Joanna was an anguished woman, tied in marriage to a man who slept with every female he could get his hands on, except his wife. Not that Paul was much better; he had done his share of tail chasing, and more.

Screwing around with the boss's wife was dangerous, for both of them, but that merely added spice to their affair. Paul had no intention of getting emotionally wrapped up with her. There were too many other women in the world to play with, and an ex-astronaut who had become a successful business executive did not have to strain himself searching for them. The son of a Norwegian sea captain and a Jamaican school teacher, Paul had charm, money and an easy self-confidence behind his gleaming smile: a potent combination.

Yet he had stopped seeing anyone else after only a few times of lovemaking with Joanna. It wasn't anything he consciously planned; he simply didn't bother with other women once he became involved with her. She had never taken a lover before, Joanna told him. 'I never thought I could,' she had said, 'until I met you.'

The phone rang while they lay sweaty and spent after a long session of lovemaking that had started gently, almost languidly, and climaxed in gasping, moaning passion.

Joanna pushed back a tumble of ash-blonde hair and reached for the phone. Paul admired the curve of her hip, the smoothness of her back, as she lifted the receiver and spoke into it.

Then her body went rigid.

'Suicide?'

Paul sat up. Joanna's face was pale with shock.

'Yes,' she said into the phone. 'Yes, of course.' Her voice was steady, but Paul could see the sudden turmoil and pain in her wide eyes. Her hand, gripping the phone with white-knuckled intensity, was shaking badly.

'I see. All right. I'll be there in fifteen minutes.'

Joanna went to put the phone down on the night table, missed its edge, and the phone fell to the carpeted floor.

'He's killed himself,' she said.

'Who?'

'Gregory.'

'Your husband?'

'Took a pistol from his collection and . . . committed suicide.' She seemed dazed. 'Killed himself.'

Paul felt guilt, almost shame, at being naked in bed with her at this moment. 'I'm sorry,' he mumbled.

Joanna got out of bed and headed shakily for the bathroom. She stopped at the doorway for a moment, gripped the doorjamb, visibly pulled herself together. Then she turned back toward Paul.

'Yes. I am too.' She said it flatly, without· a trace of

emotion, as if rehearsing a line for a role she would be playing.

Paul got to his feet. Suddenly he felt shy about getting into the shower with her. He wanted to get to his own condo. 'I'd better buzz out of here before anybody arrives,' he called to Joanna.

'I think that would be best. I've got to go to his office. The police have been called.'

Searching for his pants, Paul asked, 'Do you want me to go with you?'

'No, it's better if we're not seen together right now. I'll phone you later tonight.'

Driving along Savannah's riverfront toward his condo building, Paul tried to sort out his own feelings. Gregory Masterson II had been a hard-drinking royal sonofabitch who chased more tail than even Paul did. Joanna had sworn that she had never had an affair before she had met Paul, and he believed her. Gregory, though, he was something else. Didn't care who knew what he was doing. He liked to flaunt his women, as if he was deliberately trying to crush Joanna, humiliate her beyond endurance.

Hell, Paul said to himself, you should talk. Bedding the guy's wife. Some loyal, trusted employee you are.

So Gregory blew his brains out. Why? Did he find about Joanna and me? Paul shook his head as he turned into the driveway of his building. No, he wouldn't commit suicide over us. Murder, maybe, but not suicide.

As he rode the glass elevator up to his penthouse condo, Paul wondered how Joanna's son was taking the news. Gregory Masterson III. He'll expect to take over the corporation now, I'll bet. Keep control of the company in the family's hands. His father nearly drove the corporation into bankruptcy; young Greg'll finish the job. Kid doesn't know piss from beer.

Paul tapped out his code for the electronic lock, stepped into the foyer of his condo, and headed swiftly for the bar. Pouring himself a shot of straight tequila, he wondered how Joanna was making out with the police and her husband's dead body. Probably put the gun in his mouth, he thought. Must be blood and brains all over his office.

Feeling the tequila's heat in his throat, he walked to the big picture window of his living room and looked out at the placid river and the tourist boats plying up and down. A nearly-full Moon was climbing above the horizon, pale and hazy in the light blue sky.

A sudden realization jolted Paul. 'What are they going to do about Moonbase?' he asked aloud. 'I can't let them shut it down.'

NEW YORK CITY

Paul flew his twin-engined executive jet to New York's JFK airport, alone. He hadn't seen Joanna in the three weeks since Gregory Masterson's suicide. He had phoned her and offered to take Joanna with him to New York, but she decided to go with the company's comptroller in her late husband's plane. This board meeting would decide who the new CEO of Masterson Aerospace would be, and Paul knew they would elect young Greg automatically.

He also knew that Greg's first move as CEO would be to shut down Moonbase. The corporation had run the base under contract to the government for more than five years, but Washington had decided to stop funding Moonbase and 'privatize' the operation. Masterson Aerospace had the option of continuing to run the lunar base at its own expense, or shut it all down.

The chairman of the board was against keeping the lunar operation going, and Greg was hot to show the chairman and the rest of the board that he could cut costs. Paul had to admit that Moonbase was a drain on the corporation and would continue to be for years to come. But eventually . . . *If only I can keep Moonbase going long enough to get it into the black.*

It's going to be tough once Greg's in command. Impossible, maybe. He spent the entire flight to New York desperately wondering how he could convince Greg to give Moonbase a few more years, time to get established well enough to start showing at least the chance of a profit downstream.

It's the corporation's future, he told himself. *The future for* all of us. The Moon is the key to all the things we want to do in space: orbital manufacturing, scientific research, even tourism. It all hinges on using the Moon as a resource base.

But it takes time to bring an operation like Moonbase into the black. Time and an awful lot of money. And faith. Greg just doesn't have the faith. He never has, and he probably never will.

Paul did. It takes a special kind of madman to push out across a new frontier. Absolute fanatics like von Braun, who was willing to work for Hitler or anyone else, as long as he got the chance to send his rockets to the Moon. It takes faith, absolute blind trusting faith that what you are doing is worth any price, any risk, worth your future and your fortune and your life.

I've got that faith, God help me. I've got to make Greg see the light the way I do. Somehow. Get him to listen to me. Get him to believe.

JFK was busy as always, the traffic pattern for landing stacked twelve planes deep. Once he had taxied his twin jet to the corporate hangar and climbed down the ladder to the concrete ramp, the howl and roar of hundreds of engines around the busy airport made Paul's ears hurt.

As he walked toward the waiting limousine, suit jacket slung over one arm, the ground suddenly shook with a growling thunder that drowned out all the other sounds. Turning, Paul saw a Clippership rising majestically on its eight bellowing rocket engines, lifting up into the sky, a tapered smooth cone of plastic and metal that looked like the most beautiful work of art Paul had ever seen.

He knew every line of the Clippership, every detail of its simple, elegant design, every component that fit inside it. A simple conical shape with rockets at the flat bottom end, the Clippership rose vertically and would land vertically, settling down softly on those same rocket exhaust plumes. Between takeoff and landing, it could cross intercontinental distances in forty-five minutes or less. Or make the leap into orbit in a single bound.

Everything seemed to stop at the airport, all other sounds

and movement suspended as the Clippership rose, thundering, slowly at first and then faster and faster, dwindling now as the mighty bellow of its rockets washed over Paul like a physical force, wave after wave of undulating awesome noise that blanketed every frequency the human ear could detect and much more. Paul grinned and suppressed the urge to fling a salute at the departing Clippership. The overpowering sound of those rockets hit most people with the force of a religious experience. Paul had converted four members of the board of directors to supporting the Clippership project by the simple tactic of bringing them out to watch a test launch. And hear it. And feel it.

Laughing to himself, Paul ducked into the limousine door that the chauffeur was holding open. He wondered where the Clippership was heading. There were daily flights out of New York to Tokyo, Sydney, Buenos Aires and Hong Kong, he knew. Soon they would be adding more cities. Anywhere on Earth in forty-five minutes or less.

The Clipperships had pulled Masterson Aerospace out of impending bankruptcy. But Paul knew that he had pushed for them, fought for them, was willing to kill for them not merely because they made Masterson the leader in the new era of commercial transport. He went to the brink of the cliff and beyond for the Clipperships because they could fly into orbit in one hop, and do it more cheaply than any other rocket vehicle. The Clipperships would help to make Moonbase economically viable. *That* was why Paul rammed them past Masterson's board of directors – including the late Gregory Masterson II.

The Clipperships would help Moonbase to break into the black, if Greg Masterson III didn't kill Moonbase first.

But as the cool, quiet limousine made its way out of the airport and onto the throughway, crowded with the world's most aggressive drivers, Paul realized that the Clipperships meant even more to him than Moonbase's possible salvation. He had made the Clippers a success, true enough. But they had made a success of him, as well. Paul's skin was no darker than a swarthy Sicilian's, but he was a black ex-astronaut when he started at Masterson, all those years ago. With the accent on the black. The success of the Clipperships had elevated him to the exalted level of being the black manager of Masterson's space operations division, in Savannah, and a black member of the board of directors.

And the black lover of the dead boss's wife, he added wryly to himself.

Paul had never liked New York. As his limo headed through the swarming traffic along the bumpy, potholed throughway toward the bridge into Manhattan, Paul thought that New York wasn't a city, it was an oversized frenetic anthill, always on the verge of explosion. Even twenty years after the so-called Renaissance Laws, the place was still overcrowded, noisy, dangerous.

Electricity powered all the cars, trucks and buses bound for Manhattan. Old-style fossil-fueled vehicles were not allowed through the tunnels or over the bridges that led into the island. That had cleaned the air a good bit, although hazy clouds of pollution still drifted in from New Jersey, across the Hudson.

Police surveillance cameras hung on every street corner and miniaturized unmanned police spotter planes were as common in the air as pigeons. Vendors, even kids who washed windshields when cars stopped for traffic lights, had to display their big yellow permits or be rousted by the cops who rode horseback in knots of threes and fives through the crowded streets.

Yet the streets still teemed with pitchmen hawking stolen goods, kids exchanging packets of drugs, prostitutes showing their wares. All that the Renaissance Laws had accomplished, as far as Paul could see, was to drive violent crime off the streets. There was still plenty of illicit activity, but it was organized and mostly nonviolent. You might get propositioned or offered anything from the latest designer drugs to the latest designer fashions, fresh off a hijacked truck. But you wouldn't get mugged. Probably.

Still, the limo had to thread its way across the ancient bridges and along the narrow, jampacked streets. The windshield got washed – partially – four different times, and the chauffeur had to slip a city-issued token through his barely-opened

window to the kids who splashed the brownish water onto
the car.

He must use up the whole tank of windshield cleaner every
trip, Paul thought as the limo inched downtown, wipers
flapping away.

At one intersection a smiling trio of women tapped on Paul's
window, bending low enough to show they were wearing
nothing beneath their loose blouses. Kids, Paul realized.
Beneath their heavy makeup they couldn't have been more
than fifteen years old. A trio of mounted policemen watched
from their horses, not twenty yards away.

Paul shook his head at the whores. I've gotten this far
in life without killing myself, he thought. The girls looked
disappointed. So did the cops. Then the traffic light went
green and the limo pulled away.

By the time he got to the corporate offices in the Trade
Towers, Paul needed a drink. The walnut-panelled board room
had a bar and a spread of finger foods set up in the back, but
neither a bartender nor waitress had shown up yet. Paul did
not see any tequila. He settled for a beer, instead.

Paul had always been one of the early ones at board
meetings, but this time apparently he was the first. The
opulent room was empty, except for him. Glancing at his
wristwatch, Paul saw that the meeting was scheduled to start in
less than fifteen minutes. Usually more than half the directors
would be already here, milling about, exchanging pleasantries
or whispering business deals to one another, drinking and
noshing.

Where is everybody? Paul wondered.

He paced the length of the long conference table, saw that
each place was neatly set with its built-in computer screen and
keyboard.

He went to the long windows at the head of the conference room and gazed out at the towers of Manhattan,
thinking how much better it was on the Moon, where all
a man had to worry about was a puncture in his suit or
getting caught on the surface during a solar flare. He craned
his neck to see JFK, hoping to catch another Clippership

takeoff or, even more spectacular, see one landing on its tail jets.

'Paul.'

Startled, he whirled around to see Joanna standing in the doorway, looking cool and beautiful in a beige miniskirted business suit. He hadn't seen her since the day of her husband's suicide.

'How are you?' he asked, hurrying toward her. 'How've you been? I wanted—'

'Later,' she said, raising one hand to stop him from embracing her. 'Business first.'

'Where's everybody? The meeting's scheduled to start in ten minutes.'

'It's been pushed back half an hour,' Joanna said.

'Nobody told me.'

She smiled coolly at him. 'I asked Brad for a half-hour delay. There's something I want to discuss with you before the meeting starts.'

'What?'

Joanna went to the conference table and perched on its edge, crossing her long legs demurely. 'We're going to elect a new president and CEO,' she said.

Paul nodded. 'Greg. I know.'

'You don't sound happy about it.'

'Why should I be?'

'Who else would you recommend?' she asked, with that same serene smile.

'Greg doesn't know enough to run this corporation,' Paul said, keeping his voice low. But the urgency came through. 'Okay, we're not supposed to speak ill of the dead, I know, but his father nearly drove this company into the ground.'

'And you saved it.'

Paul felt uncomfortable saying it, but he agreed. 'I had to practically beat your husband over the head before he saw the light.'

Every major airline in the world began clamoring for Masterson Clipperships, once Paul pushed the project through its development phase. Yet Gregory Masterson II had almost

ruined Masterson Aerospace, despite the Clippership's success. Maybe because of it, Paul now thought.

And his son was eager to follow in his father's mistaken
footsteps.

'He wants to shut down Moonbase,' Joanna said quietly.
'He told me so.'

'You can't let him do that!'

'Why not?' she asked.

'It's the future of the company – of the nation, the whole
goddamned human race!'

She sat on the edge of the conference table in silence for a
moment, her eyes probing Paul. Then Joanna said, 'The first
order of business in today's meeting will be to elect me to the
board to fill Gregory's seat.'

'And then they'll elect young Greg president and CEO,' Paul
said, surprised at how much bitterness showed in his voice.

'They'll have to have nominations first.'

'Brad's going to nominate him.'

'Yes. But I intend to nominate you,' said Joanna.

He blinked with surprise. A flame of sudden hope flared
through him. Then he realized, 'To show there's no nepo-
tism.'

Joanna shook her head. 'I know my son better than you do,
Paul. He's not ready to head this corporation. He'd ruin it and
himself, both.'

'You mean you really want me to be CEO?'

'I want it enough,' Joanna said, slipping off the table to
stand before him, 'that I want us to get married.'

Paul's insides jolted. 'Married?'

Joanna smiled again and twined her arms around Paul's
neck. 'I like being the wife of the CEO. I just didn't like the
CEO very much. With you, it will be different, won't it? Very
different.'

Paul's mind was racing. CEO. Married. She doesn't love
me, not really, but if we're married and I'm CEO we can keep
Moonbase going until it starts making a profit but she's probably only doing this so Greg can grow up some and then she'll
want to turn the corporation over to him sooner or later.

Joanna kissed him lightly on the lips. 'Don't you think marriage is a good idea? Like a corporate merger, only much more fun.'

'You'd marry me?' Paul asked.

'If you ask me.'

'And nominate me for CEO?'

'You'll be elected if I nominate you.'

She's right, Paul realized. If she doesn't back her own son the rest of the board will turn away from him. Hell, I'm one of the corporation's leaders. Saved the outfit from bankruptcy. Making them all rich with the Clippership profits. Half of 'em would be afraid to vote against a black man; afraid it'd look like discrimination. And I could protect Moonbase from Greg and Brad. I could keep them from shutting it down.

'Okay,' he said, surprised at the tightness in his throat. 'Will you marry me?'

Joanna laughed out loud. 'How romantic!'

'I mean – well, will you?'

'Of course I will, Paul. You're the only man in the world for me.'

Paul kissed her, knowing that neither one of them had used the word love.

MARE NUBIUM

The edge of the sunlit day came up to meet Paul with the inevitability of a remorseless universe. One moment he was in shadow, the next in full glaring sunlight. The sky overhead was still black but now the glare reflecting from the ground washed away the few stars that he had been able to see before.

A pump somewhere in his backpack gurgled, and the air fan in his helmet whined more piercingly. He thought he heard metal or plastic groan under the sudden heat load.

Paul looked down and, sure enough, the ground was breaking into sparkles of light, like a whole field of jewels glittering for hundreds of meters in front of him. The sunshine triggered phosphorescence in the minerals scattered in the regolith's surface layer. The effect disappeared after a few minutes, but plenty of the earliest workers on the Moon had actually thought they'd found fields of diamonds: the Moon's equivalent of fool's gold.

There was real wealth in the regolith, but it wasn't gold or diamonds. Oxygen. The opiate of the masses. Habit forming substance; take one whiff and you're hooked for life.

Cut it out, Stavenger, he railed at himself. You're getting geeky in your old age. Straighten up and concentrate on what you're doing.

He plodded doggedly ahead, but his mind wandered to the first time his eyes had opened to the grandeur of the Moon. At the planetarium, he remembered. Couldn't have been more than ten or eleven. The videos of astronauts walking on the Moon, jumping in low-gravity exhilaration while the lecturer told us that one day we kids could go to the Moon and continue the exploration.

Levitt, Paul remembered. Old Dr. Levitt. He knew how to open a kid's mind. The bug bit me then, Paul realized. He had gone up to the lecturer after the show and asked if he could stay and see it again. A round-faced man with a soft voice and big glasses that made his face look like an owl's, Dr. Levitt turned out to be the planetarium's director. He took Paul to his own office and spent the afternoon showing him books and tapes about space exploration.

Paul's father was away at sea most of the time. His classmates at school were either white or black, and each side demanded his total loyalty. Caught between them, Paul had become a loner, living in his own fantasy world until the bigger dream of exploring the Moon engulfed him. He haunted the planetarium, devoured every book and tape he could find, grew to be Dr. Levitt's valued protegé and, eventually, when he reached manhood, his friend. It was Lev who secured a scholarship for Paul at MIT, who paved the way for his becoming an astronaut, who broke down and wept when Paul actually took off from Cape Canaveral for the first time.

Paul was on the Moon when the old man died, quietly, peacefully, the way he had lived: writing a letter of recommendation for another poor kid who needed a break.

I wouldn't be here if it weren't for Lev, Paul knew. Even if I die here, I'll still owe him for everything good that's happened in my life.

He knew it was psychological more than physical, yet with the Sun pounding on him Paul felt as if he had stepped from an air-conditioned building onto a baking hot parking lot. Some parking lot, he told himself as he pushed on. The dusty, gray regolith looked like an unfinished blacktop job, pockmarked and uneven. Mare Nubium, he thought. Sea of Clouds. The nearest body of water is a quarter-million miles away.

Still, it did look a little like the surface of the sea, the way the ground undulated and rolled. A sea that was frozen into rock. I guess it was a sea once, a sea of red-hot lava when the meteoroid that carved out this basin slammed into the Moon.

How long ago? Three and a half billion years? Give or take a week.

He plodded on, one booted foot after another, trying not to look at the thermometer on his forearm displays.

His mind started to drift again.

I never told her that I loved her, Paul remembered. Not then. Guess I was too surprised. Marry me and I'll make you CEO. She never said she loved me, either. It was a business deal.

He almost laughed. Marriage is one way of ending a love affair, I guess.

But Greg didn't laugh about it. Not then, not ever. I don't think I've ever seen him smile, even. Not our boy Greg.

BOARD MEETING

The other board members filtered into the meeting room in twos and threes. Greg Masterson walked in alone, his suit a funereal black, the expression on his face bleak. He was a handsome man of twenty-eight, tall and slim, his face sculpted in planes and hollows like a Rodin statue. He had his father's dark, brooding looks: thick dark hair down to his collar and eyes like twin gleaming chunks of jet.

But where his father had been a hell-raiser, Greg had always been a quiet, somber introvert. As far as Paul knew, he might still be a virgin. He had never heard a breath of gossip about this serious, cheerless young man.

Reluctantly, feeling guilty, Paul made his way across the board room to Greg.

'I'm sorry about your father,' he said, extending his hand.

'I bet you are,' Greg said, keeping his hands at his sides. He was several inches taller than Paul, though Paul was more solidly built.

Before Paul could think of anything else to say, Bradley Arnold bustled up to Greg and took him by the arm.

'This way, Greg,' said the board chairman. 'I want you to sit up beside me today.'

Greg went sullenly with the chairman of the board. Arnold was the whitest man Paul had ever seen. He looked like an animated wad of dough, short, pot-bellied, wearing a ridiculous silver-gray toupée that never seemed to sit right on his head; it looked so artificial it was laughable. Eagerly bustling, he led Greg up to the head of the table and sat the younger man on his right. Arnold's face was round, flabby, with hyperthyroid bulging frog's eyes.

Sixteen men and three women, including Joanna, sat around the long polished table. Paul took a chair across the table from Joanna, where he could see her face. The symbolism of Arnold's seating Greg next to him was obvious. Paul waited to see how the board would react to Joanna's less-than-symbolic nomination.

Arnold played the meeting for all the drama he could squeeze out of it. He began by asking for a moment of silence to honor the memory of their late president and CEO. As Paul bowed his head, he glanced at Melissa Hart, sitting down near the bottom of the table.

Silky smooth, long-legged Melissa, with skin the color of milk chocolate and a fierce passion within her that drove her mercilessly both at work and play. Most board members thought of her as an affirmative action 'twofer:' black and female. Or a 'threefer,' since she represented the unions among the corporation's work force. Paul knew her as a fiery bed partner who was furious with him for dropping her in favor of Joanna.

She had been sleeping with Gregory Masterson before Paul, everyone knew. That was how she got on the board of directors, they thought. Now, as Paul glanced her way, she did not look terribly grieved. Instead, she glared angrily at him.

Arnold next asked for a vote to accept the minutes of the last meeting, then called for reports from the division heads while the board members fidgeted impatiently in their chairs.

When it came to Paul's turn, he gave a perfunctory review of the Clippership's profits and the firm orders from airlines around the world. Paul referred to them as aerospace lines, even the ones that were not doing any true business in orbit, because the Clipperships spent most of their brief flight times far above the atmosphere. 'The way to make money,' Paul had told every airline executive he had ever wined and dined, 'is to keep your Clipperships in space more than they're on the ground.'

Ordinarily, at least a few of the board members would ask

nit-picking questions, but everyone wanted to move ahead to the election of the new CEO.

Almost everyone.

'What's this I hear about your people making giant TV screens up there in the space station?' asked Alan Johansen.

He was one of the newest board members, a handsomely vapid young protegé of Arnold's with slicked-back blond hair and the chiselled profile of a professional model.

Surprised, Paul said, 'It's still in the developmental stage.'

'Giant TV screens?' asked one of the women.

'Under the weightless conditions in orbit,' Paul explained, 'we can make large-crystal flat screens ten, fifteen feet across, but only a couple of inches thick.'

'Why, you could hang them on a wall like a painting, couldn't you?'

'That's right,' said Paul. 'It might make a very profitable product line for us.'

'Wall screens,' said Johansen.

'One of our bright young technicians came up with the name Windowall.'

'That's good!' said Johansen. 'We should copyright that name.'

Bradley Arnold turned, slightly sour-faced, to the corporate legal counsel. 'See that we register that as a trade name.'

'Windowall, right,' said the lawyer. 'How do you spell it?'

Paul told him.

'Now before we get to the highlight of this meeting,' Arnold said in his rumbling bullfrog voice, 'we have to consider filling the seat left vacant by the sudden demise of our lamented late president and CEO.' Far from showing grief, Arnold's bulging brown eyes seemed to be sparkling with pleasure.

'I nominate Joanna Masterson,' said Greg immediately.

'Second,' came a voice from farther down the table.

Then silence.

Arnold looked up and down the table. 'Any other nominations?'

Melissa looked as if she wanted to speak, but before she

could make up her mind Arnold said, 'All right then, the nominations are closed. All in favor?'

'Don't the rules call for a secret ballot?' one of the board members asked.

A brief flicker of annoyance ticked across Arnold's fleshy face. 'If the board wants it,' he said testily. 'In this instance I think a simple show of hands will do. All in favor?'

It was unanimous, Paul saw, although Melissa's was the last hand raised.

'Congratulations, Joanna,' Arnold said warmly, 'and welcome aboard.' He pushed himself to his feet and started clapping his hands. The entire board rose and applauded. Joanna remained seated, smiling politely and mouthing 'Thank you' to them all.

'Now then,' Arnold said once they were all seated again, 'to the major business of this meeting: electing the new president and chief operating officer of Masterson Aerospace Corporation.'

Paul felt suddenly nervous. What Joanna was going to do would not only cause a rift in the board, it would shatter her son, who expected to be elected unanimously. And marriage? Paul wondered. If I don't get elected will she still want to marry me? Do I really want to marry her?

'This great corporation was founded, as you all know, in the dark years of the Second World War by Elliot Masterson,' Arnold was droning in his sonorous, soporific voice. 'His son, the first Gregory Masterson took over at Elliot's retirement . . .'

In all his years as an astronaut and then a corporate executive, the idea of marriage had never entered Paul's mind. Women were plentiful, and there was no time to get hung up over one. Paul was driven by the urge to succeed. Not merely to be the best, but to get the others to acknowledge that he was the best. To get to the Moon. To make Moonbase viable. To make a success where everyone else said it was impossible.

I never really thought about marriage, Paul was saying to himself. Maybe it's time to settle down. Enough tail chasing. I haven't really wanted to, anyway, since I met Joanna. Maybe that means I really love her. But does she love me or is this just going to be a business deal? Marriage for Moonbase. Some deal.

'. . . and now that Gregory Masterson II is no longer among us,' Arnold went on, 'I believe it is in accord with the finest traditions of this great corporation that we ask his son, Gregory Masterson III, to accept the weighty responsibilities of president and chief operating officer of Masterson Aerospace Corporation.'

'Second the nomination.'

Paul swivelled his head. Melissa had seconded Greg's nomination with the swiftness of an automaton. That was a surprise.

Grinning coyly, Arnold asked, 'Any other nominations?'

'I nominate,' said Joanna, 'Paul Stavenger.'

A shock wave flashed along the table. Greg's face went white. He looked as if his mother had just slapped him. Arnold's mouth dropped open.

'Second that,' said the man at Paul's left, the corporation's comptroller.

Arnold blinked several times, looking more like a perplexed frog than ever. Finally he said, in a low angry voice, 'Any *other* nominations?'

None.

'Discussion?'

Joanna said, 'I don't want to give the board the impression that I have no confidence in my son. I simply feel that Paul has earned the right to be CEO. He pushed the Clippership program to its current highly successful status. Without the Clipperships this corporation would be in receivership.'

'That's something of an overstatement!' Arnold sputtered.

Joanna made a smile for him. 'Perhaps. But Paul's shown he can be an effective CEO. My son is young enough to wait a few years. With a little patience, he'll make a fine CEO one day.'

Greg said nothing. He glowered at his mother in silent hatred.

Paul knew what was irking Arnold. Old frog-face thought that he could control Greg. With Greg as CEO, Arnold would effectively be running the corporation his way. He had no desire to see a strong independent CEO elected.

His face florid, Arnold said to Joanna, 'But this corporation has always had a Masterson at its head. I thought that we all wanted to keep control in the family's hands.'

Joanna's smile turned slightly wicked. 'Oh, it will be in the family's hands. Paul and I are going to be married.'

Greg bolted up to his feet so hard he knocked his heavy padded chair over backwards. 'Married!' he shouted. 'To – to *him!*'

Before his mother could reply, Greg pushed past his overturned chair and stamped out of the meeting room, slamming the heavy door as he left.

Christ, Paul thought, she hadn't told him anything about this. He's just as shocked as the rest of them.

'I'm afraid,' Joanna said calmly, 'that Greg allows his emotions to overwhelm him, sometimes.'

Paul stared at her. She's like an iceberg, he thought. Implacable, unmovable. And cold as ice.

The other board members were muttering to one another. Arnold rapped his knuckles on the table to restore order. Paul saw beads of perspiration on the chairman's brow and upper lip. His hairpiece was slightly askew.

'I think, in light of this unexpected turn of events,' he said hesitantly, 'that we should postpone the election of our new CEO until we have all had a chance to think and consider carefully—'

'I disagree,' interrupted the comptroller. He was older than Paul, not as old as Arnold; a trim little man, dapper, always impeccably dressed. With just a trace of an Irish accent he said, 'We all know each other here, and we all know both young Greg and Paul Stavenger. I don't see why we should wait at all.'

Arnold started to say, 'But I—'

'Let's vote,' said another board member.

'Call for the vote,' said still another.

Visibly defeated, Arnold said, 'Very well, if that is the sense of the board. Shall we use the secret ballot?'

'I'm willing to let everyone see my hand raised,' the comptroller said.

'Then let us take a fifteen-minute recess before we vote,' said Arnold. 'I want to make sure that Greg is with us when hands are raised.'

The tension eased a little as everyone got to their feet. The comptroller patted Paul's shoulder and said loudly enough for all to hear, 'I'm sure you're going to make a grand CEO, my boy.'

Paul mumbled his thanks and made his way around the table toward Joanna. He passed Melissa, who kept her face frozen.

Joanna was walking slowly toward the big windows at the front of the meeting room. As if by instinct, the other board members drifted away from her, allowing Paul to be alone with her.

'You didn't tell Greg first?' he whispered urgently to her.

She looked up at him, her eyes tired, almost tearful. 'I tried to,' she said. 'He didn't show up until just a few moments before the meeting began.'

'But . . . before the meeting. Christ, you two live in the same house!'

'Not any more. Greg took an apartment here in New York. Just after his father's death. Didn't you know?'

Paul shook his head. 'Still . . . breaking it to him like that, in front of the rest of the board . . .'

Joanna turned to the windows. 'The Clippership from Hong Kong should be arriving in a few moments.'

'Never mind that. You should've told him! Warned him, at least.'

'I couldn't,' she said, still staring out beyond the towers of Lower Manhattan, the harbor, the gray expanse of Brooklyn and Queens. 'He hasn't spoken to me in more than a month. Not since he found out about us.'

'He knows?'

Joanna breathed out a shuddering sigh. 'He knows.'

'Then – his father must've known.' Paul was jolted by the thought.

'He probably did.'

'God almighty.'

Joanna said nothing.

'Do you think that's why he killed himself?' Paul asked her.

Joanna did not answer for a long moment. Then, 'I can't picture Gregory blowing his brains out over his wife's infidelity. Not when he'd already turned infidelity into a lifetime career.'

She sounded bitter. But Paul knew that a man like Gregory had a totally different set of values when it came to his wife's faithfulness. Still, he never would have thought that Gregory would kill himself, for any reason.

'Look!' Joanna pointed. 'There it is!'

A pinpoint high in the sky, a flare of rocket flame against the gray-blue background. Paul watched the tiny dot grow into a discernible shape as the Clippership seemed to halt in midair, slide sideways slightly, then slowly descend on a pillar of flaming rocket exhaust toward the ground until it was lost to their view.

'I still get a thrill every time I see it,' Joanna said.

And Paul thought that maybe he did love her, after all.

'Please be seated,' Arnold called from the head of the table. Looking around, Paul saw that Greg was still gone. Unable to face the music, Paul wondered, or too torn up by his mother's betrayal?

He knew about us, Paul told himself as he went back to his chair. He knew that I was fucking his mother. And if he knew, his father did, too.

Eighteen board members took their places around the long table. Arnold called for discussion of the nominations. The board members shifted uneasily in their chairs, looked at one another. No one wanted to be first.

'I presume,' Arnold said, seizing the initiative, 'that you are still in favor of keeping Moonbase going, Paul?'

Nodding solemnly, Paul replied, 'The future of this corporation is in space, and Moonbase holds the key to profitable space commerce.'

'But the government's backed away from it,' Arnold pointed out. 'If they won't do it, why should we? After all, they can print money; we have to *earn* it.' He made a rictus of a smile to indicate humor.

Paul hesitated, as if carefully considering his answer, even though he knew exactly what he wanted to say. After a couple of heartbeats he began, 'Washington is giving us an opportunity to develop this new frontier without a lot of government red tape tying our hands. The politicians have finally realized that they can't run anything at a profit. But we can! And we will – eventually.'

'How long is eventually?' one of the older board members asked. 'I don't have all that much time to wait.'

Paul smiled patiently. 'Several years, at least. We're talking about developing a new frontier here. How long did it take Pittsburgh to become the steel center of the world? How long did it take to make air travel profitable?'

'It's still not profitable!'

'The Clipperships are profitable,' Paul pointed out.

No one contradicted him.

'I know it's asking a lot to back Moonbase on our own, but believe me, this is the key to our future. I believe that as firmly as I believed that the Clipperships would make money for us.'

Joanna asked, 'Isn't the government willing to pay whoever operates Moonbase to keep the scientific work going?'

Nodding, Paul replied, 'That's right. Washington's willing to support six scientists at Moonbase. It's not very much money, but it's a baseline commitment.'

'And if we decide *not* to continue with Moonbase,' one of the other directors asked, 'what happens to those scientists?'

'Moonbase operations will be offered to any other corporation that wants to bid on the base. If nobody bids, the base is shut down and all work on the Moon comes to an end.'

'You're fully committed to keeping Moonbase open?' Joanna asked him.

'Totally,' said Paul. 'Take me, take Moonbase with me. One and inseparable.'

'Now and forever,' muttered a voice further down the table.

The vote was an anticlimax. Arnold claimed that he had Greg's proxy. The only other vote for Greg came from Melissa Hart. Paul Stavenger was elected president and chief operating officer of Masterson Aerospace Corporation by a vote of sixteen to three.

'Congratulations,' smiled the comptroller. 'Now when is the wedding going to take place?'

MARE NUBIUM

Some wedding, Paul said to himself as he sweated across the lunar regolith. Like another pissing board meeting, only bigger. The biggest society bash in Savannah. They all came out of curiosity. Too soon after Gregory's death, they all whispered. Bad taste. But they all came and sipped the champagne and ogled at the daughter of one of the oldest families in Georgia actually marrying a black man. Lawdy, lawdy, what would Miz Scarlett say?

The whole board of directors showed up for the wedding. All except Greg. And Melissa. Joanna planned every detail, even picked the comptroller to be my best man. So what? I had enough on my dish. Pissing company was in even worse shape than I'd thought. I could see right at the outset that saving Moonbase was going to be a bitch and a half.

It was always there, the race thing. Even at MIT the blacks had their own clubs and cliques. Had to. Nobody hung WHITES ONLY signs in the halls, but everybody knew who was who and what was what. The classes and labs were one thing: performance counted there. It was the social life where they cut you. And Paul got cut both ways. He wasn't black enough to suit the militants; he was too black to please most of the whites. Especially when he dated white women.

Learning to fly was something else, though. Alone in a plane Paul could get away from everything and everyone, at least for a couple of hours. More than once he would squint up at the blue sky and see the pale ghost of the Moon riding out beyond his wing tip.

'I'm on my way,' he would say to the distant Moon. 'I'll be with you in a few years.'

Something was wrong with his left boot. It was rubbing his heel raw. A pang of fear burned through his gut. He saw Wojo again, screaming as the nanobugs ate his suit and his flesh. And Tink, screeching like a terrified monkey in a leopard's jaws. Forget about the pissin' nanobugs! Paul raged silently. It's nothing but a lousy fitting boot, he insisted to himself.

He was trying not to limp, despite the pain in his left heel every time he set his foot down. It felt awkward, walking that way.

And then his boot slipped.

If he had fallen forward, just tripped and gone down face-first, he would have had plenty of time to put out his hands, stop the fall, and push himself up to his feet again. Even in the cumbersome surface suit, the Moon's gravity was so slight that he could have done that. It was an old trick among the 'Lunatics,' done to impress newcomers: pretend you're going to go splat on your face, then push yourself up to a standing position before the tenderfoot can holler, 'Look out!'

But Paul's foot skidded out from under him on a suddenly slick piece of exposed rock and he fell over backward, onto his life-support backpack and oxygen tank, banged down heavily and skidded, yowling sudden pain and fear, down a slope so gradual he hadn't even noticed it a moment before.

His head banged inside his helmet, his vision blurred. He tasted blood in his mouth. For long moments he lay panting, dizzy, blinking to clear his eyes. Gradually he took stock. He was lying on his right side, his arm pinned under him, the bulky backpack and oxygen tank pressing against the back of his suit.

Shakily he lifted his left arm to look at the displays. No red lights. Everything still in the green. He listened carefully. Nothing but the air fans whirring and his own labored breathing. No hisses. No leaks. He hoped.

He pushed himself up to a sitting position, grateful that he weighed only one-sixth of what he would on Earth.

He was at the bottom of a shallow pit with sides sloped

so gradually that you had to be inside it to realize it was a depression at all. Absently, he ran a gloved hand along the stony ground. Smooth as glass. Must be an old crater; a really old one, smoothed down by the infalling meteoric dust for Christ knows how long.

It was a struggle to get to his feet. Once erect, he saw that the pit was slightly deeper than his own height and some forty-fifty feet across. Got to get up this slippery slope, he told himself. Not going to be easy.

Shifting the backpack's weight on his shoulders, Paul crouched over and placed his gloved hands on the bare rock. Four legs are better than two for this, he told himself. Slowly, with enormous care, he picked his way up the gradual slope. It felt like walking on glass. Or ice. For a crazy moment Paul thought back to his one and only ice-skating lesson, when he'd been a teenager. Split his eyebrow open in a fall that ended his interest in skating forever.

Easy now, he commanded himself. Don't slide down. You don't have any time to waste playing around in here.

His boots slipped and skidded, barely providing any traction at all. Paul bent his face closer to the stone, looking for rough patches, bumps, anything that could provide purchase. He was grateful that the Sun was still low enough in the sky to throw long shadows; made it easier to see where he could plant his feet and get something to push against.

Just as he reached one hand across the rim of the crater his foot slipped and he started to slide backward. He clung desperately to the slightly raised edge of the crater, grabbed with his other hand and hung on to keep himself from sliding all the way back to the bottom.

For several moments he stayed there, strung out, gasping, while his booted feet searched for something to hold them. He gave it up and hauled himself upward, letting his legs go limp. He got his belly over the edge, trying not to think of what would happen if he tore the fabric of his suit. One leg over the rim. Then the other.

At last he climbed to his feet. Wish I had a marker beacon, he thought. There ought to be a warning here.

Okay, get moving. Enough time wasted.

But which direction? He turned a full three hundred sixty degrees. Mare Nubium looked the same in all directions. Flat bare plain of dust-covered rock. The hump that marked the shelter he had fled was nowhere in sight now, but neither was the next shelter, nor the ringwall mountains of Alphonsus.

'Talk about the middle of nowhere,' Paul said aloud.

He checked the GPS receiver on his suit's forearm. Nothing. The display was dark. No signal chirped in his earphones. *Satellite's too low for my suit antenna to pick up the signal.*

Paul stared out at the horizon. For the first time he felt truly afraid. He was alone and lost and miles from any possibility of help.

SAVANNAH

'Murder?' Paul felt his insides go hollow.

'That's what Greg said,' Melissa Hart told him.

It was Paul's first day in his new office as CEO of Masterson Aerospace. He had been in the midst of setting up his personal mementos on his broad ebony desk: a fist-sized chunk of Moon rock; a solid mahogany model of a Clippership in the red, white and blue colors of American Airlines; a framed photograph of Joanna smiling at him from beneath a wide-brimmed straw hat.

It had taken more than a week to get his new office suite squared away. Paul had wanted to stay at his old office, but it was in the manufacturing plant out where I-16 intersected with I-95. Corporate headquarters was in the old historic section of Savannah, down by the riverfront, where the docks and warehouses had been largely replaced by tourist hotels and upscale restaurants. At least he could walk to work, just a few blocks along Bryan Street.

He had felt uneasy about taking over Gregory's suite, but finally decided he shouldn't let old guilts stand in the way of doing his new job. So he had his secretary totally redecorate the office; a chore she delighted in, for six whirlwind days of painters and carpet installers and electricians and decorators.

And now Melissa had walked unannounced into his office, so spanking new it smelled of paint and freshly-sawn wood. She stood before his desk, arms clasped tightly across her chest, looking wired tight.

Paul sank into his stylishly modern caramel leather swivel chair, staring open-mouthed at Melissa.

'Murder?' he repeated.

She pulled up the upholstered chair in front of his desk. 'Greg's got a videodisk that his father made just before he died. He says it proves Gregory didn't commit suicide. He was murdered.'

'Holy shit,' Paul groaned.

Melissa said nothing.

'Did you see this videodisk?'

'Greg played it for me,' she said.

'What's on it?'

'Gregory's sitting at his desk. Right here in this office. It must've been late afternoon, right before he was killed.'

He was supposed to have been at the executive committee meeting, Paul remembered. But Gregory had walked out on the rest of the committee halfway through the agenda and returned to his office. Nothing unusual in that; he had done it often enough in the past. Meetings usually made him more irritable than usual, especially when there were unpleasant decisions to be made that he wanted to avoid.

'He looked drunk to me,' Melissa went on. 'Smashed. Muttering into the camera. He must've set it up on his desk.'

'What did he say?'

She made a little shrug. 'Most of it was hard to understand. He did a lot of mumbling. But he had that Magnum on his desk and he said something about somebody trying to kill him. "The gun's for protection," he said. "This gun's going to save me."'

'And?'

'That's about it. A lot of it was incomprehensible. Greg says he's going to get some experts to go over the disk and extract as much from it as they can.'

'Has he shown it to the police?'

'Not yet. He just got it himself; it was delivered through the interoffice mail.'

'It took more than a month to get a videodisk fifty feet down the hall?'

Melissa almost smiled. 'Greg's been in New York all this time. He just got back yesterday and started going through his mail.'

'Oh. I see.' Paul looked out the picture window toward the riverfront, then turned back to Melissa. She seemed tense, wary. But not angry, the way she'd been at the board meeting.

He asked her, 'Why are you telling me this?'

'Figured you ought to know.'

'You're not sore at me? About Joanna, I mean?'

A flicker of something crossed her face, but she regained her self-control almost immediately. 'It hurt when you dumped me, Paul.'

Feeling flustered, he spread his hands and said defensively, 'I didn't exactly dump you, did I?'

Her voice deathly calm, Melissa replied, 'Call it what you want. Soon's you started after the boss's wife you didn't have any time for me.'

'I fell in love,' Paul said.

Melissa swept her almond eyes around the big office in a long, exaggerated inspection. 'Yeah,' she said finally. 'I can see that.'

Paul wished he could get angry at her, but he was terribly afraid that she was right.

'Well, anyway, thanks for the news.'

'Sure.' She got up to leave and for the first time Paul noticed the forest green miniskirt that clung to her hips and her long slim legs encased in patterned green stockings.

'Who in the hell would want to kill Gregory?' he muttered as she headed for the door.

Melissa turned back toward him. 'Maybe it was the guy who took over his job. And his wife.'

Paul sagged back in his chair, stunned. 'You don't mean that!'

She shrugged again. 'That's what Greg thinks. That's what he's going to tell the police.'

For a long while Paul sat at his desk, staring out the window, looking at nothing. In his mind's eye he saw Gregory sitting in this same room, with a Smith & Wesson .357 Magnum from his gun collection in the wall cabinet sitting on the desk in front of him and a half-empty decanter of Gentleman Jack beside it.

He put the gun in his mouth and blew his head off, Paul told himself. Nobody murdered him. The bastard committed suicide, but first he made that pissing disk to leave as much trouble behind him as he could. He knew about Joanna and me. The disk's his revenge on us.

But why did Joanna have his body cremated? You can't exhume a cremated body and look for evidence of murder.

Paul shook his head, trying to clear the suspicions away. Slowly he got up from his chair and walked to the big window overlooking the riverfront. He glanced at his wristwatch, then looked past the docks and boats, past the river itself, out into the clear blue sky, just starting to darken with twilight.

And there it was, a bright gleaming star moving rapidly from west to east, cutting across the sky in silent purposefulness. The Rockledge space station. It seemed to beckon Paul like a steady, unwavering hope.

Tonight, Paul said to himself. I'll be up there tonight. I'll leave all this shit behind me and be up there where everything's clean and uncomplicated.

He had decided that, as the new CEO, he should visit all the corporation's operating divisions, starting with the research labs and prototype factory facility that Masterson rented aboard the Rockledge Corporation's space station. He had wanted to go on to the scattering of underground shelters on the lunar surface that was Moonbase, but the pressures of his new responsibilities had forced him to postpone that pleasure.

Instead, he decided to take Joanna to the space station with him.

'A honeymoon in zero gravity,' he had told her.

'Aboard a space station?' Joanna had seemed startled at the idea.

'You'll love it,' Paul had coaxed. 'Zero gravity is better than waterbeds.'

She had finally agreed. Reluctantly, it seemed to Paul.

The intercom buzzer yanked his thoughts back to the present.

'What?' he called from the window.

'Mr. Arnold to see you, sir.'

Paul turned back toward the desk. 'Send him right in.'

He started for the door, wondering why his secretary allowed Melissa to waltz in unannounced but held up the chairman of the board.

Bradley Arnold came smiling into the office, looking around at the new decor appreciatively. 'I wouldn't recognize the place,' he said in his heavy croaking voice.

Paul showed him to the round conference table in the corner, next to the built-in bar.

'Ah, this corner I do recognize,' Arnold said, lowering his chunky form into one of the chairs slowly, painfully. 'Gregory was here more than at his desk, his last few months.'

'Would you like something . . . ?' Paul asked.

'No, no, no,' Arnold replied, waving both hands vigorously in front of his face.

He protests too much, Paul thought. But he pulled out the chair next to the chairman's and sat in it.

'You're scheduled for a flight to the space facilities this evening, aren't you?' Arnold asked.

Paul nodded. 'Joanna and I are set to leave in about an hour.'

Arnold's bulging eyes widened slightly. 'Joanna's going with you?'

Forcing a smile, Paul said, 'A sort of honeymoon. Only three days, but that's all I can squeeze in.'

'A honeymoon in space,' Arnold murmured. 'Leave it to a former astronaut to think of that.'

'You ought to try it – a trip into orbit, I mean.'

'Me?' Arnold looked genuinely startled. 'In space? No thank you! I'll stay right here with my feet on solid ground. I don't even like to go to California, the ground shakes too often.'

'Do wonders for your arthritis,' Paul said. 'Zero gee can be very therapeutic.'

Shaking his head hard enough to make his toupée jiggle, Arnold said, 'I'm doing fine here on Earth.'

Paul was tempted to say that the chairman wouldn't have

to worry about his weight in zero gravity, but he bit it back. Arnold was sensitive about his poundage. In-between meals and snacks, Paul thought.

'I'll come straight to the point, Paul,' the old man said. 'You've heard about this disk that young Greg has?'

All thoughts of levity vanished from Paul's mind. He nodded in silence.

'Have you seen it?'

'No.'

'Neither have I.'

That surprised Paul. He said, 'I've heard what's on it. Gregory says somebody was out to kill him.'

'Yes, that's what I heard.'

'I guess Greg will be taking it to the police.'

Arnold's frog eyes narrowed. 'Eventually, I suppose. Don't know how believable it is. The ravings of an obviously drunken man. He was getting quite paranoid, you know.'

'Was he?' Paul said carefully.

'Yes. He had all sorts of suspicions. About everyone around him.'

Arnold did not have to say that Gregory knew his wife was having an affair with Paul. The implication was perfectly clear.

'Well,' Paul said, 'I'm not sure of what I ought to do about this. Ask Greg about it, I suppose.'

'I'd speak with McPherson first.'

The corporation's counsel. 'You really think I should talk to the lawyers?' Paul asked.

Arnold started to nod, but broke it off to say, 'Paul, you know that I nominated Greg for CEO only out of family loyalty. That's all it was, believe me. I had no idea that you and Joanna were going to be married. I was merely being loyal to the family.'

Before Paul could reply, Arnold rushed on, 'I want you to know that I'm one hundred percent behind you, Paul. One hundred percent! I think you're going to make a fine CEO and I'll do whatever I can to help and support you. Even if it comes down to a murder investigation.'

Paul looked into the chairman's earnest, florid face and did not believe a word of what he said. You'll be right behind me, all right, Paul thought. With a hatchet.

But he made himself smile and clasped his hands together in front of his face and said mildly, 'I appreciate that Brad. I really do.'

Arnold looked satisfied. 'I merely wanted you to go off to the space station with as clear a mind as possible. Don't worry about Greg at all. I'll hold the fort while you're gone.'

'I'll be back by Friday.'

'Good,' said Arnold. 'Don't worry about a thing while you're up there.'

'Sure. Thanks a lot.'

'Why did Greg show the disk to Melissa?' Joanna wanted to know.

They were in the limousine, heading for the company airfield, where a Clippership was waiting to boost them to the Rockledge space station. They both wore utilitarian coveralls: Paul's were drab green; Joanna's coral red. And form-fitting.

Paul blinked with surprise at his wife's question. 'I never even thought to ask.'

Joanna said, 'I'd have thought he'd bring it to Brad Arnold. Or straight to the police.'

'Brad hasn't seen it.'

'So he says,' Joanna muttered.

'Greg's having the disk analyzed,' Paul said. 'Wants to extract all the information he can. Make sense out of Gregory's mumblings, if he can.'

'He's not turning it over to the police?' she asked sharply.

'Not yet.'

With a shake of her head, Joanna said, 'It's going to be useless as evidence, then. Once he lets anyone tamper with it—'

'They're not tampering.'

'Legally, the disk will be compromised. The technicians can make it show or say anything they want, once they get their hands on the original.'

With a feeble smile, Paul said, 'That's your expert legal opinion, is it?'

'I could have taken a law degree,' Joanna said, straight-faced. 'I've spent enough time with lawyers, god knows.'

They drove on in silence through the deepening twilight, Paul playing his wife's question over and over in his head. Why *did* Greg show the disk to Melissa and not to Arnold? The chairman of the board would be a natural ally for Greg in this. What's the kid up to? And what's Brad up to? Are the two of them working together on this?

Then a new thought struck him: Is Melissa sleeping with Greg now? Somehow that idea bothered him.

'You have to be careful of Brad,' Joanna warned.

'I know.'

'He had just about taken over the whole corporation,' she went on, 'during Gregory's last few months. That's why he wanted Greg to be CEO; he thought he could run everything and have Greg sitting there as a figurehead.'

'Maybe he's the one Gregory was mumbling about, then,' said Paul. 'On the disk.'

'Gregory? Afraid that Brad was trying to kill him?'

'Not physically. Business-wise.'

'Then why the gun?' Joanna asked.

Paul shrugged. He had no answer for that.

'You just be careful of Brad,' she repeated. 'If he says he wants to be your friend, you don't need an enemy.'

The limo slowed at the security gate, then headed toward the airfield's terminal building. In the distance Paul could see the graceful conical shape of the Clippership outlined in spotlights against the darkening evening sky, a wisp of white vapor drifting from its liquid oxygen feed line.

Trying to summon up a confidence he didn't feel, Paul said to Joanna, 'Well, let's forget about it for now.'

'Forget about it?'

'We're on our way to our honeymoon, remember? And besides, there's not much we can do about all this. The ball's in Greg's court.'

Joanna nodded tightly. 'That's what bothers me.'

They rode the open-cage elevator to the Clippership's hatch, ducked through and climbed the ladder between the passenger rows to their reclining seats. Only six passengers this trip; Paul recognized four of them, including Hiram Tinker, the astronomer who tended the orbital telescopes that the corporation operated on contract from a consortium of universities.

'Hi, Hi!' Paul said brightly as he helped Joanna into her chair. Everyone called the man Tink, but Paul always made a pun out of his first name, even though he dreaded the flood of puns Tinker poured out in return.

'Hello boss boss.'

Paul slid into his own chair, across the ladderway from Joanna, and started strapping in before lowering the chair to its full reclining position. 'Boss boss?' he asked Tinker, over his shoulder. 'You stuttering?'

Tink had always called Paul the boss, since he worked in Paul's space operations division.

'Well, now you're my new boss's boss, aren't you?' Tink countered. 'That makes you boss boss.'

'Boss squared,' said one of the other technicians, from a back row.

'Running dog capitalist expropriator of the workers,' came another voice. Paul knew whose, without having to turn around: Alex Wodjohowitcz, tractor teleoperator and technician, on his way to a three-month tour of duty on the Moon.

Paul jabbed a finger toward Joanna. 'Here's the real boss,' he said. Then wondered how humorous the remark really was. Joanna cocked an eyebrow at him, barely smiled.

Once he was settled in the seat next to her, Joanna leaned across the aisle separating them to ask in a whisper, 'Who are those people?'

'Our employees,' Paul whispered back. 'Some of the best people in the world. In the whole Earth-Moon system, as a matter of fact.'

'And that one who called you a running dog? Why do you let him speak to you like that?'

'Wojo?' Paul laughed. 'Wojo's the most creative cusser I've ever met. I've known him more than six years now and I've never heard him resort to profanity or repeat himself. But he sure can burn your ears off.'

'Liftoff in two minutes,' came a voice from the cockpit, over the intercom speakers.

Paul knew that the astronaut pilot and co-pilot were in the cockpit strictly as redundancies. The Clippership was preprogrammed and monitored from the ground, just as it would be if it were carrying all freight and no people at all. Only if something went disastrously wrong would the human crew have anything to do. And then, Paul thought, it would probably be too late. But the government agencies had insisted on a human crew when human passengers were going aloft. Takes two paying seats out of our cash flow, Paul fumed whenever he thought about the outmoded regulation.

Then one of the astronauts came clambering down the ladder to check that all the passengers were properly strapped in and had cranked their seats back to the full reclining position for takeoff. He said a brief hello to Paul, smiled at Joanna, and then climbed back up into the cockpit and closed the hatch above Paul's head.

Paul glanced across the narrow aisle and saw that Joanna looked pale. She's never been in space before, he knew. He reached out his hand and touched her shoulder. She clasped his hand in hers. Her palm felt cold, clammy.

Grinning at her, Paul whispered, 'You'll love it.'

She nodded, but looked extremely dubious.

LANA GOODMAN

She was the first person to suffer a heart attack on the Moon.

Dr. Lana Goodman was a tiny wisp of a woman, a brilliant fifty-two-year-old with degrees in medicine, physiology, and biophysics. She was rumored to be on track for a Nobel, and could have had her pick of any university in the world. Indeed, she was teaching and conducting research in low-gravity physiology at Johns Hopkins when she applied for a position with Masterson Aerospace.

'I want to go to the Moon,' she told the corporation's astonished personnel director. 'I've always wanted to go there. I've had experience aboard space stations, but I haven't gotten to the Moon yet and I want to do it before I get too old.'

Masterson took her on as a consultant, making maximum public relations mileage out of it, and sent her on a well-publicized tour of duty at Moonbase.

Dr. Goodman was expected to look after the medical needs of the twenty-eight men and women who happened to be working at Moonbase at the time, as well as continue her own research on how the human body adapts to low gravity.

Her heart attack was totally unexpected, caused by a clot that lodged in one of the smaller coronary arteries. She was eating breakfast when she felt a terrific pain in her chest, vomited up everything in her stomach, and half-collapsed on the galley table. Her skin turned gray and sweaty.

Since she was Moonbase's resident doctor at the time, she was attended by two of the base's paramedics — both of them engineers with other duties who stood by for medical emergencies. They slapped an oxygen mask over her nose; one of them shot a load of clot-busting tissue plasminogen activator into her arm, while the other pushed aspirin and nitroglycerin tablets through her pain-clenched teeth.

The paramedics contacted Masterson's medical staff in Savannah, who plugged them in to the finest cardiac centers in Boston, Houston and even Johns Hopkins in Baltimore. Within hours Dr. Goodman was out of danger, thanks mainly to the clot-dissolving properties of the TPA.

Within three days she could walk around almost normally, in the gentle gravity of the Moon.

But she could not return to Earth.

Part of the problem was the acceleration of the rocket boost from the lunar surface, she knew, although that was only a minor part of it, since the liftoff was much less stressful than a takeoff from Earth would have been. There were gee stresses in re-entering Earth's atmosphere, too. They were greater, but she felt confident that she could handle them.

The real problem was the condition of her heart, weakened by weeks of living in low gravity and now damaged by the infarction. She feared that she would be a cardiac cripple on Earth, with its high gravity.

After days of consulting with her Earthbound medical colleagues, Goodman decided she would have to stay on the Moon for weeks, perhaps months, while slowly building up her cardiac strength through exercises specially designed to strengthen her heart muscle.

She wanted to resume her medical duties, but the corporation had sent up a strapping young M.D. to replace her as medical officer – and to watch over her while she recuperated. Looking more like a football hero than a physician, the young man supervised her exercise regimen with ruthless tenderness.

Dr. Goodman continued her research, but this was not enough to fill her increasingly boring days in the cramped underground warrens of Moonbase. She had brought her camera with her, though, and started taking photographs. Not of the busy, harried, sweaty people who lived cheek-by-jowl in Moonbase. She got into a spacesuit and went out on the surface to take photos of the grandeur of the Moon itself.

She had no intention of showing her work to anyone but her fellow Moonbase residents. But one of them electronically relayed back to Savannah a few choice shots of the Sun rising over Alphonsus's ringwall mountains. A minor executive in the public relations department showed them to an editor of a photography magazine. Within a month several other magazines were asking for her work.

She had started with ordinary color film, but soon asked her new-found friends in the world of photography to send her black-and-white film, instead. It seemed made to order for the black-and-gray world of the Moon.

With dizzying suddenness, Lana Goodman became an artist of global renown. Her photos of the Moon showed all the barren splendor of this new world in its rugged challenge. Her work adorned the covers of newsmagazines. Media personalities clamored to interview her, live, from the Moon.

The handsome young football hero of a physician left after his three-month tour ended. The next doctor was a woman, just as qualified, just as determined to see that Goodman continued her exercise routine, but nowhere near as emotionally interesting.

When medical tests showed she was physically able to return to Earth, she asked for a postponement. I'm not ready, she said. Psychologically, I'm not prepared to face the return trip.

On the first anniversary of her heart attack she decided to quit the subterfuge and asked her contacts in the corporation's personnel office to allow her to stay on the Moon indefinitely.

The decision went all the way up to Paul Stavenger, head of Masterson's space division. In full sympathy with her desire, and prodded by the corporate public relations director, he decided to allow Lana Goodman to stay at Moonbase as long as she wished.

She never returned to Earth.

Lana Goodman become the first person to live on the Moon permanently.

SPACE STATION

The Clippership took off with a thundering roar that was only slightly muted by the passenger cabin's acoustical insulation. The ship rattled hard enough to blur Paul's vision for a moment. Pressed flat against the reclined seat, he turned his head to see how Joanna was taking it. Her eyes were squeezed shut, hands clutching the armrests with whitened knuckles.

The vibration eased off a good deal, but the bellowing thunder of the rocket engines still shook his innards. Then a sharp *bang!* and the noise abruptly ceased.

Paul felt all sensation of weight disappear. One instant he was flattened against the chair, weighing three times normal, the next he was floating lightly against the restraining seat harness.

Joanna's arms had lifted off her seat's rests. Her gray-green eyes were wide open now, looking startled.

Paul grinned at her. 'We're coasting now. Zero gee.'

She smiled back at him, weakly.

Within fifteen minutes the Clippership made its rendezvous with the space station. The ship lurched slightly once, twice, a third time. Then the co-pilot opened the cockpit hatch and announced, 'We're docked. They're attaching the access tube to the main hatch.'

'Can I come up and take a look?' Paul asked, unstrapping his seat harness.

'Sure, we're all finished here,' said the co-pilot.

Paul floated up into the ladderway aisle. The other passengers were unbuckling their harnesses, bobbing up out of their chairs, opening the overhead luggage bins to haul out their gear. Straps snaked weightlessly, as if alive; travel bags and equipment boxes hung in mid-air.

Looking down at Joanna, still firmly strapped into her seat, he said, 'I'll be right back.'

She tried to smile again.

The cockpit was cramped with two seats for the astronauts shoehorned into wall-to-wall instrumentation. But there was a wide transparent port for Paul to look through.

The space station was still unfinished. Paul could see a spacesuited construction team hauling girders and curved sheets of alloy into place along the station's outermost section, so far distant that they looked like little toy figures. A welding laser flashed briefly. The construction workers all wore maneuvering backpacks so they would not need tethers to keep them from drifting off into space.

The Earth hung off to one side, huge and bright blue with parades of pure white clouds marching across the face of the broad ocean. Paul could see specks of islands and, off at the curving horizon, the wrinkled brown stretch of California's rugged coastline swinging into view.

The station was built in three concentric wheels with a docking area at the hub. Once the construction was finished the station would be spun up so that people in the widest, outermost wheel would feel a normal Earthly gravity. The inner wheels would provide one-third and one-sixth gee, while the docking hub would be effectively in zero gravity all the time. For now, though, the entire huge structure hung motionless against the utterly black sky. It was all in zero gee.

'They're making good progress,' Paul said.

'Had an accident yesterday,' the pilot told him. 'Boom operator got pinned between one of the girders and a new section of flooring they were installing.'

'Was he hurt bad?'

'She,' said the co-pilot. 'Ruptured her suit. She was dead before they could get to her.'

Paul shook his head. 'How many does that make?'

'Four this year. Six, altogether.'

'Christ, you think they'd be more careful.'

'It's the new guys, every time. They start hauling big girders around and they're weightless so they forget they still got mass. And momentum. Get hit by one and it can still cave in your ribs.'

'There hasn't been much publicity about it back on the ground,' Paul said.

The co-pilot smiled grimly. 'Rockledge has a damned tight public relations operation. No reporters up here at all.'

'Still . . . you'd think they'd be screaming about it.'

'Nah,' said the pilot. 'Rockledge insures the workers, pays off the family plenty. Nobody complains.'

'Not yet,' the co-pilot countered.

'The work's getting done on schedule and within budget, from what I hear.'

Paul asked, 'Even with the insurance costs factored in?'

The pilot nodded. 'Rockledge must've factored in a casualty rate when they decided to build this wheel.'

Yeah, Paul thought, and our rental of space in the station must be helping to pay off their insurance premiums.

'It's a tradeoff,' the co-pilot said, as if he could read Paul's face. 'The sooner they get this station finished and operating, the sooner they can rent out all its space. They must've figured that the insurance costs are worth it if they can get the job done fast enough.'

'Pretty damned cold-blooded,' Paul muttered. 'I don't think I'd push an operation that way.'

The pilot grinned at him. 'That's why we work for you, boss, instead of Rockledge.'

Masterson Corporation's space operations division – Paul's former bailiwick – had rented half the innermost wheel of the space station for research laboratories and an experimental zero-gee manufacturing facility. Once the station was completed and spun up, that innermost wheel would rotate at one-sixth gee: the gravity of the Moon's surface. The labs would shift from zero-gee to a lunar environment. The manufacturing facility would be removed from the station and hung outside as a 'free floater,' where it could remain in the weightless mode.

Part of Masterson's rented space was living quarters for its employees. Spartan at best, they were meant to house people who would spend no more than a few months aboard the station.

'It's not exactly the Ritz,' Paul said to Joanna as he slid back the accordion-fold door to their designated quarters.

It was a cubicle about the size of a generous telephone booth. No window, but a small computer terminal built into one bulkhead. Otherwise the walls, floor and ceiling were covered with Velcro and loops for tethering one's feet. A mesh sleeping bag was stuck to one wall.

'At least we're close to the toilet and washroom,' Paul said, pointing along the corridor that sloped upward conspicuously in both directions.

Hanging onto the open doorjamb while her feet barely touched the deck, Joanna looked bleary-eyed at her honeymoon suite and said wretchedly, 'I think I'm going to be sick.'

'It's not that bad, is it?'

'No, Paul,' she said, her face pasty-white. 'I'm really going—' She clutched at her middle.

Paul grabbed her by the shoulders and spun her toward the toilet area. Joanna moaned and gagged. Pushing her weightlessly down the short length of the corridor, their feet barely touching the deck, Paul slid Joanna sideways through the open doorway. She bumped gently against the wall inside.

'Just let go,' he said to her, leaning over her bowed back to start the toilet's air suction flow. 'This happens to almost everybody. I should've realized it'd hit you. I'm sorry, I just didn't think . . .'

He kept on talking while Joanna puked her guts into the zero gravity toilet.

'It's all my fault,' he kept saying. 'I'm so damned sorry. I never stopped to think that you'd be sick.' As he spoke and Joanna vomited, Paul fought to hold down the bile rising in his own throat.

Some honeymoon, Paul said to himself. Two days in orbit,

two days sick as a dog. Joanna had tried to be brave, tried
to fight down the nausea that assailed her, but whenever she
moved her head it overpowered her.

I should have known, Paul berated himself over and over.
She's never been up here before. It gets everybody, one way or
another. Damned idiot! You did your thinking with your balls.
Honeymoon in zero gravity. Upchuck city.

He spent the entire first day alternating between Joanna,
miserably sick in their cubicle, and the research labs and
manufacturing facility. The experiments on fabricating thin-
film video screens and special alloys in zero gravity and the
high vacuum of space were going well.

The director of the manufacturing facility was a sandy-
haired bespectacled Australian with degrees in metallurgy
and management from the University of Sydney. He patiently
took Paul through every step of the zero-gravity smelting and
refining system they had built.

There were hardly any other people in the area. The facility
took up more than a third of the space station's inner wheel, but
Paul saw only a handful of technicians and other personnel, all
in coveralls of one color or another, all of them busily ignoring
them as the facility director conducted the mandatory tour for
the new CEO.

'The board's very interested in the Windowall development,' Paul told the director.

'That's good, I suppose.'

Paul went on, 'Better than good. If we can manufacture
wall-sized screens on a scale big enough for the TV market,
it'll make this operation very profitable.'

The younger man shrugged. 'Thin-film manufacturing is no
great problem. Give us the raw materials and we'll make flat
screens the size of Ayer's Rock, if you want.'

Paul laughed. 'Ten feet across should do, for now.'

The director remained quite serious. 'We can do that.
But what I really wanted to show you . . .' He led Paul
to an apparatus that looked something like an oversized
clothes drier.

Peering through a thick, tinted observation port, Paul saw

an array of fist-sized molten metal droplets glowing red-hot as they hung weightlessly inside a capacious oven heated by concentrated sunlight. Tentatively, he touched the glass with his fingertips. It was hardly warm.

'The vacuum is a fine insulator,' the younger man said, with just a hint of an Aussie accent. 'Just open the far side of the oven to space and we don't have to worry about heat transfer much at all.'

Still, Paul thought it looked damned hot in there. The place *smelled* hot, liked a foundry or a steel mill. Paul realized it was all in his imagination; his brain was linking what he was seeing to memories associated with blast furnaces and smelting forges. Yet imaginary or not, he felt beads of perspiration trickling down his ribs.

The director looked youthfully cool. No perspiration stained his light tan coveralls.

'By focusing the incoming solar energy,' he was explaining, 'we can generate temperatures close to the black-body theoretical limit – better than five thousand kelvins.'

Paul already knew that, but he let himself look impressed. 'I'm surprised that you keep the droplets so small. I always pictured a big ball of red-hot metal hanging in the vacuum chamber.'

The youngster smiled tolerantly and nudged his rimless glasses back up his nose. 'It's a lot easier to handle a bunch of small spherules than one big glob. We can spin them up quicker, make them flatten out into sheets.'

'How do you spin them?' Paul asked.

'Magnetic fields. Dope the molten mix with a little iron and we spin the spherules, flatten them out into sheets, meld them together. It's straightforward and it doesn't take all that much energy.'

'So you're using centrifugal force to produce sheets of alloy.'

The kid nodded and his glasses slid slightly down his nose again. 'Then we turn off the heat and let the sheets outgas in vacuum. That drives out all the impurities while the alloy's hardening.'

'All the impurities?' Paul asked.

The director gave him a lopsided grin. 'Enough,' he said. 'Come on over here, I'll show you.'

He pushed off the oven wall with one foot and glided past a trio of workers bent over a piece of equipment that Paul did not recognize. Its access hatch was open and one of the workers – a slim Asian woman – was reaching into its innards while the two men with her muttered in low, exasperated tones. Paul didn't understand what they were saying, but he knew the tone of voice: something had broken down and they were trying to figure out how to fix it.

'Here's the final product,' the young director said, coasting to a stop in front of a long workbench. He slid his feet into the restraining loops set into the floor and pulled a thin sheet of metal, about a foot square, from a stack that was tied to the workbench with Velcro straps.

Paul flexed the thin sheet of shining metal in his hands. It bent almost double with ease.

'Higher tensile strength than the best steel alloys made on Earth,' said the director proudly, 'yet it weighs less than half of the Earth-manufactured alloys.'

Paul felt impressed. 'Detroit's going to like this,' he said. 'With an alloy like this they can make cars that are half the weight of the competition, so their energy efficiency will be double anything else on the road.'

'And the cars will be safer, too,' the youngster said, 'because this alloy's stronger than anything else available.'

'Good,' said Paul, smiling with genuine satisfaction. 'Damned good.'

'But there's a problem.'

Paul's smile evaporated. 'Cost?'

The kid nodded. 'When you figure the cost of bringing the raw materials up here to orbit, this alloy costs ten times what groundbased alloys cost.'

Paul looked around the facility. It's all here, he thought. We've got a new industrial base within our grasp. Almost. We can make billions. If . . .

Turning back to the earnest young director, he said, 'Suppose I could provide you with the raw materials at a cost twenty times lower than they cost now?'

The youngster's eyes widened behind his rimless glasses. 'Twenty times cheaper? How?'

'From the Moon.'

The kid looked as if Paul had just offered to put the Tooth Fairy to work for him. 'Sure. From the Moon.'

'I'm serious.'

'I know, Mr. Stavenger. Everybody knows you've been pushing to set up a mining operation at Moonbase. But that's *years* away, at best.'

Paul smiled tightly. 'It wasn't all that long ago that people said we were *years* away from zero-gee manufacturing.'

'Well, yeah, maybe. But—'

Stopping him with an upraised hand, Paul said, 'Orbital manufacturing doesn't make economic sense if you have to lift the raw materials from Earth. We both know that. But if we can provide the raw materials from the Moon it'll reduce your costs by a factor of twenty or more.'

The kid made a half-hearted nod. 'Okay, so the Moon's got low gravity and no air and you can shoot payloads off its surface with an electric catapult. That makes it real cheap.'

'And the raw materials are there. Aluminum, silicon, titanium, iron . . .'

'But how much will it cost to set up a mining operation on the Moon?' the youngster asked. 'How long will it take? How much will that electric catapult cost and how soon can you have it in operation?'

'As soon as I goddamned can,' Paul said. Meaning, As soon as I can get the board of directors to put up the money I need to get Moonbase up and running.

The younger man nodded, unimpressed.

'In the meantime,' Paul said, 'I want you to get the Windowall operation through development and into production. We can make enough money off that to keep your alloy processing going.'

*   *   *

Joanna was still in the sleeping bag when he returned to their quarters. She was awake, though, and looking almost healthy.

'It's all right if I keep still,' she told Paul. 'But as soon as I move my head, even a little bit, everything starts spinning.'

'I guess this was a lousy idea,' he said, hovering a few inches from her. For a moment he felt as if he were floating above her as she lay cocooned in the mesh sleeping bag, and a shudder of erotic heat flashed through him. He forced his feet into the restraining loops on the deck and his perspective shifted immediately; he was standing in front of her and she was pale and despondent.

'No, it was a *wonderful* idea. I'm just not cut out to be an astronaut.'

Paul disagreed. 'It's only a matter of adjustment. If we stayed up here for a week you'd be fine.'

'I don't think so.'

'Your body's already adjusting to zero gee. You've grown at least an inch taller.'

'Have I?'

'Look at the cuffs of your pants,' he said. Then quickly, 'No, don't bend your head down. But your sleeves are shorter now, too. See?'

'I really have grown taller,' Joanna said.

'Everybody does in zero gee. The spine unbends and you gain an inch or two. Your waist gets slimmer, too.'

'But my head feels so stuffed.'

'Mine too. The sinuses can't drain the way they do on Earth. Zero gravity means no post-nasal drip.'

'I wish there was something I could take to make me feel better,' she said.

'The transdermal patches haven't worked?'

'I don't think so,' Joanna said, fingering the flesh-colored circular patch behind her ear. 'Or maybe they are working and I'd feel even worse without them.'

He sighed. 'I could call for a Clippership to take us back tonight.'

'No,' Joanna said firmly. 'You're not going to spend a few million dollars just to pamper me.'

He grinned at her. 'Who else should I pamper?'

Before she could answer the phone buzzed. Paul reached across the tiny cubicle to the computer keyboard built into the bulkhead and tapped a key.

Bradley Arnold's florid face appeared on the display screen.

'Ah, I got the two of you together,' he said, smiling widely. 'Good.'

'What is it, Brad?' Joanna asked. Paul was surprised at the sudden strength in her voice.

'I've had a long talk with Greg. Did you know he's been – ah, seeing – Melissa Hart?'

'Is that why you called?' Paul asked, annoyed.

'No, no, no. Not at all. But Greg and I had a long talk, almost a father-son talk, you might say.'

The man is a monument to poor taste, Paul thought.

'How is he?' Joanna asked.

Arnold blinked his frog's eyes twice. 'He seems to be bearing up well. Physically, he's fine.'

Sure; he's getting physical therapy from Melissa, Paul growled to himself.

'He wants to have a meeting with you, Paul,' Arnold went on. 'To discuss the videodisk.'

'Discuss it? What do you mean?' Paul asked.

'Greg hasn't decided whether or not to take the disk to the police. He wants to talk it over with you before he makes that decision.'

Paul felt alarmed. There's more going on here than Brad's telling us.

But Joanna smiled tightly and answered, 'We'll be glad to sit down and talk it over with him. Just as soon as we can. We can leave the station right away, can't we Paul?'

Paul nodded, thinking that the few million she wouldn't spend to alleviate her own physical distress wasn't even a consideration in her mind when it came to trying to patch it up with her son.

MARE NUBIUM

Dead reckoning. Paul tried not to think of the irony in the term.

With no navigational aids to help him, Paul looked across the glassy crater that he had fallen into and lined himself up with his own boot prints, shining bright against the dark lunar regolith. Turning, he looked for a recognizable feature on the sharp horizon.

Okay, he said to himself. You head for that big squarish boulder. March.

He started off again, checking his watch to see how much progress he had made. How the hell can I tell how far I've come? he fumed at himself. Pissing suit doesn't come with an odometer. Three hours since I started. Legs still feel pretty good. No stiffness.

But his left heel hurt worse each time he set the foot down. Wonder if that's the same heel that did in Achilles?

He struggled on, doggedly aiming for the boulder, big as a fair-sized house. When I get there I'll take a break, he promised himself. Sit down in the shade and rest a spell. Just a few minutes. Don't have enough oxygen to sit around for long. Don't want the legs to stiffen up, either. Got to keep moving. But you've earned a little break. Just a little one. Just a couple minutes.

The horizon cut across his view like the edge of a cliff, much closer than on Earth, much sharper in the airless clarity of the Moon. Wonder what Columbus's crew would've thought about the horizon here. They were scared they were gonna fall over the edge when they were sailing across the Atlantic. How'd they like to walk to the edge of this horizon?

Paul turned his head slightly inside his helmet and put his lips to the water nipple. Nothing. Fear flared through him. No, wait. A few drops. He sucked harder. Damn! It was dry.

The suit had a full water tank when I put it on, he told himself. He tried to remember. He had checked out the suit in a panicky hurry, but all the indicators were in the green. He looked at the indicators now. Still green.

But no water coming through the nipple. Maybe the tube got bent when I fell down. Banged my head pretty good, might've whacked the pipe. It's only a small plastic tube. Maybe it's just kinked a little. Just needs to be straightened out. But how the hell can I fix it from inside the suit?

Think! he commanded himself. Don't make a move until you think it out. Remember what that old cosmonaut Leonov said: In space, think five times before you move a finger. In the meantime, keep moving.

Think. You can pull your arm out of the suit sleeve, you know that. Maybe worm your hand up past the collar ring and try to straighten out the tube. Maybe that'd work.

He closed his eyes to get a better mental picture of the inner workings of the surface suit. Hell, guys have smuggled women into these suits. Take a joyride up on the surface and watch the Earthlight. He remembered the first time he'd seen the night side of Earth, the glowing lights of cities and highways outlining North America. The fantastic shimmering of the aurora's pale blues, reds and greens. Very romantic.

Keep your mind on your problem, butthead! he raged at himself. The suit's loose enough to jerk off in, too, but that ain't gonna help anything.

Wait till you get to the rock. Then lean against it, take some of the weight off your legs, and see if you can worm your hand out of the sleeve and up inside the helmet here. That's what you've got to do.

It seemed as if he'd never get to the boulder. It loomed bigger and bigger, but it still seemed miles away. Until, all of a sudden, he was right in front of it.

Paul reached out and touched its stony side, smoothed by eons of meteoric sandpapering.

'Hello, rock,' he said aloud, surprised at how dry and scratchy his throat felt.

He stepped across to the shadowed side of the boulder, then leaned back carefully. Now see if you can wriggle your arm out of the sleeve. Careful! Easy does it.

It felt as if he was wrenching his shoulder out of its socket, but at last Paul got his arm entirely out of the suit's sleeve and started to work his hand up past the metal ring of the helmet collar.

He was sweating so hard his eyes stung. If you get your hand up here inside the helmet, he thought, first thing you do is wipe your eyes.

Then he realized that all this perspiration was merely draining his body of water. If I don't get this damned drinking tube fixed I won't make it much farther.

Slowly, desperately, he tried to worm his fingers up into the helmet.

SAVANNAH

Joanna recovered from her space sickness as soon as the Clippership lit its engines for the return flight from the orbiting space station to Savannah. Once they got home, she phoned Bradley Arnold and insisted that they meet with Greg at her house instead of in the corporate offices.

'It will be much more relaxed,' she said to Arnold's image in the phone screen. 'After all, it's been his home, too.'

Arnold agreed. 'I'll have him there first thing tomorrow,' he promised.

They were in Joanna's upstairs sitting room, next to the master bedroom suite. Joanna was reclined on the chaise longue. She reached out wearily to turn off the phone console on the table beside her.

Joanna turned to Paul as the screen went blank. 'We'll resolve everything tomorrow.' She smiled happily.

Sitting alone on the love seat beneath her portrait, Paul muttered, 'I hope so.'

They met in the spacious parlor of the house. It had been decorated in what Paul had always thought of as mock Gone With the Wind style: frills and doodads everywhere; long sweeping curtains of heavy silk on the tall windows; overstuffed furniture; patterned wallpaper. The house was only a few years old. Gregory had built it in a fit of conspicuous consumption. The worse the corporate profit-and-loss picture became, the more lavishly he spent, it had seemed to Paul.

So now he sat tensely on the brocade-covered sofa while morning sunlight poured through the windows and Joanna fiddled nervously with the bric-a-brac on the fireplace mantle.

It was a gas-fed fireplace, and the architect's drawing of the house that hung above the mantle concealed the room's big television screen, one of the first thin-film Windowall screens built in orbit.

Paul heard a car pull up on the driveway outside. Joanna stiffened, then hurried to a window.

'They're here,' she said, looking pleased and apprehensive at the same time. Then her face clouded. 'Greg's brought Melissa Hart with him.'

Paul's insides wound even tighter. This isn't going to be a reconciliation, he knew. It's war.

Greg still wore a black suit and tie. Paul thought his underwear might also be in mourning. Dark circles rimmed his reddened eyes. He looked somber, almost gaunt. Melissa, wearing a knee-length violet skirt and simple white blouse, seemed as tense as Paul felt. Bradley Arnold, in a rumpled gray business suit, was the only one smiling.

Greg had an attaché case with him. The videodisk must be in there, Paul thought.

'I'm glad that we could all get together like this,' Arnold said as they sat down on the two sofas that faced each other across the carved cherrywood coffeetable. Greg and the board chairman sat on one sofa, Joanna and Paul on the other. Greg clutched the attaché case on his knees. Melissa took the overstuffed armchair by the end of the coffeetable, facing the cold, empty fireplace.

The butler came in, carrying a tray of juices, coffee, tea, and a plate of toast. He deposited the laden tray on the coffeetable, then stood off to one side.

'Have you all had your breakfasts?' Joanna asked mechanically. 'Would you like anything from the kitchen?'

They all said no, and Joanna dismissed the butler.

'Now then,' she said as the butler left the room, 'I believe you've brought the videodisk, Greg?'

'It's right here,' he said, his voice low.

'Before we do or say anything else, then, I think we should all see it.'

Arnold bobbed his head in agreement. Paul glanced at

Melissa. Why did Greg bring her here, except to show me that he's got her now?

Greg opened the attaché case and took out a single, unmarked videodisk, about the size of a credit card. Paul thought it ridiculous to lug around the tooled leather case just to carry one slim disk; like using a heavy-lift booster to put a sugar cube in orbit.

Joanna started to say, 'I'll get the butler—'

But Greg got to his feet with a wintry smile. 'I know how to use the TV, mother,' he said. 'This has been my home, too, you know.'

Sarcastic bastard, Paul said to himself.

Greg flicked down the hidden access panel in the mantlepiece and powered up the TV. The architect's drawing faded away and the wide display panel turned soft gray. Then Greg inserted the videodisk and returned to his seat beside Arnold.

Paul stared at the screen. It streaked random colors for a few moments, then Gregory Masterson II's face filled the screen, bloated and distorted because it was almost pressed against the camera lens.

Gregory was mumbling something. Then he leaned back and they could see he was sitting at his desk, his face dark and grim. Paul was startled to realize how much alike father and son looked.

Joanna's hand reached into Paul's and gripped tight.

'Fuckin' sonsabitches,' Gregory muttered. 'How the fuck'm I s'posed to know if this piece of crap is in focus? Autofocus my hairy ass . . .' His voice trailed off into incoherent mumbles.

Paul saw the crystal decanter of whiskey at Gregory's elbow. He was waving a heavy old-fashioned glass as he grumbled, whiskey sloshing over its rim onto the desk. The Smith & Wesson revolver was resting in front of him, big and menacing, polished steel, long ribbed barrel and fine-grained walnut grip.

'It's killing me,' Gregory said, looking straight into the camera. 'What they've done to me . . . what they're doin' now . . . might's well be dead. Serve 'em right, the goddam' pricks.'

Paul felt his insides turning to ice. Joanna was staring fixedly at the big screen, where her late husband loomed over her. She seemed transfixed, unmoving as a statue, not even breathing, like a deer that freezes when it's caught in an automobile's headlights.

With his free hand Gregory picked up the heavy revolver. 'See this? Oughtta blow their fuckin' heads off with this. Blam! Right between the eyes. Or maybe shoot off their goddam' balls, see how they like it.'

Their balls? Paul wondered. What's he talking about?

'Get 'em before they get me,' Gregory muttered darkly. 'Only way to do it . . .' He lapsed into incomprehensible mumbles again.

Then he put the old-fashioned glass down with exaggerated care and transferred the gun to his right hand. He studied it for long moments, breathing heavily, mouth hanging open. Paul thought he might have been having trouble focusing his eyes.

'Get 'em before they get me,' he repeated thickly. 'This gun's my protection, my insurance policy. Make sure they can't hurt me anymore. Protect myself . . .'

Suddenly Gregory's eyes blazed with fury and he swung the gun madly. The picture abruptly went dead.

For several seconds no one said a word. They all stared at the blank screen.

At last Arnold spoke up. 'That's it.'

Paul pulled his eyes away from the screen and saw that Greg was staring at him accusingly.

'It's pretty much of a jumble,' Joanna said, disengaging her hand from Paul's. 'Is that the original disk or the enhanced version?'

'That's the enhancement,' Arnold replied.

'The original's in a bank vault,' Greg said tightly, 'with orders to turn it over to the police if anything should happen to me.'

Joanna gave her son a pale smile. 'Isn't that just a trifle melodramatic?'

Paul could see that Greg's hands were trembling slightly.

'No, it's not melodramatic, mother,' he answered. 'It seems very likely that someone murdered my father. Whoever did it—' he shifted his gaze toward Paul – 'might try to kill me to keep this disk out of the hands of the authorities.'

'That's stupid,' Paul snapped.

'I don't think so.'

'In the first place,' Paul said, 'the disk doesn't show anything – except that Gregory was blind drunk and had a loaded pistol in his hand.'

'And felt his life was in danger,' Arnold added.

'He said someone was killing him,' Greg said, still staring at Paul. 'He felt betrayed.'

Paul started to retort that Gregory was an expert on betrayal, but decided it would only make the situation hotter, so he bit it back.

'Are you saying,' Joanna asked her son, her voice tense, strained, 'that Gregory committed suicide because he felt betrayed?'

Greg turned molten eyes to her. 'I'm saying that my father was frantic. That his feelings of betrayal drove him to drink—'

'Then he must've started feeling betrayed twenty years ago,' Paul snapped.

'And after he passed out from drinking,' Greg went on, glowering, 'someone slipped into his office, put that gun in his mouth, and pulled the trigger.'

'Bullshit,' Paul growled.

Joanna asked, 'Who are you accusing, Greg?'

'We all know who stood to gain the most from my father's death.'

'Paul couldn't have done it,' Joanna said, so calmly that Paul wondered how she could control herself so well.

'Why not?'

'Because he was here, with me, that afternoon,' she said, her voice low but firm. 'We spent the afternoon in bed together. That's where I was when the phone call came through.'

Greg's face went white with rage.

'So if you think that Paul murdered your father,' Joanna

continued, 'then you're going to have to blame the two of us. I can't prove that we were here that afternoon. I obviously didn't want the servants to see us together.'

'I don't believe you.' Greg said. 'You're trying to protect him.'

Almost triumphantly, Joanna said, 'If Paul murdered your father, then I helped him. Go to the police with that!'

'You were sleeping with him!' Greg accused. 'You betrayed my father.'

'Your father betrayed me a hundred times and more,' Joanna said, her voice edging higher. 'Paul was the only consolation I had.'

'Paul and who else?' Greg snarled. 'How many other men have you—'

Paul jumped to his feet and leaned across the coffeetable to haul Greg up by his lapels. 'That's enough! You'd better shut your mouth.'

Greg pulled free, glaring pure hatred. Bradley Arnold, never moving from his place on the sofa, smiled and raised his hands soothingly.

'Gentlemen!' Arnold said. 'Please! Let's not allow our emotions to get the better of our judgment.'

For a long moment Paul and Greg stood confronting each other, the coffeetable between them: Greg tall and slim, Paul a solid welterweight.

'Sit down, both of you,' Joanna commanded.

'Please,' Arnold said. 'Let's try to keep this on a civilized plane.'

Paul took his place beside Joanna again. Greg sat down next to Arnold. Paul saw that Melissa looked alarmed, frightened.

'If we had wanted to go to the police,' Arnold said, 'we would have done that days ago.'

We? Paul's ears perked up. Arnold said *we*.

'The reason I set up this meeting,' the board chairman went on, 'was to try to come to some sort of understanding about all this. Keep it in the family, so to speak.'

'Then why is she here?' Joanna asked, gesturing toward Melissa.

'She's with me,' Greg said. 'If it hadn't been for Melissa these past few weeks I think I would've gone off the deep end.'

You're already in over your head, kid, Paul said to himself.

'Now, now,' said Arnold. 'Let's try to be reasonable and come up with a solution that makes some sense.'

'I don't see where the problem is,' Paul said. 'Gregory committed suicide. That's all there is to it.'

'He was murdered,' Greg insisted sullenly.

'Then show your pissin' disk to the cops and see what they make of it.'

'No!' Arnold boomed. His deep voice seemed to make the heavy window drapes flutter. 'We should settle this among ourselves.'

'Settle it how?' Joanna asked.

'Greg will refrain from showing this disk to the board of directors—'

'Refrain?' Paul snapped. 'He's got no business showing that disk to anybody.'

Arnold shook his head disappointedly. 'Paul, I'm sure you understand that even though the disk may not constitute the kind of evidence the police could use, it would certainly look very bad for you in the eyes of the board members.'

'Especially,' Melissa pointed out softly, 'with Joanna's alibi for you.'

Paul sank back on the sofa cushions. 'You sonsofbitches are going to use this disk to drive a wedge between me and the board?'

'You can resign,' Greg said. 'Just quit and leave the company and I won't have to show the disk to anybody.'

'Resign?'

'You have a golden parachute,' Arnold pointed out. 'You won't be hurting, financially.'

'Quit the company? Is that all you want?'

'No,' said Greg. 'There's one additional thing you'll have to do.'

'What's that?'

'Divorce my mother.'

Paul got to his feet again, slowly this time. 'This meeting's over,' he said through gritted teeth. 'There's the door, Greg. Get out.'

Still sitting, Greg looked up at him sullenly. 'You can't throw me out. This is my house.'

'Not any more.'

Greg's eyes widened and he looked past Paul to his mother. 'I live here, too!'

'Get out,' Paul repeated, pronouncing each word distinctly. 'You can send somebody over to clear out your things later. Now get out of here before I throw you through a window.'

Greg shot to his feet. 'Mom, are you going to let him do this to me?'

'I think it would be best,' Joanna said. 'We obviously can't live under the same roof anymore. Not now.'

'You're letting him throw me out of my own home?' Greg's voice climbed an octave higher.

Arnold lumbered to his feet. 'Come on, Greg, you can stay at my house until you find a place of your own.'

The old man pulled at Greg's jacket sleeve. Looking bewildered, hurt and angry at the same time, Greg let himself be led away toward the door.

Melissa stood up. 'For what it's worth,' she said softly, 'I told him this would happen.' Then she left, too.

LEV BRUDNOY

He was a good-will ambassador or a con man, a free spirit or a pariah, depending on your point of view. Levrentii Alexandrovich Brudnoy was a trained fluid dynamicist who somehow managed to wangle a job as a life-support engineer at the ill-starred Russian facility called Lunagrad, and then go on to become its most famous – or infamous – emissary.

The Russians had placed their base at the giant crater Aristarchus, up in the area where Mare Imbrium and Oceanus Procellarum merge, nearly a thousand miles northwest of Moonbase.

Like Moonbase, Lunagrad was originally heavily subsidized by the Russian government. After years of supporting the primitive base as basically an outpost for scientific research and further exploration of the Moon, Moscow decided (long before Washington did) to 'spin off' the base to private enterprise.

While Masterson Aerospace Corporation operated the American Moonbase under government contract, NPO Lunagrad, the corporation hastily formed to run the Russian base, sought investors all over the world. Few were willing to risk their money on a lunar base.

Lev Brudnoy happened to be in Moscow, applying for his second tour of duty at Lunagrad, when the desperate corporate personnel director caught sight of him. Handsome, red-haired, charming, young enough to appear dashing, old enough to appear knowledgeable, Brudnoy would make the ideal 'image' of the new Russian space pioneer. After all, the man *wanted* to return to Lunagrad, no?

Why did he want to return to the Moon? Some said he realized that this new frontier was humankind's great new challenge and opportunity. Others said it was to make the extra salary so he could pay his gambling debts. At least three different women were certain that handsome Lev was running off to the Moon to escape from them (although none of them knew of the other two).

No matter what his reasons, the corporate personnel chief knew a media star when she saw one. She interviewed Lev extensively, often in bed, and then unleashed him as the new Russian icon: the space traveller, the lunar explorer, the man of the future.

In his way, Lev helped to raise billions for Lunagrad. He became an international television celebrity. When he went to Lunagrad he brought virtual reality equipment with him so he could 'escort' Earthbound visitors through the facility and show them the stark grandeur of the Moon's harshly beautiful environment.

The Lunagrad that he showed was mostly a television studio's carefully prepared set, a heavily cosmeticized version of the grubby reality of the cramped, stuffy, overheated and underfinanced underground shelters that composed the true Lunagrad.

Money flowed in for Lunagrad. Not enough to really expand the base, but enough to keep it staggering along. Scientists came to the Moon and departed. Geologists and metallurgists explored the wide expanses around Lunagrad. In Moscow the board of directors, chaired now by the woman who had been personnel director, published glowing full-color brochures of the glorious future of Lunagrad.

Like many tragedies, Brudnoy's success came crashing down when he went one single step too far. He shuttled back and forth to Lunagrad so often that he became known world-wide as 'The Moon Man.' Inevitably, on a certain global television broadcast, he was asked the fateful question: When will tourists be allowed to visit Lunagrad?

'Why not now?' was his immediate, unthinking reply.

Within hours the offices of NPO Lunagrad were deluged

with requests for visits to the base on the Moon. For the first time in ages, the Russians had scored a public relations triumph over the West. Tourists to the Moon! It was fantastic. But it promised to be profitable. Even at a cost of millions, there were wealthy individuals who – bored with the Great Wall of China and Antarctica and the space stations in low Earth orbit – simply *had* to see the Moon firsthand.

Brudnoy led the first contingent himself. Their complaints started even before the booster rocket took off from Baikanour. There were no hotels! They were expected to sleep in barracks, like . . . like . . . well, like cosmonauts or scientists. Lunagrad was small, crowded, smelled bad. The food was awful. There weren't enough spacesuits for everyone to go out for a walk on the Moon's surface at the same time; they had to take turns. And the suits stank!

On and on, a litany of complaints that went all the way back to Mother Russia and over the television networks to the rest of the world.

Lunar tourism was set back twenty years. Lunagrad was exposed as a dirty, dangerous, crowded and unwholesome frontier outpost. Lev Brudnoy was accused of fronting for a fraud. Lawsuits were actually started by several of the American tourists, although the Russian government quietly quashed them – with Washington's even quieter acquiescence.

Lev Brudnoy became a pariah. He was no longer welcome in the Moscow offices of NPO Lunagrad, nor in the beds of women who had adored him only weeks earlier.

Then came the most tragic blow of all. Their finances ruined, NPO Lunagrad declared bankruptcy. Lunagrad would shut down. Permanently.

Lev was at Lunagrad when the terrible news came. Most of the skeleton crew of scientists and cosmonauts did not blame him, exactly, but they did not console him either.

Deep in his heart, Lev knew he had done nothing truly wrong. And he wanted to continue his life as a 'lunik.' So he commandeered one of the last rocket vehicles left at Lunagrad, reprogrammed its guidance computer with his own hands, and flew it in one long ballistic arc to Moonbase, where he asked for asylum.

The people at Moonbase had seen Lev on television, of course. They immediately took a liking to the big, lovable redheaded Russian. Besides, they had no way to get him back to Lunagrad; Lev's rocket transport could be refueled, of course, but somehow its guidance computer had broken down as soon as the craft had landed at Moonbase.

After somewhat frenzied discussions with Savannah, Moscow and Washington, it was decided that Lev could become a Masterson Corporation employee without losing his Russian citizenship. But it was all kept very quiet. Lev's days as a television idol were over. He became a regular visitor to Moonbase, working there six months at a time, then spending a month Earthside.

He even returned to Moscow, but only briefly. Too many women were waiting for him there.

MARE NUBIUM

A part of his mind wanted to giggle. I must be going crazy, Paul thought. Yet it was slightly ludicrous, leaning against the massive boulder, alone on the desolate lunar plain, miles from shelter, running out of oxygen while the fingers of his right hand wiggled pitifully around the metal collar of his surface suit, trying to reach the water tube.

Suppose I die like this. When they finally find me they'll think I strangled myself.

He wanted to laugh but his throat was too dry for it. Sweat stung his eyes, though. I'm not dehydrated. Not yet.

There! His thumb and forefinger grasped the slim plastic tube. It was just below his chin, out of his field of vision. Blinking the sweat away, Paul slowly, carefully slid his fingers along the tube. He could not feel a kink in it. The tube went into the metal collar ring, where it connected with the piping that ran inside the suit, across the left shoulder to the water tank in the life-support backpack.

Maybe when I fell I dislodged the connection in the collar, he guessed. Don't feel any wetness. The tube's not ruptured. He spent several precious minutes searching for kinks in the slim tube, finding none.

Must be the connection inside the collar ring, he told himself. No way to get to it.

He pushed himself up to a standing position and stared out at the sharp horizon, blazing in unfiltered sunlight. Must be at least another ten miles to go. Without water I won't make it. He held up his forearm display panel. In the shade of the boulder the temperature was a hundred eighty below zero. But just a foot away, in the sunlight, it was over two hundred above, he knew. And still rising.

His mouth was parched. Can't go ten more miles in the sunshine without drinking water. You'll dehydrate and collapse.

Okay, he said to himself. If it is to be, it's up to me. You know what you've got to do. Make it quick and do it right. You won't get two chances.

If the water tube was no longer properly connected inside the collar ring, the only way to fix the problem was to re-set the collar. Inside a shelter, or even in an airlock, Paul would have unlocked the collar seal, taken off his helmet, checked the connection to make certain it wasn't blocked or broken, then put the helmet back on and sealed it tight again.

Out here in the vacuum of the lunar surface he didn't have that luxury. But I can do most of it, he told himself. If I'm quick enough.

Painfully he wormed his arm back into its sleeve and wriggled his fingers back into the glove. Then he stood still, breathing hard, swiftly going through the emergency procedure in his mind. It works in the procedures manual, he told himself. Now let's see if it works for real.

He took one long, last breath, then exhaled slowly. Holding his breath, he clicked open the seal of the collar ring and slid the helmet half a turn, as if he were going to take it off. A slight hiss of air made every nerve in his body tighten. But he held the helmet for a moment that seemed years long, then twisted it back to the closed position and snapped the seal shut again.

The hissing stopped and Paul took a big, grateful gulp of oxygen.

Then he turned his head to the left and found the nipple of the water tube with his lips. Carefully he sipped.

Water. Just a dribble, and it was warm and flat. But it tasted better than champagne to him.

He took another sip. Still had to suck hard, but at least some water was flowing now. The connection had been dislodged when he fell and now it was back in place. Okay.

'Okay,' he said aloud, his throat not so parched now. 'Let's get on with it.'

He started off again, still using the trail of his own boot prints to point him in the right direction. The glare of the sun made him want to squint, even behind the heavily tinted visor.

'Ten more miles,' he said. 'Okay, maybe twelve. Could be less, though. Hard to tell.'

He trudged on, boots kicking up soft clouds of dust that fell languidly in the gentle gravity of the Moon. His mind turned back to Greg. Nanomachines. The sonofabitch turned them into a murder weapon. Kid's brilliant. Crazy but brilliant.

Will he turn on Joanna? Will he try to kill his own mother? How crazy is he? Or is it all a very clever scheme to get what he's always wanted – total control of the corporation. Total control of his mother. Total control of Melissa, too.

Melissa. Paul thought about her as pushed himself across the barren rocky plain. Sweet silky Melissa. I knew she'd be my downfall. I knew it, but I let it happen anyway.

SAN FRANCISCO

Paul's tour of the corporation's divisions took him to Houston, Denver, Los Angeles and finally to the struggling nano-technology division in San Jose, squarely in the dilapidated heart of what had once been called Silicon Valley.

Joanna stayed in Savannah. They had not made love since the ill-starred trip to the space station. The night after Greg's confrontation over the videodisk, Joanna had flinched when Paul had touched her in bed.

'Not now,' she said. 'I just can't.'

Trying not to feel angry, Paul leaned against the pillows and grumbled, 'You're acting as if I did kill Gregory.'

Joanna turned to face him. 'Maybe we did, Paul. In a way.'

Paul started to shake his head.

'He found out about us,' Joanna said. 'That might have driven him to kill himself. We're responsible.'

'The hell we are.'

'Why else would he do it?' she asked, her voice filled with anxiety. Yet her eyes were dry and clear. 'Unless Greg's right and somebody actually did murder him?'

'He blew his own brains out,' Paul insisted.

'But why?'

Paul thought a moment. 'Good question. I'll ask McPherson to look into it.'

'What do you mean?'

'There must have been some reason for Gregory's suicide. And I don't mean us. Let McPherson hire some investigators. There's a lot about Gregory's life that we don't know about.'

Joanna's face hardened. 'There's a lot about his life that I don't want to know about. Not the details.'

'Okay. But I want to know the details. I want to know if there's anything there that could be a reason for his killing himself.'

'Such as?'

'How the hell would I know? Let McPherson look into it.'

Joanna agreed – hesitantly, Paul thought. But they didn't make love that night, nor any night afterward until Paul left on his swing of visits to the corporation's facilities across the country.

Paul was surprised to see Bradley Arnold at the Houston division. The chairman of the board was sitting in the division manager's office when Paul arrived. He looked uneasy, his bulging frog's eyes darting back and forth between Paul and the division chief, who was coming around his desk, his hand extended to Paul.

'I didn't know you were coming here, Brad,' Paul said as he shook hands with the youthful division manager. 'I could have flown you out in my plane.'

'I'm on my way to a meeting in Tokyo,' Arnold said, fiddling with his ill-fitting toupée nervously.

'Tokyo? By way of Houston?' Paul forced himself to chuckle as he sat beside the chairman in front of the manager's desk. Arnold refused to fly in the Clipperships. He would take all day to get from Savannah to Tokyo on his private supersonic jet rather than make the jump in forty minutes aboard a Clippership.

'I wanted to stop off here and talk with you,' Arnold replied. Turning to the manager, he added, 'In private.'

The manager took the hint and excused himself. Once he shut the office door behind him, Paul asked, 'What's this all about, Brad?'

Radiating earnestness out of his florid face, Arnold said, 'I know it looked as if I were on Greg's side, back there at the house—'

'It sure did,' said Paul.

'But I'm on *your* side, Paul. I want you to understand that and believe it.'

Yeah, Paul said to himself. And Brutus loved Caesar so much he stabbed him.

'I wanted that meeting to be a reconciliation between you two. I had no idea Greg was going to make the demands he did.'

'You didn't seem terribly surprised,' Paul said.

'Oh, but I was!'

'If I remember correctly, you told me that you were going to play Greg's videodisk for the rest of the board members.'

'I had no choice!' Arnold pleaded. 'Greg's going to do it anyway, so I went along with him. How can I act as a mediator between the two of you if he doesn't trust me?'

Paul looked into Arnold's hyperthyroid eyes and saw nothing but ambition. He's playing both sides of the street; or trying to. If Greg can shove me out of the corporation, Brad runs the show. Greg'll be CEO but Brad will be pulling the kid's strings. If I hang in and beat Greg, the bastard wants me to believe that he's been on my side all along.

'All right,' Paul said calmly. 'What are you going to do about the disk?'

Arnold spread his chubby hands in a gesture of helplessness. 'What can I do? Greg's determined to show it to each and every member of the board. All I can do is try to downplay it, tell them that Gregory had turned into a paranoid alcoholic and committed suicide.'

Pouncing on that, Paul demanded, 'You'll say that to the board?'

Arnold nodded.

'In front of Greg?'

'Yes.'

Thinking swiftly, Paul said, 'All right, then. Can you call an emergency meeting of the board as soon as I get back from this trip? Let's get this out in the open and finish it, once and for all.'

Bobbing his head up and down, Arnold said, 'The quarterly meeting is due—'

'I don't want to wait for the quarterly meeting,' Paul snapped. 'Call a special meeting and play the videodisk for them all at the same time, before Greg can get to them.'

'I think he's trying to meet each board member individually,' Arnold said, 'and show the disk to each of them in private.'

'All the more reason for speed, then. Set up an emergency meeting right now.' Paul pointed to the phone console on the manager's desk.

'Yes, good thinking.' The board chairman pushed himself out of his chair and went to the phone.

Nodding, satisfied, Paul got up and headed for the door. 'Thanks, Brad,' he called over his shoulder. 'Have a good meeting in Tokyo.'

Arnold waved to Paul, the phone receiver in his other hand. But as soon as Paul left him alone in the office, he phoned Gregory Masterson III in Savannah.

Melissa Hart was also at the Houston plant. She told Paul she had come to help negotiate new work rules for the factory that was being converted from making commercial airliners to building Clipperships.

She was at the Los Angeles facility, too. And then, when he got to San Francisco, Paul saw her walk into the lounge at the Stanford Court.

No one who could afford to avoid it stayed overnight in San Jose: despite all the efforts at rebuilding the area after the economic collapse that had swept the American computer industry at the turn of the century, the slums were still dangerous and dirty. The corporation's travel office booked Paul into the Stanford Court Hotel in the heart of San Francisco.

The nanotechnology division was Greg's special baby; his father had let Greg pump money into the nascent technology even though any hope of profitability was years, maybe decades, away. The board of directors had tried more than once to admit defeat and close the division down. Then they wanted to move it away from San Jose, to a 'safer' location in Nevada.

Paul had led the fight to keep the nanotech division in San Jose; he had convinced the board of directors that the corporation had a responsibility to keep as many jobs in the region as possible. His strong moral stand – and a stiff helping of government subsidies – swayed the board to do the right thing. And take every public relations advantage of it that they could.

It was late afternoon. Paul had just arrived in San Francisco; tomorrow morning a limousine would take him to the waterfront, where a helicopter was set to fly him to San Jose for the day's meetings and inspections of the labs and prototype factory. Then, back to the airport and home to Savannah. And Joanna. And Greg.

He stopped off in the lounge for a soothing shot of mellow golden tequila. Cool and dimly lit, with soft music purring in the background, the lounge was less than half full; mostly businessmen and women finishing their day with a drink and some chat.

Then Melissa walked in, tall and beautiful. Men and women both, they all looked her over, from her slick pageboy hairdo to her slitted ankle-length skirt that opened to reveal her long shapely legs as she walked to the bar.

She went straight to the chair beside Paul.

'You following me?' he asked as she swivelled the chair and sat on it.

'I was going to ask you the same question,' she said, smiling slightly.

'I don't know of any labor negotiations set for the San Jose division,' he said.

'My office has a few complaints of discrimination,' Melissa replied. 'Thought I'd try to defuse them before they get serious.'

The bartender came by. She ordered a glass of chardonnay. Paul got a refill on his *Tres Generaciόns*.

'Discrimination?' Paul asked. 'Against who?'

Melissa took a sip of wine, then answered, 'The usual: Asians claiming the Hispanics are picking on them; Hispanics claiming the Asians won't promote them. Small stuff, but it could get nasty if we don't take care of it right away.'

A faint hint of her perfume reached him: subtle, suggestive, it reminded him of the times they had shared.

'So you're not following me, after all.'

Melissa shook her head.

'Greg didn't ask you to keep tabs on me?'

Her eyes widened with surprise. 'Greg and I are finished. Didn't you know that?'

'Finished?'

'He dumped me. Just like you did.'

'I didn't—'

'And for the same reason,' Melissa said bitterly. 'Joanna.'

'What?'

'He's jealous of you, Paul. And not just over the CEO job. He doesn't want you with his mother.'

Paul downed half his tequila in one gulp. Feeling it burning inside him, he muttered, 'The kid's crazy.'

'He needs help, I agree,' Melissa said. 'He might do something violent.'

'Violent?'

'It was scary,' she said. 'I thought he was going to turn on me.'

'Why didn't you leave him?'

She stared down into her wine. 'I . . . To tell you the truth, Paul, I was afraid to. I was almost glad when he told me he wanted to end it.'

Jesus, Paul thought. Her job is to handle cases of discrimination and sexual harassment, and she can't even take care of herself.

'He had to get real teed off about it,' she went on, almost in a whisper. 'He couldn't just tell me he wanted to end it. He had to get raving and yelling like some monster. I thought he was going to belt me.'

'Greg?' Paul couldn't believe what she was saying.

But Melissa nodded solemnly. 'Underneath all that self control he's a wild man. He's like a bomb, all wound up tight and ready to explode.'

'Maybe we ought to get the company shrink to look him over.'

'You'd have to tie him hand and foot first.'

Paul finished his tequila and motioned to the bartender for another. Inevitably he invited Melissa to have dinner with him, and they made their way – Paul just a bit unsteadily – down the stairs to the venerable Fourneau's Ovens.

'Like old times,' Melissa said, smiling at him.

'Yeah,' Paul agreed. Old times. Life was a lot simpler then. No ties, no responsibilities.

As they sat across the table from each other Paul thought, It was a mistake to get married. Joanna doesn't love me. She just wants me to run the company for her until Greg's old enough to take over. Marrying me kept it in the family, put me under her control. She doesn't love me at all. We had better sex when we were sneaking around behind Gregory's back.

Do I love her? The question startled him. He stared at Melissa, coolly beautiful, just an arm's length away. The street outside was darkening into evening, people were walking by, the sky was fading from pink to violet. He remembered their times in bed together. No holds barred; no questions asked. Just pure physical pleasure.

Do I love Joanna? he asked himself again. If you have to ask, the answer must be no. What the hell is love, anyway? Then why did you marry her? He knew the answer, or at least he thought he did. To take control of the corporation. To keep them from scrapping Moonbase.

But you must have loved her, he insisted to himself. You were wild about her. Yeah, before we got married. Before all this corporate crap got in the way. Before this mess with Greg came up.

I did love her. Maybe I still do. But Greg's between us now.

And then Paul realized the truth. I don't know if she cares more about him than me. If we get right down to the crunch, would she take me over her son?

No, he realized. Never. She picked me as a stand-in to hold things together until Greg's ready to take over. She didn't realize that he'd challenge me right off the bat. And now that he has challenged me, will she back me or him?

Paul thought he knew the answer.

And here's Melissa sitting close enough to touch, smiling and sad at the same time, talking about old times and looking at me like she needs me again. And I need her. I really do. I need *somebody*. I'm all alone in this.

'You're awful far away,' Melissa said softly.

Paul drank the last of his wine. 'Got a lot on my mind, Mel.'

She closed her eyes briefly. Then, 'You know what I wish?'

'What?'

'I wish we had a time machine.'

He wanted to laugh. 'A time machine.'

'Yes. So we could back one year.'

One year ago he and Melissa were in the midst of their affair.

'You know,' she said softly. 'Before all this other shit happened. When it was just you and me.'

'Yeah,' he agreed. 'That'd be nice.'

Neither of them said another word about it, but once they finished dinner Paul brought Melissa to his suite and slowly, deliciously took off her clothes while she nuzzled him and crooned softly and smiled as he lifted her naked body in his arms and brought her to his bed.

When Paul woke the next morning to the buzzing of the alarm clock she was gone. Not a trace of her left, except the slight musky smell of her on the pillow he had slipped beneath her hips.

That was pretty stupid, Paul told himself. If Joanna finds out – Suddenly he realized that he had done to Joanna exactly what Gregory had done. Betrayed her.

For somebody who doesn't really love her, he thought, you feel pretty damned shitty this morning.

SAVANNAH

Joanna could hear the thumping and banging from Greg's rooms, even from all the way down the hall. She had gone up to her own sitting room, part of the master bedroom suite, when Greg had shown up with two husky movers and a small van to clean out his rooms.

'I'm taking all my belongings,' Greg said tightly to his mother. 'That includes my furniture.'

Joanna simply nodded and fled upstairs to her sitting room, not wanting to be in her son's way, not daring to let him see how miserable it made her to see him moving out.

But there was no other option. Greg and Paul could not live under the same roof.

After what seemed like hours, the noise stopped. Joanna looked up from the hand-held screen of her cyberbook reader. It was only midday; Greg had taken less than an hour to remove his belongings – and the furniture that she had bought for him.

He can't leave without saying goodbye, she thought. Should I go out and see him before they drive away?

Then she heard his tap on her door. It hadn't changed since he'd been a little boy. A single gentle tap. She had always responded to it immediately.

'Come in, Greg,' she called, shutting down the screen and placing the cyberbook reader on the end table beside her.

He looked tense, quivering with suppressed anger. Yet his shirt and slacks were neatly pressed, no perspiration stains. If he had physically helped with the moving, it did not show.

Joanna remained seated in the comfortable armchair as Greg crossed the room toward her.

'Did you get everything?' she asked.

'Yes. I think so.'

'There's quite a lot of things in the basement. Mostly old toys and school papers.'

He shook his head. 'I won't have room for that. My condo's too small.'

'I'll keep it all here for you.'

Greg swallowed hard. 'I – I suppose it's time that I moved into a place of my own.'

Smiling as gently as she could, Joanna said, 'Greg, dearest, you've had a place of your own in New York for quite a while now.'

'I mean . . . moving out of this house.' His voice almost broke. 'My home.'

She held her arms out to him and he dropped to his knees and let her embrace him.

'Oh, Greg, I'm so sorry that things have worked out this way. I didn't want it to happen like this.'

'I know,' he said, his head on her lap. 'It's not your fault.'

'It's not anyone's fault.'

'It's his!' Greg snarled, looking up from his mother's lap, his eyes red and burning. 'He's done this to us!'

'If you mean Paul—'

'He murdered my father!'

Joanna stroked his midnight hair, trying to soothe him. 'Greg, I told you . . . I was with Paul all that afternoon. I really was.'

Shaking his head stubbornly, Greg insisted, 'He didn't have to do it himself. He could have hired someone.'

'He couldn't have.'

Greg looked into his mother's eyes. 'You have no idea of how low he really is, do you?'

'Now, Greg, I won't listen—'

'You think he loves you? He loves the corporation! He loves that stupid Moonbase!'

'He's my husband,' Joanna said.

'Right. Sure. And last night he was in bed with Melissa Hart. Some husband.'

Joanna's could feel her face flame. 'That's not true!'

'Isn't it? Do you think it's a coincidence that Melissa's been at the Houston and L.A. divisions the same time he's been there? Is it an accident that they both booked the same hotel in San Francisco?'

Joanna's breath caught in her chest. She could not answer.

'Why shouldn't he take his pick of younger women?' Greg went on. 'He's the top dog now, isn't he? He's an important man, thanks to you. He can have any woman he wants.'

'You're lying!'

'Check with the travel office. The two of them have been travelling across the country together. Your black CEO and his black mistress.'

'But I thought Melissa . . .' Joanna ran out of words. Her thoughts were tumbling through her head.

'Melissa's a slut who'll sleep wherever the power is. You gave Paul the power so she's gone back to him.'

'No . . .' she said weakly.

'He murdered my father and he'll spit on you now that he's got what he wants.'

'No,' Joanna repeated desperately. 'Paul's not like that. He isn't!'

'He's a cheat and a murderer.'

'No!'

'He is! I know he is! He murdered my father and now he's cheating on you.'

'But why? Why would he murder your father?'

'To get you!' Greg blurted. 'To get control of the corporation. To save his precious Moonbase.'

Trying to drive thoughts of Paul in bed with Melissa out of her mind, Joanna shook her head stubbornly.

'But he already had me, Greg. I loved him and he loved me. We were going to tell your father, sooner or later. I was going to get a divorce.'

'But if you divorced Dad, then Paul could never hope to get

control of the corporation. He had Dad murdered so he could make himself CEO.'

Joanna said again, 'No, Greg. Paul had no idea that he could become CEO. He was shocked when I told him I was going to nominate him.'

'But—'

'And that was just a few minutes before the board meeting started,' Joanna continued. 'You were there. Didn't you see how stunned he looked?'

'I was there, all right,' Greg growled.

'I know, it was a shock to you, too, dear. But I had to make Paul take over the company. I'm sorry I couldn't explain it to you beforehand.'

'He forced you into it, didn't he?'

'No, dear. He didn't know anything about it until just before the meeting started.'

'You didn't trust me to run the corporation. You still don't.'

Patiently, trying her best to mollify her son, Joanna explained, 'Greg, dearest, you're not ready yet.'

'I'm twenty-eight years old. Dad wasn't much older when he took over from his father.'

Joanna remembered. Gregory hadn't been ready, either. And he never really learned how to make the corporation profitable. Under his direction Masterson Aerospace staggered along from one crisis to another. Until Paul pushed through the development of the Clipperships. That saved us, she thought.

'Greg,' she said to her son, 'I know that Brad Arnold has been telling you he thinks you're capable of running the corporation, but Brad's merely flattering you.'

'Flattering?'

'Brad thinks that he can control you, and through you control the company. That's why I had to put Paul in charge. To stop Brad.'

'He couldn't control me.'

'He's very clever,' Joanna said. 'And much more experienced in this kind of infighting.'

'He could never control me.'

Joanna hesitated. Then she said, 'Now that I think of it, the only one who could possibly have thought he'd benefit from your father's death is Brad.'

Greg's body twitched as if a live electric wire had touched him. He looked into his mother's eyes. 'Brad?' he whispered, unbelieving.

'Paul had no idea I'd nominate him,' Joanna repeated slowly, thinking out loud. 'But Brad would have known that if your father died, he could make you CEO and run the whole company through you.'

'I told you he couldn't control me!' Greg snapped.

'Yes, yes, I know,' Joanna said quickly, stroking his hair again. 'But Brad thought otherwise, I'm certain.'

For several moments Greg remained still, his head in his mother's lap, as she stroked him soothingly.

At last he said, 'Do you really think Brad murdered my father?'

'No,' Joanna said softly. 'I think your father committed suicide.'

'But you said—'

'I said that the only one who would have profited from your father's death was Brad.' Before her son could insist he couldn't be controlled again, she added, 'At least, he was the only one who thought he might have profited.'

'Brad,' Greg breathed.

He stayed there kneeling at his mother's feet until the butler rang from downstairs to say that the moving men were waiting in their van for Greg to direct them to his new home.

Then he kissed his mother's cheek and left the house.

Joanna sat alone for most of the afternoon, trying to keep herself from phoning the travel office to see if Greg's accusation was true. Her son's voice kept ringing in her ears, half triumphant, half sneering: *Why shouldn't he take his pick of younger women? He's the top dog now, isn't he? He's an important man, thanks to you. He can have any woman he wants.*

MARE NUBIUM

The Moon turns very slowly on its axis: one complete revolution in just under twenty-eight days. That's why Paul did not have a GPS signal to guide him as he pushed himself across the mare, hoping that he was heading for the ringwall mountains of the giant crater Alphonsus.

On Earth, two dozen global positioning satellites are enough to provide pinpoint locating fixes for virtually any spot on the globe. The satellites' orbits are fixed in space while the Earth spins below them. No matter where on Earth you are, there are always at least two satellites above your horizon to give you a precise navigational fix.

To get the same kind of coverage on the Moon, with its slow rotation rate, takes many more satellites. The consortium of private companies and government agencies that had cooperatively set up the lunar GPS system had tried to strike a careful balance between practicality and cost. They had started with a network of six positioning satellites and were adding to the web from time to time.

Just my luck to be out here at a time when the two closest satellites are both too low on the horizon for my suit radio to pick up their signals, Paul grumbled. Maybe it isn't luck. Maybe Greg timed it all. Is the kid that smart?

What difference does it make? he asked himself as he plodded across the barren lunar plain. Every few minutes he stopped to turn and see if his path remained straight, but he knew that was only the roughest of guides. You could be drifting off to one side or the other and never know it.

He sucked up a mouthful of water, sloshed it around his teeth and then swallowed it.

'Hell,' he muttered, 'for all you know you're heading for the pissin' south pole by now.'

One of the GPS signals oughtta come through pretty soon. I'll straighten out my course then. In the meanwhile, keep pushing ahead.

In the back of his mind Paul knew, as every astronaut knew, that what killed people on the Moon was fatigue. More than equipment failure or ignorance or even bad judgment, simple fatigue could wear you down to the point where you forgot just one little, vital thing. And then you were dead.

Paul forgot about the dust.

That powdery, fine dust, like beach sand underfoot, was electrically charged by the constant infall of ionized particles from the solar wind. No matter how carefully you stepped, your boots stirred up little clouds of dust, and some of the stuff inevitably clung electrostatically to your suit.

Through hard experience the men and women who worked on the Moon had learned to include a hand vacuum cleaner in the airlocks of their buried shelters. After an hour or so out on the surface, the suit needed a thorough cleaning. Otherwise the dust would get into everything inside the shelter itself.

It was more than an annoyance. Gritty dust particles worked their way into the hinges of space suits. If enough dust clogged the knees or other joints the suit would stiffen up just like the Tin Woodsman of Oz, left out in the rain. The experienced astronaut listened carefully for grating noises in his suit; kept sensitive to whether or not the joints of his suit were moving smoothly.

When they weren't too tired to remember.

Paul plodded along. He knew that he had been down on all fours back at the glass-smooth crater that he had slid into. He knew, if he had thought about it consciously, that his gloves probably had a thin sheen of lunar dust clinging to them electrostatically.

But he was too tired to be wary of the dust.

Wish I had a headband, he said to himself as he tried to

blink the sweat out of his eyes. He didn't want to look at the thermometer on his forearm panel, didn't want to know how hot it really was. The Sun was broiling him, he knew that and it was enough.

The bleak plain stretched in every direction around him, nothing but rocks and dusty regolith and more rocks. In his helmet earphones he heard nothing but the precisely timed beep of his suit radio's plaintive call to the GPS satellites that were not there to answer. Like a Chinese water torture, Paul groused. Beep. Then wait. And then another beep. Where the fuck's the answering signal? At least one of the pissing satellites ought to be in range by now.

But he heard only his suit radio's patient, maddening call signal.

One foot in front of the other, Paul told himself as he pushed along. Just keep putting one foot in front of the other and you'll get there sooner or later.

His vision blurred and without thinking he wiped at his helmet visor. A film of gray smeared across the visor.

Oh crap! Just what I need, Paul grumbled to himself. The upper half of the visor was covered with dust. He had to peer through the lower half to see where he was going.

Without stopping, he fumbled in the pocket on the right thigh of his suit for an electrostatic cloth. Got to be one in there, he said to himself. If they kept the suit supplies topped off. If the cloth hasn't already been saturated.

It was almost impossible to feel anything as thin as the cloth with his gloves on, but at last Paul pulled a bright green square from the pocket. He held it up in front of his visor and inspected it as best as he could through the smear of dust. Looks good enough. Most of it was still bright green, although one corner of the cloth had turned gray. It had been used before.

Carefully folding the cloth so that the gray, used section was out of the way, Paul wiped slowly at his visor. It seemed to help, but only a little.

Ought to have windshield wipers on the damned helmets, he thought. The cloth was not doing the job it should have done. Must've lost some of its electrostatic charge while it was sitting in the pocket. It's been used before, too. Christ, it's just not working!

The gray smear seemed a bit thinner now, not as opaque. Paul could see through it as if it were a frosted window: blurry shapes and shadows, not much more.

He refolded the cloth and tried again. No improvement. All he managed to do was to smear the dust a little further across his visor.

In disgust he tossed the cloth away. It soared like a rigid sheet of thin metal in the airlessness of the Moon, spinning lazily until it sailed out of his range of vision.

'Okay,' Paul muttered. 'Now we play pissin' blind man's bluff all the way to the next tempo.'

Then he heard a sudden chatter of beeps in his earphones: the signal from a GPS satellite. Grinning, Paul remembered that blind people often gain a remarkable sense of hearing.

'I'll play it by ear,' he said aloud, and began to laugh wildly at his pun.

But he needed to look at the displays on his forearm panel to make sense of the GPS navigational signal. His laughter died as he squinted through the dust filming his visor. If he was reading the instruments correctly, he had drifted more than six miles off his course to the next underground shelter.

SAN JOSE

The manager of the nanotech division was barely out of her thirties, young and intense and obviously nervous. Yet she seemed to be the oldest person that Paul could see anywhere in the plant. Her skirted suit of charcoal gray looked as if she hadn't worn it since her first job interview. She looked uncomfortable in it, as if she longed to be in a t-shirt and jeans, as almost everyone else was.

Paul felt like an old and stuffy grandfather in his light whipcord slacks and tan sports jacket. Good thing I didn't wear a tie, he said to himself. These kids'd think I came from Mars.

'Mr. Masterson was here last week, y'know,' the manager was saying, 'and he said he was very satisfied with the progress we've made in the past six months.'

So that's it, Paul realized as they looked through the thick window into a clean room where white-smocked technicians were bent over laboratory benches. Paul saw that the techs wore white caps over their heads and even had white booties over their shoes. Or sandals, he thought, glancing at the manager's bare unpainted toes.

'Look,' he said to her, 'I'm not here to swing a hatchet, you know.'

The manager's expression clearly said she didn't believe Paul. The ID badge pinned to her jacket said Kris Cardenas. She didn't look Hispanic, though. To Paul she looked like a California surfer chick: an attractive kid with softly curled sandy hair, a swimmer's broad shoulders, wide sincere cornflower blue eyes and a deep tan. And enough brains in her head to rise to the top of this very competitive high-tech division.

Making a smile for her, Paul explained, 'You've probably heard that Greg Masterson and I are enemies, haven't you?'

She nodded warily.

'Well, even if we are that doesn't mean I want to kill this division just because he's backing it. From what I can see, you're doing a good job here.'

Cardenas seemed to be holding her breath, waiting for the other shoe to drop.

'What I'd like to know,' Paul went on, 'is whether or not you're at a stage of development where we can try some practical tests of nanotechnology.'

'We were ready to try clinical tests of tumor killers,' Cardenas said, 'but the government ruled that anything intended to go inside human patients has to go through the FDA's approval procedure, and that takes *years*.'

'I know,' Paul said. Washington's decision had sent the entire nanotechnology industry into a tailspin. It wiped out any hope of profitability for this division for years to come.

'I can show you the animal tests we've done,' Cardenas said, starting down the corridor. 'We can destroy tumors with better than eighty percent efficiency – and no collateral damage to healthy tissue, y'know.'

Following her, Paul said, 'In animals.'

She nodded vigorously. 'Pigs, rhesus monkeys, even chimps. There's no reason why the bugs shouldn't work just as well in humans. There's just no *sense* to the government's restrictions!'

With a world-weary shrug, Paul said, 'I agree, but they've made their decision and we've got to live with it.' Or die with it, he added silently.

'It's stupid,' Cardenas insisted.

'I was wondering, though, could you adapt nanotechnology to other applications?'

'Oh, sure,' she said easily, pronouncing the word *shirr*.

They had reached a set of big double doors. Cardenas pushed one open and they stepped through into a large room filled with animal cages. The walls and floor were tiled in white. The smell of animal fur and excrement was enough to make Paul's eyes water.

'Careful,' Cardenas warned. 'These floor tiles get kind of slick, y'know. The handlers have to wash them down a lot.'

'I'll bet,' said Paul.

As she led Paul past a row of cages filled with hairless lab rats, Cardenas told him, 'We're already adapting what we've developed here for other applications.'

One of the monkeys yipped at them and within half a second all of them were howling and shrieking. The din was overpowering, echoing off the tiled walls like shock waves pounding on Paul's ears.

Looking worried, Cardenas shouted over the noise, 'Maybe we'd better go someplace quieter.'

'Amen to that,' Paul yelled back.

Once they were out in the corridor again, with the heavy doors muffling most of the noise, Cardenas said, 'Just about every one of those monkeys had cancerous tumors. Y'know, really nasty carcinomas and stuff like that. The nanobugs found them inside their bodies and disassembled them, molecule by molecule.'

'So once you finally get FDA approval this division ought to be worth a good-sized fortune,' Paul said reassuringly.

'For sure.'

'In the meantime, though . . .' Paul let the thought dangle in the air between them.

'In the meantime,' she said, leading him farther down the corridor, 'we're trying to spin off the medical work into toxic waste cleanup.'

'You can program the bugs to eat toxic wastes?'

Cardenas nodded vigorously. 'It's pretty simple, really, compared to the tumor work. They can go through a waste dump, find the molecules you want to get rid of, and take them apart. Nothing left but carbon dioxide, water, and pure elements – which you can recycle.'

'Sounds good,' Paul said.

'We're trying to get the state environmental agency to participate in a demonstration we've set up.'

'Not the federal EPA?'

Cardenas wrinkled her nose. 'The feds are real assholes. My strategy is to get the state environmental guys on our side and let them convince the feds.'

Paul remembered the first man he had worked for, when he had started at Masterson Aerospace. 'Make the customer a party to the crime,' he had advised. 'Get them on your side and they'll do half your work for you.' His respect for Cardenas went up a notch.

She stopped at a locked door with a RESTRICTED ACCESS sign over it. 'At least this area will be quieter than the animal pens.'

A few taps at the electronic lock and the door swung open. Paul followed her into a small, stuffy, windowless room crammed with consoles and instrumentation. The only lights came from the display screens on the consoles. The room felt overly warm, uncomfortably so.

As Paul peeled off his jacket, Cardenas leaned over one of the keyboards and typed out a single command. A shutter slid back from the blank wall on Paul's right and he saw a window that looked into another room.

An ancient Cadillac sat in there, one of those old monsters heavy with chrome and tailfins. Bright red, where there was paint still on it. Almost half the side that Paul could see was dull bare metal. The car was up on blocks, although the rear tire was still on its hub. The front tire was gone. The hood was propped up part-way; the windshield wipers were gone.

'What's this?' Paul asked. 'A pop art exhibit?'

Cardenas grinned at him. 'It's our toxic waste exhibit. What do you think of it?'

Paul turned back to stare at the Cadillac through the thick window. 'Nanobugs are taking it apart?'

She nodded happily. 'We've got four different types of specialized gobblers in there.'

'Gobblers?'

'Nanomachines specifically designed to attack certain molecules, break them apart into their constituent atoms.'

'Gobblers,' Paul repeated.

'One set's taking out the paint,' Cardenas explained. 'Another is reducing the organic molecules in the tires to carbon dioxide, methane, and whatnot. The third is working on the engine, separating out all the tungsten and platinum in the steel alloys.'

'Tungsten and platinum?'

'They're valuable metals, y'know. We want to separate them out so we can recycle them.'

'I see,' said Paul.

'And the fourth set of nanos is gobbling the plastics in the dashboard, steering wheel, seat covers and such.'

Paul could see the sheer fervor of achievement radiating from her face. A muffled bang made him snap his attention back to the Cadillac. The one tire remaining had just blown out and now hung limply on its hub. Paul thought he could see it twitching like something alive being devoured by parasites.

'Why do you keep the car in a sealed chamber?' he asked.

'To keep the bugs from spreading, of course,' Cardenas answered. 'We keep the chamber at ten below zero, Celsius. The bugs are programmed to stop at any temperature above zero.'

'But why—'

'To make sure they won't start gobbling people!'

'Oh.' Paul hadn't thought of that.

Cardenas didn't seem the least bit condescending as she explained, 'The bugs don't see any difference between your molecules and the Cadillac's, y'know. Except temperature. We design them to immobilize themselves 'way before they get to human body temperature.'

Paul nodded slowly. 'Then how do you expect to use them in toxic waste dumps if you're worried that they might attack people?'

Her smile faded slightly. 'We're working on that problem. We've got to make them much more specific than they are now.

Much more specific. Tailor them to distinctive molecules, so they'll gobble those molecules and nothing else.'

'Can you do that?'

'In time,' she replied.

Time costs money, Paul knew. It was the old story: an exciting new possibility that could make fortunes of profit, but first you have to sink fortunes of investment into it and pray that it eventually succeeds.

'What else do you have?' he asked.

Cardenas went back to the control console, flicked her fingers across a different keyboard. Another section of shutters slid back, this time on Paul's left.

'Nanomachines can build things, too, y'know,' Cardenas said.

At first Paul thought he was looking at a child's sand castle, the kind that kids build on the beach. The chamber he was looking into was hardly larger than a phone booth, dimly lit by a single bare bulb in the ceiling. Its floor was covered with sand or a grayish brown powder of some sort. In the middle of it stood a half-built tower.

'Here we've got assemblers at work,' Cardenas said, her voice low, almost a reverential whisper.

Paul studied the tower. It was about three feet tall. It wasn't made of sand, he realized. It was gray, almost the same color as the stuff strewn over the floor, but it looked smoother, metallic.

'What is this?'

In the dim light from the display screens Cardenas' expression was difficult to read. But her voice was vibrating with barely-suppressed excitement.

'Last week Mr. Masterson phoned me with a special request. This is the result.'

'What'd Greg want?'

'That sand is from the Moon,' Cardenas said. 'We've put in a few simple assemblers and the tower is what they're building.'

'Assemblers? You mean nanomachines?'

She nodded eagerly. 'Actually, we put one hundred assemblers into the sand, five days ago.'

'And they've built the tower,' Paul said.

'They're still building it. Watch real careful and you can see new features being added.'

Paul turned and stared at the tower rising out of the lunar sand. It rose perpendicularly from a wide, low base, its flanks smooth and featureless except for small setbacks every foot or so.

'Nothing seems to be happening,' he said.

Cardenas peered at the tower. 'They stop every once in a while, like they're taking a coffee break. Then they get busy again.'

'Don't you know why they stop?'

'For sure.' She grinned. 'Each time they reach a change in the blueprint we've programmed into them, they stop until the proper members of the team are in the right position to start the new phase of the building.'

Paul's eyes widened. 'You make them sound as if they're intelligent.'

'About as intelligent as bacteria,' Cardenas replied.

Paul grunted.

'The assemblers spent the first four days building more of themselves out of the aluminum and silicon in the sand. Yesterday that tower wasn't here.'

'No shit,' Paul breathed.

'The tower is mainly titanium, y'know. The assemblers are taking titanium atoms preferentially from the sand and using them to build the tower.'

'How do they know—'

'It's all programmed into them,' Cardenas said. 'We did this sort of thing last year, as a demonstration for Mr. Masterson and his father, when they visited here. We didn't use lunar sand then; just beach sand. We built a really neat castle for them.'

Paul looked at her. 'Could you build more complex stuff?'

Without an eyeblink's hesitation, Cardenas said, 'We could build a whole base on the Moon for you, if you give us the time to program the assemblers.'

Paul saw that there were a couple of little wheeled typist's chairs by the consoles. He pulled one up and sank onto it. Cardenas took the other one, facing him.

'Instead of sending tons and tons of heavy machinery to the Moon,' she said, leaning toward him, 'all you'd have to do is send a sampling of the necessary assemblers. They'll build more of themselves out of the raw materials in the Moon's soil—'

'Regolith,' Paul corrected automatically.

'—and then they'll construct your base out of the *regolith*,' she stressed the word, 'all by themselves.'

'One shipload of nanomachines,' Paul mused.

'Could build your whole base for you,' she said.

'How long would it take you to develop the nanomachines? Specifically for Moonbase, I mean.'

She waved her hands in the air. 'Simple tasks, like building airtight shelter shells and other construction forms, that's pretty easy. When you get down to complicated equipment, like air regenerators and pressure pumps, we'll need a while to program the assemblers.'

'A while? How long?'

'Months. Maybe years. We've never tried to build anything very complicated. Not yet. It'll take some time.'

A new thought struck Paul. 'Most of the compounds in the regolith are oxygen-bearing. And there's hydrogen imbedded in the top layers of the regolith, blown in on the solar wind. Could your machines—'

'Produce water out of those atoms? For sure. That's no problem!'

'Jesus H. Christ on a motorcycle.'

'You want a motorcycle, we'll build you a motorcycle.' Cardenas laughed.

'Maybe we ought to be talking with Harley,' Paul kidded back.

'Or General Motors.' She was suddenly completely serious.

IN FLIGHT

Paul was in the company helicopter heading back to San Francisco International Airport when his pocket phone beeped.

It was Melissa. 'Delta's flight's been cancelled,' she said, 'and there's nothing connecting to Savannah until late tonight. Can I ride back with you?'

'Sure,' Paul said, knowing it was a mistake, not knowing how to say no without feeling like a jerk.

Melissa was waiting for him in the hangar where his twin-engined jet was sheltered. The same plane in which he and Joanna had made love for the first time. Melissa was standing beside the plane, looking slightly forlorn in a baggy pair of tan slacks and a light sweater that hung loosely on her.

'Sorry to impose on you,' she said as soon as Paul got to within arm's reach. 'I'd have to fly the redeye to Atlanta and then make a connection at six tomorrow morning, otherwise.'

'It's okay,' Paul said. Last night they had been in bed together. But that was last night.

Melissa picked up her single garment bag. 'I know I look a mess. This is my airline outfit. It's for comfort, not looks.'

He made a smile for her. 'You look fine, kid.'

As he walked toward the plane beside Melissa, Paul remembered his elderly grandfather on the day the news broke that the first black president of the United States had been caught in the sack with a woman who was not his wife.

His grandfather had shaken his head mournfully. 'See the trouble a man's cock can get him into?'

Yeah, I see, Gramps. But seeing ain't the same thing as doing.

Paul let Melissa sit in the co-pilot's seat as he slipped on the headset and checked out the plane's instruments. She did not say a word to him as he taxied out to the runway, got clearance for takeoff, and then shoved the throttles forward.

The engines howled joyfully and the plane surged down the runway, faster, faster, the ground blurring as Paul watched the digital airspeed display, then pulled back with an artist's delicate touch to rotate the nose wheel off the concrete. The plane seemed to leap into the air and Paul's heart soared with it.

Once they cleared the airport traffic and Paul put the twin-jet on course eastward, he slipped his earphones down around his neck and turned to Melissa.

'Too bad there's no Clippership service to Savannah,' he said.

'When will we get there?'

'Eleven-thirty, eastern time, the way things look now. We'll have to make a pit stop in Amarillo. Gas up.'

Melissa nodded. 'Beats the redeye.'

For a while neither of them said anything. Paul watched the shadows lengthening below as they flew over the mountains with the sun setting behind them.

'Lake Tahoe,' he said.

'Uh-huh.'

Time went by in silence. Then he pointed out the Grand Canyon, barely visible off in the distance in the twilight haze.

Melissa stared out the window on her side of the cockpit until a cloud bank obscured the ground altogether.

Finally, Paul said hesitantly, 'About last night . . .'

Melissa turned sharply toward him. 'Forget it,' she said.

'Forget it?'

'It never happened.'

Paul felt puzzled. 'What d'you mean?'

'You're a married man and you're worried I'm going to shoot my mouth off to Greg or somebody. Well, don't worry about it.'

'That's not what I meant.'

'Isn't it?'

'Shit, Mel, I wasn't thinking you were a spy for Greg.'

'The hell you weren't.'

'You told me you two had broken up.'

'Yes. That's right.'

Paul's befuddlement deepened. Melissa seemed irritable, almost angry.

'Look,' he said. 'I'm sorry about last night. I shouldn't have done it. I am a married man and—'

'Oh, Paul, it's not your fault. I . . .' She seemed to want to say more, but stopped.

Paul didn't know what to say. If anything. It was a stupid thing to do, he told himself. If Joanna finds out I'll have hurt her just as bad as Gregory hurt her in the past.

'Do you know why Greg and I broke up?' Melissa asked, her voice so low Paul had to strain to hear her over the muted rumbling of the engines.

'You said it was because of Joanna.'

Melissa shook her head slowly. 'That's only part of it. I mentioned the magic word, and that drove him off the deep end.'

'The magic word?'

'Baby.'

Paul wasn't certain he had heard her correctly.

'I told Greg that I wanted his baby,' Melissa said sorrowfully. 'I told him that when a man and a woman love each other they make a baby together.'

'He didn't like the idea.'

'I thought he was going to punch me out.'

'If he ever lays a hand on you—'

Melissa silenced Paul by laying a slender finger on his lips. 'I can take care of myself,' she said. 'You've got a wife to think about. You can't go around fighting my battles.'

But Paul pictured Greg hitting Melissa. Just like the spoiled sonofabitch, he thought. He doesn't love anybody except himself. If he ever touches her I'll punch out his lights, but good.

After they stretched their legs in Amarillo and took off again, Melissa curled up in one of the capacious reclining seats in the plane's cabin and fell asleep. Paul put the plane on autopilot, but stayed in the cockpit, awake, his mind churning with thoughts of Greg and Melissa and Joanna and the nanomachines that could make Moonbase a going proposition if only he could hammer the idea through the board of directors. But Greg was going to use the next meeting to accuse him of murder, or at least fornication. *How can he attack me without attacking his mother?* Then Paul realized that Greg was so furious with blind hate that he *wanted* to hurt Joanna, punish her for falling in love with a black man.

It was almost midnight when Paul finally put the twin-jet down on the company's airstrip, a few miles from Savannah. He was tired, drained physically and emotionally. Gratefully, he saw that the limo was there at the apron in front of the hangar, waiting for him.

Paul helped Melissa down the little metal ladder to the concrete of the apron. When he turned back toward the limousine, he saw that Joanna was standing beside it, staring at them.

MARE NUBIUM

Do I have enough oxygen to make it? Paul asked himself that question again and again as he struggled across the rocky undulating lunar plain, trying to make up for the time and distance he had lost by straying so far off course.

He pushed himself harder. 'Gotta get smokin' now,' he told himself. 'Gotta get there before the oxy runs out.'

Somewhere in the back of his mind he remembered an equation that showed how oxygen consumption is related to the amount of physical work the body is doing. From some aerobics class he had taken back when he was in astronaut training, a thousand years ago. Shaking his head inside his helmet, Paul tried to forget about the equation. Just keep pumping along, he told himself. Go, go, go.

At least he had the GPS signal to keep him company. Cheerful little chirp in his earphones, almost like a songbird but nowhere near as melodious. Just a monotonous steady set of peeps, repeating over and over again.

Hey, don't knock it, he told himself. Long as you can hear that boring little song you're on the right track. You can listen to Wynton Marsalis some other time.

Through his dust-smeared visor Paul could make out the bulky shape of a massive boulder rising up on the horizon ahead of him, like a ship coming in from some far-off land. Boulder big as a house, Paul thought. As he got closer to it he saw that it was as big as a shopping mall.

Got to go around it. Damn! Pissin' chunk of rock's gonna force me ten-twenty minutes outta my way.

Squinting through his dust-covered visor, Paul saw that the

huge boulder was pitted and rough, with a fairly flat top. Maybe I can climb over it. Be faster than walking all the way around it.

But a voice in the back of his mind warned, You got enough troubles out here without rock-climbing. Stay on the flat ground and walk around the damned rock.

Still, Paul studied the boulder as he came closer to it. I could climb up this side. Looks easy enough.

And rip your suit? And how do you know what the other side's like? Once you get up on top of it, you gotta climb down again.

I can do it, he insisted silently.

Don't.

'It'll save me almost half an hour,' Paul said aloud, trying to convince himself.

The voice in his head reminded him, There are old astronauts and there are bold astronauts, but there are no old, bold astronauts.

Paul reached the rock. It towered over him as he put out a gloved hand and touched its rough surface. He took a deep breath, then started climbing.

SAVANNAH

Through the whole ride back to their house, Joanna stayed coldly silent. A perfunctory peck on the cheek as Paul got into the limo, then not a word. Paul could feel icicles growing from the roof of the car.

She can't be pissed off just because she saw Mel rode back here with me. Somebody's told her about last night. Who? Who could possibly know? Unless it was all a setup! He felt his stomach go hollow, the way it does the first few minutes in weightlessness.

A setup. Melissa came on to me deliberately, and she must have reported right back to – who? Greg, most likely. Or maybe Brad; be just like the sneaky little sonofabitch to pull a trick like this.

Paul waited until they were in the bedroom. He flopped his travel bag on the king-sized bed as Joanna went around to her dresser and sat in front of its triple mirror.

'I did something I'm ashamed of,' he began, staying on his side of the bed.

Joanna looked at him in the mirror. Paul could see her face-on, and both profiles. She looked calm, unsmiling but not scowling either. If she was angry she wasn't showing it on her face. Just sat there, the ice queen: regal and cold, staring at him through the mirror, her back to him.

'I went to bed with Melissa last night,' Paul said, hoping that confession would ease the tension.

Her chin went up; her eyes flared.

'It was a stupid thing to do,' he went on. 'I had more to

drink than I should have . . .' No, he commanded himself. Don't hide behind an excuse.

'Did you enjoy it?' Joanna asked coldly.

'Not once I woke up.'

She turned to face him. 'Paul, I want the absolute truth from you.'

'You're getting it.'

'Is this the first time you've done this?'

Instantly he replied, 'I haven't slept with another woman since we first went to bed together, Joanna. Until last night.'

'You had an affair with Melissa before, hadn't you?'

'We were together when I met you. I left her for you.'

'And now you've gone back to her.'

He stepped around the bed, then sat on its edge, on her side, close enough to Joanna to reach out and touch her. Yet he kept his hands on his knees.

'Joanna, it wasn't her. It could've been anybody. I was alone. We haven't made love since we went to the space station. It—'

'So it's my fault?'

'No,' he said quickly. 'Nobody's fault but mine. Not even Melissa's, really. I should've kept my wick in my pants.'

'Your wick?' Despite herself Joanna smiled a little. 'I've never heard it called that before.'

'It was a rotten thing to do,' he said. 'It won't happen again. I promise you.'

She sighed wearily. 'So did Gregory.'

Paul gritted his teeth. You knew that was going to come up, he said to himself.

'I'm not Gregory,' he said tightly.

Joanna's shoulders slumped. 'Maybe it's me,' she murmured. 'Maybe I do something to cause this sort of thing to happen. Maybe I pick out men who'll betray me.'

Paul reached out and took both her hands in his. 'Christ, Jo, it's not your fault! I'm the guilty party here.'

She wouldn't look into his eyes.

'You knew about it, didn't you?' Paul asked. 'You knew about it before I landed.'

'Greg told me that you and Melissa were travelling together.'

'Greg.'

'I told him I didn't believe it, but he said I could check with the travel office. So I did.'

'She was in several of the same cities I was. I only saw her in the offices, though. We weren't travelling together. We weren't shacking up.'

'Until last night.'

'That was a mistake that won't be repeated.'

Joanna said nothing. She still would not meet his eyes.

'I think Greg sent her to nail me,' Paul said. 'The bitch did this just to cause trouble between us.'

With a weary shake of her head, Joanna replied, 'Greg is finished with her. They broke up. He can't stand the mention of her name.'

'That's an act he puts on.'

'No,' she said. 'I know my son better than that. He hates the sound of her name.'

'Then it had to be Brad who set me up.'

'Why does it have to be a trap?' Joanna asked. 'Why can't you accept the fact that you've made a mess of our marriage?'

'Don't say that! I don't want our marriage to be hurt.'

'It's been hurt, Paul. You've hurt it.'

'Okay. I know that. But—'

'I'm pregnant.'

It hit him like a physical blow. Paul sat there, hunched forward, holding both Joanna's hands tightly in his. He blinked several times.

'Pregnant?' In his own ears his voice sounded a full octave higher than normal.

Joanna nodded. 'It wasn't just the weightlessness that was making me sick on the space station. I've been sick every morning for—'

'We're going to have a baby?' Suddenly everything was swept away. A baby! Paul had never even considered the possibility. At his age, at Joanna's age . . .

'Will you be okay? Can you do it without endangering your health?'

Joanna smiled patiently at him. 'It's not an illness, Paul.'

'Yeah, I know. But I mean, isn't it kind of late in the game for you?'

'The obstetrician says I'm in fine condition and there's no reason why I can't bring the baby to term.'

'A baby.' Paul glowed with the wonder of it. 'I never thought I'd be a father.'

Her smile widened. 'It does happen, you know.'

He pulled her to him, sat her beside him on the edge of the bed and kissed her on the lips. 'We've got to take extra-special good care of you.'

But Joanna had not forgotten anything. 'Paul – about this thing with Melissa.'

'That was finished this morning,' he said quickly. 'And nothing like it is going to happen again. Ever.'

'I want to believe you.'

'Believe it.'

'It's just that – Gregory started womanizing when I was pregnant with Greg.'

'I'm not Gregory,' he said firmly. 'I told you that and I meant it.'

For several moments Joanna did not reply. Then, 'All right, Paul. I'll believe you.'

For now, she added silently. I'll trust you as far as I can watch you. Maybe it will all work out all right, but I'm not going to sit by and watch my second husband humiliate me the way my first one did.

And Paul was thinking, This changes everything. I'll have a kid to take care of. A son, maybe. I can't let Greg gets his hands on the corporation. Not now. It's going to be my child's inheritance. A son. I want it to be a son.

Ed McPherson was a chubby, moonfaced, baldheaded make-believe Texan who dressed like a cowboy instead of the head of a major corporation's extensive legal department. Born in New Jersey, educated at Princeton and Harvard Law, he cultivated a handlebar moustache and made a fetish of wearing cowboy boots, suede jackets and bolo ties. Word was around the office that the only time he wore a business suit was when he appeared before the Supreme Court of the United States.

Which was never. McPherson rarely strayed farther from the headquarters of Masterson Corporation than the corporation's Wall Street offices in New York.

Paul was in his office in Savannah when McPherson's call came through. He put the lawyer's image on the display screen of his desktop computer.

'Gregory had prostate cancer,' McPherson said, with no preliminary. 'Terminal.'

Paul sank back in his swivel chair. 'You're certain?'

McPherson hardly ever smiled. He tried to keep a stony, hard-bitten look on his face. It was difficult for him, despite the luxurious moustache he sported; his round cheeks and bald dome did not lend themselves to a gunslinger's beady-eyed glare.

'The agency I hired tracked down the doctor who diagnosed him. It was so advanced that no treatment was possible.'

'Christ,' Paul muttered.

'He'd been seeing half a dozen different doctors over the previous five years or so,' McPherson went on. 'He knew about the cancer, looks like, but refused to do anything about it until it was too late.'

'But there are treatments for prostate cancer,' Paul objected.

McPherson made a sour face. 'You run the risk of incontinence. And impotence. I doubt that Gregory worried much about peeing his pants, but impotence would have been a big problem to him.'

'So he just let the cancer go.'

'And it killed him. Or rather, he killed himself when he found out it was terminal. Must have been giving him a lot of pain.'

Paul thought for a moment. 'You're certain about all this? You've got documentary evidence?'

McPherson brushed an index finger across his moustache. 'I can get written statements from each of the doctors, plus all of Gregory's medical records, if Joanna will sign a form demanding them.'

'I'll talk to her about it. Thanks. That was good work.'

'Wait'll you see the bill,' McPherson said, cracking one of his infrequent smiles.

Paul blanked the screen, then sat thinking, Will Joanna be willing to sign such a form? Should I bother her with this? She's got enough on her mind, and I shouldn't be upsetting her with old stories about Gregory.

It'll come up in the board meeting, Paul told himself. There's no way I can shield her from Greg's showing that damned videodisk to the board.

But now I know what Gregory was muttering about in the video. It wasn't us. It wasn't our fault. It was the cancer that was killing him, and the gun was going to protect him from the pain. He was pissed off with the doctors, not us. He knew he was a dead man anyway; he just stopped the pain for himself.

I've got to tell Joanna. She shouldn't feel any guilt about this.

Paul nodded to himself, satisfied that he had all the necessary pieces to the puzzle.

One puzzle, he remembered. There's still the question of who got Melissa to set me up. Was it Brad? And if it was, how can I prove it?

He shook his head slowly. It's gonna be one helluva board meeting. One helluva meeting.

OVER THE ATLANTIC

Supersonic aircraft were not allowed to fly above Mach 1 over populated areas, because their sonic booms disturbed people and rattled their homes. Farmers complained of milk cows gone dry because of sonic booms. Environmentalists protested against sonic pollution.

So Bradley Arnold's flight angled out over the Atlantic after taking off from the corporation's private airstrip outside Savannah. Alone in the passenger compartment, sitting in one of the plane's luxurious padded chairs, Arnold had no time to admire the procession of deep swells on the steel-gray ocean far below him. He had expected Paul and Joanna to come with him to New York, but Stavenger had backed out at the last minute.

'We'll fly up in my plane,' Paul had told the board chairman.

'But I thought we would all be going together,' Arnold had said.

'I've got a few things to do here this afternoon. We'll fly up overnight.'

What Paul did not tell Arnold was that he wanted to tell Joanna what McPherson had dug up about Gregory's cancer. Paul had no intention of letting the board chairman in on the news, not until the directors' meeting, when he would spring it on all of them, including Greg.

Disappointed, Arnold had grumbled, 'This is going to be an extremely important meeting, Paul. We could use the time to get our strategy ironed out.'

But Paul had insisted that he could not fly with Arnold to

New York. He had other things to do. More important than a strategy session with me, Arnold groused to himself.

He doesn't trust me. Arnold frowned with the realization that despite everything he had said to Stavenger, the new CEO still did not trust him. That's Joanna's doing, he thought. She's never liked me. All the years I tried to help her husband, and all the help I've given to young Greg, and she still hates the sight of me.

Well, it's too bad for them, he said to himself as he swung out the keyboard set into the swivel table built into the plane's bulkhead beside him. He stabbed at the telephone key and as soon as the computer's smoky female voice asked, 'How may I help you, sir?' he told the phone to get Greg Masterson.

'His private line,' he added.

Greg's face appeared on the screen almost instantly, but it was only his recorded answer. With a grave smile his image said, 'I am unable to take your call right now, but please leave your name and I'll get back to you as soon as I can. Thank you.'

Nettled, fuming, Arnold blurted, 'Greg, it's me. Brad Arnold. I need to talk to you *now!* Wherever you are, call me right—'

The smiling image was replaced by a more serious Gregory Masterson III. He was sitting in front of a window that looked out on Central Park and the towers of midtown Manhattan.

'Brad? Where are you?'

'I'm on my way to New York,' Arnold replied testily. 'Where else would I be?'

'Oh. Of course.' Greg looked relieved.

'I have some upsetting news.'

Greg looked more amused than worried. 'Really?'

'McPherson's come up with evidence that your father was dying of prostate cancer.'

Greg's slightly smug smile winked off like a light turned out.

'It looks as if he committed suicide, after all.'

'No,' Greg snapped. 'That's crazy. Prostate cancer can be

treated. My father wouldn't allow the cancer to go so far that it was going to kill him.'

'My source in McPherson's office tells me that Paul's getting statements from half a dozen doctors who either examined your father or counselled him.'

'With enough money you can get anyone to say anything.'

'But Paul's going to use these medical statements at the board meeting tomorrow, to show that your father killed himself, after all.'

Greg fell silent. He glanced at his wristwatch. Then he said, 'He wants to use these statements to counterbalance the videodisk, is that it?'

Nodding, Arnold said, 'I think he's outmaneuvered us.'

Greg's expression hardened. 'Even if my father had cancer he could still have been murdered.'

'That doesn't make much sense.'

'Doesn't it?'

'I don't think so,' Arnold said. 'It doesn't seem reasonable.'

'My father would never commit suicide, Brad. I know that. And so do you.'

'What do you mean?'

'Whoever killed my father deserves to die.'

'But you don't know that he was murdered,' Arnold said.

'I know enough,' said Greg. 'I may not be entirely certain of who the murderer is, but I know enough to act.'

'You mean at tomorrow's meeting? What do you plan to do?'

Greg looked at his wristwatch again. 'Thanks for the information, Brad. It was good of you to call.'

'What? Is that all you've got to say?'

'That's all you've got time for,' said Greg.

Arnold blinked his frog's eyes, puzzled. 'What are you talking about? We've got to figure out some way—'

The plane lurched so hard that Arnold was hurled out of his seat and banged against the tabletop keyboard. The sudden pain in his middle made him feel he'd been carved in two. For an instant he hung there, then the plane pitched up sharply and he was thrown back into his chair.

'Seatbelts!' the pilot's frantic shout came over the intercom. 'We've lost power on—'

Another staggering tumble, and the plane plunged downward.

'Mayday! Mayday!' the intercom was blaring. 'Lost power on both engines. Going down!'

Horrified, pinned in his seat, unable even to lift his arms, Arnold saw the steel gray Atlantic rushing up toward him. Then a frightful shriek of tortured metal and part of the wing ripped away.

He was too terrified to scream. But Greg's face on the little screen smiled grimly and said, 'Goodbye, Brad.'

The screen went blank and then the plane hit the water and exploded.

MARE NUBIUM

Paul pulled himself onto the flat top of the huge boulder and lay on his belly panting and sweating for long minutes.

Like when we used to climb up onto the roofs of the warehouses, when we were kids, he thought. But he knew the difference. Back then he could scramble up the warehouse walls like a monkey and then spend the rest of the day running races across the flat roofs or playing hide-and-seek with his bro's among the cooling towers and other structures on the roofs. He remembered the chicken game they played, jumping from one roof to the next across the alleyways separating the buildings. One slip and it was the morgue or the hospital. And the police.

Good thing everything weighs one-sixth here, Paul thought. I'm sure in no shape to play tag now.

Slowly, carefully, he forced himself to his knees, and then to his feet. The GPS signal was still coming through loud and clear. No tears in the suit. Probably saved half an hour, at least, he told himself.

He walked across the big rock. Its top was not as flat as it had looked. It was pitted here and there with small, sharp craters, almost like bullet holes.

Then Paul got to the far side. He peered over the boulder's edge. This side was much steeper than the other had been. Looks like the pissin' rock was sheared off with a big cleaver. How the hell am I gonna get down there? There's hardly anyplace for a toehold.

I could jump, he thought. Only about thirty feet. But he knew that, lunar gravity or not, a man could break bones jumping that

far. Paul recalled a couple of wise asses who disregarded the
safety regs when they had first started working on the Moon.
One broke his leg. The other, his neck. How surprised the poor
sonofabitch looked, even through the visor of his helmet. Died
before they could get a medical team to him.

So I won't jump, Paul concluded. But how the hell do I get
down? Could go back the way I came, but that'd mean I'd have
to walk all the pissin' way around this damned rock, just as if
I never climbed up here in the first place. I'll lose an hour or
more and there's not that much oxygen left.

He rummaged through the pockets on the thighs of the suit,
and in the pouches on the belt around his waist, looking for
anything that might serve as a rope. All he found was a lot
of useless junk, and a ten-foot length of hair-thin wire. It was
used to plug the suit's microcomputer into more powerful
units, when necessary.

Too short and too frail, Paul thought. But it'll have to do.

He jammed one end of the wire into the craterlet closest
to the rock's edge, then wedged it with pebbles and bigger
stones until it looked like a miniature cairn. Might mark my
grave, after all, he told himself.

'Okay,' he said aloud. 'Down we go – one way or
another.'

The wire held his weight, but as Paul cautiously edged his
way down the sheer face of the boulder, he could feel the wire
slipping out from under the rocks he had used to weight it
down. He thought about rappelling, but figured that would
just tear the wire loose even faster.

The worst part was that he couldn't see the ground from
inside his helmet. He'd have to bend over almost double to look
down and he didn't have the time or the inclination to try.

The wire felt as if it were really slithering loose. Gotta jump,
Paul told himself. If I don't—

The toe of his left boot struck a projection. A ledge, only
a few inches wide, but it felt like an interstate highway and
international jetport runway put together.

He found the ledge with his other boot and rested there for
a moment, taking the strain off the wire.

If I can just turn around, he thought. Slowly, with infinite care, he twisted his body around in a clumsy, sweaty pirouette, never letting go of the wire dangling above his head. He only got halfway turned around. The bulky backpack of his suit stopped him from going further.

Still, it was enough. He leaned over slightly, judged his distance from the ground. Still hard to see; the dust was still clinging to his visor. Looks like more than twenty feet.

Paul turned around again until he was facing the boulder once more. He felt the wire with both gloved hands. Only another foot or so of it left.

'Okay,' he said to no one. 'Just like you're jumpin' off the warehouse roof.'

He let go of the wire, got down on one knee, planted both his hands on the ledge, then lowered his other leg over its edge. He let himself dangle for a moment, hanging onto the ledge with his fingers while he swung his boots to touch the boulder's face. Then he pushed off.

And fell.

It was like a dream, he fell so slowly. He had time to calculate, I'm almost six feet tall and the ledge was twenty feet above the ground so I'm really only dropping about fourteen feet and in the one-sixth gee it ought to be okay if I don't hit another ledge or a bump or projection or—

His boots slammed onto the ground. Like a parachutist, Paul let his knees bend deeply, using all his legs to absorb the impact. He *whoofed* out a big grunt of air, clouding his visor with his breath.

But he was standing on the ground again. No broken bones. Just a little twinge in his right ankle. Otherwise everything was okay.

He took a deep breath, turned up his helmet fan to clear the fog from his visor, and started out across the plain once again.

I must've saved at least fifteen minutes, he told himself, not daring to look at his watch or make an estimate of how much oxygen might be left in his backpack tank.

The ankle hurt enough to make him limp.

BOARD MEETING

Paul's personal jet was subsonic, so he expected to arrive in New York hours later than Bradley Arnold. He had rushed from his office to the corporation's airstrip, where Joanna was waiting for him, eager to tell her about what McPherson had learned.

But before he could start to break the news to her, Joanna asked, 'Aren't all these personal planes an expense we can cut down on?'

She was buckling herself into the co-pilot's seat, on Paul's right.

'You can bring it up as new business at the meeting,' he answered, watching over the plane's stubby nose as the ground crew disconnected the towing tractor from the nose wheel.

'Perhaps I should,' Joanna said.

Paul ran up the engines, his eyes on the indicators of the control panel, amused at the no-nonsense tone of Joanna's voice. She was taking her responsibilities as a board member seriously.

'Before you do,' he said over the muted howl of the jets, 'you ought to check out the efficiency study we commissioned last year.'

He eased off the brake pedals and the plane rolled forward. Paul slipped on his headset as he maneuvered the plane toward the end of the runway. He got his clearance from the tower, pushed the throttles to full power, and the twin-jet hurtled down the runway and arrowed into the sky.

Once they were on course for LaGuardia, Paul slipped the headset down over his neck.

'I presume,' Joanna said, 'that the efficiency report says your personal planes are the only thing standing between us and utter bankruptcy.'

He grinned at her. 'Not quite. But the report does endorse the planes. Saves the top executives a lot of time, and time is our most precious commodity.'

Joanna looked unconvinced. 'Another report that says exactly what its readers want to hear.'

'The best consultants money can buy,' Paul said.

'I'm sure.'

More seriously, Paul said, 'I got a report from McPherson this afternoon.'

'About Gregory?' Joanna tensed visibly.

'He had terminal cancer of the prostate,' Paul told her. 'That's why he killed himself.'

She was silent for a long time. Paul let her absorb the information, sort out her feelings. He looked out at the clouds below, like a range of massive white mountains, but alive, dynamic, billowing up and reaching toward them. Above the clouds everything always seemed so much better, cleaner. The sun was always shining up here. The sky was always bright blue.

'Then he didn't know about us, after all,' Joanna said at last.

'Or didn't care. He had other problems.'

'He never had much of a tolerance for pain,' Joanna murmured, so low that Paul could hardly hear her over the engines. 'His own pain, that is.'

'He killed himself to end his pain,' Paul said.

Joanna nodded, her face unreadable.

Paul heard a sudden burst of chatter in his earphone. He pulled the headset back on. 'Masterson one-oh-one,' he said crisply into the pinhead microphone. 'Repeat, please.'

'One-oh-one, this is Masterson base. Paul, we just got word that Mr. Arnold's plane has gone down.'

'What?'

Automatically, Paul reached for the intercom switch on the control panel and flicked it on, so Joanna could hear the radio transmission, too.

'Arnold's plane is down. Over the Atlantic. Coast Guard's sent out search planes, but they don't expect any survivors.'

'What happened?' Paul demanded.

'Dunno. Got one Mayday transmission that said they'd lost power on both engines.'

'Holy God.'

They flew in silence for a while, Paul's mind churning. Brad's gone. That supersonic blowtorch of his has the glide ratio of a grand piano. Must have hit the water like a bomb. Cripes, what a blow!

But a part of his mind was thinking that with Arnold out of the way Greg had no one of real importance backing him on the board of directors. This strengthens my hand. A lot, he told himself.

He looked over at Joanna. She seemed lost in thought, also. Weighing the odds, he knew. Trying to figure out how the balance of power has shifted.

Just like I am.

The board meeting went on anyway. Most of the directors had come from considerable distances to attend the emergency meeting. The old days when the rich and powerful lived in or near New York were long gone. Now the directors came from Tucson and Aspen, Houston and Sarasota, Seattle and Hilo. Several had flown in from Europe and the Asian rim.

The vice chairperson, a white-haired superannuated woman who had once been the corporation's director of personnel, seemed staggered when Paul told her that Arnold was dead.

'First Gregory and now Brad,' she whispered.

She easily agreed to let Paul run the meeting. Paul thought she was eager to escape the responsibility.

Leaving Arnold's seat at the head of the table vacant, Paul convened the meeting and broke the news to the stunned board.

'My God,' said one of the older directors, his hair white, his skin gray. 'Who's next?'

'I move that we observe a minute of silence for our late chairman,' said Greg. He sat halfway down the table, wearing his usual black business suit. He had not even glanced at Melissa, sitting at the end of the table. Paul thought that either he really did hate her now, or they were putting on a damned good act.

Once the minute of silence ended, Paul said, 'I suppose we should elect a new chairman right away.'

Heads bobbed agreement. Directors turned in their chairs, murmured to one another.

'I suggest we take a fifteen-minute break,' Paul said, 'then reconvene to hear nominations.'

They didn't even bother to vote; just pushed their chairs back and headed for the bar and snacks at the back of the meeting room. Paul saw that the directors clumped into knots of threes and fours. Plenty of whispered conversations. Plenty of sudden, desperate politicking.

Joanna came up to his side. 'Do you have a nominee in mind?' she asked.

Surprised, Paul admitted, 'No. I haven't even thought about it.'

Before Joanna could say anything more, Greg stepped between them. 'I need to talk to you,' he said to Paul, pointedly turning his back to his mother.

'You can talk to both of us,' Paul said, shifting sideways a step so that he was once more side by side with Joanna.

'Certainly,' Greg said tightly.

'So?' Paul prompted.

'You were out at the nanotech division, right?'

Paul nodded.

'Several board members want to shut it down.'

Joanna said, 'It's going to be years before it has any hope of showing a profit.'

'Just like Moonbase,' Greg snapped.

'What're you driving at?' Paul demanded.

'Just this. You vote to keep the nanotech division going and I'll vote to keep Moonbase going.'

Paul blinked with surprise. 'You'll back Moonbase?'

'If you'll back the nanotech division.'

Glancing at Joanna, Paul thought, This is the way a

corporation goes broke; everybody's got his own pet project that he wants to keep alive, so nobody kills anything and we all go down the tubes.

Almost as if he could read Paul's thoughts, Greg said, 'Kris Cardenas showed you the lunar construction demo, didn't she?'

'That's right.'

'Well, why don't we pool our interests and set up a demonstration on the Moon?'

'Demonstration of what?' Joanna asked.

'Nanotech construction,' Greg told his mother. 'Set up a construction task for the nanomachines at Moonbase. Use it to prove that we can build lunar facilities at a fraction of today's costs.'

'I don't understand,' Joanna said.

Feeling suddenly enthusiastic, Paul jumped in, 'We can send a handful of nanomachines up to Moonbase and have them construct new facilities out of regolith materials.'

'Right,' said Greg.

'Can that be done? I mean, now? Today?'

'In a few months,' Greg replied.

Paul said, 'If the demonstration works, we can cut the costs of Moonbase by half or more.'

'And prove to the world that nanotechnology has useful applications here and now,' Greg added.

Joanna looked from her son to her husband, then back again. 'Greg, that's – beautiful!'

'I think it can work,' Greg said. 'I'm *certain* it could work.'

'You might be right,' Paul admitted. 'Cripes, we could build a viable Moonbase right away and start making a profit off it within a couple of years.'

'Or sooner,' said Greg.

Joanna smiled happily. 'This is a fine idea, Greg.'

'You're right,' Paul agreed.

Greg put his hand out. 'Can we work together on this? You and me, Paul?'

Grabbing his proffered hand in his own, Paul said, 'Damned right.'

'Good,' said Greg, beaming. 'And once the meeting recon-
venes, I've got another little surprise for you.'

Paul looked at his wristwatch. 'Hey, we'd better get them
back to work.'

It took a few minutes to get the directors settled back in
their chairs around the long conference table.

'All right,' Paul said. 'Before we get into the regular
agenda, we should take nominations for the new chairman
of the board.'

Greg spoke up immediately. 'I nominate Joanna Masterson
– er, Stavenger.'

Paul stared at him.

'Second,' said the elderly woman vice-chair. She's happy
with the title she's got, Paul thought; she doesn't want any
real responsibility.

'Move we close the nominations,' Greg said.

'Second.'

Numb with surprise, Paul looked at Joanna, sitting across
the table from him. She seemed just as shocked as he was.
Automatically, he called for discussion.

'Let's go straight to a vote,' said the old man at Paul's
right.

'Let's make it by acclamation,' said the vice-chair.

'Hear, hear!'

Paul broke into a grin and got to his feet. The entire board
stood up and applauded their new chairperson. Paul went
around to Joanna and ceremonially guided her to the empty
chair at the head of the table.

The board members sat down, obviously expecting Joanna
to make a little acceptance speech. Standing there at the head
of the table, she glanced at Paul, then looked at Greg.

'Thank you,' she said, her eyes still locked on her son. 'This
is totally unexpected and a little scary.'

Paul noticed that Joanna was resting her fingers lightly on
the table top. Her hands were steady, her voice firm.

'I want you to know that I will do my very best to serve
you as chairperson of this board. I will do everything I can
to fulfill the trust you've shown in me.'

Greg's eyes were on his mother, his face blank, emotion-
less.

'The first order of business I would like to address,' Joanna
went on, 'is unity. I know my late husband's death has upset
many members of this board. And Brad Arnold's, too. But I
ask you now – all of you – to put these deaths behind us and
work together for a stronger, more productive company.'

'Hear, hear,' muttered one of the older men.

'I expect no recriminations and no accusations,' Joanna
said, still looking at Greg. 'I want cooperation and harmony.
It's useless to dwell on the past; we must look to the future.'

They all applauded, Greg the loudest of all. Paul noticed
that Joanna said not another word about Bradley Arnold, nor
did any of the other board members. Sic transit gloria mundi,
he said to himself. Gone and forgotten.

SAVANNAH

The next three months were the happiest Joanna had ever known. Her son and her husband were working together, forging a bond between them, learning to know and respect one another.

Greg dined frequently at the house. He gave up his apartment in Manhattan to live full-time in his Savannah condo. He and Paul travelled together frequently to San Jose to check the progress of the nanotech program. They had agreed that the first goal would be to have the nanomachines build a complete shelter out on Mare Nubium totally out of local raw materials from the lunar regolith.

'I think we should put the site pretty far out on the mare,' Greg suggested at one of their meetings.

Kris Cardenas arched a questioning eyebrow. The three of them were in her cubbyhole of an office, hunched around the tiny circular table she used instead of a desk.

'If anything goes wrong,' Greg explained, 'we don't want the bugs infesting any of the existing shelters.'

'What could go wrong?' Cardenas demanded.

Paul intervened. 'I think Greg is right. This is the first time we're trying this. No harm in being a little on the conservative side.'

'But we've already programmed a temperature limit into the bugs. They won't operate at an ambient higher than thirty degrees.'

'Celsius,' Paul said.

'That's what – ninety degrees Fahrenheit?' Greg asked.

'Eighty-six,' said Cardenas. 'So the bugs can't work or

multiply on the surface during the lunar daytime. Even if they somehow started to spread, you'd have two weeks of lunar night to dig 'em up and get rid of them.'

'Still,' Greg insisted, 'we ought to put the demonstration some distance away from existing facilities. Don't you think so, Paul?'

'I guess so. No harm being careful.'

Cardenas looked more angry than hurt. 'You guys act as if we're in a Frankenstein mode. We're using assemblers here, y'know, not gobblers.'

'Still,' Paul said, 'the test site ought to be remote enough so that if anything does go wrong—'

'It won't,' she snapped.

'If something unforeseen happens,' Paul went on, 'it'll happen far enough out in the boondocks so none of the existing tempos'll be threatened.'

'Tempos?' Cardenas asked.

'That's what the shelters are called,' Greg explained. 'They're supposed to be temporary shelters.'

She blinked those deeply blue eyes. 'They've been in use for nearly ten years, some of them, haven't they?'

'That's right,' Paul said.

'Some "temporary."'

With a tight smile, Paul said, 'When the history of Moonbase's first hundred years gets written, you'll see that they're temporary.'

'I should live so long,' Cardenas muttered.

'I thought your nanobugs were going to allow you to live a thousand years or so,' Paul teased.

'Once the friggin' FDA lets us start using them in human patients, they will.'

Greg leaned back in his chair and steepled his long, sensitive fingers in front of his face. 'Do you mean that you wouldn't inject nanomachines into yourself if you thought they could improve your medical condition, just because the FDA hasn't approved them?'

'If we had bugs that I knew would protect me from tumors or keep my arteries from clogging I'd swallow 'em in a hot second,' she said. 'But we haven't progressed that far yet, and we can't make much more progress on the medical end until we get an FDA okay to do human trials on the simple stuff we have developed, y'know.'

Greg looked thoughtful. 'So the medical work is on hold.'

'Right.'

'But you're making progress on the toxic waste bugs.'

'The gobblers? For sure.'

Greg nodded as if satisfied.

That evening Paul invited Cardenas and Greg to dinner at the Stanford Court, in San Francisco. She showed up with her husband, whom she introduced as the finest neurosurgeon in the Bay area.

Paul shook hands with Pete Cardenas. He was as slim as a dancer, his skin a shade darker than Paul's own. His given name must really be Pedro, Paul thought.

'So this is where you get your medical inputs,' Paul said.

'Is that supposed to be a pun?' Kris asked, pretending suspicion.

Paul felt his mouth drop open. 'I didn't mean—'

Greg guffawed. It was the first time Paul had seen his step-son actually relaxed enough to laugh out loud. And it has to be at my expense, he groused inwardly. But it was good to see that the kid at least knew how to laugh.

Greg had come into the dining room alone, even though Paul had urged him to bring a date. They had talked about it during the helicopter ride from San Jose.

But Greg had said, 'You're not bringing a date, are you?'

'Hey, I'm a married man,' Paul had replied.

'Yes,' Greg had said. 'That's right, isn't it?'

With the two men in her life working shoulder-to-shoulder, Joanna put her energies into her new position as chairwoman of the board of Masterson Aerospace Corporation.

To her surprise she found that she enjoyed the work. And the newfound respect that Masterson's employees gave her. Before, when she happened to visit the corporate offices, she was the boss's wife. Now, she was chairwoman of the board.

She couldn't exactly fire people, but she could see to it that they were fired by others.

All her life she had been the reflection of the men around her. As her father's daughter she had been one of the brightest young lights in Savannah's social scene: a fine catch for some worthy young man. Her father had married her off to Gregory Masterson II, who had a bright future ahead of him as the heir to Masterson Aerospace. Joanna's marriage saved her father's failing fortune; Masterson money propped up the old man's final years.

Then she had been the wife of Gregory Masterson II, outwardly a happily-married woman with not a trouble in the world. Except that her husband drank and whored and had the business sense of a butterfly combined with the stubbornness of a jackass. And a mean streak that could cut deep without ever raising a hand. Joanna was a leader of Savannah society – but she knew the whispers that trailed behind her back. Gregory slept with any and every woman he could get his hands on. She bore it with as much dignity as she could pretend to, not knowing what else she could do.

She was the mother of Gregory Masterson III, and the thought of how devastating to her son would be a bitterly-contested divorce stayed her hand for years, for decades. She lived for her son and tried to raise him to be the kind of man she had hoped her husband would be.

And then she met Paul Stavenger and her life turned upside-down. For the first time she let herself be loved, wonderfully, excitingly, foolishly loved by another man.

It had almost turned to ashes. Gregory's suicide and Greg's almost insanely jealous accusations had nearly torn her apart. But now Greg and Paul were working harmoniously together. Greg had finally accepted his father's suicide and his mother's new marriage.

Joanna hesitated to tell Greg that she was expecting a baby. Paul's son. Several times she had been on the verge of telling him, and each time she refrained. Wait, she told herself. Give his relationship with Paul a little more time to ripen. The two men are getting along so well together, don't throw this at Greg. Not yet.

In the meantime, she found that she enjoyed being chairwoman of Masterson's board of directors. She was a person in her own right now. Not a wife or a mother but chairwoman of the board. She was determined to be the best board chairperson Masterson had ever known.

Joanna threw herself into a complete review of the corporation's product lines. The Clipperships were the only profitable products Masterson had, although the prospects for the Windowall TV screens looked extremely bright. Still, she could see from the marketing department's forecasts that there was a disaster curve looming about three years ahead. New orders for the rocket vehicles were going to taper off dramatically in three years.

Sales of the Clipperships will have saturated the market by then, the reports told her. The corporation will have sold as many as the world's airlines wanted or felt they needed. Sales would dwindle terribly.

What then? Joanna asked herself. The other divisions – commercial aircraft, electronics, and satellite manufacturing – were barely holding their own in very competitive markets. The Windowall development might be the salvation of the orbital manufacturing group, but the nanotechnology division and Moonbase were deeply in the red and showed no prospects of profitability for years to come.

Unless Greg and Paul can pull a rabbit out of the hat with their lunar nanotech demonstration. She knew Paul's reasoning by heart. If Moonbase can be developed into a viable resource center, the costs of orbital manufacturing will drop by a factor of twenty. The two will be synergistic: as the manufacturing facilities in Earth orbit grow more profitable, their demand for raw materials will make Moonbase more profitable, too.

She looked up from the charts on her computer screen. And if we can use nanotechnology to build Moonbase faster and more cheaply, the nanotech division will begin to find markets on Earth, as well.

But it's such a gamble, Joanna knew. It's piling one shaky

bet on top of another and even a third. With that disaster curve waiting for us, just three years down the road.

She spent weeks thinking about the problem, discussing it with division managers and other members of the board of directors. She consulted experts from outside the company in finance, marketing, even forecasters of technological trends.

She did not tell either Paul or Greg what she was doing. They were happily working together and she had no intention of interfering or upsetting them.

Slowly, over many weeks, she gathered together a picture of what a prudent corporate leader would do. Sell off the divisions that were still marginally profitable, divisions that still had some market value. Drop the divisions that were not profitable. Lay off as many employees as you had to and downsize the corporation.

The only viable market that we can depend on, three years from now, is selling parts and maintenance services for the Clipperships. Maybe the Windowalls, but it's too early to bank on that. We should be preparing the corporation for a smaller market, trim off all the excess fat and get ready for some leaner years. Ten years from now there will be a market for Clipperships again: new, bigger, more efficient Clipperships. But we've got to be able to last through the lean times in between then and now.

She knew Paul would never go for it. Would Greg? A few months ago he would, but now he seems completely on Paul's side, ready to risk everything for the sake of this nanotech demonstration on the Moon.

Joanna mentally counted up the votes on the board of directors. If I suggest a downsizing plan it would pass, she realized. It would also break Paul's heart and ruin our marriage.

But it would save Masterson Aerospace Corporation.

MARE NUBIUM

The damned ankle really hurts.

Paul limped along, trying to make up for the time he had lost by drifting off course. Like being on a pissin' treadmill, he grumbled to himself. You keep humpin' along but you aren't getting anywhere. That's why he had never liked gyms or exercise equipment, even when he had first pulled duty on the old space stations that hung in zero gee and exercise was required every day.

Get my exercise in bed, Paul had bragged. Keep my heart in good shape nature's way. Keep my whole system pumpin' good. Yeah.

He was panting now and that was a bad sign. Exhaustion. How long have I been out here? He lifted his left arm as he staggered along, but between the dust clinging to his visor and the blurriness of his vision he could not see the figures on the digital clock clearly.

Long enough, he said to himself. Too long.

One foot in front of the other. But the ankle really hurts. Can't be a fracture, I wouldn't be able to put any weight on it. Chipped bone, maybe. More likely a sprain. But a sprain shouldn't hurt so much when you walk on it, should it? At least it makes me stop fussin' the chafed heel on the other foot.

He remembered his grandfather's grumbling remedy for a headache: 'Drop an anvil on your toes.'

It's really hot. Pissin' suit's cooling system must be breaking down. Feels like I'm draggin' my ass across the Sahara Desert. Worse. At least there you have air to breathe.

A pang of fear raced through him like an electrical current. How much oxygen is left? How much time do I have?

He coughed. His throat was dry and scratchy as sandpaper. No more water left. Oxygen running out. Suit's filling with carbon dioxide. I'm gonna choke to death on my own pissin' fumes.

Keep moving! he screamed at himself. Long as you can move you've got a chance. You must be getting close to the tempo. It's gotta be near here. Keep pushing.

The only good news was the chirping of the GPS signal in his earphones. Guide me in, you noisy little bird, Paul prayed silently. Keep talkin' to me, you pile of germanium. Sing me a song.

He coughed again. Gettin' hotter in here. No water left.

He stumbled on a loose rock and went down face first. Long years of training and experience took over and Paul put out his gloved hands, let his arms flex when they touched the dusty ground, and pushed himself to a standing position again.

And saw, through his fogged and dust-smeared visor, a single red light glowing just above the abrupt horizon.

It's a mirage, he told himself. You want to see it so pissin' bad your brain is painting stupid pictures for you.

But then he thought, there's no mirages on the Moon. Least, I never heard of one.

Blinking, limping, he stared at the red beacon. That's the kind of light they put on top of an antenna mast at the tempos.

'That's the tempo!' he shouted, his voice cracking into a choking, hacking cough.

He heard somebody cackling weirdly. Funniest thing in the world if you ran out of oxygen within sight of the tempo. Funniest thing in two worlds. Man, you could die laughing.

SAVANNAH

Looking back on it, Joanna realized it was inevitable that Paul would insist on going to the Moon for the nanotech demonstration.

'You don't have to be physically there,' she told her husband, time and again.

'But I want to be,' Paul always countered.

Joanna tried every tactic she knew.

'You are much to valuable to the corporation to go running off to the Moon just to watch a demonstration project.'

Paul grinned at her. 'Don't worry, Madam Chairperson; I'm well insured. The corporation won't get hurt financially if something happens to me.'

'But what about me? What about our baby?'

He hesitated at that. But then, 'This is *for* the baby. Don't you see? I want this demonstration to succeed. It's got to succeed! The whole future of the corporation depends on it.'

'It will succeed or fail whether you're there or not,' Joanna insisted.

'Maybe.'

'You've got a God complex!' she accused.

He shook his head, very seriously. 'If I stay here and the demo screws up, I'll blame myself for not being there to make sure it goes right.'

'That's a God complex,' Joanna pointed out.

'That's an experienced executive,' Paul retorted. 'The crew always works better when the captain is on the bridge. Don't you know that?'

'Sheer machismo.'

Since Greg was working so well with Paul, she turned to her son for support.

To her surprise, Greg agreed with Paul. 'I think he ought to be there. This is a crucial experiment and we've got to do everything we can to make sure it comes out right.'

His newfound professional demeanor surprised and pleased her – except that his position on the matter was opposed to her own.

At dinner one evening at the house, Paul suggested that Greg go to Moonbase with him. 'You've never been up there. You ought to see it.'

'You want me to go with you?' Greg asked. He looked as surprised as Joanna felt.

'Sure,' said Paul. 'Why not?'

'Oh no!' Joanna said. Firmly.

Paul was bubbling with preparations for the coming trip to Moonbase. *He wants to go so badly,* Joanna understood at last. *His heart is there, in that godforsaken barren desolation. Not here. Not with me.*

Greg, she saw, was nowhere near as enthusiastic about travelling to the Moon as Paul was.

'I'm not going to have both of you out there at the same time,' Joanna said. 'That's too much.'

Paul gave her a strange expression. Only later, much later, did she realize that he felt she was willing to let him risk his life on the Moon, even though reluctantly, but she absolutely would not tolerate her son taking the same risk.

'I'm going to Moonbase,' Paul said flatly.

'Greg stays here,' she answered.

Dinner was served in cold silence.

Days later, Greg took Paul aside at the corporate offices and said, 'I'd really like to go with you, but I can't worry my mother so much. She'd be frantic.'

Paul looked at his wife's son. He had a difficult time picturing Joanna being frantic over anything.

But he said, 'Yeah, I suppose you're right. I'll go, you stay and hold her hand.'

'I can keep in touch with you through the VR system,' Greg suggested.

With a wan smile, Paul said, 'Good as it is, virtual reality isn't the same as being there.'

Greg shrugged his shoulders. 'I agree. But it'll have to do.'

'Yeah,' said Paul.

Greg and Joanna went to the company airstrip to watch Paul depart for Florida and the Clippership launch to the space station that was the first step on his trip to Moonbase. A contingent of San Jose technicians were waiting for him at Cape Canaveral, and a man-sized container of nanomachines rested in the rocket's cargo hold.

'You're crying,' Greg said as he and Joanna watched Paul's plane take off.

'It's just the dust,' Joanna insisted, turning from the ramp outside the hangar toward the limousine that was waiting to take them home: Joanna to her house, Greg to his condo in town.

She actually saw more of her husband over the next few days than she had for weeks: Paul called her regularly from the space station and even from the transfer rocket that took him from the space station to the clutch of buried shelters that he called Moonbase.

'Well, I'm here,' Paul's image said to her from the display screen in her bedroom. 'Landed half an hour ago.'

'I was wondering when you'd call.' Joanna was sitting up in bed, a small mountain of pillows behind her. She had been waiting for his call for more than an hour, staring at the schedule for Paul's flight when his call finally came through, telling herself that it takes some time to get out of the landing vehicle and into the living quarters of the underground shelter, so it was silly to worry about him.

'Must be after midnight, your time, right?'

'It doesn't matter,' she said to the screen. 'I'm just glad you got there safely.'

There was nearly a three-second lag while her words hurtled

to the Moon at the speed of light and his response raced
back to her.

Paul broke into a big grin. 'Hey, it's a lot safer here than it
is in New York.'

Joanna forced a laugh. 'I suppose so. I'm glad you're all
right, though.'

Again the lag. Then, 'Well, I'll be here for a couple of days,
getting things set up. Then we go out to the remote site.'

'You'll be travelling by hopper?'

She noticed, while waiting for his reply, a good-looking
young woman in the background of the crowded underground
shelter. For an instant she thought it was Melissa, but no, this
woman was younger and either white or Hispanic.

'By tractor. We've got too much cargo to haul for a hopper
to lift. Had to throw my weight around to get one,' Paul said.
'They're all in pretty constant use.'

'The oxygen plant?'

Were there other women up there? Joanna wondered. She'd
have to check the files, she decided, and see who was with
Paul in those intimate quarters. Vaguely she recalled hearing
jokes about living conditions at Moonbase: something about
spacesuits built for two.

'Seems funny,' Paul was saying. 'The crew here is breakin'
their humps putting this oxygen facility together, and if the
nanobugs work right, we'll be able to pull oxy directly out of
the rocks and even make water with it.'

They chatted for nearly half an hour, always with that
annoying little delay between them. Paul looks so happy,
Joanna thought. He's in his element. He loves being there.
He's only playing at corporate business down here; what he
really wants is to be on the Moon. He feels free there.

Free of me, she thought. Free to sample the younger
women who have the same love for that frontier as he
does.

Finally she said goodnight, pleading a full schedule and the
need to get up early the next morning.

'Yeah,' Paul said, once her words reached him. 'We're
gonna have a busy day, too. Goodnight, Joanna.' Then he

hunched closer to the screen and lowered his voice. 'I love you, baby.'

And Joanna found that her eyes were misting again.

The following evening Joanna asked Greg to come to the house and have dinner with her.

'I'd love to,' her son replied. He arrived at the house with a big bouquet of flowers. 'To brighten up the place,' he said.

Faced with the choice of eating in the formal dining room or the kitchen's breakfast nook, Joanna chose the dining room. The butler used Greg's bouquet as a centerpiece on the long, polished cherrywood table, and set their two places with Joanna at the head of the table and Greg at her right.

'So how's he doing up there?' Greg asked as they spooned their soup.

'I haven't heard from him all day.'

'He must be awfully busy.'

'Yes. Of course.'

'He'll call later. They're on Greenwich time up there. All the space facilities are.'

'I know.'

'So it's . . .' Greg pressed a stud on his wristwatch, '. . . God, it's almost one in the morning there!'

Joanna's eyes widened briefly.

Quickly, Greg said, 'If he's out at the remote site, maybe the communications link isn't there for a transmission to Earth.'

'He could relay a call through,' Joanna said.

'If anything had happened, we'd hear about it right away,' Greg said. 'There's nothing to worry about, really.'

With a weary sigh, Joanna said, 'He knows I worry about him every time he goes into space. To him it's fun, exciting. But it frightens me so!'

'He should have called you,' Greg agreed. 'It's not very sensitive of him to leave you here worrying about him.'

Joanna studied her son from across the dining table. Greg's a grown man, she told herself. He's matured so much in the past few months. Could he take the reins of the company if anything happened to Paul? Could the two of us handle all that responsibility?

'There's no reason to be frightened,' Greg was saying. 'After all, Mom, you went to the space station with him, didn't you?'

'Once,' she said.

'It wasn't so terrible, was it?'

'I was sick as a dog every minute,' Joanna said.

Greg laughed. 'Really? I heard rumors about that but I didn't believe them. I guess it wasn't much of a honeymoon for you, then.'

'Did you tell Melissa to seduce Paul?' Joanna blurted, surprised to hear herself ask.

Greg flinched with surprise. 'Tell Melissa? Me? I wouldn't even speak to the bitch.'

'Do you really hate her that much?'

His face twisting, Greg snarled, 'She was one of Dad's concubines. Did you know that? Then she switched to Paul. And then she came on to me. She's nothing but a slut.'

'You told me that she wanted your baby,' Joanna said. 'Perhaps she really loved you.'

'Love? What's love got to do with it? It's nothing but her biological clock ticking. She'll have a baby with whoever she can talk into bed. Maybe she'll have Paul's baby.'

'I'm having Paul's baby,' Joanna whispered.

His mouth dropped open. His eyes flared. 'What did you say?'

'I'm pregnant. You're going to have a brother.'

Greg's face went white. Trembling visibly, he pushed his chair away from the table and tried to stand up. The effort seemed too much for him.

'You . . . you're going to have his baby?' Greg was panting as if he had run a thousand meters. 'His baby?'

Joanna nodded solemnly.

'Abort it! Get rid of it!'

'I can't do that.'

'You can't have his baby,' Greg seemed about to dissolve in tears. 'Don't you see? It's the last straw! The final nail in my coffin.'

'No,' Joanna said. 'It won't be like that.'

'The hell it won't! He'll want to give the corporation to his own son, not to me!' Greg howled. 'He'll push me out of the way, and you'll help him!'

Just then the butler came in with the main course.

'Get out!' Greg screamed at him. 'Get out of here!'

Wide-eyed, the butler looked to Joanna. She nodded and he disappeared back into the kitchen.

'Greg, dear,' she said soothingly, 'try to calm down. This isn't going to change anything between us.'

'It changes everything!' he snapped. 'I got Brad out of the way just to make sure. But what good is that now?'

'What do you mean? What are you talking about?'

'His baby! You're going to give him a son so he can get rid of me once and for all. He murdered my father and now you're helping him to kill me! Even after he's dead he'll still be killing me!'

Greg lurched to his feet, swung one fist across the table and knocked china and glassware crashing to the floor. Joanna jerked with sudden fear. Her son was standing over her, fists clenched, murderous rage boiling through him.

'I knew *he* was out to get me, but I didn't think you would help him!'

'No one's out to get you, Greg,' Joanna said, fighting to keep her voice calm. 'Now sit down and—'

'You're all against me! All of you! Brad, him, even you. But you'll see. I'm smarter than he is. Smarter than all of you. He'll never come back to you. Never! I'm going to be the master here, not him!'

He reached over the table and grabbed the vase with his flowers. 'I'm going to *destroy* him. Like this!' And, raising the glass vase over his head, he smashed it on the table top. It shattered into bits, water and flowers exploding from it.

Joanna sat there, paralyzed with shock and fear. Greg's insane, she thought. He's homicidal.

Shaking his fist at her, Greg bellowed, 'He's not coming back to you. He'll never leave the Moon. Never!'

Terrified, Joanna gasped, 'What are you talking about?'

'You'll see,' he repeated. 'You're either with me or against me now. You've got to decide. You get rid of my little brother and we can live just as happy as we were before Paul took you away from me. Otherwise . . .'

Joanna stared at her son, barely recognizing this wild-eyed maniac who stood over her so threateningly.

Abruptly, Greg strode out of the dining room, turning at the doorway to shout, 'It's your decision. Him or me.' Then he left.

Joanna realized the butler was standing at the doorway to the kitchen, white-faced. She shooed him back into the kitchen.

What have I done? Joanna asked herself, looking over the dripping shambles of the dining table. I worked so hard to bring them together and now . . .

Greg's gone insane. He hates me because I'm going to have Paul's baby.

Paul wants to be on the Moon and Greg hates the sight of me, Joanna said to herself. I'm all alone. They'll both leave me and I'll be all alone.

No, she realized. Not alone. I have a new life within me. I'm not alone.

MARE NUBIUM

Like a madman Paul tottered on toward the glowing red beacon atop the tempo's communications mast. Dragging his bad leg, staggering, gasping the last fumes of oxygen left in his tank, he pushed himself single-mindedly toward the safety that lay so tantalizingly just beyond the short lunar horizon.

It's just over the horizon, he told himself. You can make it. Just over the horizon.

You know what the horizon is? taunted a voice in his head. An imaginary line that recedes as you approach it.

World peace is just over the horizon. Fusion energy is just over the horizon. The answer to all your prayers – just over the pissin' horizon.

Through his smeared, fogged visor Paul saw that beckoning red eye rising higher and higher. He could not make out the mast itself against the black lunar sky, but he knew that with each step he was closer to safety.

Unless it's a pissin' star, that sardonic voice jeered at him. You could be heading for Mars, for all you know.

No, dammit, it's the tempo. Gotta be.

Gotta be.

The ground was rising slightly. His right leg collapsed under him and he pitched forward again. This time he put out his hands as usual, but didn't bother to push himself up to a standing position. Crawl, man. Like a little baby, down on all fours. You can make it. Just crawl right along.

He was getting dizzy, his vision blurring. Man, what I wouldn't give for just a ten-minute break. Even five minutes.

Wouldn't work, though. Not unless you can hold your breath for five minutes.

Suddenly he wanted to laugh, remembering a conversation with McPherson back when he had first become a division manager. The lawyer wanted Paul to make out a will. He seemed surprised that Paul had never had one.

'You've got to make arrangements for handling your estate,' McPherson had said, very serious.

'That's easy,' Paul had told him. 'I want to spend my last cent with my last breath.'

Coming up on your last breath pretty soon, he knew. If you're lucky – damned motherhumpin' shitfaced lucky – you'll suck up the last oxygen molecule in the tank the instant you get inside the tempo's airlock.

It almost worked out that way.

Paul looked up from his crawling and saw the mound of rubble that marked the buried shelter. He could even see the comm mast, he was so close. No hopper, though. Only a tractor sitting outside the airlock on four ludicrously thin, springy wheels.

Who gives a flyin' fuck? he said to himself as he pushed himself to his feet and staggered, limped, hopped on his one good foot, holding his breath, reaching out with both hands and flopped into the open airlock that stood in front of the buried shelter.

He pounded the yellow-glowing phosphorescent button that activated the lock. The outside door creaked shut, although Paul could hear no sound in the lunar vacuum. He imagined the creaking as the curving door slid shut on its track, grinding stray dust particles in its path.

Bracing himself inside the phonebooth-sized airlock, Paul heard the hissing of air and even the chug of the pump. Most beautiful sounds in the world, he thought. Beats Duke Ellington any day.

The overhead light went on and the indicator panel's green light glowed to life. Trembling, hoping this wasn't the last hallucination of a man dying of oxygen deprivation, Paul fumbled with the catch of his visor and slid it up.

Sweetest air in two worlds.

He took deep lungfuls of the stuff. Next sonofabitch complains about canned air is gonna get my knuckles in his mouth, Paul promised himself.

The indicator pad told him the pressure in the airlock was high enough for him to open the inner hatch. He knew he should clean the suit first. Must be carrying six hundred pounds of dust on me.

But he was too tired, too exhilarated, too anxious to get inside the shelter and out of this foul-smelling suit even to begin vacuuming.

He opened the inner hatch, clumped in his boots down the steps into the shelter's single compartment, wincing every time he stepped with his right foot.

It was a typical temporary shelter. A long aluminum cylinder that had been laid down in a trench scooped out by a bulldozer and then buried beneath a couple of feet of loose regolith rubble to protect it from the meteoroids that pelted the Moon's surface and the harsh swings of temperature from daylight to night. And from the radiation pouring in unimpeded from deep space.

Radiation. Paul wanted desperately to flop on one of the lovely, beckoning bunks that lined the far end of the shelter, but he knew he had to worm himself out of his suit first. And check his radiation patch.

It seemed to take hours, removing the helmet, then the backpack, the gloves, boots, leggings and finally wriggling out of the suit's torso. The dust was thick enough to make him cough. Hope it doesn't foul up the air vents, Paul thought.

His radiation patch had turned yellow. Not good, but not as bad as red would have been.

Hey, you're alive and safe with nothing worse than a sprained ankle and a radiation dose that'll take a year or so off the ass end of your life. Count your blessings, man.

He limped to the nearest bunk and flopped onto it. But before he could close his eyes he thought of Greg.

I'm not home free yet. He might still win this.

I should have known he'd try to kill me. All those weeks of

his smiling and working with me. Started when I agreed to the nanotech demonstration. He's hated me all along, every inch of the way. I should have known.

Ought to call the base, get them to patch me through to Joanna. The kid's tried to kill me. Already murdered Tink and Wojo. I ought to warn Joanna. He might turn on her, try to kill my child.

But he was too exhausted to do anything but close his eyes and sleep.

ALPHONSUS

Paul had been in good spirits when he arrived at Moonbase.

The transfer spacecraft that took him from the space station in low Earth orbit to the giant crater Alphonsus was an ungainly collection of tankage, antennas, cargo containers and a spherical passenger module with two bulbous observation ports. With its spindly, spraddling legs the craft looked like a huge metallic spider about to pounce on some hapless insect.

As the lander literally fell toward the Moon's surface, Paul commandeered a spot at one of the observation ports and hung there weightlessly, watching Alphonsus rush up at him. The crater's ringwall mountains looked deceptively soft, tired and slumped from eons of erosion by dust-sized meteorites that sandpapered their slopes to almost glassy smoothness.

It was hard to get any sense of scale staring out at the barren, pockmarked face of the Moon. He knew Alphonsus was more than seventy miles across, a crater big enough to swallow all of Greater New York, from Newark to Bridgeport. But as he hovered in free fall, watching, it merely looked like a big circle of mountains with a dimple in its middle.

The floor of the crater was cracked, criss-crossed with sinuous rilles. Once in a while a whiff of ammonia or methane or one of the noble gases would seep out from the Moon's deep interior through those cracks. It was one of the reasons Moonbase had been sited inside Alphonsus's circling mountains: one day they would drill for the methane and ammonia, valuable sources of life-supporting volatiles.

Paul saw the unfinished oxygen plant and a crew of construction technicians milling around it like spacesuited ants.

Oxygen was the most valuable resource of them all, in space. If Moonbase ever became profitable, it would be by selling oxygen to the factories and other facilities in Earth orbit.

The spacecraft tilted over so that it could land on its rocket exhausts, and the lunar landscape shifted out of Paul's view. Clasping the handgrips on either side of the port, he felt the slightest of pressures, just a gentle nudge. And then the soft thump of landing. Weight returned, but it was only a sixth of the weight he felt on Earth. This was the Moon. Paul felt as if he were returning home.

It took less than ten minutes for the spacesuited ground crew to connect the flexible tunnel to the lander's hatch. I wish the ground crews at commercial airports worked so fast, Paul thought as he made his way, slightly bent over, through the ribbed tunnel and into the main entrance of Moonbase.

It was hardly grand. Moonbase consisted of a dozen 'temporary' shelters, each buried beneath piles of regolith rubble and interconnected by tunnels barely high enough to stand in. The tempos, developed out of modules for space stations, reminded Paul of mobile homes: long and narrow, cramped and confining, buzzing with electrical machinery and the constant rattle of air pumps, lit by ghastly overhead fluorescents that made everyone's complexion look sickly, smelling of sweat and machine oil and microwaved fast food and too many people crowded too close together.

Paul loved it.

Wojo was at the receiving desk, checking out the cargo that the lander was unloading, his computer screen split between the invoice list and a camera view of the spacesuited ground crew hauling out the crates from the lander's cargo platforms.

'So you've decided to come live with the proletariat for a while,' Wojo said pleasantly. He was a bulky man, big in the shoulders, with a beer gut and the glittering eyes of a seeker after truth. Roughly Paul's age, Wojo's hair and ragged beard were already dead white and thinning. He insisted that it was from the radiation dosage he received when he worked out on the lunar surface.

'How're you doing, Wojo?' Paul asked, sliding his one travelbag from his shoulder and letting it thump softly on the plastic flooring.

'Still trying to get those narrow-minded bean counters in the insurance office to admit that the company owes me premium pay,' Wojo grumbled, not taking his eyes from his display screen.

It was an old, old argument. Wojo demanded compensation for his tractor maintenance work out on the surface, over and above the hazardous duty pay called for in his employment contract.

Paul had steered clear of the fight while he'd been Wojo's division manager. Now that he was CEO he feared that the man would ask him to intervene.

But Wojo had not done that, so far. 'They got a new manager in the so-called human resources department. A man so narrow-minded he can look through a keyhole with both eyes.'

Paul laughed. 'You don't like him?'

Wojo looked up and gave Paul a withering glance. 'He tells lies, his feet stink, and he don't love Jesus.'

'Yeah,' Paul said. 'You don't like him.'

'He'll make a ton of money for you. He's so tight-fisted his palms have never seen the light of day.'

Paul made his way past the receiving desk before Wojo could ask for any favors. Jinny Anson, pert and blonde and feisty, directed him through the tunnels to the sleeping quarters they had reserved or him.

'I tried to find you a corner that's at least a little quieter than most. No snorers on either side of you, and you can barely hear the pumps.'

'Thanks,' Paul said. 'I appreciate the special treatment.'

'Nothing but the best for our new CEO.'

'You're just trying to butter up the boss,' he kidded. Yet he realized that this was the first time the CEO had visited Moonbase.

Jinny led him through two of the interconnected shelters, down another tunnel, and along the narrow central passageway of a third tempo. She's a chipper little handful, Paul thought. Fills out her coveralls in all the right places. Then he frowned inwardly. Cut that out. You made a promise to Joanna and you're gonna keep it. Yeah, he agreed silently. But it won't be easy.

'How's the air recycling plant going?' Paul asked, trying to put his focus on business.

'Humming along fine,' Jinny replied. 'Getting close to eighty percent efficiency. Gimme another few months and I'll have the loop closed good, I betcha.'

'Really?'

'Uh-huh. Then we'll only need new oxy for what leaks through the airlocks, little stuff like that.'

'Good.'

They stopped at the last partition; Paul saw his name neatly printed on the card alongside the doorway. And Lev Brudnoy's name on the partition across the narrow corridor.

He doesn't snore, Paul thought, but he grunts a lot during the mating season. Which is always, for him.

'Not quite an executive suite, huh?' Jinny said, pulling back the accordion-fold partition to reveal a standard habitation compartment, one hundred ninety-six cubic feet that had to serve as sleeping quarters and office. No bigger than anyone else's quarters.

On a space station, in zero gee, a hundred ninety-six cubic feet was almost generous. Here on the Moon it came close to inducing claustrophobia.

Paul shrugged and gave the standard line, 'Beats sleeping outside.'

'Not by much,' Jinny replied with the standard counter.

He could smell a soft flowery fragrance. 'How do you stay so fresh in these sardine cans?'

She smiled prettily. 'I just took my weekly shower a couple of hours ago. In your honor. Ask me again in a few days.'

A vision of her lithe body glistening with sweat filled Paul's mind for an instant. 'Pheromone heaven,' he muttered.

'More like pheromone hell,' Jinny said. 'Head colds are a blessing around here.'

Paul mumbled, 'Yeah. Maybe so.'

'My cubbyhole's at the other end of this row,' she said, grinning. 'In case you get lonely.'

'I'm a married man,' Paul said quickly, thinking as he spoke that it sounded terribly nerdy.

Jinny's grin turned saucy. 'Well, just in case . . .'

Paul thanked her for the escort service and shooed her off, then went into his compartment, dropped onto the bunk, and immediately went to the desktop computer to call Joanna. But he was thinking of how pleasing it would be if Jinny really buttered up the boss; or vice versa.

'I just don't trust machines I can't see,' Wojo grumbled.

Paul and the tractor teleoperator were sitting in the galley, hunched over Paul's hand-sized computer.

'If these things work we can let them do all the construction out on the surface and you can sit down here in comfort and count your insurance benefits.'

Wojo fixed him with a baleful stare. The man's breath smelled terrible. Like the exhaust fan from a brewery, Paul thought. But where in the hell would he get beer up here?

'Just how smart are these slime-sucking bugs?' Wojo asked.

'Like ants,' said Paul.

Wojo scratched at his shaggy beard. 'Read a book once—'

'No!' Paul pretended shock.

With a small grin, Wojo said, 'You'd be surprised what I'm capable of. Anyway, this book was about army ants in South America. Every once in a while they run amok and strip the whole festering jungle right down to the bark and bone. Don't leave anything alive in their path.'

'These bugs aren't like that,' Paul said.

'How do you know?'

Paul had to think a moment. 'Well, for one thing, they're programmed to stop functioning at temperatures above thirty degrees.'

Wojo heaved his bulk up from the spindly chair and trudged over to the thermostat on the curving wall of the galley. 'It's twenty-seven degrees in here right now. Just a smidge over eighty, Fahrenheit.'

'I thought it felt warm in here.'

Walking back to their long, narrow table and settling ponderously into the little chair across from Paul, Wojo complained, 'We need more radiator surface outside. Only way to get rid of heat is to radiate it away. You know that. I know that. But your pus-infested, maggot-brained, excrement-eating systems engineers sitting comfy and cool in their air-conditioned offices in Savannah haven't seen fit to honor our humble requests for more radiators.'

'But thermal conduction—'

'Isn't worth a thimbleful of warm spit,' Wojo said. 'We're dug in nice and deep. The rock outside our shells conducts heat about as well as a politician tells the unvarnished truth.'

'So turning the thermostats down won't help?'

With a massive shake of his shaggy head, Wojo said, 'All you'd do is put an extra load on the air conditioners and the radiators. Which we need about as much as a prostitute needs an honest cop.'

'I'll get you more radiators,' Paul said.

'Thank you kindly, sir,' said Wojo. 'Now, to get back to these mechanical viruses you brought up here with you – you say they're programmed to shut down at thirty Cee?'

'That's right.'

'All that means is that they won't work out on the surface in daylight. Even at our current level of discomfort, they could be doing whatever it is they're programmed to do in here right now. How would we stop 'em?'

'Each set of the nanomachines is programmed to utilize one type of atom or molecule. When they run out of that material, they stop functioning.'

'And what materials are these bugs programmed to use?'

Paul punched up the list on his computer.

Squinting at the small screen, Wojo mumbled, 'Titanium, aluminum, silicon – for the love of sweet Jesus, they could munch their way right through the whole body of the Moon and come out the other side!'

'No, no,' Paul insisted. 'We have other safeguards.'

'You better show 'em to me.'

Tapping on the miniaturized keyboard, Paul said, 'See, a polarizing current can shut them all down immediately.'

'Long as you can get the current to them.'

Paul looked at Wojo's grizzled face. He's being extra cautious, and he's right to look at it that way. This is so new that nobody's had any experience with it.

But he said, 'Look, Wojo, if these nanobugs work we can turn this set of tin cans into a regular palace in a couple of years. Moonbase can start making profits right away.'

'But if it doesn't work—'

'That's why we're conducting the demonstration at a remote site,' Paul said, with growing irritation. 'If anything goes wrong, it'll go wrong out there and won't threaten the base here.'

Wojo nodded solemnly. 'It'll go wrong out there, all right. With you and me twenty miles from help.'

'We'll have a hopper, for chrissake,' Paul snapped. 'We could jump all the way back here in fifteen minutes, if we had to.'

Wojo nodded. 'I suppose that's true,' he said. But he didn't sound as if his heart was in it.

Nettled by Wojo's worries, Paul spent that whole afternoon deep in conference with Kris Cardenas, back at San Jose.

Sitting on his bunk, Paul said to her image in his laptop screen, 'You can see why some of the people here are scared of the whole idea.'

'Well,' she admitted grudgingly, 'the nanomachines *are* the size of viruses. They can be carried by air currents and float around. But the Moon's airless, so—'

'The interiors of our habitation modules aren't airless,' Paul pointed out.

'Yes, but you're not using the bugs in your habitation modules, are you?' Cardenas replied sharply, her blue eyes snapping. 'You're only using them out in the remote site, twenty miles from the nearest existing shelter.'

'That's true,' Paul agreed.

'So there shouldn't be any trouble. Even if there is, once daylight comes up the bugs will overheat and shut down.'

'Can they last fourteen days in a dormant condition?'

'For sure,' she said. 'But in fourteen days you ought to be able to sweep them all up.'

Paul nodded. 'I guess so.'

Cardenas smiled prettily. 'Believe me, Mr. Stavenger, we've gone through every possible scenario in our simulations. We even rented the big vacuum chamber over at Ames to simulate the lunar environment. Nothing's going to go wrong.'

'I guess so,' Paul said again.

'Mr. Masterson has been here half a dozen times, checking out every facet of the experiment,' she added.

'Greg?'

'Yes. He's triple-checked everything. And then some.'

'That's good,' Paul said lamely, adding to himself, I suppose.

But he went hunting through the underground shelters for Lana Goodman. Moonbase's so-called permanent resident was a smart scientist, Paul knew, and had no axe to grind in the matter of nanotechnology.

He found her in the photo lab that she had crammed into the minimal space between the laundry and the shower facility.

'Nanomachines?' Goodman was peering at a strip of film through a magnifying glass. Paul saw her elfin features in profile. With the light behind her, her thinning gray hair looked almost like a halo.

Paul explained what he was trying to do, and Wojo's apprehensions.

Goodman put the film down and turned her full attention to him. 'I don't know the details, but I've heard a lot about nanotechnology. Mostly wild claims by enthusiasts and equally wild predictions of disaster by opponents.'

Spreading his hands, Paul said, 'Well, that's what I'm faced with: either the salvation of Moonbase or a disaster. I'd like your opinion on which to expect.'

'Most of what I've read about deals with the medical

applications,' Goodman said, threading the film into the developing machine.

'Medical?'

'You know, an old lady like me gets interested in nanomachines that can keep the estrogen flowing.' She winked broadly.

'Oh,' said Paul. 'I get it.'

More seriously, she asked, 'If these nanomachines don't work, are you going to close down Moonbase?'

'I don't want to do that,' Paul said.

'I don't want to go back Earthside,' said Goodman. 'So maybe I'm not as unbiased in this matter as you think.'

Scientists! Paul fumed inwardly. They never give you a straight answer. Always hedging everything with all kinds of qualifications and escape hatches. He remembered a professor of economics who complained that the government always looked for 'one-armed' advisors: those who wouldn't qualify everything by saying, 'On the other hand . . .'

'Look,' he said, 'all I want is your honest opinion about whether or not it's safe to try this demonstration.'

Goodman looked up at him. 'Twenty miles out on the other side of the ringwall?'

'Twenty-five miles, actually. The site is twenty miles out on the mare from Tempo Nineteen.'

'That should be far enough,' Goodman said. 'If anything does go wrong, it shouldn't affect us here.'

That was what Paul wanted to hear.

But before he could thank her, Goodman said, 'Let me think about it, though. Ask some people I know about it. If I come up with any problems, I'll let you know.'

'We're leaving tomorrow morning,' Paul said.

'Who's going with you?'

'Wojo.'

Goodman grinned maliciously. 'Good. He's a cantankerous old brute.'

'You two don't get along?'

'I've been chasing his bod for months now, and he keeps eluding me. I think he's scared of me.'

'Wojo?'

'Maybe he's still a virgin.'

Paul stared at her for a stunned moment, not knowing whether she was serious or joking.

'Life's not easy up here for a horny old lady,' Goodman said, with only the slightest of smiles. 'Lots of nice young men, but they look on me like their grandmother. Wojo's more my age.'

'Yeah,' Paul said weakly. 'I suppose he is.'

Then he beat a hasty retreat, leaving Goodman grinning at his departing back.

TRACTOR FOUR

Paul was surprised to see Hi Tinker suiting up in the preparation chamber next to the airlock.

Three walls of the cubicle were lined with spacesuits standing on racks like displays of medieval armor. Helmets rested on shelves just above the empty suit torsos, boots on the plastic flooring next to the leggings.

Tink was already in his leggings and boots when Paul came in. He was an amiable Canadian from Toronto, lean and lantern-jawed, with a dry sense of humor and a maddening propensity for puns.

With a lopsided smile he told Paul, 'Wojo's outside already, checking out the tractor.'

'Good,' said Paul, going to the medium-sized suits.

'These nanomachines really worry him, you know.' Before Paul could reply he went on, 'You might say the bugs are bugging him.'

Paul ignored the pun. No sense encouraging the man. 'What're you suiting up for?' he asked, stepping into the leggings of the newest-looking suit he could find in his size.

'I'm going with you.'

'You are?'

Tinker nodded. 'You can use a third set of hands to set things up, and I want to scout the territory out on the mare for a telescope site.'

'What's wrong with siting a telescope here, inside the ringwall?'

'Too much radio chatter in here. I've got a grant from Caltech to look into developing a major radio telescope facility up here. It'll need someplace nice and quiet in the radio frequencies. A dome away from home.'

Why wasn't I told about this? Paul asked himself. Tinker was a consultant, not a regular corporate employee. He came up to Moonbase every three months to check out the astronomical equipment that the base operated for a consortium of universities. Still, Paul thought, if he's won a grant from Caltech I should have been informed.

Then he realized that he was the CEO now, too far above the ranks to be involved in such details. The thought stung him. Paul wanted to know every detail about Moonbase.

Aloud, he said, 'Farside would be the best place for radio quiet.'

Lifting his suit's torso over his head, Tinker wormed his arms into its sleeves and popped his head up through the metal ring of its collar.

With a grunt that might have been part laugh, he said, 'You know that, and I know that, and even Wojo knows that. But find me a university that's got the money to build a base on the farside.'

'What about the consortium?' Paul asked.

Tink shook his head sadly. 'Not even the entire International Astronomical Union can raise that kind of cabbage. When it comes to finances, astronomers are at the end of the line.'

Paul nodded, realizing that Tinker didn't make puns about his work. Be thankful for small mercies, he thought.

The two men checked out each other's suits and backpacks, then Paul followed Tink through the airlock and out onto the surface of the crater Alphonsus.

'Magnificent desolation,' Paul murmured, as he always did when he went outside.

The tired, worn ringwall mountains rose above them as far as the eye could see. Alphonsus was so wide that Paul could barely make out the tops of the peaks at the center of the crater poking above the horizon. The crater floor, cracked and rilled, seemed as dead and untouched as the first time Paul had landed here. Except for the humps of rubble marking the buried modules of the base and the angular metal framework of the oxygen plant off to the right. The ground was welted with bright cleated trails that the tractors left.

As Paul stood there, though, he saw what Moonbase could become: a whole city, domed and covered with protective rubble, to be sure, but a real city of thousands of people with open spaces beneath its wide dome and green trees and plants and grass, soaring pillars and winding footpaths and broad windows so you could look outside and see the solar energy farms and the factories open to vacuum and the spaceport where ships landed and took off on a regular schedule.

'We're ready whenever you are, boss-man.'

Wojo's voice in his earphones startled Paul out of his daydream. Turning, he saw the man standing by the tractor hatch. Wojo's spacesuit looked hard-used, grimy, its helmet scratched and dulled.

'Yeah,' he said tightly. 'Let's get going.'

It was considerably less than comfortable sitting squeezed together in the tractor's cab inside their cumbersome space-suits, but Paul knew that a stray meteoroid could crack the canopy and the cab would lose its air in seconds.

The tractor's cab was a bubble of tempered plastiglass, pressurized to the same five pounds per square inch as the spacesuits, so that in an emergency the occupants could slam down their visor helmets and go to their suit life-support systems without needing time to prebreathe low-pressure oxygen to avoid the bends.

The underground shelters also ran at five psi, for the same reason. The 'air' that the Moonbase inhabitants breathed with seventy-two percent oxygen, twenty-eight percent nitrogen. The oxygen came from the lunar regolith; until they drilled successfully for ammonia the nitrogen had to be carried up from Earth.

One of the ongoing research efforts at the base was aimed at producing a metallic glass that had the transparency of good crystal and the structural strength of steel. Someday we'll be able to ride these buggies in our shirtsleeves, Paul told himself. In the meantime, it felt reassuring to have the bulk of the spacesuit protecting him, comfort be damned. There was only one chance in a trillion of being hit by a meteoroid big enough to crack the canopy, but Paul had no desire to test the odds.

The tractor climbed laboriously up the ringwall mountain over the easiest slope, which Wojo insisted on calling 'Wodjohowitcz Pass.'

'Your name is too tough to spell for it to be used on maps,' Tinker said archly. 'It'll never *pass* the spelling test.'

Paul groaned. Wojo muttered.

Paul took over the driving chores once they got down onto the flat of Mare Nubium. Wojo stopped the tractor so they could shift places, then when they were underway again he reached carefully behind their seats and pulled out three prepackaged lunches.

'Best sandwiches this side of Chattanooga,' Wojo said proudly. 'Made 'em myself.'

Paul had to admit that they were good. One thing he had insisted on for Moonbase was top-quality food. We have to breathe recycled air and drink recycled water, but by God we'll eat decently, at least.

'Sandwiched the lunch chore in between your other duties?' Tinker punned.

It's going to be a long three days, Paul thought. Very long.

'Coming up on Shelter Nineteen,' Wojo called out, one gloved finger on the map readout glowing in the control panel's main display screen.

The man's breath stinks, Paul said to himself.

Looking straight ahead, searching for the red light atop the antenna that marked the heaped rubble mound of the shelter, Paul asked, 'What the hell are you drinking, Wojo?'

'What do you mean?'

'Water wouldn't give you a breath like that.'

With great dignity, Wojo asked, 'Are you implying that I have imbibed an alcoholic beverage?'

Tinker piped up, 'Now that you mention it, there's been a rumor about somebody running a still back at the base.'

'A still?' Paul snapped.

'An active still,' Tinker replied.

'Nothing but rumor,' said Wojo. 'Where would somebody hide a still?'

Paul had to turn almost sideways to peer around the edge of his helmet and look at Wojo's face. The man avoided his gaze.

'What do you use for ingredients?' he asked.

'Search me,' Wojo replied innocently. 'I'm no chemist.'

'There's plenty of exotic chemicals available,' Tinker said, 'from the labs and the pharmacy. From what I've heard, they might even be using some of the residual rocket propellants left in the landers' tanks.'

'This had better be a joke,' Paul muttered. 'Making booze and stealing rocket propellants isn't just criminal, it's god-damned dangerous.'

'It's a joke,' Wojo assured him.

Tinker laughed. 'We got you that time, boss boss.'

Paul made himself laugh with them. But he was thinking that a drunk could kill a lot of people very suddenly at Moonbase. *Better look into this joke when I get back.*

It was night and would remain so for seventy-five hours more. Yet the broad rock-strewn plain of Mare Nubium was clearly lit by Earthglow. Once Wojo resumed the driving chore Paul leaned as far back as he could and watched the big blue and white crescent of Earth hanging in the dark cold sky. It was in the gibbous phase, fatter than a half-Earth, glowing warm and beautiful out there.

When the Earth was in its 'new' phase, Paul could trace out the cities and highways from the lights shining in the darkened globe. But now the glare from its daylit side drowned out the night lights.

Anyway, Paul said to himself, *we've got work to do. We're not here for the sightseeing.*

'There's the spot,' Wojo said, slowing the tractor to a stop.

Paul looked at the electronic map on the control panel. The blue dot marking their location was touching the red dot marking the test site.

'Check it out with the GPS signal,' Paul said.

'Already did,' Wojo answered. 'Last fix we'll get for a while. Feeble-minded little satellite's sinking below the horizon and there won't be another in sight for a couple hours.'

Tinker helped them offload the equipment and while he and Paul set up a plastic bubble tent for their quarters, Wojo used the tractor's front blade to dig a trench big enough to hold a full-sized shelter.

'Now we see what these teeny bugs can do,' Wojo said. There were three sets of nanomachines, each sealed in an insulated cylindrical container that looked to Paul like a high-tech metallic thermos bottle. Using the tractor's communications system he established a link with Cardenas in San Jose, beaming a signal directly to a commsat in synchronous orbit above the Pacific.

The signal was weak, but Paul had Cardenas on-line as Wojo pried open the first container and gingerly carried it to the trench.

'Feel kinda like Aladdin,' Wojo muttered. 'Where's the puff of smoke and the genie?'

Cardenas took him seriously. 'You won't see anything for at least two hours,' she said. 'Just drop the container into the trench.' Paul could see tension in her face. And excitement.

Tinker spent the next two hours checking out the ambient levels of microwave radiation in the area, setting out a series of pocket-sized detectors on the dusty regolith. Wojo hauled equipment off the tractor and set up their quarters inside the plastic bubble tent.

Paul watched the trench. 'Nothing seems to be happening,' he said.

Three seconds later Cardenas's streaky image replied, 'The nanomachines are reproducing themselves. Everything's going according to the program.'

Carrying a portable communicator in his gloved hand, Paul walked over to the edge of the trench. Nothing was stirring. It's going to be a long two hours, he told himself.

Wojo came up beside him. Paul was staring so intently into the empty trench that he only noticed Wojo's presence when he heard the man's labored breathing through his earphones.

'You're out of condition,' Paul said.

'Easy thing to do, up here,' Wojo admitted.

'Better check with the medical people, let them set up an exercise routine for you.' It was a requirement in every employee's contract; if an employee did not follow the medical department's prescribed exercise regimen, it was grounds for return to Earth and perhaps even dismissal from the company.

'Right.' There were a thousand ways to evade the exercising, both Wojo and Paul knew.

Tinker joined them. 'I'm all finished with my work. Can we go home now?'

Paul ignored him.

At first he wasn't certain he actually saw it. Paul wanted to rub his eyes, but inside the spacesuit and helmet he couldn't. Yet it looked as if a tiny pool of something shiny had formed on the bottom of the trench, right where the opened container was lying. A puddle that looked almost like glassy, shining liquid mercury.

'Am I seeing straight?' Wojo asked.

'Yeah,' said Paul. 'Look! It's spreading.'

A glassy smooth film of titanium was growing across the bottom of the trench. And its sides. Fascinated, Paul watched for hours as the titanium shell slowly arched above the surface of the regolith to form a complete cylinder. Then its ends began to close.

'The next set of bugs is the real test,' Cardenas said, looking much happier and more relaxed now.

'The airlock,' Paul said. If they can build a whole airlock by themselves, they can build just about anything, he thought.

Wojo carried the second cylinder to the open doorway of the titanium shelter with a good deal more confidence than he had borne the first.

They took turns going inside the pressurized bubble tent to grab a bite of dinner. Paul could hardly tear himself away from watching an airlock assemble itself, as if by magic, literally from the ground up.

'Now give them a few hours to fill the shelter with oxygen,' Cardenas said, positively glowing once the airlock was finished, 'and you'll have a complete prefabricated, ready-to-use shelter built entirely out of native materials by my nanomachines.'

The three men slept inside the pressurized tent, in their suits. It was uncomfortable. They could not lie down; the best they could do was to lean back against rests they had brought with them, reclining at roughly a forty-five degree angle. If the tent were suddenly ruptured they could snap down their visors and turn on their backpack life support systems in a second or two.

To make it worse, Tinker either would not or could not stop making puns. Paul groaned and Wojo threatened the astronomer's life, but no matter what either of them said, Tink turned it into a maddening pun. They became very elaborate as the men prepared for sleep, climaxing with a pun based on the fact that making bowel movements in a spacesuit is a complex and miserable business.

'What we need is a special container, maybe two pints in capacity,' Tink merrily chattered away. 'I think I'll enter a class-action suit to force the corporation to supply us with special bottles for manure storage.'

'Tink . . .' Wojo growled menacingly.

Undeterred, the astronomer concluded, 'Yes, sir, that's what I'll do. Bring my request to a judge and see if he'll demand ordure in the quart.'

Before Wojo could throw anything, Paul said, 'Okay, Tink. That's enough. Not another word out of you.'

Tinker looked from Paul to Wojo and back again. The self-satisfied grin on his face faded a little. His eyes lit up as if he had thought of still another pun.

'No!' Paul said sharply, the way he would to a baby he was trying to train. Or a dog.

Tink nodded inside his helmet and pressed an upraised finger to his lips. Wojo, still looking grim, nodded his thanks to Paul.

Paul thought he would be unable to sleep, propped up inside the suit and excited about the nanomachines working away, silent and invisible out there. But he drifted off almost as soon as he closed his eyes, and if he dreamed at all he remembered none of it when he awoke a few hours later, long before his suit's alarm was set to go off.

Wojo was snoring like an asthmatic ox and Tinker was muttering in his sleep. Paul quietly refilled his backpack oxygen supply from the tanks in the tent, then slid his visor down and stepped through the tent's minimal airlock.

The shelter gleamed slightly in the Earthlight, its curved top uncovered as yet by protective dirt. Paul grappled one of the nitrogen tanks from the tractor's back and hauled it to the shelter. He examined the airlock's control panel. It was mechanical rather than electronic; rather crude but a good-enough test of the nanomachines' abilities. Cardenas had a team working on electronic assemblies, but Greg had wanted to go ahead with this test as quickly as possible and Paul had agreed with him.

He slid the outer hatch open, lugged the nitrogen cylinder inside and then stepped in himself and pulled the hatch closed. A set of four knobs projected from one side of the inner hatch. Paul turned the top one and soon heard the reassuring hiss of gas filling the airlock. Once the sound stopped he took a pressure gauge from his belt. Less than two psi, but holding steady. Oxygen pressure wasn't as high as it should be, not yet, but at least the airlock didn't seem to be leaking.

Is it really oxygen? Paul asked himself. The little portable mass spectrograph was still in the tractor. He'd have to assume the bugs were doing their work properly. For now.

Opening the inner airlock hatch, Paul stepped inside the shelter. In the light from his helmet lamp, the curving walls glistened almost as if they were wet. The pressure gauge held steady. The shelter was airtight. Paul dragged the nitrogen cylinder into the empty shelter and opened its valve. By noon tomorrow we'll be able to sit in here in our shirtsleeves, he thought happily.

'We'll eat lunch in here,' he promised himself aloud.

Paul and Tink spent the morning hauling equipment into the new shelter, while Wojo worked the tractor, carefully piling up rubble over its curving roof.

At last, a few minutes after noon, the three of them entered the shelter.

For a long moment they simply stood inside the cylindrical space. The walls still glistened as if newborn. The bunks, table and equipment they had carried in looked shiny new, never used. Tinker held the mass spectrometer in his gloved hands.

'Well?' Paul asked him.

Peering at the readout display, Tinker said, 'Seventy-six percent oxygen, twenty-four nitrogen.'

'Good enough,' Paul said.

'Pressure's just a tad over five psi,' Wojo said.

'Okay.' Paul slid his visor up and took a deep breath. 'It's not the Garden of Eden, but it'll do.'

With great relief they peeled themselves out of their spacesuits, although the stench of bodies confined inside the suits for several days was less than pleasant.

'I won't mention yours if you don't mention mine,' Wojo said, pinching his nose with forefinger and thumb.

'Okay,' Tinker answered happily. 'Let's not make a stink about it.'

Paul understood how a man could be driven to murder.

They ate lunch in their coveralls at the small table they had carried in, after heating the prepackaged meals in the microwave cooker. Tinker seemed very impressed with the nanomachines' achievement.

'We could build a radio telescope facility on the farside!' he said enthusiastically. 'These bugs are going to change everything we do up here!'

Wojo chewed his soyburger thoughtfully, then replied, 'Better make sure this shelter really works right before you go prancing off to the farside.'

'Oh, you want to work the bugs out of it?' Tinker asked, delightedly.

Wojo looked as if he wanted to spit.

*   *   *

After lunch Paul checked in with Kris Cardenas to assure her that all was going well. Then he patched through a call to Joanna. She was at home, in her sitting room.

'Are you okay?' were the first words out of Paul's mouth when he saw her stretched out on the chintz-covered chaise longue.

It took three seconds for her to smile. 'Of course I'm all right.'

'Oh, I thought maybe you didn't feel well.'

Again the delay. Then, 'Paul, it's seven-thirty in the morning here. I've been trying to call you for more than an hour.'

'Call me? Why?'

Joanna's face clouded once Paul's question reached her. 'It's Greg . . . I told him about the baby last night.'

'He wasn't pleased, I guess.'

'He got hysterical. He frightened me.'

Paul felt his insides tensing.

Joanna went on, 'He started raving about how we're trying to get rid of him, push him out of the corporation. Lord, he sounded like his father.'

'I'm not trying to push him out,' Paul said.

Joanna continued, 'He said something about getting rid of Brad. As if he did it deliberately.'

'Brad?'

Without a pause, she went on, 'And he's *furious* with you. He said he's going to destroy you. He said you'd never come back from the Moon.'

Paul saw the anguish in her face. The fear. For which of us? he wondered. Is she scared for me or is she scared that Greg's getting beyond her control?

'Paul, he's violent!'

'He didn't hurt you, did he?'

The three-second lag seemed like an infinity. At last Joanna shook her head wearily. 'No, but he was boiling with anger about you. And the baby. It was frightening.'

So all Greg's smiles and cooperation were just a front, after all, Paul thought.

He said to his wife, 'As long as he's not threatening you, it's okay.'

'He wants to kill you!' she blurted.

Paul made himself smile reassuringly. 'Well, he'll have to wait until I get back for that, won't he? He can't reach me up here.'

Joanna nodded, but she still looked fearful.

TEMPO 20(N)

Later that afternoon Paul got two warnings of danger simultaneously.

He had officially 'dedicated' their new shelter while they ate lunch, using a sprinkle of water instead of champagne to dub it Tempo 20(N): the twentieth 'temporary' shelter erected by Moonbase. The (N) designated that it had been built by nanomachines.

The three men spent the rest of the afternoon checking every square millimeter of the shelter. It was airtight. Radiation levels were well below minimums. Temperature hovered at twenty-five degrees Celsius.

They still had to use the tractor's communications gear to contact Moonbase and San Jose. There hadn't been enough capacity in the tractor to hold all the comm equipment that a shelter normally had, mainly because they had hauled the rocket hopper along with them.

Little more than a railed platform with a rocket motor beneath it, the hopper was a safety tactic, a hedge against danger. It could lift three men – and practically nothing else – as far as the next shelter, twenty miles away.

Paul was sitting on one of the bunks inside the shelter, sending the results of their checkout to San Jose, patching the link from his hand-held communicator through the tractor's comm unit. Kris Cardenas' image on the tiny screen was streaked with white hashes of snow. Suddenly it winked off altogether. Paul's portable went dead.

At that moment, Tinker came in through the airlock. He had gone outside to gather up his microwave detectors.

Sliding up the visor of his helmet, Tink said, 'Wojo's having some trouble with the tractor.'

Annoyed and puzzled at his communicator's failure, Paul looked up at the astronomer. 'What?'

'He's out there turning the vacuum blue,' Tink said, not looking particularly worried. 'Something's wrong with the tractor. I tried to give him some help, but I don't know enough about cryogenic motors.'

A tendril of fear wormed along Paul's spine. 'Maybe he needs a hand.' He got up and went for his suit.

'I think he'll need more than applause,' Tinker punned.

The suit still smelled ripe, but Paul barely noticed as he pulled it on, piece by piece. Tinker helped him into the backpack and checked all the connections.

'You are go for surface excursion,' said Tink, patting the top of Paul's helmet. The standard line sounded strange, coming from him.

Paul powered up his suit radio as he stepped into the airlock. He could hear Wojo's fervent litany of methodical, dispassionate cursing.

'. . . slime sucking, pus eating, dung dripping misbegotten son of a promiscuous Albanian she-goat and a syphilitic refugee from a leper colony . . .'

'What's the matter, man?' Paul asked, loping across the dusty ground in the gliding long low-gravity strides of the experienced lunar worker.

'Would you believe,' Wojo replied, still bent over the tractor's electric motor compartment, 'that this miserable excuse of an electrician's wet dream is completely shorted out?'

Paul had to lean far over to see the motor, inside its insulated compartment. In the light of their two helmet lamps, the aluminum coils looked blackened; some of them appeared to be bent, as if they had been pulled apart.

'What in hell . . . ?'

Wojo held up a length of narrow plastic tubing. 'Seals are eaten through. Each and every blessed seal is leaking like a busted sieve. All the nitrogen coolant's evaporated.'

'How could that happen?'

Wojo must have shaken his head inside his helmet. 'Don't know how, but it must've happened while we were sleeping. Mother-lusting motor worked fine yesterday.'

'And the back-up?'

'Same goddamned thing.'

That was the first time Paul had ever heard Wojo actually resort to blasphemy, however mild. He must be really worked up, Paul thought.

'Good thing we brought the hopper,' he said.

'Yeah,' Wojo agreed.

But the hopper was useless, too. The tubing connecting its propellant tanks to the rocket's combustion chamber was eaten through.

'It looks like it's corroded,' Paul said, completely puzzled. 'Like an iron pipe that's been left underwater for years.'

'It ain't iron and it hasn't been underwater,' Wojo muttered. 'This tubing is high-strength plastic and it looks like something's just chewed right through it.'

Gobblers! Paul's knees went weak with the realization.

'Jesus,' he moaned.

'What is it?'

'Put the tubing down!' Paul snapped. 'Drop it!'

Wojo let it fall. The length of tubing tumbled slowly and bounced when it hit the ground.

'Get away from here. Move away!'

'What's the matter, boss?' Wojo asked, his voice more flustered than fearful. 'What is it?'

'I'm not sure, but we—'

'Hey!' Wojo shouted. 'I got a leak!'

'Where?' Paul reached for the pocket in the thigh of his suit, where patches were kept.

'I can't—' Wojo's voice cut off. He started coughing.

In the light of Earthglow Paul could see the fabric of Wojo's gloves rotting away, dissolving, melting. The inner lining of metal mesh was showing through on most of his fingers.

'Get into the shelter!' Paul yelled. 'Run!'

Wojo stumbled for the airlock hatch as Paul stood between

the tractor and the hopper, immobilized by fear and the realization of what was happening.

Gobblers. Somehow gobblers have been mixed in with the nanobugs. They're eating up anything with carbon molecules in them.

Wojo was two steps from the airlock hatch when he screamed and fell face-forward to the ground. He writhed as if something was eating him alive, his screams higher and higher until abruptly they stopped altogether and he became still.

'Wojo!' Paul yelled. 'Wojo!'

The airlock hatch slid open and Tinker stepped out, fully suited.

'What the hell's going—'

He stopped and bent forward slightly to stare at Wojo, lying two paces before him.

'Did you handle any of the tubing from the tractor?' Paul shouted into his helmet microphone.

'What happened to Wojo?' Tinker started to bend down beside the fallen man.

'Get away from him!' Paul shrieked.

Tinker jerked back, staggered slightly and bumped against the open hatchway of the airlock.

Frantic, Paul demanded, 'Did you handle anything from the tractor?'

'What're you talking about? What's happened to Wojo?'

'He's dead, dammit!'

'Dead?'

Paul felt as if he had stumbled into a leper colony. He didn't want to touch anything, get near anyone.

Forcing himself to be as calm as possible, he said to Tinker, 'Something's gone wrong with the nanobugs. They've infected Wojo's suit and eaten away the insulation.'

'His suit failed?' Tinker's voice went hollow with sudden fear.

The goddamned bugs are chewing up his body, Paul knew. But there was no sense scaring Tinker more than he had to.

'Did you handle anything from the tractor?' Paul asked again. 'Or the hopper?'

Sounding confused, Tink said, 'I looked over Wojo's shoulder – God, is he really dead?'

'Did you touch anything?'

'He . . . he showed me a piece of tubing that had broken down. I looked it over.'

'Did you *touch* it?'

'Yes! Of course I touched it.'

'Get back inside the shelter and get out of that damned suit as fast as you can,' Paul commanded. 'Shove the suit into the airlock and stay inside the shelter until I can get some help here.'

'I don't understand,' Tinker said.

'Your suit's infected with nanobugs that attack carbon-based molecules,' Paul said, annoyed with the astronomer's obtuseness. 'Now *move!*'

'Carbon-based molecules? That includes me!'

'Damned right! Get out of that fuckin' suit as fast as you can!'

Tinker ducked back through the airlock at last. Paul stood frozen with terror, staring at Wojo's fallen body. His spacesuit was disintegrating before his eyes. In the soft light from Earth overhead, Paul watched as the arms of Wojo's suit slowly disappeared, layer by layer: fabric, insulation, the neoprene gastight bladder. They'll be down to his skin and flesh; like maggots.

Tinker's first scream turned Paul's blood cold. Tink either hadn't taken off his helmet, or he had left his suit radio on while he was getting out of the spacesuit. Either way, Paul heard him screaming and screaming and screaming. Wojo had died of decompression when the bugs had eaten through his suit. Tinker was devoured alive, screaming until his voice went hoarse.

Paul stood alone out on Mare Nubium, his two companions dead, the area infested with killing nanobugs, the nearest shelter twenty miles away.

Greg, he knew. Greg's done this. He's the only one who

would even think of it. Slipped a sampling of gobblers in with the assemblers. He's trying to murder me. He's killed Wojo and Tink.

I'm next. If I let him.

SHELTER 19

Paul was struggling with an invisible demon. He couldn't see it, but he could feel it clutching at his throat, tearing at his flesh. He thrashed madly, grappling with it, trying with every ounce of strength in him to push it away, to get it off him.

His eyes snapped open. Above him curved the rounded ceiling of Tempo 19. Air circulation fans hummed softly and a pump chugged faithfully in the background.

I'm safe, he told himself, lying in his sweaty coveralls on the bunk. I'm okay.

For how long?

'Long enough,' he said, his voice a grating, harsh rasp. Wincing when he put his weight on his right foot, he limped to the food freezer and microwave oven that comprised the shelter's galley. The sink was beside it. Paul took a plastic cup from the rack over it and filled it with water. He drank it down slowly; it was warm and flat and the best drink he had ever tasted. He savored it, relished it, gloried in the way it eased the sandpaper feeling in his throat.

He pulled out a plastic container of frozen soup and popped it into the microwave. Then he limped to the communications console and called Moonbase.

Impatiently he reported the deaths of Wojo and Tinker. The guy on comm duty quickly called the base's director, and Paul had to repeat the news to her.

'The nanomachines killed them?' her hard-bitten face radiated surprise, disbelief.

'And damned near killed me, too,' Paul said wearily. 'Now patch me through to Savannah. I want to talk to my wife.'

'Just a minute,' said the base director. 'I need to know a lot—'

'Later,' said Paul, putting iron into it. 'I want to talk to my wife. Now. On a private link.'

'Okay,' the director said. 'I'll put together a team to go out there and get the bodies.'

'No! Nobody goes anywhere *near* that site until I've had a talk with the San Jose troops. That whole area is quarantined as of now.'

The director's eyes went wide for a moment. Then she nodded. 'Understood.'

Paul was glad that Joanna was in her office at corporate headquarters. From the looks of the little urban park outside her window it must have been late afternoon.

She was smiling as her face appeared on the tabletop display screen before Paul, but her smile froze the instant she saw his haggard, bleary-eyed face.

'Paul, what's happened?'

He had spent twenty minutes setting up a direct laser link to Savannah. Anybody at Moonbase could tap into his transmission from the shelter, if they dared, but from Moonbase's laser to the receiver on the roof of the headquarters building, no one could eavesdrop.

'Greg tried to murder me,' he said, then waited three seconds for the shock to register in her face.

'Greg? How . . . ?'

'He put a mix of gobblers in with the nanobug assemblers. Two men were killed and he damned near got me.'

'Gobblers?' Joanna echoed.

'Nanobugs that take molecules apart. Long-chain carbon molecules. Like spacesuit materials. Like human flesh.'

Joanna gasped, 'Oh no.'

'There's a tractor outside this shelter. I'm going to ride back to Moonbase and then head home.'

He could see the conflicting emotions battling within her. 'What should I do? About Greg, I mean?'

'Nothing!' Paul snapped. 'Stay away from him. He's a murderer and I don't want him anywhere near you.'

Joanna did not reply, but Paul saw what she was thinking.
He's my son.

That's the long and the short of it, Paul told himself. I'm her husband, the father of the child she's carrying. But Greg is her son and she'll try to protect him even if he tries to kill her.

I've got get back there, he realized. Quick as I can. Got to get there and protect her.

Joanna could see the determination in Paul's exhausted face. He wants to get back here so he can accuse Greg. Greg tried to murder him.

Without consciously thinking about it, she tapped the phone console on her desk and called out her son's name. In a few seconds Greg's darkly handsome face appeared on the display screen.

'Could you come over to my office, Greg?' Joanna asked.

'I'm in the middle of—'

'Right now,' Joanna snapped. Then she added, 'Please.'

Annoyance flashed across his features, but he held it in check and answered, 'Certainly.'

He looked more apprehensive than annoyed when he stepped into Joanna's office. She had hardly changed anything in the big corner room since taking it over from Bradley Arnold. There had been no time; Joanna had been much too busy learning her new responsibilities to deal with interior decorators.

Warily, with the same expression he had worn as a little boy when he'd been caught doing something he shouldn't, Greg walked across the richly patterned Indian carpet and took the leather chair in front of Joanna's desk.

'What's happened?' he asked softly.

'I just got a call from Moonbase,' said Joanna.

His brows rose. 'Oh?'

'It was Paul. He's still alive, but the two men working with him were killed.'

Greg let out a long sigh. 'Too bad.'

'The nanomachines killed them.'

'Yes.'

'You know all about it, don't you?'

'Nanotechnology is very new, Mom. Untried. Accidents will happen.'

Joanna stared at her son. 'Paul thinks you tried to murder him.'

'That's just like him.'

'Did you use nanomachines to kill Brad?' Joanna heard herself ask.

The hint of a smile ghosted across Greg's lips. 'That pompous old fool.'

'Did you?'

Greg shifted slightly in the chair. 'When I was in San Jose a few months ago I saw a demonstration of what they call gobblers – nanobugs that can take the platinum atoms out of an old-fashioned automobile's catalytic converter.'

'What's that got to do with Brad's death?'

He shrugged carelessly. 'I've heard that jet engines have a lot of blades that are coated with platinum and tungsten and other metals. To resist heat, I think. If those metals erode away the engine blades break up.'

'And that's what happened to Brad's plane?'

'At supersonic speed a sudden loss of power can be very dangerous,' Greg said. Then he added, 'So I'm told.'

'Paul isn't dead,' Joanna said. 'He's coming back here and he's going to accuse you of murder.'

For the first time something like fear showed in Greg's face. 'He's got no proof . . .'

Joanna said, 'Don't you think he'll find proof? Don't you think he'll find someone in the San Jose division who gave you a sampling of nanomachines? What do you call them, gobblers?'

Irritated, Greg answered, 'I suppose the corporation's CEO can find employees who'll tell him what he wants to hear.'

'Greg, two men have died!'

'Three,' he said smugly, 'counting Brad. More, come to think of it: there's the crew of his plane, too, isn't there?'

She stared at her son. I did this to him, Joanna thought. It's my fault as much as his. More. I've allowed my happy little boy to turn into a sick, sick man.

'You need help, Greg,' she said.

'Yes,' he said. 'I suppose I do. Are you going to help me, Mom?'

'All that I can.'

He leaned forward in his chair. 'Then get rid of that monster you're carrying in your belly and get a divorce. You and I can run this corporation. Just the two of us. We don't need him or his spawn.'

Shocked by his sudden intensity, Joanna could say nothing except, 'I can't do that.'

'Then I'll have to kill him.'

Joanna studied his face. 'Will you kill me, too?'

He seemed surprised at the thought. 'I could never harm you, Mom. I've always tried to protect you. Even against Dad.'

'Against . . . your father?'

'He deserved to die. He even *wanted* to die. But he was too weak to do it himself.' Greg smiled the way he had when he brought home good marks from school. 'So I helped him.'

Joanna sank back in her swivel chair. Bradley Arnold's chair. Her son continued to smile at her as charmingly as the little boy who used to offer her flowers he plucked from their garden.

MARE NUBIUM

Paul was thinking how different everything looked from the driver's seat of the tractor. The barren landscape rolled by, not without jounces and bumps, but it was sure easier than walking. The tractor was a small one, without an enclosed cab. He had to keep his suit buttoned up against the vacuum. But it beat walking by about a thousand lightyears.

Up ahead he could see the tired old mountains of the Alphonsus ringwall rising to meet him. Too far away to make out the winding ruts that marked Wodjohowitcz Pass, but he'd be there soon enough. The thought of Wojo and Tink tore at his memory. He'll pay for what he did, Paul promised himself. He'll pay if I have to kill him myself. He could feel the muscles of his jaw and neck tense. Whose side is Joanna going to take? Paul knew the answer. She'll protect the kid all she can.

Some kid. He's a homicidal maniac.

The sudden shrill alarm in his helmet earphones startled him. Looking down at his forearm display he saw a red light blinking. Oxygen supply critical.

How the hell can that be? I topped off the tank before I left Tempo 19.

More annoyed than afraid, Paul followed the standard practice and plugged his auxiliary oxygen line into the tractor's standby tank. The shrilling in his earphones stopped.

What the hell happened to my backpack tank? he wondered. Or is it just a sensor crapped out?

He kept his real fear buried deep in the back of his mind. He knew it was there, knew what it was, but he didn't want to face it, deal with it, admit that it even existed.

For nearly half an hour he continued riding along the bleak, pockmarked plain. The ringwall mountains were really looming before him now. He could see the notch where they had come across on their way out.

The tractor's oxygen supply was okay, he saw with a glance at the control panel. He reached around with one hand to check the hose from his backpack tank. *Maybe it came loose, all the bangin' around I did out there.*

The plastic hose fell apart in his gloved hand. Paul felt it crumble, breaking into pieces at his touch.

He pulled his hand back as if it had been scalded. A ragged chunk of plastic was in the palm of his glove, part of the oxygen hose.

It can't be the bugs, he told himself. *I didn't touch anything that was infected. Besides, we're still in daylight; it's too pissin' hot for the bugs to work.*

Yet his insides trembled and burned.

What else could make a hose fall apart like that? Gotta be the bugs. Desperately, Paul tried to remember if he touched Wojo or anything out there when Wojo was cussing over the infected tractor. *What difference does it make?* he raged at himself. *You're either infected with 'em or you're not.*

How to tell?

He reached back again and pulled off another chunk of the plastic hose, about the size of his palm. Keeping one hand on the steering lever, he placed this new chunk of hosing on his thigh, alongside the first piece. They were roughly the same size. Satisfied, Paul placed the new piece atop the dashboard, in full sunlight. The first piece he tossed to the floor of the cab, deep in shadow.

Now we'll see.

Paul had to gear down the tractor as it began climbing the laborious winding trail that threaded through the ringwall mountains. The rounded, worn peaks averaged about ten thousand feet, but the trail notched through at least a thousand feet lower. Paul could see the tracks in the dust left by previous tractors. Like those old pioneer trails across the prairie, he thought. A hundred years later you could still see the ruts their wagons made in the ground.

Someday we'll have a monorail system to cross the ringwall, he told himself. Or maybe we'll tunnel right through the mountains. Connect the crater floor with Mare Nubium. Someday.

For now, he had to steer the tractor slowly, carefully, up the gentle mountain slope. The tracks of earlier trips faded at the higher elevation, where there was little dust to register them. The rock surface was bare and slick here, almost glassy. Paul geared down again to maintain traction.

It took more than an hour, but at last he reached the crest of the mountains. Peering over the front of his tractor, Paul could see the cluster of humps in the crater's floor that marked the buried shelters of Moonbase.

Automatically he pressed down the accelerator. The tractor surged forward. But then Paul looked down on the floor at the piece of hosing lying in the cold shade.

He stomped on the brake. The tractor slewed slightly as it ground to a stop. With trembling hands Paul reached down and picked up the scrap of plastic. He placed it alongside the other piece, still in sunlight on the dashboard.

The piece from the floor was less than half its original size.

They're here! In the tractor!

He leaned down and pawed at his dust-caked leggings. The outer fabric of his surface suit was already eaten through. His boots, too. Paul could see the metal mesh layer that underlay the fabric.

They can't get through the metal if they're designed to eat carbon molecules, he told himself. Yeah? They got through the metal in Wojo's suit. Must be different kinds. Different kinds.

He wanted to run. He felt unclean, infected, his skin crawling and his heart pounding so loud he could hear it in his helmet earphones.

And suddenly the enormity of it hit him. I'm going to die! Even if I get to Moonbase, I'll just be carrying the damned bugs with me. They'll infect the whole base, tear apart everything. Kill everybody.

That's what Greg's been after, all along! Not just me, but everything I stand for. He wants to wipe out Moonbase altogether!

Paul sat there inside his failing suit, blinking at the vision of Moonbase, everything he had worked for, everything he wanted, being utterly destroyed.

Strangely, the realization calmed him. He knew what he had to do now. There were no other options, no excuses, no escape clauses. It was finished.

At least I'm close enough to reach them with the suit radio, he thought.

Jinny Anson was at the communications desk when he called in.

'We'll send a team up to get you!' she said when Paul told her where he was.

'No!' he snapped. 'I'm infested with nanobugs and you can't run the risk of bringing them into the base. They'll kill all of you.'

'But what can we do? We can't just leave you out there. You'll . . .' Jinny's normally chipper voice faltered, went silent.

'It's too late to do anything for me. Call Kris Cardenas in the San Jose division and get her to come up here and personally lead a decontamination team to clean up this mess.'

'But what about you?'

Paul said, 'Get my wife on the line for me. Private link. No eavesdropping.'

Paul could not see Joanna's face, but he pictured it in his mind. She was beautiful. Whether she loved him or not didn't matter now. Whether she placed Greg before her husband didn't matter, either. Not any more.

'Where are you, Paul?' her voice asked. 'Why can't we establish a visual?'

'I'm out in a tractor, at the summit of the ringwall.'

He waited for her reply. 'You're on your way back to the base, then?'

'I was,' Paul answered. 'But I'm not going to make it.'

The three seconds stretched, stretched. Then, 'What do you mean? What are you talking about? How long can you stay outside?'

'For the rest of my life,' he said. 'The nanobugs are in my suit. They stopped their activity while I was in sunshine, it was too hot for them. But they must've chomped away on my suit while I was in the tempo and I can't bring them into the base; they'll eat up everything.'

Joanna was already talking before he finished, 'You *can't* just stay out there until you run out of air! They've got to get you, save you!'

'There's no way to do that,' Paul said. 'If I go down to the base I'll be killing everybody there.'

'No, Paul! No!'

'Listen to me. Be quiet and listen!' he shouted into his helmet microphone. 'It's all up to you, now. You've got to keep it all together. Don't let them shut down Moonbase because of this. This isn't an accident; we both know that. Don't let Greg or anybody else use this as an excuse to shut down Moonbase.'

He waited for her response. 'I understand,' Joanna said at last. From the sound of her voice, she was fighting for self-control. 'I'll . . . take care of everything.'

'Good,' he said, feeling suddenly bone-weary, exhausted physically, emotionally.

'Paul, isn't there anything . . . ?'

'I wish there was. I didn't want it to end like this.'

That long wait again. Then, 'I love you, Paul. I love you.' Joanna broke into sobs.

'I love you too, Jo. I guess you're the only woman I've ever really loved.'

Instead of waiting for more from her, Paul snapped off his radio. No sense dragging it out, he said to himself. We've said all we have to say. There's nothing left for either of us now but pain.

He got up from the tractor seat and clambered down to the ground. Walking to the edge of the narrow trail he looked

down once again at the pitiful heaps of rubble that marked
Moonbase.

Like Moses on the pissin' mountain, Paul thought. I can see
the promised land but I'll never get to live in it.

He thought again of what Moonbase could become, someday. He saw a future that beckoned, with humankind spreading
across this new frontier and heading outward for new worlds. A
future that would never happen if Moonbase was destroyed.

Paul sighed. 'If it is to be,' he said softly, 'it's up to me.'

With a sudden, quick move he yanked open the visor of
his helmet.

SAVANNAH

It had been two days since Joanna last slept. Most of that time she had spent on the videophone with Kris Cardenas in San Jose, making arrangements for a team to be sent to the Moon to deactivate the nanomachines that had killed her husband and the two other men.

And she made other arrangements, as well.

'I want to know who allowed those killer machines to be mixed in with the other nanobugs,' Joanna said, as implacable as an ocean tide.

Cardenas' image in the phone screen nodded somberly. 'I've already started an investigation. That kind of stupidity verges on the criminal.'

'It *is* criminal,' Joanna said. 'But I don't intend to press charges or bring the law into this. I just want to know who those people are.'

'You won't press charges?' Cardenas brightened.

'No. I want them transferred to Moonbase, once we find out who they are.'

Cardenas blinked her cornflower blue eyes. 'Why would you send them to Moonbase?'

Grimly, Joanna replied, 'So they can see the consequences of stupidity. So they can live in a place where one little mistake, one moment of stupidity, can kill you.'

'How long will they have to stay?'

Joanna shook her head. 'Until my husband comes back to life.'

She still had not slept when she had her meeting with Greg.

Joanna had decided to meet her son at the house, rather than the office. She sent two hefty security guards to escort him to the meeting.

Greg looked subdued when he stepped into the living room, flanked by the two uniformed men. Joanna dismissed them and told her son to sit on the sofa, facing her.

'You killed Paul,' she said, once she was certain that they were alone.

Greg evaded her eyes. 'Suppose I did. What of it? It's over and done with. You can't bring him back and that's that.'

Joanna studied her son. He seemed tense, but the fury that had exploded in him now was gone, spent, dissipated.

'What do you intend to do now?' Joanna asked calmly.

Greg cocked an eyebrow. 'Take my rightful place as president and CEO.'

'Really?'

He leaned forward intently, suddenly flushed with prospects for the future. 'Don't you see, Mom? Now it's just you and me, the way it ought to be. We can run everything together, just the two of us. It'll all work out, you'll see.' He even smiled that same old boyish smile at her.

'But there's not just the two of us,' Joanna said.

Greg pulled back from her slightly. 'What do you mean?'

'I'm carrying Paul's baby. Paul's son.'

'Oh, that.' Greg flapped one hand in the air dismissively.

'You don't care anymore?' Joanna asked, caught unprepared for his casual attitude. 'A few days ago you wanted me to abort it.'

'I was foolish,' Greg said. 'I wasn't thinking straight.'

'Really?'

'By the time he grows up enough to join the corporation I'll be ready to retire,' Greg said.

Be careful, Joanna told herself. He knows how to play on your feelings.

'Greg, you're a murderer.'

For an instant she saw fear in his eyes. But then his smile returned. 'Are you going to turn me over to the police?'

'I'm getting the names of the people who allowed those

killer machines to be sent off to the Moon. They'll implicate you to save themselves.'

'So you *are* going to hand me to the police, after all.'

Joanna shook her head. 'I should,' she said. 'But I can't. I can't hurt you more than you've already been hurt.'

'I knew it!' he said triumphantly. 'It's going to be just the two of us! I knew it would work out this way!'

'Greg . . .' Joanna took in a deep breath. This is going to be painful, she knew. 'Greg, I'm sending you to a place where they can help you.'

His brows knit. 'Sending me? Where?'

'It's like a hospital. Very private. Very discreet. They'll be able to help you there.'

'I don't need anyone's help! I'm not sick!'

'I'm not asking for your opinion,' Joanna said firmly. 'I'm telling you. You're going there and that's all there is to it.'

'I want to be with you!'

Joanna felt her heart clutch within her. 'I know, Greg. I know. I'll come and visit you. Often.'

'I want to be with you all the time!'

'Later,' Joanna said. 'When you're better.'

He sat there, looking perplexed, for several moments. Then, sullenly, 'You want to play with your new baby and forget about me.'

'No!' Joanna blurted. 'I could never forget you. You're my baby boy and I'll love you forever, no matter what.'

'Then don't send me away.' Greg fell to his knees in front of his mother and buried his face in her lap. 'Please, Mom, don't send me away.'

A wild thought raced through Joanna's mind. 'What if . . .' She hesitated, searching for an answer. 'Greg, what if you stayed here at the house, with me?'

'Yes!' he said fervently.

'And I can bring the doctors and their assistants here to stay with us.'

'Yes! Yes!'

'And we'll be together while they help to make you well again.'

'Anything,' Greg sobbed, 'as long as we can be together.'

Joanna stroked her son's midnight dark hair, thinking, That will be the best way. Keep him here, where I can watch him. Bring the medical help to him.

She realized that Greg had fallen asleep with his head cradled in her lap. He probably hasn't slept for the past couple of days, either, Joanna thought.

I can't turn him over to the police. What good would that do? It won't bring Paul back and it will destroy Greg completely. Not the police. No scandal. No one must know what he did.

She sighed. It'll be difficult, especially when the new baby comes. Douglas. She already had his name picked out. Greg will be insanely jealous of the baby. But I can protect him. I can do it. I can take care of both my sons. I can. I will.

PART II:

Hero Time

FILE:
GREGORY MASTERSON III

The subject is a twenty-eight-year-old male in good physical health. He is deeply disturbed and potentially violent, although like many schizophrenics he can cloak his misapprehensions and delusions with extremely logical and plausible-sounding rationalizations. He is in private care at the home of his mother. Deep hypnotherapy is recommended, together with chemosuppressants to regulate his mood swings.

After two years of hypnotherapy the inescapable conclusion is that the primary focus for the subject's neurosis is the morbid fear of losing his mother. Although the Freudian concept of an Oedipus Complex has long been discredited, the subject sees his mother as a symbol of safety and well-being, hence an object of intense desire. While this desire is primarily connected to his fear of loss of maternal protection, there is also decidedly a sexual component involved.

The subject is now thirty-five years old and freely able to admit that he has harbored murderous rages against the men with whom he was forced to share his mother's affection: i.e., his father and his step-father, both of whom are now deceased. Even in deep hypnotherapy sessions he evades any mention of his seven-year-old half-brother who, quite obviously, has also taken a share of his mother's attention and affection.

SAN JOSE

'I don't like the looks of this,' said Kris Cardenas.

She was standing on the roof of the two-story nanotechnology building, her chief of security beside her, watching
the stream of picketers being whipped up into an angry
mob.

At the security chief's earnest suggestion, she had sent
most of the working staff home when the mob began to
gather outside the main gate. She hadn't really believed
him when he warned her there was going to be trouble;
now, hours later, she realized that she hadn't wanted to
believe.

From up on the roof, with the warm wind at her back, she
couldn't hear what the woman with the bullhorn was telling
the picketers, but by the way they surged around her and
roared incoherently every few minutes Cardenas knew she
was working them up into a frenzy.

And more demonstrators were arriving, cars and minivans
and even busloads of them.

'This is organized as all hell,' Cardenas muttered.

Her security chief scanned the growing crowd with
electronically-boosted binoculars, his mouth set in a grim
line.

'Take a look,' he said, looping the strap of the binoculars
around Cardenas' neck. Then he fished a palm-sized phone
out of his shirt pocket.

'Got those fire hoses ready?' he asked into the phone.

Cardenas searched through the placards that bobbed drunk-
enly in the sea of bodies. Professionally printed, she saw.

NANOTECH IS THE DEVIL'S WORK
NANOBUGS TAKE JOBS FROM REAL PEOPLE
NANOTECH KILLS!

Jesus, she thought, this isn't just one gang of nut cases. They've got organized labor, religious zealots – it's a coalition of pressure groups.

'Look!' the security chief shouted.

Cardenas lowered the binoculars to see where he was pointing. A black pickup truck was speeding across the nearly empty parking lot, straight for the crowd. The people parted like the Red Sea, on cue she thought, and the truck raced straight up to the main gate of the wire security fence and crashed through. One of the uniformed guards was knocked down as the truck roared by without slowing, jounced over the circular plot of flowers in front of the building's front entrance and smashed into the glass doors of the building's lobby.

The crowd poured through the open fence, roaring like a white-water river.

'Get the fire hoses on 'em!' the security chief screamed into his phone.

Cardenas' legs felt rubbery. If that truck had been filled with explosives it would've killed us all!

Streams of high-pressure water were spraying the oncoming crowd, knocking people off their feet, pushing them back away from the shattered entrance to the building. But other groups were skirting around the sides of the building, flanking movements. Cardenas knew that the back doors and the loading gates were not protected as well as the front entrance.

She shook herself. It's a battle now, she realized. A battle to save the labs.

They lost the battle. Police helicopters eventually arrived to evacuate Cardenas and the few remaining security people from the roof. The building was gutted: lab equipment smashed, computers professionally destroyed by magnetized wipers that jangled disk memories into useless hash, offices torn apart.

The news headlines that evening concentrated on the three demonstrators who were injured by the streams from the fire hoses. Masterson Aerospace was going to be sued for police brutality and excessive force. The security guard who died as a result of being hit by the pickup truck was hardly mentioned at all.

FILE:
GREGORY MASTERSON III

It has become possible – and even desirable – to transfer at least part of the subject's feelings for his mother to a desire for security and self-esteem through success in the world of business and commerce. Therefore he has been encouraged to restart his career in Masterson Aerospace Corporation and to establish his own residence near his place of employment.

At age forty, this sublimation procedure is proceeding with apparent proficiency, although careful watch must be maintained since the subject is intelligent enough to know what his therapists desire and to parrot the responses they wish to observe – even under hypnotherapy.

However, his relationship with his twelve-year-old half-brother has apparently stabilized. The subject spent the Christmas holidays at home with his mother and sibling. Post-holiday interviews and testing showed no outward manifestations of hostility, although latent resentment is of course still present.

It has been four years since the subject's last hypnotherapy encounter. As expected, his success in the corporate world has enabled him to build a new structure of self-esteem. His sexual feelings for his mother have not been eradicated, of course, but now he is able to usefully channel such feelings into accomplishment and respect from his peers. Although he still has some difficulties in forging relationships with peers, it is recommended that all therapy sessions be discontinued, and the subject merely visit this practitioner on a semi-annual basis.

Two years of semi-annual visits have convinced this practitioner that the subject can function adequately in society. He is still something of a 'loner,' and will undoubtedly need more time to adjust his feelings toward women who might be sexual partners, but it is apparent that he is now a competent, even quite extraordinarily competent, fully functional adult. His relationship with his mother is, at least outwardly, quite normal. His relationship with his eighteen-year-old half-brother, while strained, is apparently no worse than most family relationships under similar circumstances.

MOONBASE

Douglas Stavenger visited Moonbase for the first time on his eighteenth birthday.

His mother had been against it. She would not say why, but Doug knew her reason. His father had died on the Moon before he had been born. It was an accident, as far as Doug knew, a freak accident involving nanomachines that had been improperly programmed.

'That was eighteen years ago,' Doug pleaded with his mother. 'And besides, I won't be using nanobugs. I just want to see Moonbase with my own eyes.'

Joanna offered him a trip around the world, instead. But Doug insisted on Moonbase.

Not that he had quarrelled with his mother. Doug never quarrelled. Since elementary school he had made his smiling way through bullies among the students and the faculty alike, never fighting, never raising his voice, never losing his temper. He seemed to lead a charmed life. Everything came his way, seemingly without his needing to raise even a finger. People wanted to please him.

It wasn't merely the fact that he was extremely wealthy. Everyone he knew came from wealthy families and most of them were miserably unhappy, absolutely no fun to be with. Like his brother Greg. Half-brother, actually. No matter how hard Doug tried, ever since childhood Greg had been a dark, sullen shadow across his life. He saw his half-brother only rarely, yet the room chilled when Greg was in it. Doug could feel the tension pulling between his mother and her other son. There seemed to be some deep, dreadful secret

between them, a secret that neither of them chose to share
with him.

Doug accepted it as a fact of his life, something that had
always been there. Someday he would find out what it was,
why his mother and half-brother were so guarded and uptight.
In the meantime, he had his own life to live.

Doug got along well with almost everyone simply because
he thought farther ahead than the rest of them, and saw options
that no one else considered. He was very bright and very
adventurous. He had inherited his father's compact, solid build
and quick reflexes, his mother's intelligence and endurance.

Captain of his prep school's fencing team, shortstop on the
baseball squad, Doug also discovered the thrills of jetbiking.
When his mother objected he smilingly turned his fancy
to rocket-boosted gliders that surfed the stratosphere's jet
streams. He took risks, plenty of them, but only after he had
calculated all the odds and convinced himself that the risks
were survivable. He knew he sometimes worried his mother,
but he did not think he was foolhardy.

Still he did well enough academically to win acceptance by the top universities. His mother chose the University of Vancouver, where Kris Cardenas now headed the
nanotechnology department. He accepted her decision, with
the proviso that she allow him to visit Moonbase.

'Just for a few days,' he urged. 'A weekend, even.'

Reluctantly, she gave in.

Doug had visited Masterson's factories in Earth orbit. He
had experienced zero gravity before. But in preparation for
his Moonbase jaunt he spent a week in Houston, at the
corporation's lunar simulator, teaching himself how to walk
in one-sixth gee without stumbling and bouncing and making
a fool of himself.

He was prepared for everything to be expected at Moonbase.
Everything except meeting Foster Brennart.

His visit was something like a command performance.
The son of the corporation's board chairwoman was given
a thorough tour of the base.

'Moonbase is built into the flank of the mountainous

ringwall of the crater Alphonsus,' his tour guide recited.
She was a sloe-eyed brunette with a soft Savannah accent, an
assistant to the base director. Like all the other base personnel,
she wore a utilitarian one-piece zippered jumpsuit. The only
differences in clothing Doug could see were the color codes
that marked the four main departments. Her coveralls were
sky blue, for management. So were his.

'The base consists of four parallel tunnels,' she continued as
they walked along. 'The tunnels have been carved out of the
basaltic rock of the ringwall mountain by plasma torches—'

'You didn't use nanomachines to dig out the tunnels?'
Doug asked.

The young woman blinked at him as if coming out of a
trance. 'Nanomachines? Uh, no . . . nanobugs are only used
out on the crater floor, to harvest hydrogen out of the regolith
and, um, to process regolith silicon into solar cells for the
energy farms.'

'Then these tunnels were burned out of the mountain by
plasma torches? That must've been something to see!'

She nodded, frowning slightly as she tried to pick up her
interrupted recitation. Once she remembered where she'd been
stopped she resumed, 'Living quarters, offices, laboratories
and work stations have all been carved out of the rock . . .'

She walked Doug through each of the four tunnels, opening
almost every door along the way. Junior technicians and
engineers took time off from their normal duties to show
him every laboratory, every control station, the intricate
plumbing of the plant where water was manufactured out
of lunar oxygen and hydrogen, the humming pumps of the
environmental control center where oxygen was combined
with nitrogen imported from Earth to make breathable air
at normal pressure, the hydroponics farm where food crops
– mostly rows of soybeans – were grown under precisely
controlled conditions, even the waste processing center where
precious organic chemicals were extracted from garbage and
excrement for recycling.

'When do I go outside?' he asked his guide after several
hours of trudging through the underground facilities.

'Outside?' She looked alarmed.

'Yes,' he said pleasantly. 'I want to see what it's like out on the surface.'

It took some doing. Apparently the word had been sent up from Savannah to be especially careful with their young visitor, to take no chances with his safety. But the word had also been to show him whatever he wanted to see, and treat him with every courtesy. So his tour guide referred Doug's request straight to Moonbase's safety chief and the chief spent fifteen minutes trying to talk Doug out of a surface excursion.

'You can see anything you want to on the monitors at the control center,' the chief said. He looked quite old to Doug, a little gray mouse of a man who had once been a little dark mouse of an astronaut.

'I could do that back on Earth,' Doug replied gently, standing relaxed in front of the safety chief's desk. 'I've come a quarter of a million miles; I don't want to go back home without putting my boot prints on the lunar surface.'

Wishing that the kid would go away, or at least sit down like a normal person, the chief answered, 'Oh. I see.' He ran a hand through his thinning, close-cropped iron gray hair and took a deep sighing breath. At last he said, 'Well, I suppose it wouldn't hurt to let you walk around a bit on the crater floor.'

Doug broke into a pleased grin.

'With somebody escorting you, of course,' added the chief.

The safety chief personally led Doug out to the garage where the tractors were housed and maintained. It looked like a big cave to Doug, which is what it had once been. The garage was fairly quiet; most of the tractors were out on the surface, working. Only off in a far corner was there a knot of technicians tinkering with a pair of the spindly-wheeled machines.

'That's the main airlock.' The chief pointed to a massive steel hatch, big enough to drive a fully-loaded tractor through. Off to one side Doug saw a row of spacesuits hanging on a rack, with a row of gas cylinders standing behind a long bench.

Somehow the bench didn't look strong enough to support a man's weight; its legs were frail and spaced too far apart. Then Doug grinned to himself and realized that a two-hundred pound man weighed only thirty-four pounds here.

They selected a spacesuit for Doug from the rack of suits waiting empty by the airlock. Although all the suits were white, they looked grimy and hard-used, their helmets scratched and pitted. It took an hour for Doug to suit up and then prebreath the low-pressure mix of oxygen and nitrogen that the suits used. The safety chief explained the need for prebreathing in minute detail, eloquently describing the horrors of the bends, despite Doug's telling him that he understood the situation.

A taller figure already suited up clumped toward them in thick-soled boots. His visor was up, so Doug could see the man's face and piercing electric blue eyes. His spacesuit looked brand new, sparkling white with red stripes down the sleeves and legs, like a baseball uniform.

'Oh, Foster, there you are,' said the chief. 'This is Douglas Stavenger.'

With the breathing mask still clamped over his lower face, Doug got up from the bench where he'd been sitting and extended his gloved hand. The spacesuited man was almost a full head taller than he.

'Foster Brennart,' he said, in a surprisingly high tenor voice. Then he turned to the safety chief. 'Okay, Billy, I'll take it from here.'

Foster Brennart! thought Doug. The greatest astronaut of them all! The first man to traverse Mare Nubium in a tractor; leader of the first mission across the rugged uplands to visit Apollo 11's Tranquility Base; the man who rescued the European team that had gotten itself stranded inside the giant crater Copernicus.

'I'm pleased to meet you,' Doug managed to say from inside his breathing mask. It was like saying hello to a legend. Or a god.

Brennart shook Doug's hand without smiling, then reached behind the bench to take one of the breathing masks resting atop the gas cylinders and held it to his face.

'It's okay, Billy,' he said to the chief through the mask. 'I'll take him out as soon as we're done prebreathing. You can go back to your office now.'

The little man nodded. 'Right. See you in an hour or so.'

Doug realized it was the chief's way of telling Brennart to make their surface excursion a short one.

'Or so,' said Brennart casually.

As the safety chief walked hurriedly toward the hatch that led back to the offices and living quarters, Brennart asked Doug, 'How much longer do you have to go?'

Feeling confused, Doug asked, 'Go where?'

'Prebreathing.'

'Oh!' Glancing at the watch set into the panel on his suit's left forearm, Doug said, 'Twelve minutes.'

Brennart nodded inside his helmet. 'That ought to be enough for me, too.'

'Only twelve minutes?'

'I've been outside all day, kid. There's not enough nitrogen in my blood to pump up a toy balloon.'

The time crawled by in silence with Doug wanting to ask a half-million questions and Brennart standing over him, holding the plastic breathing mask to his face, sucking in deep, impatient breaths.

At last Doug's watch chimed. Brennart pulled his mask away and slid his visor down, then helped Doug to take off his mask and fasten his visor shut.

'Radio check,' Doug heard in his helmet earphones. He nodded, then realized that Brennart couldn't see it behind the heavily-tinted visor.

'I hear you loud and clear,' Doug said.

'Ditto,' said Brennart. Then he took Doug by the shoulder and turned him toward the personnel hatch set into the main airlock. 'Let's go outside,' he said.

Doug's heart was racing so hard he worried that Brennart could hear it over the suit-to-suit radio.

SAVANNAH

The years had been kind to Joanna Masterson Stavenger. Eighteen years older, she still was a handsome, vibrant woman. Her hair had always been ash blonde, she joked, so the gray that came with chairing the board of directors of Masterson Aerospace Corporation hardly even showed. She had put on a few pounds, she had undergone a couple of tucks of cosmetic surgery, but otherwise she was as lithe and beautiful as she had been eighteen years earlier.

'I'm not ready for nanotherapy yet,' she often quipped, even when assured that exclusive spas in Switzerland were quietly using specialized nanomachines that could scrub plaque from her arteries and tighten sagging muscles without surgery. Such therapy was impossible almost anywhere else on Earth; public fear of nanomachines had led to strict government regulation.

Yet she remained close to Kris Cardenas, even after the former head of Masterson's nanotech division had left the corporation in frustration at the red tape imposed by ignorant bureaucrats and the increasingly violent public demonstrations against nanotechnology. Cardenas had accepted an endowed chair at Vancouver and from there won her Nobel Prize.

Joanna's office had changed much more than she in the eighteen years since she had become Masterson Aerospace's board chairperson.

There was no desk, no computer, no display screen in sight. The office was furnished like a comfortable sitting room, with small Sheraton sofas and delicate armchairs grouped around Joanna's reclinable easy chair of soft caramel brown. The

windows in the corner looked out on the shops and piers of
Savannah's river front. The pictures on the walls were a mix
of ultramodern abstracts and photographs of Clipperships and
astronomical scenes.

At the moment, the room's decor was a cool neocolonial
classicism: muted pastels and geometric patterns. At the touch
of a button the hologram systems behind the walls could
switch to bolder Caribbean colors or any of a half-dozen
other decoration schemes stored in their computer memory.
The pictures could be changed to any of hundreds catalogued
in electronic storage or be transformed into display screens.
Even the room's scent could be varied from piney forest to
springtime flowers to salt sea tang, at Joanna's whim.

Sitting comfortably in her chair, Joanna could be in touch
with any part of the Masterson corporation, anywhere in the
world or beyond.

But her mind was on her sons. Greg was getting along well
enough, running the corporation's Pacific division out in the
island nation of Kiribati. It wasn't exile so much as one more
test to see if he really could function, really could build a
halfway normal life for himself. So far, Greg was doing fine.
But she always found herself using that term *so far* wherever
Greg was concerned.

It was her younger son, Douglas, who worried her. Joanna
realized that Doug was at the age where he sought a quest, a
way of proving his manhood. Naturally enough, he looked to
the Moon.

An adventurous eighteen-year-old never thinks that pain
or injury or death can reach him. When she found that he
was planning to jetbike all the way to Seattle she absolutely
forbade it.

'Come on, Mom,' Doug replied with his father's winning
smile. 'I'll be all right. What can happen to me?'

During his first visit to Vancouver she learned that he had
taken part in a power surfing jaunt to Victoria. 'What could
have happened to me?' he asked when she phoned, appalled
at the risks he blithely took on.

She hoped that attending the university, under Cardenas's

tutelage, would calm Doug down. Lately he had taken to flying rocket-boosted soarplanes. 'Riding the jet stream!' he chirped happily, all eagerness and enthusiasm. 'What a blast!'

And now he was at Moonbase, celebrating his eighteenth birthday a quarter-million miles from home. From her.

How like his father Doug was, she thought. The same burning drive, the same restless urge to break new ground, to push the edges of the envelope. He had his father's radiant smile and quick wit. His skin was lighter than Paul's had been: a smooth olive complexion, with blue eyes that sparkled youthfully.

Paul must have been just like that at eighteen, Joanna realized; impatient to prove himself. Willing to take on risks because he doesn't think for an instant that he could be harmed. The impervious confidence of youth.

And now he's on the Moon, just as Paul was. Why? she asked herself. What is it about that harsh unforgiving country that draws men like that?

Joanna had never told Doug all the details of his father's death. Nor anyone else. As she pictured her younger son's eagerly beaming face, she was wondered again if she had been right to keep the truth from him.

ALPHONSUS

The outer airlock hatch swung open at last and Doug stepped out onto another world.

He forgot about the pounding of his heart, forgot about Foster Brennart standing beside him, forgot about everything except the eerie grandeur that now stretched before his hungry eyes.

He forgot about making bootprints in the lunar dust. If Brennart said anything, he didn't hear it. If he himself spoke or made any sound at all he was unaware of it. His whole being filled with the vision of the lunar landscape: stark, somber, silent. The ground before him was flat, pockmarked with little craters, glaring brightly in the unfiltered light of the Sun. The mountains that marched off to the sudden horizon on either side of him looked somehow soft, rounded, old and tired. Easy to climb, Doug thought. Their folds and slopes made shadows that were impenetrably dark, utter blackness side-by-side with the bright glitter of their sunlit flanks.

The horizon was sharp as a knife edge, cutting off the world where it met the infinity of space. Gray and black, Doug saw. The Moon was a hundred shades of gray, from gleaming bright almost-white to the somber charcoal of the pitted ground beneath his booted feet. And black, shadows darker than the deepest pits of Earth, and the even blacker expanse of endless space. An uncompromising world, Doug thought: brilliantly bright in sunlight or unconditionally dark in shadow, sharp and clear as the choice between good and evil.

The only touches of color Doug could see were the dayglo-painted tractors working silently at their tasks: bulldozers scraping up the regolith, backhoes piling the dirt into waiting trucks, which carried it to a small man-made hill. That's where the nanomachines extract oxygen and hydrogen from the regolith, Doug told himself. On Earth they'd be roaring and grunting, their gears would be grinding away. Here on the Moon they do their jobs in perfect silence.

It's quiet here, he thought. Peaceful. A man can hear himself think.

He turned and looked out toward the horizon once again, framed by the curving ringwall mountains and dimpled almost exactly in its middle by the tips of the crater's central peaks, barely visible above the slash that separated sunlit ground from the endless void of space. Doug strained his eyes, but couldn't see any stars at all.

'I thought there'd be stars even in the daytime,' he said.

'Slide up your outer visor,' Brennart told him, 'but be careful not to look at the Sun.'

Doug did it, yet the sky remained dark and empty.

'Cup your hands around your eyes. Cut off the ground glare.'

Doug pressed his cupped hands to his visor, but nothing changed.

'Give it a few seconds . . .'

And there they were! Stars appeared out of the darkness, not merely the pinpoints of light that Doug was accustomed to, but swarms of stars, oceans of stars, stars strewn so thickly across the heavens that the darkness was banished. Doug tottered as he stared out at the universe, felt himself getting dizzy.

'When I behold your heavens, O Lord,' he whispered, 'the work of your fingers . . .'

'I know that one,' Brennart said. 'Some psalm from the Bible, isn't it.'

'Yes,' Doug said.

'You're Paul Stavenger's son, aren't you?'

'You knew my father?'

'Knew him?' Brennart laughed, a high-pitched giggle. 'Like the man says, we were practically hatched from the same egg. The times we had up here! And back Earthside!'

'What was he like?' Doug asked.

'You look a lot like him,' said Brennart. 'Come on, I want to show you something.' And he took off in long, loping, low-gravity strides across the crater floor.

As Doug followed him, the two of them galloping along like a pair of tailless kangaroos, Brennart began happily relating tales of the days when he and Paul Stavenger and a handful of others were digging the first temporary shelters of Moonbase.

'Would you believe old Billy-boy was one of us, then? A real hell-raiser, too.'

'The safety chief?' Doug guessed.

'Yep. He changed an awful lot once they put him behind a desk. You're never going to see *me* vegetate like that!'

They were skirting the edge of the solar energy farms now, where the ground gleamed with acre after acre of glassy solar cells. Along the far edge of the glittering field Doug could see a dark oily film; it looked alien, out of place, almost hostile. Nanomachines, he realized, working ceaselessly to convert lunar regolith into more solar cells.

'Up there . . .' Brennart was puffing; Doug could hear his labored breathing in his earphones.

Up ahead was a machine of some sort: a big, boxy, heavy metal contraption resting on what looked like caterpillar treads. It had once been painted white, Doug saw, but now it was streaked with smears of dusty dead gray.

'What is it?'

Brennart slowed to a walk as they approached the abandoned machine. He seemed to twist inside his suit, adjusting the bulky life-support pack on his back. 'Damned LSPs never stay in place like they should,' he muttered.

'What is this thing?' Doug asked again. Now that they were close enough to touch it, he saw that the machine was really massive, taller than even Brennart himself.

'This poor dumb beast,' said Brennart, 'is what we used in the old days to make the solar farms, before we had nanomachines to do the work.'

'It must weigh fifty tons,' Doug said.

'Forty-two, on Earth.'

'That's a lot to lift.'

'Yep. The nanobugs are a lot better. But once upon a time, my boy, this beast was the height of modern technology. A tele-operated, self-sufficient, solar powered mechanical cow. Grazed on the regolith. Took in silicon, aluminum, et cetera in its front end, digested them and put them together, and shat solar cells out its backside.'

'And that's how the first solar energy farms were made.'

'More or less. Damned dumb beasts kept breaking down, of course. Nobody knew how bad a problem the dust was, back then. We spent more time repairing these stupid cows than anything else.'

'Out here in the open?'

'Sure. Didn't make any sense to trundle 'em all the way back to one of the tempos. Anyway, we didn't have a garage in those days, so we'd have to work in the open one way or the other.'

'What about the radiation?'

'That's why we're all prematurely gray,' Brennart said. 'Even your dad, although on him it looked good. He was a handsome devil. The women flocked around him.'

'Really?' Doug had never heard that before.

'I could tell you stories . . .' Brennart broke into a low chuckle.

'What happened to the other cows?' Doug asked.

'Scrapped them. We left this one out here and converted it into an emergency shelter.'

Doug turned, frowning, and saw that the airlock in the ringwall mountains was hardly a half-mile away.

'We also use it for other purposes,' Brennart added, before Doug could ask. 'It's fitted out with a double bunk inside and certain other, ah . . . amenities.'

Doug saw that someone had scrawled in luminescent red just above the machine's hatch *If this van's rocking, don't come knocking.*

'Oh!' he said, with sudden understanding. 'This is the Moonbase Motel.'

Brennart guffawed. 'Pree-cisely!'

He started walking again, out at an angle away from the carcass of the mechanical cow and the glittering solar farms.

'So what're you doing up here, kid? Why'd you come to Moonbase?'

Doug almost shrugged, but the spacesuit made it too difficult. 'I wanted to see it firsthand. All my life I've heard about Moonbase, and how my father worked to make it viable. He died here.'

'He let himself die in order to protect the base.'

'Yeah.' Doug was surprised at the lump in his throat. 'So . . . I had to see the place.'

'Now that you've seen it, what do you think?'

'The inside's a lot smaller than I thought it'd be,' Doug replied. 'But the outside . . .' He stretched his arms out to the horizon. 'This is – well, it's terrific!'

'You like it out here, do you?'

'It's like all my life I've waited to get here and now that I'm here, I'm home.'

For a moment Brennart did not reply. Then, 'Are you running away from something, son, or running toward something?'

'What do you mean?'

'Are you running away from your father's ghost, or maybe trying to get away from your mother? Is that why you came here?'

Doug thought it over. 'No, I don't think it's that.'

'Then what?'

He hesitated another moment, sorting out his feelings. 'All my life I've heard about my father and Moonbase. Now that I'm here, I can see what he saw, I can understand why he'd give his life for it.'

'Why?'

Looking around at the barren landscape one more time, Doug answered simply, 'This is the future. My future. Our future. The whole human race. This is the frontier. This is where we grow.'

He could sense Brennart nodding approvingly inside his helmet. 'That's exactly how your dad felt.'

'This is where we grow,' Doug repeated, convinced of the truth of it.

Brennart said, 'Now let me tell you about something even more exciting.'

'What?'

'The most valuable real estate on the Moon – in the whole solar system, in fact. It's down by the south pole . . .'

They walked side by side farther out into the giant crater's floor, out toward the area where sinuous rilles cracked the surface, Brennart talking nonstop.

'There's a mountain down there that's in sunlight all the time, twenty-four hours a day, every day of the year.'

'*That's* the place for a solar farm!' Doug said excitedly.

'And there's fields of ice down in the valleys between the mountains,' Brennart went on. 'Water ice.'

Doug's breath caught. He calmed himself, then asked, 'That's been confirmed?'

'It's top secret corporate information, but, yes, it's been confirmed.'

'Then we could—'

'Look out!'

Doug felt Brennart clutch at his shoulders and yank him backwards from the edge of the rille he was about to step over. As the two men staggered backward several steps Doug could see that the rille – a snaking crack in the ground – was crumbling along its edge, just where he was about to plant his boot.

'Didn't mean to scare you,' Brennart muttered.

'What's happening?'

'I'm not sure, it might – Look!'

Thousands of fireflies seemed to burst upward, out of the rille. Glittering coldly blue and bright green, the cloud of glistening light expanded in the sunlight, twinkling, gleaming, filling Doug's vision with ghostly light. He was surrounded by the sparkling lights; it was like being inside a starry nebula or a heaven filled with angels.

Doug saw nothing but the lights, heard nothing but his own gasping breath. Tears filled his eyes.

'An eruption,' he heard Brennart say, his voice filled with awe.

'What is it?' Doug managed to whisper.

'Ammonia, methane. From down below. It seeps up through the rilles every now and then. Someday we'll mine the stuff.'

The cloud grew and grew, enveloping them in its flickering light. Then it dissipated. As quickly as it had arisen it disappeared, wafted away into nothingness. The landscape went back to its dead grays and blacks.

'I've been coming up here more than twenty years,' said Brennart, his voice hollow, 'and I've never seen an eruption before.'

Doug could not reply. He was thinking that it was an omen, a sign. My welcome to the Moon, he said to himself.

'You must lead a charmed life, kid.'

'It was . . . beautiful,' Doug said lamely.

'That it was. It certainly was.'

For long moments they stood in silence, each secretly hoping that another seepage of gas would envelope them in the colorful fireflies once again.

'I hope the monitoring cameras caught that,' Brennart said at last. 'The science people'll want spectra and all that.'

'The cameras run all the time?'

'Right.'

At last Doug gave it up. There would be no more. Strange, he thought, how sudden elation can give way to disappointment so quickly.

'Guess we should start back to the base,' Brennart said. He sounded dismayed, too.

'Tell me more about this south pole business,' Doug said, as much to cheer their conversation as any other reason.

'We've got to claim that territory,' Brennart said, his tone brightening immediately. 'I want to lead an expedition down there and . . .'

SAVANNAH

'There's ice down there at the pole!' Doug said, brimming with enthusiasm. 'Water ice! Mr. Brennart wants to lead an expedition there and claim it for us.'

'I've seen his proposals,' Joanna said, feeling weary at her son's insistence. She leaned back in her reclining chair. 'Brennart's deluged me with video presentations, reports, survey data.'

'I want to go with him,' Doug said.

Joanna had known he would. Of course he would. That was why she had hesitated, ever since her son had returned from his brief visit to Moonbase, bubbling with excitement about joining Brennart and trekking off to the south lunar pole. Now he sat in her office, facing her, burning with enthusiasm, hardly able to sit still as they waited for Brennart to show up. She saw Paul's features in her son's face, Paul's boundless energy and drive. And she remembered that Paul had died on the Moon.

Brennart's proposed expedition to the lunar south pole had worked its way up through the corporate chain of command and now sat on Joanna's desk. She could approve it or kill it. She knew that if she approved it, her son would stop at nothing to be included in the mission.

Misunderstanding her silence, Doug said, 'Mom, all my life I've heard about my father and Moonbase. I want to carry on in his footsteps. I've got to!'

'Your freshman classes start in September.'

'We'll be back by then. It's my legacy, Mom! All my life I've wanted to get to Moonbase and continue what he started.'

All his life Joanna, thought. All eighteen years of his life.

'It's the frontier,' he told her excitedly. 'That's where the action is.'

Joanna countered, 'Moonbase is a dreary little cave that's only barely paying its own way. I've come close to shutting it down a dozen times.'

'Shutting it down? You can't shut it down, Mom! It's the frontier! It's the future!'

'It's a drain on this corporation's resources.'

Doug started to reply, then hesitated. With a slow smile he said, 'Mom, if you won't allow me to go to Moonbase, I'll get a job with Yamagata Industries. They—'

'Yamagata!'

'They're looking for construction workers,' Doug said evenly. 'I'll get to the Japanese base at Copernicus.'

That was when Joanna realized how utterly serious her son was. Behind the boyish enthusiasm was an iron-hard will. Despite his pleasant smiling way, he was just as intent as his father had been.

'Douglas,' she said, 'there's much more at stake here than you understand.'

He jumped to his feet, startling her. Pacing across the office, Doug replied, 'Mom, if we can get water from the ice fields down at the south pole we can make Moonbase profitable. We can even sell water to Yamagata and the Europeans.'

'No one's ever gone to the south pole. It's mountainous, very dangerous—'

Doug grinned at her. 'Come on, Mom. Foster Brennart's going to head the expedition. Foster Brennart! He's a living legend. He's like Daniel Boone and Charles Lindbergh and Armstrong, Aldrin and Collins all wrapped up in one!'

Joanna knew Foster Brennart quite well. On the Moon Brennart had distinguished himself as a pioneer trailblazer: he had been there from Moonbase's earliest beginnings, side by side with Paul. On Earth, especially here at corporate headquarters, Brennart was a constant aggravation. He always had some wild scheme to promote, some adventure that he swore was crucial to the survival of Moonbase and the profitability of Masterson Aerospace Corporation. More often than not, his treks into the unknown cost far more than they could ever return. And he was getting wilder, more adventurous with the years. Reckless, Joanna thought. Brennart took chances that seemed outright foolish to her.

Now he was pushing for an expedition to the lunar south pole. He had been at it for nearly two years, wheedling and cajoling every time he visited Savannah. And now he had enlisted Doug in his campaign. Joanna felt simmering anger at that. Brennart had taken advantage of the eighteen-year-old's natural enthusiasm and now Doug was as frenzied as a religious convert. Brennart had made the Moon's south pole into a holy grail, in Doug's young eyes.

The trouble was, this time Brennart seemed to be right. The more Joanna studied the possibilities, the more inevitable the idea looked to her. Still, it was chancy – even dangerous.

I can't keep Doug on a leash, Joanna told herself. But it all sounds so damnably dangerous.

Doug couldn't sit still. He paced between the two little Sheraton loveseats to the window, glanced out at the cloudy afternoon, then turned expectantly toward the door.

'He ought to be here any minute,' he said.

'Relax. Foster's never been late for a meeting,' said Joanna. 'I'm sure he'll be on time for this one.'

Her intercom chimed. 'Mr. Brennart here to see you,' said her private secretary.

'Send him right in,' Joanna said, leaning back in her chair. Doug was practically quivering as he stood by the window.

Foster G. Brennart was accustomed to dominating any room he entered. Tall, athletically lean, he had a thick mane of curly golden hair that he allowed to flow to his shoulders. His eyes were pale blue, and although they often seemed to be gazing at a distant horizon that only he could see, when they focused on an individual, that person felt the full intensity of Brennart's powerful character.

He wore a simple sky blue velour pullover shirt and pale blue slacks. Joanna noticed that he was shod only in leather sandals; no socks.

'Foster,' she said with a gesture toward Doug, 'You've already met my son—'

'Hello, Doug,' said Brennart, extending a long arm. 'Good to see you again.'

Doug was surprised by Brennart's sweet high tenor all over again. He somehow expected the lanky six-footer to sound deeper, more manly. Still, Doug smiled with pleasure as he shook Brennart's hand. The older man sat in the loveseat facing Joanna.

'I presume the subject of this meeting is the south polar expedition,' he said.

'Of course,' said Joanna.

'The Aitken Basin down there is most valuable real estate on the Moon,' Brennart said.

'I've watched your proposal disks several times,' Joanna said. 'And read all the tons of material you've sent.'

Turning toward Doug, still standing by the window, Brennart touted, 'There's a mountain down there – Mt. Wasser – that's in daylight all the time. We can generate electrical power at its summit constantly, twenty-four hours a day. And use the power to melt the ice down in the valleys and pump the water back to Moonbase.'

'We're producing enough water for Moonbase with the nanomachines,' Joanna said.

'Barely,' said Doug.

Brennart smiled at the lad. 'At Moonbase you have to build twice the solar power capacity that you really need, because the area's in night for two weeks at a time. At Mt. Wasser we can provide electrical power constantly.'

'Once you put up the solar panels,' said Joanna.

'We can use nanomachines to build a power tower on the mountaintop.'

'And transmit the energy back to Moonbase by bouncing a microwave power beam off a relay satellite,' Doug added eagerly.

Shaking her head slightly, Joanna said, 'Moonbase is only marginally profitable. This expedition—'

'Can put Moonbase solidly into the black,' said Brennart.

'There's enough power and enough water at the south pole to allow Moonbase to grow and prosper.'

'But the cost.'

'Mom,' Doug said, 'if we don't claim the polar region somebody else will.'

Joanna started to reply, then hesitated.

'He's right,' said Brennart. 'Yamagata's planning an expedition, we're pretty certain. And the Euro-Russians aren't fools, they know the value of that territory.'

No corporation could claim it owned any part of the Moon. No nation could claim sovereignty over lunar territory. Treaties signed almost a century earlier prevented that. But, after people had actually begun building bases on the Moon and digging up lunar resources, the earthbound lawyers had to find some legal method of assuring some form of property rights.

They cloaked their decisions in clouds of legalistic verbiage, but what it boiled down to was that any 'entity' (which was defined as an individual or a combination of individuals) which could establish that it was utilizing the natural resources of a specific part of the Moon's surface or subsurface was entitled to exclusive use of that territory. It was not first-come-first-served, exactly; it was the first to show *utilization* of a chunk of lunar real estate who could expect legal protection against others who wanted to use the same area.

'Well,' said Brennart as he sat facing Joanna, 'like the man says, there it is. We can reach the Aitken Basin first and use those resources to make Moonbase a real city. Think of what we can do! A year's worth of tourist income would more than pay for the expedition.'

'Tourists?' Joanna snapped. 'Tourism destroyed Lunagrad.'

'Aw, Mom, that was years ago,' Doug replied. 'Tourists go to the space stations, don't they? If we could build reasonable facilities for them, they'd spend their money at Moonbase.'

'They could plant their bootprints where no one has ever stepped before,' Brennart said. 'If we built a big-enough enclosure and filled it with air at Earth-normal pressure, they could fly like birds.'

'On plastic wings that we rent to them,' Doug added.

Suppressing an urge to laugh, Joanna said, 'That's all in the future.'

'Yes,' said Brennart, 'but the future starts now. The resources at the south pole can make Moonbase into a true city. Or maybe Yamagata or the Europeans will get there first, and Moonbase will never be able to grow much beyond where it is now.'

Joanna recognized the threat. 'There's only one detail that still bothers me.'

Brennart leaned forward slightly and fixed his pale blue eyes on her. 'And what might that be?'

Turning slightly, Joanna said, 'My son, here. He wants to go along with you.'

Brennart looked over at Doug and smiled broadly. 'You do, eh?'

'You bet!' said Doug. 'I've been spending every minute I can in lunar simulators. I can handle a tractor or a hopper and I've got the rest of the summer free.'

Brennart laughed his high-pitched giggle. 'You want to come along to the lunar south pole for your summer vacation?'

Grinning back at him, Doug said, 'I know it won't be a vacation. But, yes, I very much want to go.'

'He wants to go so much,' Joanna said, unsmiling, 'that he's threatened to go to Japan and take a job with Yamagata Industries.'

Sobering, Brennart said, 'Yamagata's people don't give soft jobs to Americans, you know. Only the dog work, basic construction labor, stuff like that.'

'I know,' said Doug. 'But it'll be on the Moon.'

'You want to get to the Moon that bad?'

'I want to be at the frontier. I want to go places where no one's been before.'

With a solemn nod, Brennart admitted, 'I know the feeling.'

'If I approve your planned expedition,' Joanna asked, 'will you take Doug with you?'

'If I say no, will you still approve the expedition?'

She looked into those ice-blue eyes, then said, 'I might approve it more easily if you say no.'

'I mean it, Mom,' Doug said. 'I'll go to Yamagata.'

Brennart smiled again. 'I like his spirit. Reminds me of his father.'

'If I approve,' Joanna cut off any reminiscences, 'I want Doug under your direct supervision. I want you to keep your eyes on him every moment. Both eyes, Foster.'

Brennart hesitated a moment, as if marshalling his thoughts. 'We'll have to find some useful task for him. There'll be no room on the expedition for anyone who can't pull his own weight.'

'I can be the legal recorder,' said Doug. 'You don't have anyone in your group who's responsible for recording the corporation's legal claim to the polar region. I can do that for you.'

Brennart rubbed his chin. 'We were going to take turns recording everything with vidcams, but I suppose it makes some sense to have somebody assigned that responsibility specifically.'

Joanna said nothing, but she realized that Doug had thought all this out very carefully.

Grinning, Brennart asked, 'You've really put in time in lunar simulators? You're certified for tractor operation? And hoppers?'

'Nearly fifty hours!' said Doug.

With a shrug, Brennart said, 'I've got no objections to your coming with us.'

'Then I can go?'

Joanna sank back in her chair and closed her eyes briefly. 'Yes,' she said reluctantly, 'you can go.'

But she sat up straight again and levelled a finger at Brennart. 'He's your responsibility, Foster. I don't want him out of your sight.'

Brennart nodded easily. 'I'll treat him as if he was my own son.'

'Don't worry, Mom,' said Doug, almost dancing with excitement. 'I'll be fine. What can happen to me?'

Joanna stared at Doug, grinning from ear to ear. Just like his father. Who died on the Moon.

MOONBASE

'I hate his guts,' said Jack Killifer.

'Who? Brennart?'

'Naw. Little Douggie.'

'Doug Stavenger?'

'That's right,' Killifer said sourly. 'Mama's boy.'

'How can you hate him? You haven't even seen him yet. He's not due to arrive until—'

'I don't have to see him,' Killifer snapped. 'The little pissant's already screwed me over.'

Killifer and Roger Deems were sitting in Moonbase's galley, a cavern large enough to hold the entire regular staff of fifty, plus a dozen or so visitors. At the moment, in the middle of a work morning, they were the only two people seated at the tables. A few others drifted in now and then, made their way down the line of automated dispensing machines, then headed back to their offices or workplaces.

Known to the regular Lunatics as The Cave, the galley had been carved out of the rock of Alphonsus's ringwall mountains by the same plasma-torch crews who had dug the tunnels that now served as living quarters, laboratories, offices and workshops for Moonbase.

They had left The Cave's ceiling rough-hewn, unpolished rock: hence its name. The walls were smooth, though, and the floor was planted with the toughest species of grasses that could be found on Earth. Twelve square plots of grass, forbidden to step upon, tended constantly and lovingly by the agro team, formed a green counterpoint to the tables and chair scattered across The Cave's floor.

Full-spectrum lamps spanned the rock ceiling, keeping The Cave as bright as noontime on an Iowa summer day. The Lunatics joked that you could tell how much time a person spent in The Cave by how tanned he or she was. Ceiling, walls, and the smooth rock walkways and floor beneath the tables were all sprayed with clear airtight plastic.

'Why're you pissed with the kid?' asked Roger Deems.

He was sitting across the small table from Killifer. Both men had mugs of what was supposed to be vitamin-enriched fruit juice before them. Both had laced their drinks liberally with 'rocket juice' from Moonbase's illicit travelling still.

The two men were a study in contrasts. Killifer was lean, lantern-jawed, his face hard and flinty. His light brown hair was shaved down almost to his scalp. His eyes were deepset, piercing, suspicious. Deems was large, round, plump, his dark locks curling down to his shoulders, his soft brown eyes wide. He always seemed startled, like a deer caught in a car's headlights.

Killifer took a long sip from his mug, then placed it down on the table. 'I'm supposed to be second-in-command on this expedition, right?'

'Right.'

'Yeah, but Brennart's put this snotnosed Douglas Stavenger in ahead of me.'

'But Douggie's only aboard as an observer,' Deems protested. 'And Brennart *had* to bring him in. Orders from Savannah!'

'Yeah, I know. Orders from Mama. She's the real pain in my ass.'

'She's the boss.'

'Damned bitch.'

Deems tried to make light of his companion's mood. 'Hey, you don't know her well enough to call her names like that.'

'I know her,' Killifer muttered. 'How d'you think I came up here to the Moon in the first place?'

Deems blinked uncertainly.

'She sent me. Fuckin' *exiled* me. Five years I had to spend

up here before she'd let me come back. Just because I tried
to help her son.'

Now Deems was very confused. 'Tried to help Douggie?'

'His half-brother. Greg.' With great disgust Killifer explained,
'It was eighteen years ago. I was working for the San Jose
division then, not much more than a kid myself. Greg
Masterson – his father was the bitch's first husband – he
asked me for a favor.'

'What kind of a favor?'

Killifer shrugged his bony shoulders. 'He wanted a sample
of nanomachines. He was a big mucky-muck with the corporation, the president's son, for chrissakes. So I gave him
a sample like he asked for and it turned out bad, her new
husband got killed up here. And I got blamed for it.'

'I didn't know,' Deems said, awe in his voice.

'She said I could work on the Moon until she was ready to
let me come back or she'd fire me and sic the police on me. I
was too scared to realize that she couldn't rat me out without
turning in Greg, too. So I spent five years digging tunnels.'

'No shit?'

'No shit. By the time she was willing to let me come back
Earthside I was so adapted to one-sixth gee I had to spend
another six months doing special exercises to build up my
muscles and bones. My heart, too.'

'But you made it back okay?'

'Yeah. Except the everything I had on Earth was gone by
then. My girl had married somebody else. My parents died
within a couple of years. My career in nanotech – forget it!'
Killifer snapped his fingers. 'Nanotech was dead in the States
and everywhere else except a few universities. And you don't
lose five years in a field like that and then boogie back in get
a university slot. I came back here. Been a Lunatic ever since,
a rock jock.'

'No wonder you're pissed.'

Killifer leaned across the little table menacingly. 'I don't
want you telling anybody else about this, understand? Not
a word.'

'Okay, okay.' Deems backed away slightly. Smoothing the

front of his wrinkled jumpsuit, he said, 'But it seems a shame to take it out on little Douggie.'

'Who cares? He's his mother's son.'

'Still . . .'

'*She's* the one who forced Brennart to take the kid along. Stuck him on top of me.'

'He's not on top of you. He's just an observer. On the org chart—'

'He's a snoop from Mama in Savannah,' Killifer growled. 'Little bastard's only eighteen years old and they put him in ahead of me.'

'But—'

'Don't try to bullshit me, pal! He's the boss's son, for chrissakes. Everybody'll be falling all over themselves to be on his good side.'

Deems shrugged. 'I talked to him yesterday. He seems like a nice-enough kid.'

'See what I mean?'

Looking more startled than usual, Deems shook his head in denial and disbelief.

'I'll fix him,' Killifer grumbled. 'Put the kid ahead of me, huh? She'll pay for that. And everything else she's done to me.'

Doug Stavenger knew that his mother was worried about him. She thinks I'm just a kid, he knew. She thinks an eighteen-year-old isn't smart enough to take care of himself.

But my father wasn't much older than that when he flew his first solo. And what's age got to do with it, anyway.

As soon as Doug arrived in his quarters at Moonbase – a standard cell along one of the tunnels carved out of the rock, not even as large as the smallest compartment aboard a cruise ship – he put in a call to his mother in Savannah.

At first he merely assured her that he was all right and the trip to the Moon had been safely uneventful. Soon enough, though, they began to talk about the coming expedition to the south polar region.

'I'm going to make a point of meeting everyone who's going on the mission,' he was saying.

'Douglas, I don't want you taking unnecessary risks,' she said sharply to her son.

Doug's image in her phone screen grinned at her as soon as her words reached him.

Trying to sound business-like, Joanna said to her son's smiling image, 'You're going along on this expedition for one reason only: to make certain that all the proper claims are made and all the legal forms filled out exactly right. That's your job. I don't want you traipsing around on some adventure when you should be tending to the legal formalities of this expedition.'

His smile did not fade an iota while he waited for her words to reach him on the Moon.

'I know, Mom. Don't worry about it. Masterson Aerospace will have a full and legal claim to operate in the Basin, don't worry about it.'

'We're not the only ones interested in that region,' Joanna warned.

But Douglas had not waited for her reply to him. He kept right on, 'And we'll be the first group there, don't worry about it. Nobody else is going to contest our rights.'

'Don't take foolish risks,' she said, sounding more like a worried mother than she wanted to.

This time he listened, then replied, 'I'll be okay. Mr. Brennart is about as experienced as they come. He's a living legend, really. We'll be in good shape, don't worry. What can happen to us?'

But even as she promised her son that she wouldn't worry, Joanna wanted to reach out across the quarter-million miles separating them and bring him back safely to her side. She worried about Brennart. It seemed to her that the man was working too hard at increasing his reputation, taking risks needlessly.

Doug said good-bye to her at last, and she blanked the phone screen, then sank back into her caramel brown chair. It subtly molded its shape to accommodate her. In its armrests were controls that could massage or warm her, if Joanna wanted.

All she really wanted was her son safely by her side. Both her sons.

Trying to drive away her fears and apprehensions, Joanna concentrated on her work for hours. Long after darkness fell, long after the corporate headquarters building had emptied of everyone else except its lone human guard monitoring the security sensors and the robots patrolling the hallways, Joanna remained in her office, studying reports, scanning graphs, speaking with Masterson employees scattered all around the globe and aboard the corporation's space facilities in orbit.

It was almost one in the morning when she wearily got up from her chair and went to the closet next to her personal lavatory. Joanna felt growing tension as she took off her dress and stripped down to her bra and panties. She reached into the closet and pulled out the sensor suit. It hung limp and lifeless, gray and slightly fuzzy-looking, in her hands.

He always called precisely on time, and she was slightly behind schedule. Quickly, Joanna stepped into the full-body suit and pressed closed the Velcro seals at its cuffs, ankles, and running down its front. The suit felt itchy on her skin, as it always did.

Taking the helmet from its shelf in the closet, she went back to her recliner chair and sat down. As she plugged the virtual reality suit into the chair, her wristwatch announced that she had one minute to spare. One minute to try to calm down a little.

She pulled the helmet over her coiffure, but left the visor up. This must be what a spacesuit's helmet is like, she thought. Or a biker's.

The phone's chime sounded in her earphones. Joanna slid the visor down and said, 'Hello, Greg.'

Her son had not changed much outwardly in the eighteen years since Paul's death. Still darkly handsome, pale skin stretched over high cheekbones and strong, stubborn jaw. Eyes as dark and penetrating as glittering obsidian. Just a touch of gray at his temples; it made him look even more enticing, in her eyes.

'Hello, Mom,' he said somberly.

Even on this tropical Pacific beach he wore dark slacks
and a starched shirt. His shoes and slacks will be soaked by
the surf, Joanna thought, then reminded herself that Greg was
actually in his own office, quite dry and probably amused at
the flowered wraparound *pareo* and oversized mesh shirt that
she had programmed into her virtual reality costume.

They were standing on the white sand beach on the lagoon
side of Bonriki. The airport was hidden by the high-rise office
towers of the town, but out in the lagoon Joanna could see the
floating platforms and work boats of the sea-launched rocket
boosters. Almost on the equator, Tarawa lagoon was an ideal
launch point for Pacific traffic into orbit. The island nation
of Kiribati was getting rich on its royalties from Masterson
Aerospace.

'Happy birthday, Greg,' Joanna said. She embraced her son
and felt his arms fold around her briefly. 'I'm sorry I couldn't
come in person.'

'That's okay,' he replied, trying to smile. 'VR's the next
best thing.'

'How are you?' she asked.

'Fine. The operation here is going very well. They're
even talking about setting up an amusement park to draw
in tourists.'

Joanna shook her head. 'That's a good way for them to lose
money.'

Greg laughed. 'The more they blow, the more dependent
they'll be on us. I'm already working out better terms for our
contract renewal.'

'I'm very proud of what you've accomplished here,' Joanna
said.

'Thanks, Mom.'

Neither of them spoke of what stood between them. Greg
had gone through years of intensive therapy after his maniacal
rage had led him to murder. For years Joanna had watched
him every day, trusting him only as far as she could see him,
protecting him against the pain and pressures of the world
beyond the walls of their home.

Only gradually, when it became clear that the focus of his

murderous fury had abated, did she allow him to return to the real world. Greg learned to control himself, learned to calm the bitter tides that surged through him, learned even to accept the fact that he had to share his mother with his younger half-brother.

In time, Joanna allowed him to return to the corporation. Gradually, slowly, the leash on which she kept her son grew longer, more flexible, until now he lived thousands of miles away and directed an important new operation of the corporation.

Yet despite his outward calm Joanna always felt the volcano seething beneath Greg's surface. Even in the tropical tranquility of this Pacific atoll he was all tension and wary-eyed pain. Even in the relaxed mores of Micronesia he had not taken a lover; as far as Joanna could determine he did not even have a steady girlfriend, neither native nor corporate.

He doesn't even have a tan, she realized. He's in his office all the time, driving himself constantly. The only time he gets to the beach is in VR simulations for meetings with me.

Joanna had kept Greg and his half-brother Douglas separated as much as possible. Over the years it began to seem almost normal that Doug would be away when Greg visited home, and Greg would not be there when Doug was. It was as if she had two different families, one son in each. There were holidays when the three of them were together, briefly, but they were always filled with tension and the fear that Greg might suddenly explode.

He never did. And Doug learned to get along with his older half-brother. It was difficult to dislike Doug; he had his father's charm. Greg could even laugh with Doug, on rare occasions.

Now, as Joanna and Greg walked ankle-deep in the gentle virtual surf of the lagoon, with the dying sun painting the towering cumulus clouds fabulous shades of pink and orange, Greg seemed lost in thought.

'What's the matter?' she asked, looking up into his somber eyes.

Greg let out a sigh, like a man in pain.

'What is it, dear?' Joanna repeated.

He stopped and turned to face her, his back to the glorious sunset. 'Have I done an adequate job here?'

Joanna had to shade her eyes to look up at him. 'More than adequate, Greg. You've made me proud of you.'

'All right,' he said. 'Then I want to move up to the next challenge.'

'The next . . . ?'

'Moonbase,' Greg said.

For a moment Joanna wasn't certain that she had heard him correctly.

'I want to be put in charge of Moonbase,' he said, his voice calm. But she could sense the depth of his desire, even through the virtual reality interface.

'Moonbase,' she repeated, stalling for time to think.

'Anson's due to rotate back to Savannah when her tour is finished,' Greg said. 'I'd like to be named to replace her for the next year.'

Doug is on the Moon, Joanna thought swiftly. But he'll be coming back once Brennart's expedition establishes an operational facility at the south pole.

'Mom? Did you hear me?'

'Yes, of course I heard you. It's just . . . unexpected. You've caught me by surprise, Greg.'

He broke into a cheerless smile. 'That's the first time *that's* happened!'

'I never thought you'd want to go to Moonbase,' she said.

'It's the next logical step, isn't it? A year at Moonbase and then I can move up to head the entire space operations division.'

Joanna made herself smile back at him. 'Director of Moonbase is a big responsibility.'

His smile evaporated. 'You don't trust me.'

'Of course I trust you!' she blurted.

'But not enough.'

'Oh, Greg—'

'I know. You've got every reason not to trust me. But it's not like I'm looking to be made CEO, or even asking for my old seat on the board of directors.'

'There's going to be a vacancy on the board next year,' Joanna said. 'I was planning to nominate you.'

If that pleased him, Greg did not show it. 'Mom, I want to *earn* my way. Moonbase is always tottering on the brink of collapse. I want to spend a year there and make the tough decision.'

'The tough decision?'

'To close it down, once and for all.'

'You can't do that!'

'Somebody has to,' he snapped. 'We can't let Moonbase keep draining the corporation, year after year.'

'But it's making a profit . . .'

Greg's expression turned sour. 'You know that's not true, Mom. Oh, sure, the bookkeeping shows a small profit, but when you figure in all the seed money we've put in for research that's off the books and all the other hidden costs, Moonbase is an expense we can't afford.'

Joanna drew in her breath. That's what he's really after. He wants to kill Moonbase. He wants to put an end to Paul's dream.

'Let me put in a year up there,' Greg insisted. 'I'll do my best to find a way to make the base really profitable, without bookkeeping tricks. But if I can't, after a whole year, then I'll recommend we close the operation for good.'

'Do you think you can make that decision?'

'After a year of hands-on management up there, yes.'

'What do you see as a potential profit-maker?' Joanna asked. 'If anything.'

'I don't know!' he said, agitated. 'They've been using nanotechnology up there. Maybe we can turn Moonbase into a nanotech research center.'

'We've been through this before, Greg,' Joanna objected. 'The public resistance to nanotechnology is too strong. People are frightened of it. The San Jose labs were trashed. We even had to close down the nanofactory in Austin because of the public pressure.'

'Yes, yes, I know,' Greg said impatiently. 'And I heard the Vice President's speech last week, too.'

'He's asking for a U.N. treaty to ban *all* nanotechnology all over the world!' Joanna said.

'He'll be president after November,' said Greg gloomily. 'He's certain to win.'

'A man like that in the White House.'

With a sardonic smile, Greg said, 'He won't be the first ignoramus to get there.'

'But he's violently opposed to nanotechnology; he's making it a religious issue.'

Joanna did not add that the deaths on the Moon caused by 'runaway' nanomachines were still prime ammunition for the anti-nanotech Luddites. She did not have to.

'Ambitious politicians always play to the peoples' fears,' Greg replied impatiently. 'Since when do we let that determine corporate policy?'

Joanna shook her head. 'It's like the fear the public had of the old nuclear power plants. It's irrational, but it's very real. It generates political power, more power than we can challenge.'

'I don't agree.'

'We can't invest major resources in nanomanufacturing, Greg. We haven't even been able to put medical nanoproducts on the market, and they've been proved to save lives. The government, the public, the *media* – they've stopped us every time we've tried.'

Greg countered, 'But maybe if we do it in space . . . on the Moon or in orbit. Everybody's afraid of nanobugs getting loose and running wild, so we do it all in space where they can't get loose.'

'But what will they build? What can you make in space that we can sell here on the ground?'

'I don't know,' Greg admitted. 'Not yet. That's why I want to spend a year at Moonbase, to see what they can do.'

Joanna stared at her son. He was serious, intent, perhaps even confident. Even though she was afraid of his unconscious desires, she couldn't refuse him.

'If you can find a product that could make Moonbase profitable,' Joanna said slowly, 'or even if you have the strength to recommend closing the base – you'll have earned your place on the board of directors.'

'You mean you'd nominate me?'

She could see all the hope, all the need in him. He's been through so much, Joanna thought. But another part of her mind asked, Can you really trust him? Do you dare to let him shoulder so much responsibility? Can he handle it without breaking down?

'Let me talk with a few people,' she temporized. 'In the meantime, I'll see about getting you the Moonbase job.'

'That's the best birthday present you could give me,' Greg said.

Doug is at Moonbase, Joanna reminded herself. I don't want them both up there at the same time.

'I love you, Mom.'

Joanna felt sudden tears blurring her vision. 'I love you too, Greg.'

She knew that she meant it with every fiber of her being. She hoped that Greg meant his words, too. Yet she was always afraid that he still didn't understand what love really was.

He had been so sick, so terribly mixed up. He had never seen a loving relationship in his home until I met Paul, and then . . .

Joanna shut her eyes inside the VR helmet and refused to cry. This is a step in Greg's recovery, she told herself. I can't refuse to let him go to Moonbase.

Then she realized, If we close Moonbase it will be the end of all Paul's dreams. Greg will be killing him all over again. And I'll be helping him.

MOONBASE

It was easy for experienced Lunatics to spot newcomers to the Moon. They walked funny. Unaccustomed to the one-sixth lunar gravity, they stumbled or even hopped when they tried to take a step.

But not Doug Stavenger. Even though he had already been to Moonbase once, briefly, he left Savannah a week early and spent the time at the main Masterson space station, in orbit around the Earth, living in the wheel that spun to simulate lunar gravity. So when he arrived at Moonbase he did not need weighted boots. Once in a while he forgot himself and went soaring off the floor when he merely wanted to take a long stride. But by and large he fit into the underground life of Moonbase quite smoothly.

Until he ran into the linear football game.

It was almost midnight. Although most of the offices and labs were closed for the night, the tunnels remained as brightly lit as always. Doug had spent the evening in the workshop that Foster Brennart had converted into his office, going over details of the expedition. Brennart was a stickler for detail; he seemed to know every part and piece and item of equipment that had been assembled for the trek to the south pole. He could account for every gram of food, oxygen, water, even the aluminum chips that were used as fuel for the expedition's rocket craft.

Doug was determined that he would know as much about the expedition as Brennart did; especially the people. He copied all the personnel files and now, carrying the microdisks in his coverall pockets, he was heading for his own quarters and some sleep before setting out to meet each person slated to go on the expedition.

He heard shouting from down the tunnel. And scuffling. A fight?

The tunnels curved slightly, and had emergency air-tight hatches every twenty yards that remained open unless the sensors detected a drop in air pressure. Stepping through one of the open hatches, Doug jogged along the tunnel until he saw a half-dozen men and women tussling, pushing, kicking – and laughing.

'Outta the way, tenderfoot!' one of the group hollered as he kicked a small round object in Doug's direction. It was flat and black, like a hockey puck. As it skittered toward him, Paul saw that it was the plastic top from a container.

It bounced off a wall and the whole gang of men and women raced after it.

'Watch out!' yelled a young Asian woman, short and stocky, grinning toothily.

The commotion boiled right into Doug. They were all young people, he saw, not much more than his own age. The coveralls they wore were mostly the pumpkin orange of the science and exploration group, although there was a medical white and even a management blue among them, the same as Doug's own jumpsuit. One of the guys brushed past him, pushing him into the rock wall.

'Linear football,' the young woman gasped, by way of explanation. Then they were past him, kicking the black plastic lid down the corridor.

Doug trotted after them. The game seemed to have no rules. Everybody tried to kick the lid; they all scrambled to reach it, pushing and elbowing and laughing every inch of the way. Somebody kicked it into the slight niche of a doorway and they all whooped wildly. In an instant, though, the game continued down the tunnel.

Doug followed them and before he knew it he was part of the game, too. It became obvious that the object was to kick the lid into a doorway. There were no teams, though; it was all against each. And the scorekeeping was casual, at best.

'That's eight for me!'

'The hell it is!'

'You've only got six.'

'No, eight.'

'What's the difference? Are we playing or doing arithmetic?'

The tunnel ended at the closed hatch that led into the main garage, where the surface tractors were stored and serviced. The six men and women collapsed against the walls and slid to the floor, panting, sweating, all grins. Doug sank into a crouch with them.

'You're Doug Stavenger, aren't you?' asked the Asian woman.

He nodded, trying to catch his breath.

One of the young men puffed, 'For a tenderfoot . . . you run . . . pretty good.'

Doug said, 'Thanks.'

After a few minutes, one of the women said, 'Hey, it's past midnight already. I've got to be on the job at oh-eight hundred.'

'That's where you sleep, isn't it?'

'A comedian, yet.'

Slowly, laboriously, they clambered to their feet and started trudging back toward the living quarters.

'I'm Bianca Rhee,' the Asian woman said. Built like a fireplug, she barely came up to Doug's shoulder. 'The brilliant and beautiful Eurasian astrophysicist.'

Doug must have gaped at her, because she laughed out loud. Soon they were talking like old friends as they walked along the tunnel.

'Doesn't anybody complain about the noise you guys make?' Doug asked. 'People are sleeping on the other side of some of those doors.'

'Oh, we wake them up, I guess. But the game moves past them so fast that by the time they're really awake we've moved down the tunnel.'

'Nobody's ever complained?'

'Oh, sure. But we don't get up a game *every* night.'

They walked in silence for a while. 'You're an astrophysicist, you said?'

Bianca nodded. She had often used that 'beautiful Eurasian' line to see what kind of reaction it would cause. In truth, her beauty was not physical. Short, thick-waisted, with a face as round and flat as a pie pan, Bianca was the daughter of a Korean-American father and Italian-American mother. She claimed that she grew up on sushi parmigiana.

She was bored with the astronomical work she was doing at Moonbase. It was strictly routine photometry, using the wide-field Schmidt telescope to make painstakingly accurate measurements of the positions of galaxies. Adding another decimal point or two to the details. The kind of work that they stick graduate students with, while the major players get to do the exciting stuff, like scoping out black holes in galactic cores or searching for extraterrestrial intelligence.

Her work was so routine that she had set up a computer program to run the telescope and catalogue the results, and began to spend her time calculating how to build a giant telescope using liquid mercury for its mirror. And – when she was sure no one else could see her – practicing ballet in the low lunar gravity.

But suddenly, with Douglas Stavenger walking beside her, she got another idea.

'You know,' she said, 'I could use your help.'

'Mine?'

'I'd like to come along on Brennart's expedition.'

Doug stopped walking and looked at her. 'Why?' he asked. 'Why should Brennart take an astrophysicist along? What good would that do for the expedition? Or for you, for that matter?'

Bianca answered with one word. 'Farside.'

Before she could start to explain, he said, 'You want to set up an astronomical observatory on the farside, and the expedition to the south pole can be a sort of training mission. Is that it?'

'Exactly!' She was impressed with how quickly he grasped the idea.

With a slow grin, Doug went on, 'That's a pretty flimsy excuse, don't you think?'

Damn! she thought. He sees right through me. But she found herself grinning back and admitting, 'True. But it's the only one I could think of.'

By the time they reached her door Doug had promised he would speak to Brennart about her. Bianca wanted to kiss him, but decided it was too soon for that. Sternly, she reminded herself that this good-looking young man was five years her junior. She also remembered that men attain the peak of their sexual potency around the age of eighteen.

Doug did not seem to have any romantic intentions. So they merely shook hands, and then he headed down the tunnel toward his own quarters. She dreamed about him that night. She dreamed she was a slender and graceful ballerina and he was hopelessly in love with her.

Almost everyone in Moonbase wore utilitarian coveralls with nametags pinned to their chests. Yet even though Brennart wore a one-piece jumpsuit just as most others did, he needed no nametag. Although he belonged to the exploration and research group, he insisted on wearing pure white coveralls, clean and crisp as if they had just been laundered and pressed, and decorated with shoulder patches and chest emblems from the dozens of missions he had undertaken during his years as an astronaut and lunar explorer.

Doug Stavenger did not consciously think of Brennart as a father figure, but the older man's single-minded drive to establish a working base in the south polar region of the Moon impressed Doug forcefully.

'Do you really think Yamagata's planning an expedition to Aitkin Basin, too?' Doug asked.

'No doubt in my mind about that,' said Brennart, in his sweet tenor voice. 'They'd be damned fools not to.'

It was the morning after the football game, and Doug's meeting Bianca Rhee. He and Brennart were hunched over a display table in Brennart's workshop/office, studying the latest satellite photos of the Mt. Wasser area.

'After all,' Brennart went on, 'we're going out there, aren't we? The Japanese are just as smart as we are. That's why we've got to get there first. Like the man said, the side that wins is the one that gets there firstest with the mostest.'

Doug nodded as he straightened up. Brennart's office was one of the largest rooms in Moonbase, but still it felt hot and cramped. Most of the equipment that jammed the office was already crated and ready to be loaded on the ballistic lobbers. Doug saw a tousled cot in one corner, and realized that Brennart was sleeping in this room, too.

Brennart tapped the satellite display with a fingernail. 'This is where we'll put down. Right here, at the foot of the mountain. Close as lovers in a spacesuit built for two.'

Doug looked down again. 'It's hard to make out details of that area. It's too heavily shadowed.'

'It's an ice field,' Brennart said.

Doug stepped over to the end of the table and worked the keyboard. False-color infrared imagery of the region appeared over the satellite picture.

'Not ice,' he murmured. 'The spectrographic data shows anorthosite rock. Typical highlands profile.'

Brennart straightened up and stretched his arms over his head. His hands bumped the smoothed rock ceiling. 'Been coming up here more than twenty years and I still can't get used to how low the ceilings are,' he muttered.

'That area might be too rough for a landing,' Doug suggested. 'But over here—'

'We want to be as close to the mountain as possible,' Brennart interrupted. 'We land where I said we'll land.'

Doug looked up at the older man. There was iron in his tone. Brennart seemed totally convinced of his decision and completely unwilling to consider any alternatives.

Then he smiled down at Doug. 'I know you're concerned about safety, son. So am I. Be a fool not to. Like the man said, there are old astronauts and bold astronauts, but there are no old, bold astronauts.'

'Uh-huh,' Doug mumbled, for lack of anything better to say.

'I'm an old astronaut, son. If the landing area looks too spooky as we approach it, I'll simply goose the lobber a bit and land in the clear field, a little further from our goal.'

Returning his smile, Doug said, 'I see. Okay. I should have thought of that.'

'Nothing to worry about,' said Brennart. Then he added, 'Except coming in second to the Japanese.'

A little later, Doug asked Brennart about taking Bianca Rhee along with them.

'An astrophysicist?' Brennart seemed startled at the suggestion. 'Why on earth should I take an astrophysicist along? This isn't a tourist excursion, you know.'

'We have room for her,' Doug said. 'I've checked the logistics program and we could handle six more people, if we needed them.'

'Yes,' Brennart said, 'but I need an astrophysicist like a nun needs condoms.'

'She could be useful,' Doug said.

'Doing what?'

'She's a good technician. I've looked up her personnel profile and she's qualified for electrical, electromechanical, and computer repairs and maintenance.'

'I already have all the technicians I need.'

'But think of the longer-range situation,' Doug said.

Brennart glanced down at him. 'What longer-range situation?'

'Somebody's going to build an astronomical center on the farside, sooner or later. She could help you get the experience you need to lead that mission, when the time comes.'

Brennart pursed his lips. 'Farside.' His eyes looked off into the future.

'Farside,' Doug repeated, knowing he had won Bianca a spot on the team.

They celebrated that night with as festive a dinner as could be obtained at Moonbase: prepackaged turkey with holiday trimmings, microwaved somewhat short of perfection. Bianca invited all her friends, and they pushed tables together in The Cave, careful not to tread on the semi-sacred grass.

Although there was talk around the table of a mysterious still that produced 'rocket juice,' the high spirits of the gang did not come from alcohol. When at last the crowd broke up, Doug escorted Bianca to her quarters. She gave him a peck on the cheek and then swiftly went inside and slid the accordion-fold door shut.

He's too young, she told herself. Probably a virgin. No, she contradicted herself immediately. Not with those looks. But why should he be interested in you? He's the son of the corporation's chairwoman. He's young and good-looking and rich and kind and . . .

She stared at her image in the full-length aluminum mirror on the rock wall of her room. You used him and he was kind enough to let you do it. He's not interested in you sexually. Who would be?

Bianca did not cry. But she wanted to.

Doug was too keyed up to go back to his quarters and go to sleep. Instead, he jogged up the tunnel to the main garage and asked the security guard on duty for permission to go up to the surface.

The garage was quiet and shadowy, tractors parked in precise rows along the faded yellow lines painted on the rock floor, barely visible in the dim nighttime lighting.

The guard cocked a doubtful eye at him, then checked Doug's record on his display screen.

'You've been here three days and you've already spent six hours on the surface?'

'Yes, that sounds about right,' said Doug.

'You some kind of scientist?'

Shaking his head, Doug said, 'No. Not yet, at least.'

'Says here you're okay to go out alone,' the guard said, still dubious. 'But you stay inside camera range, understand? If I've gotta wake up a team to go out and find you, your ass is gonna be in deep glop. Understand?'

'Understood,' said Doug, grinning. Obviously the guard thinks I'm some kind of freak, going out alone in the middle of the night. Even though it's full daylight outside.

Doug went down the row of lockers where the surface suits hung like empty suits of armor, looking for one his size. After he got it all on, Doug spent an hour reading through the logistics list for the expedition on his hand computer while he pre-breathed the suit's low-pressure mix of oxygen and nitrogen. Finally the security guard came out of his cubicle long enough to check out the suit's seals and connections.

'Your suit malfunctions, it's my ass,' he muttered. Once he completed the checklist, though, he pointed Doug to the personnel airlock and said cheerfully, 'Okay kid, now you're on your own.'

Through the sealed visor of his helmet Doug said, 'Thanks for your help.'

The guard simply shook his head, obviously convinced this strange young visitor was crazy, even though his record said he was qualified for solo excursions on the surface.

The massive steel hatch for the vehicles was tightly closed; Doug used the smaller personnel airlock set into the rock wall beside it and stepped into the brilliant glare of sunlight. The cracked, pockmarked floor of Alphonsus stretched out before him all the way to the strangely close horizon. The worn, rounded ringwall mountains slumped on both sides like tired old men basking in the sun.

Doug smiled. 'Magnificent desolation,' he muttered, remembering Aldrin's words. But he did not see desolation in this harsh lunar landscape. Doug saw unearthly beauty.

And more.

He paced out across the dusty crater floor, carefully counting his steps, knowing that the safety cameras were watching him. At one hundred paces he stopped and turned back to face the cameras, the airlock hatch, Moonbase.

Off to his left the ground was scoured bare and blasted by rocket exhausts. The expedition's four ungainly-looking ballistic lobbers stood on the base's four landing pads, the most visible mark of human habitation. The base itself was barely discernible. Just a few humps of rubble marked the various airlocks. Most of the base was dug into the mountain wall, of course.

Mt. Yeager. Doug looked up to its summit, gleaming in the sunlight. More than twelve thousand feet to the top, Doug knew. I'll have to climb it before I go back home.

He turned a full circle, there alone on the crater floor except for the automated tractors patiently scooping up regolith sand and the distant glistening slick of the tiny, invisible nanomachines quietly building new solar cells out of the regolith's silicon and trace metals.

Doug saw the future.

Where I'm standing will be just about a tenth of the way along the main plaza, Doug said to himself. The plaza floor will be dug in below the surface, of course, but its dome will rise more than a hundred feet over my head. We'll plant it with grass and trees, get it landscaped with walking lanes through the shrubbery and even a swimming pool.

It'll be a real city, he thought. With permanent residents and families having babies and everything. We'll set up a cable car system over Mt. Yeager, out to Mare Nubium. That'll be easier than trying to tunnel through the mountain, especially in this gravity. We'll have to move the rocket port further out, but we'll connect it with tunnels.

For more than two hours Doug paced out the structures he visualized, the city that Moonbase could become. We can do it, he told himself. If I can get Mom to agree . . .

Then reality intruded on his dream. 'Mr. Stavenger, this is security. You've been outside for two hours. Unless you have some specific duties to perform, standard regulations require that you return to the airlock.'

Doug nodded inside the helmet of his spacesuit. 'Understood,' he said. 'I'm coming back in.'

But he brought his dream with him.

LEV BRUDNOY

They had disconnected all the life-support tubes and wires. Lana Goodman knew she was dying and she was tired of fighting it. She was nothing but a shell of a creature now, fragile, shrivelled, each breath a labor.

Lev Brudnoy sat at her bedside in Moonbase's tiny infirmary, his expressive face a picture of grief. Behind him stood Jinny Anson, gripping the back of Brudnoy's chair with white-knuckled intensity.

'You know the one thing I regret?' Goodman's voice was a harsh, labored whisper.

Brudnoy, tears in his eyes, shook his head.

'I regret that you never made a pass at me, Lev.'

For once in his life, Brudnoy was stunned into silence.

'You came on to just about every other woman in Moonbase,' Goodman wheezed, 'except me.'

Brudnoy gulped once and found his voice, 'Lovely woman,' he said softly, 'I was too much afraid of being rejected. You have always been so far above me . . .'

Goodman smiled. 'We could have had some times together.'

'Never in my wildest fantasies could I hope that you would be interested in a foolish dog like me,' Brudnoy muttered, letting his head sink low.

'You're a good old dog, Lev. No fool.'

He spread his hands. 'I'm nothing but a peasant. I spend all my time in the farm now.'

'I know,' Goodman whispered. 'The flowers . . . they cheered me up.'

'The least I could do.'

'I want you to bury me in your farm,' Goodman said.

'Not return to Earth?'

'This is my home. Bury me here. In the farm. Where what's left of me can do some good.'

Brudnoy turned toward Jinny Anson. 'Is that allowed? Is it legal?'

'I'm a witness,' Anson said. 'I'll see that the forms are properly filled out.'

'In the farm.' Goodman's voice was so faint now that Brudnoy had to bend over her emaciated form to hear her. 'Always did believe in ecology. Recycle me.'

Then she sighed and closed her eyes. For a moment Brudnoy thought she had fallen asleep. But then the remote sensors started shrilling their single note.

A doctor appeared at the foot of her bed. Brudnoy struggled to his feet, a big lumbering man, weathered but still handsome, slightly paunchy, his shoulders slumped and his hair graying. There seemed to be new lines in his face every year; every day, he sometimes thought. A ragged gray beard covered his chin.

He felt Anson's hand on his arm as he shambled out of the infirmary, leaving behind its odor of clean sheets and implacable death.

The tunnel was bright and cheerful, by contrast. People strode by as if nothing had happened on the other side of the infirmary's doors. Young people, Brudnoy realized. All of them younger than I. Even Jinny.

'Well,' he said, trying to straighten up, 'now I'm the oldest resident of Moonbase. I suppose I'll be the next to go.'

Anson smiled up at him. 'Not for another hundred years, at least.'

'At least,' Brudnoy murmured.

'Come on, let me buy you a drink. We could both use some rocket juice.'

'You?' Some of the old playfulness sparkled in Brudnoy's sky-blue eyes. 'You, the base director? You speak of illegal alcoholic drinks?'

Anson grinned wickedly at him. 'What kind of a director

would I be if I didn't know about the still? Besides, I won't be director much longer. My relief is due in another two weeks.'

She led Brudnoy to her own quarters, where she uncovered her stash of 'rocket juice:' a gallon-sized thermos jug she kept under her bunk. She and Brudnoy had shared that bunk more than once; but that was years ago.

Now, as they sat on the springy wire chairs that Anson had made from scrap metal, Brudnoy sipped the homebrew thoughtfully.

'Is it legal?' he asked.

'The booze? Of course not. But as long as people don't drink during their work shifts, there's no sense trying to find the still and knock it apart. Damn little else to do for entertainment around here.'

Brudnoy shook his head. 'I meant Lana's request to be buried in the farm.'

Anson said, 'As long as I'm in charge here we'll honor her last request. There's probably some relatives back Earthside; if they want her they'll have to get a court order.'

'I'll see to the burial, then,' Brudnoy said.

'How soon?'

'I'll talk with the medical people. Tomorrow, I imagine, would be good enough.'

'I'll be there. I'll get the word out, a lot of the old-timers will want to come.'

'Old-timers,' Brudnoy echoed. 'Yes, that's what we've become.'

Anson quickly changed the subject. 'How's the farm doing?'

'Lunar soil is very rich in nutrients,' Brudnoy said. 'What we need is more earthworms and beetles.'

She took a sip of her drink, then replied slowly, 'We've got to be *very* careful about introducing any kind of life forms here. That's why I brought that team of biologists up here. I don't want any runaway populations of *any* kind.'

Brudnoy sipped also. 'Your biologists spend more time at my little farm than I do.'

'That's what they're paid to do.'

'All I wanted was to grow some beautiful flowers.'

'Yeah, but we should be growing more of our own food.'

'Someday.' He winked mischievously. 'Once we have enough worms and beetles.'

'Ugh,' said Anson.

'How long will you be Earthside?' he asked.

Anson took a breath. 'I don't think I'll be coming back, Lev.'

'No? Why not?'

'I'm going to get married,' she said. 'Would you believe it?'

'You mean you've been carrying on a romance Earthside? For how long?'

'Two years now.'

'Two years! And you never told me.'

'You're the first one I have told,' Anson said. 'It's time for me to settle down. No more gypsying. He's a university professor with two daughters from his first marriage. Very stable guy.'

'Well . . . good luck.' Brudnoy said it with enormous reluctance.

'Thanks.' She took a larger swallow from her cup. 'I just wish this Brennart trip had started sooner. Hate to leave while they're out on their own.'

'Who will your replacement be?'

She shook her head. 'Should be O'Rourke.'

Brudnoy made a sour face.

'He's good at his job,' Anson said.

'Yes,' Brudnoy said. 'And about as much fun as a flat rock.'

Anson laughed. 'He's not a high-flier, that's for sure.'

'Perhaps you should stay until the expedition returns,' Brudnoy suggested.

'No can do,' said Anson. 'I've got a husband to catch.'

'Ahhh,' Brudnoy sighed. 'Too bad. We used to have such good times together.'

'Well,' she said, drawing the word out languidly, 'we have two weeks before I have to leave.'

Brudnoy's brows shot up. 'But you're about to be married!'

'For old times' sake,' Anson said, leaning toward him. 'Besides, I don't want to be out of practice.'

It was more than an hour later when Brudnoy finally left her quarters. Out in the tunnel, blinking in the overhead lights, he smiled to himself. For an old dog you performed rather well. But then he saw that the people striding along the tunnel all looked so young. So fresh. When Jinny leaves I'll be the only old dog left here. He realized that there were hardly any people left in Moonbase that he knew very well. All the old friends have gone, Brudnoy said to himself.

He felt very old and tired as he walked slowly toward the farm.

'We leave tomorrow,' Doug said happily.

Even from a quarter-million miles away, Joanna could see his excitement. She leaned back in her embracing leather chair and studied her young son's smiling face.

'The expedition shouldn't take longer than two weeks,' he was saying, not waiting for her to reply. 'We've got the nanobugs all set, all the equipment's checked out. Of course, we're carrying supplies for a month, just in case. And we can always be resupplied by rocket lobber . . .'

As he prattled on eagerly, Joanna wondered if it would be wise to tell him about Greg now or wait until he was safely back from the polar expedition.

'. . . so this time tomorrow we'll be at the south pole,' Doug finished.

'Your brother's coming up to Moonbase,' Joanna heard herself say. 'He's going to be the new director when Anson leaves.'

Then she held her breath for three seconds until her words reached him.

Doug's eyes widened slightly. 'Greg? The new director?'

'Yes,' said Joanna. 'He asked for the position and I think he's earned it.'

She could see the wheels spinning in Doug's head. 'He's coming up here to close down Moonbase, isn't he?'

No sense trying to lie to him, she thought. 'He's going to spend the coming year trying to find some way to make Moonbase truly profitable. But if he can't, then, yes, we'll have to shut it down.'

Doug's smile had faded but not disappeared. He seemed to be mulling over the possibilities. 'If we can come up with a profitable product, then he'll keep the base open?'

'Yes, of course.'

In the three seconds it took for her reply to reach him, Doug seemed to brighten. 'Clipperships are still the corporation's most valuable product, aren't they?'

'They're just about our only profitable product,' Joanna admitted. 'And the Windowalls, of course.'

But Doug didn't wait for her answer. He went on, 'Then why don't we start to build the next generation of Clipperships here at Moonbase?'

'That's foolishness, Doug,' she said. 'Why build the ships on the Moon when we can build them perfectly well at our plants here in Texas and Georgia?'

He waited, grinning, as if he knew what she would say. Then he replied, 'Because here we can build them out of pure diamond, using nanomachines.'

'Diamond?'

'Diamond is lighter, stronger than any metal alloy,' he said, without pausing. 'We can build Clipperships that will outperform anything you can make on Earth, at a fraction of your manufacturing costs.'

'Using nanomachines,' Joanna murmured. Then she thought aloud, 'But to make diamond you need carbon. There isn't any carbon on the Moon, is there?'

'Not much,' Doug admitted. 'Nowhere near enough. We'll have to snag one of the Earth-crossing asteroids and mine it for carbon.'

'Mine an asteroid?'

Doug rolled right along, hardly drawing a breath. 'We can convert one of the transfer ships to make a rendez-vous with a carbon-bearing asteroid. There's plenty of them in orbits that come close to the Earth/Moon system; no need to go out to the asteroid belt, that's 'way out past Mars.'

'Do you really think you can build Clipperships out of diamond?' Joanna asked.

When her question reached him, Doug replied easily, 'Why not? It's just a matter of programming nanomachines.'

'And a diamond ship will be better than the ones we're manufacturing now?'

Doug waited patiently, then answered, 'They'll be lighter, much stronger, capable of carrying heavier payloads with the same rocket thrust, safer, more durable. What else can you ask for?'

'Cheaper to manufacture,' Joanna replied.

He nodded once he heard her response. 'Not only cheaper to manufacture, but the aerospace lines will be willing to pay more for them, since they'll perform so much better than today's ships.'

Despite herself, Joanna felt almost breathless at the sweep of Doug's vision. 'We could use nanomachines to manufacture other things, too, couldn't we?'

'Aircraft,' Doug said.

'Automobiles!'

'Houses,' Doug added, grinning hugely.

'All by using nanomachines for manufacturing,' said Joanna. 'Masterson Corporation could become the biggest, most powerful company in the solar system.'

Joanna felt the same excitement her son did. But then she remembered the realities. 'People are afraid of nanotechnology, Doug. There are powerful forces opposing it.'

His cheerful grin didn't shrink by a millimeter when he heard her doubts. 'But don't you see, Mom? This will show everybody that nanotechnology works! It'll knock the opposition flat!'

'And it will save Moonbase,' Joanna said.

'Right!'

If it works, Joanna thought. If the nanoluddites don't prevent us from doing it. If Greg doesn't try to stop his brother from trying.

BALLISTIC VEHICLE 1

The liftoff wasn't exactly silent. When the rocket ignited Doug could feel a surge of vibration in his bones that rumbled in his ears almost like sound. Still, the lack of thundering noise made Doug feel slightly eerie. And of course the thrust he felt was minuscule compared to a Clippership liftoff from Earth.

The excitement of the previous night's conversation with his mother hadn't worn off, exactly. The thought of going out to capture an asteroid and then using its carbon to build Clipperships out of diamond still tingled in the back of Doug's mind. But that was for the future. This flight to the Moon's south pole was *now*.

He had spent an hour in the main airlock, big enough to accommodate full-sized tractors and dozens of people, prebreathing the oxygen-nitrogen mixture that they would be using throughout the expedition. Moonbase ran on 'normal' air: almost eighty percent nitrogen and twenty oxygen, with traces of carbon dioxide and water vapor, all at 14.7 pounds per square inch, almost exactly like the clean dry atmosphere of a desert region on Earth. The surface suits still worked at five psi, with a 72/28 ratio of oxygen to nitrogen.

Moonbase safety regulations called for prebreathing the spacesuit mix for an hour before going outside, to get the excess nitrogen out of the blood stream and prevent the bends.

Now, strapped into the bare metal seat in the ballistic lobber, his suit buttoned up tight, Doug felt weird as the rocket engines blasted them off the floor of Alphonsus in almost total silence.

The lobbers were modified versions of the transfer space-craft that shuttled passengers and freight from Earth orbit to the Moon. There was nothing aerodynamic about them, since they never flew in an atmosphere. They were utilitarian assemblies of silvered tankage, rocket engines, bulky cargo containers, pressurized personnel pods, and spindly legs that jutted out from the four corners of the spacecraft's main platform.

Doug felt the rockets' vibration through the metal frame of the vehicle; it was almost sound, like a thunder so distant and faint you wonder if you've heard anything at all. The spacecraft rose quickly enough; Doug could see through the transparent bubble of the passenger pod the slumped mountains of the ringwall whiz past and then nothing but the darkness of space. But there was hardly any palpable acceleration, none of the heavy forces that pushed you down in your seat when you lifted off from Earth.

And then all sense of thrust disappeared. The vibration ceased, too. Engines have cut off, Doug knew. We're coasting on a ballistic trajectory now, like an artillery shell.

His suit helmet cut off his view of Bianca Rhee, sitting beside him. There were four others crowded into the plastiglass bubble of a passenger module, plus Brennart and Killifer up in the cockpit module. The eight other expedition members were in the second lobber. The other two rocket vehicles carried only cargo; unmanned, they were guided remotely.

'How do you like it?' he asked Bianca.

Her voice in his helmet earphones sounded strained. 'If I could walk, I'd do it.'

Doug laughed. 'This is a lot easier than walking. And safer.'

'It's the free-fall,' said Bianca. 'Makes my stomach want to turn inside out.'

'Well, try to relax. We'll be back on the ground in about half an hour.'

'Can't be too soon.'

The spacecraft tilted forward a few degrees, enough so that they could look down at the cratered mountains sliding below them, dwindling as the lobber headed for the peak of its ballistic trajectory. Bianca groaned aloud.

'Isn't that Tycho?' Doug said, tapping a gloved finger against the plastiglass canopy. 'Over there, near the horizon.'

The crater was unmistakable: big and sharp, with bright rays of debris streaking out of it for hundreds of miles. One of the newest big craters on the Moon, Doug said to himself. Not even a billion years old.

'Tycho,' Bianca said, awed. 'Wow, I've never seen it so close.'

'It's beautiful, isn't it?' said Doug.

'Sure is.'

She leaned over until her helmet visor was touching the canopy's plastiglass. Doug knew that Tycho marked the midpoint of their half-hour flight. He hoped it would keep Bianca fascinated long enough to make her forget about barfing.

Foster Brennart sat up in the lobber's cockpit, a separate and smaller bubble that projected out to one side of the lobber. Jack Killifer was in the co-pilot's seat. Panels of instruments and controls surrounded them at waist height. Above the panel the bubble was clear plastiglass.

Killifer took a wire from one of the pouches in his spacesuit's belt, plugged it into an access port in the side of his helmet, then plugged the other end into the similar port in Brennart's helmet. Now they could talk to one another without using their suit radios, which might be overheard.

'Smooth liftoff,' Killifer said.

If Brennart was flattered by the praise, his tone failed to show it. 'Check the other craft, see how their takeoffs went.'

'Right.'

Killifer dutifully called the second ballistic craft as he checked the instrument readouts for the two unmanned vehicles.

'No problems. Just like four tennis balls,' Killifer said to the expedition commander.

'Tennis balls?' Brennart sounded puzzled.

'That's where the term *lobber* comes from, Foster. These ballistic birds go like a tennis ball that's been lobbed up in the air.' He gestured with his gloved hand. 'Up, up, up, and then down, down, down.'

Brennart was silent for a few moments. 'Never played tennis,' he said at last. 'Never had the time.'

'I used to, a little,' said Killifer. 'Back when I was in California.'

The memory ached in his gut. Nanotechnology had not expanded much in the eighteen years since he'd been forced out of the field. Still, he told himself, I could've been an executive, a rich man, a leader in the field. I could have taken Cardenas' spot when she left the corporation. Instead, here I am, a quarter-million miles from anything worthwhile, second-in-command on a loony expedition to the ass end of nowhere. With Joanna Stavenger's son stuck into the pecking order ahead of me.

Deftly, Brennart fired the attitude control jets, just a slight puff to tilt the craft enough so they could see the ground sliding by far below them. Rugged mountains, peppered with craters.

'No one's ever set foot on that territory,' Brennart said. 'Not yet.'

Killifer grunted. He was still thinking about his younger days in California.

'We've only begun to explore the Moon. There's a whole world waiting for us to put our bootprints on it,' said Brennart.

Killifer smiled inside his helmet. 'Wasn't this expedition your idea?'

'It certainly was,' Brennart answered immediately. 'It took the better part of two years to convince Mrs. Stavenger to let us go. It wasn't until I showed her that Yamagata's preparing an expedition that she finally gave her okay.'

'That's what I thought.'

Brennart turned toward him. In the spacesuit it required him to move from the waist, torso and shoulders, so he could look at his second-in-command. What he saw was the reflection of his own helmet in Killifer's visor.

'You know how hard I worked to convince her. Of course this expedition is my idea. Who else's?'

'Nobody,' Killifer replied. 'Only . . .'

'Only what?'

'Why'd she send her kid along?'

'Douglas?'

'Yeah.'

'He's like a kid with a new toy, all excited about being on the Moon and working with me,' Brennart said happily.

'Oh,' said Killifer. 'Yeah.'

It only took a couple of seconds for Brennart to ask, 'Why, are you worried about the kid?'

'Not about him.' Killifer put just the slightest stress on the word *him*.

'Who, then?'

'Aw, nobody. Forget it. I'm just being a geek.'

'What do you mean?' Brennart insisted. 'What's eating you?'

'It's just that – well, do you think the Stavenger woman would send her son up here just to do a job that any brain-dead clerk could do?'

Brennart did not answer for a while. Then, 'Why else?'

Killifer took a breath, then, with apparent reluctance, he answered, 'Well . . . maybe, I don't know . . .'

'What?' Brennart demanded.

'Maybe she wants him to get the credit for your work. Her son, I mean.'

'Get the credit?'

'Once we've established legal priority and we set up the power tower and everything,' Killifer said in a rush, '*he'll* get all the credit with the board of directors. And the news media. You do the work but he'll be the hero.'

'That's crazy,' Brennart snapped.

'Yeah, I guess so.'

'How could he get the credit for what I do? I'm the mission commander. I'm in charge.'

'Yeah, I know.'

'He can't take the credit away from me. That's impossible.'

'Sure,' said Killifer.

Brennart lapsed into silence. After a few moments he muttered, 'So that's why he was so hot to get up here with me.'

'Maybe it's not him,' Killifer said. 'Maybe it's all his mother's idea.'

'Either way,' Brennart growled. 'Either way.'

Killifer smiled behind his helmet visor. He thought he could see smoke rising from his commander's spacesuit.

Joanna cast a knowing eye over the guests who filled her spacious living room. The party was going well; she could tell that with her eyes closed: the chatter of conversations and laughter filled the room and spilled over into the hallway and the library, as well. The clink of ice cubes added a background counterpoint.

Joanna had been nursing the same tall fluted glass of champagne for almost an hour now. Gowned in a magnificent silver and taupe brocade jacket over a filmy chiffon skirt, she searched the crowded room. Men in immaculate white dinner jackets, women in glittering jewels and the latest fashions. But the one man she wanted to find was nowhere to be seen.

Slowly she made her way through the crowd, chatting briefly with a couple here, smiling as she passed a group there. Across the hallway and into the library she went. Still no sight of Quintana. He wouldn't have left so early, she thought, especially without saying good night to his hostess.

Through the French windows of the library she saw a solitary figure out on the patio, the gleam of a cigar smoldering in the dark Georgia night. Quintana. Still smoking, despite all the laws against it.

Joanna slipped through the open doorway and approached Quintana, her high heels clicking on the patio tiles.

'What you're doing is illegal, Carlos,' she said softly, smiling as he turned toward her.

He smiled back. 'In Mexico we have much more freedom.'

'You also have much more pollution. And cancer.'

Quintana waved his long, slim cigar. 'The price of freedom. Will you call the police?'

Laughing, Joanna said, 'No. But I'd prefer that you throw that thing away.'

'It's barely started.' Quintana examined his cigar like a man admiring a fine work of art. 'But for you, beautiful one, I make the sacrifice.' He let the cigar drop to the patio floor and ground it out with the heel of his highly-polished shoe.

Even in the shadows of the night Joanna could see his gleaming smile. Carlos Quintana was the kind of man for whom the word *dashing* had been coined. A mining engineer who parleyed intelligence and daring into a considerable fortune, he was a champion polo player, a yachtsman of note, and a key member of Masterson Aerospace's board of directors. Handsome, suave, he had the kind of classic Latin male good looks that would remain virtually untouched all his life. No one knew his true age; the guesses ran from forty-five to seventy.

'My party bored you?' Joanna asked as they strolled side by side toward the garden. Overhead a sliver of a Moon was rising and stars glittered in the dark sky.

'No, I just felt the need for some nicotine,' Quintana said. 'And I knew that as soon as I lit up you would come running at me with a fire extinguisher.'

'You're hopeless,' she said, laughing again.

'On the contrary, I am a man filled with hope.' His voice was soft, gentle, easy to listen to.

Joanna arched a brow at him. 'Hope springs eternal?'

'Why not? The world is young, the night is beautiful, and I adore you.'

'*I'm* not young, Carlos. Neither are you.'

'I feel young,' he said. 'You make me feel rejuvenated.'

Joanna wished she could say the same to him. Instead, she changed the subject. 'I'd like your advice about something, Carlos.'

'Anything.'

'You know my son Greg?'

'I've met him once or twice.'

'It's time to appoint a new director for Moonbase.'

He hesitated only a heartbeat. 'I thought that decision has already been made.'

'I'm reconsidering it. Greg has asked for the job.'

'Ahh.'

'What do you think about it?'

This time Quintana's hesitation was considerably longer. 'There are several people on the board who would like to close Moonbase.'

'I know.'

'You've always fought to keep it going, even though it's a drain, financially.'

'Moonbase is in the black,' she said firmly.

'Barely,' Quintana answered easily. 'And when you consider all the little extras that somehow get put into the pot . . .' He sighed. 'Joanna, you know I support you unstintingly, but if we did an honest bookkeeping job, Moonbase would be in the red.'

'Perhaps,' she murmured.

'So you want to send your son there to make certain we keep it going.'

'Quite the contrary, Carlos. Greg wants to spend his year there deciding whether or not to shut the base down.'

'Really?' In the darkness she couldn't see his brows rise, but she heard it in his voice.

'He wants to make a thorough, unbiased assessment of the base's prospects and then make a recommendation to the board, one way or the other.'

It was several moments before Quintana replied, 'Well, he's certainly got the qualifications, based on the work he's done with the Pacific division.'

'Yes, I think so too.'

'Would he really recommend closing the base? And if he did, would you agree to it?'

Now Joanna hesitated. But she finally said softly, 'Yes, to both.'

'Isn't he a little old for Moonbase? Most of the personnel we send there are quite a bit younger.'

'He's forty-six.'

Quintana glanced up at the crescent Moon, just clearing the sycamore trees. 'There's always seemed to be – some sort of shadow on his history. Some scandal or something that everyone knows is there, but no one knows what it is. A family disagreement?'

Tensing, Joanna answered, 'You might say that.'

'It must have happened before I joined your board of directors.'

'Yes. A long time before.'

'That's why he's been kept off the board and away from headquarters all these years?'

'I think,' Joanna said, 'that it's time to put all that in the past. As you say, it's family history and it doesn't necessarily involve the corporation at all.'

'Doesn't necessarily involve the corporation?' Quintana's voice was filled with questions.

'Carlos, I'm his mother. I think I know Greg's limitations and his capabilities. I think he can handle the Moonbase job. But I might be too emotionally close to be seeing clearly.'

'I understand,' Quintana replied. 'I think I am too emotionally close to you to render an unbiased judgment.'

'But if you can't help me, who can I turn to?'

He sighed again. 'Joanna, I have always considered your intelligence to be of the highest order. Do what you think is best. I will certainly back you on the board, whatever you decide.'

'Thank you, Carlos,' Joanna said. But she was thinking that unqualified support was no real help at all.

MT. WASSER

'There it is! Look!' Doug cried out.

Turning awkwardly in her spacesuit to follow his pointing hand, Bianca Rhee saw a tall, wide pinnacle of rock jutting up into sunlight from the rugged shadowed mountain range below their ballistic lobber.

'That's Mt. Wasser?' she asked.

'Got to be,' Doug said, nodding inside his helmet. He studied the sunlit jut of rock carefully. Slightly taller than Everest, Mt. Wasser just happened to be situated so close to the south pole that its uppermost reaches were always in sunlight.

And down below, in those shadows, there're fields of ice, Doug knew. Areas that are always in shadow, where the temperature is always at least a hundred below zero. Water, covered with dust from the infalling meteoroids, kept frozen in the cryogenic dark.

Water and sunlight. The two most important resources of the Moon. Water for life. Sunlight for electrical power. Brennart is right, Doug told himself. That's the most valuable real estate on the Moon, down there. He felt the excitement building in him all over again.

In the lobber's cockpit, Brennart was scanning the readouts on his panel displays.

'What are the others doing?' he asked Killifer.

'Right on track. Following us like nice little puppies.'

'Superb.' Brennart's gloved fingers flicked along the control panel. 'Okay. We're going in.'

The lobber tilted back to its original vertical orientation.

Killifer punched up the camera view of the ground on the main display screen.

'Awful dark down there,' he muttered.

'Infrared,' Brennart snapped.

The image on the display screen did not change much: still dark, with vague suggestions of shapes looming in the shadows.

'Braking in ten seconds,' Killifer read from the flight plan display.

'I know.'

'Altitude twenty.'

'I know!'

Killifer realized that Brennart was jumpy. They both peered hard at the camera display.

'Lights,' Brennart ordered.

'Too high to do much good,' Killifer muttered, but he turned on the powerful lamps that had been installed on the underside of the lobber's main platform.

Brennart's gloved thumb hovered over the keypad that would override the rockets' firing. The shadowy ground was rushing up toward them. Killifer could see a jumble of shapes glittering in the reflected light of the landing lamps.

'Boulders!' he yelped. 'Big ones.'

Smoothly Brennart ignited the main rocket thrusters. Killifer felt a sudden surge of weight, but before he could even take a breath it disappeared and they were falling again.

'Goldman!' Brennart called into his helmet microphone. 'Jump the boulder field. Follow me!'

'Following,' came Goldman's voice in their earphones, professionally unperturbed.

'Reset the braking program,' Brennart commanded.

Killifer tapped the keyboard. 'Reset.'

The camera view showed a smoother stretch of ground beneath them. Still a great deal of rocks strewn across the area, but they were smaller, less dangerous.

The hard stony ground rushed up at them, stopped momentarily, then came at them again. The image on the display

screen blurred; rocket exhaust, Killifer knew. Then he felt a
thump and the familiar sensation of weight returned.

'We're down,' he said to Brennart. And realized he was
sweating inside his suit.

'Number two?' Brennart called into his helmet mike.

'Hundred-twenty . . . seventy . . . touchdown. We're about
fifty meters off your left rear. About seven o'clock in relation
to your cockpit.'

Both men turned in their seats but could not see the second
spacecraft from their position.

'The drones,' Brennart said.

The two unmanned vehicles were programmed to follow
Brennart's craft at a preset distance, and to land a hundred
meters on either side of it.

Killifer glanced at the radar display. 'Coming in now,' he
said, pointing to the blips their beacons made.

They could see one of the robot craft descending, its braking
rockets winking on and off against the dark shadows of the
mountains.

'Override!' Brennart snapped. 'It's coming down in the
boulder field.'

But it was too late. The unmanned lobber touched one of
its outstretched legs on a boulder almost as big as the vehicle
itself. The other three landing pads were still a good ten meters
above the ground. The attitude-control thrusters tried to keep
the vehicle from tipping over for several wobbling, twitching
seconds, but they gave out and the spacecraft tilted, tilted and
finally struck the ground with a soundless crash. Killifer saw
the landing legs crumple and the cargo pods split open; an oxygen tank blew apart in a silent burst of frost-glittering chunks.

From the passenger module, Doug saw the crash. His first
reaction was, My God, that could've been us! Then he
wondered how much equipment they had lost.

'Well, we're down safely, at least,' he said to the others in
the bubble.

They muttered replies, voices hushed, subdued.

'I think my telescope was in the pod that broke open,'

Bianca said worriedly. 'I'll have to go over and see if it survived the crash.'

By the time the six of them unstrapped from their seats and wormed through the hatch to stand on the ground, Brennart was already striding toward the crashed craft. Everybody's spacesuit was basically white, although some of them had been used so hard they were gray with imbedded lunar dust. But Brennart was easy to spot, even in a suit. His was sparkling new, gleaming white, and had red stripes down the arms and legs. For recognition, he had said.

Doug followed Brennart and his second-in-command, Killifer. He caught up with them as they reached the edge of the wreckage. It was impossible to see their faces, behind their heavily-tinted visors, but Brennart clearly radiated disgust, fists clenched on his hips.

'See whose equipment's on this ship and get them to check out this mess,' Brennart commanded. 'Determine if any of it's still usable.'

'Right,' said Killifer.

'Is there anything I can to help?' Doug asked.

Brennart wheeled and leaned down slightly to read the name tag printed on the breast of Doug's suit.

'Oh. Doug. I suppose you're going to remind me that you wanted to land farther out, aren't you?'

Surprised at the sarcasm in the older man's voice, Doug said, 'No sir, it hadn't entered my mind.'

'No,' Brennart said. 'Of course not.'

'Were any of our life-support supplies on this ship?' Doug asked.

Brennart huffed. 'Of course there were! The only question is how much of it have we lost. Jack, check it out.'

'Right,' said Killifer.

'What can I do to help?' Doug asked again.

'Just keep out of the way,' Brennart snapped. 'Like the man said, leave the real work to the professionals.' Then he started walking back toward the first spacecraft, leaving Doug puzzled and feeling more than a little hurt.

*   *   *

The base that Yamagata Industries established at the beautiful and prominent crater Copernicus, on the Sea of Rains, was called Nippon One. Admittedly, this was an unimaginative name of no intrinsic grace, and would be changed to something more poetic in time. For now, however, its utilitarian nature mirrored the character of the base itself. Nippon One was small, crowded, and unlovely: little more than a collection of huts buried beneath protective regolith rubble, much as Moonbase had been nearly twenty years earlier.

The worst part of serving at Nippon One was the lack of water for bathing. Even with nanomachines to ferret out atoms of hydrogen imbedded in the regolith and combine them with lunar oxygen, water was scarce and precious. Yamagata engineers had developed an ultrasonic device which, they claimed, cleaned the skin more efficiently than detergent and water. Nippon One's inhabitants complained that its ultrasonic vibrations gave them headaches, its vacuum suction sometimes plucked hair painfully from one's body, and it did nothing to relieve the body odors that made lunar living so unpleasant.

Still, it was a great honor to be assigned to serve at Nippon One, even if only for a few months. Yamagata's brightest young men and women eagerly sought lunar postings; this new frontier was the key to rapid advancement up the corporate ladder.

Miyoko Homma was the daughter of an old and honored Japanese family. Trained in astronomy and mathematics, she was determined to prove to her elders that a woman can add luster to the family name, just as a man can. She had jumped at the chance to work at Nippon One.

That was four months ago. Now, sitting in a cramped cubicle, feeling sweaty and filthy in fatigues that she had been wearing for several days on end, all she truly wished for was a steaming hot bath and just a bit of privacy.

She was checking the telescopes sitting up on the surface of Mare Imbrium, a chore she did daily, patiently studying the images they showed on her display screen as she ran each instrument through its checkout procedures to make certain that it was operating within its designated parameters. Her mind was wandering, though, to thoughts of home and comforts that she would not know for another two months.

Sitting next to her, close enough to touch shoulders, was Toshihara Yamashita, one of the communications technicians, headphone clamped to his ear.

'Have you heard the news?' Toshi asked. 'The Americans have sent an expedition to the south pole.'

That jolted Miyoko out of her reverie. 'No!' she said.

'It's true. The chiefs are trying to decide if we should put up a reconnaissance satellite to watch them.'

'But we're sending a team to the pole, aren't we? I've heard about the preparations for weeks now.'

'The Yanks have beaten us to it,' said Toshi. 'Somebody's head will roll.'

'Have they gone to the Bright Mountain?' Miyoko asked.

'Where else?'

'Ah, that's too bad. Now they'll set up a base there, won't they?'

'Of course. That's what we wanted to do.'

'And there's water ice there, too,' Miyoko murmured. 'Now the Americans will claim it all.'

Toshi leaned back in his spindly chair, shrugging. 'If the ice fields are big enough we can send a crew out there and stake our own claim. Maybe there's enough for more than one.'

Miyoko felt doubtful. 'Even if there is, the Americans will want it all, they're so greedy.'

Laughing, Toshi replied, 'We would too, if we got there first.'

'I don't believe—' The image on Miyoko's screen suddenly caught her eye. Glancing down at the monitor displays, she saw that she was looking at a real-time image of the solar x-ray telescope.

'Look at that,' she said.

Toshi glanced at the screen. 'At what? It looks like a bunch of noodles, all twisted together.'

'That's a sunspot field,' Miyoko said. 'It's gaining energy

very rapidly. I'll bet there's going to be a solar flare erupting within a day or so.'

'So what?' Toshi said carelessly. 'We're safe down here.'

'Yes, of course. But no one should be out on the surface if the flare's plasma cloud reaches the Moon.'

Toshi's face grew serious. 'The Americans.'

'Someone should warn them.'

'They have their own observers, don't they?'

'Yes, I think so. Still . . .'

'You'd better let the chiefs know. Let them decide what to do.'

SAVANNAH

'The expedition took off at fifteen-twenty-two, Eastern time.'

Jinny Anson's image on Joanna's wall screen looked tired and tense. She's lost enough weight over the past few months for it to show in her face, Joanna thought. Is she ill?

'The two crewed ships landed safely in the Mt. Wasser area,' Anson went on, 'but one of the freighters crashed on landing.'

'What?' Joanna nearly came out of her chair.

Anson had not waited for her reply. She continued without a break, 'About half of the cargo was damaged or destroyed in the crash. Mostly scientific instruments and life-support supplies. We will have to either cut the mission short or resupply much sooner than anticipated in the mission plan.'

Almost as an afterthought she added, 'There were no injuries to the expedition personnel.'

Joanna relaxed a little. 'I want to be included in the decision on cutting the expedition short or resupplying.'

She could see that Anson was waiting for her response. When it came, the base director nodded as if she had expected it. 'Of course. We'll need to talk it over with all the top division management, as well.'

'How did the crash happen?' Joanna asked.

They discussed the situation haltingly, impeded by the three-second lag between Earth and Moon. Joanna had always found the communications lag annoying; this day it was maddening. Doug was out there in the open, more than a thousand miles from shelter, and the expedition was already in trouble the instant it touched down.

'Jinny,' she said finally, 'I have a favor to ask of you.'

Anson's normally pert face, now drawn and weary, showed a sudden flicker of curiosity once Joanna's words reached her. 'A favor?'

'I'd like you to stay on a few weeks longer up there. Until the expedition returns. I don't think it's a good idea to change base directors while that team's down at the south pole.'

Anson's expression went from curiosity to alarm. 'I'm afraid I can't do that, Mrs. Stavenger.'

Surprised, irritated, Joanna snapped, 'Why not?'

For three infernally long seconds she waited for the answer. 'I'm getting married. All the arrangements are made.'

'Is that all?' Joanna eased back in her chair. 'The arrangements can be changed. I'll personally pay for whatever it costs you. I want you at Moonbase until the expedition safely returns.'

I can't have Greg up there while Doug's out in the wilderness, she told herself. It's a chance I won't take.

But Anson replied firmly, 'Mrs. Stavenger, it's not my fault that the expedition departed nearly three weeks late. I'm going to get married in San Antonio two weeks from tomorrow. I am leaving Moonbase on the first of the month, eight days from now, as planned. I'm afraid I can't change those plans.'

Her temper flaring, Joanna replied, 'As long as you're an employee of Masterson Aerospace you will follow the directives of your superiors. I want you at Moonbase until that expedition comes back!'

The two women stared at each other from a quarter-million-mile distance until Anson's image on the wall screen stiffened noticeably.

She took a visible breath before replying. Then, with deliberate calm, she answered, 'Mrs. Stavenger, if I have to resign from Masterson Aerospace, I will. I'm getting married on the seventh of next month in San Antonio, in the Alamo, and *nothing* is going to stop my wedding.'

Joanna's immediate instinct was to tell the ungrateful little snot that if she thought she was going to travel back to Earth for her stupid wedding on a Masterson spacecraft she had another think coming. But Joanna stifled that response. You catch more flies with honey than with vinegar, she told herself.

'I would appreciate it very much,' she said to the image on the wall screen, 'if you would reconsider your position. I will be happy to get you the Alamo for a future date. Or the Grand Canyon or the Taj Mahal, if you prefer. And I will of course want to give you and your husband a substantial wedding gift, since you are such a loyal and valued employee of this corporation. Please think it over.'

Before Anson's stubborn-faced image could reply, Joanna clicked off the connection. I'll give her a wedding gift, she said to herself grimly. And then I'll send her to our African division and let her play with the tse-tse flies for the rest of her career.

She didn't have to call up the list of waiting messages to know that Greg was impatient to talk with her. He had flown in from Kiribati, fully expecting his mother to name him the new director of Moonbase. Greg has his own sources inside the board of directors, Joanna realized. He knows I've been planting the seeds for him.

Over the years, the space operations division had become the tail that wagged the corporate dog. Sales of new Clippership models were the mainstay of the corporation's profits. When Clippership sales were strong, the stockholders received dividends. When Clippership sales sagged, workers were laid off. But the orbital manufacturing end of the space division had never broken clearly into the black. Even with raw materials supplied by Moonbase, the metal alloys and pharmaceuticals produced in the space stations were still too expensive to compete in the marketplace, except for the Windowalls, and even their profits were declining as the market for them saturated.

Joanna and the board of directors had looked into several reorganization plans that would separate the Clippership production from the orbital manufacturing work. A dozen bright young executives wanted to be named head of the Clippership program; nobody wanted to be stuck with orbital manufacturing.

Well, Joanna told herself, if Greg can actually find the strength to shut down Moonbase, all our orbital manufacturing will go down the drain with it, except for the Windowalls, and their costs will jump. Paul's dream will be dead. But maybe it will be for the best. I've given it nearly twenty years; how long can I keep on hoping for a miracle?

And there was even more trouble with the nanotechnology division, which was also tottering on the brink of collapse. Nanomachines were used on the Moon to produce water and build solar cells, but their uses on Earth had been slowed to a crawl by government regulations and a massive public relations campaign of demonstrations and protests, based on ignorance and hysterical fear, in Joanna's view. Medical applications of nanomachines had been brought to a standstill by so-called safety regulations, although those who were rich enough went to nations such as Switzerland; the Swiss government's regulations did not apply to foreigners, especially very rich foreigners, who quietly bought their nanotherapies there.

Joanna herself had been toying with the idea of accepting nanomachines to keep her arteries clear of plaque. And there was always the temptation to use the bugs to tighten up sagging muscles, renew wrinkled skin, even break up fatty deposits and harmlessly flush them out of the body.

Kris Cardenas had gotten herself into legal hot water by using nanobugs on herself to restore her failing eyesight. No glasses, no contact lenses, no surgery. The bugs restored her natural lenses to their youthful flexibility and strengthened the muscles that controlled them. Twenty-twenty vision, from only a few injections over a three-week period. Followed by three years of hounding by government lawyers and endless hearings in courts and the Canadian parliament. And Cardenas had all the prestige and authority of a Nobel Prize backing her.

Joanna shook all that out of her thoughts as she phoned the chief of the Space Operations division and asked him to come to her office.

'Why not use the virtual reality system?' Ibriham Rashid asked playfully.

Joanna was not amused. 'Omar, you're no more than fifty yards down the hall from me. Get your butt over here. In person.'

'Now?' he teased.

'At your earliest convenience,' Joanna answered, with as much sarcasm as she could muster.

'Harkening and obedience,' said Rashid.

Ibriham Muhammed al-Rashid had been born in Baltimore, third son of second-generation Palestinian-Americans. For all of his forty-two years he had balanced a firm belief in Islam with a firm belief that science and technology were gifts of Allah to help men in their struggle for existence. From his earliest childhood it was apparent that he was extremely intelligent and even more extremely motivated to rise high in the world. Johns Hopkins and MIT honed his intelligence. And his diplomatic skills. At school he was quickly dubbed 'Omar the Tentmaker.' Instead of becoming angry at the derogatory nickname, Rashid turned it into a badge of honor.

His career with Masterson Aerospace had been little short of meteoric. As head of the space operations division, he knew that the corporate knives were being sharpened behind his back. Space operations was the corporation's largest division, thanks to the Clipperships, a profitable cash cow that various reorganization plans sought to carve up into smaller sections and remove from Rashid's control. He resisted those attempts with a mixture of deft corporate maneuvering and unfailing loyalty from his division staff. He also used his urbane charm wherever it would do the most good – especially with the chairwoman of the board.

Joanna enjoyed his attentions, as she did those of Carlos Quintana and several others. It amused her to watch the male ego at work, and to manipulate their testosterone-driven ambitions toward goals of her own choosing.

Rashid stepped into Joanna's office and looked around appreciatively. He was short and compact in build, rather like Paul, thought Joanna, although slimmer. A trim black beard framing his oval face, Rashid had movie-star looks: huge soulful dark brown eyes and a smile to die for. He was smiling now as he sat in the delicate little loveseat, facing Joanna's personal chair.

'Desert golds and tans,' he said, noticing the decor. 'And a scent of jasmine. Are you trying to make me homesick?'

Joanna laughed. 'For Baltimore?'

'Racial memory,' Rashid bantered. 'Jung claimed that we all have primitive memories stored in our subconscious minds.'

'Maybe my ancestry goes back to the desert,' Joanna said. 'I like this color scheme. And I love the Southwest.'

'Arabs prefer cities. My people are great architects.'

Joanna decided they had chatted enough. Time to get down to business. 'Omar, how would you feel if I suggested that my son Greg be the next director of Moonbase?'

Rashid did not seem surprised. He eased one arm across the back of the loveseat and crossed his legs. 'O'Rourke is slated for that position.'

'I know, but . . .' She let the sentence dangle.

'O'Rourke is very competent. Unimaginative, true, but very competent.'

'I asked Jinny if she'd stay on until the polar expedition came back and she refused,' Joanna said.

The slightest of tics twitched at the corner of Rashid's mouth. 'You should have spoken to me first. I would have told you she'd refuse. She's going to be married.' His voice was soft, yet Joanna heard his disapproval. She had gone over his head to speak directly to Anson.

'My other son's out there at the south pole with Brennart.'

'Yes, I am aware of that.'

'I don't like the idea of changing base directors while the expedition's out there.'

Rashid shrugged elaborately. 'It really makes almost no difference whatsoever. The base director is in no position to help or harm the expedition.'

'Really?'

'The expedition is rather self-sufficient. Brennart knows what he's doing.'

'Even with one of the cargo ships crashed?'

Again the shrug. 'They'll resupply earlier than scheduled. It's not a major problem.'

'So you don't think Anson's leaving will be a problem?'

'Of course not. If I did, she wouldn't be leaving, believe me.'

Joanna studied his handsome face. Rashid seemed completely at ease, totally confident.

'Then allowing Greg to take over . . . ?'

He spread his hands. 'It shouldn't be a problem. O'Rourke has more experience, but your son has shown quite remarkable leadership qualities.'

Almost, Joanna blurted her fear that Greg still hated his younger half-brother. You're being irrational, Joanna told herself sternly. Yet the fear was still there, gnawing inside her.

'This must be a very difficult decision for you,' Rashid said softly, smiling at her from an arm's length away.

Joanna's thoughts snapped back to the here-and-now.

'No,' she said. 'No, it isn't difficult at all. Unless you are actively opposed, Greg Masterson will replace Jinny Anson as the director of Moonbase.'

'Effective on the first of the month?' Rashid asked.

'Yes. But I want Greg to get up there right away and spend Jinny's final days at Moonbase getting oriented.'

'How soon . . . ?'

'Today,' Joanna snapped.

Rashid dipped his head slightly. 'Harkening and obedience.'

MOONBASE

Jinny Anson felt her teeth grinding together as she looked over the graph on her desktop screen.

'Solar flare,' she said, almost accusingly.

The technician who had been monitoring the astronomical instruments in Bianca Rhee's absence nodded unhappily.

'And it's going to be a big mother, is it?'

'Class Four flare. Maybe a Five.'

Anson leaned back in her creaking plastic chair and glared at the young tech. 'How soon?' she snapped.

The technician was barely into his twenties, still an undergraduate student who had taken a year off to make money by working at Moonbase. Standing in front of Anson's desk in his baggy, frayed coveralls, he shuffled his feet uncertainly.

'Hard to say,' he replied. 'I've checked with Tucson. Next twenty-four hours, for sure. Could be a lot sooner, though.'

'Great. I'll have to alert the surface crews.'

'And, uh – Brennart's people?'·

'Yes, them too. They should have their shelters dug in by now. Will the radiation hit them?'

The young man looked miserably unsure of himself. 'Hard to say,' he repeated. 'Oh, they'll get the first pulse sure enough: the ultraviolet and x-rays. But the heavy stuff – that depends on how the interplanetary magnetic field's twisted up.'

Rankled, Anson said, 'So you don't know when the particle cloud will hit or how heavy it'll be.'

'Nobody could tell you that,' the kid said defensively. 'Not this far in advance.'

'Okay,' Anson squinted at his nametag, 'Albertson. Thanks for the bad news.'

The kid fled her office as if afraid for his life.

A Class Four solar flare, she thought. Maybe a Five. Just what we need. Angrily she punched her keyboard to call up the communications center. Got to get all the surface workers inside. And warn Brennart's people.

As she spoke to the comm center, Anson pictured in her mind what they were going to be facing. The most violent event the solar system can produce, an explosion on the Sun with the force of a hundred billion megatons of TNT. More energy than the whole world consumes in fifty thousand years. Hardly a quarter-second's worth of the Sun's total energy output, but enough to kill anyone caught in its lethal plasma cloud. Enough to wreck unprotected equipment.

'What about cislunar traffic?' the comm technician asked.

'What's it look like?' Anson asked back.

The tech's face disappeared from her desktop screen and a visual display of the Earth-Moon traffic showed four green arrows representing unmanned freighters heading for the factories in Earth orbit and a single violet arrow of a passenger vehicle on its way to the Euro-Russian base at Grimaldi. There were three yellow arrows, as well: Yamagata spacecraft, two inbound, one heading Earthward.

As she watched, Anson saw a new red arrow appear on the screen. A passenger-carrying craft was leaving Earth orbit, heading for Moonbase.

'What's that new blip?' she asked. 'I don't recall anything scheduled today.'

The technician's voice answered, 'Message just came in; it's in your voice mail. Your replacement is on his way.'

'O'Rourke's coming now?' Anson felt puzzled, annoyed.

'It's not O'Rourke,' the tech's voice replied. 'It's Gregory Masterson III.' The technician pronounced the three-part name with appropriate awe in her voice.

'Shit on a shingle!' Anson exploded. 'Get that poor dumb boob on the horn and tell him to abort his flight and get his butt back home where it's safe. That's all I need, having the boss's son fried!'

'It's ice, all right, but I'm afraid it's pretty thin,' said Roger Deems.

He, Brennart, Killifer and Doug Stavenger were jammed into the analysis lab of the expedition's main shelter. Deems was still in his cumbersome spacesuit, minus only its helmet, which made the little cubicle even more crowded. The only light came from one of the computer screens.

Doug could hear the grating patter of regolith rubble being piled on the shelter's curving roof. Outside, the expedition's minitractors were struggling to dig up enough surface dirt to provide the necessary coverage for radiation protection and thermal insulation. The regolith here in the south polar highlands was thin and hard, its normally powder-like texture vacuum welded into the consistency of concrete. The remotely-operated little tractors were having a hard time digging up enough of it to cover the expedition's four shelters. Brennart had to send people out to jury-rig some of their aluminum and oxygen rocket propellants to burn into the hard rock and break it into manageable chunks.

'We should've brought a couple tons of plastic explosives,' one of the tractor operators grumbled.

Deems's job, immediately upon landing, had been to lead a team to the ice field that the unmanned probes had identified and take samples.

Peering at the computer screen where the spectrograph's analysis of the ice was displayed, Brennart said heartily, 'Looks good enough to drink!'

'A lot of dissolved minerals,' Doug said, tracing a calcium line with his outstretched finger.

'You could say the same about Perrier!' Brennart snapped.

Killifer said nothing, standing between Brennart and Doug, his face in shadow.

Turning to Deems, Brennart asked, 'Did you get a chance to map any of the ice field?'

'We didn't do any mapping,' Deems said, almost apologetically. 'Our mission plan called for digging some preliminary cores and bringing back the samples taken. Mapping comes later.'

'I know the mission plan,' Brennart said impatiently. 'I wrote it.'

Deems glanced at Killifer, who said nothing.

'So?' Brennart demanded. 'What about the cores you dug?'

'We drilled three cores. You see the analysis of the ice. It's water, all right.'

'Is it drinkable as is, or will we have to treat it?' Doug asked.

'Looks perfectly drinkable to me,' said Brennart.

'The ice is only ten centimeters deep,' Deems said. Then he added, 'Where we dug.'

'Which is at the edge of the field, right?' Brennart said.

'A hundred meters from the edge,' said Deems. 'That's what we figured was a safe walk-back distance, what with the darkness and the slick surface – even with the dust on it, there's not much traction to walk with.'

'That field is more than ten kilometers across, isn't it?' Brennart said, more of a statement than a question. 'And there are a dozen or more other ice fields scattered about the area.'

Deems nodded. 'That's right.'

'But how deep does it go?' Doug wondered aloud.

'That's what we're here to find out,' Brennart said.

'Right,' said Killifer.

Brennart straightened up, his golden hair almost brushing the curving roof of the shelter. 'All right, we've made a good start. Jack,' he turned to Killifer, 'I want a complete inventory of the supplies we lost in the crash on my screen by the time I come back in for supper.'

'No problem,' said Killifer.

'I'm going outside to set a little fire under the digging. Roger, you did well out there. I'm pleased.'

Deems's normally half-frightened expression slowly evolved into a shy, delighted smile.

'Doug,' Brennart snapped, 'shouldn't you be registering our time of arrival and summary of activities?'

'I've already done that,' Doug replied, biting back the instinct to add, sir.

'And our schedule for tomorrow?'

'I'm set to transmit that as soon as we send out the nanotech team tomorrow morning.'

Brennart looked down on Doug with something approaching displeasure. 'Do it now. Right now.'

'But legally—'

'Get it into the record!' Brennart insisted. 'Tell them you'll send confirmation when the team actually starts out tomorrow. Exact time and all that.'

'Very well,' said Doug.

They squeezed out of the analysis cubicle like four men getting out of a phone booth. This is no place for a claustrophobe, Doug thought as they marched single file up the narrow central aisle of the shelter.

The cylindrical shelter was divided by thin plastic internal walls that could be load-bearing only in the gentle gravity of the Moon. Brennart and Deems headed for the airlock; Brennart to suit up for the surface, Deems to put his helmet back on and go to a well-deserved rest break in the shelter that housed his bunk. The digging team had not yet linked the four shelters with connecting tunnels.

Doug followed Killifer to the comm center, another cubicle that was hot and overcrowded with two people in it. The communications technician was at his post, headphone clamped to his ear.

'I'll take over,' Killifer said. 'Go take a leak.'

The guy grinned appreciatively and surrendered his flimsy plastic chair to Killifer, who took the headset and slipped it around his neck.

'Anything expected in?' Killifer asked his departing back.

'Nope,' said the technician as he squeezed past Doug. 'Everything's quiet until the next satellite comes over.'

The expedition included six miniature communications satellites in polar orbit, following one another endlessly like soldiers on perpetual parade. Moonbase's regular commsat, hovering at the L-1 libration point above the lunar equator, could not 'see' the deep valleys of the mountainous south polar region, so the polar orbiting minisats were necessary.

Doug had suggested twelve satellites, so there would be continuous coverage, but Savannah had decided that the expedition could do with fifteen-minute breaks between satellites, and doubling their communications costs was not worth the additional coverage.

While Killifer began punching up the inventory of supplies and equipment carried aboard the crashed lander, Doug sat at the other display and tapped out his legal report for Moonbase and the World Court at The Hague. He could feel the heat that their bodies and the computers and communications sets were generating. Sweat trickled down his ribs.

They were sitting close enough to be touching shoulders, but for nearly half an hour neither of them said a word. Doug finished his task and set up tomorrow's work, then – for lack of anything else to do – called up the inventory Killifer was working on.

'You checking up on me?' Killifer snapped.

Startled, Doug said, 'No. Of course not.'

'Then why're you looking over my shoulder?'

With a shrug, Doug answered, 'I don't have much of anything else to do at the moment.'

'Then get outta here and give me some space.'

Doug stared at the older man. 'You don't like me much, do you?'

'Why should I?'

'What do you mean?'

'You were stuck into this mission on orders from Savannah. Your so-called job could be done by a trained baboon. You're nothing but a snoop from corporate headquarters.'

'A snoop?' Doug wanted to laugh. 'What's there to snoop about? I'm here because I thought this expedition would be exciting.'

Killifer glared at him. 'Exciting? You must be crazy.'

Doug waved a hand. 'Don't you find all this exciting? The first people here at the south pole and all that?'

'Christ, you're worse than a snoop. You're a frigging dilettante.'

'Well,' said Doug, 'I'm sorry you think so. I hope to be as helpful as I can.'

'Great. Just stay out of the way and we'll get along fine.'

With a laugh, Doug replied, 'It's not going to be easy to stay out of each other's way, cooped up in these tin cans.'

'Then why don't you go outside and take a nice long walk?'

Getting to his feet, Doug said, 'That's not a bad idea.' And he left Killifer alone in the comm cubicle.

Killifer watched him leave, then turned back to his tedious inventory task. He heard a piercing note from the earphone on the headset draped around his neck and quickly clapped the set over his close-cropped hair.

'Moonbase to Brennart. Emergency notification. A major solar flare is expected in the next twenty-four hours. We don't know if it will impact your area or not, but you should take all safety precautions.'

It was a recorded message, transmitted by the minisat that had just come up over their horizon. Killifer duly noted it into the computer log and then started to call Brennart, out on the surface.

His fingertip hovered over the keypad. I'll tell Brennart when he gets back in. No sense shaking him up right now. Plenty of time before there's any danger.

Too bad it won't hit while the Stavenger kid is outside, he thought.

LUNAR TRANSFER VEHICLE

Before this flight to the Moon, Greg had never been farther than the space stations in Earth orbit. He had been nervous about spending a couple of days in weightlessness, but so far the medication patch behind his right ear seemed to be working: he felt a little queasy, but under control.

The lunar transfer vehicle was basically a freight carrier; the maintenance gang at the space station had added a crew module especially for him. It was a small bubble of alloy and plastiglass, barely big enough for the mandatory human pilot and co-pilot and a pair of passengers.

The bubble was pressurized, but safety regulations required the humans to stay in spacesuits for the duration of the two-day flight. If a stray meteoroid punctured the module's skin they could slide their visors down and ride the rest of the way buttoned up in their suits.

The other 'passenger,' tightly strapped in to the seat next to Greg, was a drum of lubricating oil. Not romantic, but very necessary for the machinery at Moonbase. With the bulky steel-gray drum beside him and the two pilots sitting in front of him, Greg's main view was overhead. He cranked his seat back as far as it would go, and realized that in zero-gee 'overhead' was a matter of opinion. He felt almost as if he were standing and looking straight ahead.

What he saw was the Earth, glowing blue and white against the empty blackness of space, dwindling imperceptibly as the lunar transfer vehicle coasted toward the Moon. Two days inside this spacesuit, Greg thought. We're going to smell ripe when we finally put down at Alphonsus. Staring at the

Earth, he realized with the force of a physical sensation that he was leaving the world and heading for a place that had no air or water or life of its own. He shuddered inwardly at the thought.

'Mr. Masterson, sir?'

Greg could not tell whether it was the pilot or co-pilot speaking to him. Their voices sounded virtually identical in his helmet earphones.

'We have a problem, sir. Ground control reports an imminent SFE. We're ordered to reverse course and return to the station.'

Astronauts and their jargon, Greg thought. 'What's an SFE?'

'Solar flare event. Extremely high levels of ionizing radiation. Very dangerous.'

'Lethal,' said the other astronaut.

Alarmed, Greg asked, 'How much time do we have?'

'Unknown, sir. The flare could burst out any time within the next twenty-four hours.'

'The radiation could increase to killing levels within a few hours afterward,' the other astronaut said.

It was annoying to be talking to the backs of two helmets. Greg still could not tell from the voices in his earphones which astronaut was speaking.

'Can't we get to Moonbase before the flare erupts?' he asked.

'Standard safety procedure is to return to the orbital station we started from.'

'The space stations orbit below the geomagnetosphere,' said the other voice.

'What's that got to do with it?' Greg demanded.

'The geomagnetosphere is like a magnetic umbrella, sir. It offers protection from the heaviest levels of radiation.'

'Still, all personnel on each station have to evacuate to the ECPM during the peak radiation influx.'

Before Greg could ask, the other astronaut explained, 'Emergency Crew Protection Module, that is.'

'I see,' said Greg. 'But if the flare is still a day or so away, why can't we go on to Moonbase?'

'There's no telling when the flare will burst out.'

'Could be in another few minutes.'

'But even so,' Greg insisted, 'you said it would be several hours after that before the radiation levels got dangerous.'

They hesitated before one of them answered, 'That's true, but standard procedure—'

'Can't we juice this vehicle and get to Moonbase sooner?'

Again they hesitated. Then, 'We'd have to re-light the main engine.'

'But that would actually cost us less delta-vee than reversing back to LEO.'

Greg tried to sort out their jargon. 'You're saying that it would be *easier* to speed up and get to Moonbase?'

'Yessir.'

'But we'd have to file a new flight plan and get it approved by traffic control.'

'And undergo another three or four gees of thrust for a few minutes.'

The takeoff from Earth had been slightly less than three gees for several minutes, Greg recalled.

'I can crunch the numbers and then check 'em out with ground control.'

'Do that,' Greg commanded.

For several minutes the two astronauts hunched their helmeted heads together, fingers flicking over the keyboards in their control panel. Greg realized they were talking to ground control, back at Savannah. He tapped the channel selector on the wrist of his suit until he found their frequency. Listening in on their chatter was pretty much a waste of time, though: Greg could barely understand half of their technospeak.

But at last he heard, 'Trajectory alterations are approved. You are cleared for high-thrust burn to Moonbase.'

'Cleared for Moonbase. Roger,' said the pilot.

Greg heard the radio link click off. Then, 'Yahoo!' yelled one of them, loud enough to make Greg's ears ring.

'Light 'er up and move 'er out!'

As a heavy hand of acceleration pressed Greg back in his

seat, he realized that the astronauts were more than happy with his insistence on pushing ahead to the Moon.

Killifer's main assignment was to remain inside the head-quarters shelter of the expedition's base camp and monitor all surface activities. Thus the communications center was his principal station.

He had quite deliberately erased Moonbase's warning message from the comm system's computer memory. He waited calmly underground until Brennart came in. Then Killifer hurried to the airlock, where Brennart was carefully removing his suit and vacuuming the dust from it.

Sitting on the slim-legged bench next to Brennart, he spoke just loudly enough to be heard over the buzz of the hand vacuum.

'We got a warning of an imminent solar flare.'

'When?'

'About two hours ago. I didn't say anything about it; didn't want to shake up the team.'

Brennart looked down at him, his brows knit in thought. They made an odd pair: the tall, golden-haired leader and his dark, lantern-jawed aide.

'I might have exceeded my authority,' Killifer confessed. 'I erased the warning from the log.'

'Why?'

'I didn't want anyone but you to know about it. You're the expedition commander. You should be the one who makes the decision on what to do. If the comm tech or Doug Stavenger or somebody else found out about the warning, they'd be blabbing it to everybody and nobody'd want to be outside.'

Brennart nodded slowly. 'That's true enough.'

'I hope I did the right thing,' Killifer said, with as much humility as he could muster.

'Yes, you did. A warning of an imminent flare poses no immediate danger and we still have a lot of digging to do out there.'

'The connectors?'

With a shake of his head, Brennart said, 'We're behind

schedule, I know. You don't have to remind me. The ground out there is all rock. Hardly any regolith over it at all.'

Without the tunnels to connect them, the expedition members would be stuck in the four separate buried shelters when the flare's radiation reached them.

'What do you plan to do, then?' Killifer asked.

Frowning, Brennart said, 'I'd better put everybody into the digging. We don't even have enough rubble to adequately shield the four shelters yet, let alone the connecting tunnels.'

For the first time, Killifer felt alarmed. But he hid it and said merely, 'You always know what's best.'

It was dark out on the surface, menacingly, cryogenically dark with the high mountains blocking out any chance of light or warmth. Yet Doug found it thrilling. More than thrilling; it was the most exciting thing he had ever known. To put your bootprints down where no human being has ever stood before. To see what no human eyes have ever gazed on. Danger and wonder and the lure of the unknown, all mixed together. That's what the frontier is all about, Doug told himself. God, it must be habit-forming, like a drug.

He took a deep breath of canned air, realizing with a grin that it was an artificial mixture of oxygen and nitrogen at unnaturally low pressure. Every breath we take, every step we make, all depends on the machines we've developed.

So what? he asked himself. How long do you think humans would've survived on Earth if they hadn't developed fire and tools? We're machine makers, and with our machines we can expand throughout the universe.

Then he chuckled to himself. Throughout the universe, huh? Maybe you ought to just concentrate on this little base camp you're building here at the south pole of the Moon. Get that done before you start challenging the rest of creation.

Starlight guided his steps across the rocky ground. The hard unblinking stars were strewn across the black sky like dust; even through his heavily tinted visor Doug could see thousands of them staring back at him. They lit the ground like pale moonlight on Earth.

He walked to the edge of the ice field. Staring at its dark flat expanse, Doug felt disappointed that the dust-covered ice did not reflect the stars. It looked almost like a dead calm sea, flat and still and gleaming slightly, as if lit from within. Then he looked up as high as he could from inside his helmet and realized that he could not see the Earth. From Moonbase the Earth was always hanging overhead, warm, beckoning, friendly. The sky down here was empty, lonely.

Turning, he saw Mt. Wasser, its flat-topped curving peak bathed in glowing sunlight, shining against the darkness like a disembodied beacon. Tomorrow we start up the mountain, Doug told himself. With the nanomachines. With any luck, we'll be building the power tower within thirty-six hours.

We're making history here! The thought exhilarated him. Kids will read about this expedition in their schoolbooks.

He looked out at the ice field again and suddenly, without even deciding consciously to do it, he ran to the edge of the softly gleaming ice with long, loping lunar strides; almost like flying. Then he felt his boots on the ice and he glided along like a skater, spinning and turning, laughing inside his helmet like a boy at play.

His earphones chirped. Then he heard Brennart's unmistakable voice, 'This is your expedition commander. I want every person suited up and outside to help dig the connector tunnels. The only personnel excluded from this order are the second-in-command and the communications technician now on watch. Everybody else get to the digging. This includes you, Mr. Stavenger. Get moving. Now!'

MOONBASE

'A peasant,' muttered Lev Brudnoy to himself. 'That's what I am. Nothing but a dolt of a peasant.'

He was kneeling between rows of fresh light green shoots that would become carrots, if all went well, bent over the dismantled pieces of a malfunctioning pump. Stretched all around him for a full hectare, one hundred meters on a side, were neatly aligned hydroponic troughs in which carrots, beans, lettuce and black-eyed peas were growing. And row after row of soybeans. Plastic hose lines ran above the troughs, carrying water enriched with the nutrients the plants needed to grow. Strips of full-spectrum lamps lit the underground chamber with the intensity of summer noon.

Off in a corner of the big cavern was a carefully boxed-in plot of lunar sand, dug up from the regolith outside and turned into a garden of brightly-hued roses, geraniums, daffodils and zinnias – all lovingly pollinated by Brudnoy's own hand. Moonbase's agrotechnicians and nutritionists were responsible for the hydroponics crops; the plot of soil-grown flowers was Brudnoy's alone.

Sweating, Brudnoy sat on the rock floor amid the strewn pieces of the pump. For the life of him, he could not see what had gone wrong with it. Yet the pump had stopped working, threatening the farm's carrot crop with slow withering death. Brudnoy had wanted to fix the pump before the agrotechs realized it had malfunctioned. Now, instead of becoming a hero, he felt like a dunce.

'Lev!' a voice rang off the farm's rock walls. 'Lev, are you in here?'

He scrambled to his feet. Two of the biologists were standing uncertainly at the airlock, several rows away. They started toward him.

'I thought you were leaving today,' Brudnoy said as they approached.

'Flight's cancelled. Solar flare coming up,' said Serai N'kuma.

'Oh.'

'So we thought we'd take you out to dinner,' Debbie Paine added.

N'kuma was tall, leggy, lean as a ballet dancer, her skin a glistening deep black. Paine was blonde and petite, yet with an hourglass figure that strained her coveralls. Brudnoy had fantasized about the two of them ever since they had first arrived at Moonbase, even after he realized that they preferred each other to men.

'I can't leave here until this wretched pump is fixed,' Brudnoy said. Spreading his arms, he added, 'You see before you a true peasant, chained to his land.'

The women ignored his heartfelt self-pity. 'What's wrong with the pump?' Paine asked.

Shrugging, Brudnoy replied, 'It won't work.'

'Let's take a look at it,' said N'kuma, dropping to her knees to examine the scattered pieces.

'I've taken it apart completely. Nothing seems wrong. Yet it refuses to do its job.'

'Engineer's hell,' Paine said, grinning. 'Everything checks but nothing works.'

'In the old days we would have it shot,' Brudnoy grumbled.

'And then you'd have no pump at all,' N'kuma said, from her kneeling position.

Paine ran a finger along the hose that carried the water and nutrients. 'Is the pump getting electricity okay?'

'There's nothing wrong with the electrical power,' Brudnoy said.

Plucking at the wire that ran along the hose, Paine said, 'Except that the insulation on this wire is frayed and the bare aluminum is touching the metal pipe fitting here.'

N'kuma popped to her feet. 'It's shorting out.'

Peering at the slightly scorched metal fitting, Brudnoy said, 'I don't think the wire we make here at the base is as good as the copper stuff they make Earthside.'

'Didn't you smell the insulation burning?' Paine asked.

Brudnoy scratched his thatch of graying hair. 'Now that you mention it, there was a strange smell a while ago. I changed my coveralls the next day and the smell went away.'

Both women guffawed. In short order Brudnoy produced a new length of wire, Paine spliced it into the line while N'kuma reassembled the pump with hands that were little short of magical. Brudnoy watched them admiringly.

Once they were finished he insisted, 'Now *I* will take *you* to dinner. It's all on me! My treat.'

They laughed together as they left the farm. Meals at the galley were free, part of the corporation's services for Moonbase's employees.

Brudnoy laughed the hardest. Hardly anyone in the base knew that these two young women were lovers. *All the men will choke on their food when they see me with these young lovelies on my arms. Some of the women will, too.*

Not bad, for an old man, he thought.

'Welcome to Moonbase,' said Jinny Anson.

Greg Masterson's nose wrinkled at the strange smell of the place: human sweat mixed with machine oil and a strange sharp burnt odor, as if someone had been firing a gun recently.

But he made himself smile and took Anson's proffered hand. 'Thanks. It's good to get here ahead of the flare.'

Anson had gone down to the receiving area dug into the floor of Alphonsus adjacent to the rocket port. Little more than a rough-hewn cavern beneath the crater's floor, the place was called 'The Pit' by veteran Lunatics. It was connected to the main section of the base by a single tunnel, nearly two kilometers long. There were plans to put in an electrified trolley line along the tunnel; for now, a stripped down tractor did the job, its finish dulled and dented from years of work on the surface.

She kept a hand on his arm as Greg hip-hopped like any newcomer to the Moon until he was safely seated in the tractor.

'I brought you a present,' she said, climbing into the driver's seat next to him.

'A present?'

Reaching behind the seat, Anson pulled out a worn-looking pair of boots. 'Moon shoes. They've got weights built into them so you won't go bouncing around when you try to walk. Remove one weight per day while you're here, and inside of five days you'll be walking like a native.'

It was a standard line among the Lunatics. So far there were no natives of the Moon. Women got pregnant occasionally; they were gently but firmly transferred back Earthside as soon as their condition was discovered.

'I was surprised to see a working elevator,' Greg said as he took off his slippers and pulled on the weighted boots.

The tractor was programmed to run the straight tunnel without human guidance. Anson hit the starter button and its aged superconducting electric motor whined to life.

'We just put it into operation last week,' she said. 'Makes it much easier to load and unload cargo, once you get the crates through the airlock.'

'Takes a lot of electrical power, though,' Greg said as the tractor jolted to a start.

Anson waved a hand in the air. 'Electricity's cheap. The nanomachines chomp up the regolith and lay down solar cells. Our solar farms are constantly getting bigger.'

'I've seen the reports,' Greg said. 'And the projections.'

'Good.' They were tooling along the tunnel now at nearly twenty miles per hour. The overhead lamps flicked past, throwing shadows across Greg's sculpted face like phases of a moon hurtling by.

He's really a handsome devil, Anson told herself. But there's something unsettling about him. The eyes? Something. He looks . . . she struggled to define what was bothering her. At last she thought, He looks as if he could be cruel.

*   *   *

Miyoko Homma felt that she should be standing at attention, like a soldier. As it was, she had bowed deeply to the chief manager of Nippon One upon entering his cubicle and then remained standing with her arms rigidly at her sides and her face as blank as she could make it.

'The solar flare that you predicted has not come,' said the head chief. He was old for Nippon One, in his forties. His belly was beginning to round out, although his face was still taut and his eyes piercing.

'Sir, it will come,' Miyoko said flatly. 'It is only a question of time.'

'How much time?' the chief demanded. 'We have kept everyone inside. The work that must be done on the surface is suspended because of this flare that was supposed to erupt. It's been more than twelve hours now! Twelve hours of lost work! How much longer must we wait?'

Miyoko took a small breath before answering, 'I do not know, sir.'

'But you are our astronomer! It is your job to know!'

'Sir, no one can predict the eruption of a solar flare with such precision. The configuration of magnetic field lines that I saw when I first issued the warning was typical of an imminent flare, one that would burst out in twenty-four hours or less.'

'Twelve hours have gone by,' said the chief. With a glance at the digital clock on his desk he added, 'Twelve hours and eighteen minutes.'

Miyoko felt like a small mouse trembling between the paws of a very large cat. 'Sir, I can only report to you what my instruments show. Any other astronomer in the world would have reported exactly the same as I did. It is unfortunate that the Sun is not cooperating with us.'

The chief settled back in his chair and rubbed his stubbled chin. 'The Americans are apparently not afraid of your flare. Our reconnaissance satellite shows them working very busily on their base.'

'But they must know!' Miyoko blurted.

'Or they know better.'

Miyoko clamped her lips shut.

The chief stared hard at her. 'It is a great problem. Do I send the surface crews back to work or not? It is most inefficient to have them sitting cooped up in here when they should be working on the surface. Yet . . .'

'Sir, may I make a suggestion?'

He nodded assent.

'When the flare actually erupts there will be at least an hour before the heavy particle radiation begins to build up. If the surface crews are willing to accept the first burst of relatively light radiation, it should be possible to get them inside to safety before the truly dangerous radiation builds up.'

Immediately the chief said, 'Tell me about this first burst of relatively light radiation.' Miyoko could detect no trace of sarcasm in his words.

She said, 'When the flare erupts it throws out a burst of high-frequency radiation – mostly ultraviolet and x-rays. This arrives in our vicinity within eight point three minutes, since it travels at the speed of light.'

'How serious is this radiation?'

'To a person already protected by a spacesuit it is not dangerous. In Tokyo the radiation from space averages about four-tenths of a rad per year. On the Moon's surface it is closer to twenty-five rads per year. The initial burst from a solar flare will increase this dose by a factor of ten.'

'H'mmm,' said the chief. Miyoko thought he was trying to hide the fact that he did not know what a rad was, nor how dangerous it could be.

'When the flare's plasma cloud arrives, however,' she went on, 'the radiation will increase to more than a thousand rads in a few hours. Worse than the radiation dose at Hiroshima.'

That startled the chief. 'Worse than Hiroshima?'

'Yes.'

'But the first pulse is not so bad?'

'The surface crews can be brought inside after the first pulse hits,' Miyoko said again.

'We have a full hour before the heavy radiation builds up?'

'At least an hour, sir.' She hesitated a moment, struggling

with her own conscience, then added, 'In truth, sir, we have no way of knowing whether the heavy radiation will strike us at all, even after the flare bursts forth. The plasma cloud that carries the radiation may miss us entirely.'

'Miss us entirely? Is that possible?'

'Yes, sir. But we have no way of predicting that quickly enough to save men working on the surface. That is why we must get them all inside once the flare erupts.'

The chief sat muttering to himself for several moments. Then a slow smile of understanding spread across his normally-scowling features.

'This is like predicting the path of a typhoon, isn't it? You know the storm is approaching, but you cannot tell exactly where it will strike.'

'Yes, sir.' Miyoko jumped at his analogy, feeling a rush of relief. 'Very much like a typhoon. An invisible typhoon that cannot be felt, but can kill a person just as swiftly.'

MT. WASSER

'What's the latest word on this flare?' Brennart asked.

Killifer pushed his little wheeled chair away slightly from the comm console. 'No word. The flare hasn't appeared yet.'

The two men were alone in the comm cubicle. Brennart was on his feet, towering over the seated Killifer. Every other member of the expedition was out digging, even the ostensible communications technician. Brennart knew the mission schedule was in a shambles but he would sort that out and get things going properly again as soon as this flare threat was over.

'What does Moonbase say about it?' he asked Killifer.

His aide made a sour face. 'They say the flare ought to have popped by now. Could pop any minute. They just don't know.'

'With that and five dollars I could buy a cup of coffee.'

'They also say,' Killifer added caustically, 'that their regular astronomer is here in the boondocks with us, instead of at her instruments at the base.'

Brennart glowered. 'That was Stavenger's idea, bringing her along with us.'

Killifer said nothing, but his sardonic smile spoke volumes.

'We can't just sit here and wait for a flare that might not even happen,' Brennart muttered.

Nodding, Killifer said, 'Oh, by the way, Moonbase reported that Yamagata sent up a recce satellite six hours ago. It's in a very eccentric polar orbit.'

'With its longest dwell time right over us,' Brennart guessed.

'Right.'

'Damn! They'll be sending a team down here to make a claim on the mountain before we can.'

'I don't see how—'

'They could drop a kamikaze crew on the other side of the mountain and use hoppers to get up to the top,' Brennart growled angrily. 'Stick a sheet of solar panels up there and claim first use. Then we're screwed.'

'But aren't they just as worried about the flare as we are?'

Brennart looked down at his aide with a withering expression. 'You don't know what kamikaze means, do you?'

'Something from history, isn't it? Last century?'

'Right. History.'

Killifer sat on the uncomfortable little chair and craned his neck to look up at his boss. Brennart liked to be known for making decisions, but now he seemed hesitant, caught on the horns of a dilemma, hung up with uncertainty.

'If only we knew when the flare will erupt,' he muttered, kneading his right fist into the palm of his left hand.

'Or if it will erupt at all,' Killifer suggested.

Brennart whirled on him. 'If? You think the whole thing might be a false alarm?'

'I don't know. I'm not an astronomer.'

'The goddamned astronomer's out here digging ditches instead of at her post with her instruments!'

Killifer shrugged. 'Douggie wanted her along.'

'The flare should have erupted by now, if there's going to be one,' Brennart thought out loud.

'Even if the flare does come, isn't there a couple of hours before the radiation really gets serious?' Killifer knew the answer to his question.

'Yes, that's right,' Brennart said.

'Enough time to get down off the mountain, using our hoppers?'

Brennart stopped his frustrated kneading and sat on the chair next to his aide. 'We could jump up to the summit of Mt. Wasser, plant the flag and start the nanobugs working on the power tower, and get down again before the radiation buildup even begins.'

'Christ, that's brilliant,' Killifer said.

'I'm going to suit up,' Brennart said.

'You?'

'I can't ask my people to do something that I'm not prepared to do myself. I take the same risks they do.'

'Yeah, but—'

'How many people will we need for a dash to the summit?'

Killifer swivelled his chair to the screen and tapped on the keyboard. 'Mission plan calls for six.'

'Strip it down. How many do we actually *need*?'

Studying the list on his screen, Killifer said, 'Two to handle the nanobugs, one to pilot the hopper.'

'Martin and Greenberg are the nanotechs,' Brennart said.

Thinking swiftly, Killifer said, 'Maybe we oughtta leave one of them here. No sense taking both of them up to the summit.'

'One person can't physically handle the task,' Brennart objected.

'All you need is an extra pair of hands. A warm body will do. Either Greenberg or Martin can direct the warm body, and you haven't risked both your nanotechs.'

Brennart pondered it for all of three seconds. 'Right. I'll take Greenberg. He's the more experienced of the two. Who can we spare to help him?'

'The astronomer?' Killifer suggested.

'Put her to some useful work,' Brennart muttered.

'You oughtta take Stavenger, too,' Killifer pointed out. 'Let him make a legal record of the claim.'

'Perfect!'

Killifer stayed in the comm cubicle as Brennart marched off to the airlock, where the spacesuits were stored. With a little luck, he said to himself, they'll all break their friggin' necks.

Doug felt excited when Brennart came out and told him they were making a dash to the summit of Mt. Wasser. He had been spraying plastic sealant along the tunnel walls just dug out by the others; the sealant made the tunnel airtight. It was dull and clumsy work, inside his spacesuit, with no light except from his helmet lamp. The sealant was doped with a weakly glowing phosphor, so that any gaps in its application would be easily seen.

It was the safest job Brennart could find for him. The more experienced expedition members were handling the flammable aluminum/oxygen propellant mixture out on the surface, desperately working to break up the rock-hard ground enough to allow the tractors to scoop it up and dump it on the shelters and tunnels.

Scrambling out of the tunnel at Brennart's command, Doug checked the equipment pouches on his belt while two of the other expedition members topped off his oxygen tank from the supply on the undamaged cargo ship. Yes, the miniature vidcam was there. Doug pulled it out and checked that its battery was fully charged. Not that he had used it, digging tunnels and sealing them.

He was surprised to see a short, stocky spacesuited figure join Brennart and Greenberg. Sure enough, the name stencilled on the chest of her suit was Rhee.

'We're making a dash to the summit,' Brennart told them as they lifted the spindly-legged little hopper from its hold in the cargo ship. 'Rhee, you assist Greenberg here. I'll pilot the hopper.'

'What's my assignment?' Doug asked.

'Official record keeper,' said Brennart. 'Unless you know how to handle a hopper.'

Why is he so hostile to me? Doug asked himself. Aloud, he replied, 'I've never actually flown one, but I've put in a lot of hours in simulators.'

'Fine,' Brennart snapped. 'You can be my co-pilot. Just don't touch anything.'

Doug helped Greenberg and Bianca Rhee to wrestle the tall canister of nanomachines onto the platform of the little hopper. Then they began strapping it down. The rocket vehicle looked too frail to take the four of them, Doug thought, even in the Moon's light gravity. The hopper was little more than a platform with a podium for its controls and footloops to anchor a half-dozen riders. There was a fold-down railing, too, with attachments for tethers.

To Doug it looked like a great way to break your neck. Racing jetcycles seemed safer.

'Come on, come on,' Brennart urged, pushing between Rhee and Greenberg to help finish the strapdown. 'We don't have a moment to lose.'

'Why the sudden rush?' Doug asked. 'This isn't on the mission schedule.'

'No, it's not,' Brennart snapped. 'But maybe Yamagata isn't waiting for our schedule.'

'Yamagata? They've got a team here too?'

'On its way,' Brennart said.

'You're certain?' Doug probed.

'Certain enough.'

'Has it been confirmed by—'

'Who's in charge of this expedition, Stavenger? You or me?' Brennart bellowed.

His ears ringing, Doug said, 'You are, of course.'

'Then climb aboard and let's get going.'

Doug dutifully stepped up the rickety little ladder and started to slide his boots into the foot loops alongside Brennart.

'Lift up the railings,' Brennart ordered, 'and see that everyone's safely tethered to them.'

'Aye-aye, sir,' said Doug snidely. Brennart paid no attention.

The tethers won't be much help if we crash, Doug thought as he snapped the flimsy railings into place. By the time he returned to Brennart's side and clicked his own tether to the rail, Brennart had powered up the hopper's systems. All the controls showed green, Doug saw.

'Ready for takeoff,' Brennart said.

Doug heard Killifer's answer in his earphones. 'You are cleared for takeoff.'

Brennart nudged the T-yoke of the throttle forward a bit. The platform beneath Doug's boots quivered and leaped upward.

There was no sound, no wind, but the dark, rocky land fell away from them so rapidly Doug felt his breath gush out of him.

Their little base dwindled quickly: four humps of shelters surrounded by spacesuited figures and a pair of minitractors, all digging tunnels and pushing rubble over the shelters like busy, scurrying ants. The brief flare of propellants burning into the rock strobed like a miniature lightning stroke.

Looking upward he saw the bare flank of Mt. Wasser coming near, sliding past dizzyingly as the hopper continued to rise. The rock face of the mountain looked glassy smooth, sandpapered by dust-mote-sized micrometeoroids for billions of years.

Suddenly they were in sunlight, brilliant, almost overpowering sunlight. The mountainside glittered like glass, like crystal, as it rushed by. Doug heard his suit fans whir faster, and something in his backpack groaned under the sudden heat load. He gripped the railing with both gloved hands.

'This is flying!' he said appreciatively. 'Like being on a magic carpet.'

He heard Brennart chuckle softly. 'You like it, eh?'

'It's terrific!'

Neither Greenberg nor Rhee said a word. Doug wondered how Bianca was taking the flight. At least they weren't weightless for more than a few seconds at a time; Brennart kept goosing the little rocket engine, pushing them higher in short spurts. But the lurching, spasmodic flight was starting to make Doug's stomach gurgle.

Brennart took the little hopper up above Mt. Wasser's flat, U-shaped summit, looking for a safe place to land, checking the actuality against the satellite photos they had studied.

'Flat area over to the left,' Doug said. 'About ten o'clock.'

'I see it,' said Brennart.

A minuscule puff of thrust from two of the maneuvering jets set along the corners of the platform and they slid over sideways until they were just above the relatively flat area. It was clear of boulders, although Doug saw the sharp-rimmed edge of a crater big enough to swallow their hopper, clearly etched in the harsh sunlight.

His stomach told him they were falling. Then a burst of thrust. Falling again. Another burst, lighter, and Brennart put them down deftly on the bare rock.

It was like being on the top of the world. Doug unhooked his tether and pulled loose of his foot restraints, then turned around in a full circle. All around them stretched peaks of bare rock, as far as the eye could see. They seemed to be floating on a sea of darkness, the land below them in perpetual cryogenic night.

'We made it.' Bianca's voice sounded breathless in Doug's helmet earphones.

We're up higher than Mt. Everest, Doug thought.

'Let's get to work,' Brennart ordered. 'Stavenger, I want you to record every move we make. Hop down and start taping us as we unload the nanobugs.'

'Right,' said Doug. He slapped down the railing and jumped from the hopper's platform, floating gently to the bare rock. His boots slid; the rock was smooth as glass.

Pulling out his vidcam, Doug put its eyepiece to his visor and was just starting to record when Killifer's voice grated in his earphones:

'Killifer to Brennart. We just received word that a solar flare broke out at seventeen-twenty-six and forty-one seconds. Moonbase advises all surface activity be stopped and all personnel seek shelter immediately.'

MOONBASE

Greg asked, 'Are they going to be all right?'

'Brennart's as experienced as they come,' said Jinny Anson. 'He knows how to take care of himself and his people.' But the worried frown on her face belied her confident words.

They were in the base control center, a big low-ceilinged room crammed with control and communications consoles. Every pump, valve, airlock hatch, air fan, sensor, heater, motor, and other piece of equipment in the base and outside on the surface was monitored from the consoles and could be manually controlled whenever it was necessary to override the automatic programming. One whole wall of the darkened, intensely quiet control center was an electronic schematic map of Moonbase, glowing with colored lines and symbols that showed everything in the base and its environs.

Anson had rushed down the tunnel from her office, with Greg in tow, the instant she heard that the flare had erupted. The focus of the center was a U-shaped set of communications consoles, with a trio of operators sitting within fingertip touch of a dozen different display screens. On those screens Greg saw several sections of the underground base, mostly labs and workshops, a lot of plumbing and pumps, and one chamber that looked like a hydroponics farm. There were also views of the surface outside on the floor of Alphonsus. The transfer rocket that had brought Greg to the Moon still sat out there, unattended. Tractors were pulling into the main airlock, trundling slowly across the crater floor to get into the garage and safely sheltered from the expected radiation cloud.

One screen seemed to be looking in on an office Earthside.

Greg could see a window with trees outside, behind an earnest-looking middle-aged man in a tweed jacket.

Anson pulled up a spindly wheeled chair at one end of the consoles and worked the keyboard there. The tweedy graying man's face appeared on her screen.

Standing behind her, Greg tried to figure out where on Earth he might be. Then he noticed a saguaro cactus poking its stiff arms into the bright blue sky amid the trees on the hillside beyond that window. It had to be Arizona.

Noticing him behind her, Anson handed Greg a headset.

'. . . Class Four,' he heard the man saying as he slipped on the earphone. 'Almost a Class Five.'

'Yes,' Anson said, 'but will it hit the Earth-Moon region?'

'Still hard to tell, Jinny. If we had warning satellites inside Mercury's orbit, as I've been begging for over the past ten years, we'd be getting data right now. As it is, we'll have to wait for the plasma cloud to reach Venus's orbit before we get any hard numbers.'

'How long will that take?' Anson asked.

'Judging from the microwave measurements, about another two hours.'

'It's moving fast, then.'

'Faster than a speeding bullet.'

'Okay, thanks. Keep us informed, please.'

The gray-haired man nodded. 'Certainly.'

Anson blanked the screen, then turned to Greg. 'Well, they've got at least a few hours before the heavy radiation hits. If it hits at all.'

Greg asked, 'It might miss us altogether?'

'There's a chance. The flare spits out a big cloud of plasma, mostly very energetic protons. Bee ee vee protons.'

'Bee ee vee?'

'Billions of electron volts. Killer particles. Fry your butt in a few minutes.'

Doug's out there, Greg said to himself. He hardly knew his half-brother. Over the past eighteen years he had seen Doug in person fewer than a dozen times, and then always with their mother between them.

'A couple meters of dirt is enough to stop the particles,' Anson was assuring him, 'so as long as they're inside the shelters they've dug they'll be fine. Just like we are.'

'But you said the cloud might not even reach here.'

She nodded vigorously. 'The cloud's a plasma; ionized gas. That means it's steered by the interplanetary magnetic field. The field is weird; it gets all looped up and tangled by the Sun's rotation. So until we start getting radiation data from the satellites we've got between us and the Sun we won't really know if the cloud's going to come our way or not.'

Greg murmured, 'I see,' as he watched Anson's face closely. She was telling him pretty much what he already knew about solar flares, but to her this was no dry astronomical colloquy. This was as real and vital to her as breathable air.

'They'll be okay,' Anson said, trying to smile. 'Your brother will come through this fine, I betcha.'

'Of course he will,' Greg said, wondering if that's what he wanted. Doug's only eighteen, he told himself. He's no threat to me. But another voice in his mind countered, Not yet. He's no threat at present. But he's out there on the Moon's surface getting experiences that you've never had. Sooner or later he's going to challenge you for control. Sooner or later. And Mom will be on his side. You know that. She'll be helping him.

'Hey, he's going to be all right!' Anson repeated, mistaking Greg's withdrawn silence. 'Really! You'll see.'

'Of course,' Greg said.

'Come on.' Anson got up from her chair. 'There's lots more to see around here.'

'Now?' Greg asked, surprised. 'With the flare and all?'

'Nothing we can do about the flare,' Anson said, almost cheerfully. 'It either hits or it doesn't. In the meantime there's a lot for you to learn about and not much time to get it all in.'

'But I—'

'I'm not going to miss my own wedding because you haven't been completely briefed,' Anson said. She was smiling, but her tone was far from gentle. 'Come on, we can start at the water plant.'

Feeling just a little dazed, Greg followed her out of the control center and down the long tunnel.

'We've got to go all the way down to the end and then cut across,' Anson said.

Feeling awkward, almost embarrassed in the weighted boots, Greg asked, 'Aren't there any cross tunnels? Besides the one up at the main airlock?'

'Two,' replied Anson, 'but they're for emergency use only. They carry piping and electrical lines.'

Greg glanced up at the color-coded pipes and electrical lines running along the ceiling of the tunnel. 'You mean that everybody has to walk the length of one tunnel to get to the next?'

'That's what they're supposed to do. Officially.'

'And in reality?'

She grinned at him. 'They take shortcuts.'

'Then why don't we?' He made himself smile back at her.

'It's kind of cramped.'

'I'm not afraid of getting my coveralls dirty,' Greg said.

She seemed delighted. They ducked into the first cross-tunnel and Greg saw that it was indeed narrow and low enough to make him keep his head down. But he followed her along its dimly-lit length, noting idly that a fat person would have a difficult time squeezing through. Anson was not fat. She filled out her coveralls very nicely, but she was certainly not overweight.

'The EVC is all the way at the back of the base, as deep inside the mountain as we could put it,' she told Greg.

'EVC?'

'Environmental control center,' she explained. 'That's where we regulate the air's CO_2 content, the temperature and humidity and all. It's not a hundred percent closed-loop, though. We have to add oxygen and nitrogen from time to time, keep the balance right.'

'Oh,' said Greg.

She went on, 'We wanted to get the maximum of protection for the EVC. We can go for a couple of days without water, but if the air goes bad – *blooey*, everybody in the base is dead in an hour or so, I betcha.'

'But the water plant's up front, near the main airlock?'

'Yeah,' Anson replied. 'Plumbing's easier that way. Cost an arm and a leg to dig the EVC in so deep. We had to run big exhaust tunnels through the solid rock. Corporation decided once was enough, so when we built the water plant we put it where we had easy access.'

Greg nodded. He knew all about the exorbitant costs of digging new living and working spaces on the Moon.

'I've been talking to some people at the University of Texas,' Anson said, 'where my husband-to-be teaches. They think our water recycling system might be useful for big cities like Houston and Dallas.'

'Really?'

'Really,' Anson said, with just a hint of sarcasm at Greg's doubting tone. 'I'll be talking with some people from Houston when I get back Earthside.'

Despite himself, Greg was impressed. 'You could start a whole new product line for the corporation,' he said.

'Water recycling systems for major cities,' Anson chirped happily. 'We could make a mint on it, I betcha.'

Once in the adjacent tunnel she led him to its front end.

'Main airlock is through that hatch.' Anson pointed. 'That's where we garage the tractors and decontaminate surface equipment.'

'Decontaminate?'

'Vacuum off the dust, mostly,' she said, leading him away from the hatch. 'Freakin' dust gets into everything, especially moving parts. It's a real pain in the butt.'

They walked along the front face of the tunnel until they came to another airtight hatch. Greg saw WATER FACILITY stencilled on the smoothed rock wall next to the metal hatch. Beneath the neatly stencilled letters someone had daubed in orange dayglo, *You make water; we make water.* And over the hatch, another graffito: *Recycling is a piss-poor way of life.*

'You leave them there?' Greg jabbed a finger at the graffiti.

With a half-smile Anson replied, 'We scrub them off every now and then. Matter of fact, I was going to have the whole base cleaned up in your honor, but you got here too quick. These are new, though.'

Greg snorted with disdain.

'Don't knock it too much,' Anson said. 'Graffiti help people let off steam. And cleaning them up takes water that's better used for more important things. Like living.'

He kept his silence as Anson showed him through the maze of pipes on the other side of the hatch.

'Everything in here is fully automated, so it's not built for human comfort. Operators monitor the equipment, of course, but it runs by itself most of the time.'

'You need access for repair personnel, don't you?' Greg asked.

'Sure. This is it, where we're walking.'

The chamber was dimly lit, its ceiling oppressively low. Narrow walkways threaded through the convoluted piping. The place felt cold, but not dank, as a cave on Earth would. The pipes were all wrapped in insulation, Greg saw. Not a molecule of water was being wasted.

'Oxygen from the nanoprocessors comes in there,' she stretched an arm toward the shadowed recesses between the largest pipes, anodized green. 'It's in gaseous form, of course. Hydrogen comes in along those red lines. They're mixed in those vats and the water is pumped out to the rest of the base along the blue pipes.'

'And the yellow pipes?' Greg asked.

'Used water coming in for recycling. Never eat yellow snow and never drink from a yellow pipe.'

Greg nodded in the shadowy dimness. Grinning, Anson seemed to be waiting for a reaction from him. After a few moments, though, her grin faded and she resumed her explanations.

'Hydrogen's getting more and more expensive,' she said.

'How come? The nanomachines—'

'We have to go farther and farther out from the base to find hydrogen. We've picked the regolith clean of the stuff nearby.'

'Really?'

'Hey, we're talking about individual atoms trapped in the regolith. There's just not that much hydrogen out there. One hundredth of a percent, by mass, tops.'

'Still, the cost should be negligible.'

'Nanomachines ain't cheap,' she said. 'We have to produce them here and they won't let us build the kind that can reproduce themselves. Scared of runaways that could eat up the Moon, or some equally buttheaded scenario.'

Greg kept silent. He knew all about the reasons for the strict safety regulations.

'So the bugs are designed to operate only during the lunar night. After a few day-night cycles they break themselves down and we have to produce another batch.'

'But they can't cost very much. A few kilograms can produce their weight in hydrogen thousands of times over, from the reports I've seen.'

Anson waved one hand in the air. 'Yeah, but at our current rate of consumption we'll have cleaned out the whole crater floor of hydrogen in another five years. Then it'll be cheaper to import hydrogen from Earthside.'

'But you recycle . . .'

'Sure, but recycling isn't a hundred percent efficient, of course.'

Greg thought a moment. 'That's why Brennart's mission to the south pole is important.'

'Water's valuable, even if it's a thousand klicks away. We can use nanomachines to build a pipeline easily enough.'

'I wonder how much water they've found down there,' Greg said.

'Enough to last us until we're ready to scoop volatiles from passing comets, I hope.'

Greg knew about the comet-scooping idea; it had been relegated to the realm of far-future projects that had neither funding nor anything else except the sketchiest of conceptual drawings.

'Won't that be expensive?' It was the usual question, expected.

Anson laughed. 'Sure it will, but then we won't have to depend on Earthside for water. Our goal is to be self-sufficient.'

That surprised Greg. 'Self-sufficient? When was that made a goal?'

'It's *our* goal,' Anson said, 'not the corporation's. The goal of the Lunatics who keep coming back here no matter how many times they return Earthside.'

'Self-sufficient,' Greg repeated. It was a distant dream, he knew. These people are kidding themselves.

'Self-sufficient,' Anson repeated firmly.

'Then why aren't you drilling for ammonia?' Greg asked.

The sudden shift of subject caught Anson by surprise. 'Huh? Ammonia?'

'Nitrogen is your biggest import from Earth. The reason this base is sited at Alphonsus is that there have been seepages of ammonia and methane from below the crater floor. If you want to be self-sufficient you should be drilling for the ammonia.'

'That's in our long-range plan,' Anson said defensively.

'Maybe we should move it up,' said Greg. 'The methane could provide carbon. And hydrogen, too.'

'Not a helluva lot, according to our geological probes.'

'Shouldn't you say selenological, rather than geological?'

She planted her fists on her hips. 'I hope you're joking.'

Greg let a ghost of a smile cross his lips. 'Certainly.'

'Good. Come on, it's almost time for dinner and we've got a lot of cost comparisons to do.'

The Cave was less than half full when they came in and got into line for the meal dispensers. Greg noticed that Anson studied her choices carefully before selecting soyburgers, salad and fruit drink. He punched the same buttons she did, and they carried their trays to a small table off in a corner by a pair of potted ficus trees.

They chewed through numbers with their meal, Anson pulling a palm-sized computer from her thigh pocket to call up data from the base's main files. Greg quickly saw that while her immediate priorities were to keep costs as low as possible, her long-term goal was to make Moonbase independent of life-support imports from Earth.

She may be getting married, Greg thought, but she really intends to come back here. I wonder if her future husband understands that?

'That's the only way to make this rat's nest really profitable,' she insisted. 'Cut the umbilical from Earthside. Moonbase has *got* to become self-sufficient.'

'Even if you have to go out and scoop volatiles from comets?'

'Hey, don't knock it. Even teeny little comets spew out thousands of tons of water vapor and other volatiles per hour.'

'I understand—'

'Less than the cost of imports, once we get the program started. It's the design and test phase that soaks up the money. Operations should be cheap: just the cost of the fuel and the teleoperators in the command center. Peanuts.'

'How soon do you see this happening?'

She picked at her salad. 'Not for years, of course. Maybe ten or more. Too far out for the corporate five-year plan.'

Greg shifted gears again. 'When is the mass driver going to be finished?'

She was ready for that one, though. Probably expected it. 'When the freakin' corporation bumps its priority up closer to the top. We're not getting much support from Savannah on it, y'know.'

'Why not?'

'Rocket fuel's cheap enough. The nanomachines produce enough aluminum and oxygen; we don't need an electrical slingshot.'

'A mass driver would reduce launch costs by a factor of ten or better,' Greg said. Then he added, 'It should have been completed years ago.'

Anson scowled across the little table at him. 'Sure it should, but with practically no corporate support we have to stooge it along on our own resources.'

'Even using nanomachines, it's going so slowly?' Greg asked. It sounded accusatory and he knew it.

'Nanomachines.' Anson snorted. 'Some people think they're like a magic wand. Just throw in some nanomachines and *poof!* the job's done for you, like the shoemaker's elves.'

Despite himself, Greg smiled at her. 'It doesn't work that way?'

'Building something as complex as a mass driver is a tough job, even with nanomachines,' she said. 'Freakin' job's turned into a nanotechnology research program. We're learning a lot about how to develop the little critters; we're producing a helluva lot of research papers and graduate degrees. But the mass driver's more than a year behind schedule.'

'I know,' said Greg.

'It'll get done,' she promised. 'But not on the schedule set up in Savannah.'

'Can you do it entirely out of lunar materials? Even the superconducting magnets?'

'Yeah, sure. And we don't need superconductors. We dropped that in favor of cryogenic aluminum magnets. Keep 'em cool and they're almost as good as superconductors.'

'But they draw some current, don't they?'

Anson shrugged. 'Not much. And electricity's cheap here. We just set up a few extra acres of solar cells. Keep the magnets shaded from the Sun and the liquid nitrogen stays cold. That's another advantage we've got here.'

'Realistically, when do you think the mass driver will be up and working?'

She looked up at the rock ceiling, thinking. 'Maybe during your year,' she said. 'More likely, not until the next director replaces you.'

'That's not very good, is it?' Greg criticized.

Anson sighed – almost a huff – and returned her attention to what was left of her soyburger. Then she looked up, her face sad.

'Look,' she said, 'I know there's great things just waiting to be done here. Tremendous things! But I'm leaving. I'm just an employee and I've had to stay strictly within the limits the corporation's set for Moonbase. You can do a helluva lot better, I know.'

'I didn't mean—'

Tears were welling in her eyes. 'Don't you think I can see what Moonbase can be, if we really dig in and give it our best? I'm supposed to squeeze a profit out of this place, not plow the profits back in to make it self-sufficient. That's for *you* to do. That's why your mother's sent you up here, isn't it?'

Greg realized his mouth was hanging open with surprise. Is that why Mom's sent me here? No. It was my idea to come here; she was against it. Or was she, really? Has she been manipulating me all along? Does she think that a few months up here will turn me into an advocate for Moonbase?

Before he could formulate an answer for her, Anson's personal computer chimed. She tapped the comm button and they both heard:

'Word just came up from Tucson. The plasma cloud will engulf cislunar space in less than two hours. Radiation levels will exceed four hundred rads per hour for at least twenty-four to thirty-six hours.'

Anson acknowledged the message, then looked at Greg again. 'You're in luck. Nothing's going to be moving on the surface for a while. There'll be a flare party starting before long. Hope you brought your dancing shoes.'

MT. WASSER

Doug heard Killifer's voice in his earphones, 'Word just came in from Moonbase. Radiation cloud's due in less than two hours.'

'Radiation cloud?' Doug blurted.

Brennart's spacesuited figure straightened up the way a man does when he's been slapped in the face. 'How much less than two hours?' he demanded.

'Unknown. Less than two hours is the best they can give us.'

'What radiation cloud?' Doug asked.

'Solar flare,' said Brennart.

'A flare?' Rhee's voice sounded shocked, scared. 'Why wasn't I told about it?'

'Why?' Brennart snapped. 'Could you stop it?'

'But . . .'

Ignoring her, Brennart asked Killifer, 'How's the digging?'

Killifer replied, 'Coverage complete on shelters one and two. About half done on three and four. Tunnels are all complete, but they're not deep enough to be safe without additional rubble on them.'

Brennart sighed. 'All right, get as much done in the next hour as you can, then get everybody inside. We're going to deploy the nanomachines and then return.'

'Right.'

Doug turned to look at Greenberg and Rhee, who had just opened the canister in which the nanomachines were stored. Inadvertently, his glance took in the Sun, hanging low above the worn, rounded mountain peaks. His heavily-tinted visor blocked most of the glare, but still the Sun's mighty radiance dazzled him.

'We've got to get back to shelter right away,' Rhee was saying. 'Flares are dangerous!'

'Don't panic,' said Brennart. 'We've got an hour, at least.'

Doug was trying to remember how much radiation a flare put out. Enough to kill, he knew.

'Get this on tape!' Brennart ordered. 'It's the reason we're here.'

Dutifully, Doug walked around the slippery rock summit until the Sun was at his back, then aimed the vidcam at Rhee and Greenberg. Bianca was gripping the big canister in her arms as if she were hugging it, while the nanotech carefully slid a long narrow metal tube from its interior. Brennart stepped into the picture to explain what they were doing. And get the credit for it, Doug thought.

The nanobugs they were using here were of a special type, designed to work in the blazing heat of unfiltered sunlight. They would extract silicon, aluminum and trace elements from the mountain's rock and use them to build a tower of solar panels that would be in sunshine perpetually. The tower would provide continuous electrical power for the machines down in the darkness of the ice fields that would grind up the ice, liquify it, and pump it back to Moonbase.

The equipment to extract the ice and pump water would be sent by a follow-up expedition. So would the nanomachines to build the pipeline. Brennart's task was to determine if there was enough ice in the south polar region to be worth the investment – and to make certain that Moonbase established an unshakable legal claim to the territory.

Thus Doug taped the first step in starting the nanomachines' construction of the power tower. Legal precedence. He grimaced as he squinted through the vidcam's eyepiece. If Brennart was correct, Yamagata was also providing a witness to their claim, with their recce satellite.

Greenberg opened the tube and placed several even thinner tubules on the bare rock.

'That's it,' the nanotech said. 'The first set of nanomachines

for construction of Moonbase's solar power tower have been
put in place at,' he lifted his left arm to peer at his watch,
'nineteen hundred hours and eight minutes.'

'Got it,' said Doug. 'The tape has a time and date setting,
too, so the timing will be verified.'

'Very well,' Brennart said. 'Transmit the imagery to
Moonbase.'

Doug switched his suit radio's frequency to the channel for
the minisats. No response. Checking the schedule he had taped
to his forearm, he went back to the suit-to-suit frequency and
said to Brennart, 'No commsat over our horizon for another
eleven minutes.'

He could hear Brennart huff impatiently. 'All right,' the
expedition leader grumbled. 'Call in eleven minutes. Now
let's get out of here. Quickly.'

'Right,' said Bianca. 'Let's get under shelter.'

Bianca sounded frightened, Doug thought. She knows more
about flares than any of us; if she's scared she must have good
reason to be.

'This is what you do when there's a flare?' Greg asked.

After an intense hour or so in her office, making certain
the base was battened down for the incoming radiation storm,
Jinny Anson had led Greg back to The Cave. It was already
filled with nearly every person in Moonbase. The tables had
been pushed to one wall, raucous music was blaring from the
overhead speakers, people were laughing, talking, drinking,
couples were dancing on the smoothed rock flooring between
the squares of grass.

'There's not much else to do,' Anson replied, her voice
raised to be heard over the thumping beat of the music, 'except
eat, drink and be merry. Until the radiation outside goes back
to normal.'

Greg consciously tried to keep from frowning, yet he
could feel his brows knitting. Okay, the people who work
on the surface ought to be brought safely inside, he told
himself. But that's only a handful. Most of the base personnel work indoors; they could go right on with their jobs,

even though a solar flare is bathing the surface with lethal radiation levels.

'Relax!' Anson said. 'This is just about the only excuse for a party we ever get up here.'

She led him to the row of food dispensers lined against The Cave's far wall, stainless steel with glass fronts, seven feet tall. Not much of a selection, Greg saw. Most of the offerings were preprocessed soybean derivatives of one sort or another.

'You mean all work stops while the flare's going on?' Greg heard the brittleness in his own voice as he selected something that looked somewhat like finger sandwiches.

Anson shrugged. 'Might as well. All the surface equipment is shut down. Even the scientific instrumentation outside takes a beating from the flare, so a lot of the researchers got nothing much to do.'

'What about communications?' Greg asked.

'The comm center is always manned,' she said easily, pulling out a soyburger on a bun and heading for the microwave ovens. 'Even during a party.'

'Doesn't the flare interfere with communications?'

'We can always go to the laser comm system if the microwave gets too hashed up.'

'I didn't mean communications with Earth,' Greg said. 'I meant with the expedition.'

Her face went serious. 'We've got six minisats in polar orbit. They're hardened, of course, but if the radiation levels exceed their hardening—'

'Then those people are cut off.'

'Right,' she conceded.

'Then what happens?'

'We've got two more minisats as backups. We send them up after the radiation dies down. Not much more that we can do.'

Greg thought hard for a few moments, then had to admit, 'I guess you're right.'

The microwave pinged and Anson pulled out her steaming soyburger. 'Come on, let me introduce you to some of the gang. Are you straight or gay?'

Greg nearly dropped his plastic dish. 'What?'

'Gay or straight? Who'd you like to dance with?'

Sex, Greg realized. It all comes down to sex. That's what this party is all about. The solar flare is an excuse for these people to have a gene-pool enrichment. Just like neolithic hunting tribes that came together once a year to exchange virgins.

Anson was looking at him with a positively impish expression. 'Have I embarrassed you?' she asked.

'No . . .'

'We get pretty close to one another, living cooped up in here for months on end,' she said. 'I forgot that most people Earthside aren't as open as we are. I'm sorry.'

'It's okay,' Greg said, trying to adjust his outlook. 'And I'm straight.'

'Great!' Anson said, with seemingly genuine enthusiasm. 'Then you can dance with me.'

Riding down the mountain was like dropping down a long dark shaft. Brennart fired the hopper's main rocket engine once to lift them off the summit, then used the maneuvering jets to nudge them away from its slope. After that it was a long slow fall into the darkness below.

Doug felt his stomach fluttering and wondered how Bianca was handling it. Brennart stood at the podium, his gloved hands on the controls, like a sea captain of old at the helm of his storm-tossed ship. Instead of a sou'wester he was encased in a bulky spacesuit. And instead of the heaving and rolling of the waves, their hopper was falling smoothly in the shadows of the massive mountains, plummeting swiftly, silently, like a pebble dropped down a deep, deep well. This is what the old-time explorers must have felt like, Doug told himself. Danger and excitement and the thrill of doing things nobody's done before. He grinned inside his helmet. This could become habit forming!

His earphones chirped with the signal from one of the minisats. Quickly, Doug plugged his vidcam into the comm port on the belt of his suit and played the tape at top speed. He heard a brief screeching in his earphones, like a magpie on amphetamines, then a verifying beep from the satellite. The data-compressed signal had been received.

'What about transmitting our claim?' Brennart asked before Doug could report to him.

'Just did it,' he said. 'Squirted the tape to the minisat. When it comes over Moonbase's horizon it'll transmit the whole scene to the base.'

'How soon will that be?'

Doug made a quick mental calculation. 'The satellite orbit is one hour. Should be in forty, fifty minutes.'

Brennart huffed again. 'Plasma cloud might hit by then.'

'The commsats are hardened, aren't they?'

'Up to a point.'

'Is there a chance the radiation could knock them out before our message reaches Moonbase?'

'Ever heard of Murphy's Law?' Brennart replied.

'Yes, but—'

'It's all a matter of degree. There's no such thing as absolute hardening. The minisats are built to withstand a certain level of radiation. If the plasma cloud's levels are higher, then the satellites will be kaput.'

'Then we'd be cut off from Moonbase.' Bianca's voice, filled with apprehension.

'Until they pop up more satellites, after the storm is over.'

'I wonder how hardened the Yamagata snooper satellite is,' Doug mused.

Brennart made no answer and when Doug tried to talk to him he realized that the expedition leader was talking to the ground on a different frequency. Doug switched to that channel.

'. . . landing lights haven't been set up yet,' he heard Killifer's voice, almost whining. 'You told me to get everybody inside—'

'Never mind,' Brennart snapped. 'Turn up the radar beacon to full power. I'd like to have *some* idea of where the ground is!'

'Right.'

Doug knew there were no lights beneath the hopper's platform. We could crash in this darkness, he realized.

The little cluster of instruments on the control podium included a laser altimeter, and Doug saw that its digital readout was falling so fast the numbers were almost a blur. Still Brennart did not fire the rocket to slow their descent. It's like parachute jumping, he thought. See how long you can stay in free-fall before you chicken out and pull the ripcord.

He felt his heart racing as he clutched the flimsy railing with both hands and marveled at Brennart's cool while the hopper plunged deeper and deeper into the eternal darkness.

'Are we there yet?' Bianca's voice bleated in his earphones. She's trying to make light of it, Doug thought, but this long free-fall must be bothering her. I wonder how she did on the trip to Moonbase from Earth? She must have been in misery all the way. Greenberg had said nothing since they'd climbed aboard the hopper and damned little before that. Doug realized that the nanotech engineer was as closed-mouthed as anyone he had ever met.

Straining his eyes, Doug peered over the railing into the darkness below. He could make out vague shapes in the darkness, like monsters from a child's nightmare reaching up to snare him.

Then a lurch of thrust nearly buckled his knees and the landscape below was briefly lit by the rocket's silent flame, like a scene suddenly illuminated by a lightning bolt's flash. Before Doug could blink it was inky dark again and they continued to fall.

Then another flash and surge of thrust. Then a gentle bump and Doug felt the comfortable reassurance of weight once more. They were on the ground.

'Don't just stand there,' Brennart commanded. 'Get off and into the shelter.'

For a moment Doug was transfixed, immobilized with admiration for Brennart's piloting. The man really is as good as all the stories about him.

'Move!' Brennart bellowed.

Almost laughing, Doug knocked down the hopper's railing and jumped softly to the ground.

'Which shelter?' Greenberg asked. He had turned on his

helmet lamp, Doug saw. So had Brennart. He did the same, then Bianca followed suit.

'Number four,' said Brennart, pointing with a long arm. 'The others are already occupied.'

They trooped to the airlock, Greenberg in the lead. He may not say much, Doug thought, but he sure makes it clear that he wants to get safely inside.

'Don't take off your suits,' Brennart commanded. 'Go right through the lock and into the shelter. Leave your suits on.'

Doug waited for Bianca to go in, then turned toward Brennart.

'Go on, go on,' the expedition commander shooed impatiently. 'We don't have all damned day.'

Doug ducked through the airlock hatch, waited for it to recycle, then stepped into the shelter. Bianca and Greenberg were sitting awkwardly on the edges of two facing bunks, still encased in their bulky spacesuits, looking like a pair of hunchbacked giant pandas. There were no internal partitions in this smaller shelter; it was merely a dugout for sleeping and eating.

The pumps chugged and the inner airlock hatch opened to let Brennart step through. He had to bend over slightly to keep the top of his helmet from scraping the shelter's curving ceiling.

'Not enough rubble on top of us to provide full shielding,' he explained, 'so we stay in the suits until the radiation dies down.'

'That could be days!' Rhee blurted.

'We'll need the extra shielding the suits provide,' Brennart said calmly. 'It'll be uncomfortable but better than getting fried.'

'And the backpacks?' she asked.

'We can take off the backpacks and breathe the air in here, but otherwise we will stay buttoned up. Like the man says, better safe than sorry.'

'What about eating?' asked Doug.

Brennart turned toward him slowly, his helmet visor staring at him like a blank-eyed cyclops. 'We'll take a quick meal now, before the radiation builds up. After that, I'll decide when and if it's safe to open our visors for food.'

After a heartbeat's span of silence, Brennart added in a more relaxed tone, 'A little dieting won't hurt any of us.'

So they grabbed prepackaged meals from the shelter's food locker and took turns sticking them in the tiny micro-wave oven.

'Stand back from the oven. You don't want to get exposed to any radiation that leaks through,' Greenberg said, so solemnly that Doug couldn't tell if he was joking or serious.

Brennart raised his visor to eat his meal, and Doug could at last see the man's face. If Brennart was worried, he didn't show it. He looked calm; thoughtful, but certainly not jittery.

'That's our guide,' he said, pointing to the radiation meter built into the airlock control panel. 'That, and our suit patches, are the only way we have of telling how high the radiation level is.'

The suit patches were cumulative, Doug knew. They changed color with dosage, going from green through yellow to red. Once they turned red you were supposed to get inside shelter, no matter what you were doing out on the surface. He looked down at the patch on his right arm and was startled to see it had already turned a sickly greenish yellow. Just from the work we've done outside today, he thought. What color will it be when the radiation cloud hits?

How can they eat this garbage? Greg wondered as he chewed on the little sandwich. It tasted like sawdust and glue, with a core of hard rubber.

He felt uncomfortable at the flare party, and most of the people around him seemed uncomfortable in his presence. Jinny Anson was perfectly relaxed, apparently, but the others stiffened visibly as he approached them. They were friendly enough, but Greg saw them put their drinks down or try to hide them behind their backs. Laughter died out as he came up to a knot of party-goers. People became polite, their smiles strained.

The new boss, Greg figured. They know I'll be in charge

here in a week, the board chairwoman's son, and they don't know what kind of a boss I'm going to be. Inwardly, Greg frowned at the irony of it. *I don't know what kind of a boss I'm going to be, either. Obviously there's alcohol in most of those drinks, even though nobody's offered me any. What else is going down?*

He had made a sort of ragged circumnavigation of The Cave, and ended up back near Anson, who was deep in conversation with a tall, ragged-looking old simp with a mangy beard and sad, baggy eyes. Greg left his dish of unfinished finger sandwiches on the nearest table and went toward her.

'Here he is,' Anson said as Greg approached them. She waved Greg toward her, then introduced, 'Greg Masterson, Lev Brudnoy.'

The legendary Lev Brudnoy! Greg realized that Brudnoy's legend was more than twenty years old now. *The poor geezer must be pushing sixty, at least.*

'How do you do,' said Brudnoy gravely, extending a calloused hand. His coveralls were a faded olive green, splotched here and there with stains. He was about Greg's own height, though, and wider across the shoulders.

'I'm very happy to meet you,' Greg said perfunctorily. Brudnoy's grip was strong; Greg got the feeling he could have squeezed a lot harder if he'd wanted to.

'So you are going to be our leader for the next twelve months,' Brudnoy said.

'That's right.'

'I knew your stepfather, Paul Stavenger. He was a good man.'

Trying not to bristle, Greg said, 'I thought it was my father who gave you permission to join Moonbase.'

With a slow smile, Brudnoy answered, 'Quite true. But I never met your father. He never came here and I was never invited to meet him when I visited Earthside.'

'Oh. I see.'

'I am most indebted to him, of course. And to your lovely mother – whom I also have never met.'

Feeling awkward, Greg tried to change the subject. 'I suppose you've been here at Moonbase longer than anyone else.' It was inane and he knew it, but Greg couldn't think of anything else.

'More than twenty years,' Anson said.

'Not all that time has been spent here on the Moon, of course,' said Brudnoy. 'I visit Earthside each year, as required by our health regulations.'

Greg knew the regulations. They were based on the idea that living on the Moon deconditioned the body for living in Earth's heavier gravity. Every Moonbase employee was required to undertake an exercise regime to keep muscles and bones strong enough for an immediate return Earthside.

'Yet,' Brudnoy went on, almost wistfully, 'my trips Earthside grow shorter and my stays here grow longer. This is my true home. Earth is a distant dream.'

With a sardonic smile, Greg said, 'The food's better on Earth.'

'Quite true,' Brudnoy agreed.

'What we grow in our farm is for nutrition, not gourmet taste,' Anson snapped.

'Mostly soybeans,' said Brudnoy. 'What little variety we have comes from them.' Before Greg could comment, he went on, 'And green vegetables, of course. We recently introduced carrots, but they aren't doing too well.'

'Everything else we have to bring up from Earthside,' Anson said defensively. 'We have to go for the highest nutritional values per kilo, not taste.'

'That's obvious,' said Greg.

Looking nettled, Anson turned to Brudnoy. 'He'll fit right in here; up here ten minutes and he's already complaining about the food.'

'I can prepare for you a fresh salad,' Brudnoy said, completely serious.

'A salad?'

'After all my years of adventuring, I have become a farmer. My true calling: to be a peasant.'

'I'd like to see your farm,' Greg said.

'Lev's got a green thumb,' said Anson. 'He'll turn us all into vegetarians one of these days.'

'Can't we bring meat animals up here?' Greg asked. 'Fresh meat would be good.'

'Oh sure,' Anson replied sarcastically. 'We've got the wide open prairies around here; get some cowboys and a herd of cattle.'

Greg felt his face redden. 'Maybe something smaller? Chickens?'

'Or rabbits,' Brudnoy said. 'I remember reading somewhere that rabbits have a high ratio of protein to bone.'

'Okay,' said Greg. 'Rabbits.'

'We have to be very careful about what we bring in here,' Anson said sternly. 'This is a closed ecology and we can't afford to endanger it.'

'But rabbits—'

'Look what they did to Australia.'

'Jinny, my dear,' said Brudnoy, 'we would not allow them to run wild and breed at will.'

'We could control them, couldn't we?' Greg asked.

Looking completely unconvinced, Anson said, 'Well, you're going to be director. You look into it.'

Turning to Brudnoy, Greg asked, 'Could you look into it?'

'Certainly,' said the Russian. 'I would be most happy to.'

Anson's face eased into a smile. 'You're going to be okay, Masterson. Delegating responsibility already. That's the mark of a successful manager.'

Greg couldn't tell if she was being sarcastic or sincere.

'Rabbits will be the salvation of Moonbase,' Brudnoy said, with a happy grin on his bearded face. 'And I have found my calling!'

'You have?' Anson asked, looking askance at the Russian.

'To feed the hungry masses!' Brudnoy said. 'To end the dreariness of packaged foods. I will not be a lowly peasant. I will become the master of cuisine for Moonbase.'

'A noble calling,' said Anson.

'Thank you!' Brudnoy said to Greg. 'You have given me a new purpose in life.'

And he clasped Greg in his long arms with a Russian bear hug.

'Now what can I do for you in return?' Brudnoy asked once he had released Greg from his embrace.

Gasping slightly, more with surprise than anything else, Greg stammered, 'I . . . I don't really know.'

'I am yours to command,' Brudnoy said. 'Call upon me at any hour and I will be at your side.'

With a sloppy military salute, Brudnoy turned abruptly and strode off into the crowd.

'Is he for real?' Greg asked.

Anson smiled knowingly. 'Lev is as real as they come. If you need any advice about anything, ask him. He's a lot smarter than he lets on.'

Greg nodded, not knowing how much he could believe. He looked at the party-goers, still talking and laughing and drinking.

'I didn't know that liquor was allowed in the base,' he said.

'It isn't,' Anson replied.

'Do you mean to tell me that there's no alcohol in those drinks? Nobody's popping pills or snorting anything?'

'What I'm telling you,' Anson said firmly, 'is that company regulations do not allow alcohol or any other substances that impair judgment or reflexes. We're even careful with aspirin up here.'

Greg smirked at her. 'Sure. And if I tested a random sampling of your employees' blood levels—'

'It doesn't work that way,' she snapped. 'Not here. We judge people by their performance, not by some numbers set down in a book of regulations.'

'So you wait for somebody to kill himself. And the people around him.'

'Not at all.' Anson's voice was calm, reasoned, but beneath it there was stainless steel. 'We live and work very close to one another. If somebody sees that someone is too – out of it, let's say – to do his job, then they don't let that person start working.'

'They report him sick?'

'They send him back to his quarters. Or her. They call for a replacement.'

'And that's all?'

'We pay for performance here. If a person needs a replacement more than twice in a three-month span, we send him back Earthside.'

'Or her?'

'Or her,' Anson agreed. 'It happens now and then, but not often enough to be a real problem.'

'And that's the way I'm supposed to handle the situation? No matter what the company regulations say?'

Anson made a small shrug. 'That's the way things have been handled here for years. If you want to change it, that's your prerogative. You'll have to do your job in your own way, of course.'

'Of course,' Greg said. 'But your way has been working fine, is that it?'

Anson smiled prettily. 'Don't fix it if it ain't broke.'

MOONBASE

The party showed not the slightest sign of slowing down. Greg watched, a stranger among the revelers, feeling like a pale and vapid ghost, almost invisible, noticed by the others just enough to make them feel uneasy and move away from him. Even Anson got tired of him and danced off with one of the younger men.

Terribly self-conscious and ill at ease, Greg made his way through the partying throng to the main exit from The Cave. Stepping through the airtight door into the empty tunnel outside was like stepping from bedlam into blissfully peaceful silence. It felt cooler out in the tunnel, easier to breathe.

Greg thought for a moment, then strode toward the control center. Make certain it's really adequately manned, he told himself. Check on the status of the radiation storm, maybe talk with the astronomers back at Tucson.

The control center was quiet. The big electronic map of the base glowed in the darkened room just as it had before the flare erupted. All three positions at the U-shaped set of comm consoles were occupied. Several of the screens were badly streaked with interference, others were altogether blank. But the three communications technicians were at their jobs, sober and quietly intense.

The woman in the middle chair turned and saw Greg standing over her. 'What do you think—' Then she saw the nametag on Greg's coveralls. 'Oh! Mr. Masterson, it's you. I figured it was too soon for my relief.'

'How's the link with Brennart's team?' Greg asked quietly.

'Something coming through now,' she said, pointing to one of the working screens.

Bending over her shoulder, Greg saw a pair of spacesuited figures in brilliant sunlight pulling a tube or something from a large gray canister.

While they fiddled with the tube on the bare rocky ground, another figure in a gleaming white spacesuit with red stripes down its arms and legs walked into the picture.

'That's it,' one of the spacesuited figures said. 'The first set of nanomachines for construction—'

Suddenly the picture on the screen wavered, distorted into wild zig-zags of color, and then broke up completely. The screen dissolved into hissing streaks of black and gray.

'Switch to backup,' said the tech on the operator's right.

The screen showed the figures in spacesuits for the briefest flicker of an instant, then broke up into electronic hash.

'Three? Four?'

The technician shook her head. 'All gone.'

'Five and six?'

'All of 'em.'

Greg asked, 'Can't you regain contact?'

She pointed to a hash-streaked screen. 'Not now. The satellite links are down.'

'But there were six satellites, weren't there?'

'Yessir, but the storm's knocked all six of them out. Bing, bing, bing, one right after another. All six gone.'

'I have to go to the toilet,' said Bianca Rhee.

She whispered the words to Doug, leaning the helmet of her spacesuit against his so she wouldn't have to use the suit radio.

They had been sitting in the half-covered shelter for several hours with nothing much to do except stare at the blank curving walls. Doug knew that the plumbing in the suits was different for women, and the suits were not meant to be worn for more than twelve hours at a time. From what he knew about solar flares, they would be in their suits for at least another twenty-four hours, perhaps considerably longer.

'If your urine collector is full you can void it into the chemical toilet,' Doug said to her, 'without getting out of the suit.'

'That's not my problem,' Rhee said.

'Aren't you wearing—'

'No,' she said. 'Are you?'

Wonderful, Doug thought. People have been using space-suits for a century and still nobody's come up with anything better than a plastic bag you stick on your bare butt. What do they call it? FC-something: fecal containment system? Some system. And you have to slap it in place before you zip up your suit, of course.

'It's not safe to get out of your suit,' he said.

'But I've got to!'

'The radiation level's still too high.'

'I can't do it in my pants.'

Why not? Doug thought. But from the sound of Bianca's voice, even muffled through the helmets, there was no debating the issue.

He turned to Brennart and clicked on his suit radio. 'Sir, do we have anything that we can rig up as temporary shielding in the john?'

'What are you talking about?' Irritated.

'Rhee's got to get out of her suit for a few minutes. Can we put up some temporary shielding in the toilet compartment for her?'

For a long moment Brennart didn't reply, and Doug could only guess what was going through his mind. At last he said gruffly, 'Pull off the leggings of your suit and hold them on your lap.'

This has happened before, Doug realized, almost smiling. Bianca's not the first one with the problem.

'And be quick about it,' Brennart added. 'Every minute you're out of the suit you're exposed to ten times the radiation you'd get in a year Earthside.'

There's no problem of depressurization, Doug knew. They were already breathing the shelter's air. The suits were just for protection from the radiation.

Rhee headed for the toilet compartment, too embarrassed to say anything. Doug thought about asking her if she needed help getting her boots and leggings off, then thought better of it. Funny, she'd rather risk the radiation exposure than mess her pants. She'd rather die of radiation poisoning than embarrassment.

Then Doug realized that before the radiation died down they'd all have to use the toilet.

'Sir, have you been in this kind of situation before?' he asked Brennart.

'Have I?' The expedition leader's voice took on a new tone: lighter, almost eager. 'This is a piece of cake compared to the fix we were in back when we were digging the first shelters in Alphonsus. The first time we were hit by a solar storm . . .'

A quarter-hour later Rhee returned from the toilet. Brennart was still spinning out yarns about the old days. Greenberg slinked to the compartment while Brennart kept on talking. And talking. And talking.

'. . . so we started vacuum breathing contests; you know, opening the visor of your helmet out on the surface to see how many seconds you could go before you closed it again. See what kind of guts you had. When you felt your eyes starting to pop you sealed up again. Well, one night there were just three of us out there, Jerry Stiles, Wodjohowitcz and me . . .'

Slowly, Doug realized what Brennart was doing. He's not just helping to pass the time away; he's calming us down, making us realize that he's been through this kind of thing lots of times, telling us that we'll live through it. Doug looked at his spacesuited leader with new respect. That's what leadership is really all about, he thought: keeping the fear at arm's length.

After making certain that communications with Earth were still intact, Greg went to his quarters and called his mother.

His quarters were a standard single cell, no bigger than a third-class stateroom on an ocean liner, since there had been so little time for the Moonbase staff to prepare for his arrival. Once Anson left, Greg would be moved to the director's more spacious suite: two whole rooms, with a private toilet and shower stall.

For now, Greg slouched on his bunk and watched his mother's face in the slightly grainy image on the screen built into the compartment's smoothed stone wall.

'Has all communication with Brennart's team been cut off?' Joanna was asking.

Nodding, Greg assured her, 'For the time being. But they're all safe inside their own shelters. They had plenty of time to dig in.'

'Yes,' she said once she heard his response. 'Of course.' But her face belied her words.

She's looking at me, Greg thought, she's talking to me. But she's thinking about Doug.

'How is Anson treating you? Is she being friendly?'

Almost laughing, Greg answered, 'She danced with me.'

Before his mother received his reply, the phone chimed. Greg tapped his keyboard and the display screen split. Jinny Anson's face appeared on the second half, her brows knit with concern.

'Danced with you?' Joanna started to say. 'What do you mean?'

But Greg's attention was on Anson. 'What's happened?'

'Thought you ought to know. Nippon One's just launched a ballistic lobber toward the south polar region. Must be a crewed vehicle, I betcha.'

'Now? With the radiation storm at its peak?'

'Now,' Anson replied flatly.

'Where are you?'

'In my office.'

'I'll be right down there.' He clicked Anson's image off his screen.

'What is it, Greg?' Joanna was demanding. 'What's going on?'

'Yamagata's just launched a vehicle toward the pole. We don't know if it's manned or unmanned.'

It took three seconds for the news to reach Joanna. When it did, she flinched with shock. 'What are they up to?'

'That's what I intend to find out,' Greg said. 'I'll call you when I've learned something.'

Brennart was running out of tall tales. Doug wondered if he'd start in on camp songs next. He remembered a counselor, when he'd been six or seven, who knew only a half dozen songs and repeated them endlessly every night around their gas-fed campfire.

'I wonder how the other shelters are doing?' Doug asked when Brennart took a breath.

'They're all right,' Brennart said. 'One and two are better off than we are; they've got more room and they can sit in their shirtsleeves.'

Getting to his feet carefully inside the cumbersome suit, Doug stepped over to the airlock hatch and the cluster of instruments built into its metal frame.

'Radiation level's down slightly,' he said. 'We might be past the worst of it.'

He could sense Brennart shaking his head inside his helmet. 'Don't kid yourself, son. The radiation levels will fluctuate up and down for hours. When it starts to tail off you'll see a pretty rapid drop, not those little jiggles.'

The voice of experience, Doug said to himself.

'As soon as we can get through to Moonbase,' Greenberg said, 'we've got to request another shipment of machines.'

'Another?' said Brennart.

'You mean more nanomachines?' Rhee asked. 'Why?'

'The ones we left on the mountain are all dead by now.'

'What?'

The nanotechnician's voice was flat, as unemotional as a surgeon discussing a patient who had died on the table. 'Don't you understand? The nanomachines are the size of viruses. They're being bombarded with high-energy protons. At their scale, it's like you or me being clobbered by an avalanche of bowling balls.'

'They'll be deactivated,' Doug said, feeling suddenly hollow inside, as if he had scaled a rugged mountain only to find higher and steeper peaks ahead of him.

'All of them?' Brennart asked.

'All the ones we exposed on the mountaintop,' Greenberg replied calmly. 'The ones still in the canister might be okay; the canister's pretty good shielding for them.'

'Why didn't you tell me this before we went up there?' Brennart demanded, his voice rising.

Without a flutter, Greenberg answered, 'You wanted to get our legal claim in, didn't you? So we got there and did it. Nobody told me we were going to be hit by a radiation storm.'

'But don't you understand? The legal claim isn't worth a termite fart if the goddamned bugs aren't *doing* anything!'

'Huh?'

Doug said, 'The legal claim is based on utilization of the area. If the bugs are dead, inactive, then we're not using the area and our claim is null and void.'

Greenberg was silent for a moment. Then he mumbled, 'I'm an engineer, not a lawyer.'

'Christ on a surfboard,' Brennart growled. 'We've got to go up there again and start the other bugs working.'

'That's not possible,' said Greenberg. For the first time Doug detected a slight nervous waver in his voice.

'What d'you mean, not possible?'

Greenberg took a breath, then explained, 'There are nine different sets of nanomachines in the mix, each programmed to do its own part of the job. We put out the first set. If they're dead, the second set won't have the substrate it needs to build on. And the third set, and so on.'

'You mean *none* of them will work?'

'Not until we get replacements for the first set.'

'We brought backups with us.'

'The backup canister was on the cargo rocket that crashed. The canister split open and the bugs spilled out. I deactivated them.'

Brennart was close to exploding. 'Deactivated our backup?'

'Standard operating procedure. Once they're loose you can't get 'em back in their containers again. And you don't want them chewing up the equipment around them. So I sprayed the area with the UV laser. Standard procedure.'

'That's what you were doing,' Rhee said. 'I thought you were looking for something that you'd lost.'

'Nope. Killing loose bugs. You can't see the ultraviolet light from the laser, of course.'

Rhee seemed unconvinced. 'You mean the bugs can take unfiltered sunlight but a little UV laser can kill them?'

'It's not the power of the beam, it's the intensity. That little laser's ten times brighter than the Sun in that one ultraviolet wavelength.'

'Douglas,' Brennart asked, 'does this really nullify our legal claim?'

Doug let several heartbeats pass before he answered. 'I'm afraid it does. I'll check with the corporate legal experts in Savannah as soon as communications are restored, but from what I know of the legalities, if we're not actively using the site we have no valid claim to it.'

'Christ on a surfboard,' Brennart muttered again.

Thinking hard, Doug said, 'The only other way to establish a claim is for at least two Masterson employees to be actively working at the site.'

'Two?' Brennart pounced on the information. 'For how long?'

'Length of stay doesn't matter, as long as they're actively engaged in utilizing the site's natural resources – and there's a working device of some sort running at the site when they leave. Either that, or more human employees replace them.'

'Two of us,' Brennart muttered.

'We've got to be doing something that leads to useful utilization of the area,' Doug warned. 'We can't just be camping there.'

'What in the world could we be doing up there?'

Rhee blurted, 'We're not going up to the summit again?'

'Two of us are,' said Brennart, with no hesitation whatso-ever. 'As soon as the radiation begins to die down.'

'But won't that be risky?'

Brennart chuckled quietly, then said, 'Sure it's risky. Like the man said, working out on the frontier is nothing more than inventing new ways to get killed.'

RAYBURN HOUSE OFFICE BUILDING

Representative Ray Underwood steepled his fingers in front of his face as he studied the earnest young man sitting on the other side of his desk.

'I'm afraid I don't understand, Mr. Eldridge,' he said.

Eldridge smiled pleasantly. 'Are we being recorded?'

Underwood feigned indignation. 'Certainly not! I wouldn't stand for that kind of thing. It's not only illegal, it's immoral.'

'Yes, of course,' said Eldridge. He was a bland young man, his sandy hair already receding, his eyes a pale blue. He was dressed casually: lightweight Madras jacket over an open-necked white shirt; inexpensive dark blue slacks; black athletic shoes.

Underwood was twenty years older, but still looked trim and fit in his tan sports jacket and darker brown slacks. There was a touch of gray at his temples, but otherwise his hair was dark, his face taut and tanned from ski vacations back home in Colorado.

'Our conversation will be strictly between us,' Underwood assured his visitor. 'Absolutely private.'

'Good. For your sake, as well as mine.'

That took Underwood aback somewhat. 'Just what is it that you're after?' he asked. 'In plain language, please.'

Eldridge hunched forward a little in his chair. 'As you know, Congressman, I represent a coalition of religious organizations—'

'The Christian Brethren, I know.'

'Not merely the Brethren,' said Eldridge. 'Not anymore. We have several Orthodox Jewish groups with us now. And the Muslims, as well.'

Underwood suppressed a gasp of surprise. Instead, he let himself chuckle. 'Well, if you can keep *those* people together you're a better politician than I am.'

'The Lord moves in mysterious ways, Congressman.'

'I suppose he does. But what is it that you want?'

'Your support on the nanotech bill.'

There. It was finally out in the open. Now I can deal with it, Underwood thought.

'What nanotech bill?' he parried. 'I'm not aware of any such bill being considered—'

'There will be, in the next session. After our vice president is elected President of the United States.'

Underwood leaned back in his swivel chair and steepled his fingers again, a tactic he used to gain time. 'He's not in my party,' he said mildly.

'But he will win the election in November,' said Eldridge flatly. 'One of his campaign promises is to introduce legislation that will ban *all* nanotechnology. That's one promise he will keep.'

'I'm not against nanotechnology,' Underwood said carefully. 'From what my aides tell me, a lot of good can come from it.'

'I'm sure you know more than your aides tell you,' said Eldridge mildly.

Underwood smiled to cover the slight pang of alarm that tingled through him. 'And what do you mean by that, Mr. Eldridge?'

'Carter. My first name is Carter.'

'Carter.'

'You're in remarkably good health for a man who suffered a heart attack just a year ago,' said Eldridge.

Damn! Does he know or is he just fishing?

'It was only a mild cardiac arrest. And I've had excellent medical care.'

'The best in the world, from what I hear.'

'Those people in Bethesda—'

'Don't you mean Basel?'

'Basel?'

'In Switzerland. And your attack was a massive infarction that would have left you a cardiac cripple.'

Forcing himself to grin, Underwood waggled a finger at the younger man. 'Carter, you've been watching the tabloids! They exaggerate everything.'

'You were flown to Basel and operated on by Dr. Wilhelm Zimmerman, one of the few doctors left who still deals with nanotherapy.'

'That's not so!'

With a patient sigh, Eldridge asked, 'Do you want me to recite the flight number to you? Your room number at the Basel Marriott? The date and hour on which Zimmerman operated on you?'

Underwood growled, 'You have no proof of that.'

'What further proof do we need? The people who leaked this information to us will be happy to speak to the news media – anonymously, of course.'

Underwood could feel his insides sinking.

Leaning forward, Eldridge said, 'You had nanomachines injected into your body. They repaired your damaged heart muscle and scrubbed out the plaque in your coronary arteries. Very likely you also had some cosmetic touches done, didn't you?'

The Congressman said nothing.

'You used your position of influence and power to cover up the fact that you obtained for yourself nanotherapy that is illegal in the United States.'

'It's not illegal in Switzerland.'

'It will be soon,' said Eldridge flatly. 'But that isn't the point. The point is that you availed yourself of nanotherapy that your constituents can't have.'

'I told you I'm not against nanotechnology. That's a matter of public record.'

'Yes, but you're about to change your position. On this

crucial issue of outlawing all nanotechnology, you are going
to vote on the side of the angels.'

'Meaning your side.'

'You're damned right!' snapped Carter Eldridge.

MOONBASE

As soon as Greg reached Anson's office she scooted around from behind her desk and led him on a half-run back to the control center. She soared along the tunnel on ten-foot leaps while Greg bounded along after her awkwardly, hopping and stumbling despite his weighted boots.

'Too much happening now to pipe through my desktop,' she called over her shoulder as they hurried along the tunnel. 'I need to see everything that's going down.'

Greg was puffing as he skidded to a stop at the control center's airtight door. Anson slid it open and went through without waiting for him.

She rousted one of the comm techs out of his seat, then took in all the working screens in a swift scan of the U-shaped console assembly.

'Power holding steady?' she asked, punching up a multi-colored graph on the screen directly in front of her.

The woman seated in the middle chair nodded, headset clipped across her close-cropped hair. 'Fading slowly, but within allowable limits. Power team's already brought the nuke on-line, just in case solar cell degradation exceeds allowable.'

'Good,' snapped Anson, her attention already turning else-where.

Greg had forgotten that there was a standby nuclear power generator buried halfway across Alphonsus. With the high-energy protons of the radiation storm beating up on the solar cells spread across the crater floor, the nuke had to be able to provide electricity without fail or they'd all quickly choke to death.

'All right now,' Anson was saying, 'where's that freakin' Yamagata lobber?'

The chief tech tapped on her keyboard and Anson's main screen suddenly showed an image of the Moon with a single red dot winking, slightly northwest of Alphonsus's position.

'That's the radar plot from L-1,' said the comm tech. 'She's got a nice bright beacon on her.'

Anson grinned fiercely. 'Show me our visual horizon.'

A thin yellow circle appeared on the Moon's image, centered on Alphonsus. The blinking red dot was well within it.

'Hot spit!' Anson yelped. 'We can get the big 'scope on her.'

'The telescopes are all working on preprogrammed routines—'

'Screw the astronomers! This is important. I've got to see if that lobber's crewed or not.'

With a sigh of reluctance the chief tech began tapping on her keyboard again.

'Humpin' astronomers're all down in The Cave, anyway,' Anson said, to no one in particular. 'They can complain to me tomorrow.'

'Here it is,' said the technician.

Greg bent over Anson's chair to see her main screen better. It showed a smear of streaks, then slowly the streaks settled down into the pinpoint lights of stars. And at the center of the image was the big metal spider of a ballistic rocket, a lobber.

The image enlarged. Greg saw bulbous tanks and other shapes wrapped in reflecting foil. And a single bubble of what looked liked plastiglass glinting in the sunlight.

'Crew module,' Anson said. 'I knew it! Yamagata's sending a team to the pole.'

'In this radiation storm?' Greg couldn't quite believe it.

Without turning toward him Anson bobbed her head. 'In this storm. They're probably wearing specially armored suits. Yamagata's people are smart, not suicidal.'

'Maybe the radiation level's gone down,' Greg thought out loud.

With a short, sharp laugh, Anson said, 'I don't think so.'

And she pointed to one of the screens on the far side
of the U.

Greg saw an image of the Earth, half daylit, half in shadow.
But something was wrong with the picture: flickering streaks
of pale colors were messing up the image of the northern
hemisphere.

'That's the northern lights you're seeing,' Anson explained.

Shifting glowing pale greens and reds, Greg saw. 'It can't
be the aurorae,' he objected. 'They're too far south – almost
in Florida, for God's sake.'

Anson looked up at him smugly. 'Still think the radiation
level's gone down?'

Greg stared at the screen. Northern lights glowing all the
way down to Florida, just about. It must be a monstrous flare,
he realized.

Anson yanked a telephone handset from the console desktop
and punched a single number. 'Security?' she said into the
phone. 'Pull Harry Clemens out of The Cave right away and
tell him to bring his best team with him. Meet me in my office
in three minutes.'

She slammed the phone down and fairly leaped out of her
chair. 'We've got to get a comm link with Brennart right
away,' she said to Greg, 'and that means launching a shielded
minisat.'

She made a dive for the door, calling over her shoulder,
'Come on, Greg! We don't have a second to spare!'

*Working out on the frontier is nothing more than inventing
new ways to get killed.* Brennart's easy tone belied the truth of
his words, Doug thought. He's lived with this kind of danger
so long that he's accustomed to it. Maybe he's even become
dependent on it.

'Question is,' Brennart was saying, 'what can we *do* back
up at the summit there to preserve our legal claim?'

And he turned his spacesuited figure toward Doug.

Stalling for time to think, Doug said, 'You're assuming that
Yamagata's going to try to dispute our claim, is that it?'

'Of course,' said Brennart. 'Always assume the opposition

will make the move that'll hurt you the most. That way you're never surprised, always prepared.'

Doug saw the reflection of his own helmeted figure in the blank visor of Brennart's suit. He tried to imagine the expression on the older man's face. He's enjoying this, Doug thought. This is how he gets his kicks. And Doug had to admit that it was exciting, hanging your butt out on the line, seeing how far you dared to go.

'So, young Mr. Stavenger,' Brennart called out, 'what can two of us do up there at the top of the mountain that will satisfy the Earthside lawyers?'

'If we could set up some kind of solar cells,' Doug mused, 'and connect them back down here – even just a few kilowatts . . .' He had no details to back the bare idea.

Brennart's cyclops figure turned toward Greenberg, sprawled in his cumbersome spacesuit on the bunk closest to the toilet.

'Well, Greenie, what about it? Can we jigger your nanobugs to produce solar cells without the rest of the power tower to hold them up?'

'Sure,' answered Greenberg, 'if I had a laboratory and a couple weeks to reprogram them. Not here, though.'

A gloomy silence filled the shelter.

Bianca Rhee broke the quiet. 'What about the cargo ship that crashed? Didn't it have a power system? Maybe we could cannibalize it.'

'Fuel cells,' Brennart said gloomily. 'Not solar panels. They were destroyed in the crash, anyway.'

'What pieces of our equipment do have solar cells?' Doug asked.

He could sense Brennart shaking his head inside his helmet. 'Nothing much. We knew the base camp down here would be in shadow all the time. The nanobugs were supposed to build the solar tower up on the summit for our electrical power.'

'You mean there's nothing?'

'A few portable radio units with standard solar batteries. But they run on milliwatts; you can't get away with pretending they're providing power for the base.'

'Wait a minute,' Rhee said. 'Why do we have to use the

summit for a power station? Why can't we set up a monitoring station up there?'

'Monitor what?' Brennart asked.

'Solar flux,' said Rhee. 'I've got the instrumentation for it.'

'What good—'

'We can set up an astronomical station at the summit,' Rhee said, excitement raising her tone a notch. 'That'd be a legitimate use of the area, wouldn't it?'

Doug said, 'Sure, why not? We could even claim we're making measurements to determine how much electrical power we could generate with solar cells.'

They both turned to Brennart. 'Pretty thin,' he muttered.

'But it'll hold up until we can get replacement nanomachines to actually start building the power tower,' Doug countered.

'You're sure?'

'Nothing's sure where lawyers are involved,' Doug said. 'But it's the best idea I've heard so far.'

Brennart muttered, 'Lawyers,' as if it was the vilest word he could think of.

'The Yamagata lobber's landed.'

Anson stared hard at her desktop screen. It was split in half: the right side showed the frenzied activity of Clemens' launch team as they laser-welded extra sheets of shielding around a grapefruit-sized minisatellite. Behind them a rocket booster stood impassively, little more than a squat tube crammed with powdered aluminum and liquified oxygen. Once the armored minisat was mated inside its nose cone the booster would be winched up the surface and fired toward the south pole.

The chief communications technician's worried face filled the left side of Anson's desktop screen.

'Landed?' Anson snapped. 'Where?'

'On the other side of Mt. Wasser from where our people are,' replied the tech. 'At least, that's where L-1 lost their radar transponder signal. Near as we can make it out, they put down right smack in the middle of the biggest ice field in the region.'

'Shee-yit,' Anson hissed.

Greg was sitting on a flimsy plastic chair alongside her desk, feeling useless as all the activity swirled around him.

Anson turned to him. 'Yamagata's people are on the ice down there. Now the question is, will they try to get to the top of the mountain right away or wait for the radiation to die down?'

'What do you intend to do with the minisat?' Greg asked.

'Tell Brennart that the Yamagata team's in his back yard, what else?'

'Won't that make it seem as if we're pushing him to take bigger risks than necessary?'

Avoiding Greg's eyes, Anson replied, 'Brennart's no feeb. He'll know how much risk he can handle.'

'Can the minisat operate in this level of radiation?'

'The satellite's only got to work for a few minutes,' Anson said. 'Just long enough to tell Brennart that the Japs are in his lap. He's got to know that! It's vital.'

Greg wondered what Brennart would do with the information. It's just going to put more pressure on him, Greg thought. Might push him to take risks he wouldn't ordinarily take. Doug is out there with him. This might put Doug in even more danger than he's in already.

Greg felt frozen inside, not daring to let his true emotions show, even to himself.

'I think my ribs are broken,' said Keiji Inoguchi.

Yazaru Hara heard the pain in his co-pilot's voice. He himself had been unconscious for at least several seconds. The landing in the mountainous darkness had been a disaster. Their craft had touched down on what had seemed like smooth ice, but somehow the craft had tumbled at the last moment and come crashing down on its side.

Now, as the two men sat still strapped into their seats, bundled in their heavily armored spacesuits, Hara thought how like a dream the crash had been. Everything had happened so slowly, gracefully almost, like a kabuki dancer's delicate movements. But the pain was real. His head throbbed and he tasted hot salty blood in his mouth. He could hear Inoguchi's ragged, shallow breathing in his helmet earphones. Every breath must be an agony for him, Hara thought.

A dream of pain and darkness. A nightmare. What was it that the old lamas said, 'What if this life is nothing more than a dream within a dream?' Yes, what if?

At least he didn't seem to be bleeding anywhere except inside his mouth. He had banged his head hard on the inside of his helmet, but thankfully the helmet was well-padded. Nothing broken, Hara said to himself. But if I have a concussion I'll be vomiting soon. That should be delightful, inside the helmet.

Inoguchi groaned, forcing Hara to ignore his own fears.

'Can you move your arms at all?' he asked his companion.

'Yes, a little.' In the dim emergency lighting of the cockpit Hara saw Inoguchi's arms move feebly.

He tried to think. 'We might as well stay where we are, Keiji,' he said. 'At least until the radiation goes down and the base puts a commsat over us.'

'Yes,' said Inoguchi, painfully. 'I don't think I'll be of much help to you.'

'That's all right. We'll just sit here and call for help when the satellite queries us.'

'At least we don't have to worry about fire,' Inoguchi said, trying to sound brave. 'When I flew on Earth, fire was my one persistent fear.'

Hara nodded at the man's confession, but did not reveal his own. Ever since coming to the Moon, Hara had suffered nightmares about choking to death for lack of air.

MT. WASSER

'Killifer to Brennart,' Doug heard in his earphones.

'Go ahead, Jack,' said Brennart. His voice sounded tired to Doug. Scratchy and strained.

'Just got a blast from Moonbase,' Killifer said. 'Yamagata's landed a team on the other side of Mt. Wasser.'

Doug felt a jolt of shock and saw Brennart's spacesuited figure stiffen. Their communications gear was in the first shelter, where Killifer presided.

'Play it for me,' Brennart commanded.

Over the suit-to-suit frequency Doug heard, 'Anson to Brennart. Yamagata lobber has landed on the far side of Mt. Wasser from your position. Definitely a crewed ship. They're obviously going to try to make a claim for the area. Foster, the safety of your team is of primary importance, as you are aware. But I thought you should know about this move of Yamagata's. As soon as the radiation drops to an acceptable . . .'

Harsh ragged static drowned out her words.

'That's all we got,' Killifer said.

Brennart huffed. 'That's plenty.'

'There's another message, though,' said Killifer. 'Piped in parallel with Anson's.'

'What is it?'

'It's for Mr. Stavenger.'

'For me?' Doug blurted. Brennart said nothing.

'Doug, this is Greg.' Doug was astonished to hear his brother's voice. 'I'm at Moonbase. I'll be taking over the director's slot when Anson leaves. I don't want you to take any unnecessary chances out there. Do you understand me?

Play it safe and come back alive.'

Doug felt embarrassed. 'My brother,' he mumbled to Brennart and the others. 'Half-brother, actually.'

'He'll be the director of Moonbase in a few days,' Brennart said, his voice flat.

'I had no idea,' said Doug.

A dead silence fell upon the bare little shelter. The four of them sat on the bunk edges, the only places to sit, staring at each other like a quartet of cyclops.

'We've got to get back to the mountaintop before the Japanese do,' Brennart said at last.

'Do you think they'd try it while the radiation's still so high?' Doug asked.

'They sent the team here while the radiation flux is pretty damned near maximum,' Brennart pointed out. 'They must have hardened suits.'

'And equipment,' Greenberg chimed in.

'And we don't,' said Rhee.

Doug turned to face Brennart. 'What should we do?'

For a long moment Brennart said nothing. Finally, 'You said that legally we need two people at the summit?'

'That's only if we intend to keep a team there. The minimum number is two,' said Doug. 'That's what the Moscow Treaty calls for.'

'But if we're just going to set up a monitoring station?' Rhee asked.

Doug spread his gloved hands. 'As long as the station can function automatically it doesn't matter how many people are used to set it up.'

'All right, then,' Brennart said. 'I'll go alone.'

'You can't!' Doug snapped.

Brennart planted his fists on the hips of his spacesuit. 'Do I have to remind you, *Mr.* Stavenger, that I'm in command here? Even if your brother's going to be my boss in a few days, I'm still in charge of this team.'

Trying to keep his voice light, Doug replied, 'We all know that, sir. I simply meant that the radiation out there will kill you before you could get the job done.'

'Maybe,' Brennart admitted. 'But the job's got to be done.'

'You have to kill yourself for the corporation?' Rhee asked.

Brennart turned toward her. 'Like the man says, everybody dies, sooner or later. Do you think my life would be worth much if Yamagata gets to claim this whole territory?'

'That's crazy,' Rhee said.

While Brennart and Rhee argued, Doug went to the shelter's computer terminal and called up the medical file.

'It's my job,' Brennart was saying. 'My responsibility.'

Rhee said, 'Oh, I get it. Machismo.' Her voice dripped loathing.

'No,' said Brennart. 'It's very practical. I get paid for results. If Yamagata takes this territory I might as well be dead, professionally.'

And he doesn't have any other life, Doug realized, tapping out numbers on the screen. Rhee might despise the idea, but for men like Brennart this is a way of life. It's all they've got. The time in-between missions is waiting time, limbo, useless. Call it machismo or stubbornness or even stupidity, but it's the hard-headed ones like Brennart who got the job done. My father must've been like that, Doug thought. He died rather than endanger the rest of the people in Moonbase.

'The question is,' Doug said – for himself as much as for Rhee and the others, 'is the claim to this region worth risking your life over?'

'Let's stop this right here,' Brennart said. 'Somebody's got to get back up that mountain and I've decided that I'll do it. End of discussion.'

'Wait,' Doug said.

'I said *end of discussion*,' Brennart growled.

'But I think there might be a way we can get this job done at much lower risk.'

'How?'

Pointing to the numbers on the screen, Doug said, 'I've just calculated the exposure doses, based on the background data in the medical file and a rough estimate of the time needed to get up to the mountaintop again.'

Brennart came across the shelter and leaned over Doug's shoulder to peer at the screen.

Doug said, 'To get this job done, somebody's got to find the astronomical equipment, load it onto the hopper, refuel the hopper, jump up to the summit, set up the equipment, and then fly back down here. Right?'

'Right.'

'Okay, here's my estimate of the times involved for each task.'

'Pretty rough estimates.'

Smiling inside his helmet, Doug said, 'It's the best I could do. I've tried to include the shielding our suits provide—'

'It adds up to more than a lethal dose,' Rhee saw. Greenberg got off his bunk and joined the rest of them, but said nothing.

'But what if we break the job down into its component tasks and let different people handle each task?' Doug suggested.

'What of it?' Rhee asked.

Working the keyboard as he spoke, Doug said, 'That way, each individual gets only a fraction of the radiation exposure that one person would get if he tried to do the whole job by himself. See?'

'Whoever flies the hopper up to the mountaintop still gets a big dose,' Rhee pointed out.

'But it's not a lethal dose,' said Doug. 'At least, that's what the numbers show.'

'If everything goes exactly as you've plotted it,' Rhee countered.

'No, it won't work,' Brennart said. Doug could sense him shaking his head inside his helmet. 'I can't ask people to take that kind of risk.'

'But look at the numbers,' Doug insisted. 'We can do it!'

'Those numbers are shakier than a nervous guy with palsy in an earthquake,' Brennart grumbled.

'You'll be killing yourself otherwise,' Doug said. 'That's the one really solid number we've got. If one man tries to do the whole job, he gets a lethal dose. No doubt about it.'

Brennart rested his gloved hands on the thighs of his suit.

'Listen up, people. I've taken risks like this before and lived through them. Truth is, I don't really give a damn if I live or die. I've had a full life and I've got nothing much to look forward to except retirement. Like the man says, I'd rather wear out than rust out.'

'More machismo,' Rhee muttered.

'Bianca,' Doug asked, 'where are your astronomical instruments?'

She hesitated a moment. 'I carried them into the shelter as soon as it was put up. Before we got the order to help with the digging.'

'Which shelter?' Brennart asked.

'The first one.'

'Okay,' Doug said. 'So you could go to shelter one and get your hands on the instruments.'

'Sure.'

'Isn't the second hopper right outside that shelter?'

'About fifty yards from the airlock,' Brennart said.

'So Killifer or somebody else could dash outside and load the instruments onto that hopper. No need to refuel the one we've already used.'

'I'll do it,' Greenberg said, surprising Doug. 'I'll go with Bianca and load the instruments. It'll only take a couple of minutes and then I've got an excuse to stay in shelter one. Let one of those guys pull on a suit and sit out here for a while.'

'Good,' said Doug, turning to Brennart. 'Then you and I can hop up to the summit—'

'You're not going,' Brennart said.

'I've got to,' Doug answered firmly. 'The numbers prove it. Two people can get the job done before the exposure adds up to a lethal dose. One can't.'

'You are not going,' Brennart said, emphasizing each word. 'I'm not going to risk my future boss's brother.'

'Half brother,' Doug said.

'I'm not going to risk either half of you,' replied Brennart.

Doug grinned inside his helmet. He made a joke. Good!

'Besides,' Brennart went on, 'I made a promise to your mother.'

Doug jumped on that. 'You promised not to let me out of your sight. How can you keep that promise if you go up to the mountaintop without me?'

Brennart was not amused. 'Don't split hairs with me, kid. I can't allow you to take that risk.'

Very seriously, Doug replied, 'And I can't allow you to go by yourself.'

'Stavenger, I'm the commander here. I *order* you—'

'Besides, I can pilot the hopper if I have to,' Doug said, actually enjoying the excitement.

'This is getting weird,' Rhee said. 'Now we've got two macho flangeheads.'

'I'm not going to let you take the risk,' Brennart repeated firmly.

'I'm not going to let you kill yourself,' Doug answered.

Brennart got to his feet and loomed over Doug. 'Now listen—'

'A dead body doesn't constitute a legal claim,' Doug said.

'What?'

'If you die up on the mountaintop before you get the instruments set up the corporation won't be able to make a legal claim to the area,' Doug said.

Tapping the numbers on the screen, Doug added, 'And if you try to do this all by yourself you're going to die.'

For a moment there was silence in the bare little shelter. Doug heard nothing but his own breathing and the faint whir of the air fans in his suit.

Then Brennart broke into a low chuckle. 'All right, you're dead-set on risking your neck. We'll do it your way.'

Rhee repeated, 'Two macho flangeheads.'

Greenberg said nothing.

'I don't know about you,' said Jinny Anson, 'but I could use a few hours' sleep.'

Greg realized he had been awake more than twenty-four hours straight. The last six hours he had spent in Anson's office, anxiously watching, waiting for some word from Brennart's group. Nothing had come through, and the radiation from the solar flare was still lethally intense up on the surface.

'I'll go down to the control center, I guess,' he said.

Anson got up from her desk chair. 'Don't you want to catch a few winks?'

Shaking his head, Greg replied, 'I'm too keyed up to sleep.'

'Go back to the party, then.'

'Is it still going on?'

With a grin, she leaned across her desk and stabbed at the keyboard. The display screen showed The Cave still jammed with dancing, drinking, chatting, laughing party-goers.

'They'll stay at it till the radiation level starts to decay.'

Greg felt his brows knitting into a frown. 'They'll be in some shape for working, won't they?'

Anson stiffened slightly. 'The party breaks up when the radiation starts going down. It takes several hours, at least, before the radiation's low enough to go out on the surface. They'll be ready for work by then.'

Greg almost admired her. She could be a tigress when it came to defending her people.

'Okay, maybe I'll drop in at the party. I'll stick my head in at the control center first, though.'

'Whatever,' said Anson. She headed for the door, thinking, What this guy needs is to get laid.

Greg followed her out into the tunnel. Anson walked off toward her quarters; Greg went the other way, toward the control center.

He was surprised to see Lev Brudnoy there, hovering morosely in his faded, stained coveralls over the three technicians working the comm consoles. There were two men and one woman sitting at the consoles, none of them the same as the crew he had seen several hours earlier. Nearly half the screens were still blank or so streaked with interference that they were useless.

'What are you doing here?' Greg asked, realizing how tactless it was as he spoke the words.

Brudnoy made an elaborate shrug. 'I worry.'

'Me too,' Greg admitted.

'I understand that a Yamagata vehicle has landed near Brennart's team.'

'Yes,' said Greg, feeling slightly annoyed that this guest, this . . . farmer, knew as much about the situation as he did. Probably a lot more.

Brudnoy read his face. 'There are very few secrets in Moonbase, my friend.'

'Really?'

'We are too small, too crowded to keep secrets,' Brudnoy said. 'It's a good thing, I think. Governments back on Earth, they thrive on secrecy. Not here. Here we are like a mir, a village; everyone knows everyone.'

'And everyone knows everybody else's business,' Greg added.

Brudnoy smiled charmingly. 'Within limits.'

'Such as?'

Brudnoy placed a hand on the shoulder of the technician sitting nearest him. 'For example, even if I knew who this lout of an electronics man was sleeping with these days, I would not broadcast the news. It would be impolite.'

'And damned dangerous,' said the tech, glaring up at Brudnoy with mock ferocity.

'Like a village,' Greg muttered.

'Yes, like a village,' said Brudnoy. 'You probably think of Moonbase as a subdivision of your corporation, with its organization chart and its lines of authority. Please throw that image out of your head. Think instead of a village. People come and go, it is true, but the social structure remains the same. In your country you call it a small town, I think.'

'Winesburg, Ohio,' Greg said, almost sneering.

'Oh no!' Brudnoy answered immediately. 'I read that decadent work when I was first studying your language. No, not like Winesburg. More like Fort Apache – without the Native Americans.'

Greg blinked with surprise. 'Fort Apache? Who's our John Wayne, then?'

'Why, Brennart, of course. And you will be the stiff-necked commandant of the fort, if you pardon a personal reference.'

Greg automatically glanced down at the three technicians, to see how much of this they were taking in. All three of them were bent intently over their screens, which made Greg think they were listening to Brudnoy for all they were worth, despite the headsets clamped to their ears.

'You think I'm stiff-necked?' Greg asked coldly.

'Of course. Everyone is when they first come to Moonbase. It takes time to adjust to our village mentality, our small town social structure.'

Greg relaxed only slightly. 'Fort Apache,' he repeated.

'An outpost on a vast and dangerous frontier. That's what we are.' Brudnoy seemed to relish the concept.

'Message coming in from Tucson,' interrupted the chief technician. 'Voice only. Radiation levels beginning to decrease slightly around Venus's orbit. We can expect the storm to end in five to ten hours.'

'Great!' Greg almost wanted to grab Brudnoy and hug him. Instead he said to the chief tech, 'How can we get the word to Brennart?'

The technician shook his head. 'There's nothing working in polar orbit right now.'

'What about the armored satellite they sent up?'

'Crapped out in the radiation. We don't know if it even got its message down to Brennart.'

'Can't you reactivate it?'

'It's dead.'

'Then we've got to send up another one.'

Another head shake. 'By the time we could get the last satellite hardened and launched the radiation levels'll be getting low enough for Brennart's people to figure it out for themselves.'

'Dammit,' Greg snarled, 'I want a commsat put up!'

Unperturbed, the technician said, 'Only the base director can authorize that.' Then he added sardonically, 'Sir.'

Greg turned to Brudnoy. 'I'll have to wake Anson up.'

Now Brudnoy shook his head. 'I wouldn't do that, my friend. She would not appreciate it.'

Greg wanted to push past him and storm down the tunnel
to kick Anson's door down. He wanted to tell Brudnoy in
no uncertain terms that he was the next director of this
base, not some snivelling technician or farmer afraid of
incurring Jinny Anson's wrath. I'm Joanna Masterson's son,
goddammit, he wanted to shout. I'll run this whole corporation
one of these days.

But he said nothing. He fought it down and remained quiet.
It was a struggle; he felt certain that Brudnoy could see the
inner battle raging in his eyes.

Brudnoy reached out and grasped his arm lightly. 'I understand your impatience and your desire to inform your brother
of the good news. But the technician is right. Even if we started
this instant, by the time we got a commsat over the pole the
radiation would already be dying and they would know it for
themselves.'

'Yèah,' Greg said, not trusting himself with more than one
syllable at a time. 'Right.'

'But it's crazy,' Killifer said.

Brennart's voice came over the comm console's speaker.
'Sure it's crazy, Jack,' he said lightly. 'But it's vital to the
success of this mission. We've got to go.'

'You and Stavenger,' said Killifer. Deems and two of the
women were crowded behind him as he sat in the tiny comm
cubicle. He could feel their breaths on the back of his neck.
And smell them.

'We'll need your help. Greenberg and Rhee are coming to
your shelter to pick up the astronomical equipment and load
it onto the hopper.'

'Okay.'

'Jack, I need you to check out the hopper, make certain it's
ready for flight.'

'You want me to suit up and go outside?' Killifer asked.
'With a zillion rads out there?'

'Doug's done some rough calculations on the exposure
levels. You should be all right.'

'Yeah, sure.'

'I can't order you to do it,' Brennart said. 'I'm asking you to.'

Killifer grimaced. Yeah, sure, he can't order me. But if I don't I'll be broken down to tractor maintenance or cleaning toilets.

'Okay,' he said. 'I'll suit up.'

'Thanks, Jack!' Brennart's voice sounded sincerely grateful.

Killifer turned in the little chair and got slowly to his feet. 'Rog,' he said to Deems, 'you take over here.'

'You're going outside?' Deems' normally startled expression had graduated to outright fear.

'That's right,' Killifer said sourly. 'You're gonna see the fastest friggin' checkout of a hopper in the history of the solar system.'

The women made room for him to pass and head up the shelter's central aisle toward the airlock and the spacesuits. Brennart wants to be a big-ass hero and I've gotta risk my butt for him. Will I get any of the credit? Shit no. He's the superstar; I'm down in the noise. Nobody'll even know I was here.

Him and the Stavenger kid, Killifer fumed as he began to pull on the leggings to his spacesuit. The two of 'em. He tugged on his boots and sealed them closed. Then a new thought struck him.

The two of them. Going up to the mountaintop in the hopper, in all this radiation. What if they don't make it back?

For an instant he felt a pang of remorse about Brennart. But then he thought, friggin' butthead wants to be a hero, what better way is there than to die up there on top of the mountain?

As Doug lifted the uncrated spectrometer onto the platform of the hopper that stood outside Shelter One, he noticed that the radiation patch on his sleeve had already turned bright yellow.

This is going to be hairy, he thought. We'll both get enough radiation to put us in the hospital.

The telescope was already on the hopper's metal platform, a man-tall tube supported on three spindly legs.

A stocky spacesuited figure toted a telemetry transmitter with its solar power panels folded up like the wings of a bird and shoved it onto the hopper's platform. Doug jumped up onto the metal mesh decking and started lashing down the instruments securely.

'Is that you, Bianca?' he asked the spacesuited figure.

'No, it's not Bianca.' Killifer's voice.

Surprised, Doug asked, 'What're you doing out here?'

Clambering up onto the hopper to help with the tie-downs, Killifer's voice rasped, 'I'm out here getting my *cojones* fried because you talked Brennart into being the big hero, that's why I'm here.'

'I didn't talk—'

'Fuck you didn't,' Killifer snapped.

Doug's usual reaction to hostility was to try to laugh it off. But he knew it wouldn't work with Killifer.

'Look,' he said while he tied down the instruments, 'I checked out your file and I understand why you're sore at me.'

'You went into my personnel file?'

'I went into everybody's files, everybody who's on this expedition.'

'Who the fuck gave you authority for that?'

Doug was tempted to reply that his mother had given him the authority. Instead he answered mildly, 'It's part of my job.'

'The hell it is.'

'I saw the order transferring you to Moonbase and all your appeals.'

Killifer grunted as he lashed down the equipment on the deck.

'The transfer was signed by my mother. Your appeals were all bucked up to her and she rejected them.'

'That's right.'

'What on Earth did you do to get my mother so pissed at you?' Doug asked. 'She practically exiled you up here.'

'None of your friggin' business.'

'Whatever it was, it wasn't fair,' Doug said, without looking up from the straps he was locking down. 'I wish there was some way I could make it up to you.'

Killifer stopped working and straightened up. 'Yeah. Sure you do.'

'I mean it,' said Doug.

'Then give me back the eighteen years she stole from me.'

Doug sighed. 'I wish I could.'

Killifer jumped down from the deck, floating slowly to the ground. Doug noticed that there was hardly any loose dust at all for his boots to kick up.

'Okay, then,' Killifer said as he headed back toward the shelter, 'there *is* something you can do for me.'

'Name it.'

'Drop dead while you're up there on that friggin' mountaintop.'

Safely back inside the buried shelter's airlock, Killifer slowly wormed out of his spacesuit and then ducked through the open hatch into the main section of the shelter. He saw Greenberg huddling with Martin, and Rhee standing worriedly next to the galley, munching on a protein bar. They were both happy to be out of their spacesuits after so many hours.

Once free of the spacesuit, Killifer strode past them swiftly and slipped into the tiny communications cubicle, where Deems still sat at the console. Standing behind Deems, he saw in the main screen the hopper outside where Brennart -- with Doug Stavenger standing beside him – quickly ran down the hopper's abbreviated checklist.

'Ready for takeoff,' Brennart said, his voice edged with tension.

'Clear for takeoff,' said Deems, his own voice high, quavering.

The little hopper disappeared from the screen in a burst of white, smokey rocket thrust.

Killifer smiled to himself as the aluminum vapor swiftly dissipated in the lunar vacuum. In the leg pouch of his spacesuit was a four-inch square of reinforced cermet, the

covering for the hopper's electronic controls for the liquid
oxygen pump.

Bon voyage, Killifer said silently. He hadn't rubbed a magic
lamp, but he felt certain that his dearest wish was about to
come true.

ACAPULCO

Carlos Quintana stood before the sweeping window of his clifftop hacienda and stared out into the limitless blue of the Pacific. White cumulus clouds were building out over the horizon, towering up into thunderheads: so beautiful to look at from a distance, so treacherous to fly through.

He held a heavy cut crystal glass of exquisite single malt Scotch in his left hand, a slim black cigar in his right.

Cancer of the lung.

The words had sounded like a death sentence at first. Cancer had taken his father, both his uncles, even his older brother. But that had all happened before Carlos had built his fortune. Now he had the money to bring a few specialists to Mexico and let them inject nanomachines into his lung.

The thought disturbed him, almost frightened him. Nanomachines had killed Paul Stavenger and several others on the Moon. Nanomachines were illegal in the United States, in Mexico, in almost every nation on Earth. They didn't always work the way they were supposed to. That's what people said. They ran amok and killed Paul, up on the Moon.

He sipped at the whisky, then inhaled a long delicious drag from the cigar. And coughed.

But we've used nanomachines on the Moon for years now. They work as designed. Maybe whatever went wrong back then has been fixed now.

Yes, he argued with himself, but the corporation's nanotech division has closed, except for the work they're doing at Moonbase. It's almost impossible to run a nanotech laboratory in the open – on Earth. And now there's talk in the U.N. about outlawing nanotechnology entirely.

As the sun slowly settled onto the ocean horizon and then dipped below it, Quintana stood alone at the window, watching but not seeing, alternately sipping and puffing, wondering if he trusted the scientists enough to let them inject invisible machines into his body.

He knew the answer, of course. Despite his fears of nanomachines, cancer of the lung frightened him more.

The fact that he would have to break the law to receive nanotherapy never impinged on his consciousness. Neither did the fact that a few hundred thousand of his fellow Mexicans would die this year of lung cancer because they were too poor to afford nanotherapy.

MT. WASSER

The jump up to the summit was smoother this time. Standing beside Brennart, Doug realized that the man had entered the distance and altitude from their first flight into the hopper's minuscule computer. Still, it took good piloting. One rather longish firing of the hopper's rocket engine and they were soaring up, up the face of the mountain, breaking into brilliant sunlight, riding as smoothly as if they were on an elevator.

Everyone else was safely tucked inside the shelters. On Brennart's orders, Rhee and Greenberg had been allowed to move into shelter one with Killifer and Deems. The two women who had been there had grudgingly pulled on their spacesuits and gone off to the fourth shelter, still only partially covered with protective rubble from the regolith.

Doug knew he should be worried about the radiation he was receiving, especially when they broke out of the shadows of the mountains and into the glaring sunlight. Yet somehow that danger seemed unreal compared to the thrill of flying up to the mountaintop again, the excitement of beating Yamagata to the claim for this rich territory.

This is fun! he told himself. We're doing something nobody else would do.

Besides, the more sober part of his mind added, I made the rad dose calculations as conservative as I could. The numbers are okay. We'll make it. We'll be all right.

Their flimsy craft seemed to hover a hundred meters or so above the mountain's summit, and Doug marvelled again at Brennart's finely-tuned piloting. Without saying a word,

Brennart crabbed the craft sideways slightly and let it down almost exactly where they had landed before.

'That was terrific,' Doug said with genuine awe.

Brennart peered over the console at the ground and the hopper's broad round feet. 'Missed our old landing spot by a good meter,' he muttered unhappily.

Doug laughed.

'All right,' said Brennart, slapping down the platform railing on his side of the hopper, 'we've got to be quick now.'

Doug knocked down the railing on his side and they both bent to untie the astronomical instruments. Within a few minutes Doug was setting up the telescope and spectrometer while Brennart, kneeling beside him, unfolded the solar panels of the telemetry unit and began plugging wires from its base to the instruments.

It was clumsy work. Doug felt as if he were wearing thick mittens instead of the most flexible gloves that spacesuit engineers could design. He saw that the radiation patch on his sleeve was a deep orange. Brennart's too.

'Ready to power up?' Brennart's voice crackled in his earphones.

Doug swallowed hard and nodded inside his helmet. 'Ready.'

The tiny display panels on the instruments lit up and the telescope swung automatically to focus on the Sun. Doug had to duck out of the way of its moving tube.

'Okay,' he said. 'They're working. Let's drag our butts out of here.'

'Get it on tape,' Brennart said. 'Make our claim legal.'

Fumbling with the vidcam in his hurry, Doug quickly panned across the little assembly of instruments with Brennart standing tall and unmistakable in his red-striped spacesuit beside them.

'Okay, got it,' he said, tucking the hand-sized vidcam back into his thigh pouch. 'Now let's get back to the shelter.'

'Wait one tick,' Brennart said. 'I thought I saw something as we were coming in for the landing . . .' And he loped off toward the edge of the summit in long lunar strides, almost soaring.

'Where're you going?' Doug called, more puzzled than annoyed or frightened.

'Come here, quick!' Brennart motioned with one long arm.

Doug tried to imitate Brennart's lunar glide and hopped clumsily to the older man's side.

'Down there. Can you see it?'

Doug peered into the inky blackness far below. 'See what?' he asked.

'Lights. Like landing lights on a spacecraft.'

Doug stared. Far, far below he thought he saw two tiny gleams of lights, one red, one white. But when he looked directly at them, they disappeared.

'Masterson Aerospace to Yamagata lander,' he heard Brennart calling. 'Can you hear me?'

That's the Yamagata lander? Doug wondered. Down there?

'Masterson to Yamagata. Do you read?'

Doug was about to turn back to their hopper when he heard in his earphones, 'Yamagata to Masterson. We read you.' The voice was weak, strained.

'We've just established legal claim to the mountaintop and we have a working base down at the ice field,' Brennart said, gloating happily. 'You boys might as well pack up and go home.'

'We can't. We crashed on landing. Both injured.'

Doug suddenly heard the pain in the man's voice.

Brennart's attitude changed instantly. 'Does your base know of your condition?'

'No. Communications impossible in radiation storm.'

'We'll try to get a team to you as soon as we can,' Brennart said.

'We are protected from radiation, but one of us is badly injured and needs medical attention.'

'We'll do our best,' said Brennart. 'Sit tight.'

'That is all we can do.'

Doug grabbed at Brennart's arm. 'Come on, we've got to get out of here.'

'We'll get help to you as soon as the radiation dies down,' Brennart said. 'Hang in there, guys.'

'Thank you.'

Without another word Brennart turned and loped back to the hopper. Doug ran alongside, almost matching his long gliding strides. They jumped up onto the platform together and Brennart slid his boots into the foot restraints and pushed the throttle forward in one motion, not even bothering to put up the railings.

But the hopper did not move.

Doug slid his boots into the foot loops and grabbed the edge of the console to support himself.

But the hopper did not move.

MT. WASSER

'Christ on a surfboard,' Brennart yelled. 'It's dead.'

'What's wrong?'

Brennart swiftly scanned the meager control panel. 'Everything's in the green, but the goddamned engine won't light.'

Doug felt cold sweat breaking out on him.

'Damn!' Brennart tugged at the throttle again. Nothing happened.

'What's wrong?' Doug asked again.

Brennart turned toward him. 'No time to check it out. Come on.'

And he jumped off the hopper's platform. Doug followed him without questioning. Brennart was unfastening the empty cargo pod.

'Undo the oxy tank,' he commanded. 'Get it down on the ground. Fast!'

Doug found the clips that held the bulbous green tank and clicked them open, then rolled the tank off the edge of the platform into his waiting arms. Shocked at how heavy it felt, he let it slip and thump onto the rocky ground. He felt immense gratitude that it didn't burst apart.

Turning, he saw that Brennart was rolling the canister of nanobugs along the bumpy ground. He wedged it against the hopper's other side.

'Get under the platform,' Brennart urged, dropping to all fours. 'Come on!'

Doug dropped to his hands and knees and crawled beneath the hopper's platform, between the oxygen tank and the nanomachine canister, nearly banging his helmet on the dangling nozzle of the defunct rocket engine.

'How are we going to fix it from under here?' he asked Brennart. There was barely room enough to turn on his side, Doug saw. They could never get onto their backs, not with the life-support backpacks they carried.

'We're not going to fix it,' the older man said. 'We're going to sit out the storm down here. This is our own little radiation shelter. Cozy, huh?'

'We're going to stay here?' Doug heard a tinge of fear in his own voice.

'Nothing else we can do,' Brennart said calmly. 'Can't poke around trying to check out the hopper's systems, not in this radiation flux. We'd be fried by the time we figured out where the malf is.'

'Malf?'

'Malfunction.'

'Oh.'

'So we pull down as much mass as we can to shield us from the sides and we hope the platform and rocket plumbing is thick enough to shield us overhead. And we wait.'

'But how can we tell when the radiation's gone down enough—'

'When we hear a satellite signal. Either our minisats will come back on the air or Moonbase'll put up a new commsat to re-establish a link with us.'

Doug puffed out a breath. 'And in the meantime?'

'We wait.'

Stretched out prone beneath the hopper's platform with a couple of tanks and cargo pods. It didn't seem like much protection to Doug.

'Snug as two bugs in a rug,' Brennart said.

'Not quite.'

'Well, we're better off than those Japs. Crashed on landing. And they need medical attention.'

'So will we,' Doug said.

For a moment Brennart did not reply. Then, quietly, 'Yeah, I suppose we will.'

'What do you think happened to the hopper?' Doug asked.

Brennart's shoulders wormed slightly inside his suit. 'Something simple, most likely. Radiation knocked out some primary system, like the computer control or the oxidizer pump.'

'Isn't the hopper shielded against radiation?'

'Sure, but that doesn't make much difference now, does it? Like the man says, this is where we're at.'

'They should've been back by now,' Bianca Rhee said to no one in particular.

Roger Deems looked frightened, as usual, as he sat at the silent communications console.

'Shouldn't they?' Bianca turned to Killifer, standing with Greenberg behind her.

Killifer slowly nodded, looking grim. 'Yeah. Something must've gone wrong.'

'Can't we talk with them?' Rhee pleaded.

Deems said shakily, 'Up there on the mountain, they're out of line-of-sight from our antenna, and we don't have any working commsats to relay a signal to them.'

'But there must be *something* we can do!'

'Wait,' said Killifer.

Rhee stared at him, aghast.

'That's all we can do,' Killifer said, almost gruffly. 'Unless you want to kill yourself, too.'

'You think they're dead?'

Killifer grunted, then answered, 'As good as.'

'The radiation is definitely receding,' the main communications technician said to Greg. 'In another five or six hours it ought to be almost down to normal.'

Greg nodded curtly. He'd been hearing 'another five hours' for the past six hours, at least.

'You'd better get some rest.'

Turning, Greg saw it was Jinny Anson who had just entered the control center.

'You look like hell,' Anson said cheerfully. She herself was fresh and bright-eyed.

'I'll wait here,' said Greg.

'Get to bed before you fall down and hurt yourself,' Anson said firmly. 'That's not advice, it's an order.'

Greg smiled tiredly at her. 'You're ordering me?'

'I'm still director of this rat nest. Get your butt into your bunk. Now.'

For a moment Greg wondered how far he might go in showing her who the real boss was. How far might she go? he asked himself. She'd call security and have me carried to my quarters, he realized, staring into her steady, unwavering steel-gray eyes.

'Okay,' he said, his voice slurring slightly, 'but you call me—'

'The instant anything happens,' Anson promised.

Greg trudged off to his quarters, not certain he remembered exactly where they were. He found the door eventually and flopped fully clothed on the bunk.

He dreamed, not of Doug and the others trapped in the radiation storm, but of his mother. The two of them were in The Cave, at the flare party, dancing together.

'Did you mean what you said back in the shelter?' Doug asked.

Lying prone beside him, Brennart said, 'What did I say?'

'That you didn't care if you lived or died?'

The older man hesitated a moment, then replied, 'Yeah, I meant it.'

Doug couldn't believe it. 'Really?'

'Everybody dies, kid. Sorry I let you come along, though. You shouldn't have been involved in this.'

'You think we're going to die?'

'I'm already dying,' Brennart said. 'Cancer in my lymph nodes.'

Shocked, Doug blurted, 'But how could they let you keep on working?'

With a low chuckle, Brennart said, 'Because they don't know. I have my own doctor, my own physical. The corporation records are . . . well, doctored.'

'Falsified?' Doug had never dreamed such a thing was possible.

'Friends in high places,' said Brennart. 'It happens when you've been around long enough.'

'You really have cancer?'

'Terminal – unless the radiation treatment we're getting right now burns it out of me.' He laughed sardonically.

'Cancer,' Doug repeated.

'It's kind of an occupational disease when you spend a lot of time up here.'

'But,' Doug's mind was churning, 'but there are treatments. Nanotherapy could—'

'Find me a nanotherapy clinic that's still open and I'll go to it,' Brennart said bitterly. 'The ones that haven't been shut down by the lawyers have been burned down by the mobs.'

'Even in Switzerland?'

'Switzerland, Thailand, Argentina – the only people I could find doing nanotherapy now are crooks and frauds. Black market; you pay in advance and you take what you get. Not for me.'

'But my mother's talked about clinics in Switzerland.'

'Your mom's a very rich woman, Doug. I don't have that kind of money. Or clout.'

'I do,' Doug said.

For a few moments Brennart was silent. Then he said, 'I appreciate it, kid, but I think it's too late for me even with nanotherapy.'

'How do you know—'

'Hey, I've had a damned good life. They'll put up a statue to me here on the Moon after I'm gone. What more could I ask for?'

'How old are you?'

'Fifty-one, in September. If I make it that far.'

'I'll be nineteen next January.'

'Maybe not.'

'Yeah.'

'I'm sorry,' Brennart said. 'I shouldn't have let you talk me into bringing you along.'

'I'm not sorry about it,' Doug said. He realized that he meant it truly. 'I would've kicked myself for the rest of my life if I hadn't come up here with you.'

Brennart made a noise that might have been a snort. Or a suppressed laugh. 'You know what we used to say about test pilots, back when we still used test pilots? More guts than brains.'

Doug laughed out loud. 'Yeah, that's us.'

'That's what it boils down to. You know what you're doing is dangerous, but it's so damned inviting! Like a really nasty-looking woman you see at a bar. You know she's trouble, but you can't help yourself.'

'I've never heard it put that way before,' Doug said.

'Yeah.' Brennart almost sighed. 'You can't turn it down, so you tell yourself you can handle the danger, you're prepared for it.'

'My father must've been like that.'

'He was one smart turkey, let me tell you. He knew when to hold 'em and when to fold 'em. Never took a chance he hadn't calculated out to six decimal places.'

'I never knew him,' said Doug. 'He died before I was born.'

'That's what impressed me about you, kid. You didn't just decide to run up this mountaintop for the glory of it. You calculated the odds, first.'

'I didn't calculate on our hopper dying, though.'

'Like the man says, you can't win 'em all.'

Doug nodded, blinking at perspiration that was trickling into his eyes.

'If we get through this without being totally fried,' Brennart asked, 'what do you want to do with your life?'

'You mean the ten minutes I might have left?'

'Come on, seriously. Have you thought about it?'

'Not much.'

'You ought to. A guy in your position has all sorts of opportunities open to him. You ought to start thinking seriously about them.'

'I've sort of been following my father's footsteps,' Doug admitted. 'I've never thought about anything but Moonbase.'

'You could do a lot worse,' said Brennart. 'Your father knew which way was up.'

'I sort of thought I'd like to study architecture.' It was something of a confession. Doug had never told anyone about that, not even his mother.

'Architecture?'

Shrugging inside his spacesuit, Doug replied, 'Lunar architecture, you know. I want to build a real city here.'

'Oh-ho,' Brennart said. 'You really have the bug, don't you?'

'Maybe it's genetic.'

'No,' said Brennart. 'It's the frontier. It gets to you. Like Mark Twain said, "When it's steamboat time, you steam."'

'Steamboat time?'

'In Twain's era the steamboat was the exciting thing. Another generation of kids wanted to be railroad engineers. Then came airplanes, and any self-respecting youngster wanted to be a pilot.'

'And then came the Moon,' Doug said, 'and they all wanted to be astronauts.'

'And now you want to be a lunar architect.'

'If we get out of this,' Doug pointed out.

Ignoring that, Brennart went on, 'You want to build, to add something to the world. Like your dad. That's good. Everybody should leave his mark on the world.'

'You've certainly left yours,' Doug said. 'They really will build a statue to you.'

'I've had a helluva lot of fun doing it,' Brennart said. 'Too bad it's got to end.'

'Like the man says,' Doug quoted him, 'everybody dies.'

They fell silent again.

Eventually, Doug said, 'I wish I could have had a life like yours.'

With a low chuckle, Brennart replied, 'You can have it, kid. It's not all that much, you know.'

'But you're a real legend! You've done so much!'

'Except the one thing I really wanted.'

'What was that?'

'Mars.'

'You wanted to go on the Mars mission?' Doug felt stupid as he heard his own words. Of course Brennart wanted to go on the Mars mission. Who wouldn't?

'The lead American astronaut was a friend of mine, Pete Connors,' said Brennart. 'Pete's a good guy, but I'm a better one.'

'Then why didn't they pick you?'

'Bunch of academics made the selections.' Brennart said the word *academics* very much the way he pronounced *lawyers*. 'I work for a dirty old profit-making corporation. Pete always stayed with the government program.'

'And that's why they didn't take you?'

'That's why.'

'But that's rotten! They must've been a bunch of brain-dead turds!'

Brennart laughed softly. 'Pete did a good job. They got back okay.'

A second Mars expedition was being put together, Doug knew. Moonbase was supplying all their oxygen and Masterson orbital factories were building spacecraft and electronics assemblies. On government contracts, for a fixed fee.

'It's a damned shame,' Doug mumbled.

'Yeah. But I'll get a statue and Pete won't.'

'They ought to put your statue right here, up at the summit.'

'No, no! I want it at Moonbase,' Brennart objected. 'Nobody'll see it if you put it here.'

Doug replied, 'We'll run special tours to Mt. Wasser to see your statue.'

He could sense the older man grinning. 'Make more money that way, huh?'

'Might as well.'

'Why the hell not? Good thinking.'

Hesitantly, Doug asked, 'Is there anyone . . . do you have any family . . . ?'

'Nope. I was an only child and I never had any kids of my own – that I know of.'

Before Doug could answer, Brennart added, 'I've been sterile for a lot of years. Another occupational hazard up here.'

'Damn,' Doug said. 'It's just not right for them to shut down nanotechnology. With nanomachines in your body, things like sterility and cancer could be stopped before they started. The nanobugs would destroy cancerous tumors and rebuild tissue that was damaged by radiation.'

'Maybe so,' said Brennart. 'But it's not going to help me.'

'It's criminal to prevent nanotherapy!'

'Yeah, maybe so. But they've got their reasons, you know.'

'Religious fanatics,' Doug complained. 'And politicians without enough spine to stand up straight. Nanoluddites.'

'Now, don't go getting all righteous and indignant,' Brennart said.

'Why not? What they've done—'

'Take a look at Earth. Take a good look. Going on ten billion people down there, with no end to population growth in sight.'

'What's that got to do with it?'

'Last thing in the world those governments need is people who live two or three hundred years. They're barely holding things together as it is, and you want them to let people extend their lifespans indefinitely? Get real.'

'You don't think that the world's leaders use nanotherapy for themselves?'

'Even if they do, they can't let it out where everybody can use it. They're already up to their armpits in starving people; give 'em nanotherapy and they'll all go under.'

'No,' Doug said. 'I don't believe that.'

'Believe it, kid. You've lived in a nice comfortable cocoon all your life. The rest of the world's poor, hungry, ignorant – and violent.'

Doug had no reply for that.

'Who'd pay for nanotherapy, anyway?' Brennart went on. 'Only a handful of people could afford it. You think the poor majority would sit back and watch the rich folks live forever? Hell no!'

'That's why they've burned down nanolabs,' Doug said with new understanding.

'They'd burn down your house, with you and your mother in it, if they thought you guys were using nanotherapy that they couldn't have.'

Doug thought about that. Then he replied, 'Yes, I imagine they would.'

'The little guys always try to bring down anybody who gets ahead of them. Greed isn't only for the rich, you know.'

'You're talking about envy.'

'Yeah, maybe so.'

Doug thought for a moment, then, 'Maybe that's what a frontier is really for.'

'What?'

'To get away from the little guys, the small minds, the people who don't want any changes, any new ideas.'

'The escape valve,' Brennart said.

'Right. That's what the frontier is: our escape valve.'

'Don't let them take it away from us, kid. We need a frontier.'

Doug nodded silently inside his helmet.

'How do you feel, kid?'

'Okay, I guess.' It was less than the truth. Doug felt feverish; perspiration was oozing out of him, trickling along his back, down his ribs.

'I'm kinda tired. Think I'll catch a few zees.'

'Nothing better to do,' Doug agreed.

But he could not sleep. Stretched out prone beneath the scanty protection of the flimsy hopper, he rolled over as far to his left as his backpack would allow him. That took some of the strain off his neck, but not much. Methodically, Doug checked each frequency of his suit radio. Nothing but harsh static grating in his earphones.

I'm going to die here, he told himself. He found that he was not afraid of the idea. He really didn't believe it. The idea of dying on this mountaintop, killed by radiation that he could neither see nor feel, seemed almost ludicrous to him. As if someone were playing an elaborate practical joke on him.

Sooner or later somebody's going to pop out and yell *April Fool!* Doug told himself.

And then he tasted blood in his mouth.

I must've bit my tongue, was his first reaction. But he knew that he hadn't. And he also knew that bleeding gums were one of the first symptoms of radiation poisoning.

Doug flicked his radio back to the suit-to-suit freak. Brennart wasn't snoring, but Doug could hear the man's steady, slow breathing. Vaguely he remembered some old astronaut telling him, when he was just a kid, 'Never stand when you can sit, never pass a toilet without taking a piss, and never stay awake when you can sleep. Those are the three basic rules of long life.'

Long life, Doug thought. The blood in his mouth tasted warm and salty. He turned his head to find the water nipple, took a long sip, and swished the water in his mouth. There was no place to spit it out, so he swallowed it.

That feels better, he told himself. But a few minutes later the warm salty taste of blood came back.

As soon as Greg awoke he checked with the control center.

'Radiation levels haven't started down yet, Mr. Masterson,' said the young woman on his phone screen. 'We expect them to start diminishing within the next hour or so.'

'Thank you,' Greg said tightly. Within the next hour or so. How long have I slept?

He tapped the keyboard next to his bunk and the screen showed he'd been asleep a little more than four hours. Feeling grimy, he stepped into the shower stall. But no water came from the shower head. 'Christ!' he bellowed. 'Doesn't anything work right around here?'

Naked, he stormed back to his bunk and pounded the keyboard. 'Maintenance,' he told the phone's computer.

A bored-looking kid in repulsive sickly green coveralls appeared on the screen. 'Got a problem?'

'My shower's not working.'

The kid glanced off to his left. 'Room two twenty-three, right?'

'Right.'

'No shower until Tuesday. Sink water only.'

Greg raged, 'What do you mean—'

'Water rules,' the kid said, with the finality of unshakable regulations on his side. 'Got a problem, take it up with administration.'

'I'm the next director of this base!' Greg roared.

The kid was far from impressed. 'Then you oughtta know the rules.' The screen went blank.

Defeated but still steaming, Greg sponged himself as best as he could in the tiny stainless steel sink, pulled out a fresh pair of dark blue coveralls from his travel bag, then put through a call to Savannah.

'The radiation level will be back to normal in about an hour,' Greg told his mother as he pressed the Velcro seal of his coveralls front.

And heard her saying, as soon as she saw his image on her screen, 'The radiation level will be back to normal in about an hour.'

Greg laughed and so did Joanna.

'They're going to be okay,' he said.

This time she waited for his words to reach her before replying, 'Have you heard from them yet?'

'Not yet,' Greg said. 'I'm going down to the comm center now. I'll have them patch you in to their transmission when it comes through, if you like.'

Joanna answered, 'No, that won't be necessary, just as long as you can tell me they're all right. I can talk to Doug later, when things calm down and get back to normal.'

Pleased with her response, Greg said, 'Okay, Mom. I'll let you know the instant we re-establish contact with them.'

'Fine,' she said.

But once the screen went dark again Greg wondered, Why doesn't she want to talk with Doug as soon as we make contact again? Is she worried that I'd be jealous? Or will she be making her own contact, direct from Savannah, without letting me know?

*   *   *

Doug's eyes snapped open. He hadn't realized he'd fallen asleep until he woke up. He had been afraid to go to sleep, he realized. Despite everything he had been telling himself, deep within him lurked the fear that once he shut his eyes in sleep he would never open them again.

Well, he said to himself, that was feeble.

He found himself lying on his right side and tried to roll back onto his stomach again. The effort left him gasping, dizzy.

I'm weak as a kitten, he said to himself.

Brennart was still asleep, stretched out beside him. Doug twisted over and looked around. It made his head swim. For several minutes he simply lay still, panting, trying to fight down the fear and nausea that rose inside him like an inexorable tide. Hang on, he demanded of himself. Hang in there; the storm must be almost over by now. Help will be on the way soon.

But not soon enough, a sardonic voice in his head replied.

His world was constrained to this metallic nest beneath the hopper, with a few containers and tanks around them. The nozzle of the hopper's main engine hung between him and Brennart like a bell in a church spire.

An old tune sprang to his mind: *It's a Small, Small World.* Idiot, Doug snarled to himself. You're being fried by a solar flare and you're thinking about childhood songs.

His earphones chirped.

By reflex, before he realized what it meant, Doug tapped the radio channel selector on his wrist.

'Moonbase to Brennart. Do you read?'

He heard Killifer's overjoyed voice, 'Loud and clear, baby! Are we glad to hear you!'

'We're working on reactivating the minisats that the storm knocked out. We have two of them working so far.'

'Great!'

'What is your condition?'

'We're all okay, except Brennart and Stavenger. They've been up at the top of Mt. Wasser for . . .' Doug sensed Killifer checking a clock, '. . . almost seven hours now.'

A different voice came on. 'Seven hours? In the open?'

'Right.'

'Brennart himself? And the Stavenger boy?' It sounded like Jinny Anson's voice. Urgent. Demanding. Doug didn't much like being called a boy.

'Right,' Killifer said again.

'What's happened to them?' Now it was Greg's voice. Unmistakable.

'Don't know,' said Killifer. 'We haven't been able to contact them.'

'This is Stavenger,' Doug said, shocked at how weak his own voice sounded. 'Can you hear me?'

'Stavenger!' Anson shouted. 'How are you?'

'Alive . . . barely.'

'And Brennart?'

'Sleeping. Or unconscious.'

'We'll get help to you as soon as we can,' Anson promised.

Greg came on again. 'Killifer! Get somebody up to that mountaintop and bring those two back to your base camp. Now!'

'Hey, we've got a few problems of our own. Power cells are running low, our one remaining hopper needs refueling—'

'Get them as quickly as you can,' Anson said. Her voice was cool, but there was no mistaking the implacable tone of her command.

'Right,' said Killifer. 'We're on our way.'

'And shoot us a complete rundown of your own status,' Anson added. 'All systems.'

'Doug,' Greg called. 'Doug, how are you?'

'I feel kind of sick, but I'm still breathing.' He reached across and shook Brennart's shoulder. No response. 'I think Mr. Brennart's unconscious.'

'We'll get help to you right away,' Greg said.

'Good,' said Doug.

Anson came on again. 'Killifer, it's going to take us several hours to get a resupply lobber to you. Storm beat up our surface facilities pretty good and we'll need some time to get 'em all back on line.'

'Understood,' Killifer replied. 'We're all okay here, except for Brennart and Stavenger.'

'How long can your power supplies hold out?'

'Fuel cells are down about forty percent. We can power down if we have to, stretch 'em out till the resupply arrives.'

Doug heard Greg's voice in the background urging, 'You've got to send a medical team down there. Right away!'

'Stavenger,' Anson called, 'can you put your medical monitoring system on frequency three? We can start checking out your medical condition.'

'Okay. And Mr. Brennart's, too.'

'Right. Of course. But you've got to be quick. The satellite won't be above your horizon much longer.'

'I understand,' Doug said. 'Now, which of these plugs is the medical system?'

'It's marked with a red circle.'

Doug held his left arm up in the light of his helmet lamp. It brushed the underside of the hopper's platform. He squinted hard to keep his vision from blurring. Either the lamp's running down or my eyesight's going, he thought.

'Okay, found it.'

'Toggle the microswitch and then press the keypad for frequency three,' Anson directed patiently.

It seemed to take forever, but Doug finally got it right.

'Okay, good,' Anson said. 'Data's coming in.'

'What about Brennart?'

'Do the same for him, if you can.'

Puzzled by the *if you can*, Doug pushed himself closer to Brennart, found the right switch and punched frequency three on his radio keypad.

'We've only got another fifty seconds before the satellite drops below your horizon,' Anson said. 'Killifer, get a team up to those two immediately.'

'Will do.'

'We hope to re-establish a link with you in fifteen minutes.'

'Right.'

The contact broke up into crackling static. Doug clicked off the noise. The universe went silent, except for the sound of the suit's fans and his own breathing. It sounded ragged, labored. A wave of nausea was surging up his throat. Doug fought it back. The last thing he wanted was to upchuck inside the helmet.

Panting, sweating, feeling sick and dizzy, he clicked on the suit-to-suit frequency, to check on Brennart's breathing.

Nothing. Doug held his breath and listened hard. He could not hear anything at all from Brennart.

BASEL

Wilhelm Zimmerman rocked slowly in his desk chair. It creaked under his weight. He was a fat, bald, unkempt man in a wrinkled gray suit that looked as if he had been sleeping in it for a week.

The woman sitting in front of his desk looked distraught. She was well into her seventies, lifeless white hair hanging straight, skin wrinkled and brittle-looking, obviously her blood circulation was poor. Too bad, thought Zimmerman, she must have been something of a beauty once.

'I don't want to die,' she said, her voice cracking.

'Neither do I,' said Zimmerman softly. 'No one does. And yet . . .' He shrugged elaborately.

'I've heard . . . some of my friends have told me . . . that it is possible to reverse the effects of aging.' She looked at him piercingly, her diamond-hard blue eyes belying the hesitancy in her voice.

Zimmerman rested his hands on his considerable paunch. She wants to live. So do I.

'Madam, what your friends have told is unkind. There are no miracles.'

'But . . . I thought that your work here at the university,' she said. 'What is it called? Nano-something or other.'

'My research is on nanotechnology, yes,' he replied. 'But procedures on human subjects is absolutely forbidden. The laws are very strict. We are not allowed to deal with human patients.'

'Oh!'

'In fact,' Zimmerman said, 'for the past several years we

have worked only on non-medical aspects of nanotechnology. The animal rights movement has made even animal experiments too difficult to continue.'

The elderly lady took a tissue from her tiny purse and dabbed at the corners of her eyes.

Pointing a chubby finger at the graphs on his office wall, Zimmerman said with some distaste, 'As you can see, Madam, our most recent work has been on new manufacturing processes for solar panels and long-range electrical distribution lines.'

'Oh my,' said the elderly lady, 'I haven't the faintest idea of what that means.'

'For an organization called OPEC,' Zimmerman explained, frowning. 'To generate electricity in the desert and send it here to Europe.'

The woman's eyes went crafty. 'But isn't it true that you also do therapeutic work – but you're not allowed to let people know about it?'

Zimmerman shook his head hard enough to make his cheeks waddle. 'No!' he said firmly. 'That would be against the law. The university would not stand for it and neither would the authorities.'

'But I was told—'

'Madam, you were misinformed. I am sorry, but do I look like the kind of man who would risk his career and his good name by breaking the law?'

Dubiously, she replied, 'I suppose not.'

For another half hour she tried to get Zimmerman to admit that he could use nanotherapy to help her. When at last she gave up and left, Zimmerman called a friend from the forensic medical department who came to his office, grinning, and lifted several excellent fingerprints from the armrests of the chair on which she had sat.

It took more than a week for Zimmerman's connections in the Swiss national police to get the information to him. The elderly woman was the mother of a bureaucrat in Berne who was in charge of monitoring all nanotherapy work in the nation.

'An agent provocateur,' Zimmerman said to himself. 'Next they will close down all nanotechnology work, even research, the way they've done in the United States.'

He wished there was somewhere in the world where he could continue his work in peace.

MOONBASE

'It'll take at least twelve hours to get a lobber properly loaded with the supplies they need,' Anson said over the din in the garage.

Tractors were starting up, the whining shrill of their electrical engines echoing painfully off the rock walls of the cavernous garage area. Men and women were scurrying across the polished rock floor; the big steel inner hatch of the airlock itself was groaning on its bearings as it slid shut for the twentieth time in the past two hours.

'They need help now,' Greg insisted. 'My brother's dying, for chrissake.'

Anson shook her head. 'No sense killing more people by going out there half-cocked.'

'Can't we send a medical team right now?' Greg pleaded. 'I don't care what it costs—'

Anson whirled on him. 'You think I'm worried about cost?'

Greg backed a step away from her sudden fury. 'What I meant was . . . dammit, send a medical team now. Right away! Consider that an order from the board of directors.'

'I take my orders from Ibriham Rashid, in Savannah,' Anson said, striding away from Greg.

He pushed past two technicians waving hand-held computers at each other as they argued.

Grabbing Anson by her shoulder, Greg said, 'Send the medical team now. Don't wait for the rest of the stuff they need. Do it now! I'll take the responsibility.'

Anson glared at him. 'We don't have any medical staff to

send! One doctor and a couple of part-time technicians, that's
our medical staff. They won't be able to do anything for him
down there anyway.'

'But—'

'It isn't a matter of responsibility or cost or anything else
except the fact that we don't have the personnel we need up
here. And it takes *time* to fuel up a rocket vehicle, goddammit
to hell and back! It takes *time* to bring our radars and other
surface instruments back on line after the pounding they
just took.'

'I know, but—'

'I can't just wave a freakin' magic wand and have a fully
loaded and properly crewed lobber jump off to the freakin'
south pole!'

'But you can send out a lobber as soon as the goddamned
equipment is back on line, can't you?' Greg yelled back. 'Get
him here as soon as you can.'

Anson pulled in a deep breath and stood there in the middle
of the bustle and noise, staring hard at Greg. He saw her nostrils
flare angrily and thought for a moment that she was going to
charge him, like an enraged bull.

Instead, her shoulders relaxed slightly and she said, just
loud enough to be heard over the clanging, yelling, screeching
cacophony, 'Yeah, you're right. I can.'

Before Greg realized what she had said, she added, 'And I
will.'

She turned abruptly and started off in a half trot, yelling over
her shoulder, 'C'm'on, we've got to get out to the rocket port
and light some fires under some butts.'

As soon as she heard Doug's voice over the satellite link,
Bianca Rhee ducked out of the cramped comm compartment
and raced down the shelter's central aisle to the airlock, where
the spacesuits were stored. Without bothering even to think
about what size she was grabbing, she pulled on the first pair
of leggings she came to and plopped down on the floor to tug
on the boots.

'What d'you think you're doing?'

Rhee looked up and saw Killifer standing over her, looking displeased.

'We've got to go up there and get them!' Rhee said, scrambling to her feet once the boots were sealed.

'You know how to run a hopper?'

'No,' she said, 'but you do. Come on, hurry!'

Killifer grunted unhappily. 'That's my suit you're putting on.'

'Oh!' She felt confused for a moment. 'Look, there's no time for me to get out of these and into my own. We're about the same size. Use my suit.'

'Plumbing's different,' Killifer said. But he reached for Rhee's suit, hanging next to his.

'We won't be out long enough for that to matter,' Rhee said. Then she added, 'Will we?'

Killifer almost laughed.

Is he dead? Doug wondered. Brennart didn't seem to be breathing and all Doug's prodding and poking hadn't awakened the astronaut.

Maybe it's just a coma, Doug told himself. The radiation hasn't killed me, why should it kill him?

But he had to admit that he felt very sick. His head was spinning and waves of nausea made him feel weak and feverish. The bleeding in his mouth seemed to have stopped, though. Maybe I just bit my lip or something, he tried to reassure himself.

Doug didn't realize he had drifted into sleep until a sudden voice jerked him awake.

'Brennart! Stavenger! We're here!'

Someone was rolling the canister of nanomachines out of the way.

'Under here,' Doug called weakly. 'We're underneath the hopper.'

Someone pulled him by the arms. 'Careful,' he heard. 'Don't rip his suit.' Bianca's voice? Doug couldn't be sure.

'Brennart,' Doug mumbled. 'Get him. He needs help.'

'Like you don't.'

Doug felt himself carried a short distance and then laid down on his side. He fought back the nausea that burned up into his throat. Don't vomit, he commanded himself. Not inside the helmet.

'Strap him down, I'll go get Brennart.'

'Can you carry him by yourself?'

'If I need help I'll holler.'

'Vidcam,' Doug said weakly. 'Make certain the vidcam's in my pocket.'

'Don't worry about that now.' Definitely Bianca's voice, he thought.

'No, it's important. Our legal claim. Got to have it. Otherwise Yamagata . . .' He had to pause for breath.

'It's okay,' Bianca said. 'The vidcam's there in your thigh pouch.'

'You take it,' Doug gasped. 'Hang onto it. Take care of it.'

She pulled the vidcam out of his thigh pouch and held it up so he could see it. 'I've got it. I'll take care of it. Now relax, Doug.'

Relax. The word seemed to echo in Doug's mind. Relax. Relax. There's nothing more that you can do. You've done everything you could. It's up to them now. Up to them.

The sudden pressure of takeoff startled him out of his drowsiness. Doug realized he was strapped down like a patient on a surgical table. And then the long, falling emptiness as the hopper descended back to their base camp. Got to tell them about the Yamagata team, Doug thought. We've got to rescue them. They're hurt. Got to tell them about it.

But the falling sensation overpowered every thought in his head and Doug held himself as rigidly as possible, forcing himself not to give in to the nausea burning up into his throat. The only thing he could see was the flank of the mountain, twinkling like crystal in the sunlight, gleaming so brightly that it hurt his eyes and he had to squeeze them shut.

Weight returned. We've landed, Doug knew. Darkness all around him. He was being lifted again, moved.

'We're down,' Bianca's voice said tenderly. 'We'll have

you in the shelter and out of your suit in a few minutes.'

'Barf bag,' Doug mumbled.

'What is it?' He sensed Bianca bending low over him, as
if that would improve their suit-to-suit radio link. 'What do
you need?'

'Barf bags,' he repeated, raising his voice as loud as he
could. 'Plenty of them.'

Joanna sat tensely in the rear seat of the company jetcopter.
Greg's face on the tiny pop-up display screen built into the
seat's armrest looked tired and strained.

'He's taken a massive radiation dose,' Greg was saying.
'The data they're transmitting from his medical sensors
aren't good.'

Greg continued speaking, but Joanna ignored his words and
said, 'Get him back to Moonbase as quickly as possible. I'll
get a team of specialists up there right away.'

She saw Greg stop in midsentence to hear what she was
saying. 'I expected as much,' he said. 'Jinny Anson's already
sent off a lobber to get him. It should be landing at their base
camp in half an hour or so.'

'Good,' said Joanna. 'I'm coming up there, too.'

Even in the minuscule screen she could see the displeasure
on Greg's face. 'There's nothing you can do to help him.'

Nothing you can do. The words echoed in Joanna's mind. *I
let this happen to Doug. The Moon killed his father and now
it's going to kill him.*

Misunderstanding her silence, Greg said, 'We're doing
everything possible.'

'I'm already on my way to the rocket port,' Joanna
said firmly.

When her words reached him, Greg nodded wearily. 'I'm
not really surprised, even though I think it's a waste of
your time.'

Joanna bit back an angry retort and said instead, 'Greg, if
this had happened to you, I'd be on my way to Moonbase just
as fast.'

His face brightened a little. But only a little.

Joanna saw the yellow message light beside the screen start to flicker.

'Greg, I've got to end this call,' she said. 'I've been trying to reach Kris Cardenas all morning and she's finally returning my calls.'

It seemed to Doug that he spent a thousand hours or more weaving between consciousness and a restless feverish sleep that brought him neither rest nor relief from the waves of pain and nausea that were washing through him.

But it couldn't have been all that long, because when he opened his eyes he saw Bianca Rhee still bending over him. And she was still in her spacesuit; only the helmet was gone.

'How's Brennart?' Doug croaked. His throat was raw from the bout of vomiting that he had surrendered to as soon as they had removed his helmet.

'He's dead,' said Rhee.

Killifer's face appeared beside her, unshaven, dark circles beneath the eyes. 'Poor bastard strangled on his own puke while the two of you were laying under the hopper.'

'Oh no.' Doug gagged on the bile burning up into his throat again. Rhee grabbed a vomit bag and pushed it into Doug's hand. He retched miserably.

When he lay back on the bunk again, his eyes were watery and he felt as if every molecule of strength had been drained out of him.

'Brennart must have been unconscious when it happened,' Rhee said. 'Totally out of it.'

'You're lucky to be alive,' Killifer said dourly. 'You took a helluva dose out there.'

'I would have died if Brennart hadn't rigged up a shelter for us.'

'You might still die, kid,' said Killifer. 'You're not out of the woods yet.'

Doug grinned weakly. 'Thanks for the news.'

Killifer walked away.

Does he blame me for Brennart's death, Doug wondered. He turned to Bianca. 'What about the Yamagata people?'

'What Yamagata people?'

'The men in the lander . . . on the other side of the mountain.'

Rhee shook her head. 'Don't worry about them. You've made the claim to the mountaintop. I've got your vidcam.'

'No . . . you don't understand.' Doug tried to raise his head but the effort left him dizzy, exhausted. 'They crashed. They're hurt. They need help.'

Rhee's eyes widened. 'They crashed?'

'We talked to them. They need medical help.'

'Wait,' Rhee said. 'I'll tell Killifer.'

She disappeared from Doug's sight. He lay on the bunk, too weak to do anything else.

Bianca returned with Killifer, who looked more annoyed than usual.

'What's this about the Yamagata team?'

Doug told him. Killifer eyed him suspiciously. 'You sure about this? Maybe you were delirious out there and dreamed it up.'

'I'm sure,' Doug said, too weary to get angry.

'Well,' Killifer groused, 'they've probably re-established communications with their own base. Let the Japs take care of their own; we've got enough on our hands.'

'No,' Doug protested. 'Go get them.'

Glaring, Killifer said, 'Get real, kid. Why should we help the competition?'

Trying to pull together enough strength to get a whole sentence out, Doug said, 'Because . . . if we rescue them . . . it wipes out any hope Yamagata might have . . . of making a claim . . . to any part of this region.'

Killifer stared at him for a long moment.

'Do it,' Doug urged, his voice little more than a whisper. 'It'll impress . . . management.'

'Think of it as a working vacation,' Joanna was saying to the tiny display screen.

Kris Cardenas looked distinctly unhappy.

Glancing up at her window, Joanna saw that the jetcopter was approaching the landing circle at the far end of the Savannah rocket port. A Clippership stood waiting on Pad Three, a thin wisp of white vapor wafting from the liquid oxygen hose connected to its LOX tank.

'Kris, I don't have time for pleading with you. My son is dying from a massive radiation dose. If you tell me there's nothing that nanotherapy can do for him, all right, I'll have to believe you. But if there's the slightest chance that you could help him . . .' Joanna ran out of words. For the first time in years she felt on the verge of crying.

'But I'm not the one you want,' Cardenas replied. In the minuscule screen of the armrest her face still looked earnest, intent.

'Then who?'

'Zimmerman, at the University of Basel.'

'I've never heard of him.'

Cardenas almost smiled. 'He keeps a very low profile. But he's the best there is at this kind of nanotherapy.'

'Can you get him for me?' Joanna asked. 'I'm leaving for Moonbase in a few minutes.'

'You mean, talk him into going to the Moon?'

Nodding briskly, Joanna said, 'Offer him anything he wants. The sky's no limit.'

'I don't know—'

'Get him to Moonbase,' Joanna commanded. 'And quickly.'

Cardenas looked bewildered by the idea. 'I'll try.'

'You come, too,' Joanna said. 'Both of you. And any equipment you need. I'll get my people to contact you, make all the arrangements.'

'I'll try,' Cardenas repeated lamely.

'Thanks, Kris,' Joanna said as warmly as she could manage. Then she cut the connection and immediately called Ibriham Rashid, back at the office in Savannah.

The jetcopter was settling on the ground in a flurry of rotor-blown dust and the high keening wail of its engines as Rashid's dark bearded face appeared on Joanna's screen.

'Omar, I don't have time for details. I'm leaving for
Moonbase. Get Kris Cardenas and Zimmerman, at the University of Basel, off to Moonbase as soon as possible. They've
got to be there in twenty-four hours or less. I'll call you from
the Clippership with more. Understand?'

Rashid nodded as if he had been expecting such a call.
'Harkening and obedience,' he said.

Bianca Rhee finally left Doug's bunk and trudged wearily to
the airlock hatch. She slumped tiredly to the plastic flooring
and started to unseal her boots.

'Need help?' Roger Deems asked.

'Thanks,' she said, letting him tug the boots off her.

Slowly she got to her feet and, with Deems' help, lifted the
upper half of the suit over her head. Deems hung the empty
torso on its rack.

'You've been wearing Killifer's suit,' he said, noting the
name stencilled on the chest.

'Seems like I've been wearing it all my life,' Rhee said
tiredly.

'It's only been a couple of hours.'

She started worming out of the lower half of the suit.

'Do you think Doug will live through this?' Deems asked,
his soulful brown eyes looking almost tearful.

Rhee shook her head slowly. 'He's awfully sick. So pale,
like there's no blood in him.' Suddenly she wanted to cry.

'It's a shame,' Deems said.

'Yeah.'

Rhee finally worked her legs out of the suit and hung it
on the rack. Without another word to Deems she padded in
her stockinged feet to the toilet. When she came out, Deems
was gone. She was alone with the row of empty suits. No one
could see her sobbing quietly.

After a few minutes she tried to pull herself together.
The vidcam, she remembered. Doug was worried about the
vidcam.

She went to the leggings she had just hung up and searched
through the thigh pouches. Sure enough, Doug's vidcam was

there. As she pulled it out, Rhee thought, This is what all the mess is about. Doug put our legal claim on disk. This is what's killed him.

There was something else in the thigh pocket. Thinking it might be a part of the vidcam that had somehow worked loose, Rhee took it out. It was a flat square of reinforced cermet, about four inches on a side, anodized flat white on one surface, and gleaming gold on the other.

Rhee felt puzzled. This isn't part of the vidcam, she told herself. But she took it along with her, back to her bunk, where she stuck both the vidcam and the strange piece of cermet into her personal bag for safekeeping, until they got back to Moonbase.

VANCOUVER

'Do I really have to do this?' Kris Cardenas asked.

Greg Masterson's image in her desktop phone screen smiled gravely. 'How long have you known my mother, Kris?'

'I owe her, I understand that. But I can't just pop off to the Moon like I'm going to the mall for groceries.'

On the wall behind her desk hung the round gold seal of the Nobel Prize. The rest of the wall was covered with photographs, mostly family – husband and children who had grown to adulthood and now had children of their own. A few of the photos were not family, although each of them had Cardenas in them, together with a former President of the United States, a six-time Oscar-winning actress, a group of scientists posing before a splendid vista of the Alps.

Cardenas herself looked much younger than her fifty-eight years. Much younger. Her hair was still a sandy light brown, no trace of silver. Her bright blue eyes still sparkled youthfully. She looked as if she could spend the day surfing or skydiving or skiing down those snow-covered Alps, rather than delivering lectures to university students.

Greg's smile looked strained, she thought. He was saying, 'Look, Kris, we're talking about my half-brother here. Mom will kidnap you if she has to.'

'But I can't do anything for him! Zimmerman is the man she wants.'

For almost three seconds she waited for Greg's reply. Finally, his smile transformed itself into a knowing smirk. 'Zimmerman's on his way here.'

'He is?'

Greg continued, not waiting for her reply, 'A Masterson Clippership lifted him and four of his assistants half an hour ago on a direct trajectory to Moonbase. They'll arrive here in about ten hours.'

Dumbfounded, Cardenas asked, 'How on Earth did she swing that?'

When her question reached him, Greg actually laughed. 'Simplest thing in the world. She just threatened to reveal to the media that he's running a nanotherapy clinic for wealthy foreigners right on the university campus.'

'Blackmail!'

'Black and green,' Greg replied after the lag. 'She's also making a hefty donation to his department at the university.'

Cardenas said, 'She hasn't offered me anything.'

When Greg heard her words, he replied, 'Come on up here, Kris. Bring your husband if you want. Even if it's just to hold her hand, she needs you. She's not as strong as she'd like everyone to believe, you know.'

Who the hell is? Cardenas asked herself. To Greg's image in the phone screen she said, 'I'll get there as soon as I can.'

Doug swam in and out of consciousness. He seemed to be floating, but that couldn't be. He dreamed he was drifting in the ocean, bobbing up and down on the long gentle swells of the open sea. Yet somehow he was stretched out on the desert sand, broiling in the sun, every pore sweating and Brennart lay beside him saying, 'Like the man says, working out on the frontier is nothing more than inventing new ways to get killed.'

When he opened his eyes Bianca Rhee was always hovering over him, gazing down at him with an expression that mixed tenderness with desperate fear.

Is this real or am I dreaming? Doug asked himself.

'We're on our way back to Moonbase,' Rhee said to him at one point. 'They're bringing specialists up from Earth to take care of you.'

Embalmers, thought Doug. Undertakers. Bury me on the Moon, he wanted to say. And don't forget Brennart's statue.

'The Yamagata team?' he heard himself croak.

'Killifer went out to get them,' Rhee replied gently, sooth-ingly. 'Moonbase agreed with you: rescuing them blocks any claim they might have tried to make.'

'They're okay?'

'We don't know yet. Killifer hasn't reached them yet.'

'I get all the shit jobs,' Killifer grumbled.

Deems, wedged into the cramped cockpit beside him, shrugged resignedly. 'Well, you're not alone, are you.'

They were piloting one of the lobbers over Mt. Wasser, searching for the crashed Yamagata ship. Killifer had been ordered to do so directly by Jinny Anson, Moonbase's direc-tor.

Two big lobbers had arrived at their south polar camp from Moonbase, filled with oxygen and other supplies, but without a single human being aboard. Killifer had to guide their landings remotely and use the expedition's remaining personnel to unload them. Instructions – orders, really – from Anson back at Moonbase crackled along the satellite relay system: Get Doug Stavenger back to Moonbase *immedi-ately*. Then go find the wrecked Yamagata lander and save its crew.

Killifer had loaded the Stavenger kid onto one of the lobbers. The astronomer, Rhee, volunteered to go with him. Volunteered hell, Killifer thought. Nobody could tear the little gook from the kid's side.

The expedition was a mess, but from what Anson told him, the corporation would have a valid claim to the area as soon as Stavenger's vidcam pictures were verified. As he monitored the lobber's automated takeoff for its return flight to Moonbase, Killifer almost hoped that the radiation had ruined the vidcam and the disk would be a blank.

What the hell, he told himself. It rankled him, though, that even if he died young Stavenger would be a fucking hero. Especially if he died.

'I'm getting a transponder signal,' Deems said.

The summit of Mt. Wasser was below them. Glancing down through the cockpit's transparent bubble, Killifer could glimpse the telescope and other gear that Brennart and Stavenger had left on the mountaintop.

'Show me,' he said to Deems.

With the tap of a gloved finger, Deems brought up the transponder signal on the cockpit's starscope display of the deeply shadowed ground below them. The screen showed not much more than a blur, with a red dot winking at them.

'Let's take it down to five hundred and hover,' Killifer said.

'That'll burn up a lot of propellant.' Deems' face was covered by his helmet visor, but his voice sounded scared.

'We gotta see the ground before we set down on it,' Killifer said. 'Friggin' starscope sure isn't showing much. Switch to infrared.'

'It's too cold down there in the dark,' said Deems. 'Must be two hundred below, at least.'

'Switch to infrared,' Killifer repeated, louder.

Silently Deems touched the keypad and the cockpit's main screen showed a false-color image of the ground below: mostly deep black.

'That must be ice,' Killifer said.

'Yeah, it's absorbing the infrared.'

'And the transponder signal's right in the middle of it.'

'They must've landed on the ice,' said Deems.

Killifer nodded inside his helmet. 'Landing jets melted the ice under them and they splashed in. Dumb bastards.'

'Good thing the ice isn't too deep.'

'Nah, it must've refrozen as soon as they turned off their rocket engines.'

'Then they must be stuck in it.'

'Yeah,' Killifer said disgustedly. 'And we better make sure we don't get caught in the same stupid trap.'

Killifer was not primarily a pilot, although over the years at Moonbase he had trained in both lobbers and hoppers and flown them many times. But setting down in pitch darkness in totally unfamiliar territory – no wonder the Japs crashed, he said to himself.

Hovering above the ice field while Deems worriedly stared

at their fuel gauge, Killifer jinked the lumbering spacecraft
sideways, searching for solid ground to land on.

'Ice field's a lot bigger on this side of the mountain,' he
muttered.

'But they won't be able to claim it once we rescue
them, huh?'

'That's the theory.' The only ground the infrared display
showed looked too rough for a landing, strewn with boulders
the size of houses.

The radio speaker crackled. 'Anson to Killifer. Yamagata
just launched a lobber from Nippon One on a trajectory for the
polar region. Must be their rescue party. Where are you?'

'Looking for a place to land without breaking our asses,'
Killifer replied.

'It's important that you get to the Yamagata team before
their rescue party does,' said Anson.

'Yeah, I know. But there doesn't look like much room to put
down safely. That's why the Japs crashed in the first place.'

'There must be someplace!'

'When I find it I'll let you know.' Killifer punched the radio
off. Turning to Deems, he added, 'If we can find a landing spot
before we run out of fuel.'

Deems said, 'How about right on the edge of the ice?'

'We'll melt it, just like they did.'

'Okay, but it can't be real deep there. Must be solid ground
underneath.' Before Killifer could object he added, 'And if
there's boulders big enough to give us trouble, they'd probably
be poking up above the surface of the ice.'

'Probably,' Killifer muttered.

'I don't see any other way,' said Deems. 'Do you?'

Killifer stared at the polished visor of Deems' helmet. He
could only make out the vaguest outline of the face inside. For
a scared rabbit, Killifer though, he's getting pretty gutsy.

'Otherwise we're just going to run out of propellant jerking
around, looking for a flat spot that isn't here.'

Unaccustomed to bold ideas from Deems, Killifer grunted
and mumbled, 'Maybe you're right.'

MOONBASE

It was unusual for a Clippership to land at Moonbase. Usually the big commercial spaceliners went only as far as the space stations that hugged Earth in low orbits.

Greg watched the main display screen at the spaceport flight control center as the big, cone-shaped *Maxwell Hunter* settled slowly, silently on its rocket exhaust. More than a dozen others had crowded into the flight control center, too. Like a cruise liner landing in some out-of-the-way port, Greg thought. The natives go down to the dock to watch.

A flexible access tube wormed its way to the Clipper's main airlock while the ship stood on the blast-scarred landing pad, gleaming in the sunlight. Greg knew that the Clipper carried Professor Wilhelm Zimmerman and four of his top aides. Kris Cardenas was on her way to Moonbase, also. And Mom. It's going to be a busy few hours here, he said to himself.

Greg was shocked when Wilhelm Zimmerman pushed through the airlock hatch at the underground receiving area. He was grossly fat, almost as wide across his soft sagging middle as he was tall. Bald, jowly, wearing a gray three-piece business suit with the unbuttoned jacket flapping ludicrously, the first thing he did upon setting foot on the underground chamber's rock floor was to reach into his jacket pocket and pull out a long, black, evil-looking cigar.

'You can't smoke in here!' Greg shouted, lunging toward him.

Zimmerman scowled from beneath bushy gray eyebrows. 'So? Then where?'

'Nowhere in Moonbase. Smoking is strictly prohibited. For safety reasons.'

'Nonsense!' Zimmerman snapped. 'Like the laws in Switzerland. Pure nonsense.' He fished in his side pocket and pulled out a gold lighter.

Greg gently took the lighter from him. 'This is a totally artificial environment,' he said. 'Smoking is not allowed.'

Zimmerman's scowl deepened. 'You drag me up here to this . . . this . . . cavern, you ask me to perform a miracle for you, and you deny me my only vice?' His English was heavily accented but understandable.

'I'm afraid so, Professor.'

'Professor Doctor!'

'No smoking,' Greg said somberly, 'no matter how many titles you have.'

Zimmerman looked as if he wanted to turn around and go back to the spacecraft that had brought him. But then he broke into a fleshy grin.

'Very well,' he said, suddenly amiable. 'Since I have no choice, I will refrain from smoking. But you can't stop me from chewing!' And he clamped his teeth on the fat black cigar.

Greg raised his eyes to the rock ceiling. 'Come this way, please,' he said softly, pointing to the tractor that was waiting to take them to Moonbase proper. 'And be careful—'

He realized that Zimmerman was walking perfectly well alongside him. Looking down, Greg saw that Zimmerman's feet were already shod in weighted lunar boots.

His grin turning triumphant, Zimmerman said grandly, 'I am not a complete . . . how do you say it, tenderfeet?'

'Where did you get them?' Greg asked. 'I didn't know they were available on Earth.'

'Mrs. Stavenger had them aboard the ship that took me here. My abductor is very kind to me.'

'Abductor?' Greg asked as he helped the obese old man up into the tractor.

'You think I would come to this bunker of my own volition? I have been kidnapped, young man, by a powerful, vicious woman.'

Greg gave him a wintry smile. 'My mother,' he said as he climbed into the driver's seat.

'So?' Zimmerman looked briefly surprised. 'But your name is not hers.'

His smile disappeared. 'She remarried after my father . . . died.'

'Ah.' Zimmerman nodded, making his jowls jiggle. As Greg put the tractor in gear and started down the long tunnel, he asked, 'You have prepared the tissue samples for which I asked?'

'The medics will have them for you by the time we get to the infirmary.'

'And blood – whole plasma, hemoglobin, this you have available?'

Greg shook his head. 'The blood bank here is very small. We're lining up volunteer donors who have the proper blood type.'

'We will probably have to replace his entire blood supply.'

'Then we'll need more brought up from Earth,' Greg said. 'In the meantime, you can examine him and get started on your procedures.'

Zimmerman grunted. 'I will have time to wash my hands, perhaps?'

'It's my half-brother who's dying, Professor Doctor. We've got to act quickly.'

'Ah,' the old man said again. 'Very well. The tissue samples are needed so that we can imitate them on the surface of the nanomachines. Otherwise what is still functioning of his body's immune system will attack the machines when they are injected into his blood stream.'

'I see.'

'You don't want his damaged immune system attacking the machines that are trying to save him.'

'I understand.'

'Blood transfusions immediately. By the time my associates have analyzed the tissue samples the transfusions must be complete. Then we inject the nanomachines.'

'I see,' said Greg.

Zimmerman lapsed into silence, folding his hands over his ample belly and letting his many chins sag to his chest. He seemed asleep. Mom must've had him yanked out of his bed, Greg thought. She probably would've really kidnapped him if he hadn't agreed to come up here. She's frantic over Doug. Would she be just as frantic, just as determined, if it was me in the infirmary, dying?

'Contact light,' Deems said, his voice quavering slightly.

'Okay,' said Killifer. 'We're down.' He was perspiring; cold sweat made his palms slippery, stung his eyes.

They had landed at the edge of the ice field, as Deems had suggested. The ice partially melted beneath the blast of their rocket exhaust and the lobber's landing feet sank into a mushy cold swamp. For an instant both men had felt their vehicle sinking, then it hit solid rock and came to a halt, tilted slightly but safely down.

Killifer reached into his thigh pouch for a reusable sponge-like sheet of plastic to wipe his face. He saw that Deems was doing the same. Scared shitless, Killifer thought.

'Okay,' he said, after taking a breath. 'Check suits. Prepare for surface excursion.'

'I don't see their lights,' Deems said.

'They're over the horizon, about four klicks out on the ice.'

'We both going out?'

'Damned right. We'll hook a tether to the winch.'

Deems said, 'All right,' without much enthusiasm.

Killifer stuffed his wiper back into the pouch on the thigh of his suit. Then he realized that the cermet hatch cover from Brennart's hopper was not in there. He groped in the other thigh pouch. Not there, either.

'What's the matter?' Deems asked.

'Nothing,' Killifer snapped. 'Let's get going.'

The astronomer. Stupid little gook put on my suit when she went up the mountain to get Stavenger. She's got it!

Panic surged through him. If she understands what it means – No, he told himself. She wouldn't. How could she? It's just a hunk of cermet to her. I'll have to get it back from her, though.

'You okay?' Deems' voice sounded worried in his earphones.

'Yeah. Let's get moving.'

I'll have to get it back from her, Killifer told himself again. Because if she figures it out, I'm dead.

Zimmerman terrified the meager infirmary staff. Only one M.D., a very junior young woman, and three technicians who split their time between medical duties and elsewhere, the staff was meant to deal with injuries and minor illnesses. Big problems were sent Earthward, either to one of the space stations or to a hospital on the ground.

'Equipment, this is? Junk, this is!' Zimmerman bellowed when they showed him the infirmary. 'It is impossible to work with Tinkertoys! Impossible!'

None of the youngsters could please Zimmerman in the slightest. He bullied them, swore at them in German and English, told them what incompetent swine they were. He cursed their teachers, their progenitors, and predicted a dim future for the human race if such *dummkopfs* were allowed anywhere near the practice of medicine.

When Greg tried to intervene, Zimmerman turned on him. 'So? Now you are an expert, also? How can I work here? Where are my facilities that your blackmailing mother promised me? Where is the blood for transfusion? How can I perform miracles without the tools I need? Even Christ had some water when he wanted to make wine!'

'Willi, Willi, I could hear you out at the airlock.'

Greg turned and saw Kris Cardenas, bright and blonde and perky, striding into the narrow confines of the four-bed infirmary.

'Kristine, *liebling*, no one told me you were coming here!'

Zimmerman's demeanor changed as abruptly as the dawn transforms the dark lunar night.

'Willi, you mustn't let yourself get angry at these people,' Cardenas scolded cheerfully. 'They're trying to help you.'

'Ach, with such help a man could die. I'd rather have Hungarians on my side.'

'It's bad for your heart to get so worked up,' Cardenas said, smiling sweetly. She was wearing a light blue sweater and slightly darker knee-length skirt. If Greg didn't know better, he would have sworn she wasn't much older than thirty-five.

Zimmerman's fleshy face turned puckish. 'Ah, this will be like the old days, won't it? You were my best student, always.'

'And you were always my favorite professor,' Cardenas returned the compliment.

With a shake of his head that made his jowls waddle, Zimmerman spread his stubby arms in a gesture of helplessness. 'But look around at this place! There is not the necessary equipment! There is not the trained staff! How can I—'

Cardenas silenced him by placing a fingertip gently on his lips. 'Willi, I'm here. I'll assist you.'

'You will?'

'And the four people you brought from your clinic.'

'Clinic?' The fat old man looked startled. 'I have no clinic! My research facility at the university is a laboratory, not a clinic.'

'Yes, I know,' Cardenas said. 'Forgive my error.'

His beaming smile returned. 'For you, *liebling*, no forgiving is necessary. Now let us get to work.'

MOONBASE

'Welcome to Moonbase, mother,' said Greg.

Joanna did not look haggard. Not quite. But the tension in her face was obvious. She's frightened, Greg realized. Frightened and frustrated because there's nothing more that she can do for Doug. Nothing but wait and hope that Zimmerman can perform a miracle.

'Take me to him, Greg,' she said, her voice strained. 'Please.'

She had changed into standard lunar coveralls on the trip up, Greg saw. White, the color code for medics, rather than management's sky blue, such as he wore. And she was already wearing weighted boots.

Without another word, Greg led her to the tractor and started down the tunnel toward the main part of the base. I'm getting to be a taxi driver, he grumbled to himself.

'How is he? Is he in pain?'

'They've wrapped him in cooling blankets to bring his body temperature down as far as they dare,' Greg reported. 'Zimmerman and his team are programming a set of nano-machines to repair the damage to his cells that's been done by the radiation.'

Joanna nodded tensely.

Glancing at her as they drove down the long tunnel, Greg added, 'They're giving him massive blood transfusions, but the damage is pretty extensive, I'm afraid.'

'I'll give blood,' Joanna said immediately. 'You can, too.'

Greg turned away from her. 'I don't know if Zimmerman's bugs are going to be able to save him.'

'If he can't, no one can,' Joanna said.

'Careful!' yelped Yazaru Hara. 'His ribs are broken.'

'Got to get him out of the seat,' Killifer said.

The unconscious Japanese was dead weight made extra heavy by his bulky armored spacesuit. Killifer grasped him under his arms while Hara, turned awkwardly in his seat, lifted his companion's legs so that the American could slide him out of the spacecraft cockpit.

'How long's he been unconscious?' Killifer asked, panting with the effort.

'Many hours,' said Hara. 'He was still breathing, though, when you arrived.'

'Yeah.' Slowly Killifer pulled Inoguchi's inert form through the cockpit's emergency hatch and out onto the black ice.

Deems had rigged a makeshift stretcher out of honeycomb panels from the side of the Yamagata craft. Killifer lowered the spacesuited Japanese onto it. He heard a groan from the Jap.

'He's still alive!' Hara shouted.

'Yeah,' said Killifer, thinking, Great. Now we gotta carry this dead weight back over four klicks of ice. Lucky if we don't all wind up with busted bones.

'How much longer will it take?' Joanna demanded, nervously pacing up and down Jinny Anson's office.

Greg, sitting on the couch jury-rigged from scavenged spacecraft seats, shook his head. Zimmerman and his staff had been working for hours in Moonbase's nanolab. The grumpy old man hadn't even looked at Doug yet.

'It takes time,' Kris Cardenas said. She was sitting behind Anson's desk. Anson herself had rushed down to the control center to pipe Doug's vidcam disk to The Hague, registering Masterson Corporation's claim to the Mt. Wasser region. She had graciously turned over her entire suite to Joanna, saying she could stay in smaller quarters until her tour of duty was finished and she left for Earth. In truth, she wanted to keep as far away from Joanna as she could.

'But Doug doesn't have time,' Joanna said. 'He's dying!'

Cardenas got up from the desk chair. 'I'll get back to the lab and see if I can help speed things up.'

'Yes,' said Joanna. 'Good.'

The instant the door closed behind Cardenas, Greg got up from the couch, took his mother by the hand, and made her sit down where he had been. Then he sat beside her.

'There's no sense getting yourself sick over this,' he said. 'You should try to get some rest.'

Joanna shook her head. 'How can I rest?'

'I could get something for you, to help you sleep.'

'No! I . . .' She stopped, as if confused, suddenly uncertain of what she wanted to say, wanted to do.

'I'll let you know the instant something happens,' Greg promised.

'Don't you see!' Joanna blurted. 'It's my fault! All my fault! I should never have allowed him to go to Moonbase. I knew he was too young, too careless.' She broke into tears.

Greg put his arms around his mother and let her sob on his shoulder. 'It's not your fault; it isn't. And he wasn't careless. Nobody could have predicted the flare.'

'First the Moon killed Paul, now it's killed him. And it's my fault, all my fault.'

Coldly, Greg said, 'The Moon didn't kill Paul Stavenger. We both know that.'

Joanna pulled slightly away from him. Her eyes were red, filled with tears. 'I was a terrible mother to you, Greg. What happened was my fault as much as anyone's.'

'Mom, that's all in the past. There's no sense dredging it up again.'

'But if only I had been—'

'Stop it,' Greg said sharply. 'I've spent years working my way through this. I don't want to hear any more about it.'

Joanna stared at him, but said nothing.

'It's not your fault. None of this is. What's happened has happened. Now all we can do is wait and see if Zimmerman can save him.'

But he was thinking, Would she cry over me? He tried to

remember back to his own childhood, all those years, he could
not recall his mother crying for him. Not once.

Joanna pulled herself together with a visible, shuddering
effort. 'I can't stay here,' she said, jumping to her feet too
hard in the unaccustomed lunar gravity.

Greg had to grab her, steady her. 'Be careful, Mom! You'll
hurt yourself.'

'Take me to him,' Joanna said.

'Doug? He's in—'

'No. Zimmerman. I want to see him. I want to find out what
he's doing.'

Zimmerman sat sweating on a rickety swivel chair that seemed
much too fragile to support his weight. He had draped an
ancient lab smock over his gray suit; the coat had once been
white but now, after so many years of wear and washings, it
was beyond bleach.

Beads of perspiration on his lip and brow, he chewed
anxiously on his black cigar, his fourth of the long, trying day.
One of his assistants had thoughtfully converted a laboratory
dish into an ashtray for him. It sat on the lab bench at his
side, filled with the shredded and soggy remains of three
earlier cigars.

On the other side of the clear plastiglass wall, his four
assistants bent over lab benches. Their lab smocks looked
very new, starched and pressed.

The airtight door of the nanotechnology laboratory sighed
open and Kris Cardenas came through.

'How's it going?' she asked.

Zimmerman's bushy brows contracted into a worried frown.
'What takes weeks in Basel we are trying to do in hours
here.'

'Is there anything I can do to help?'

'Turn up the air conditioning! Must I suffer like this?'

Cardenas shrugged. 'I think the temperature is centrally
controlled.' To her the lab felt comfortably warm; perhaps
a bit stuffy. She smiled and added, 'If you would lose some
weight . . .'

'Camouflage,' Zimmerman said, slapping his belly.

'Camouflage?'

'Do you think the politicians and their spies suspect me of working on nanotherapies when I am so gross? Hah?'

Cardenas felt her jaw drop open. 'Is it that bad? Even in Switzerland?'

'I take no chances,' Zimmerman said.

'Do you need anything?' Cardenas asked.

Zimmerman's cheeks waddled slightly. 'No. The equipment here is surprisingly good. Not precisely what we require for medical work, but good enough, I think. We are adapting it.'

'They use nanomachines here quite a bit.'

'But not for medical purposes.'

'No, I think not.'

'How is the patient?' Zimmerman asked.

Cardenas shrugged. 'Last time I checked he was fairly stable. Sinking slowly, but they've lowered his metabolic rate as far as they can.'

'H'mm.'

The airtight door slid open again and Joanna Masterson strode through, followed by Greg.

Zimmerman scowled. 'This laboratory is in use. Find yourselves—'

'This is Joanna Masterson,' Cardenas said quickly.

Pushing himself up from the creaking little chair, Zimmerman clicked his heels and bowed slightly. 'My abductress. The woman who has blackmailed me.'

Joanna ignored his jibe. She looked at the rumpled obese old man, noting that he was several inches shorter than she.

'How soon will you be ready?' she asked.

'As soon as we can,' Zimmerman said.

'Please don't play games and don't patronize me. My son is dying. How soon can you begin to help him?'

Zimmerman's tone changed. 'It's a matter of programming. We are moving ahead as quickly as we can.'

'Programming,' Joanna echoed.

Waving a pudgy hand, Zimmerman explained, 'We are adapting our little machines to seek out damaged cells and repair them. They will remove damaged material, molecule by molecule, and repair the cells with fresh material, molecule by molecule.'

Joanna nodded. Greg, standing slightly behind her, folded his arms across his chest.

'The problem is that your son has sustained massive damage. His case is very different from merely getting rid of accumulated fat cells or breaking down plaque along blood vessels.'

'Can you do it?' Joanna asked.

'We will do it, Madam,' said Zimmerman. 'Whether we will be able to do it in time, before he is too far gone even for the nanomachines to help him, remains questionable.'

'Is there anything else that you need? Any other assistants?'

'Nothing and no one that could be brought here in time.'

Greg asked, 'How much of a chance does he have? I mean—'

'If I had even one single week this would be no problem.'

'But we've only got a few hours.'

Zimmerman sighed hugely. 'Yah. This I know.'

Killifer clumped wearily to the comm cubicle of the buried shelter, still in his spacesuit, minus only the helmet. The young woman at the communications console rose to her feet.

'You did a fine job out there,' she said, eyes gleaming. 'You saved two lives.'

With a crooked grin, Killifer said, 'I saved the corporation from any competition to their claim, that's what I saved.'

The young woman smiled knowingly. 'You're just being modest.'

Killifer shook his head and took the emptied chair, thinking, Hey, now I'm a friggin' hero. I'll have to look her up when we get back to the base. Might be worth some sack time.

'Moonbase says the Yamagata craft has shifted its trajectory and asked for permission to land here and pick up their men.'

'They're welcome to 'em. I hope they brought medics. One of them's in a bad way. Busted ribs.'

As he spoke, Killifer opened the channel to Moonbase. Jinny Anson's face appeared on his screen, surprising him.

'I'm living in the control center until things settle down,' Anson told him. 'Mrs. Stavenger's come up here to be with her son.'

'She's there? At Moonbase?'

'Yep. She's going to be pretty damned thankful to you for getting him down off the mountain, I betcha.'

Like I had any choice, Killifer thought.

'And for getting those two stranded Japanese guys. Yamagata's people have been falling all over themselves thanking us.'

'Really?'

'That's their way of admitting that they messed up any claim they might have made. Heads are going to roll over at Nippon One, I betcha.'

Who gives a fuck? Killifer said to himself. Then he remembered, and a pang of sudden fear flared through him.

'How's the Stavenger kid?' he asked.

Anson shook her head. 'Not good. The Dragon Lady's brought a team of nano specialists up here, but I don't know if they can save him. He's pretty far gone.'

It took a conscious effort for Killifer to unclench his teeth. 'And the astronomer? Rhee? How's she doing?'

Anson looked mildly surprised. 'I don't know. She was hanging pretty close to Doug Stavenger but she ought to be back at her job by now.'

Killifer nodded. I'll have to track her down when we get back to the base.

'I'm going to start breaking the camp here, soon as the Yamagata ship lands and picks up their guys.'

'Right,' said Anson. 'The expedition didn't go the way we planned, but at least we've got a valid claim to the territory. Next time we go back, you'll be in charge.'

Killifer made himself grin. 'Yeah? That's great.' But he knew that his newfound status as a hero and leader could be destroyed by a single small square of cermet. I've gotta get it away from her, he told himself. Got to.

INFIRMARY

'That's it?' Joanna whispered harshly. 'All these hours have been spent to make something that doesn't even fill a single hypodermic?'

Standing beside her, Kris Cardenas nodded without taking her eyes off Zimmerman's bulky lab-coated form, bending over Doug's infirmary bed.

'That's all he'll need,' she whispered back, 'if it works right.'

Doug lay unconscious, his face pallid as death, covered to his chin in cooling blankets. Another hypothermic wrap was wound around his head. Like the undergarment of a spacesuit, the pale blue blankets were honeycombed with fine plastic tubes that carried refrigerated water to keep Doug's body temperature as low as possible. Intravenous lines fed into his arms and an oxygen tube was fixed to his nostrils.

Joanna couldn't tell if her son was breathing or not. The monitoring instruments above the bed showed his life signs: their ragged electronic lines looked dangerously low to her. She glanced at Greg, standing on her other side. He stared grimly through the plastiglass window that separated them from the infirmary bed.

'Shouldn't we have a medical team to stay with him? I could bring—'

Cardenas silenced her by placing a hand on Joanna's shoulder. 'Zimmerman's an M.D. as well as a Ph.D. And two of his aides are also physicians.'

Zimmerman straightened up. For a moment he gazed down at the unconscious patient, then he turned and went to the door.

Stepping into the observation cubicle where the others waited, he dropped the syringe into the waste recycling can.

'It is done,' he said, his voice loud enough to startle Joanna. 'Now we wait.'

'And rest,' Cardenas said. 'You look like you could use a nice nap, Willi.'

In truth, his fleshy face looked ravaged.

Greg spoke up, 'We should all get some sleep.' Turning to Zimmerman, he asked, 'How long before we see some results?'

The old man blinked his pouchy eyes. 'Twelve hours. Maybe more. Maybe a little less.'

'Nothing's going to happen for eight to ten hours, at least,' Cardenas said briskly. 'So let's all get a decent sleep.'

Greg agreed. 'I'll get the people on duty to call if there's any change in his condition.'

Joanna said, 'I can sleep here, on the chair.'

'No,' Greg said firmly, taking her by the arm. 'You sleep in your quarters, on a bunk. Doctor's orders.'

Reluctantly, Joanna allowed her elder son to lead her out of the observation room and toward the suite that Anson had vacated for her. She almost felt grateful to Greg for his forceful tenderness.

Small as viruses, millions upon millions of nanomachines flowed through Doug's blood stream like an army of repair personnel eager to get to work. Blind, deaf, without the intelligence of an amoeba, they were tuned to the chemical signatures that cells emit. In their world of the ultrasmall, where a bacterium is as gigantic and complex as a shopping mall, they were guided by the shapes of the molecules swarming around them.

Built to seek out specific types of molecules, they quickly spread through the enormous labyrinthine ways of Doug's failing body. With receptors barely a thousand atoms long they touched and tested every molecule they came in contact with. Hardly any of them were of interest to the nanomachines; they merely touched, found that the molecule did not fit precisely into their receptor jaws, and left the molecule behind. Like a lock seeking its proper key, each nanomachine blindly searched the teeming liquid world within Doug's wasting body.

When they did find a molecule that nested properly in their receptors, they clamped onto it and tore it apart into its individual atoms: carbon, hydrogen, nitrogen, oxygen and the rarer metals and minerals. Then other nanomachines seized the freed atoms and combined them into new molecules, new nutrients for the cells that were damaged and dying.

Deep into the cells they penetrated, into the nucleus where the huge double spiral DNA molecules worked as templates for building vital proteins. Here was where the most crucial damage had been done. The links between the two intertwining spirals, the base pairs that were the genes themselves, had been heavily damaged by the ionizing radiation. Where the nanomachines saw a break in this vital linkage, where base pairs had been broken or mismatched, the nanomachines rebuilt the bases and linked them correctly. Like vastly complex three-dimensional jigsaw puzzles, the DNA molecules were put together properly by the busily hurrying nanomachines, much as Doug's own natural enzymes were valiantly trying to do. Together, the polymerases and the nanomachines worked frantically to repair the massive DNA molecules.

They worked with blinding speed, although time meant nothing to them. In this nanometer universe a thousandth of a second stretched like years and decades. In microseconds they repaired damaged cells and then flowed onward, seeking, testing, destroying damaged areas, rebuilding molecules for the growth of healthy new cells. DNA repair was more intricate, more demanding. It took whole tenths of seconds to repair a damaged DNA molecule. Millions of cells and DNA molecules were repaired each minute. But there were so many billions more to reach.

Killifer was not accustomed to being a hero. He was surprised to see that Jinny Anson and more than a dozen others were waiting for him at The Pit when he led his weary team out of their lobbers. Anson pounded him on the back and insisted on taking him to The Cave for a drink. She even provided the booze.

'You did damned fine out there,' Anson said, leaning back in her chair, grinning across the table at Killifer.

Unshaven, grimy, Killifer relished the glow of the rocket juice that laced his coffee. And the glow of her approval.

'Yep,' Anson said, 'now I can turn over the job to Greg Masterson and leave on schedule and get myself married.'

Shocked, Killifer blurted, 'Married?'

'The Dragon Lady wanted me to stay on until the expedition got back. So now you're back and I can head for San Antone with a clear conscience.'

'I'll be damned,' Killifer said.

Anson's expression sobered. 'Shame about Brennart, though.'

'Yeah.'

'What went wrong with his hopper, do you think? Why'd it die out there?'

Shifting nervously in his chair, Killifer said, 'Radiation must've knocked out the electrical system. Something like that.'

'Somebody'll have to check it out when you go back there,' said Anson.

'Yeah. Right.'

'But we've got the polar region, that's what's really important.'

'How's the Stavenger kid?'

She shrugged. 'They're working on him.'

'Is he gonna pull through?'

With a shake of her head, Anson replied, 'Damned if I know. They've dragooned some high-priced talent here to try nanotherapy on him, but nobody knows if it'll work.'

Killifer was silent for a moment. 'And, uh, the astronomer . . .' Don't look too anxious, he warned himself. 'What's her name?'

'The Korean? Rhee. Bianca Rhee.'

'Yeah. How's she doing?'

'Okay, I guess. Why're you so interested in her?'

'I'm not,' he said quickly. 'Just – she flew out with Stavenger, I wanted to make sure she's okay.'

'She's probably on duty right now. Check the astronomy dome if you want to see her.'

'Yeah,' Killifer said. 'Maybe I will. After I clean up some.'

Anson grinned lopsidedly. 'Do I detect a romance?'

'Naw,' Killifer said. Then wished he hadn't.

It made no difference. Anson, her mind turning toward her own marriage, said, 'Don't be coy, Jack. You're a hero now. You can have your pick of the love-starved women of Moonbase, I betcha.'

Killifer grinned at the idea. Yeah, he told himself. I'm a big friggin' hero. As long as nobody finds out what I did to Brennart and Doug Stavenger.

She wasn't at the astronomy dome. The place was empty. Nothing there except a half dozen display screens and a computer humming to itself.

Killifer slipped into the empty chair and used the computer to find where Rhee's quarters were. He phoned; no answer.

Maybe I can duck in there, he thought, and find the cermet cover. Then when we go back to Mt. Wasser I can stick it back onto the hopper and nobody'll ever know what happened.

He headed for Rhee's quarters.

Bianca Rhee was at the infirmary, staring through the observation room's window at Doug's inert form, still swathed in the light blue cooling blankets. The medic on duty told her that Doug wasn't expected to come out of his hypothermic coma for days. But with oriental patience, Rhee sat as immobile as he was and watched over him.

The accordion-fold door was locked but Killifer got past it easily enough, using his plastic ID card to spring the bolt. Rhee's one room looked as neat as a real-estate model. Everything in place. Bed, desk, bureau: standard issue, same as every other apartment in Moonbase. The only signs of individuality were a set of framed photographs on the bureau, family from the looks of them, and a delicate small lacquered vase with an imitation flower in it.

Killifer went swiftly through the desk drawers. It wasn't there. Then the bureau. Nothing but clothes. And a pair of toe shoes, for god's sake, beat up as hell and just as smelly. The closet. Not there either.

He stood for an agonized moment in the middle of the room, so small that he could almost touch its opposing walls by stretching out his arms. It's got to be in here someplace, he told himself. Where? He checked under her sink. Nothing.

Where the hell is it? She can't be carrying it around with her. Can she?

Then he saw it. So obvious that he knew she wasn't trying to hide it. She was using it as a base, beneath the flower vase. Its gold plating complimented the deep burgundy of the vase nicely. Killifer felt his pent-up breath ease out of him. Feeling enormously relieved, he slipped the cover out from under the vase and tucked it into the back pocket of his coveralls.

Cautiously, he cracked the apartment door open. Two people were coming down the tunnel, talking earnestly. Killifer let them pass, then eased himself out behind them, closed the door and heard its lock click, then walked swiftly in the other direction.

With the cermet cover in his pocket.

'It's been almost twelve hours,' Joanna said to Zimmerman. 'Shouldn't we see some change? Some improvement?'

She and Greg, the Swiss scientist and Cardenas were in the infirmary's observation room again. A young oriental woman had been sitting there when Joanna entered, but she got up and left so swiftly that Joanna didn't even get the chance to ask her who she was. She was wearing the pumpkin orange coveralls of the scientific staff; maybe she was working for Zimmerman, Joanna thought.

'There is improvement,' Zimmerman said, pointing a stubby finger at the monitors above Doug's bed. 'Look at his vital signs. Heartbeat is stronger. Blood pressure is almost normal. Kidney function is returning.'

'But he hasn't moved,' Greg said, peering through the window.

'That's to be expected,' Cardenas said softly. 'He's using all his energy internally.'

'I believe,' Zimmerman said, pulling out another long black cigar, 'that it will be possible to remove the hypothermic blankets in another two hours.' He chomped on the cigar with relish. 'Three, at most.'

'And then?' Joanna asked.

With a sloppy shrug, Zimmerman said, 'And then, sooner or later he will wake up and ask for food. He will be very hungry. Very!'

'He'll be cured?'

'If that's the word you want to use, yes. He will begin to function normally again.' Zimmerman grinned around his cigar.

Joanna looked from his florid, fleshy face through the window at her son. Doug will be cured! This nightmare will be over. Even Greg looked pleased, she thought.

'He'll be all right,' Cardenas said to her. 'The nanomachines are working inside him.'

For an instant Joanna wanted to throw her arms around Zimmerman and kiss him. But she controlled herself and the moment passed. As calmly as she could, she said to him, 'Dr. Zimmerman, I want to find some way to repay you. What can I do?'

'Let me go home,' he snapped.

Laughing, Joanna said, 'Of course. Of course. As soon as Doug regains consciousness – although I suppose you'll want to see him after he's on his feet again.'

'Yes, yes. You have virtual reality equipment here. I can examine him using VR.'

'But won't you want to see him in person?' Joanna asked. 'In the flesh?'

Zimmerman shook his head violently, making his cheeks waddle. 'I am not coming back to this cavern! Never!'

'All right. Doug can see you in Basel, then.'

'That will be impossible, I fear.'

'Why not?'

'A young man who is carrying millions of self-replicating nanomachines in his body would not be a welcome person on Earth. I doubt that he would be able to get past your own customs and immigration inspectors.'

Feeling confused, Joanna sat down on the couch facing the observation window. 'I don't understand.'

Cardenas sat next to her. Zimmerman remained standing. Greg was staring at him now.

'Your son is carrying nanomachines,' Zimmerman said. 'He would not be permitted to land on Earth. Every nation has laws against nanomachines in the human body. They are all afraid of nanomonsters.'

'But the bugs will flush out of his system once they've finished their work,' Joanna said, then added, 'Won't they?'

Zimmerman would not meet her eye.

Joanna turned to Cardenas. 'What's he talking about?'

With a careful sigh, Cardenas said, 'You know about the laws against injecting nanomachines into human patients, don't you?'

'Oh, *that* stupid stuff.'

'It's stupid, all right, but it's still the law. If Doug still has any trace of nanomachines in his system, he'll be stopped by the immigration inspectors at any rocket port on Earth. They're terrified of nanobugs running amok and killing people.'

'But—'

'May I point out,' Zimmerman interjected, 'that perhaps these laws are not so stupid after all. How many military establishments have supported research into nanoweapons? Nanotechnology could make biological warfare look like child's games.'

'But there are laws against military applications of nano-technology,' Greg objected. 'International treaties.'

'Yes, of course. Those are precisely the laws that do not allow nanomachines to be injected into human patients.'

'But Doug isn't going to hurt anybody!' Joanna said.

'Still, he will be carrying these self-replicating nano-machines for as long as he lives.'

'What?' Startled, Joanna snapped, 'You didn't tell me that—'

'That,' said Zimmerman, bending to put his cigar-clenched face close to hers, 'is the payment I extract from you.'

'Payment? What are you talking about?'

'Your son is my living laboratory, Madam; my lifetime experiment. He carries self-replicating nanomachines within his body. Forever.'

'What have you done?' Joanna cried.

'I have given your son a great gift, Madam,' Zimmerman replied.

Before Joanna could say anything, Cardenas said, 'You've enhanced his immune system.'

Zimmerman took the soggy cigar from his mouth. 'Yah, but there is more to it than that.'

'What?' Joanna demanded.

Almost smirking, Zimmerman said, 'Frankly, I do not know. No one can know. We have no experience with self-replicating nanomachines in the human body.'

'You've turned my son into—'

'An experiment. A living laboratory,' Zimmerman said. 'A step toward the perfection of nanotherapy.'

Before Joanna could reply, Cardenas said, 'It's a great gift, really! His immune system is now so enhanced he'll probably never even catch a cold anymore.'

Zimmerman nodded. 'Perhaps. The machines should be able to adapt to destroy microbes and viruses that invade his body.'

'But you don't know for certain what they'll do,' Greg said, his voice hollow.

'They should also repair effects of aging and any injuries he might incur,' Zimmerman added, still speaking to Joanna. 'Your son will most likely live a long, *long* time, Frau Stavenger.'

Greg muttered something too low for Joanna to hear.

'But that doesn't mean he can't return to Earth,' Joanna said.

'Yes it does,' said Cardenas. 'They'll never let him off the rocket.'

'They don't have to know.'

'They already know,' Zimmerman said. 'I have informed my colleagues and by now the authorities know.'

'You informed . . . why?' Joanna wanted to scream, yet her voice was barely a whisper.

'I have my own fish to fry, Madam. My own agenda. Your son will be a living advertisement that nanotherapy is *not* dangerous and *not* undesirable. I will see to it that his case is broadcast all over the world. Some day, sooner or later, he will become the *cause cèlébre* that will lead these ignorant politicians and witch doctors to lift their ban on nanotherapy.'

Feeling fury rising within her, Joanna said, 'I don't want a *cause cèlébre*. I want a normal, healthy son!'

'Healthy, he will be,' said Zimmerman. 'Normal, never.'

Trying to cool her down, Cardenas said, 'Think of it, Joanna. He'll never get ill. He might never even get old! And if he's ever injured, the nanomachines will repair him.'

Joanna thought of it. And turned to Greg, who stood mute and deathly pale, staring through the observation window at his half brother.

Slowly Doug woke from a long, deep dream. He had been swimming with dolphins the way he'd done when he was a kid visiting Hawaii except that the water was cold, numbingly cold and so dark that he could only sense the dolphins swimming alongside him, big powerful sleek bodies gliding effortlessly through the cold black waters. Don't leave me behind, he called to them, but somehow he was on the Moon and it was Brennart standing beside him whispering something, the secrets of the universe maybe, but Doug could not hear the man's words.

And then his eyes opened.

He saw that he was in some kind of hospital room. Moonbase. The infirmary. Low rock ceiling painted a cheerful butter yellow. A wide mirror took up almost the whole wall on one side of his bed. He could hear the humming and beeping of electronic monitors over his head.

The door opened and Bianca Rhee stepped through.

'You're awake!' she said, looking happy and surprised and awed and curious, all at once.

Doug grinned at her. 'I guess I am.'

'How do you feel?'

'Hungry!'

Bianca's smile threatened to split her face in two. Before she could say another word, a medic in crisp white coveralls pushed through the door angrily.

'What're you doing in here?' he demanded of Rhee. 'No one's allowed in here without—'

'Shut up!' Doug snapped. 'She's my friend.'

The man glared at Doug. 'No one is allowed inside this cubicle without specific permission from the resident M.D., friend or not.'

Over the next ten minutes, Doug learned how wrong the young medic was. Rhee dutifully left his cubicle, but his mother, Greg, and several strangers poured in, including a funny-looking fat older man with an unlit cigar clamped ludicrously in his teeth.

His mother fell on his neck, crying for the first time he could remember. Greg smiled stiffly. The others stared at the monitors while they checked his pulse, thumped his chest, and performed other ancient medical rituals.

'How do you feel?' everyone seemed to ask.

'Hungry,' Doug kept repeating. But no one brought him anything to eat.

Gradually he began to piece it together from the babbling of their chatter. Nanotherapy. He was alive and well. And would be for a long time to come. It was a lot to take in over a few minutes. It seemed to Doug as if just a few minutes ago he was dying from radiation poisoning. Now they were telling him he would live forever, just about.

'Could I just have something to eat?' he shouted over their voices.

Everyone stopped and stared at him.

'I'm starving,' Doug said.

'You see?' said the old fat guy. 'Just as I told you!'

INFIRMARY

Bianca Rhee came back, shyly, almost tiptoeing into Doug's cubicle after everyone else had left. He had eaten a full dinner, napped a short while, then asked for another dinner. Its remnant crumbs were all that was left on the food tray when Rhee entered and smiled happily at him.

'How do you feel?' she asked, sitting on the edge of his bed because there was no chair in his cubicle.

'Fine,' said Doug with a big grin. 'I feel as if I could run up to the top of Mt. Wasser in my bare feet!'

'The nanotherapy is really working.'

'I guess it is.'

'Do you feel – different?'

Doug thought about it for a moment. 'No,' he answered. 'Not different, exactly. Just – a little tired, but good, just the same. Like I've just won my fifth gold medal in the Olympics.'

'That's wonderful,' she said.

'What about you?' Doug asked. 'Have you been checked over? Are you okay?'

She shrugged. 'We all took more of a radiation dose than we should have, but I'm okay. No obvious medical problems.'

'Obvious?'

'Oh, I might have a two-headed baby someday.' She tried to laugh.

'And your chances of getting cancer?' Doug asked.

'A few percent higher.'

'Oh.'

'But that won't happen until I'm old and gray,' she said.

'Besides, there's no history of cancer in my family.'

'That's good,' Doug said, but he thought, There will be now, most likely.

Then he noticed that her coveralls were sweat-stained, and there was a fine sheen of perspiration on her forehead.

'Are you sure you're okay?' he asked. 'You're perspiring.'

'Oh.' Rhee looked more embarrassed than worried. 'I – I was exercising a little.'

'Exercising?'

She nodded, keeping her lips clamped tight. This isn't the time to tell him I practice dancing, she decided. He's a nice guy, but he'd laugh. The fat little gook in ballet slippers, pretending she's a ballerina in the low gravity of the Moon. Anyone would laugh.

So they talked about the expedition, about Brennart and what heroism was all about. Doug told Bianca that Brennart was already dying of cancer and had nothing much to lose by his daring.

She shook her head. 'I still think it was a real bonkhead thing to do. Just because he wanted be a hero was no reason for you to take such a risk.'

'We would've been okay,' Doug insisted, 'if the hopper hadn't broken down.'

'Sure.'

'Well, anyway, I appreciate your coming out to get us. You saved my life.'

Bianca blushed. 'I didn't do much. The radiation was back to normal by then.'

'Still, you must've volunteered. Didn't you?'

'Well . . . yes, I guess I did.'

'And my vidcam,' Doug went on. 'You saved that, too, didn't you? The corporation owes you a lot.'

Her expression changed. 'I didn't do it for the corporation,' Bianca said, so low that Doug could barely hear her.

'Still,' he said, 'you're as much a hero as anybody.'

She shook her head. 'Not really.'

Doug sensed that something had gone slightly off track.

Bianca had been smiling and friendly up to a moment ago, but now she seemed to be almost sad, almost – disappointed.

'Tell me all about it,' he said. 'Tell me exactly what happened.'

'It was all in a rush, you know,' she said, still looking unhappy, almost bitter. 'Kind of confused. Killifer was pretty nervous, really wired tight. He got pissed off because I grabbed his suit by mistake.'

Doug listened as she haltingly told him what they were doing while he and Brennart were stuck underneath the hopper on the mountaintop.

'. . . and when you started mumbling about the Yamagata people, he didn't want to believe you.'

'Killifer?'

'Right. He didn't like the idea of going out again to find them. He didn't like it *a lot*.'

Doug let out a sigh. 'I guess I don't blame him.'

Rhee's face contracted into a puzzled frown. 'And there was something semi-weird, too.'

'Semi-weird?' Doug grinned at her.

'When I got your vidcam, there was another piece of something . . . a flat oblong hunk of ceramic or metal. I don't think it's part of the vidcam. It was all white on one side and gold on the other.'

'Doesn't sound like anything from the vidcam.'

'No. Besides, the vidcam looked intact to me. Maybe it was something Killifer had on him. I was in his suit, remember. Maybe he already had it in his pocket.'

Curious, Doug asked, 'How big was it?'

She shaped it with her hands. 'Oh, just about fifteen centimeters long, I think. Maybe half that wide.'

'White on one side and gold on the other?'

'I took it along with your vidcam, and then left it in my quarters,' Rhee said, looking even more puzzled. 'But it's disappeared.'

'Disappeared?' Doug sat up straighter.

'It was on my bureau yesterday, but now it's gone.'

'Are you sure—'

'Of course I'm sure!' she snapped.

'I didn't mean it that way,' he said. 'Has anybody else been in your quarters?'

Rhee shook her head. But before she could say anything, the door to Doug's cubicle slid back and Joanna stepped through. Even in ordinary blue coveralls she radiated power and decision. Zimmerman waddled in behind her, still in his rumpled three-piece suit with the lab coat thrown over it.

Rhee hopped off the bed. 'I'm glad you feel so well, Doug,' she said. Impulsively, she darted forward and gave Doug a peck on the cheek, then rushed past Joanna and Zimmerman and left the room.

'Who's that?' Joanna demanded.

'The woman who saved my life,' said Doug.

Joanna frowned, while Zimmerman smiled bemusedly.

'Does that give her the right to kiss you?' Joanna asked sharply.

'Oh come on, Mom! It was just a friendly little smack.'

'You don't have to feel obligated to somebody for doing their job,' Joanna said.

Doug laughed lightly. 'Simmer down, Mom. She's just a friend. I hardly even know her, actually.'

Zimmerman eyed him thoughtfully. 'Perhaps the nano-machines enhance your sexual attractiveness, hah?'

Doug frowned at the old man. 'You must be Dr. Zimmerman, right?'

'Yah.' Zimmerman clicked his heels and bowed slightly, his paunch making it difficult to go farther.

'How soon can I get out of here?' Doug asked. 'I feel fine. Terrific, in fact.'

Glancing at the monitors over Doug's bed, Zimmerman said, 'Another few hours. There are some tests I must do. Then you get out of bed and I leave this glorified cave and return to civilization.'

Joanna paced over to the other side of the bed. 'Do you really feel fine?'

'Like I said, terrific. Really.'

His mother looked across the bed at Zimmerman. Doug saw tears in her eyes. 'You've saved him.'

The sloppy old man shrugged, suddenly too embarrassed to say anything.

And Doug realized the enormity of what had happened to him. I would have died, he told himself. Under any normal circumstances I would be dead now.

He looked at Zimmerman with different eyes and saw a man of strength and vigor and the kind of passion that dares to challenge anyone, everyone who stands in the way between him and his life's work. Governments had outlawed nanotherapy. Ignorant mobs had burned nanolabs and killed researchers. But Zimmerman plugged doggedly ahead, despite all of that. Doug understood that even a fat old man can be heroic.

'You've given me life,' Doug said.

'No,' Zimmerman said, shaking his head slowly. 'Your mother gave you life. I have merely helped you to keep it. And perhaps prolong it.'

'If there's anything we can do,' Joanna said stiffly, 'you only have to name it.'

'I have already informed you of my price, Madam.'

Joanna's expression hardened. 'Yes, you have, haven't you?'

'What I have already gained will be payment enough. Plus transportation back to Basel, of course.'

'Of course,' said Joanna. She was positively glaring at the old man now.

Doug realized that their conversation, back and forth across his bed, dealt with things he didn't know about.

'What's the price?' he asked. 'What are you two talking about?'

Joanna tore her gaze from Zimmerman and looked down at her son: so young, so innocent and unknowing.

'She is referring, young man, to the fact that you will not be allowed to leave the Moon.'

'For how long?' Doug asked.

'Forever,' blurted Joanna.

'You are a walking nanomachine factory now,' said Zimmerman. 'No nation on Earth will allow you entry.'

Doug turned from Zimmerman, who looked gravely concerned, to his mother, who looked angry and fearful and almost tearfully sad.

'Is that all?' he asked. 'I have to stay here on the Moon? That's what I wanted to do anyway.'

It was supposed to be Jinny Anson's going-away party. And it was supposed to be a surprise. But when Anson stepped into the darkened biolab, led by the hand by Lev Brudnoy, and they snapped on the lights and everybody yelled, 'Surprise!' Anson took it all in her stride.

'You are not surprised,' Brudnoy said, disappointed, as well-wishers pressed drinks into their hands.

Anson fixed him with a look. 'What kind of a base director would I be if I didn't know what you guys were plotting?'

'Ah,' said Brudnoy. 'Of course.'

She was surprised, though, when a dozen of the women started handing her wedding presents. Little things, made at Moonbase of lunar raw materials or cast-off equipment. A digital clock set to Universal Mean Time that told when lunar sunrise and sunset would be. A hotplate of cermet salvaged from a junked lander. A vial of lunar glass filled with regolith sand.

Halfway through the wedding gifts, Jack Killifer showed up and the party quickly centered around the new hero. Just as Anson had predicted, the women clustered around Jack, who had shaved and showered and put on a crisp new jumpsuit for the party.

Even as she continued to unwrap presents, Anson scanned the growing crowd for the astronomer, Rhee. No sign of her. Busted romance? she wondered. Or is the kid too shy to come to the party? She sneaks off every now and then. I thought she just wanted to be alone, but maybe she's already got a boyfriend tucked away someplace.

Not likely, Anson thought. Rhee's not much of a looker and she's too timid to go out and grab a guy for herself.

One of the lab benches had been turned into a bar. Anson wondered if the illicit still had been stashed in this lab all along; certainly they had all the right equipment for it, plumbing and glassware and enough chemical stores to plaster the whole base. The noise level climbed steadily: people talking at the top of their lungs, laughing, drinking. And then somebody turned on a music disk. The display screens along the walls all began to flash psychedelic colors and the lab quivered under the heavy thumping beat and sharp bleating whine of an adenoidal singer.

Couples paired off for dancing. Killifer seemed to be having the time of his life. Anson staggered away from the ear-splitting music, out into the tunnel where the party had spilled over.

Brudnoy was sitting on the floor with half a dozen others. Anson put her back to the wall and let herself slide down to a sitting position, careful not to spill a drop of her beaker of booze.

'You are not reigning at your own party?' Brudnoy asked. Even out here in the tunnel he had to half-shout to be heard over the music.

'Everybody's having a great time,' she said.

'Are you?'

'Sure.'

'Truly?'

'Yes, of course.'

Brudnoy looked at her with his sad, bleary eyes. 'I think you will miss us.'

'Of course I'll miss you.'

'Will your husband come up here with you?' Brudnoy asked.

Anson shook her head. 'I'm not coming back, Lev. I told you that. I'm starting a new life.'

'In Texas.'

'Just outside of Austin, actually,' she said, straining her throat to get the words out over the party noise. 'In the hill country.'

'The land of enchantment, they say.'

'That's New Mexico.'

'Oh.'

'But the Texas hill country is beautiful. Air you can breathe. Mountains and valleys and land that goes on forever. Flowers! When the bluebonnets bloom it's gorgeous. And a blue sky with white clouds. Clean and wonderful.'

'Not like Moonbase.'

'Not at all like Moonbase.'

'And you really want to leave all this behind you?' Brudnoy made a sweep with his arm.

Anson knew he was kidding. Half kidding, at least. That sweep of his arm took in not merely this crowded underground warren of labs and workshops and cramped undersized living quarters. It took in the ancient ringwall mountains and the cracked crater floor, the vast tracts of Mare Nubium and the Ocean of Storms, the slow beauty of a lunar sunrise and the way the regolith sparkled when the sunshine first hits it, the sheer breathtaking wonder of standing on this airless world and planting your bootprints where no one had ever stood before, the excitement of building a new world, even that crazy mountain down at the south pole that's always in sunshine.

She pulled in a deep breath. 'Yes, I'm really going to leave all this behind me. I'll miss you guys, but I've made up my mind.'

Anson was surprised that she had to force the words past a good-sized lump in her throat.

Doug found that he could not lie idly waiting for the medics to start their tests. He asked for a computer and, once the technician on duty wheeled a laptop machine to his bed on a swing-arm table, he searched through the literature program for something to read.

Nothing appealed to him. In the back of his mind a question simmered, making him restless with pent-up curiosity. An oblong piece of ceramic or metal, about fifteen centimeters long and half as wide, gold on one side and white on the other.

There must be an inventory program, Doug told himself. He started searching the computer files for it.

BIOLAB

The party was winding down. Jinny Anson had gone back inside the biolab, Lev Brudnoy at her side. Only about a dozen and a half people remained, most of them paired off into couples. The music had gone softly romantic, dancers held each other in their arms as they shuffled slowly across the cleared space behind the lab benches.

As Anson tipped over the big cooler of fruit punch to get its last dregs into her plastic cup, Greg Masterson showed up at the door, looking somber as usual. Anson frowned inwardly. He's going to have to unwind if he expects to make it as director up here. Otherwise he's going to have a mutiny on his hands.

She giggled to herself. Captain Bligh, she thought. Who would be Fletcher Christian and lead the mutineers?

Brudnoy saw Greg, too, and made his way past the dancers and the lab benches toward him. Jinny followed the Russian, drink in hand, feeling a little annoyed. Greg's a wet blanket, he's going to rain on my parade, she thought, mixing metaphors in her slightly inebriated condition.

'Better late than never,' said the Russian, smiling.

Greg's face remained somber. 'Is my brother here?'

'Your brother?' Anson asked. 'I thought he was in the infirmary.'

'He was. He just disconnected all his monitors and walked out.'

Anson glanced at Brudnoy, who looked as puzzled as she felt. 'He hasn't shown up here.'

Greg's frown deepened. 'He's got to be someplace.'

'Want to call security?'

'No,' Greg said. 'I don't want to get my mother upset. She's asleep, but—'

'We can search for him,' Brudnoy volunteered. 'After all, this place isn't so big that he can hide from us.'

'Why would he want to hide?' Anson wondered.

'Where the hell is he?' Greg growled.

Doug was prowling the tunnel that led to Jack Killifer's quarters. He had put aside his search of the computer's inventory program when the medics came in to run their infernal tests. After they left, he booted up the program again and found what he'd been looking for.

The cermet piece that Bianca Rhee had described was a cover for a hopper's electronics bay. The electronics bay held, among other items, the electrical controls for the main engine's liquid oxygen pump.

Doug's mind had leaped from one point to the next. Remove the cover and the electronics systems are exposed directly to the radiation from the solar flare. Knock out the rocket engine's propellant pump and the engine can't ignite. A dead engine keeps the hopper on the mountaintop, where the radiation will build up to a lethal level in a couple of hours or less.

He killed Brennart! And he damned near killed me. Once Doug was convinced of that, he pulled off his monitor leads, bolted out of bed and ran out of the infirmary in nothing but his flapping pale blue hospital gown.

Killifer kept the cover in his spacesuit pocket, Doug reasoned as he trotted down the nearly-empty tunnel. It was past midnight, the lighting was turned down to its late-night level. Still, the few people he passed in the tunnel stared at Doug in his loose gown and bare feet.

Bianca found the piece and thought it might have something to do with my vidcam. She kept it in her quarters and Killifer went in there and took it back. Good thing she wasn't there when he broke in; he might have killed her, too.

There it is. Doug saw J. KILLIFER stencilled on the name card beside the accordion-pleat door. He banged on the door frame and called Killifer's name. No answer. Either he's sound

asleep or he's not in. Doug pulled on the door handle. Locked.
He braced one bare foot on the door jamb and pulled hard.
The flimsy catch gave way and the door jerked open, nearly
toppling him.

Doug padded into Killifer's quarters. Empty. The bunk was
a mess, hadn't been made in days, from the looks of it. The
place smelled of unwashed clothes and sweat. Doug closed
the door as far as it would go. He's got to come back here
sooner or later. I'll wait.

He didn't want to sit on the grubby tangle of the bed.
There was a slim molded plastic chair at the room's desk.
When Doug sat on it he realized that his hospital gown left
a lot to be desired. The chair felt cold and sticky on his
partly-bare rump.

He jumped up and went to Killifer's closet. Two clean pairs
of olive green coveralls hung limply there, but once Doug held
them up against his own frame he realized how small Killifer
really was. No wonder Bianca took his spacesuit by mistake;
he's not much bigger than she is.

So he waited for Killifer in his loose hospital gown, pacing
up and down the tiny room in four strides. Suddenly an idea
struck him. The cermet cover must be here someplace, hidden
in this room. Doug started to search through the drawers of
Killifer's desk.

It was the best night Jack Killifer had ever had on the Moon.
There's something to this hero business, after all, he laughed
to himself as he headed back toward his quarters, weaving
slightly along the tunnel.

The party had been great fun, and just like Jinny had said,
there were several women falling all over him. He danced with
them all, then picked the one who had snuggled the closest
and walked her back to her quarters. Sure enough, she made
no objection when he stepped into her place with her and as
soon as he slid the door shut she was unzipping her jumpsuit
for him.

When he left her quarters, Killifer thought briefly about
heading back to the party, see who's still there, maybe go for

a double-header. But as he started along the tunnel to the biolab
he ran into Jinny and Lev Brudnoy and Greg Masterson.

'Have you seen Doug Stavenger?' Jinny asked him, very
serious and concerned.

'Little Douggie?' Killifer wanted to laugh but held it in.
'He's in the infirmary.'

'No he's not,' snapped Greg. He showed no recognition of
Killifer whatsoever. They hadn't seen each other in more than
eighteen years, but Killifer recognized Greg instantly.

'We're trying to find him,' said Brudnoy, also looking so
damned sober.

Killifer ignored Greg. He wants to be a stranger, fuck him.
Suddenly it all seemed awfully funny: little Douggie out on
the loose. Maybe he'll fall down and break his neck. But
he made a serious face and shook his head gravely. 'Nope.
Haven't seen him.'

They hurried on past him. Killifer stood in the tunnel,
blinking with thought. Douggie's not in the infirmary. They
lost their little Douggie.

Then a thought hit him hard enough to snap him into
sobriety. The cover! Suppose the little sonofabitch has figured
it all out and he's looking for the cover. I'd better hide it,
and quick.

He started running down the dimly-lit tunnel toward his
quarters.

Doug almost laughed at the pathetic stupidity of it. Under
the mattress. Killifer had hidden the cermet cover beneath his
mattress.

Maybe it wasn't so dumb after all, Doug thought. It had
taken a real effort of will to work up the strength to touch
Killifer's roiled, sweaty bunk.

Doug held the cover in his hands. The murder weapon. He
stepped over to the desk and placed it down on its surface,
gold side up.

And the door flew open.

Killifer's eyes were so wide Doug could see white all the
way around the irises. The man stared at Doug, then his

eyes flicked to the gold-plated cermet cover, then back to Doug again.

'Why did you want to kill Brennart?' Doug asked quietly. 'Or was it me you were after?'

Killifer slid the door shut behind him. 'It was you. Brennart—' he shrugged. 'Couldn't be helped.'

'Couldn't . . . be . . . helped.' For the first time in his life Doug felt real anger, a fury that threatened to shatter his self-control.

'He wanted to be a big-ass hero, now he is one,' Killifer said. 'So what?'

Before he knew what he was doing, Doug lashed out with a stinging left that snapped Killifer's head back and a hard straight right, blurringly fast. Killifer slammed back against the rock wall and crumpled to the floor, blood gushing from his nose.

Doug bent down and grabbed the front of his coveralls. Yanking Killifer to his feet, Doug cocked his right fist again.

And stopped. Killifer made no move to protect himself. His arms hung limply at his sides. Blood streamed down his chin, spattering his coveralls and Doug's hand, still gripping the coverall front.

Doug pushed him onto the bunk.

'Why?' he demanded. 'Why did you do it? Why did you want to kill me?'

'Because you killed me, you snotty sonofabitch.'

'Me? I never even saw you until ten days ago.'

'Your mother,' Killifer snarled. 'She killed me. She took away everything I ever had. She exiled me to this goddamned cavern in the sky.'

'I know that,' Doug said. 'But why? Why would she do that? What did you do to make her hate you so much?'

Killifer stared at him, wiping at his bloody nose. Slowly a crooked smile worked its way across his face.

'You don't know, do you?' he asked, grinning at Doug. 'You really don't know.'

All of a sudden Doug felt slightly ridiculous, standing over this beaten smaller man in a dangling hospital gown that barely covered him.

Killifer was cackling with laughter. 'You don't know! You don't know a friggin' thing about it! She never told you, did she?'

'Never told me what?'

'About your brother! She never told you what your brother did!'

'Greg?' Doug felt suddenly uneasy, as if he were teetering on the edge of a tremendous precipice. 'What's Greg got to do with this?'

'He killed your old man!' Killifer roared. 'He murdered your father, kid.'

'That's a lie,' Doug snapped.

'The hell it is. Your brother salted the nanomachines your father was using. The nanos didn't malfunction. They did exactly what they were programmed to do.'

Inwardly Doug was falling off that precipice, dropping like a stone into the darkness. He heard his own voice, hollow with shock, 'They were programmed to destroy the spacesuits?'

'Yeah. Your brother asked me for a sample of nanobugs that could eat carbon-based molecules. I didn't know what the fuck he wanted 'em for, but he was big shit with the corporation so I gave him what he wanted.'

'You gave him—'

'Gave him the bugs that killed your old man, that's right. Nobody else knew. Just your big brother Greg and me. But your mother figured it out and shipped me up here.'

Feeling his legs trembling, Doug pulled up the plastic chair and sat on it. Hard. 'But why would she send you here to Moonbase?'

'To get me outta the way, wise ass! She didn't want me where I might rat out her son.'

'Greg.'

'That's right.'

'Greg murdered my father and you helped him.'

'Hey, I didn't know what he wanted the friggin' bugs for. Not until after it happened.'

'You were just following orders,' Doug muttered.

'Right.'

For what seemed like hours Doug sat there, running the story around in his head, over and over again. Mom protected Greg. She knew he'd killed my father and she protected him. And she never told me.

Never told me.

Never told me.

'So, whatcha gonna do now, kid?' Killifer taunted. 'Beat the crap outta me? Kill me?'

Slowly Doug got to his feet. Killifer cringed back on the bunk, his bravado suddenly evaporated.

'Get out of here,' Doug said quietly.

'What?'

'Get off the Moon. Quit Masterson Corporation. Take early retirement and go back to Earth.'

'And if I don't want to . . . ?'

Doug looked down at him. 'If I see you here after tomorrow I'll kill you.'

From the look in Killifer's eyes, Doug knew the man believed him.

ALPHONSUS

Doug walked alone across the floor of the giant crater, his boots stirring clouds of dust that settled languidly in the gentle lunar gravity.

He had lost track of time. For hours now the universe had narrowed down to his spacesuit, the sound of his own breathing, the air fans softly whirring, the bleak cracked, pitted ground. He passed the rocket port, where an ungainly transfer ship sat on one of the blast-scarred pads, waiting for tomorrow's launch Earthward. Past the solar farms he walked, where nanomachines were patiently converting regolith silicon and trace metals into spreading acres of solar panels that drank in sunlight and produced electricity. Off in the distance he could barely make out the dark bulk of the half-finished mass driver, a low dark shadow against the horizon.

Turning, he looked through the visor of his helmet up at the worn, rounded mountains that ringed the crater floor. Mount Yeager, he saw. And the notch in the ringwall near it that everybody called Wodjohowitcz Pass.

My father died up there. Greg murdered him and my mother covered it up, kept it even from me. Protected him, protected my father's murderer. My half-brother. Her son. He's just as much her son as I am and he murdered my father. And got away with it.

'Doug? Is that you?'

The voice in his earphones startled him. He would have turned the suit radio off, but the safety people had fixed all the suits so that you couldn't.

A small tractor was approaching him, kicking up a plume

of dust that looked almost silvery in the sunlight. Must be the safety guys, Doug thought. I guess I've wandered too far out for them. Broke a rule.

'Doug, are you all right?'

He realized it was Bianca Rhee's voice.

'I'm okay,' he answered as the tractor approached him. Sort of, he added silently.

He stood there as the tractor pulled up and stopped in a billow of dream-slow swirling dust.

'Where've you been?' Rhee asked, stepping down from the tractor. It was a two-seat machine with a flat bed for cargo: the lunar equivalent of a pickup truck.

'I needed some time by myself,' he said.

'Oh! I'm interrupting—'

'No, it's okay. I was just about to start back anyway.'

'Everybody's looking for you. Your mother's just about to roast the infirmary staff under a rocket nozzle for letting you walk off like that.'

Doug looked at Rhee's stubby, spacesuited figure and felt glad that their helmet visors hid their faces. He did not want anyone to see his expression right at this moment. Nothing but an impersonal, faceless figure encased in protective plastic, metal and fabric.

'How'd you find me?' he asked.

'I like to be by myself sometimes, too.'

'And you come out here?'

'No . . .' Her voice faltered. 'I, uh, I find some cubbyhole where I'm alone and I . . . dance.'

'Dance? By yourself?'

'Ballet,' Rhee said, her voice so low Doug could hardly hear her. 'You know, with an orchestra disk.'

'Ballet,' said Doug. 'Sure! Here on the Moon it must be terrific.'

'I'm not very good, even in low gravity.'

'How do you know, if you don't let anybody see you?'

'Every time I fall down, I know!'

Doug didn't laugh. He could tell from the tone of her voice that this was very precious to Rhee.

Softly, he said, 'I hope you'll let me see you dance sometime, Bianca.'

He waited for her reply, but she said nothing. So he said, 'You're the only one in the whole base smart enough to find me.'

'I checked with the airlock monitors,' she said, sounding relieved. 'They keep a record of everybody who goes out.'

'And comes in,' Doug added. The crew monitoring the main airlock didn't know that Doug was supposed to be in the infirmary. They had allowed him outside after only a cursory check of the computerized files.

'You must be feeling awfully good to come out here,' Rhee said cheerfully, clambering back up to the driver's seat.

And Doug realized, She must feel awfully strong about me to come out looking for me. It can't be impersonal, after all. It never is.

'Bianca,' he asked as he climbed up into the tractor beside her, 'how long are you going to be here at Moonbase?'

'My tour's over at the end of the month. That's when the new semester starts.'

'Well,' Doug said carefully, 'we've got a couple of weeks to get acquainted, then.'

He could hear her breath catch, over the suit radio. Then she said, 'That'd be fine.'

I can't tell her anything, Doug knew, but at least I can have a friend to unwind with. Somebody to help keep me sane.

'Uh . . .' How to say it without hurting her feelings? 'You know, it's good to have a friend here. I really don't know anyone else in Moonbase.'

'There's Killifer,' she said lightly.

'He's leaving tomorrow.'

'Really?' She sounded completely surprised.

'Really.'

'Well, your brother's here now, isn't he?'

'Half brother.' Doug felt his insides clench. 'And I hardly know him. He's always . . . we've never been close.'

He heard her chuckling. 'What's so funny?'

'Oh, I was just thinking about some of the other women here. They'll be green with envy.'

'Bianca, it isn't going to be like that.'

'They'll say I'm robbing the cradle,' she went on, happily ignoring him. 'After all, I'm almost five years older than you.'

Doug shook his head inside the helmet. 'I've aged a lot since coming to Moonbase,' he said. And he hoped that he could keep her as a friend without crushing her dreams.

'You never told me about Greg.'

Doug could see the sudden alarm in his mother's eyes. They were having dinner together in the suite Anson had turned over to Joanna: a sparse microwaved meal of bland precooked veal that Joanna had commandeered from the stores at The Cave.

'What about Greg?' she asked, from across the round table that Anson had used for conferences in her office.

Despite the roaring emotions blazing in him, Doug still had an appetite. He chewed carefully on a thin slice of veal while his mother watched him, waiting.

Doug put his fork down and said, 'Greg murdered my father.'

She did not look surprised. Only tired. Suddenly his mother looked utterly weary.

'He did, didn't he?' Doug asked, keeping his voice low, not screaming out the accusation the way he wanted to.

'He was terribly sick,' Joanna said. 'He didn't really understand—'

'Don't lie for him,' Doug snapped. 'He killed my father. Killifer helped him. I know the whole story.'

'The whole story? Do you? Do you know what kind of childhood Greg had? How abusive his father was to both of us? Do you know how hard he's struggled over these past eighteen years to atone for what he did?'

'Atone?'

'Greg's gone through hell and purgatory to overcome the feelings that led him to . . . to—'

'Murder,' Doug said, uncompromising.

Tears were glimmering in Joanna's eyes but she fought them back. 'That's right, murder. He killed your father. My husband. The man I loved.'

'The father I never knew.'

'*I* knew him. I loved your father.'

Doug saw what she wanted to say. 'But you loved Greg, too. You couldn't let your son be arrested for murder.'

'He was so sick,' Joanna said, suddenly pleading. 'Don't you understand, he would never have done anything like that if he'd been well. He was in torment every day of his life.'

'So you helped him.'

'I protected him. I got him the best medical help on Earth. He worked, Douglas. He went through hell—'

'And purgatory.'

She shook her head. 'You just don't know. How could you? For years and years and years Greg struggled and worked to overcome his feelings. He's accomplished so much! He's come so far.'

'He's come to the Moon.'

'He's your brother,' Joanna said.

'Half brother.'

'You're both my sons. I love you both. I don't want you to hate him. That's why I never told you.'

'Didn't you think I'd find out one day?'

Joanna waved one hand in the air, still clutching her fork. 'One day, yes. Some day. But I didn't think it would happen so soon.'

'Is that why you kept us apart all these years? Because you were afraid I'd find out?'

'I don't know,' Joanna said. 'No, I don't think so. At first, when you were an infant, I worried that Greg might be jealous of you. He was in heavy therapy then and I felt it was best to keep him away from you. Later . . .' Her voice died away; she seemed lost in the past.

'I've told Killifer to resign and take early retirement,' said Doug flatly.

'All right. Fine.'

'What are you going to do about Greg?'

She looked at him sharply. 'What do you mean?'

'I'm stuck here at Moonbase indefinitely. Greg's the new base director.'

'I can't send Greg back to Earth. It would look as if I had fired him as director before he even started.'

Doug spread his hands. 'So we're going to be here together then.'

From the expression on her face it seemed to Doug that his mother hadn't thought about it before. She was silent for long moments.

'You're right,' she said at last. 'I'll have to stay here, too.'

'You?'

Nodding as if she had made up her mind irrevocably, Joanna said, 'I'll resign as chair of the board of directors and live here. For the coming year, at least.'

Doug stared at her and saw the determination in her eyes. 'To keep between Greg and me.'

'To bring the two of you together,' Joanna said, almost desperately. 'I love you both and I don't want you to hate each other.'

'You're asking a lot.'

'Don't you see, Doug? It was my fault, too. I'm his mother. Whatever Greg's done, I bear a responsibility for it.'

'You didn't murder anybody.'

'But I didn't stop him from doing it! I didn't raise him well enough to keep him from murder.'

'That's like blaming Hitler's mother for the Holocaust,' Doug snapped.

'I didn't pay enough attention to him. And when I met your father – how betrayed Greg must have felt.'

'The criminal as victim,' Doug muttered.

Joanna pointed at him with the fork. 'Douglas, if you hate your brother for what he did, you'll also be hating me. He's my son, as much as you are, and what he did is my fault, too.'

Doug felt drained, exhausted, almost the way he had felt up at the mountaintop with Brennart. *My father, Brennart, even Zimmerman's leaving me. I can't lose her too; I can't drive*

my mother away from me. She wants to live up here, to be
with me. And Greg, too, but still . . .

With a slow shake of his head, Doug replied, 'I don't hate
Greg.' He hoped it was true.

'Do you mean it?' his mother asked.

'It's just – all this is new to me. I never thought—'

Joanna got her feet and came around the table to sit at the
empty chair beside him.

'I love you, Douglas. I don't want to lose you. You and
Greg are the only people in the world I care about.'

'I know,' he said. And he let her put her arms around him
and hold him close. It felt awkward for a moment, but then
he melted into his mother's embrace and it felt warm and safe
and soothing.

Joanna could feel the tension between her two sons, crackling
like an electrical spark between two electrodes of opposite
polarity.

The three of them were standing in Anson's former office.
Now it was Greg's office. Joanna had moved into her own
quarters.

It had been a long day. They had seen Anson off and
Greg had formally taken the directorship of Moonbase. Now,
the little cluster of people who had crowded the office to
congratulate their new boss had left. Greg stood behind his
desk, Joanna at his side, Doug in front of the desk.

Even in the sky-blue coveralls that designated management,
Greg looked darkly somber. Doug, wearing the pumpkin
orange of the research and exploration group, seemed as
bright and youthful as a freshly-scrubbed cadet. Joanna wore a
flowered dress, insisting that she would not limit her wardrobe
to the utilitarian jumpsuits that everyone else wore.

Doug smiled at his half-brother and put his hand out over
the desk.

'I haven't had a chance to congratulate you, Greg,' he said.
'Best of luck as director.'

Greg took his hand and smiled back. 'Thanks.'

'And I want you to know,' Doug said as their hands

separated, 'that I understand what happened . . . about my father.'

Greg turned his startled gaze to Joanna.

'She didn't tell me. Killifer did.'

'Killifer?'

'He left Moonbase a couple days ago. It's all over with. Finished.'

'Is it?' Greg asked. 'Just like that, you find out about your father's death and you don't *care?*'

Doug looked toward Joanna, too, then turned back to his brother. 'I care, Greg. But it's all . . . kind of abstract. I never knew my father. He died before I was born. Maybe I ought to be angry, furious – but I can't seem to work up the emotion.'

Greg just stared at him.

'It's all in the past,' Doug said. 'I don't like it, but then I guess you don't either.'

With a quick glance at his mother, Greg said, 'No, I'm not happy about the past.'

'Then let's make the future something we can both be happy about. All of us,' he quickly amended.

'Okay,' Greg said guardedly. 'Sounds good.'

Doug caught the slight but definite stress on the word *sounds*.

'What do you have in mind?' Joanna asked.

Doug shrugged indifferently. 'I've got a lot of learning to do. I'm signed up with the research and exploration group. We'll be going back to Mt. Wasser and building the power tower.'

Greg cleared his throat and said, 'Yes, I've got the mission plan on my list of action items. Top priority.'

'I hope you approve it,' said Doug.

'Don't worry about it,' Greg replied.

Joanna watched her two sons, thinking, Maybe they can work together. Maybe they'll learn to trust one another and become as close as brothers. But I'll have to watch them. Closely. For a long time to come.

'Once we get the water flowing back here,' Doug was

saying, 'we can start thinking about expanding the base, turning it into a really livable town.'

Greg said nothing. He was thinking, Doug knows! He knows what I did. He says he doesn't care, he says it's all in the past, but he hates me. He'll do whatever he can to destroy me. He's already challenging me. He'll want to keep Moonbase open. He'll want to be director, sooner or later. Sooner, most likely. I'll have to keep a couple of jumps ahead of him. I'll have to make certain that Mom doesn't give him unfair advantages.

I'll have to make certain that Moonbase is shut down for good. When I leave here, Moonbase will be history.

PART III:

Legacy

MANHATTAN

It was more like a comfortable little lounge than a confer-ence room, thought Carlos Quintana. Richly appointed and furnished with quiet, understated elegance. These diplomats do all right for themselves, he reminded himself.

The Secretary-General gestured him to sit beside her on the bottle green leather sofa. Quintana had known the woman since before she had been Ecuador's ambassador to the U.N., back when she had been a shy and frightened newcomer to the world of international politics.

She introduced him to the acting president of the Security Council and the chairwoman of the General Assembly, a comely African whose skin glowed like burnished ebony. The Security Council president was from Bangladesh, one of the poorest nations on Earth, yet he was quite overweight and his thick fingers were heavy with jewelled rings.

Nothing is done swiftly among diplomats, Quintana already knew. The four of them had a drink, chatted amiably, and only gradually got down to the reason for which the meeting had been arranged.

'Yes,' Quintana said quietly, once he had been asked, 'I am a beneficiary of nanotherapy. I had lung cancer. Now it is gone.'

'You had the therapy illegally?' asked the General Assembly chairwoman.

Quintana smiled. 'It is a gray area. Nanotherapy is illegal in many nations, including Mexico. But in Switzerland appar-ently the authorities allow it to continue.'

'Not for Swiss citizens, however,' said the Security Council president, who had been a lawyer. He had rolls of fat instead of a neck, the glistening skin of his round face seemed stretched tight like an overinflated balloon.

'But you did it anyway,' said the Secretary-General.

Still smiling, Quintana said, 'It seemed better than surgery or radiation treatments.'

'Or chemotherapy.'

'Or death,' Quintana added wryly.

For a moment they were silent. Then the Secretary-General smoothed her skirt and said, 'So you are a supporter of nanotechnology, then.'

'Yes. Very much.'

'And you would speak against the current treaty being negotiated?'

'To outlaw all nanotechnology research? Yes, I am against it.'

'Would you speak publicly against it?'

'If I must.'

'Wouldn't that involve some element of danger for you, personally?'

Quintana shrugged. 'There is always the chance of some fanatic. I can hire bodyguards.'

The Security Council president cleared his throat ostentatiously. All eyes turned to him.

'Isn't it true,' he asked, in an accusing voice, 'that you are a member of the board of directors of Masterson Aerospace Corporation?'

'That's no secret,' Quintana said evenly.

'And isn't it true that Masterson Corporation will suffer greatly if all nanotechnology work is prohibited?'

Quintana nodded. 'It would mean the end of their base on the Moon. They could not survive up there without nanomachines to process oxygen for them and maintain their solar power farms.'

'It is also true, is it not,' the president continued, 'that your corporation stands to make indecently enormous profits from nanotechnology manufacturing.'

'If we manufacture any salable products with nanomachines,

the manufacturing will most likely be done in space, not on Earth.'

'The *profits* will be made on Earth.'

'Yes, certainly.'

'So you are not exactly unbiased in this matter.'

Quintana put his glass down on the marble-topped coffee table. 'I am a living example of what nanotherapy can accomplish. As you can see, I am not a monster and the nanomachines that were put into my body have done me nothing but good.'

'But—'

'But nanotechnology can do more than heal the sick, that is true,' Quintana went on. 'Nanomanufacturing can bring a new era of prosperity to Earth. I should think that nations such as Bangladesh and Zaire would welcome such an opportunity.'

'At the cost of ruining our existing industries!'

Quintana laughed disdainfully. 'Your existing industries are keeping your people poor. If I were you, sir, I would embrace nanotechnology instead of trying to outlaw it.'

The president said nothing. Silence hung in the elegant little room for many heavy moments.

At length, the Secretary-General said, 'Thank you for sharing your views with us, Carlos.'

Knowing he was being dismissed, Quintana got to his feet, bowed slightly to her. 'Thank you for inviting me.'

He got as far as the door, then turned back to them. 'Take my advice. Don't fight nanotechnology. The best thing you could do, right now, would be to buy Masterson stock.'

And, laughing, he left the three of them sitting there.

He was still smiling as he stepped out of the elevator at the U.N. complex's underground garage level. He walked to the dispatcher and asked him to call his limousine.

As he lit up a thin cigar, a man in grimy coveralls stepped up to him and pushed the muzzle of a nine-millimeter automatic into Quintana's midsection.

'Antichrist,' he snarled. And he emptied the gun's magazine into Quintana's midriff and chest, smashing him back against the dispatcher's booth. The shots rang deafeningly through the garage.

Quintana felt no pain, but the world seemed to tilt into a crazy lopsided scene of concrete ceiling and staring faces. The man with the gun stood calmly over him.

'Let's see your devil's bugs cure you of *that*.' And he spat on Quintana's shattered, bleeding body.

MOONBASE DIRECTOR'S OFFICE

'This nanotech treaty has got to be stopped!' Joanna said.

Greg nodded tightly. He had been director of Moonbase for slightly more than six months. What had been Jinny Anson's office was now his, and he had transformed it considerably. His desk was an ultramodern curved surface of gleaming lunar glassteel, a new alloy from Moonbase's labs that was as transparent as crystal yet had the structural strength of high-grade concrete. A long couch of lunar plastic sat against one wall and comfortable webbed chairs were scattered across the floor, which was covered with soft, sound-absorbing tiles manufactured in one of Masterson Corporation's space station factories in orbit around Earth.

The air in the room was pleasantly cool, like an air-conditioned office of a major corporation back on Earth. Greg had insisted on paving a large section of Alphonsus' floor with new radiators that allowed the environmental control system to work more efficiently and made all of Moonbase's underground facilities much more comfortable. It was his major accomplishment, to date.

The office walls were lined with precisely spaced Windowall display screens. Most of them showed artwork from the world's great museums, although Greg could, at the touch of a keypad, turn them into views of virtually any part of Moonbase or the surface of Alphonsus' crater floor.

Behind Greg was a giant Windowall that presently showed a restful silk scroll landscape of mountains and mist by the thirteenth-century Chinese master Kao K'o-Kung. It lent the office an air of serenity that neither Joanna nor her two sons felt.

'Will the United States sign the treaty?' Doug asked, from his seat on the couch against the far wall.

Joanna, sitting on the webbed chair closest to Greg's curved desk, had noticed that Doug always picked that couch to sit on. It was farthest from his brother.

'Yes, of course they will,' Greg said, frowning darkly. 'The whole idea of the treaty came from Washington.'

'But they *can't* outlaw nanotechnology completely,' Joanna said. 'Not entirely.'

'Yes they can,' said Doug. Joanna knew he was just as concerned as his older brother, yet Doug looked at ease, relaxed, lounging back in the long couch as if this were nothing more than a computer game. She almost expected him to put his feet up and stretch out for a nap.

'But if they do, they'll want us to stop using nanomachines here at Moonbase, too. We can't allow that.'

Greg shook his head. 'If and when the U.S. signs the treaty, its provisions will be like federal law. And we'll be bound by them just like any flatlander down Earthside.'

'You'll have to stop work on the mass driver,' Joanna said.

With a tight nod, Greg said, 'We'll have to stop everything that we use nanomachines for.'

'That means closing Moonbase,' she said.

Greg started to nod but Doug interrupted with, 'As long as we remain an American corporation.'

'I've thought about that,' Joanna said. 'But Venezuela, Ecuador, all the European nations – they're all going to sign the treaty.'

'What about Kiribati?'

Greg looked sharply at his brother. 'Kiribati?'

'Don't you have enough clout with them to keep them from signing, Greg?' Doug asked.

'What good would that do?' Greg almost growled the words.

Joanna turned to her elder son hopefully. 'We could transfer our articles of incorporation to Kiribati.'

Greg shook his head dismissively. 'And get half a dozen federal agencies jumping all over us. They'd take us to court and the courts would decide against us. We'd be in real trouble. They'd send federal marshals up here to shut down all our nanomachines.'

Doug still looked strangely unperturbed. 'Suppose we start up a new corporation,' he suggested. 'In Kiribati. And Masterson sells the Moonbase operation to them.'

Greg's somber face paled. 'Sell Moonbase to them?'

Doug was grinning now. 'Sure. Moonbase and all our Earth-orbital stations.'

'All the corporation's space operations?'

'That could work,' said Joanna.

'It's an obvious attempt to circumvent the treaty,' said Greg.

'But it's legal,' Doug replied. 'I checked it out with both the federal and international law programs.'

'Did you?' Greg grumbled.

Joanna smiled a little. 'Rashid won't like living in Tarawa, though.'

Doug replied, 'He can stay in Savannah and be in Tarawa with a virtual reality connection any time he wants to. Just the same as you attend board meetings without leaving here, Mom.'

Greg objected, 'The board of directors would never go for it.'

'Setting up a dummy corporation and selling the space division to it,' Joanna mused. 'It *would* take some explaining.'

'It'll never work,' said Greg.

'Why not?' Doug challenged. 'You spent all those years out there in Kiribati. Don't you think you can get them to play along with us?'

'Of course I could, but—'

Joanna interrupted with newfound enthusiasm, 'I'll call Carlos right away.'

'Why not the board chairman?' Doug asked.

Greg answered sourly, 'Because Quintana is the real power on the board – present company excepted, of course.'

'Of course,' Joanna agreed. 'Can you put the call through for me, please?'

Frowning slightly, Greg touched the keyboard built into his desk with one long slim finger and said merely, 'Carlos Quintana.' The comm system's voice recognition circuitry searched automatically for Quintana's number and made the connection.

'Johansen is just a figurehead,' Joanna was explaining to Doug as the communications computer established the link with Savannah. 'He looks good for public relations, but he's—'

The wall screen showing Monet lilypads changed abruptly to display a harried-looking young woman brushing at her dishevelled hair.

'I want to talk to Carlos,' Joanna snapped, unaccustomed to having underlings answer her calls.

'He's dead!' the young woman bawled, bursting into tears. 'He's been shot!'

Joanna fell back against her chair's webbing, feeling almost as if a bullet had hit her heart.

Ibriham al-Rashid felt perspiration beading his brow and upper lip despite the nearly-frigid air conditioning of the small control room.

Beyond that window, he knew, inside that gleaming metal sphere is a small man-made star, so hot and dense that its very atomic nuclei are being fused together.

The plasma physicist tapped him on the shoulder and pointed to the power gauges lining the control room's side wall. Rashid nodded, too awed to speak.

The control room was almost silent. Nothing but the faint electrical hum from the monitoring consoles.

'How long has it been running?' Rashid asked in a whisper. It seemed the proper tone of voice, this close to a miracle.

'Tomorrow will make four months, exactly,' said the plasma physicist. Even he kept his voice hushed.

He was a fellow Moslem, even a fellow native of Baltimore; a man Rashid had known in his youth. Now he was a paunchy overweight academic with thinning hair and a light brown beard and eyes that blinked behind oversized, tinted glasses. Now he was a plasma physicist at Johns Hopkins University who just happened to have invented the world's first practical nuclear fusion generator.

'And it has been producing power like this for all that time?' Rashid whispered.

The plasma physicist nodded. 'As long as we keep it supplied with helium-three.'

Rashid stroked his beard and turned back to stare through the safety glass at the small metal sphere. It was almost hidden inside a maze of magnet coils and cooling pipes and heavy tangles of multi-colored electrical wires. In his imagination, Rashid could see inside the sphere, see the blinding hot plasma that was fusing atomic nuclei together, forcing mass to transmute into energy, imitating the processes that made the stars shine.

By the Prophet, Rashid thought, Allah is offering us a gift beyond price.

But not beyond cost.

The plasma physicist gestured toward the door and, once out in the laboratory's hallway again, Rashid drew a deep breath. 'It really works,' he said, almost in a normal tone.

'It really works,' the plasma physicist echoed. 'And much better – and cheaper – than that monstrosity up in Princeton.'

'But it requires helium-three for fuel, which the Princeton machine does not.'

'The Princeton machine is designed to produce new Ph.D.s,' the plasma physicist grumbled. 'My generator is designed to produce megawatts.'

The plasma physicist led him up the hallway toward his own cluttered office. 'Helium-three and deuterium,' he said. 'The deuterium is easy to get from ordinary water. There's enough deuterium in an eight-ounce drinking glass of water to equal the energy in half a million barrels of oil.'

Rashid smiled wanly. 'Our brothers in OPEC will not be happy with you.'

The plasma physicist shrugged his soft shoulders. 'They're busy building receiving farms for the solar power satellites. The deserts will still be energy centers.'

'But once fusion comes on line . . .'

'It never will.'

'What? Your work—'

They reached his open office door. The room looked just as chaotic as when they had left it, an hour earlier.

'My work may win me a Nobel Prize,' the plasma physicist said, plopping himself in his creaking desk chair, 'although the Princeton people will try to sabotage that.'

Rashid took the only other chair that didn't have piles of journals or reports on it.

'But my fusion system will be nothing but a laboratory curiosity, I'm afraid.'

'Why? How?'

'For two reasons.' The plasma physicist raised two chubby fingers. Rashid noticed that his nails were dirty.

'First,' he said, 'is the matter of the fuel. Helium-three is vanishingly rare. We have to produce it in nuclear accelerators, which makes it cost more than the power that the fusion generator produces.'

'Helium-three exists on the Moon,' Rashid said.

'So I've been told,' said the plasma physicist, as if Rashid had said he could produce helium-three by rubbing a magic lamp. 'But there's a second problem.'

'What is that?'

'Energy conversion.' When he saw the puzzled expression on Rashid's face, the plasma physicist added, 'Converting the heat and particle energy of the fusion reaction to electricity. It's electricity you want, not hot plasma and energetic neutrons.'

His brows knitted, Rashid said, 'But the gauges in your control room; weren't they measuring electrical energy?'

The plasma physicist smiled slyly. 'The gauges are something of a trick. They show how much electrical energy the generator would produce, based on an algorithm I devised from the amount of heat and kinetic energy inside the reactor.'

Rashid felt as if he'd been pushed out of an airplane without a parachute. 'You mean that there's no way for your generator to produce electricity? Then what good is it?'

Raising a single finger this time, the plasma physicist said, 'I invited you here because I think there is a way. Magnetohydrodynamic power conversion is *perfect* for this task.'

'Mag . . . what?'

'Call it MHD,' said the plasma physicist.

'Tell me about MHD, then.'

Hunching over his desk enthusiastically, the plasma physicist began, 'Those dolts up in Princeton and the bigger dolts funding them in Washington, they're all trying to make a conversion system based on turbines. Turbines! Just like Edison did, a century and a half ago.'

'I don't understand,' said Rashid.

Impatiently, the plasma physicist answered, 'They want to use the heat energy from fusion to boil a fluid, probably liquid sodium, Allah protect us. That would keep the overall efficiency of the system down below forty percent; no better than a uranium-fueled generator and not even as good as a coal-fired one!'

Struck with new understanding, Rashid blurted, 'That's why their fusion system is more expensive than ordinary power plants!'

'Yes, exactly. They are using a man-made star as a tea kettle.'

For hours the plasma physicist rattled on, jumping out of his chair to rummage through bookshelves for old reports, grabbing chalk to draw schematic diagrams on his board, making the chalk shriek so often that Rashid winced and felt his blood running cold.

But slowly, Rashid began to see the picture. The fusion generator could produce electrical power with sixty percent efficiency or even better if it could be teamed with an MHD conversion system. And if it could obtain helium-three fuel.

Rashid thanked his boyhood friend and promised him he would carefully consider funding his effort to match an MHD power converter to his fusion generator.

'Keep this as quiet as you can,' his friend pleaded as he walked Rashid out to his waiting limousine. 'I may have to leave the university once they find that I'm being funded by your corporation.'

Rashid raised his brows questioningly.

The plasma physicist smiled unhappily. 'Oh yes, there are lots of knives in the dark here. Even the New Morality people have questioned what I'm doing. They say it's against God's will to try to imitate the stars.'

Rashid snorted disdainfully. 'What do they know of the One God?'

'Believe it or not, there are Moslems among them.'

Shaking his head, Rashid promised that he would keep very quiet about what he had seen and heard.

Once in his plane and heading back to Savannah, Rashid smiled to himself. Very quiet indeed. I could channel some of my discretionary funding to him, to get him started on this MHD business while I begin to prepare the board of directors for a full-scale fusion development program.

Helium-three, he mused. It's imbedded in the lunar regolith, just like the hydrogen atoms they take up to make water. We could set up nanomachines to harvest helium-three and ship it to Earth easily enough. My division could open an entirely new line for the corporation: fusion power systems.

Instead of simply supplying raw lunar materials to the corporations that want to build solar power satellites, we could have a monopoly on the fuel for fusion power.

All the way back to Savannah Rashid dreamed about turning Masterson Aerospace into the world's leading energy company. Fusion power. Enough energy to irrigate the world's deserts, to light the world's cities, to bring the poorest of the poor into the glow of the modern world. All based on helium-three from the Moon. All developed by Masterson Corporation's space operations division. By me.

He pictured himself as president and CEO of Masterson

Aerospace. As the most important and powerful man in America; in the world; in the whole Earth-Moon system.

One small cloud troubled his vision. The helium-three would be produced by nanomachines, and there was enormous resistance to anything touched by nanotechnology. Still, Rashid assured himself, if we have to we can extract the helium-three by older methods. It will raise the price somewhat, but not too much.

He smiled again, satisfied that even the New Morality could not stop his inevitable rise to wealth and fame and power.

Doug left the meeting with Greg and his mother in a turmoil of conflicting emotions. They shot Quintana. Some New Morality fanatic gunned him down at the U.N. building. Because he was against the treaty. Or was it because he was living proof that nanotherapy can cure cancer? Maybe both reasons. Probably both.

As he strode down the tunnel he realized all over again that he could not return to Earth. Even if they let me through customs I'd be a marked man. Every nutcase in the world would come after me.

With a shake of his head, he tried to clear his mind of Quintana's assassination and think through the idea of moving Moonbase's legal ownership to Kiribati. With a half-bitter smile, Doug remembered an economics professor from his first year at Caltech telling the class, 'Figures don't lie, but liars sure can figure.'

Let them make their treaty; we'll find a way around it. Kiribati will have the highest per-capita income on Earth, just from the bribes Mom and Greg will spread around.

We can't let them stop us from using nanomachines here. We can't! It would be like stopping New York City from using elevators. The city would die.

One way or another we've got to keep on using our nanomachines. Otherwise we'll have to shut down Moonbase. And then what about me? They'd have to let me come back Earthside. But if I do I'll be a target for every brain-dead New Morality zealot who can get his hands on a gun.

Doug tried to push that fear out of his mind and concentrate on what had to be done.

For the past six months Doug had worked on the Mt. Wasser power tower project and building the pipeline from the ice fields at the south pole back to Moonbase. Negotiations were under way to sell water to Yamagata's Nippon One and the Euro-Russian base over at Grimaldi.

But Doug knew that the ice fields were limited. He had helped to map them, down in the perpetual shadows of the polar mountains, and to probe their depths. There's enough water there to provide for all three of the bases on the Moon; with recycling, the water should last for decades, maybe half a century, even. But there's not enough to allow us to grow! That's the problem. It's a no-growth solution – which means no solution at all. Moonbase has *got* to grow. Or eventually die. Somehow, we've got to figure out how to get water and the other life-support volatiles we need from elsewhere in the solar system.

Grow or die. Just like any living organism, any society. You either grow or you wither away and disappear.

He realized his fists were clenched as he marched along the tunnel. Passersby were giving him strange looks. Doug tried to smile at them, tried to appear relaxed. But inside he was stretched tight.

There's going to be a split with Earth, Doug knew. This nanotech treaty is just the beginning. They must know, down there, that we can't exist without nanomachines. It would've taken years to build a pipeline from the south pole, instead of months. The cost of building the power tower would have been out of sight if we didn't have nanomachines to do the work.

How can we prevent the split? How can we keep connected with Earth, at least until we're fully self-sufficient?

He pushed back the door to his room, forming a scenario in his mind: Okay, we establish the legalities that we're a corporation based in Kiribati and the Kiribati government doesn't sign the nanotech treaty. But suppose the U.N. or the World Court doesn't accept that? Suppose they insist that we've got to give up our nanomachines? And we can't, of course. Suppose they send Peacekeeper troops up here to enforce their demands!

Doug sagged onto his bunk. Jeez, we've got to figure out a way to prevent that from happening. But how?

Without thinking consciously about it, he flicked on the Windowall screen hanging opposite his bunk. Instantly the screen seemed to turn into a big picture window that looked out at the floor of Alphonsus. Doug stared out at the scene for a few moments, then went to his desk and pecked at his keyboard. The 'window' showed Victoria Falls, then an underwater scene from a tropical reef. Not satisfied, Doug finally got a live view from the top of Alphonsus' ringwall mountains that looked out across Mare Nubium.

'Magnificent desolation,' he murmured. The barren plain was empty, not a sign that a human being had ever set foot on it, except for the faint glow of a handful of red beacons that marked the sites of the old temporary shelters marching off to the sudden horizon.

If Greg looked out there, Doug thought, he'd see nothing but barren wilderness. But I see beauty. I see freedom. I see the opportunity to explore and learn and grow and build the future. How can I make Greg see it the way I do?

He was still wondering about the problem as he put on his VR helmet and data gloves, booted up his computer and linked with his afternoon class from Caltech.

ROCKET PORT

Doug always asked permission to come into the rocket port's flight control center. It was a tiny cubbyhole burned out of the lunar rock by plasma torches back in the earliest days of Moonbase, barely large enough for two controllers sitting shoulder to shoulder at their consoles. It always reminded Doug of an old-time submarine's command compartment, compact and crowded, jammed with equipment that hummed and glowed and gave off heat. Despite Greg's swath of new radiators, the flight control center was stuffy and sweaty.

It even had a conning tower, sort of. There was a vertical tunnel that led up to a minuscule observation bubble, barely big enough for a person to stick his head up above the surface of the crater floor for a visual inspection of the rocket pads outside.

The controllers had never refused Doug permission to come into the center, tight though it was. Usually Doug clambered up the ladder to the observation bubble, leaving the controllers to huddle over their glowing display screens.

Traffic was seldom heavy. The lunar transfer vehicles plied the route between Earth orbit and Moonbase on a monotonously steady schedule. Rarely were there two spacecraft on the pads at the same time, even though Moonbase boasted four pads for LTVs to land on, spaced equidistantly from the observation bubble.

Standing on the narrow platform of the observation bubble, his chin barely above the crater floor's surface and his hair brushing the transparent dome, Doug watched the lander come down slowly, silently, its dirty-white rocket exhaust splashing on the smoothed rock pad, blowing dust and pebbles that rattled against the bubble's glassteel dome. Doug could barely see the actual touchdown, when the big ungainly lunar transfer vehicle settled on its outstretched spindly legs like an old, old man sinking into a favorite easy chair.

From below he heard the chatter of the controllers as they remotely manipulated the access tunnel to lock against the LTV's personnel hatch. To Doug it looked like a giant gray worm blindly groping for its prey.

The spacecraft that transited between Earth orbit and Moonbase had a human pilot aboard only when they were carrying passengers. Even so, the pilot was merely a redundancy required by archaic safety regulations. The controllers landed the craft remotely, as they did all the unmanned cargo carriers.

Once the access tunnel was connected and pumped up with air Doug slid down the ladder in dreamy lunar slow motion, without touching his feet to its rungs, and landed softly behind the two controllers.

'Thanks, guys,' he said, despite the fact that they both happened to be women on this shift. Without waiting for them to reply, he ducked through the hatch and padded quickly in his softboots down the tunnel that led to The Pit, the receiving area.

The airlock's inner hatch was just swinging open as he got there. Two men stepped over the hatch's steel lip, both dressed in the olive green coveralls of the mining and manufacturing group. The next, another man, wearing the pumpkin orange of the science and exploration group, tripped over the coaming. A newcomer, Doug realized. Despite his weighted boots he stumbled and floundered, arms flailing. Doug went to him, grabbed him, straightened and steadied him.

'I'm okay,' the man said. Like most of the short-timers, he was in his twenties.

'It's a little strange, your first time,' Doug said. 'Especially after a couple days of zero-gee.'

'I'm okay,' he repeated, scowling as he pulled free of Doug's supportive grasp.

Doug watched him walk awkwardly away, as if he were stepping on land mines. He'll never make it here, Doug said to himself. Too uptight to accept help; probably too self-centered to give help when it's needed.

Turning back to the hatch, he saw Bianca step carefully through, also in orange. Her round face broke into a wide grin at the sight of Doug.

'Welcome back!' Doug said, striding up to her, arms outstretched.

'Hi!' she said, shifting her travel bag so they could embrace in a welcoming hug.

Half an hour later they were in The Cave, sipping fruit punch and catching up on the months since Rhee had last been at Moonbase.

'I'm not just a grad student slave this time,' she said proudly from across the narrow table. 'I'm here to do my thesis work.'

'No kidding?'

'If I don't run into any snags, I'll be *Doctor* Rhee this time next year.'

'Terrific,' said Doug.

He liked Bianca. Ever since their experience together on the first south polar expedition – which was known now as the Brennart Expedition – Doug had felt that Bianca Rhee was one of his best friends. She had come to Moonbase twice in the past six months, for a month each time. They had eaten together, joined others for parties or meals, talked endless hours about their hopes and plans for the future. Nothing more. Sometimes Doug got the feeling that Bianca might be feeling lonely at Moonbase; sometimes he thought he saw something in her eyes, in her voice, that made him feel as if she was – what? Disappointed? Sad? Uncertain?

Maybe she's a frustrated ballerina, Doug thought, remembering her shy confession about dancing. She had never brought up the subject again, so he hadn't asked about watching her dance.

Doug couldn't figure it out, and didn't feel that he wanted to probe Bianca's psyche that deeply. Is it sex? he wondered.

But she's older than I am and she's got her own life back Earthside. Probably boyfriends or lovers. Maybe her family's already picked out a husband for her. She's never brought up the subject and it's none of my business. We're friends and that's fine; no sense getting it all tangled up with sex.

Doug was not a virgin, but he was far from experienced. He had dated now and then during his year on the Caltech campus. Despite the so-called New Morality that the politicians, the media, and even the university administration constantly drummed on, several times his dates had ended in bed. He had never had to push it, he just went along with the tide. He never considered that being good-looking, athletic, easy-going – and extremely wealthy – made him attractive to young women. Doug simply did what came naturally.

At Moonbase it was the same, yet different. There was a core of some two hundred long-term Moonbase employees, plus a couple of permanent residents such as Lev Brudnoy and his mother. The long-term Lunatics tended to form solid, long-term relationships, for the most part, although there were a couple of loose cannons of both genders. Rumor had it that Brudnoy himself was quite a Romeo, or had once been.

It was among the short-timers, the men and women who visited Moonbase for a month or so at a time, that most of the action took place. Doug had enjoyed a couple of flings, nothing major, nothing more than fun and games.

'So what's your thesis about?' he asked.

'Well, originally I was going to do it on brown dwarfs; you know, superlarge planets that're almost real stars. With the equipment up here I've been able to do a real thorough search for them.'

'Have you found any?'

'I've got six candidates, but I'd need some ultrasensitive infrared equipment to definitely identify them as brown dwarfs. They've got to be radiating at the wavelengths predicted by Chartrand's theory.'

'Sounds heavy,' said Doug.

She grinned again. 'Too heavy. Too big a subject. My thesis advisor wouldn't let me tackle it.'

'So?'

She took a quick breath and then said, delightedly, 'So I'm going to analyze the chemical compositions of the Earth-crossing asteroids, using the observatory here at Moonbase.'

Doug was immediately interested. 'Now that's something we can use right here. One of these days we're going to want to go out and grab an asteroid that's rich in carbon—'

'I remember you talking about that last time I was up here,' Rhee said. 'That's one of the reasons I picked that topic. I thought it might help you.'

'It'd be a terrific help, Bianca. When we actually start the project, you could be part of our team.'

She beamed at him.

'If we ever start it,' he added, more soberly.

'If?'

'I'm learning economics the hard way,' Doug said. 'I want to get an asteroid and mine it so we can use nanomachines to build Clipperships from asteroid carbon, make them out of pure diamond.'

'Diamond?'

Nodding eagerly, Doug said, 'Diamond's got a strength-to-density ratio fifty times better than the aluminum alloys we make at the space stations.'

'And nanobugs can produce pure diamond?'

'Out of the carbon we mine from the asteroid, sure: atom by atom.'

'Wow!' Rhee said. 'That's brutal!'

'But it takes money to get started. Capital investment. And Moonbase isn't making enough profits to swing it.'

'Won't the corporation—'

Doug interrupted, 'The board of directors won't sink any risk capital into Moonbase, not with the U.N. working up an international treaty that'll ban nanotechnology completely.'

'That would shut Moonbase down!' Rhee said, alarmed.

'Maybe,' Doug replied. 'But whether it does or not, the corporation isn't going to provide the capital we need for the asteroid project.'

Rhee stared glumly at her half-finished drink. 'And I was ready to come up here full time.'

'Full time? Really?' Doug asked. 'I mean, I know you've got family and school and everything back Earthside.'

'There aren't that many jobs for astronomers back there,' she said. 'I couldn't even get a teaching assistant's position this semester.'

'Well, I'm sure we could fit you in here.' Then he added, 'If this flipping nanotech treaty doesn't shut us down completely.'

'You don't think that could happen, do you?'

Doug smiled reassuringly. 'No way. We'll keep Moonbase going and we'll use our nanomachines no matter what laws they pass down there.' Then he added, 'I hope.'

'It's really getting sick back home, you know,' she said, suddenly glum. 'The New Morality people keep passing new laws and the Supreme Court lets them get away with it. They've even shut down the national art museum in Washington!'

But Doug's mind was looking outward. 'If only we could start the asteroid program now. If there was only some way I could get Greg to go for it.'

'I could stay here,' Bianca said. 'I wouldn't mind staying here with you indefinitely.'

'You want to become a real Lunatic?'

'Why not?'

'You're sure?'

She nodded gravely. 'I'm positive.'

Again Doug caught a hint of something more going on than her words revealed. But he pushed that out of his thoughts. How can we can get the asteroid-grabbing program started right now? he asked himself.

Looking up, he saw that people were filing into The Cave, lining up at the food dispensers for their evening meals. He spotted Lev Brudnoy's tall, gangly form meandering through the rapidly-filling tables, a tray of food in his hands and a bemused, almost puzzled look on his grizzled face.

'Mr. Brudnoy,' Doug called out, getting to his feet. 'Would you care to join us?'

'Why? Are you falling apart?'

'Huh?'

Brudnoy smiled sheepishly as he approached their table. 'Forgive me. It's an old Groucho Marx line and it's become something of a conditioned reflex in my silly little brain.'

Doug didn't quite understand. 'Marx? Like, with Lenin?'

With a sigh, Brudnoy said, 'Please ignore my foolishness. And, yes, I would like to join you. I hate to eat alone.'

'You were an astronaut, weren't you?' Doug asked as Brudnoy put his tray down on the table and folded his lanky frame into the chair between himself and Rhee.

'A cosmonaut,' Brudnoy corrected. 'The same thing, but in Russian.'

'What do you think of the possibilities of going out and finding a carbonaceous asteroid and moving it into an orbit around the Moon?'

Brudnoy slumped back in his chair and puffed out his cheeks, then let out a long, slow whistle. 'Ambitious. It would take a lot of delta vee.'

'Change in velocity,' Doug explained before Rhee could ask.

'I know that!' she hissed.

'Even for the Earth-crossing asteroids,' Brudnoy said, half musing, 'you would need a tremendous expenditure of propellant to change their momentum into a lunar orbit.'

'Suppose we use the asteroid's own materials as propellant?' Doug challenged.

Brudnoy's shaggy brows went up. 'It would have oxygen, wouldn't it.'

Rhee said, 'Carbonaceous chondrites contain water.'

'Yes, of course.'

'Hydrates,' she said, 'chemically linked to the rock.'

'It would take energy to get the water from the rock.'

'There's plenty of solar energy,' Doug said. 'And we can use nanomachines to do the separation.'

'I see. Once you have water, of course, you have hydrogen and oxygen for rocket propellants.'

'Right.' Doug nodded eagerly.

'Of course, the trick is not to use up all the asteroid's valuable chemicals merely to get it into an orbit around the Moon. You want its water for us to use here, don't you?'

'And its carbon,' said Doug.

'Carbon?' Brudnoy's shaggy brows rose. 'For life support?'

'For making spacecraft out of diamond, using nano-machines,' Doug said.

'Diamond,' Brudnoy whispered.

'Stronger, lighter, more heat-resistant,' said Doug. 'And cheaper to manufacture, with nanomachines.'

Brudnoy nodded, deep in thought, his dinner tray untouched. At last he asked, 'Why bring the asteroid into lunar orbit?'

'So we can mine it,' Doug said.

'You can mine it while it remains in its own orbit around the Sun. Then all you need to bring back here are the materials you really want. Why drag the entire asteroid here? It's inefficient.'

Doug thought about it for a moment. 'Yes . . . that could work.'

'You see, my young friend, in space distance is not so important as the amount of energy you must expend to get the job done.'

Doug nodded agreement. 'And it would take much less energy to bring the raw materials we want from the asteroid to Moonbase than it would to move the whole asteroid into a lunar orbit. I see.'

'Much less energy,' said Brudnoy, smiling approvingly at Doug. 'Which means much less rocket propellant.'

'Which means much less money,' said Doug.

Brudnoy patted Doug's shoulder. 'You understand it very well.'

Rhee pointed to Brudnoy's tray. 'Your dinner's getting cold.'

Glancing down at the plastic dishes, Brudnoy said, 'It's almost criminal how the cooks take the fruits of all my hard labor and turn it into unappetizing mush.'

'Maybe we need a good chef up here,' Rhee said, grinning.

Brudnoy nodded dolefully. 'We certainly need someone who can create something better than this. Look, even the salad is soggy and lifeless.'

But he stuck a fork into it anyway. 'I raised these sad little leaves. They were crisp and cheerful when I handed them over to the cooks.'

Doug had never given much thought to the quality of the meals. He ate what was available.

Munching thoughtfully, Brudnoy swallowed and asked, 'What will you use for a spacecraft?'

'Adapt a lunar transfer ship, I suppose,' Doug replied.

'You will need a team of engineers and technicians.'

'We already have an astronomer to pick out the most likely asteroid.' Doug jabbed a thumb in Rhee's direction.

'Congratulations.' Brudnoy lifted his tea mug to her. 'But if you don't mind my saying so, you're going to need more than the three of us to accomplish this task.'

'Three of us? You mean you're willing to help us?'

'Of course.'

'Terrific!' said Doug, tremendously pleased.

They clinked their cups together.

'We'll take one of the LTVs and have it modified for the mission,' Doug said, his insides beginning to tremble with growing excitement.

'Do you have the facilities for modifying spacecraft here?' Rhee asked.

'No, but the corporation has space stations that can do that kind of work. In Earth orbit.'

Brudnoy's enthusiasm was muted. 'Why do it at a space station?' he asked, jabbing at another piece of salad on his tray. 'Why not do it here?'

'We don't have the facilities here,' Doug said.

'We could adapt what we do have,' said Brudnoy. 'We have the talent, too, if we use our people properly.'

Doug gaped at him. 'Modify the LTV here,' he muttered.

'Do the entire job here at Moonbase,' Brudnoy said firmly.

'Do you think we could build the Clipperships here at Moonbase?' Doug asked.

'Why not? The nanomachines don't care where they are.'

'That would mean turning Moonbase into a major manufacturing center.'

'Why not?' the Russian repeated, smiling patiently. 'After all, I can feed you *lapin à la Brudnoy* now, although I shudder to think of what the cooks would do with it. Why not take the next step forward?'

'From a mining center to a manufacturing center,' Doug mused.

'A natural step in the evolution of a frontier settlement. It will allow us to expand from a town into a city.'

'Wow,' said Rhee. 'This is getting awesome.'

But Doug sagged back in his chair. 'We'd need a lot of additional capital investment.'

'Of course.'

Rhee sensed Doug's sudden change of mood. 'The corporation won't put up the money?'

'Not with this nanotech treaty hanging over us. The whole scheme depends on nanotechnology.'

'But you said we'd keep on using nanotechnology regardless of the treaty.'

'If we can. We'll have to fight Washington over it.'

'And Moscow,' said Brudnoy. 'And London and all the other world capitals. Even in Paris the couturiers must submit their fashion designs to a censorship board before they are allowed to go ahead with them.'

Doug began to wonder if Kiribati could withstand the international pressure, despite the best Greg could do.

'Could we do this without the corporation knowing about it?' Rhee asked.

Doug began to shake his head.

But Brudnoy said, 'Perhaps it would be possible to "retire" one of the older transfer craft and then modify it.'

'We'd have to take people off other jobs to do it,' Doug said. 'It would show up in the base's bookkeeping.'

'There is a technique,' said Brudnoy, 'known as midnight requisitioning. You must learn to be as creative in your bookkeeping as you are in your engineering.'

'Moonlight the whole project?' Rhee asked.

'Why not?' Brudnoy replied. 'Or perhaps we should call it Earthlighting, considering where we are.'

'Instead of capital investment from the corporation,' Doug mused, 'we get people to invest their own time and talents into helping us. That's a form of capital that doesn't involve money.'

'Or the company's bookkeepers,' Brudnoy added.

Doug said, 'Greg would have to be in on this. We couldn't hide it from him.'

A sly smile crept across Brudnoy's bearded face. 'Fort Apache,' he muttered.

'What?'

'Oh, nothing,' said Brudnoy. 'I was just recalling a conversation I had with your brother when he first came up here.'

'What we're proposing is to bring Moonbase up to the next step toward self-sufficiency,' Doug said.

'By mining an asteroid?' asked Rhee.

'If this scheme succeeds, Moonbase will have developed the means of supplying itself with carbon and nitrogen and all the other volatiles we now import from Earth,' Doug said, feeling the excitement rising in him again.

'If we succeed,' Rhee said.

'But if we can do it,' said Doug, 'then it won't matter what treaties or laws they pass Earthside. We can survive without them.'

'By mining asteroids,' Rhee repeated.

'By lifting ourselves up by our own bootstraps,' said Brudnoy.

'Operation Bootstrap,' Doug said, breaking into a huge grin. 'We do it without letting Savannah know what we're up to.'

'Can we get away with it?' Rhee asked.

'Why not?' said Brudnoy.

'We'll need Greg's help,' Doug said. 'And my mother's.'

The other two fell silent.

Doug pushed his chair back from the table. 'They'll help,' he said, with a confidence he did not truly feel. 'I'm going to tell them about it right now.'

JOANNA'S QUARTERS

All employees were treated equally as far as their living space in Moonbase was concerned. Even the director, who had a two-room suite, received no more living space than anyone else: the director merely had an office that connected to the living quarters, which were no larger than any other one-room dwelling space, within the tolerances of practical lunar architecture.

It took energy and manpower to carve out new quarters with plasma torches that vaporized the lunar rock. No one was going to get a bigger living space than anyone else. Utilitarian rules prevailed. Besides, standard-sized quarters prevented jealous comparisons and arguments.

However, Joanna Masterson Stavenger was not a Masterson employee. So while everyone was treated equally, Joanna was more equal than anyone else. Her quarters were a two-room suit: two ordinary living spaces that had been connected by a plasma-torched doorway.

At her own expense, Joanna had brought up furniture from her home in Savannah and turned one of her cubicles into a crowded little sitting room, the other into the most luxurious bedroom in Moonbase, with a real bed of actual wood – polished lustrous rosewood – and a thick cushiony mattress with pillows and flowered sheets and even a comforter that was strictly for ostentation in the climate-controlled environs of the underground base.

There was no space in the bedroom for the two massive wardrobes full of clothes that Joanna had brought with her; there was barely enough space to inch around the massive bed. So Joanna had requisitioned a pair of technicians to build storage space under her bed; the drawers formed a sort of platform that was high enough to require steps to get up onto the bed itself.

The bed on its 'throne' – and who might be sharing it with the 'queen' – quickly became the most talked-about item in Moonbase.

'You must tell Greg about this,' Joanna said to Doug as she reclined on the smaller of the two couches in her sitting room. She was wearing casual pale green silk slacks and a loose cashmere sweater of slightly darker green.

Doug had noticed that some of the women among the long-term Lunatics had taken to wearing more stylish clothes since his mother had come to Moonbase. Some women had started modifying their coveralls, snipping out pieces along the sleeves or shoulders or legs, adding trinkets or decorative patches. Eye candy, one of the guys called it.

Doug enjoyed the fashion trend. The women were adding color to the drab underground surroundings. Like the flowers that Brudnoy grew and the pictures that the Windowalls offered. Women wore perfume more often now, too. Even Bianca had added a trio of tiny gold pins to her collar as soon as she had arrived from Earthside: two cats on one side and some kind of fish on the other.

Doug remembered how Brennart had decorated his coveralls with mission patches and emblems. Yet none of the men had followed his lead. Doug himself wore his plain sky blue coveralls as he sat on the spindly armchair next to his mother's delicate little upholstered couch, leaning forward intensely, elbows on knees.

'I wanted to run it past you first,' he said, 'to make certain there aren't any obvious holes in the plan.'

The corners of Joanna's lips curled slightly. 'I might even detect a subtle flaw, if there are any.'

Doug grinned sheepishly. 'Aw, Mom, you know what I mean.'

'What you're trying to do is to make Moonbase as self-sufficient as possible.'

'And as soon as possible.'

'Without letting the corporate management know what you're doing.'

'Or the board of directors,' Doug added.

Joanna studied her son for a long moment. Then she said, 'The board's in a turmoil since Carlos' assassination. They're all jockeying for power down there.'

'Will it affect you?'

She smiled grimly. 'Of course it will. The trick is to make certain it enhances my position on the board rather than detracting from it.'

'Will you have to go back Earthside?'

'I don't think so,' Joanna answered slowly. 'The VR link's been good enough – so far.'

Doug saw the shadow of uncertainty on her face. 'I don't want to start new problems for you, but—'

'No, I think your scheme could be a good insurance policy for us, in case they really do try to stop us from using nanomachines.'

Doug nodded.

'In fact,' Joanna said, smiling slightly, 'if all the other major corporations are prevented from using nanotechnology by the treaty, Masterson could become very wealthy. Extremely wealthy.' Her smile widened. 'We should support the nanotech treaty!'

'We can't do that,' Doug snapped. 'It'd be immoral.'

With a small shrug, Joanna said. 'I suppose so. But still . . .'

'Will Greg go along with us?'

Joanna's smile vanished. 'Well,' she said carefully, 'it's a lot to swallow in one bite, for him.'

'He wants to shut down Moonbase, doesn't he?' Without waiting for his mother's response, Doug went on, 'And I want to enlarge it, turn it into a manufacturing center, make it profitable so it can grow and prosper. That's what Operation Bootstrap is all about . . .'

Joanna saw the intensity in her son's face. Operation Bootstrap, she thought. A theatrical name for a pretty daring idea.

We've been talking about making Moonbase self-sufficient for years. Paul wanted to do it, even back then. And now Doug's found the way to do it, if we can only get it started. Greg will be dead-set against this, though.

Aloud, she told her son, 'Let me talk to Greg about it first. Alone.'

Doug nodded as if that was what he had expected. Maybe what he had hoped she would say.

'I think he'll take it better if he hears it from you, Mom.'

Joanna sighed. 'I think so too.'

Doug got to his feet and Joanna stood up beside her son. It always surprised her that Doug was so much taller than she, taller than his father had been. He looks so much like Paul, she thought, solid and compact. But he's really much bigger. Almost Greg's height.

And he's still growing, she realized. Mentally. He's challenging Greg already, although he doesn't really understand that. Greg does, though. Greg will see exactly what this means.

I mustn't let them clash over this Operation Bootstrap. I've got to get them to work together, not against one another.

Wilhelm Zimmerman almost toppled off his bar stool as he flinched away from his friend's blazing anger. His huge bulk teetered on the swivelling stool. He had to grab the edge of the bar with both hands to steady himself.

Verban took no notice of his obese friend's struggle to stay on the stool.

'Are you mad?' Verban hissed, his teeth showing. 'Do you want to ruin us all?'

The bar was of the American type, in the old Osborne Hotel where the tourists stayed. Verban had insisted on their meeting there, rather than the ratskeller next to the campus where they usually had their seidels of beer.

It was late in the afternoon, yet the place was almost empty. Muted bland music issued thinly from the speakers in the ceiling. A few elderly couples, obviously tourists from Japan or one of the Asian rim tigers, sat together at one circular table, their heads together over a vidcam as they viewed their day's videodiscs.

Verban had suggested this hotel bar as a place where they would not be seen. Zimmerman thought they looked as obvious as a syphilitic chancre on a nun's face. How much better he would have felt in the noisy fellowship of the beer hall!

Zimmerman steadied himself, then said, 'No one is going to be ruined just because I occasionally help a wealthy foreigner.' He whispered in the quiet, almost deserted bar.

'Madness!' Verban repeated. 'Sheer madness.'

Zimmerman had known the man for nearly thirty years. Verban had always been the jittery type, scarecrow thin, nervous, given to smoking illicit cigarets when he thought no one was watching. He was a professor in the university's law school, on the verge of graduating into the bliss of a professor emeritus' well-earned retirement.

'I've been doing it for so many years,' Zimmerman said. 'Why does it upset you now?'

'Because the pressures are stronger now than ever! Don't you watch the news? Don't you see what's going on around you – all over the world!'

'You mean that assassination in New York?'

'That's only part of it.'

'And the treaty that the United Nations is sponsoring.' Zimmerman smiled at his old friend. 'You see, I do keep an eye on events outside my laboratory.'

'Switzerland will sign the treaty.'

Zimmerman shrugged and reached for his glass of beer, a delicate thing that held only a fraction of a seidel's worth. It was almost empty. At their favorite haunt the barmaids always made certain that the mugs were topped off regularly.

'So Switzerland will sign the stupid treaty. So what? The authorities have never bothered me.'

'They will now,' Verban whispered harshly. 'They will close your laboratory entirely.'

'No, they won't stop research—'

'Yes they will! And they'll come looking for you first of

all, you with your proud announcement that you saved that boy's life on the Moon with nanotherapy.'

'But it's true,' Zimmerman insisted. 'I did.'

'And you had to tell the world about it?'

'I had to tell the world that nanotherapy is useful, therapeutic, and – used properly – it isn't harmful.'

'So now you are a marked man. They will close your laboratory.'

Feeling sudden panic, Zimmerman blurted, 'But what am I to do?'

'Retire as gracefully as you can. You certainly have enough money to live well.'

He shook his fleshy head. 'Not really. Most of my income I spent on new research, once the university stopped funding nanotechnology work.'

'It's over, Willi,' Verban said, half annoyed, half sorrowful. 'You mustn't fight against them. Just take this peacefully and go off into retirement.'

'Never!'

'You'll get the entire university shut down, you fool! Don't you understand what kind of power they have?'

Zimmerman wanted to laugh. 'They can't shut down the entire university.'

'They can and they will, if you try to struggle against them.'

'But . . .' Zimmerman's words died in his throat. He stared at his old friend. Verban was terrified. If the university shut down, who would pay out his pension?

His voice suddenly heavy, Zimmerman said, 'What they are doing is terribly, terribly wrong.'

'Yes, I know it,' said Verban. 'But they have the power. And they will use it mercilessly.'

'I can't stop my life's work. I won't! There must be some university, somewhere. Perhaps in America.'

'Hah!'

'Or Canada?' Zimmerman asked hopefully.

Verban shook his head.

Zimmerman realized he was perspiring. A fear reflex, he

knew. They're making me afraid. He felt a sudden surge of hatred for the faceless people who ladled out fear as part of their power.

Verban said, 'It's all finished, Willi. Nanotechnology – even theoretical research on the subject – will be outlawed once the treaty goes into effect.'

'There must be someplace . . .' Zimmerman muttered.

'Nowhere on Earth,' said Verban sadly.

Zimmerman heaved an enormous sigh. But then he remembered that his protegé, Kris Cardenas, was now living in Canada. Vancouver, he recalled. Perhaps she can help; after all, she won the Nobel Prize. She must have some influence.

CHELSEA, MASSACHUSETTS

She was good-looking. Older than Killifer would've liked, but a real stunner despite her age. Skinny, though. Her arms were rail-thin and he guessed her legs were, too, beneath the tight ankle-length skirt she wore. No way of telling how much of a figure she had under that severe outfit. It was plain dull gray from the choker collar down to her plain dull gray shoes. Killifer almost wondered why she didn't wear gloves, every other part of her body was covered. No jewelry at all.

But her face was enough to kill for. A sculptor's dream. The kind of face video stars wished they had. A black Venus, a chocolate-cream-colored goddess of beauty.

As she walked up to Killifer, he was totally unable to stop himself from staring at her. Automatically he got up from the bench where he had been waiting. But then he saw something in her eyes that almost frightened him. Her eyes were pained, haunted, rimmed with red like the fires of hell.

'Jonathan Killifer?' she asked needlessly. Her voice was smokey, low, inviting.

'Jack,' he managed to choke out.

'I'm Melissa Hart. Pleased to meet you, Jack.' Without a smile, without any change in those burning eyes. 'Would you follow me, please?'

Killifer wanted to tell her he would follow her off the edge of a cliff, but her eyes stopped him. In silence he walked beside her down the busy corridor. He noticed that all the people here dressed in gray, men and women alike, the only difference was that the men wore trousers while all the women wore tight ankle-length skirts. Well, Killifer

thought, they sure can't run away from you in those hob-
bles.

He expected her to lead him into her office, or maybe a
conference room. Instead he followed her to the end of the
hallway, up a narrow flight of stairs, and then through a
metal door out onto the building's roof. The open sunlight
made Killifer's eyes water.

'We can speak freely here, Jack,' she said.

That worried him. Wiping at his eyes, he asked, 'Whattaya
mean? Is your office bugged?'

Melissa gave him a cool smile. 'Jack, the Urban Corps
doesn't believe in private offices, not even for General
O'Conner. I thought that we could have our first chat here,
without anyone else to bother us.'

'How'd you find me?' Killifer asked.

'We have sources of information.' She walked slowly
toward the brick parapet along the roof's edge. 'Isn't it a
beautiful day?'

Following her, Killifer could see that the building was on a
hill and the whole city of Boston was laid out before them,
beneath the bright cloudless sky. After so many years at
Moonbase, the deep clear blue almost hurt. Everything was
so dazzling: the green of the trees, the red brick buildings, the
glittering glass facades of the soaring downtown high-rises.

Killifer took in a deep breath of real air. It smelled great,
with the salt tang coming in off the harbor. He could
almost taste it.

'You were born in Boston, weren't you?' Melissa asked
him.

He nodded and pointed. 'Winthrop. Out there by the old
airport.'

A Clippership took off from the airport, like a toy at this
distance, the thunder of its rocket engines nothing more than
a muted rumble.

'Do you remember what Chelsea used to be when you were
growing up in Winthrop, Jack?'

Killifer grinned sourly. 'A dump. We used to make jokes
about Chelsea. It was the bottom of the barrel.'

'That's right,' said Melissa Hart, like a schoolteacher pleased with her student's answer. 'For generations Chelsea was the bottom of the barrel.'

'And now?'

'Now it's a model community. The Urban Corps has transformed Chelsea. We brought new industry into the community, new businesses. People have jobs now. They have hope. Crime is down. The schools are turning out model citizens.'

'I thought it was the New Morality did that.'

'We're part of the New Morality. The Urban Corps, the Angels of God, the Disciples of Allah, St. Michael's Battalion – there are dozens of organizations within the New Morality structure.'

'Uh-huh.'

'We want your help, Jack.'

'Mine? What for?'

'You've worked for years at Moonbase. We need to know all about Moonbase, what they're doing up there, how they operate, what they're planning.'

'Why?'

Melissa looked disappointed. 'Jack, they work with nano-machines at Moonbase, don't they?'

'They've got to,' he said.

'Nanomachines will soon be illegal,' she said. 'We've got to know how the people at Moonbase will react to the new law.'

Killifer turned away from her and looked out at the city again. It was so shining and lush it almost looked unreal. It all seemed clean and fresh. And quiet. Hardly any noise from street traffic. No boom boxes blasting away. No voices raised.

'What's in it for me?' he asked, still without looking at her.

If his self-centered questioned bothered her, Melissa Hart gave no hint of it. She immediately answered, 'We'll hire you as a consultant at fifteen hundred a day, with a guarantee of a minimum of one hundred consulting days per year.'

A hundred-fifty thousand per year, Killifer realized.

'That should augment your Masterson Corporation pension very nicely,' she added.

'My pension, yeah.' He wanted to spit.

'It's a very generous offer, Jack.'

'For how many years?'

Sounding slightly disappointed again, she replied, 'Oh Jack, I can't promise you more than this one year. If everything goes the way we expect it to, Moonbase will be shut down by the end of that time.'

'And then what happens to me?'

'We'll see,' she said simply. With a glowing smile. But her eyes still radiated pain.

Killifer thought it over briefly. 'What the hell,' he said. 'Why not?'

'Then you agree?'

'If you'll come to dinner with me.'

She seemed to think it over with great care. At last Melissa said, 'I'd be happy to have dinner with you, Jack. But only dinner.'

'Sure,' he said. 'Just dinner.' It was a lie and he knew that she knew it.

The North End of Boston had once been an Italian preserve, but over the decades it had evolved into Little Asia. Vietnamese, Malay, Thai, Indian and a dozen varieties of Chinese now occupied the narrow twisting streets where once a patriot had climbed the Old North Church bell tower to signal Paul Revere.

Over spicy Hunan platters Killifer found himself spinning out his life story to this beautiful black woman with the haunted eyes. As if he couldn't stop himself, he spilled out the bitterness, the rage and frustration of his wasted life.

'But why did you spend all those years in Moonbase,' Melissa asked sweetly, chopsticks held gracefully in her long slim fingers, 'when you had such a promising career in nanotechnology?'

'*She* did it,' he growled. 'Masterson's widow. Then she married Stavenger. She stuck me in Moonbase.'

'But you could have resigned and come back to Earth, couldn't you?'

He hadn't intended to tell her about the nanobugs and Greg Masterson and Paul Stavenger's murder. He had never intended to speak of that at all. But by the time dinner was finished and they were walking the crowded, brightly-lit streets, he had revealed himself to her almost completely.

'Greg Masterson murdered his stepfather?'

There was something in the way she said it that brought Killifer up short. Something in her voice.

'You know Greg Masterson?'

She nodded. In the harsh glare of the street lamp her face looked like frozen stone. 'I knew him. Long ago.'

They walked in painful silence down to the waterfront, where the streets were emptier. And darker.

'My apartment's up there.' Killifer pointed to an apartment block across the street from the piers.

'You must have a nice view,' Melissa said absently, sounding as if her thoughts were a quarter-million miles away.

'Come on up and see it,' he suggested, taking her by the arm.

She disengaged effortlessly. 'No, Jack,' she said. 'It doesn't work that way.'

'Come on,' he wheedled. 'Just have a drink with me.'

With a smile that might have been sad, or perhaps pitying, Melissa said, 'You don't understand, Jack. I'm celibate.'

'You're what?'

'I've been celibate since I met General O'Conner, many years ago.'

'Celibate?'

'It's part of our creed.'

'You mean everybody I saw in your building . . . ?'

She nodded.

'That's hard to believe.'

'Believe it, Jack. Celibacy removes one of the great causes of pain in this life.'

'But . . . but you're so beautiful! It's a damned shame. A waste.'

Her eyes flared. 'No, it's not a waste. I know what pain can be caused by the attractions of sex. I was caught in that web, once, years ago. It led to nothing but pain and evil, drugs and self-destruction. I nearly killed myself before General O'Conner found me.'

'General O'Conner.'

'He wasn't the general then; he hadn't even founded the Urban Corps yet. But he saved my life. He made me dedicate my life to the New Morality and all that it stands for.'

'And you've gotta be celibate?'

'It simplifies your life, Jack. It allows you to concentrate your energies on the things that really matter.'

'Still seems like a damned waste to me,' Killifer grumbled.

'No, Jack. It makes life so much easier. Cleaner. Come back to the office tomorrow, Jack. I want you to join us. We need your help.'

Killifer thought, Maybe this celibate crap is just her excuse. After all, we just met this afternoon. Give it time, she'll pull her pants down sooner or later.

'Okay,' he said lightly. 'See you tomorrow morning.'

'Nine sharp,' said Melissa.

'Right.'

He left her at the street corner and went into his apartment building. She didn't seem to have the slightest fear of being alone on the dark street.

Jinny Anson stared at her husband. 'What do you mean?' she demanded.

'Just what I said,' he replied calmly, his teeth clamped on his favorite briar pipe.

'You've got to submit your syllabus to a freakin' committee?'

His studied composure irritated her. 'It's not as if this is the first time,' he said.

'But this committee's got nothing to do with the university,' she said.

Her husband shrugged. 'It's a local citizens' group. They call themselves the Moral Watchdogs or something like that.'

'Moral dipshits,' Anson muttered.

Her husband gave her a disapproving frown. He was obviously afraid his young daughters might hear her language, even though the door to their bedroom was firmly shut and the kids were down in the rec room watching video on their new wall-to-wall Windowall screen.

Quentin Westlake was a sweet, gentle professor of English literature at the University of Texas. It had taken him ten years to work his way from various outlying campuses in the vast hinterlands of the state to the main campus at Austin. Along the way he had married, fathered two daughters, and divorced when his first wife fell in love with an investment broker from Chicago.

Jinny Anson had met him at a seminar in Lubbock, where she had been invited to participate in a panel discussion of 'Literature in the Space Age.' Jinny had been the only panel member who was not an English lit professor and Quentin had been the only one among them who had treated her with kindness.

It was a different kind of romance, with Jinny commuting every few months from Moonbase to Texas, and Quentin trying to convince his two pre-pubescent daughters that he wouldn't marry anyone who would turn into a wicked stepmother. When Jinny took her regular annual leave from the directorship of Moonbase the commute became easier: merely from Savannah to Austin. By the time she returned to the Moon they had decided to get married.

Their wedding was at the Alamo, as scheduled, with Quentin's two daughters serving as bridesmaids and Joanna Stavenger among the guests. Joanna's best wedding present was to allow Jinny to transfer to the corporation's manufacturing facility in Houston; she could commute to work now on the high-speed levitrain from Austin. In addition to her regular duties, Jinny was supervising construction of a model water recycling center for the city of Houston, based on the technology perfected at Moonbase. It made for very long days, but at least she was home each night with her husband. Most nights.

For nearly six months now Jinny had lived in his three-bedroom ranch-style house in suburban Austin, getting acclimatized to raising two half-grown daughters and to the intricate jealousies and competitions of a major university's faculty. She quickly fell in love with the girls; the other faculty wives and women professors – and administrators – she felt she could gladly do without.

Now, as they were undressing for bed, Quentin told her about the new committee that would be reviewing his work. She knew he was concerned about it, despite his easy-going attitude. He wouldn't have brought up the subject if it didn't bother him.

'But what right does a self-appointed gaggle of uptight New Morality people have to pass judgment on your syllabus?' Jinny asked, aggrieved.

Quentin smiled wearily and rubbed the forefinger of his right hand against its thumb. 'Money talks, sweetheart. Some of those committee members are among the biggest contributors to the university.'

'It's an invasion of academic freedom!' Jinny snarled.

'Sure it is,' he agreed amiably. 'But what can I do about it? The Jews don't like "The Merchant of Venice," the Africans don't like "Othello." The Baptists say "Hamlet" is smutty and the feminists complain about "Macbeth," for lord's sake! What can I do?'

That stopped her. What *could* they do about it if the university administration and the faculty leaders permitted it? Probably a lot of New Morality members among them, she realized.

'You know the old Chinese advice about getting raped,' Quentin said softly, as he took off his trousers.

'You shouldn't relax,' she said, from her side of the bed. 'And you sure as hell shouldn't enjoy it.'

Naked, he flopped onto the bed. 'Ah, love, let us be true to one another, for this world has neither certitude nor peace nor help for pain,' he misquoted slightly.

Jinny sat on the bed beside him. 'This world,' she replied.

DIRECTOR'S OFFICE

'Operation Bootstrap?' Greg echoed, from behind his desk. 'Are you joking?'

'No,' said Doug. 'It's not a joke.'

The two of them were alone in Greg's office: Doug in his usual spot on the couch by the door, Greg sitting upright behind his desk.

With a shake of his head, Greg said to his brother, 'When Mom told me about it I thought perhaps it was some kind of prank you and Brudnoy had cooked up.'

'Greg, it's something we have to do,' Doug said earnestly.

'Really?'

'Sooner or later.'

'It won't be sooner.'

For all the urgency in his words, Doug looked calm and relaxed, almost insolently at ease, Greg thought. His young half-brother slouched back in the couch all the way across the office. He expects me to get up from my desk and go over to him, Greg told himself. No way.

I'm the director of Moonbase. I called him here into my office; he's not going to make me jump through his hoops.

'Look, Doug, I asked you to come here without Mom so we could talk over this crazy idea of yours—'

'It's not a crazy idea,' Doug said.

'Come on, now . . .'

'I've worked out the numbers, Greg. We can build Clipper-ships that'll outperform anything that's ever flown. And that's just the beginning. There's aircraft, automobiles – we can transform the whole world!'

Greg frowned at his half-brother. 'Pie in the sky. Nothing but pipedreams.'

'Look at the numbers!' Doug urged. 'I can bring them up on your computer.'

'I'm sure you can put numbers on a screen that say anything you want them to say,' Greg replied, acidly. 'But that doesn't mean I'm going to get as crazy as you are.'

'It's not crazy!'

'Operation Shoelace,' Greg sneered.

Doug jolted to his feet and strode up to the curving desk. Greg had to look up at his younger half-brother, leaning both fists on the desk top menacingly.

'Operation Bootstrap will not only save Moonbase, Greg,' Doug said, as calm and implacable as a brick wall, 'it'll make Masterson Aerospace the most powerful corporation on Earth.'

'Sit down,' Greg snapped.

Doug pulled up the nearest webbed chair and sat in it.

'Now listen to the realities,' Greg said, tapping a fingernail on his desk top.

Doug smiled slightly. 'Okay, I'm listening.'

'I've spent the past six months searching for a way to keep this base afloat—'

'Operation Bootstrap is the way to do it!'

'All that you'll accomplish,' Greg countered annoyedly, 'is to push Moonbase into the red deeper and faster. It's nonsense! Absolute nonsense!'

'But it's not—'

'For chrissake, Doug, we can't even get the mass driver finished!'

'I know that.'

'It's taking every bit of energy and manpower that I can spare. I've got to get the mass driver built and still show a profit every quarter. Do you know how tough that is? Do you have any idea of the pressures I'm under?'

'Okay,' Doug said, raising his hands in a gesture of surrender. 'Forget everything I just said, then.'

'Good.'

'But we've got to do Operation Bootstrap if we're going to keep Moonbase alive.'

'Moonbase is a continuing drain on the corporation's finances.'

'Greg, this isn't about money! It's much more—'

'Don't be childish,' Greg snapped. 'It's always about money. There isn't anything else.'

'But—'

'But nothing! If I don't show a profit the board will shut us down, just like that.' Greg snapped his fingers. 'Is that what you want?'

'No,' said Doug quietly. 'But it's what you want, isn't it?'

Greg stared at him.

'You didn't take the directorship here to save us, Greg. You came up here to kill Moonbase.'

Doug saw his brother flinch at the word 'kill.' I shouldn't have said it, he told himself. But it's too late now.

'Moonbase is Mom's pet project,' Greg said slowly, his voice low and trembling. 'She's been nursing it along for more than twenty years now. But there's no rationale to keep it going. It's a drain on the corporation.'

With a shake of his head, Doug replied, 'There's more involved here than the quarterly profit-and-loss statement, Greg.'

'You *still* don't see—'

'No, *you* don't see,' Doug said, raising his voice slightly. 'Moonbase has been tottering on the brink of extinction ever since it started. I know that. I also know that if we're limited to supplying raw materials for the orbital factories we'll always be on the ragged edge. Always!'

'What do you mean, limited?'

'We've got to expand our operations! We've got to make ourselves self-sufficient and move beyond just being a mining operation. Being self-sufficient means more than just having enough water to go around, Greg. We've got to be able to manufacture everything we need, right here at Moonbase, without needing imports from Earthside.'

'In your dreams,' Greg muttered.

'We can do it! I know we can! But we've got to start now. We've all got to work together on this.'

Is he really that naive, Greg wondered, or is he just trying to manipulate me?

Taking a deep breath and sitting up straighter, Greg said firmly, 'When my term here is over, I'm going to recommend to the board that Moonbase be shut down.'

'But we can turn things around,' Doug urged.

Exasperated, Greg burst out, 'Do you have any idea of what you'd need to mine an asteroid? This isn't some game! Get real!'

Strangely, instead of getting angry, Doug smiled. 'Greg, I've calculated every detail of the job. I've run it through our logistics and engineering programs. I can even tell you the exact date on which we'll make rendezvous with 2015–eta.'

'With what?'

'That's the best asteroid for our purposes. When you trade off its nearest-approach distance against the eccentricity and inclination of its orbit—'

Doug blathered on about the asteroid while Greg sat, seething. I didn't want Mom here, he reminded himself, because she'd side with him and not me. I wanted to confront him face-to-face, all by ourselves. But now he's pulling out all this technical garbage to show how much more he knows than I do.

'Hold it!' Greg snapped.

Doug stopped in mid-sentence.

'Now listen to this and believe it: Nothing new is getting started at this base. I'm willing to let the mass-driver job continue, but that's just because we might be able to sell the facility to the Japanese once it's finished.'

'Sell it?'

'Or sell the know-how. Yamagata could buy the nanobugs and build their own mass driver for themselves.'

'Maybe Yamagata will want to buy Moonbase,' Doug thought aloud. 'The whole base.'

'Maybe,' Greg agreed, with a cold smile. 'I hadn't thought of that possibility. They just might be fanatic enough.'

'But otherwise you'll shut down Moonbase.'

'What choice do we have? The U.N.'s nanotech treaty will wipe out the base anyway.'

'So the deal with Kiribati is just a fake?' Doug asked.

'I'll take care of the Kiribati deal. You don't have to worry about it.'

'You're just doing it to keep Mom happy.'

'I'm doing it,' Greg said icily, 'so that we'll have a place to continue nanotech work, despite the U.N. treaty.' Before Doug could reply he added, 'We don't need Moonbase or even space stations to use nanotechnology. I can make Kiribati a very wealthy nation, using nanotechnology.'

'If the U.N. doesn't pressure them into quitting,' Doug said. 'Or the New Morality doesn't bomb the islands.'

Greg glared at him.

'So you're really going to shut down Moonbase,' said Doug.

'That's right. And you can run to Mom and tell her all about it. I don't care. My mind's made up.'

'You're making a mistake, Greg. A horrible mistake.'

Raising his voice nearly to a shout, Greg insisted, 'Doug, I won't have it! Stop this crap here and now! Moonbase is history! It's dead!'

Doug looked shocked. For the first time since he'd sauntered into the office, he looked upset, almost fearful. Greg nodded, satisfied. That wiped the self-satisfied smile off his face.

'I've made my decision and that's it,' Greg said. 'Moonbase is history and there's nothing you or Mom or anyone else can do to save it.'

Doug studied his older brother's face for several silent moments. There's no sense arguing with him, he realized. His mind's made up. He's in no mood to consider the facts.

'All right.' Slowly, Doug got up from the web chair. 'You're the boss.'

Greg's smile widened slightly. 'I'm glad you understand that.'

Doug walked to the door. He knew he shouldn't, but he

turned back and said, 'But if Moonbase is dead, it's because you've murdered it.'

Greg wanted to scream at the impudent young snot, but for just a flash of a second he thought he saw Paul Stavenger standing at the door and not his son. Looking at him accusingly. Greg blinked and it was Doug again. With the same accusing stare.

Before Greg could reply, Doug opened the door and stepped through.

'It's always darkest just before the dawn,' Doug muttered to himself. It didn't cheer him one bit.

Surprised and stung by Greg's stubborn refusal to listen to reason, Doug did what he often did when he felt troubled. He went to the main airlock, pulled on a space suit, and went out for a walk on the crater floor.

The Sun was down; dawn would not come for another several hours, but it was never truly dark at Alphonsus' latitude. The Earth hung up in the sky, glowing warm and bright, deep blue oceans and swirls of clean white clouds. Doug saw that Earth was nearly at its full phase. He could clearly see the southwestern U.S. desert and the cloud-shaded California coast. On the other side of the Pacific the tight spiral of a powerful typhoon was approaching the Philippines.

Greg's acting like he's brain-dead, Doug told himself. He's made up his mind and he doesn't want to be bothered with the facts.

A tractor trundled past him, kicking up dust.

'Need a lift?' Doug heard in his helmet earphones.

'Thanks, no.'

The tractor lumbered past him, on its way out to the mass driver site. Doug walked slowly in that direction, thinking that up until a few months ago you could walk almost anywhere you wanted to out here on the crater floor and be happily alone. Except for the rocket port, of course, but you could avoid that easily enough if you wanted to.

Not anymore, he saw. The mass driver project was turning

this part of the crater floor into a busy, bustling conglomeration of tractors and nanotech crews in dust-spattered space suits.

The mass driver. An electric catapult more than two miles long that accelerates packets of lunar ore to more than a hundred gees in a few seconds. With luck, they'll finish it just in time to close down the whole base.

Tractors with bulldozer blades on their fronts were smoothing a road between the main airlock and the mass driver site, scraping aside the dark top layer of the regolith to reveal the bright, new-looking stuff beneath. Doug followed the churned-up turmoil of their tracks until he could clearly see the driver itself rising from the dusty, pockmarked ground like a low metal finger pointed at the horizon.

They were having trouble with the nanomachines, Doug knew. Not enough iron in the regolith to process into the structural steel they needed. And every atom imported from Earth raised hell with Greg's quarterly profit-and-loss figures.

What a waste, Doug thought sadly. Finish the job so we can sell it to Yamagata. What would the men and women working on this mass driver think if I told them Greg's going to close the base? That all their work is for nothing. That the best they can hope for is to sell the fruit of their labor to Yamagata.

It's not right, he knew. It's just not right. We ought to be building for the future, reaching out to the asteroids, the other planets, eventually to the stars. Not retreating, not slinking back to Earth as if we can't meet the challenges out here.

Briefly Doug wondered what it'd be like to be launched off the Moon by the mass driver. A hundred gees. He laughed to himself. In the first second you'd be smeared into a thin bloody pulp. Take the nice slow rocket; it's safer.

He could see the driver clearly now, its dark metal bulk marching straight as an arrow off into the distance while machines and spacesuited figures crawled over and around it like mechanical acolytes at some vast alien altar.

Greg doesn't have the vision, Doug knew. He just doesn't see the future at all. To him, tomorrow's just like today. He's making the deal with Kiribati so the corporation can become more profitable by using nanotechnology on Earth. He doesn't even see the forces down there that'll try to crush him and nanotechnology, together.

Okay, Doug said to himself. Do you see the future? Are you so dead-certain that you know what's right?

He answered himself immediately. Yes. I know what we've got to do. I can see the path the human race has to take. Grow or die. It's that simple, that stark. If we don't grow beyond the confines of Earth we're going to sink into an overcrowded, overpolluted fishbowl of a world without freedom, without hope, a world of poverty and despair and global dictatorship.

As he trudged along the dusty crater floor, Doug tapped a gloved finger into the palm of his other hand, ticking off the points he wanted to make.

The mass driver's important. It can lower our launch costs and make us profitable. But only if the factories in Earth orbit can build products that we can sell.

We've got to get out to that asteroid. We've got to show them that we can make Clipperships of diamond and revolutionize the aerospace industry. More than that, we'll be producing a product with nanotechnology that everyone on Earth will want. We'll be striking a blow against the nanoluddites and the New Morality. And even more than *that*, we'll be moving Moonbase from a mining operation to a manufacturing center. From a marginal town to a growing city. That's the most important thing.

That's what we've got to do! We've got to! And we've got less than six months to do it.

Doug stared off into the dark endless sky. I can't let Greg shut down Moonbase. I've got to get Operation Bootstrap going despite him. Behind his back, over his head, any way I can. We've got to push Operation Bootstrap whether Greg likes it or not.

But how? How can I mobilize the people here when Greg's dead-set against it? How can I move us toward the asteroid mining effort if the base director won't permit anyone to work on the program? It'll be a direct challenge to Greg, almost a mutiny.

Can I really fight him? Mom wants us to work together,

but Greg doesn't want that. He just doesn't see what we have to do. He doesn't have the vision. He's acting as if he's still sitting in Savannah or New York. That's where his mind is. That's where his attitudes are.

Doug turned away from the busy work scene stretching out along the miles-long track of the mass driver, turned his back to all that and looked across the emptiness of the pockmarked crater floor toward the softly rounded old mountains of the ringwall.

'It's always darkest before the dawn,' he repeated to himself. Scant consolation, he thought.

It certainly was dark out there. With the Earth behind him, the airless sky looked black as infinity, specked here and there by a few stars bright enough to see through the heavy tinting of his helmet visor.

Dark and empty, Doug thought.

But as his eyes adjusted to the darkness, Doug realized that there was a faint glow rising above the tired old mountain that poked its head up in the middle of the giant crater. Out beyond the brutally close horizon, the sky was slowly brightening.

They're wrong! Doug told himself. They're all wrong! It's not darkest just before the dawn. Not on the Moon, at least.

For out in the star-flecked blackness beyond the weary mountains, a pale hazy glow was beginning to light the predawn hours. The zodiacal light, Doug knew. Sunlight reflected off dust particles floating in space, the leftovers from the creation of the solar system. Here in the airless sky of Moonbase they light up the heavens long before the Sun comes into view.

Doug raised his arms to the ancient motes of dust that brightened the predawn hours. They're like friendly little fireflies out there in space, he told himself. They bring us the message, the promise that the light is on its way, the Sun will rise, a new day will dawn. Have hope. The darkness will end. It's a good omen.

Feeling excited again, energized, he said to himself, I've got to talk with Brudnoy again. And Bianca. Maybe they can get me together with a few people who can get Operation Bootstrap started.

And Mom? Doug wondered about that as he started trudging back toward the main airlock. No, Mom will side with Greg. She's a businesswoman, and Greg can make a stronger case for the bottom line than I can.

Still, Doug broke into a broad grin as he hurried back toward Moonbase. Greg's got profit-and-loss statements and projections of inventories and all that puke. All I've got is a broken-down former cosmonaut and maybe a few other people who might want to help me with Operation Bootstrap.

And a vision for the future.

He began to leap across the barren dusty ground, soaring in twenty-yard strides across the crater floor.

'Hey, where you goin' in such a hurry?' a construction worker's voice called in his earphones.

'Into the future!' Doug sang back.

BIANCA'S QUARTERS

'All right, quiet down!' Bianca Rhee shouted.

They all stopped talking and looked at her expectantly. Doug counted fourteen people crammed into Bianca's quarters, five of them squeezed on the bunk, the others crowded on the floor. Most of them were long-termers, men and women on year-long work contracts. Several had been working at Moonbase for many years, shuttling back and forth to Earth.

Lev Brudnoy had appropriated the desk chair and placed one of the female student-workers on his lap. He sat there with a satisfied smile on his grizzled face, one long arm around the young woman's waist, his other hand grasping an insulated flask of rocket juice. The others clutched a motley assortment of cups, glasses, bottles, even zero-gee squeeze bulbs. It was a BYOB party.

The ostensible reason for the party was to show off the new wallscreen that Doug had bought for Bianca. It almost filled the wall opposite her bunk, turning the blank stone into a window that could look out on the world, wherever vidcams could go. For the first hour of the party they had hooted and catcalled through a production of a Masterson Corporation-sponsored drama set on a corporate space station where romance and intrigue flourished in zero gravity.

Now the video was finished and the Windowall showed a satellite view of the great rift valley of Mars. Bianca perched herself on the desktop, her legs too short to reach the floor. She asked Doug to come up and sit beside her. They all wore workers' coveralls, color-coded to show their departments. Doug saw mostly the pumpkin orange of the research department and the olive green of mining, although there were a couple of medical whites in the crowd; one of the women medics wore hers unbuttoned almost to the waist, showing plenty of cleavage. He wore the only management blue.

Seeing that she had their attention, Bianca said more softly, 'Doug's got something important to tell you.' And with that, she turned to him, grinning.

'Thanks for the glowing introduction,' Doug joked weakly. A few chuckles from the people looking up at him. He knew most of them, at least the long-termers. Of course, each coverall carried a nametag.

'I need your help,' Doug began. 'I want to start moving Moonbase along the road to self-sufficiency as rapidly as we can manage it.'

As he began to outline his plans for Operation Bootstrap, Doug studied their faces. At first they looked amused, as if they expected this to be an elaborate joke of some kind. But then they started getting interested, and began asking questions.

'You really expect us to modify an LTV in our spare time?'

Doug answered, 'A couple of extra hours a day from five technicians who know what they're doing can get the job done in ten weeks, from what the computer estimates tell me.'

'But we won't get paid for the extra work.'

'No, it'll be strictly voluntary. Your pay will come as a share of the profit we make from the asteroid ore.'

'Work first, pay later. Huh!'

Bianca said, 'Hey, you're always complaining there's nothing to do up here except drink and screw around.'

'What's wrong with that?' one of the guys piped up.

Everyone laughed.

But Doug went on seriously, 'I know it's a lot to ask, and you might put in a lot of work for nothing if the mission isn't successful. But if we do succeed . . .'

'How much money we talking about?'

'The calculations work out to about five times your hourly wage, if we get the amount of ore we're hoping for.'

'And the corporation'll give us this money as a bonus?'

'Right.'

'But the corporation doesn't even know we're doing this . . . this Bootstrap thing? How does that work?'

Doug replied, 'We're all taking a chance. You're risking your time. Once we've got the ore from the asteroid, though, the corporation will pay you a bonus along the lines I've calculated.'

'How can we be sure of that?'

'You have my word on it,' Doug said.

'No offense, pal, but how much weight does your word have with the management?'

Doug smiled. 'Good question. Let me put it this way: If the corporation won't come up with the money, then I will. Personally.'

'Or we can sell the ore to Yamagata,' one of the women said.

No one laughed.

Lev Brudnoy said, 'I hate to be the bearer of evil tidings, but there is a rumor that the base will be shut down at the end of this director's term.'

'Yeah, I've heard that buzz.'

Several others nodded.

Doug had to admit it. 'That's the director's current plan. I'm hoping we can make him change his mind.'

'He's your brother, isn't he?'

'My half-brother.'

'Does that mean he's only half as heavy?' asked one of the women. 'You know, "He ain't heavy, he's my brother."'

Doug made a rueful grin for her. 'He's twice as heavy, believe me.'

'So you want us to stick our necks out when the base director's ready to shut down the whole humpin' operation?'

'I want to save Moonbase,' Doug replied.

'Wait a minute. Where are you going to get an LTV to modify?'

'I'll handle that,' said Doug. 'None of you has to do a thing or commit yourselves to a minute of extra work unless and until I get an LTV for us.'

They glanced at each other, muttering.

'Whatever happens,' Bianca said, without waiting for them to come to a group decision, 'this little meeting here ought to be kept secret for the time being.'

'Secret? From who?'

'Whom,' corrected one of the students.

'From management,' said Doug. 'I want to present this as a *fait accompli* before my brother knows what we're doing.'

Someone whistled softly.

'Look,' Doug said, 'we can't expect any support from the corporation. That's why we've got to do this on a volunteer basis and hope to get our payback at the end of the asteroid mission.'

'Sounds awfully risky.'

'Sounds like a good way to get fired.'

'You can't be fired for working overtime on a voluntary basis,' Doug said. 'Read your employment contracts.'

'Well,' said Bianca, 'I don't know about the rest of you turkeys, but I'm ready to put in a couple of extra hours for this.'

Brudnoy said, 'It should be more interesting than spending your spare time in The Cave, waiting for the menu to change.'

They all laughed. Doug thought maybe half of them would actually volunteer to work on their own time. But this meeting would never be kept a secret. The word about Operation Bootstrap would spread through Moonbase with the speed of sound.

Which was what he was counting on.

'I've never been out this far before,' said Brudnoy.

His voice sounded strange in Doug's helmet earphones. Subdued. Almost reverent.

'I hardly ever come out here myself,' Rhee said. 'Just for these regular maintenance checks.'

The astronomical observatory was on the opposite side of Alphonsus' central peak from Moonbase. It had been placed out there to shield it from any stray light or dust or chemical pollution from the spacecraft landing and taking off at the rocket port. This meant a two-hour tractor ride across the crater floor, but Doug and Brudnoy had decided to accompany Rhee to see the instruments she used to track near-Earth asteroids.

Now Rhee led them through a jungle of metal shapes, all pointed skyward. Wide-angle telescopes, spectrometers, infrared and ultraviolet and even gamma-ray detectors. Doug easily recognized the wide dishes of the four radio telescopes off in the distance, but one shape puzzled him: it looked like a huge but stubby wide tub mounted on tracked pivots. It was easily twenty yards across.

'The light bucket?' Rhee said when he asked. 'That's the Shapley Telescope, two-thousand-centimeter reflector. The most powerful telescope in the solar system.'

'You use it for deep space observations?'

Rhee replied cheerfully, 'I don't use it at all. It's reserved for the Big Boys back Earthside. But yes, they use it for cosmological work. Quasars and redshifts, stuff like that.'

Brudnoy asked, 'Wasn't there talk of building an even bigger "light bucket," using liquid mercury instead of a glass mirror?'

'The Shapley's mirror is aluminum,' Rhee answered. 'No need for glass in this gravity.'

'But the mercury telescope?'

'Maybe someday. Probably be easier to make really big mirrors with mercury, but it tends to vaporize into the vacuum.'

Doug watched their two spacesuited figures as they spoke: Brudnoy taller than Rhee by more than a helmet's worth.

'Couldn't it be covered with a protective coating?' the Russian asked.

'Sure, but that cuts down on its reflectivity.'

'Ah.'

Doug asked, 'Which ones do you use for tracking the asteroids?'

'Over here.' Rhee pointed and Doug followed her out-stretched gloved hand with his eyes.

'The two big ones are Schmidts,' she explained. 'Wide field

'scopes. Schmidt-Mendells, actually; they've been specially built for lunar work. And those over there are tracking individual asteroids, getting spectrographic data on their compositions.'

'For your thesis,' Doug realized.

'Right.'

'Don't you use radar to detect asteroids?' Brudnoy asked.

Doug could sense her nodding inside her helmet. 'Sure. One of the radio telescopes converts to radar sweeps twice a day. When we pick up something new we track it long enough to determine its orbit and then turn one of the spectrographic 'scopes on it.'

'What happens to all this equipment if Moonbase shuts down?' Doug asked.

'The university consortium will keep them running as long as they can, I guess,' Rhee answered. 'The data gets piped back Earthside automatically, as it is. Maybe they'll be able to send a maintenance crew up here every six months or so, keep it all going.'

'It would be a shame to lose all this,' Brudnoy muttered.

Doug nodded agreement even though they couldn't see him do it.

It took three hours for Rhee to complete all her maintenance checks and make the necessary adjustments in the instruments. Then they climbed back into the open tractor and trundled toward Moonbase. Brudnoy and Doug got off at the rocket port and Rhee drove alone back to the main airlock and the garage inside it.

'So this is the one you want to buy,' Brudnoy said as they walked slowly to the lunar transfer vehicle sitting on one of the smoothed rock pads.

'It's been in service for ten years,' Doug said, looking up at the ungainly spacecraft. 'The corporation would sell it for about twice its scrap value, I think.'

The LTV looked rather like a pyramidal shaped skeleton. It squatted on four bent, flimsy-looking legs that supported a metal mesh platform. From the platform rose gold-foiled propellant tanks, darker odd-shaped cargo containers, pipes and plumbing with gray electronics boxes wedged in, it seemed, wherever they could be fitted. Up at the top, some thirty feet above Doug's head, was the empty plastiglass bubble of a passenger/crew compartment.

'Well,' Brudnoy said, sighing, 'we won't need the passenger bubble.'

'Replace it with more cargo holds,' said Doug.

'No, I think the mining equipment should go there.'

'Oh, right,' Doug agreed hastily. 'I almost forgot we'll need that.'

For nearly an hour they clambered over the aging LTV, awkward in their cumbersome surface suits. The spacecraft stood stoically on the pad, like a dignified old gutted building being inspected by skeptical prospective buyers.

'Metal fatigue,' Brudnoy muttered time and again. 'This whole section must be replaced.'

Doug took notes on his hand-held computer.

Finally the Russian was satisfied. 'Not as good as I wanted,' he said as he and Doug climbed back down onto the scoured ground again. 'But not as bad as I feared.'

'Can we get into shape?' Doug asked.

'Of course,' Brudnoy answered. Then he added, 'The question is, how much will it cost to get it into shape?'

'We've got some homework to do,' Doug said as they headed for the main airlock.

Once inside, and out of their suits, Doug said, 'Come on down to my quarters and we'll start figuring out the cost numbers.'

He started striding down the tunnel. Brudnoy lagged behind him.

'I could use a good night's sleep,' the Russian said.

Doug saw that Brudnoy's pouchy eyes had dark circles under them. He glanced at his wristwatch. It was nearly midnight.

'Oh. Okay,' Doug said as they approached the double-sized hatch of the farm. 'Actually, I've got a few hours of studying to do; got an exam tomorrow.'

'On what subject?'

'European architecture. I'll have to build either a classical Greco-Roman temple or a Gothic cathedral.'

'With your bare hands?' Brudnoy asked.

Grinning, Doug replied, 'They'll let me use a computer.'

'Very kind of them.'

'I've still got to put in a few hours at the screen, though,' said Doug.

Brudnoy stopped a moment at the farm's entrance. The airtight hatch was closed, as usual.

'I should check on my rabbits,' he said, yawning. 'The automatic feeder has been cranky lately.'

'I'll help you,' Doug offered.

'No, not now. I'm too tired. Tomorrow will be good enough.' And he started walking down the tunnel again.

Doug slowed his own pace to keep in step with the Russian.

'You never get tired, do you?' Brudnoy asked.

'I don't feel tired, no.'

'Is it the natural buoyancy of youth, I wonder? Or do the nanomachines in you give you this preternatural endurance?'

'Preternatural?' Doug laughed.

Just as they reached the cross tunnel, two young women came around the corner. They stopped and stood uncertainly in the tunnel, both in crisp new white coveralls. Doug saw that they were wearing weighted boots. Newcomers.

'Oh!' said the taller of the two. 'We're looking for the farm.'

She was a good-looking brunette. Her companion was stockier, curly red hair clipped short, with a bosom that strained the front of her jumpsuit.

Brudnoy stroked his bearded chin. 'The farm? Why should two such lovely ladies be looking for the farm at this time of night?'

'We just got off our shift,' said the brunette.

'And we heard that you keep bunny rabbits down here,' said the redhead.

Brudnoy's weariness seemed to disappear. Before Doug's eyes the tired old man turned into a smiling, boyish swain

with large, liquid eyes that blinked at the two women long-
ingly.

'Ah, yes, the bunny rabbits. One of them just gave birth,
this very afternoon.'

'Really?' they squealed in unison. 'Can we see them?'

'Of course,' said Brudnoy. 'Right this way.'

'It's not too late?'

'For such lovely newcomers to our humble farm, how could
it be too late?' Brudnoy glanced at Doug and rolled his eyes.

'I've got to be going,' Doug said.

Smiling wolfishly, Brudnoy said, 'Then I shall have to show
the rabbits to these young ladies all by myself?'

'Well,' said Doug, 'maybe I can hang around for a little
bit.'

'If it's not too much trouble,' the brunette said.

'No trouble at all,' Brudnoy answered grandly. 'Just follow me.'

Doug laughed to himself as he followed Brudnoy and the
two women back toward the farm and the rabbit pens. No
wonder Lev likes to keep the rabbits, he said to himself. And
here I thought he only had our nutritional needs in mind.

Well, Doug mused, maybe we can recruit these two for
Operation Bootstrap. If nothing else.

MT. YEAGER

'Well, what do you think?' Doug asked.

He could hear his mother's excited breathing through the suit radio. From their vantage atop Mt. Yeager they could see almost the entire floor of Alphonsus before the sharp lunar horizon cut off their view. In the other direction, Mare Nubium stretched out like an endless undulating frozen sea of rock, dotted with smaller craters and the glowing red beacon lights of the old temporary shelters.

'You were right, Doug,' Joanna said in a hushed, awed voice. 'It's breathtaking.'

She had never been out on the lunar surface before. Doug quietly insisted that she make an excursion with him; they both knew his motive was to get her alone, away from Greg, so they could talk without interruption, without eavesdropping.

Joanna had been upset and impatient during the hour they spent getting into the spacesuits and prebreathing their low-pressure mix of oxygen and nitrogen. Then Doug had requisitioned a hopper and taken his mother – who made it clear she was frightened half to death – up to the top of the tallest mountain in Alphonsus' ringwall.

'There's the mass driver,' Doug said, pointing at the dark line laid out across the crater floor. 'And the rocket port. You can see the solar energy farms . . .'

But Joanna's eyes were turned the other way. She stretched out a gloved hand toward the red beacons marching straight out toward the brutally close horizon.

'Those are the tempos, aren't they?' she asked.

Doug nodded inside his helmet, then grasped his mother's shoulders gently and turned her slightly to the left.

'That's Wodjohowitcz Pass,' he said, pointing to a rounded cleft in the ringwall. 'That's where my father died.'

He heard the breath catch in her throat.

'Would you like to see the plaque there?' Doug asked.

'No,' Joanna said, her voice husky. 'I know what it says.'

'We put one like it at the top of Mt. Wasser,' he said. 'For Brennart.'

'I know.'

'We really ought to put up a statue for Brennart,' Doug went on. 'He deserves it.'

'Not until there are tourists to spend money to see it,' Joanna replied firmly.

Doug laughed lightly. 'Right.' More seriously, he added, 'Brennart and I were just getting to know each other . . . respect each other . . .'

'And you lost him.'

'We all lost him. Mom, if he were still here he'd be pushing Operation Bootstrap even harder than I am.'

'All right,' Joanna said. 'Tell me what it is that you didn't want to say in front of Greg.'

Doug went to scratch his chin, but his gloved hand bumped into his helmet, instead. 'Well,' he said, only slightly startled, 'I need to buy an LTV.'

'A lunar transfer vehicle? Buy one?'

'Would the corporation let us modify one of their LTVs for the asteroid mission? Would Greg?'

'No,' she said. 'Of course not.'

'Then I'll have to buy one. I've thought it all through a thousand times,' he said, exaggerating only a little. 'I've worked it out with Lev Brudnoy and a couple of other people who don't want their names used, not yet, anyway—'

'You've got a real conspiracy going!' Joanna said, sounding shocked.

'A cabal,' Doug answered lightly. He immediately added, 'But it hasn't done any harm to Moonbase. Or to Greg. No harm at all.'

'Really?'

Doug returned to his subject. 'We need an LTV to get out to the asteroid.'

'But you'll have to modify the spacecraft. You can't use it as-is to make a rendezvous with an asteroid.'

'That's right.' Doug nodded.

'And where will you make these modifications?'

'I'd like to do it right here.'

'At Moonbase?'

'Right.'

'Do you have the facilities here?'

'Not really.'

'The proper personnel?'

'Sort of.'

'And how do you propose to get the facilities and people you need without your brother knowing about it?'

Doug spread his arms out wide. 'That's the tough part of it. But I figured once we actually acquired an LTV he'd *have* to let us go ahead and modify it.'

'Have to?' Doug could hear the amusement in his mother's voice. 'Greg would more likely fire everyone connected with your – what did you call it, cabal?'

'He wouldn't fire anyone if you were on our side,' Doug said.

That stopped her. Joanna fell silent. The time stretched and stretched.

'I can't be on your side,' Joanna said at last, her voice almost a whisper. 'And I can't be on Greg's. I don't want you two to oppose each other.'

'I know you don't, Mom,' Doug said. 'But you're going to have to choose.'

'No!'

'You can't avoid it,' Doug said firmly, knowing that it was going to come down to this, hating the need but fully certain that there was no other way, there'd never been any other way, she was destined to choose between the two of us since these mountains were raised up, since the beginning of time.

'It's not just Greg or me,' Doug explained. 'It's Moonbase.

It's the future of humanity. Either Moonbase expands and becomes self-sufficient or it dies. My father knew that. You know it! We've got to move beyond being a mining town and grow into a community that's physically and economically self-sufficient. That's what the diamond Clipperships are all about, but Greg's too close-minded to see the entire picture, to grasp the fullness of the future.'

'And you do understand it?'

'I honestly think I do, Mom. Either Moonbase grows or it dies. And if Moonbase dies, if we close this little foothold on the frontier, humankind folds back in on itself. The whole human race will sink into poverty and despair – and the kind of mind-controlling dictatorship that the New Morality is aiming at.'

'What about Yamagata and Europeans?'

'They can't open the frontier the way we can. They're government-run, they'll stay small and stick to scientific research.'

'I don't see where—'

'Dictatorship is already on the march back Earthside, Mom. It's already happening!' Doug insisted, pleading with her. 'Now they want to shut down all nanotechnology. They've been censoring books and video for years. They're taking control of the universities. Don't you see, Mom? They're trying to control the thought centers! Once they've got them under control they can take over governments. And then the corporations.'

'But even if that's true, what's it got to do with Moonbase?'

'We can be free of them,' Doug said. 'And as long as there's one place that's free the rest of the human race has a chance. We can be an example of what people can accomplish when they're free to think and build and grow.'

For a few moments Joanna was silent. Doug strained to see her face through her visor, but all he saw was the reflection of his own blank helmet.

'Those are fine words, Doug,' she said at last. 'And I know you believe them—'

'You believe them, too, don't you?'

'I don't know.' She turned away from him, looked out across Mare Nubium again.

'My father believed it,' Doug said. 'He died for it. So did Brennart.'

She stood stock-still, facing the vast Sea of Clouds and the tiny red beacons still glowing out where the old buried shelters stood.

'I need your help, Mom.'

'So does Greg.'

'Then you'll have to choose between us.'

'No,' she whispered.

'Yes,' Doug insisted. 'Him or me. My father's dream, or . . .' Doug found that he couldn't finish the sentence.

But Joanna could. 'I either help you build Paul's dream or I help his murderer. That's what you're saying.'

'That's where it is, Mom.'

She turned back to face him. 'Buy your damned LTV,' Joanna hissed. 'Do what you have to do. I'll try to get Greg to listen to reason.'

'Thanks.' Doug was surprised by the bitterness in her voice, and even more shocked at the resentful anger he felt welling up inside him.

I've won, he told himself. Why does it feel so awful?

VANCOUVER

'Isn't this city beautiful?' Kris Cardenas asked. 'I'm going to hate to leave it.'

She and Wilhelm Zimmerman were strolling along a curving path through Stanley Park's harborside garden, dazzling with flowers. Above them the sky was a perfect blue, dotted with puffs of cumulus. In the distance the snow-capped peaks of the coastal range floated like blue-white ghosts disconnected from the ground.

'Christchurch is just as beautiful,' said Zimmerman, in his wretchedly accented English. 'Almost.'

'I've been very happy here,' Cardenas said wistfully. 'Pete's been able to do really useful work among the poor.'

'Are you safe here?' Zimmerman asked. 'There have been murders, you know.'

Cardenas laughed lightly. 'Safer than Switzerland, Willi. Canadians are the least violent people on Earth, I think.'

'But Canada will sign the U.N.'s treaty,' Zimmerman said heavily.

'New Zealand's so far away!'

Although he was not that much older than she, Zimmerman looked to passersby like Cardenas' father or at least a paunchy elder uncle as they walked slowly along the meandering garden path. Puffing away on a foul-smelling cigar that earned him several angry stares, the Swiss biophysicist was sloppy and grossly overweight, his suit jacket flapping in the sea breeze like a loose sail. Cardenas still looked like a California surfer, curly sandy hair and broad in the shoulders, decked in jeans and a light beige sweater.

But her bright blue eyes did not sparkle.

'How does your husband feel about New Zealand?' Zimmerman asked.

She waggled a hand in the air. 'A good neurosurgeon can work wherever he goes. That's no problem.'

'And the children?'

Cardenas smiled at him. 'Grandchildren, Willi.'

'No!'

'Of course. What did you expect? My oldest will be thirty in another few months.'

Zimmerman puffed hard on his stogie. 'How many grandchildren are there?'

'Two, so far. My daughter's expecting in November. That's why I want to stay until the end of the year.'

'Well,' said Zimmerman bravely, 'Christchurch is less than an hour away from here, if you use the rocket.'

Cardenas smiled wanly. 'I know. But still . . .'

'Yes, I know. I understand. I will miss Basel, also. The pastries. And the good beer. More than half of my staff refuse to leave Switzerland. I can't blame them. Some of them worry about their pensions, others have family they don't want to leave.'

'It's not an easy choice, Willi.'

'For you and me, it is. We go where they allow us to work. As long as New Zealand doesn't sign the *verdammt* treaty—'

Her phone buzzed. Only the immediate family had access to it, so Cardenas hurriedly pulled the palm-sized instrument from her shoulder purse.

'Yes? Pete?' Zimmerman watched her face relax. She was worried about her pregnant daughter, obviously. 'Joanna Stavenger?' She glanced at Zimmerman. 'Why in the world would I travel to Moonbase, just to examine her son? That's ridiculous . . . No, I'll call her myself when we get home.'

Her husband said more, and Zimmerman saw Cardenas' jaw clench. 'Oh no! Oh my god.'

He waited as patiently as he could, standing there in the winding garden pathway as couples and families passed

them, casting frowns at his cigar, while Cardenas' face
grew whiter.

At last she folded the phone and put it back in her
shoulder bag.

'Bad news?'

'New Zealand's just announced that they'll sign the treaty,
after all.'

'No!'

'Their government is under tremendous pressure from the
party that's backed by the New Morality movement. To stay
in power, they've decided to sign the treaty.'

Zimmerman flung his cigar butt to the brick walk and
stamped on it, swearing in German. Cardenas couldn't understand the words but she recognized the tone easily enough.

'Well,' she said, her breath fluttering, 'Pete really didn't
want to leave Vancouver anyway. And the kids are all here . . .'
Her voice tailed off.

'The only concession you must make is to give up your
career,' Zimmerman said scornfully. 'That's all.'

There were tears in her eyes. 'You too, Willi. They've
stopped us both.'

'Never! I do not stop.'

'Where are you going to go?' Cardenas asked rhetorically.
'There's only a couple of tiny nations that won't sign the treaty
and they don't have the facilities or the trained personnel
you need.'

'Where will I go?' Zimmerman grasped her by the shoulders
and turned her to face toward the distant mountains. The pale
curve of the Moon hung above the bluish snow-clad peaks.

'There!' said Zimmerman firmly. 'I will give up wiener
schnitzel. Sausage and pastries and even beer I will give up.
Even cigars! But not my work. Never! I will *not* give up my
work, even if I have to live like a cave man!'

MOONBASE CONTROL CENTER

'The first day or so when I came up here,' Greg was telling his mother, 'I spent more time in this spot than anyplace else.'

'I remember,' Joanna said.

'The radiation storm.'

'You told me they had a big party going on in The Cave.'

Greg nodded as he walked along the row of consoles. Each was occupied by a man or woman; they all had earphones clamped to their heads, but there was no tension in the room, no excitement. Most of the technicians looked bored as they watched their screens.

The big electronic map of Moonbase that covered one wall of the control center glowed softly. No red lights and only a few amber ones. Everything was under control; no major problems in sight. The base was functioning smoothly.

'We haven't had a big flare like that one since then,' Greg said. 'We're about due for one.'

Greg made his rounds of the base once each day, walking from his office out to the main airlock, then down the ladder that led to the tunnel that went past the farm, then back along the next tunnel to The Cave, and finally to the control center. The fourth tunnel was entirely living quarters, and Greg saw no need to inspect it every day, although he strolled its length at least once a week, just to check things out.

The control center was the nerve nexus of Moonbase, of course. From its consoles every electronic circuit, every valve, every pump and drop of water and whiff of air was monitored both by the base's mainframe computer and the human technicians who constantly watched the display screens and the big glowing wall map.

Joanna was following him on this afternoon's inspection tour, seeking a way to tell him of what Doug wanted to do without causing an explosion.

'So what did you and Doug talk about out there on the mountaintop?' Greg asked, making it sound so casual that she knew he was blazing with curiosity. Or more.

'Operation Bootstrap,' she replied honestly.

'Is he still harping on that nonsense?' Greg complained as he strolled slowly along the row of consoles. 'I wish he'd grow up.'

'I think Doug—'

'Do you know what he's doing?' Greg interrupted, a sly smile on his lips. 'He and Brudnoy want to get their hands on one of our old LTVs and convert it for this idiotic asteroid mission he's dreamed up. He's behaving like a sneaky little kid.'

'Do you think Brudnoy's behaving childishly, too?' Joanna asked mildly.

Instead of answering, Greg stopped and bent over one of the technicians' shoulders to look closely at the monitor display. Joanna wondered if he actually were interested in the display or just doing it for effect.

When Greg straightened up and resumed pacing behind the seated technicians, Joanna said, 'I think Doug has a good idea – it's too good to throw away.'

'Not you too!'

She stopped, forcing him to stop too and turn to face her.

'Greg, we've got to move on this while we still can. If we wait, the U.N. or the New Morality or somebody might try to stop us.'

With exaggerated patience, Greg said, 'Mom, look: I've lined up Kiribati for us. We'll be able to continue developing nanotechnology there in the islands. You ought to be making certain that the board is solidly behind us on this maneuver.'

'Don't worry about the board.'

'Then we can forget about this Bootstrap business, can't we? We can forget about Moonbase altogether. We won't need it as long as Kiribati is cooperative.'

'And how long will that be?'

'Long enough for me to build the first diamond ship,' Greg said.

Shocked, Joanna blurted, 'What?'

Smiling icily, Greg said, 'We have plenty of carbon on Earth, Mother. We don't have to build Doug's dream ships up here. We can do it in Kiribati; much more cheaply, too. And once I demonstrate the prototype to the major aerospace lines, they'll clamor to buy them, treaty or no treaty.'

'But what about your brother? What about Moonbase?'

'Doug will have to return to Earth when I shut this base down.'

Joanna took a breath. 'But Doug can't return to Earth! They'll kill him just like they killed Carlos!'

'He can live in the islands. We can protect him there.'

Glancing at the men and women attending the consoles, Joanna said, 'Greg, we shouldn't be discussing this here.'

But he planted his fists on his hips and demanded, 'Why not? I'm going to recommend to the board that we shut down Moonbase for good. There's nothing we're doing up here that we can't do in Kiribati and you know it!'

My god, Joanna thought, his mind's made up and he won't listen to any alternatives. He doesn't care what happens to Doug. He doesn't care about anything at all.

She heard herself reply, 'Very well, then, Greg. I'll fight you every inch of the way on this. And in the meantime I'm going to buy an LTV and pay for adapting it for the asteroid rendezvous.'

The blood seemed to drain from Greg's face. 'You're going . . . to buy . . .' He couldn't choke out the rest of the words.

'With my own money,' Joanna said. 'It'll be a private venture.'

'You can't . . .'

'Yes I can,' said Joanna, trying to keep her voice down, hating having to say this within earshot of so many strangers.

'And I can rent space from Moonbase for doing the necessary refurbishing work on the LTV.'

Greg visibly struggled to regain control of himself. Some color returned to his cheeks. His eyes seemed to calm down somewhat.

'It's your money,' he said. Then he pushed past his mother and strode back toward the door to the control center, leaving Joanna standing there.

Spend Christmas on Christmas Island, Ibriham al-Rashid grumbled to himself. Only an advertising executive who's never left Manhattan could come up with such an idiotic idea.

It had been three months since Rashid had been named chief operations officer of the new Kiribati Manufacturing and Entertainment Corporation, a weirdly structured company that included luxury vacation centers alongside all of Masterson Corporation's former space operations division, including Moonbase.

Just like that, with little more than a few strokes on a keyboard, he had been removed from his directorship of Masterson's space division and made chief operating officer of this ridiculous new corporation. His work with the fusion energy system was put on hold. 'No need for that if we can still use nanotech in space, or out there on the islands,' the corporate president told him. 'Don't look so grim! This is a promotion for you.'

A promotion, Rashid thought bitterly. They're throwing away the fusion development and sticking me here on this miserable little island. I've been destroyed by corporate politics.

As part of their deal with Kiribati, Masterson Corporation was setting up the new company with seats on the board of directors for each of the council chiefs. In addition to transferring Moonbase and the entire space operations division to the new corporation, Masterson was funding construction of two major tourist complexes, with hotels and casinos and all the amenities, one on Tarawa and another on Kiritimati –

the atoll that Westerners still called Christmas Island. 'Spend your holidays on Christmas Island,' was going to be their advertising slogan.

Rashid stood on the atoll's highest point, Joe's Hill, all of twelve meters high, and stared at the devastation that last week's typhoon had left. The sandy islands had been scrubbed clean by the ferocious winds and a storm-driven tide that had surged completely across them, leaving nothing standing but a few battered palm trees.

The islanders had been moved to safety days before the storm struck, of course, and now were trickling back from the shelters to which they had scattered, most of them thousands of miles away, across the broad Pacific.

There were more construction workers than natives on the atoll now, and Rashid's ears rang with the grating whine of power saws and the incessant thumping of electric staple-drivers. Huge trucks groaned and rumbled all over the tiny island.

They were building a luxury casino hotel, an amusement center, and an airfield that could handle Clippership rockets as well as supersonic jets. International relief crews would be arriving soon to start helping the returning natives to rebuild their homes, but the corporate task of turning this smashed atoll into a vacation paradise was moving ahead without delay. Every gram of building materials had to be flown in. Four thousand palm trees were due to arrive today, Rashid knew. Tomorrow's Clippership cargo would include enough sod to grass over the 'championship eighteen-hole golf course' that the advertising brochures promised.

It would almost be as easy to build a resort complex at Moonbase, Rashid thought sourly.

Construction had been behind schedule when the typhoon struck. Now it was seriously lagging. Rashid, who hated to leave Savannah, and actually preferred New York, had rocketed out to Tarawa once the storm had spun away, and then flown on a corporate jet to what was left of Christmas Island.

Not this Christmas, he knew. There'd be no tourists visiting this atoll for many months to come.

His only consolation on this trip was the new assistant he
had hired, a tall, sleek dark woman named Melissa Hart who
had gladly accompanied him on this depressing journey to this
miserable little lonely island.

Rashid had been impressed with her good looks and smooth
self-confidence when she had first appeared at his office
seeking a job on his staff. Her personnel file said that she
had been a faithful Masterson employee for more than ten
years, with an excellent record.

She was older than the women Rashid usually went after.
And rather too thin for his taste. Yet she was alluring: cool
yet tempting, proper in dress and demeanor while her smile
seemed to suggest everything a man could desire. She spoke
modestly, worked efficiently, and smiled deliciously. When
she agreed to accompany him as his assistant on this trip to
the Pacific, Rashid's fantasies kept him awake and sweating
for the entire flight.

Now, with the sun setting and the infernal racket of the
trucks and construction crews beginning to ease off, Rashid
walked along the sandy beach toward the little tent city that
had been put up to house the workers. The largest tent of all had
been erected for him. Melissa slept in a tent with three other
women, all construction workers, all bigger, more muscular,
and much tougher-looking than Rashid himself.

Yet he grinned as he walked along the curving beach. At
least now that the construction crews were knocking off for
the evening he could hear the hiss and boom of the surf. There
would be a moon tonight. Very romantic, looking out across
the lagoon at the night sky.

And Melissa had agreed to have dinner with him. In his
tent. Just the two of them, alone. Rashid felt like a sheik of
old as he prepared his mind for the night's pleasure.

Melissa Hart had not been surprised at how easy it was to
get close to Rashid. New Morality cohorts in Masterson's
personnel department had faked a record for her, and Rashid
hadn't bothered to check any of the recommendations that
were signed by department heads from across the continent.

No, the man had taken one look at her and hired her with a wolfish smile.

Sex is a weapon, Melissa told herself. But a weapon is powerful only when it's used wisely. Keeping Rashid wanting her was the important thing; as long as his desire was alive, she had the power. Allowing him to have her would diminish that power, she knew. She would give Rashid smiles and glances, even kisses and fondling. But they would consummate his lust only when it suited Melissa's goal.

Tonight we have dinner in his tent, she told herself as she clipped on a pair of faux pearl earrings. One of them was a microminiaturized radio that would transmit every word of their conversation to the solid-state recorder hidden beneath her cot.

'Big night with the big shit boss, huh?' said one of the construction workers with whom Melissa shared the tent. She was a short, burly woman with a good-natured laugh and a vocabulary from the docks. The other two had not come in yet.

Melissa nodded as she studied her image in the only mirror she had, a small hand-sized one.

'How do I look?' she asked.

The woman eyed her critically. Melissa was wearing flowing light pink silk harem pants slitted from hip to cuff, with a loose long-sleeved overblouse.

'Good enough to eat,' the construction worker said, grinning.

Melissa smiled back at her. The woman began to pull off her grimy tee-shirt. 'Watch out for him,' she warned. 'He's got ideas about you.'

'Don't worry about me,' said Melissa. 'I've handled men like him before.'

'Sure.' And the woman made an up-and-down movement with her fist.

Melissa laughed at the crudity. I should give her a lecture on morality, she thought, but I don't have the time.

As she started out of the tent, the woman said, 'I'm damned fuckin' jealous, you know.'

Surprised, Melissa blurted, 'You'd want to have dinner with the boss?'

'Uh-uh,' she replied. 'I'd rather have you.'

'Oh,' was all that Melissa could think to reply. But as she left the tent she thought that she would certainly have to give her a morality lecture. Then she wondered if she'd be safer in Rashid's tent overnight than with the three other women.

Joanna felt miserably alone as she walked along the tunnel toward her quarters.

Instead of bringing them together I'm driving them further apart, she said to herself. I want Greg and Doug to work in harmony, and here I've as much as told Greg I don't trust his judgment and I'm siding with Doug.

But what else can I do? Doug's right and Greg's simply refusing to pay attention to what he's trying to accomplish. This whole Kiribati business could blow away at any time; Greg thinks he's being so clever in setting it up, yet it could be a house of straw.

Well, she thought as she slid open the door to her suite, it's done. I've told Greg what I'm going to do. Now I'd better tell Doug. At least he'll be happy about it. I hope.

The message light on her computer was blinking. Joanna closed her door, then said in a clear, firm voice, 'Computer, read messages.'

The screen lit up with the words as the computer announced in a synthesized contralto voice, 'Dr. Kristine Cardenas returned your call at 1435 hours today.'

Joanna slid into her desk chair as she asked, 'Did she leave a message?'

'Yes.'

'Read it, please.'

Again, the words spelled on the screen as Kris Cardenas' slightly shaking voice said, 'Mrs. Stavenger, I've been thinking about your request that I come to Moonbase to examine your son. Professor Zimmerman is with me, and we would both like to come, if that can be arranged.'

'End of message,' said the computer.

Joanna sat at the blankly glowing screen, thinking hard. Zimmerman! He swore he'd never come back here again. But

Switzerland's going to sign the nanotech treaty. Canada, too. Could it be . . . ?

'Phone,' said Joanna. 'Call Kristine Cardenas.'

Their conversation was brief, cool, and to the point. Kris Cardenas and Wilhelm Zimmerman would leave from Vancouver for Moonbase on the next available flight. Joanna checked the schedules and saw that they could get to an Earth-orbiting transfer station on the next day. Then they'd have to wait for four days before an LTV was scheduled to make the weekly run to Moonbase.

She shook her head. They're too important to sit around for four days. The authorities might even try to detain them, especially if they wait in Vancouver instead of the space station.

Joanna ordered a special flight to meet them at the orbital station and take them immediately to Moonbase. They'll be here in three days, she told herself.

The corporate comptroller called an hour later to ask if she knew how much a special lunar flight cost and how thin Moonbase's profit margin was already.

'I'll have to clear this with the division head,' he said, glowering out from the screen at Joanna. 'And he'll probably want to check it out with the director of Moonbase before he okays it.'

Joanna sighed. 'Put it on my personal account, Lester,' she said.

Once her words reached him, his eyes went wide. 'You're going to pay for it out of your own pocket?' He looked as if she had threatened some fundamental tenet of his inner faith.

'Yes,' Joanna snapped. 'And while I've got you on the link, I want to buy a lunar transfer vehicle. A used one, if possible; one that's about to be retired, if there are any such available. But used or new, I want an LTV. Put *that* on my personal account, too.'

She thought the man would faint.

SPACE STATION
MASTERSON

Like most of the major complexes in permanent Earth orbit, *Masterson* was a combination of several purposes: part manufacturing facility, part scientific research laboratory, part observation platform, part maintenance and repair center, and part transfer station for people and cargo heading onward to Moonbase.

Orbiting some two hundred fifty miles above the Earth, at first glance *Masterson* looked like a disconnected conglomeration of odds and ends, a junkyard floating in space. The modules where personnel were housed spun lazily on opposite ends of a two-mile-long carbon filament tether, like two oversized aluminum cans glinting in the sunlight, connected by a string so thin and dark it was for all practical purposes invisible. Outside the circumference of the housing modules' arc floated the factories, labs, repair shops and transfer center, their angular utilitarian shapes dwarfed by huge wings of solar panels and radiators, massive concave solar mirrors that collected and focused the Sun's heat for smelting and other processing work, and forests of antennas and sensors – all in zero gravity, or the nearest thing to it.

Spacesuited figures bustled from module to module, some of them jetting along in solo maneuvering units, others riding the bare-bones shuttlecraft that the station personnel called broomsticks.

Jinny Anson shook her head as she peered out the observation port. It had been almost nine months since she'd last been in zero gee, and she was testing her reactions. She felt a little woozy, but nothing she couldn't handle.

Not so bad for an old lady, she told herself. Just don't make any sudden moves.

There was a lunar transfer vehicle floating out there next to the repair sheds, she saw. It wasn't the regular LTV, which wasn't due back from its run to Moonbase for another thirty-six hours. As far as Jinny knew, the LTV had no business being there. But a maintenance crew was working on it, and she could see propellant lines feeding into its tanks.

'Are you ready for the inspection tour, Ms. Anson?'

Jinny pushed off the smooth surface of the observation port with her fingertips. The plastiglass felt cold, a reminder that there was nothing on its other side but empty infinity.

Turning toward the earnest young man who was to be her guide through the chemical processing plant, Jinny smiled and resisted the reflex to correct him. I'm still Ms. Anson on the company's files. I'm only Mrs. Westlake in Austin.

'Let's get it done, son,' she said.

He pushed off the handgrip projecting from the bulkhead and floated through the hatch. Jinny followed him into the access tube leading out of the observation center, saying, 'Take it slow, huh? It's been a while since I've been up here.'

The kid grinned over his shoulder at her.

As far as Masterson Corporation was concerned, Jinny was visiting the space station as part of her duties as quality control manager of the Houston division. The station manufactured the alloys and most of the electronics components that Houston used to build Clipperships. The station itself was now the property of the new Kiribati corporation, but its new ownership seemed to make no observable difference on the station staff or the work they did.

There had been a rumor that some day they would start using nanomachines to build the Clippers out of pure diamond, but Jinny discounted that as the usual shop-floor outgassing. If nothing else, the nanotech treaty would scuttle that idea.

Unofficially, Jinny had come to the station to hitch a ride to Moonbase. It wasn't as simple as catching a bus, of course, but for a former director of the base and a pretty important company official, the rules could be stretched a little. She only wanted to visit Moonbase for a day or so, just long enough to talk with Joanna Stavenger face to face. Jinny was convinced that what she had to ask Joanna couldn't be done any other way. *I've got to see the whites of her eyes when I pop the question to her.*

'What's that LTV out there doing?' she asked as casually as she could.

The youngster turned lazily as he floated along the access tube so he could look back at her. 'Special job,' he answered. 'Rumble is that there are some big gasbags coming up from Savannah, on their way to Moonbase. Ultra VIP. They pooched out a backup LTV just to take them up to the base, quickie-quick.'

'How many?' Jinny asked.

'Dunno,' the kid said. 'Two or three, from what I heard. Could be more, but not enough to fill a whole passenger pod.'

Jinny smiled to herself. *There's my ride. Quickie-quick.*

It was startlingly easy to talk her way onto the special LTV. Most of the crew at the station knew her; most of the senior crew, at least. There was plenty of spare capacity aboard the nearly-empty LTV, and an extra body visiting Moonbase for a couple of days wouldn't raise too many eyebrows – especially when the body was a former base director.

Jinny was supposed to get permission from the current base director, of course, but she knew how to get around that problem. She simply accessed the proper file from the station's mainframe and okayed her own trip, using the computer codes that hadn't been changed since she'd been running Moonbase. Easy.

I'll say hello to Greg Masterson when I get there, she told herself. *See his eyes pop.*

There were only two other passengers in the LTV's personnel pod. Jinny recognized the fat old guy as Professor Zimmerman, the nanotech whiz who had saved Doug

Stavenger's life after the big solar flare the previous year. The woman with him looked familiar, but Jinny couldn't place her. She had 'California' written all over her sandy-haired, tanned features. They ignored Jinny almost completely, talking to each other with deep seriousness as the LTV's co-pilot ducked in to make sure they were buckled safely into their seats.

Silly safety regulation, Jinny thought. This bucket won't put out enough thrust to slosh the coffee in a cup, even on a high-energy burn to Moonbase. Still, when the red light came on and the rockets lit, she felt herself squeezed back into her seat.

It was impossible to eat, sleep and go to the bathroom over the thirty-six-hour length of their flight without saying anything to the other passengers. When Jinny went past them to get to the meal dispenser, she hovered weightlessly by their seats long enough to say hello to Professor Zimmerman. The old man didn't remember her at first, but when he started to unstrap and politely get up from his chair, his face went pale.

'Please, stay in your seat,' Jinny pleaded. 'The rules of etiquette are different in zero gee.' Inwardly, she wanted to make sure that the flatlander didn't puke all over her.

With an effort to maintain his dignity even while seated, Zimmerman introduced Professor Kristine Cardenas to Jinny.

Soon the three of them were talking together the way passengers on a trip will, strangers yet shipmates. Jinny found that Cardenas was also an expert in nanotechnology and they were both going to Moonbase at the personal request of Joanna Stavenger.

She also learned that their *real* reason for allowing Joanna to coax them up to Moonbase was almost exactly the same as Jinny's own motivation.

'Perhaps we should pool our resources,' Zimmerman said. He was obviously uncomfortable in zero gee; Cardenas looked a little green, too. Jinny had gone to the meal dispenser for them and brought them prepackaged trays. And slow-release anti-nausea patches, which they both stuck behind their ears.

'What do you mean?' Jinny asked. It was impossible to eat

in zero gee without spraying crumbs and droplets all around. The compartment's air circulation sucked them up – slowly – into the ventilator grids along the ceiling.

Zimmerman started to gesture with his hands, then thought better of it. 'You know the Stavenger woman much better than I or even Kristine. You could help us to convince her to allow us to remain at Moonbase indefinitely.'

'I work for her,' Jinny said, 'but I can't say that I know her very well. Not socially.'

Kris Cardenas said, 'Still, if we all want the same thing, we ought to present a united front.'

'Fine by me,' said Jinny, delighted to have a Nobel prizewinner and her mentor as unexpected allies.

Greg's face looked like a storm cloud when he stepped into the reception area beneath the rocket landing pads.

'What's the matter?' Joanna asked him.

'Jinny Anson,' he snapped.

'Jinny?'

'She's on the incoming ship, with Cardenas and Zimmerman.'

'But she's supposed to be in Houston.'

'She's on the ship. She thought she'd sneak in here without my knowing it. Thought I wouldn't bother checking the LTV's manifest.'

Joanna immediately recognized the problem. Naturally Greg would be suspicious of having the former director of the base suddenly pop in for a visit. Especially when she hasn't told anyone she's coming or even asked permission to make the trip.

'They'll be coming down in a few minutes,' Greg said, in a tight-throated whisper. 'Flight control has locked in on them.'

Joanna nodded wordlessly, wondering what she could do or say to ease his misery.

'Where's Doug?' Greg asked her.

'He went up to the observation bubble,' she said. 'He likes to watch the spacecraft land.'

Greg made a sour face. Everything's a game to Doug; just a big entertainment. Impatiently he went to the wall panel beside the hatch and flicked on the intercom.

'Fifteen . . . right down the pipe,' said the flight controller's voice. 'Ten . . . five . . .'

'Green light,' a different voice announced. The spacecraft's pilot, Greg assumed.

'Touchdown confirmed.'

'Shutting down.'

'Base power connected. The snake's on its way.'

Greg paced impatiently across the small room. Doug came in through the door from the flight control center.

'Hi, Greg,' he said.

His half-brother gave him a dark look in return. Joanna thought how strange it was that they could both wear the same color coveralls, but Doug's sky-blue jumpsuit looked bright and sunny while Greg's seemed somehow darker, more ominous.

'This is your doing, isn't it?' Greg snapped.

'My doing? What?'

'Bringing Anson here.'

'Jinny Anson?' Doug looked genuinely surprised. 'She's aboard this ship?'

Greg waved a finger in Doug's face. 'Don't play innocent with me, Doug. I know what you're doing, you and your Operation Bootblack.'

'I didn't know Jinny Anson was coming here until this moment,' Doug said evenly.

'You're a liar!'

Joanna's breath caught in her throat. Greg stood red-faced before his half-brother, slightly taller but much slimmer. Doug seemed stunned by the accusation, his face frozen with shock, his hands clenching into fists at his sides.

'That's quite enough,' Joanna said, stepping between them. 'I won't stand for you two fighting like this.'

But Doug smiled and stepped back, his hands relaxing. 'Honestly, Greg, I'm just as surprised as you are that Jinny's come here. As for Operation Boot*strap*, okay, we're trying to make Moonbase profitable without costing you any cash flow. It's all to your benefit, really.'

'Really?' Greg sneered.

'Really,' said Doug as pleasantly as a springtime breeze.

The airlock hatch's signal chime interrupted them. Joanna and her two sons turned to the heavy metal hatch as the indicator light on its panel turned from red to amber and one of the mission controllers came hustling into the reception area. She was a petite, almost frail-looking young woman, wearing the gray coveralls of the transportation division. Why do they give the heaviest jobs to the smallest kids? Joanna wondered. The hatch had to be swung open manually, and even though there was a pilot and co-pilot on this flight, standard procedure was for one of the controllers to be on hand to open the hatch from this side, if necessary.

It wasn't necessary. As soon as the indicator light went from amber to green, the heavy metal hatch swung open. Joanna felt a slight stir of air in the reception room; the air pressure on the other side of the hatch had not exactly matched the pressure on this side.

The pilot pushed the hatch all the way open, grinning at the mission controller. 'See,' he said, 'there *is* a reason for carrying us up from Earth orbit, after all.'

'Then you ought to get paid as a doorman,' said the controller.

He wasn't all that much bigger than she, Joanna realized. The pilot's eyes widened when he recognized Greg. 'Hey,' he said to the controller, 'don't talk that way in front of the boss.'

Greg forced a smile for them as they passed him, on their way to the flight control center. They didn't recognize Joanna, apparently; at least the pilot didn't.

Then Jinny Anson stepped through the hatch. Right behind her came Kris Cardenas and, finally, the lumbering form of Wilhelm Zimmerman.

For an awkward moment no one knew what to say. Greg looked like a smoldering volcano, Doug seemed nonplussed, and Joanna herself wondered what was going to happen.

Then Zimmerman broke the silence. 'We seek asylum,' he said, with great dignity.

DIRECTOR'S OFFICE

'Let me get this straight,' Greg said. 'You're seeking political asylum? Here at Moonbase?'

'You are now under the legal jurisdiction of the nation of Kiribati, is that not so?' Zimmerman asked.

'Legally, yes,' said Greg.

'So! We seek asylum. Me from Switzerland, she from Canada.'

The six of them sat around the circular conference table in Greg's office, where Greg had taken them immediately after their arrival. Joanna sat between her two sons, facing Anson across the table. Cardenas' and Zimmerman's luggage was still at the reception area, out at the rocket port.

'I don't know if it's political asylum or what,' said Kris Cardenas, 'but we want the freedom to continue our research—'

'And our teaching,' interrupted Zimmerman.

Cardenas nodded. 'And our teaching.'

'And you can't do it Earthside?' Doug asked.

'Not once this treaty goes into effect,' said Zimmerman heavily. 'All research on nanotechnology will be banned. Teaching also.'

Joanna saw the despair in his fleshy face. She had never considered how the nanotech treaty would affect researchers like Zimmerman and Cardenas.

Greg steepled his fingers before his face and looked at Anson. 'Jinny, don't tell me you're seeking asylum, too.'

She grinned mischievously. 'Nope. I just wanted to talk to you – and Mrs. Stavenger – about getting transferred to someplace where my husband can teach without the New Morality on his back.'

'What does he teach?' Joanna heard herself ask.

'English literature,' Anson replied. 'Specializes in Marlowe – the Elizabethan, not the detective.'

No one laughed.

'Why don't we invite him here?' Doug asked.

'Here?' Greg demanded. 'To Moonbase? We can't afford to carry nonproductive people here. What would we do with an English lit professor?'

'Start a university,' said Doug.

'What?'

Gesturing toward Zimmerman and Cardenas, Doug said, 'We have two of the world's greatest nanotech researchers, don't we? Let Jinny's husband teach English lit from here. Bring up a few other teachers and researchers. Moonbase can start its own university and people will pay good money to study here.'

'But the transportation costs,' Joanna pointed out.

Doug gave her a patient smile. 'Mom, I'm studying at Caltech and the Sorbonne and the American University in Rome – all without leaving Moonbase. People on Earth can study with our faculty the same way.'

'Electronically.'

'Virtual reality, when you need it,' said Doug.

Greg seemed intrigued despite himself. 'You mean we could make a profit out of a university?'

'Of course!' said Zimmerman. 'We can make this miserable collection of caves into a great intellectual center!'

Greg turned to his mother questioningly.

Joanna leaned close enough to whisper into his ear, 'Don't fight it. Take the credit for it.'

He smiled and thought, As long as Kiribati doesn't sign the U.N. treaty, I can start the university here and transfer it to the islands when I close Moonbase.

Melissa had easily eluded Rashid's attempts at romance during their first dinner together in his tent. She had talked nothing but business, and learned more about the rumors of building a new type of Clippership out of diamond, using nanomachines. Rashid, ardently wanting to impress her, had blithely laid out everything he had heard about the scheme at her feet.

His reward was a brief kiss goodnight and the vague promise of delights to come.

Melissa dared not report back to General O'Conner or her cohorts at the Urban Corps headquarters in Atlanta. The only communications links on the storm-ravaged atoll belonged to Masterson Corporation; she wasn't prepared to take the risk of being overheard.

Instead, she tried to think out a plan of action for herself. The nanotech scheme had to be stopped, preferably nipped in the bud. Greg Masterson must be behind it, she reasoned. He always was fascinated with nanotechnology. Another reason to ban it everywhere.

If they actually succeeded in making this breakthrough in spacecraft manufacturing with nanotechnology it would be a body blow to the U.N. treaty. Greg could sit up there at Moonbase and build spacecraft and make billions. These people here in Kiribati would get rich. Then they would start using nanomachines to manufacture other things: automobiles, perhaps; aircraft, certainly. Who knew what else?

The nanotech treaty would be a shambles, a mockery. All because this little island nation could be bribed into resisting the will of the people, the mandate of God.

All because of Greg, she knew. He's sitting up there, above us all, laughing at us. Laughing at me. I've got to stop Greg, Melissa told herself. I've got to tear him down from his throne in the sky. I've got to wipe out Moonbase.

Her only tool, she realized, was Rashid.

He invited her to dinner the next night, but she refused. Again the following night, and she refused again. But by the third night, Melissa had done enough research into Rashid's own personal and corporate life so that the beginnings of a plan had started to form in her mind. When he oh-so-casually asked her if she would like to keep him company during dinner, she accepted.

His answering smile pleased her.

In place of candles, Rashid's tent was lit by battery-powered fluorescent lamps. His table was still meager, supplies had to be flown in from Hawaii, yet Melissa could see the effect he was trying to create: a romantic dinner for two, alone from the rest of the world.

Instead of the usual slacks and shirt, Rashid wore a flowing white robe with gold embroidery, and a cloying musky cologne that made Melissa's nostrils twitch. She half expected to hear reedy Middle-eastern music; instead, the background was the rhythmic beating of the surf against the reef out beyond the island.

'And how is your wife today?' Melissa asked coyly as they sat at the folding table facing each other.

Rashid smiled blandly. 'I've been much too busy to speak with her today. I'll call tomorrow.'

Nodding understandingly, she asked, 'Moslems are allowed four wives, aren't they?'

He seemed pleased that she knew. 'The Koran allows four, yes. But the laws of the United States make polygamy illegal.'

With a slight frown, Melissa said, 'Secular law shouldn't be placed above religious law. Don't you agree?'

'In this case, I agree wholeheartedly!'

Melissa looked down at her dinner, a prepackaged meal heated in the portable microwave oven. We might as well be aboard an airliner, she thought. The natives who had returned to the island were catching fresh fish in the lagoon, although the papaya and mango and other fruit trees had been stripped by the typhoon's winds, if not flattened altogether.

Rashid did not offer wine; neither of them imbibed. Instead they drank clear water produced by the desalting plant that had finally gone into operation.

Slowly, as they ate and chatted, Melissa brought the subject around to Moonbase.

'I just don't understand how the corporation can risk so much of its resources on a totally unproven scheme,' she said.

'Unproven?'

'The idea of manufacturing Clipperships with nanomachines,' Melissa said. 'Nanotechnology isn't really that reliable. It's dangerous, in fact.'

'They use nanomachines at Moonbase all the time.'

'Yes, of course,' she said, 'but only for the simplest of tasks, like taking oxygen out of the regolith. When it comes to trying to build the mass driver, they're having trouble, aren't they?'

Rashid's eyes narrowed slightly. 'You're very well informed.'

'I am your assistant,' said Melissa. 'It's my job to know what you need to know.'

'Yes.'

'And it worries me,' she went on, 'that your whole standing in the corporation hangs on this crazy scheme. How on Earth did you ever agree to be part of it?'

His brow knit more deeply. 'I really had no choice. I was transferred here on the orders of Joanna Stavenger.'

'Isn't she Greg Masterson's mother?' Melissa asked innocently.

'Yes. And he's the director of Moonbase.'

'But you're his superior. He reports to you in the corporate chain of command.'

His nostrils flaring slightly, Rashid muttered, 'Not for long, I imagine. He'll be sitting on the board of directors before I do, no doubt.'

'Because of his mother?'

'Why else?'

'But she's retired, hasn't she? She's living up at Moonbase, too.'

'She's still on the board of directors. And still very powerful.'

Melissa took a sip of water, then asked, 'So because of this woman you must risk your career?'

Stiffening, Rashid replied, 'I wouldn't put it just that way.'

'But suppose Kiribati decides one day to sign the U.N. treaty? What happens then?'

'That won't happen.'

'No one expected New Zealand to sign the treaty, but they did. What if Kiribati does, too?'

Rashid puffed out a breath. 'The whole scheme collapses like a house of cards.'

'And yet you have the key to the corporation's salvation in your hands, don't you?'

'I do?'

'Fusion power,' said Melissa. 'The secret of the stars, brought to Earth.'

'Ah, yes! Fusion. Yes, I had great hopes for it.' His face darkened again. 'Before I was assigned to the Kiribati Manufacturing and Entertainment Corporation.' He pronounced the words with clear disgust.

'And what's happening with the fusion development program?' Melissa asked.

'Nothing. It's dead in the water. If the corporation would only put some funding behind the effort . . .'

She reached across the table to put her hand on his. 'Why don't you move in that direction?'

'I can't,' he said. 'I've got to get this miserable resort complex up and going.'

'Wouldn't the board back you, if you made a strong presentation about the benefits of fusion energy?'

Rashid blinked at her several times as he stroked his trim dark beard. 'With Quintana gone,' he muttered, 'the balance of power on the board is rather shaky.'

'Moonbase has always been such a marginal operation,' said Melissa eagerly. 'Why not cut it entirely and devote our resources to developing fusion? That way there won't be any problems with the U.N. treaty to worry about, and you can end this farce of a resort complex here in these godforsaken islands.'

'But the fusion generator requires helium-three.'

Melissa waved an impatient hand. 'One trip to the Moon per year could scoop up enough helium-three to run a hundred fusion generators. You don't need a permanent base on the Moon for that.'

'Are you certain?'

She nodded. 'Make fusion work and you can forget about Kiribati.'

Rashid laughed shakily. 'I could go home to Savannah.'

'You could be elected to the board of directors!'

'And solve the world's energy problems.'

'You could become the most powerful man in the corporation,' Melissa urged. 'The most powerful man on Earth!'

He laughed again, stronger. 'I could live in a Moslem nation, where a man is allowed his proper number of wives.'

'And concubines,' said Melissa, deliciously.

For an instant Rashid looked as if he would toss the table aside and seize her in his arms. But then the fire in his eyes dimmed, shifted. His face fell.

'Greg Masterson,' he muttered. 'And his mother.'

'But they're a quarter-million miles away,' Melissa said. 'You can outmaneuver them.'

He shook his head. 'Joanna is a powerful woman. And Greg – he must be the one behind this diamond Clippership concept.'

Melissa took a deep breath, then said, 'Why don't you let me deal with them?'

'What do you mean?'

Very seriously, Melissa replied, 'Let me go to Moonbase and speak to them directly. Let me try to convince them that shutting down Moonbase is the right thing for the corporation to do.'

'How on Earth can you possibly do that?'

With a knowing smile, Melissa said, 'Oh, there are ways to convince people of almost anything.'

'Are there?'

'Yes, of course. Especially if you know things about them that they would prefer to keep others from knowing.'

THE FARM

'I am honored that you have come to see my humble patch of weeds,' said Lev Brudnoy, quite seriously.

He had been bent over one of the miniature lime trees that he had planted in a row of pots filled with lunar sand. Getting the cuttings to start the miniature citrus orchard had been relatively easy; people brought them up from Earthside, and, after an intense inspection by Moonbase's environmental protection scientists, they were carried in sealed containers to the farm. The little orchard was another step in Operation Bootstrap.

Joanna cocked a brow at him. 'Come off it, Lev. We're not in old Mother Russia anymore.'

Brudnoy pawed awkwardly at his shock of graying hair. 'But you are such a great lady, and I am only a sort of peasant . . .'

'Lev,' said Joanna sternly, 'how long have we known each other?'

He screwed up his eyes, thinking. 'About nine months, more or less.'

'How much actual work have you seen me do in that time?'

'Work?' He spread his hands. 'Your work is far removed from the kind of thing I do.'

'Not any more,' said Joanna. 'If we're going to make a success of this Operation Bootstrap that you helped hatch up—'

'Me?'

'Yes, you. Maybe it was entirely Doug's idea, but I have a feeling that you at least aided and abetted him.'

Brudnoy spread his arms in a gesture of helplessness. 'I am part of the cabal, I confess it freely.'

Joanna's expression relaxed into a smile. 'Very good. So am I, from here on. I'm here to help you. What do you want me to do? Weeding? Picking? Name it.'

He swallowed visibly. 'Well, we don't have weeds. So far, we've been able to screen them out before we accept a new batch of seeds or cuttings. But pruning is important . . .'

Joanna rolled up the sleeves of her blouse and made a mental note to wear regular coveralls the next time she came to Brudnoy's farm.

'Look, I know how I'd feel if I was still the base director and my predecessor showed up all of a sudden,' said Jinny Anson.

Seated behind his curved glass desk, Greg eyed her suspiciously. 'Do you?' he retorted.

Anson gave him a disarming smile. 'I don't want your job, Greg! Honest. Been there. Done that. All I want is a place where my husband can work in peace.'

'Doug suggested he come up here.'

'With two teenaged daughters?' Anson shook her head. 'You don't want that, I don't want that, and they don't want that.'

'Then what?' Greg demanded.

'Damned if I know,' Anson admitted. 'There's gotta be someplace on Earth where Quentin can teach without being hounded by the New Morality bigots.'

A slow smile crept across Greg's lips. 'You could move to Kiribati.'

Anson blinked. 'Kiribati.'

'The islands are really lovely,' said Greg. 'I wish I were there, right now.'

'Kiribati,' she repeated.

Three extra people at Moonbase strained the living accommodations. Zimmerman got the base's only unoccupied quarters. Anson and Cardenas had to share one room, and a ninety-day contract employee, a young nanotech engineer working on the mass driver, reluctantly agreed to give up his quarters and double up with one of the other short-timers for the remainder of his stay.

Anson called her husband in Austin as soon as the crew that delivered the extra bunk to her quarters had shut the door behind them.

'Kiribati?' Quentin's placid face crinkled into a mild frown. 'Where the hell's that?'

Knowing that she was taking her husband's career in her hands, she said, 'Way out in the middle of the Pacific. They used to be called the Gilbert Islands, I think.'

Once her words reached him, his frown dissolved. 'The Gilberts? Robert Louis Stevenson lived there! He loved it! Said it was the best place on Earth.'

'Really?'

They chattered back and forth – with three-second lags – for more than an hour. Quentin pulled up a geography program that showed them both the modern Kiribati: palm-fringed atolls in the tropical Pacific; small towns with happy, crime-free people.

'It'll be a better place to raise the girls than Austin,' said Quentin, with real enthusiasm.

Jinny worried about tropical islanders' ideas about sex, but said nothing.

'I could start the English department for this new university,' Quentin went on. 'I could really—' Suddenly his voice cut off and his big smile vanished.

'What is it?' Jinny asked.

Before her words could reach him, Quentin said, 'But what about you? You'll have to leave your job with Masterson Aerospace if we move to the islands.'

Jinny relaxed. 'Don't sweat it,' she said easily. 'I've got a new job all picked out. I'm going to be president of the new university, whatever we decide to name it.'

His eyes widened once he heard her response. 'President? Wow.'

'Damn' right,' said Jinny. 'I'm gonna be your boss, sweetheart!'

*   *   *

She couldn't get what she wanted without going to bed with him. Melissa decided that she had played Rashid as far as she could; the next step had to involve sex.

Rashid was no fool. He realized that the only way for him to get out from under this Kiribati farce was to move the fusion development forward. He had to get the board of directors hot for fusion energy, divert their attention – and their funding – from Moonbase and nanotechnology.

Both Rashid and Melissa assumed, automatically, that Greg Masterson was behind the diamond Clippership scheme. And Melissa urged, almost begged, Rashid to send her to Moonbase to deal with Greg.

Yet Rashid was wary of allowing Melissa to go to Moonbase. He wanted to know how she could possibly stop Greg Masterson and, even more difficult, his mother.

She told him, part of it, in bed.

They had their usual dinner in his tent. This time, though, instead of keeping him at arm's length Melissa let Rashid hold her, kiss her, undress her. She almost laughed at the way his hands trembled as he fumbled with the old-fashioned hook-and-eye at the back of her blouse's collar.

It wouldn't do to tell him outright, she knew. Her story would have much greater impact if she seemed to reveal it to him reluctantly, overpowered by his masculine mastery, her resistance melting away under the fierceness of his passion.

So she let him paw her and walk her to his double-sized cot and run his hands and lips over her naked body. She felt almost nothing, she kept herself in rigid control. But she moaned for him and writhed and gasped and heaved when he entered her.

At last it was finished. She wanted to leap out of the narrow bunk and run to the lagoon for a cleansing swim in the warm enfolding waters. Instead she lay at Rashid's side, breathing softly.

He turned toward her and propped himself on his elbow. Looking down at her in the darkened tent, he asked, 'Was that enjoyable for you?'

Melissa made a sigh. 'The best I've had in years and years,' she said languidly. Truthfully.

He laughed gently. 'How many years?'

'Ever since . . .' Melissa let her voice fade away into the shadows.

'Since when?'

'I shouldn't tell you,' she whispered. 'I shouldn't let anyone know.'

'Know what?'

For long moments she remained silent, waiting for his curiosity to grow unbearable, knowing that the best lies were always based on truth.

He leaned over her, grasped her by the shoulders almost menacingly. 'What is this great secret? Tell me.'

Melissa let the breath sigh out of her. 'It was so long ago, so many years have passed . . .'

'You can confide in me,' he said more gently. 'I won't tell anyone else.'

'Years ago – a lifetime ago—' She hesitated.

'You must have been only a girl,' he said.

'Yes,' Melissa replied. 'I was very young. And I fell in love.'

'Ahh.'

'With Greg Masterson.'

Even in the darkness of the tent she could see his eyes go wide. 'Greg Masterson?'

'I was his lover,' said Melissa, in a little girl's voice. 'But he cast me aside. He nearly destroyed me.'

Rashid dropped onto his back and lay beside her. 'Greg Masterson,' he muttered.

'Greg Masterson,' she repeated.

'And you want to go to the Moon to be with him again.'

'I want to go to the Moon,' whispered Melissa, 'to repay him for the way he treated me.'

'You no longer love him?'

'I've hated him for nearly twenty years.'

Rashid was silent for a long time. At last he asked, 'And what can you do to him on the Moon that you can't do from here on Earth?'

'I can confront him. And his mother. His mother is at Moonbase. She's protected him all these years.'

'Protected him? From what?'

'From—' Melissa stopped herself. She had no intention of telling Rashid everything. 'From me,' she said. 'I was carrying Greg's baby when he sent me away. I had an abortion. All my life I've had to live with the knowledge that I murdered my own child.'

It was a clever variation of the truth. But it was enough to convince Rashid.

'So you want to go to Moonbase to confront Greg and Mrs. Stavenger.'

'Yes. I want them to know that if they don't shut down Moonbase I'll tell the whole world about him, how he abandoned me, how he made me commit murder.'

Rashid thought it over for a few moments. 'But that all happened almost twenty years ago, you say.'

Melissa pulled her trump card. 'There is no statute of limitations on murder. The law says abortion is murder. I'm willing to stand trial for what I did. I deserve to be punished. But Greg will have to stand trial beside me, as an accomplice to murder.'

'My god!'

'That's the law now in America,' she said.

'It would ruin him,' said Rashid.

'It would force him to return to Earth to face trial,' Melissa said.

'His mother would never allow that.'

'Do you think she would shut down Moonbase instead?'

'Yes,' said Rashid. 'I think she would. The old tigress would blow up Moonbase and all the people in it before she'd let her son be humiliated and destroyed like that.'

Melissa nodded in the darkness. What would Mrs. Stavenger do once she knew that her precious son would have to stand trial for the murder of his stepfather?

'Then you'll send me to Moonbase?' Melissa asked.

He hesitated. 'There's a board of directors meeting coming up next week. I've asked to be put on the agenda, to make a presentation about the fusion program to them. Let's see how that goes. It might not be necessary to . . . go to all that trouble.'

Melissa knew that she should not press him too far. 'You're thinking of me, aren't you? Trying to save me the pain, the suffering of confronting them.'

'If the board allows me to push the fusion development, then why go to all that trouble?'

'But if the board decides against you . . . ?'

'Then,' Rashid said, his voice cold and hard, 'yes, I will send you to Moonbase like a guided missile.'

'Good,' said Melissa.

'You *want* to go?'

'I want to help you,' she said quickly. 'I want to see you gain the power and recognition that you deserve.'

'But you must return to me,' he said, excited by the future parading before his eyes. 'I will become the most powerful man in the corporation, once Moonbase is closed.'

'And I will be one of your loving slaves,' Melissa lied.

It aroused Rashid just as if it were the truth.

BOARD OF DIRECTORS

Good things always happened to Alan Johansen. Never a deep intellect, he had at least been clever enough to pick extremely wealthy parents. He also inherited their good looks: Johansen had the chiseled blond features of a Nordic warrior of old, although his slim, almost delicate build was more like that of a dancer than a Viking. With his slicked-back hair and thin-lipped smile he looked like a chorus boy from the Roaring Twenties.

He was, in fact, chairman of the board of Masterson Aerospace Corporation. And very confused and troubled.

It was bad enough that Joanna Stavenger insisted on attending Board meetings electronically, instead of in person. Her image appeared on the wallscreen at the end of the conference table, floating above their heads like the magic mirror in Snow White. At least Carlos Quintana was able to keep things running smoothly, even with that infernal delay whenever she wanted to say something.

Now Quintana was gone, and half the board members were scheming and trying to make alliances against the other half, and to top it off they had set up this dummy corporation on some tropical islands out in the South Seas to take over all their space operations. It sounded awfully tricky to Alan, maybe even illegal.

And on top of everything else, the man they had sent out to those islands was pestering him with some crack-brained idea about nuclear energy, of all things. Why, nuclear energy was as dead as the horse-and-buggy. People *hated* nuclear! It was full of dangerous radiation.

Alan sat at the head of the polished board room table, watching Rashid's video. In the big Windowall that stretched almost the length of the entire room, a smallish metal sphere stood, humming slightly, doing nothing.

'As you can see from the power gauges,' Rashid's voice was saying, 'this one small generator can produce enough electrical energy to power an entire city the size of Savannah.'

'And this is nuclear fusion?' asked one of the white-haired men sitting halfway down the table.

'Yes,' Rashid's voice replied. 'Fusion, not fission. No uranium or plutonium is involved. The fuel basically comes from water and the waste product is helium: inert and safe. You can use it to blow up balloons for your grandchildren.'

A few snickers of laughter went down the conference table.

'I thought you said we needed fuel from the Moon to make this work,' said one of the women directors.

'One shipload per year will fuel as many fusion generators as we can profitably build,' Rashid answered.

'So we wouldn't need to keep Moonbase open?'

'No. We could even process the helium-three without nanomachines, if we must.'

'Now wait a minute,' Johansen interrupted. 'I thought you said the helium was a waste product. Now you're saying it's the fuel? I don't understand.'

Patiently, Rashid tried to explain, but Johansen felt more confused than ever.

'But the point is,' said the comptroller, 'that we could get the fuel we need from the Moon without keeping Moonbase open.'

'That is correct,' said Rashid.

'Then why have we started up this dummy corporation in Kiribati?' asked Johansen.

Rashid's voice answered from the screen, 'The Kiribati Corporation exists specifically to allow Moonbase to continue using nanotechnology in spite of the U.N. treaty.'

'In other words, we're sinking all this money into those islanders just to keep Moonbase poking along?'

Rashid's voice replied, 'Without nanotechnology, Moonbase could not exist.'

Joanna's face, in the screen at the far end of the room, hardened as soon as she heard the question. 'We're keeping Moonbase *poking along*,' she said, with steel in her voice, 'because we will soon be able to manufacture spacecraft out of pure diamond, using nanotechnology.'

'Who needs a diamond Clippership?' asked one of the women. 'The Clipperships we have now work just fine, don't they?'

Johansen twiddled his fingers impatiently until Joanna's response came from the Moon:

'Diamond ships will be lighter, yet far stronger, than anything made of metals. Therefore they will be safer yet more economical to operate. They will be cheaper to manufacture, yet the market will pay more for them than they do for today's Clipperships. Our profits will be double, or even greater.'

'You mean Moonbase will actually start showing real profit, after all these years?'

Again that agonizing wait.

Then Joanna replied, 'I mean that diamond Clipperships, built by Moonbase, will make this corporation more profitable than it's ever been.'

'Then why do we need this fusion thing?' Johansen asked, almost surprising himself that he spoke his thoughts out loud.

The Windowall view of the fusion reactor vanished and Rashid's trimly bearded face loomed over them. 'Because, with fusion generators Masterson Corporation can become bigger than the old petroleum companies were!'

'We can't sink risk money into both these new ideas,' said the comptroller, sitting at Johansen's right hand. 'It's just too chancy.'

'Suppose the World Court decides that our Kiribati Corporation is nothing but a subterfuge to get around the U.N. treaty?' Rashid threatened.

But before anyone on the board could respond to that, Joanna countered, 'How long will it take to make this fusion process practical? And profitable?'

Rashid hesitated. 'Well, the power conversion system needs to be developed.'

'Power conversion?'

'Magneto—' Rashid cut his words short. 'MHD is what it's called.'

'How long will *that* take?' asked the comptroller. 'And how many bucks?'

Before Rashid could reply, Joanna said firmly, 'We're not asking for a penny of corporate risk funding on our new Clippership development.'

All heads turned to her image.

'Moonbase will build a prototype diamond Clippership on our own. It won't cost the corporation a cent.'

The board broke into a dozen conversations at once.

Joanna's voice stilled them all. 'But once that prototype ship is demonstrated and the aerospace lines start placing their orders, I'll expect every Moonbase employee who worked on the program to get a share of the profits.'

Johansen wished for the hundredth time that Quintana were still there. He'd know what to say. As it was, the board sat in stunned silence for what seemed like half a lifetime.

Finally the comptroller spoke up. 'Mrs. Stavenger, if your people up there can build a diamond Clippership without additional funding from the corporation and sell the concept to the aerospace lines, I'm sure we can work out an equitable profit-sharing plan.'

Rashid, in an agonized voice, asked, 'But what about the fusion program?'

Johansen spoke up. 'Let's wait before we make a decision about that. Let's see what Moonbase can actually do for us, first.'

Sitting in his bare little office in the concrete building on Tarawa, Rashid sank back in his chair. The board of directors nodded their heads – white haired, bald, silvery gray – and agreed with Johansen's idiotic decision.

Angrily, Rashid punched his desktop keyboard and blanked the display screen on the office's wall.

Melissa Hart got up from her chair at the side of the desk

and stepped behind Rashid. Gently she massaged his shoulders as she whispered, 'Let me go to Moonbase. Let me use the sword of vengeance against them.'

Rashid closed his eyes as her deft fingers kneaded the tension out of him.

'Yes,' he said. 'You go to Moonbase on the next available ship.'

ROCKET PORT

This one was different. Doug could hardly contain his excitement as he stood in the rocket port's observation bubble and watched the LTV come down. *The* LTV. The one they were going to modify for the asteroid mission.

He spotted the puffs of rocket exhaust against the dark sky as the controllers made their final adjustments, then the LTV took shape, big and lumpy with tanks and pods, and then the main engine fired its final braking burst and the ungainly vehicle settled down on its rickety-looking legs in a dirty white cloud of gaseous aluminum oxide and blowing lunar dust.

Doug just stood there, practically on tip-toes, his hair brushing the curved plastiglass of the bubble, and admired the spacecraft. This wasn't a worn-out cripple, ready for the scrap heap. This LTV was practically new; his mother had insisted on getting quality for her money.

To his surprise, the personnel access tube was worming its way toward the hatch in the passenger pod. Were there passengers aboard the ship?

Doug slid languidly down the ladder into the flight control center and asked the two controllers on duty.

'One passenger. VIP from Tarawa,' said the chief controller.

Surprised, Doug said, 'Well, I might as well go down and greet him.'

'Her,' the controller corrected. 'Personal representative from the chief operating officer of the Kiribati Corporation.'

'Oh,' said Doug. 'The new owners.'

He ducked out of the flight control center and slid down the ladder into The Pit. He walked briskly to the airlock hatch and waited for the indicator light to turn green. As soon as the hatch cracked open, Doug grabbed it and helped to swing it all the way.

'Welcome to Moonbase,' he said. The words almost stuck in his throat. The LTV's pilot and co-pilot both were holding the arms of a very beautiful dark-skinned woman who looked as if she were dying.

It had been a miserable flight for Melissa. Worse than hell, forty-eight hours of weightlessness. She had never been in space before, and the nausea of free-fall simply overwhelmed her, despite all the medication. She puked her guts out during the first few hours of the flight and had the dry heaves the rest of the way.

The only thing that kept her going was the mantra she repeated to herself all the long, exhausting way to the Moon. It was a mantra of hate. She filled her mind with a vision of Greg Masterson. The man who had betrayed her so brutally. All men were betrayers, of course, but Greg had been the worst. She had loved him, once. She had conceived his baby. Now for nearly twenty years she had survived by hating him. His betrayal had driven her into self-loathing and a life so foul it had nearly killed her, just as she had killed the unborn child within her, but Melissa fought for her life with one burning goal set before her pain-filled eyes: to make Greg pay. To make him feel the agony she had felt. To make him suffer as she had suffered.

It was not a worthy goal, she knew. General O'Conner and the others would be horrified if they could see into her soul. But it was the goal that had kept Melissa sane all these years. And now she was close to achieving it.

Hate can move mountains, she said to herself. Faith, hope and hate. And the greatest of these is hate.

Now her long journey was over. With at least some sense of weight to anchor her stomach, she looked with watery eyes at a bright-faced young man beaming a ridiculous greeting to her.

'I'll take care of her,' Doug said. The two crewmen looked enormously relieved.

'Come on,' he said, taking Melissa by the arm. 'You're okay now. You just need to clean up a bit and get some food into you.'

Melissa groaned at the thought of food. 'I must look a mess,' she said.

Grinning, Doug admitted, 'A shower and a change of clothes would help.' She smelled so bad his own stomach wanted to heave.

He led Melissa to the waiting tractor and the co-pilot dumped her one travelbag on the back seat. As they trundled along the dimly-lit tunnel, Doug accessed the central computer and found the room assigned to Melissa. She must be a real VIP, he thought, to get the personnel department to push another short-timer into doubling up.

Fortunately Melissa's assigned quarters weren't far from the main airlock. Doug walked her there and told her to take a shower.

'I'll wait out in the tunnel and take you to lunch when you're ready,' he told her.

Melissa was too miserable and weak to debate with the stranger. She stumbled into what looked like a cell carved out of rock, found the shower stall, and stepped in fully clothed. The water was tepid, at best, but it felt good. Slowly she stripped off her soggy clothing as the water sluiced over her.

She was looking for soap when the water stopped. Blinking drops from her eyes, she turned the controls. Nothing. Suddenly blasts of air pummeled her from vents in the ceiling and sides of the stall. She shivered, but as the air evaporated the droplets on her skin it began to feel warm, even hot.

And then it, too, suddenly stopped. Melissa shook her head, feeling like a hamburger in an automated oven. As she stepped out of the shower she realized that her nausea was gone. She shook her head again. No wooziness at all.

Leaving her soiled clothes in the shower, she opened her bag and got dressed: crisp clean ivory slacks and a pullover blouse of metallic gold. It was a struggle, though; every move she made seemed too big. She nearly toppled over onto the bunk when she tried to step into the slacks. Of course, she told herself. You're on the Moon. The gravity's much less here. Carefully, she finished dressing and slipped on a pair of soft-soled espadrilles.

No jewelry, only her wristwatch. She looked at herself in the shadowy reflection of the desktop computer screen; there was no mirror in the room. Warmed-over shit, she appraised herself. Well, girl, that's as good as it's going to get.

Wondering if the nice young kid was still waiting out in the hall, she stepped cautiously to the accordion-pleat door and slid it partway open.

Doug saw her peeking out. 'Hi!' he said. 'Feeling better?'

The shock of recognition almost knocked her legs out from under her. Standing there grinning at her was a young Paul Stavenger. Bigger than Paul, lighter skinned. But it was Paul's eyes she saw looking at her; Paul's irresistible smile.

Then it flashed into her mind: Paul's son, Douglas, lived here at Moonbase with Greg and their mother. Paul's son. Joanna's son.

She pushed the door all the way open and stepped out into the tunnel, very carefully.

'We'll have to get you a pair of weighted boots,' Doug said, offering her his arm. 'First stop, though, is The Cave.'

Melissa clung to his arm and let him do the talking. She learned that The Cave was some sort of cafeteria or galley where Moonbase people took their meals. The thought of eating felt better to her now that her stomach was in place. She actually felt hungry. Ought to be, she told herself. You lost everything you had in there and then some.

'You haven't told me your name,' she said as they walked slowly down the tunnel.

'Doug Stavenger,' he answered. 'And yours?'

She covered her emotions quickly. 'Melissa Hart,' she said, not trusting herself to say more. Joanna's baby. Greg's half-brother.

Then she remembered that this was the young man whose body swarmed with nanomachines. This was the symbol of wickedness that General O'Conner was sworn to destroy. Almost, she disengaged from his arm. The thought of those evil machines inside his body frightened her. But he looked normal enough, and she was afraid that if she let go of his arm she'd stumble and fall.

'You didn't have any trouble working the shower, did you?' he asked as they walked down the tunnel.

'The water shut off on me.'

'Oh, sure. There's a timer. Water's pretty precious, still, so there's an automatic cutoff in all the showers.'

'And air driers?'

Doug nodded easily. 'We generate a lot of heat, most of it's too low-grade to be put to anything useful, but we can save a lot of towel laundering by using some of it to dry off in the shower.'

'I see,' Melissa said.

'Not that we use water for the laundry,' he added.

'No?'

'Don't have to. Just take the dirty laundry outside; the dirt dries out almost immediately in the vacuum, so you can shake it off.'

Melissa wondered if he were telling her the truth or pulling her leg.

'And the ultraviolet out there sterilizes everything, too, of course.'

He seemed quite serious. Melissa realized that Doug Stavenger was a bright, good-looking, charming young man. Paul's son in every way. Once they were seated at a small table in The Cave and Melissa no longer had to worry about walking in the feeble gravity, she could study his face, feel his intensity. He had Paul's infectious enthusiasm, the same drive that could sweep you up and carry you away, despite yourself.

'. . . so you've actually brought us the LTV we're going to use for our asteroid mission,' he was saying.

Melissa paid scant attention to his words. She saw Paul again. And the whole sorry mess of twenty years ago played itself out in her mind. All the pain and rejection and fury boiled up inside her, burning worse than the bile she had vomited on the way to the Moon.

'Your brother is the director of Moonbase, isn't he?' she asked, struggling to keep her voice from shaking.

'Greg. That's right.'

'And your mother lives here, now, doesn't she?'

Doug nodded eagerly. 'In fact, there she is now.' He stood up and waved.

Melissa turned in her chair and saw Joanna: older, a bit thicker in the middle, her hair more gray than ash-blonde now, but unmistakably Joanna. While the other women in The Cave wore mostly coveralls, Joanna was in a midnight blue pantsuit set off by a flowered silk scarf at her throat. She doesn't need weighted boots to hold her down, Melissa thought; those bracelets and necklaces must be heavy enough to do the job.

Doug saw that his mother had spotted him and pulled up a third chair for her. Joanna smiled as she approached their table, but her smile froze once she recognized who was sitting with her son.

It's Melissa Hart! Joanna realized as she neared Doug's table. She looks as if she's been through hell and back. Painfully thin. And her eyes – as if she hasn't slept in years. What's she doing up here?

'Melissa,' she said as she put her tray on the table. 'Whatever brings you here?'

'She came up on the LTV you're buying,' said Doug.

'Really?' Joanna sat down between them.

'I'm here as the representative of the new corporation's COO,' Melissa said cooly.

'Omar? You're working for him?'

'For Mr. Rashid, yes.'

Doug sensed their mutual hostility. It was as obvious as the snarling of a pair of lionesses arguing over a bleeding chunk of fresh meat.

'I didn't know you were still with the corporation,' Joanna said.

'I dropped out,' Melissa replied, 'but I'm back now.'

'And in such a key position, too.'

Melissa said, 'Mr. Rashid seems pleased with my work.'

'I'm sure,' Joanna murmured.

Doug broke in, 'Just what are you doing here, Melissa? Why've you come to Moonbase?'

Before she could think of a reply, Joanna said, 'Rashid is pushing the idea of developing nuclear fusion power.'

'Using helium-three?' Doug asked.

'You know about it,' said Melissa, impressed.

'I've looked into it. Power conversion is the key to its economic success.'

Turning to Joanna, Melissa lied, 'I was hoping to get your support for the fusion development.' This isn't the time or place to confront her, she told herself. I want to see Greg. He's the one I've come for.

'I suppose we could program nanomachines to glean helium-three out of the regolith,' said Joanna.

'You don't really need nanomachines to do that,' Melissa said.

'We're fully committed to nanotechnology here,' Joanna replied icily.

'But the U.N. treaty—'

'Won't be signed by Kiribati. You know that.'

'Still,' Melissa said, 'the fusion program shouldn't be dependent on nanotechnology.'

Doug said, 'We want to show the world that nanomachines aren't harmful, despite all the hysteria down there.'

Melissa kept herself from replying.

'After all,' Doug went on, 'nanomachines can do a lot more than scour the regolith for raw materials. The medical applications of nanotech are the greatest thing they've got going for them.'

'Are they?' Melissa countered. 'Nanomachines killed your father, didn't they?'

Doug felt as if she had slapped his face. He saw that his mother had gone white, too.

'That was twenty years ago,' Joanna said stiffly. 'Nothing like that has happened again.'

'Are you sure?'

'Positive.'

'Nanomachines saved my life,' Doug said, recovering somewhat. 'If it weren't for nanotech I'd have died of radiation poisoning.'

'And now you can live forever, is that it?'

'Really,' Joanna started.

But Doug silenced her with a gesture. 'I don't know how long I'll be able to live. But wouldn't you want to extend your lifespan, if you had the chance?'

'That's just it, isn't it?' Melissa retorted. 'Of all the billions of human beings on Earth, how many of them will get the chance to live forever?'

'Answer the question,' Doug insisted. 'If you, yourself, had the chance to extend your lifespan indefinitely, would you take it?'

'No,' Melissa said honestly. 'I don't want to extend this misery one minute longer than I have to. Life is pain, don't you understand that? The sooner we're out of it, the better off we are.'

DIRECTOR'S OFFICE

'Melissa? Here?' Greg stiffened at the news. 'What does she want?'

Joanna was too nervous to sit down. 'She wants to see you.'

'But why?'

'Who knows? She says she's here to ask our support for Rashid's fusion program.'

'You don't think that's the truth?'

Joanna glared at her son. 'Do you?'

Greg leaned back in his desk chair and stared at the ceiling. The bare rock seemed lower than usual, heavier, inching down to crush him.

'You're going to have to see her,' Joanna said.

'Yes,' he said, feeling the desperation creeping into his bones. 'Yes, I suppose I will.'

'Would you like me to be with you when you do?'

What to answer? Greg wondered. I can't tell my mother that I'm afraid to see Melissa by myself. But I am! I don't want to see her, I don't want to be anywhere near her. She's bringing me nothing but pain, I know it, I can feel it.

'Well?' Joanna insisted.

'Yes,' Greg blurted. 'I think it would be better if you were present when I talked with her.'

'Good. I do too.'

Doug didn't forget about Melissa, but he relegated her presence at Moonbase to a corner of his mind. He had more important things to do.

He brought Bianca and Lev Brudnoy to his room and imaged on his Windowall the LTV sitting on its pad.

'She's a beauty,' Doug said, beaming at the picture on the screen. 'Only been used for seventy-two flights; practically new.'

Brudnoy scratched at his beard. 'I've always wondered why Americans tend to personalize their machinery. It looks like any other LTV, to me.'

Bianca was more practical. 'Okay, how long are we going to let it sit out there?'

'I've requisitioned a dome for it,' said Doug. 'The machine shop's putting it together now.'

'So we put up the dome over the landing pad?'

'No, that'd interfere with the rocket port operation too much. We put up the dome a half-mile away from the pad and tow the LTV to it.'

'We're going to work on the ship in spacesuits?' Brudnoy asked.

'No, the dome will be pressurized.'

'But we'll need suits to get to and from, won't we?' asked Bianca.

Doug admitted it with a shrug. 'Can't be helped. There's no space inside the base to work on it.'

'The main garage? Is the ceiling high enough?'

'I checked. Ceiling's okay, we can just about squeeze her in, but there's not enough room for the LTV when all the tractors are inside.'

'But at least half of them are left outside, usually,' said Brudnoy.

Shaking his head, Doug told them, 'I know. I asked Greg about it, but he just scrolled up the regulations on his screen. The main garage's got to be able to house *all* the tractors in an emergency.'

'What kind of emergency?' Brudnoy asked.

'Solar flare,' Bianca and Doug answered in unison.

'So your technicians will have to spend an hour getting into spacesuits and then walk or ride half a mile past the rocket port to work on our LTV,' said Brudnoy.

'They can work in their shirtsleeves once they're inside the dome,' Doug pointed out.

Brudnoy sighed. 'And then spend another hour getting back into their suits to go home again.'

Doug spread his hands helplessly. 'What else can we do, Lev? You know how much work it takes to carve out extra space underground. We can't blast out the space we need with plasma torches; it'd take too long and too much effort. The dome's our best bet.'

'I presume you've run all the numbers through your computer,' Brudnoy said drily.

'Frontwards and backwards,' said Doug. 'I've gone through every option I could think of. The dome's our best choice.'

'I just hate all that extra work of getting into the suits,' the Russian muttered.

'It's the prebreathing that takes most of the time,' Bianca said. 'If the suits ran at the same pressure that the base does we could zip into them in half the time.'

'Well, they don't,' said Doug, 'and it takes time to breathe the excess nitrogen out of your system.'

Brudnoy's pouchy eyes looked even sadder than usual.

With a grin, Doug added, 'When I'm director of Moonbase I'll start our people working on suits that run at normal base pressure, so you'll be able to hop into them in a couple of minutes.'

Bianca shook her head. 'You'd think after all these years somebody would've already done that.'

'Not much need for it,' said Doug. 'What kind of an emergency could come up so suddenly that you need to jump into a suit in a few minutes?'

Brudnoy nodded. 'True enough. I've been here more than twenty years and I've never seen such an emergency.'

Doug nodded.

'On the other hand,' the Russian went on, 'it's going to slow down our work tremendously. Isn't there some way we can put up a pressurized access tube to the dome?'

'A mile-long tube?' Bianca asked.

'Wait!' said Doug. 'Why don't we pressurize one of the

tractors? Couldn't we put the crew module from the LTV itself onto a tractor? That way we can take three or four people at a time out to the dome in their shirtsleeves.'

'Yeah!' Bianca cheered. 'That could work.'

Brudnoy was more reserved. 'Check it out on your computer, my friend. Don't celebrate until the engineering program tells us it can be done.'

'It's good to see you again, Greg,' said Melissa.

'It's been a long time,' he said, staring at her from behind his desk. *She looks awful*, Greg thought. *Her face is still beautiful, but it's like a death mask, a skull, her skin is stretched so tight over the bones it's a wonder she can open her mouth. And she's so thin! As if she's been a prisoner of war all these years.*

She wore a shapeless gray pants suit, its jacket falling halfway to her knees. When she sat in front of Greg's desk and crossed her long legs, he saw that the trousers ended in stirrups that looped under her weighted boots.

It was Melissa's eyes that frightened Greg. He saw fury in them, hot red rage. He remembered the last time he had been with Melissa, when he had told her they were through. Her eyes were red then, too, but with tears and pleading. *I turned my back on her and she's never forgiven me for it,* Greg realized. *All these years she's been hating me.*

He turned to his mother, sitting beside Melissa. Joanna was outwardly cool and controlled, but Greg knew that she was just as tense as he was. He could see it in the way Joanna was nervously fingering the ends of the flowered silk scarf she was wearing.

Greg had to swallow before he could bring his voice back. 'I understand that you're working for Rashid now, with the new corporation.'

Melissa's chin dipped a bare centimeter. 'That's right.'

Greg opened his mouth again but no words came out. He didn't know what to say. He looked up at the ceiling, menacingly low.

Joanna prompted, 'Rashid's pushing the fusion program, isn't he?'

'I'm not here to talk to you two about Rashid or his programs or anything like that,' Melissa said, her eyes flaring.

'Then what?' asked Joanna.

She focused those laser-beam eyes on Greg. This is the man who abandoned me, she thought, staring at him. The man I begged to stay with me. The man I thought I loved. The man whose child I was going to have. A wave of self-loathing swept over her, made her shudder visibly. I pleaded with him! I got down on my knees and begged him! And he turned his back on me. He walked away, the cold-hearted sonofabitch. He knew I was pregnant with his baby and he just walked away from both of us.

'Murder,' she whispered.

I murdered my own baby. You made me do it, the two of you. You threw me out like so much garbage. I aborted the baby. I committed murder.

'What are you talking about?' Joanna demanded.

Greg knew.

Melissa pointed a skeletal finger at him. 'You murdered Paul Stavenger. You used nanomachines to kill him.'

'That's nonsense!' Joanna snapped.

'Is it?'

Greg couldn't answer. He couldn't speak. He gripped the armrests of his swivel chair and stared in growing horror at Melissa. It's all coming back. It's all rising up again, all around me, walling me in, smothering me.

'I have Jack Killifer's sworn statement,' Melissa was saying, her voice cold and hard as ice. 'He gave you a sample of nanomachines that attacked long-chain carbon molecules. Gobblers, he called them.'

Joanna blustered, 'That doesn't mean—'

'You put them in with the nanomachines that Paul was using up here on the Moon, didn't you, Greg? They killed Paul and two other men.'

'My husband died in an accident,' Joanna insisted.

'He was murdered. By your son. And I can prove it.'

'That . . .' Greg choked out the words, '. . . that was, for god's sake, that was twenty years ago, almost.'

Melissa smiled thinly. 'There's no statute of limitations on murder.'

'You haven't got a shred of evidence,' Joanna said. 'Even if this Killifer person gave Greg a set of nanomachines, what of it? You can't prove murder in a court of law.'

'Can't I? Criminal courts have become much tougher over the past few years.'

'We'll have the best lawyers in the world.'

'Fine. Hire all the lawyers you want. A big, scandalous trial will be perfect. The public will love to watch the two of you, week after week. It'll be the entertainment highlight of the year.'

'Two of us?' Joanna asked.

'You aided and abetted your son, Mrs. Stavenger. Didn't you? Accessory after the fact.'

'Now wait . . .' Greg started.

Melissa silenced him with a glance. 'Mrs. Stavenger, it was you who covered up the evidence of the murders. It was you who sent Jack Killifer to Moonbase, so he wouldn't be available to tell anyone what he'd done until nearly twenty years afterward.'

'You can't be serious,' Joanna said.

'I've never been more serious in my life,' Melissa replied. 'The murderer son and his accomplice mother. Think how that's going to look on video back home.'

Greg stared at her. *The bitch is trying to ruin my life. She's trying to ruin both our lives.* He thought how easy it would be to get up from this chair, walk around the desk, and snap her neck like a brittle stick.

Then he gasped with the sudden realization that Doug had ordered Killifer out of Moonbase. *And I let him do it!* Greg raged at himself. *Doug knew exactly what he was doing. He knew Killifer would testify against me once he got back to Earth! He's been against me from the very beginning. Doug, Melissa – all of them!*

Joanna took a deep breath, then asked Melissa, 'What do you want?'

'Justice,' said Melissa.

'And what do you think would be just, in this case?'

Melissa turned away from Joanna's cool gray-green eyes to look squarely at Greg once again. 'Shut down Moonbase,' she said flatly. 'Put an end to all the nanotechnology you're using here.'

Greg blinked at her. 'And what else?'

Melissa shook her head. 'First things first. I want an end to this evil of nanotechnology. An end to this place where rich people can escape the problems of Earth.'

With a shaky laugh, Greg asked, 'That's all? Just shut down Moonbase?'

'And any nanotech operations you might have elsewhere,' Melissa said.

'And for that, you'll forget about this murder business?' He couldn't believe it.

Melissa smiled again, this time showing teeth. 'Oh no, Greg. You misunderstood me. Moonbase has to be shut down. But you'll still have to stand trial for murder. In Atlanta, I imagine. In the federal court in Atlanta.'

'You little bitch! You want to destroy me!'

'That's right,' Melissa said calmly. 'I'm going to destroy you. And Moonbase with you. And the nanotechnology that you're protecting.'

For the first time, Joanna looked alarmed. 'My son's life was saved by nanotherapy. He can't return to Earth.'

'He'll have to. He'll have no other choice.'

'But they'll murder him! One of your fanatics will kill him just the way they killed Carlos Quintana.'

Melissa replied coolly, 'Surely, Mrs. Stavenger, you have enough money to protect your son. Even if you go to prison, the family fortune will still be there for him.'

'To live behind walls all his life?' Joanna said, her voice almost pleading. 'To live separated from the rest of civilization?'

'What's he doing here?' Melissa retorted. 'A quarter-million miles from civilization.'

Greg watched and listened, the horror within him freezing his insides. They're worrying about Doug when she wants to put me on trial for murder. She wants to destroy me and Mom's thinking of Doug! Mom doesn't care about me; it's Doug she's trying to protect.

'All right!' he shouted, leaping to his feet. 'You want to kill me? You want to wipe out Moonbase? All right, I'll help you!'

Joanna's face went white. 'Greg, what are you—'

He came around the desk, swift as death, and grabbed Melissa by her bony wrist.

'I'll show you!' Greg roared, dragging Melissa toward the door. 'I'll show you all!'

ZIMMERMAN'S QUARTERS

'So? You have come to see my monastic little cell?' Zimmerman asked as he stepped aside and allowed Doug to enter his room.

Stepping past an unopened garment bag thrown carelessly on the floor, Doug said, 'I think we can make the room feel a lot bigger if we put up a couple of Windowalls for you.'

'Windowalls?'

'Big flat-screen display panels. You could show videos of scenes you like, make it seem as if you're looking out a window.'

Zimmerman bobbed his fleshy jowls. 'Yah, that would be an improvement.'

'I'll let you have one of mine until we get some new ones brought up,' said Doug.

Zimmerman gave Doug a crafty look. 'You didn't come here to discuss my interior decorating problems, hah?'

'No,' Doug admitted cheerfully. 'I've come to enlist your help.'

'Sit,' said the professor, gesturing to the desk chair as he eased his bulk onto the sagging bunk. 'What help do you need from me?'

'We want to build Clipperships out of pure carbon – diamond – using nanomachines.'

Zimmerman's shaggy brows rose. 'So? That would make them much stronger than metal ships, no?'

'And lighter,' Doug said.

'My experience has been mostly in medical uses of nanotechnology, not rocket engineering.'

'It would help us enormously if you'd work with the technicians here. Just look over their shoulders a bit. Encourage them.'

'Stick my nose in.'

'You'd be an inspiration to them.'

Zimmerman shook his head. 'I'd be an old man bothering your young people. The one you want is Professor Cardenas. She has experience in engineering programs.'

'I intend to ask her, too. But I wanted to ask you first.'

'Why first?'

'Because I respect you so much,' Doug replied. 'I owe my life to you.'

Zimmerman slouched back on the bunk until his head rested against the cushioned wall. 'The Chinese believe that if you save a man's life, you are responsible for him ever afterward,' he said gloomily. 'I have the feeling that you are going to find many things for me to do.'

Doug laughed. 'I'm not Chinese. But I do want your help on this.'

'I suppose—'

The ceiling lights flickered.

'What was that?' Zimmerman sat up rigidly on the bunk.

'Don't know,' said Doug. 'The lighting system must've switched—'

They flickered again.

'Does this happen often?' Zimmerman looked decidedly worried.

'No, never,' Doug said, puzzled. 'I don't know what's going on.'

From outside in the tunnel they heard the ceiling speakers paging, 'DOUGLAS STAVENGER, PLEASE CALL THE BASE DIRECTOR'S OFFICE. DOUGLAS STAVENGER, PLEASE CALL THE BASE DIRECTOR'S OFFICE.'

Feeling uneasy, almost worried, Doug tapped the phone key on Zimmerman's computer keyboard.

Joanna's face appeared on the screen, strained, distraught. 'Doug! Where are you?'

'I'm with Professor Zimmerman, in his quarters.'

'Your brother's snapped! He's run off with Melissa Hart somewhere, screaming that he's going to destroy everything.'

'Greg? What do you mean?'

Then he heard the unmistakable thud of an airlock hatch slamming shut.

'EMERGENCY,' blared the speakers out in the tunnel's ceiling, loud enough to be heard clearly through the flimsy accordion door. 'EMERGENCY. AIR PRESSURE DROP IN MAIN GARAGE. ALL AIRLOCKS HAVE AUTOMATI-CALLY SHUT. FOLLOW EMERGENCY PROCEDURES. UNLESS YOU ARE WITH SECURITY OR ENVIRON-MENTAL CONTROL GROUPS, REMAIN WHERE YOU ARE. DO NOT MOVE FROM YOUR PRESENT LOCA-TION UNTIL NOTIFIED BY BASE ENVIRONMENTAL CONTROL.'

The sad sweet strains of the Rose Adagio from *Sleeping Beauty* filled her mind as Bianca Rhee floated through a nearly-perfect *grand jeté*, higher in the air than any prima ballerina could possible achieve on Earth, arms extended, toes pointed properly, when the loudspeakers bellowed out their warning.

She landed on her toes, stumbled off-balance, and staggered against the flimsy partition that closed off her little practice area from the rest of the main garage. Almost angrily she yanked out the earplug and snapped off the miniature chip player clipped to her belt.

'EMERGENCY,' the automatic warning repeated.' AIR PRESSURE DROP IN MAIN GARAGE. ALL AIRLOCKS HAVE AUTOMATICALLY SHUT. FOLLOW EMERGENCY PROCEDURES. UNLESS YOU ARE WITH SECURITY OR ENVIRONMENTAL CONTROL GROUPS, REMAIN WHERE YOU ARE. DO NOT MOVE FROM YOUR PRESENT LOCATION UNTIL NOTIFIED BY BASE ENVI-RONMENTAL CONTROL.'

Bianca didn't feel any air-pressure drop. Some stupid sensor's gone down, she thought. But she padded in her ballet slippers to the edge of the partition and looked out at the main garage. People were hustling for the hatches that led into the base's four main tunnels.

And she felt a breeze.

Bianca had screened off this unused part of the main garage to serve as her practice hall. It was as far away from everything – and everyone – else as it could be, a good hundred meters from the nearest airlock.

There was definitely a wind surging through the main garage. She could see dust swirling along the floor. Somehow one of the airlocks to the outside must have been opened and the air was rushing out into the vacuum. A pang of fear shook her. I'll never get to one of the tunnel hatches in time!

A rack of six spacesuits stood a few meters away, hanging like empty suits of armor against the rock wall. There were racks like this spotted throughout the garage, standing ready against a possible emergency.

Bianca dashed to the nearest suit, ducked under its torso and wormed her way into it. As soon as her hands wiggled into the gloves attached to the arm cuffs, she reached overhead and grabbed the helmet, desperately hoping that the backpack's tanks were filled with breathable air. She clapped the helmet down on the neck ring and sealed it, then took a deep breath. The seal mechanism automatically activated the air flow.

Okay, she told herself shakily. The gasket around the waist of the torso shell will hold your air; you've got a couple of minutes to get into the leggings. It was awkward bending inside the hard shell of the suit's torso, but she ripped off her ballet slippers and got into the leggings faster than she had ever done before. Then she sat on the floor and pulled on the boots.

I did it! Bianca exulted. I got into the suit. Then she remembered that if she stayed in the suit for more than a few minutes she would get decompression sickness: the bends.

Greg had dragged Melissa from his office, down the tunnel toward the rear of the base.

'You want to destroy everything?' he had screamed at her. 'I'll show you how to wipe them all out! All of them!'

Melissa tried to keep up with him but her legs wouldn't work right in the low lunar gravity. She stumbled, flailed her free arm to regain her balance, then tripped again and fell to the floor. Greg hauled her along, skidding and scraping on the cold rock floor.

Two women and a young man, all in the olive green coveralls of the mining division, rushed up the tunnel toward them.

'What's the matter?' one of the women asked. 'What's going on?'

'Get out of my way!' Greg roared. 'Get out! Now! Leave us alone!'

The two women glanced at Melissa, sitting on the tunnel floor with her legs drawn up, glaring up at them.

'I'm the base director,' Greg bellowed, banging the nametag on his chest with his free hand. 'Get out of my goddamned way.'

'Call security,' said the young man. 'Let them take care of it.'

They hesitated a moment longer, staring at Greg's wild-eyed expression and Melissa, her arm still hanging in his grasp.

'Come on,' said the young man. The three of them hurried up the tunnel.

'Assholes,' Greg muttered after them.

Melissa yanked her wrist free of Greg's grasp. He turned on her, hand raised to strike.

'I'll help you,' she said, climbing slowly to her feet. 'You don't have to drag me. I'll go with you willingly.'

'You bet you will,' Greg said. And he started down the tunnel again.

'Where are we going?' Melissa asked, trying to keep up with him without stumbling again.

'EVC,' he muttered.

'What?'

'Environmental control center. The air pumps.'

Breathlessly, Melissa answered, 'Good.'

Greg felt lightheaded, almost giddy, as he hurried down the tunnel. Don't run, he warned himself. You might trip yourself and fall. You don't want to look foolish in front of Melissa. He thought about the veteran Lunatics he had seen taking yards-long strides in the gentle gravity, soaring along like ballet dancers. I'll show those wiseasses, he thought. I'll show them all. Let's see how far they can jump when there's no air left to breathe.

For the first time in his life Greg felt free, totally, absolutely free. It didn't matter what anyone thought or said or did. This is the end of it all. At last it'll all be over with, finished. The end of everything. No more fear. All my worries are behind me now.

To Melissa, this tunnel seemed longer than the others. As she struggled to keep up with Greg, she saw that they had passed the area where laboratories and offices lined the tunnel on both sides. Now the doors were farther apart and the labels on them proclaimed MAINTENANCE STORES and ELECTRONICS SPARES.

At the end of the tunnel was a dull metal hatch with an electronic security pad alongside it.

'Rank has its privileges,' Greg said, almost giggling as he tapped the keyboard with his index finger. 'All the base director has to do to open any hatch, anywhere, is punch in his personal code.'

Greg's eyes were aglow. Melissa thought he looked – happy. I've freed him, she said to herself. I've freed us both.

The hatch clicked but did not open. Greg grasped its metal wheel, gave it half a turn and then pushed.

Inside was a shadowy cavern that throbbed with the sound of pumps.

As Greg, suddenly solicitous, helped Melissa over the hatch's coaming, he explained, 'All the base's air supply is routed through here. That's the recycling equipment . . .' He pointed to a clump of bulky metal shapes connected by a maze of piping. 'We'll take care of them later.'

He pushed the hatch shut, then spun its wheel, locking it.

'Find a tool box,' he ordered Melissa. 'There's got to be tools stashed here someplace.'

'What about those lockers?' She pointed to the row of metal lockers a few feet down the wall from the hatch.

'Right,' said Greg. He yanked the lockers open, one after the other, and slammed each door shut again with a disgusted clang. 'Emergency space suits, emergency oxygen tanks, extra coveralls – where do they keep the fucking *tools?*' His roar echoed off the bare rock walls.

'Here.' Melissa called from a workbench on the other side of the hatch.

Greg rushed to her. 'Right!' He yanked open the metal boxes lining the back of the workbench and lifted out a heavy wrench. 'Just what I need.'

Grinning madly, he went back to the hatch and lifted the back cover off the security pad. Then, raising the wrench over his head like a spear, he jammed it into the electronic works of the hatch's security pad. Sparks crackled, throwing blue-white highlights against his grimacing face.

'There,' Greg said triumphantly. Then he jammed the wrench into the hatch's wheel, to prevent it from being turned. 'Now if they want to get in here they'll have to blast.'

He whirled around, eyes blazing. Melissa felt her heart thundering beneath her ribs. We're going to do it! she said to herself. We're going to tear it all down! We're going to put an end to all of it, at last!

There was a computer at the end of the workbench. Greg strode to it, bending over the keyboard.

'One system at a time,' he muttered. 'First the lights.'

The computer screen lit up. Greg worked the keyboard, fingers moving in staccato rhythm. Melissa thought the sparse overhead lights flickered, but the lighting was so dim in this cavern that she couldn't be sure.

'Damn! The backup nuke comes on-line automatically and there's no way to shut it down unless the solar farms come back on.'

He pecked at the keyboard again, harder. 'Shit,' he muttered. 'Shit, shit, shit.'

'You can't do it?' Melissa asked, looking at the incomprehensible alphanumerics scrolling up the display screen.

'I can do it,' Greg growled. 'I just can't do it through the damnable computer. Too many redundancies and backups.'

'Then what—'

'The main airlock!' Greg crowed. 'I can open the main airlock long enough to blow all the air out of the garage! Emergency decontamination procedure. Look!'

Melissa saw another jumble of symbols on the computer screen, but overhead loudspeakers immediately blared out a warning that echoed through the big cavern.

'That's just a start!' Greg shouted.

He ran back to the workbench, picked up another wrench, and waved it in the air. 'I'm going to wipe them all out! I can do it! Watch me!'

Melissa followed him down the narrow walkway between man-tall metal shapes that throbbed and chugged ceaselessly.

'I don't need the computer system,' Greg railed, banging his wrench angrily on the metal domes of the pumps as he passed them, making the cavern ring. 'I don't need the fucking computer! I'll do it the hard way!'

'Do what?' Melissa asked.

Instead of answering her, he turned and pointed back to the workbench. 'Get every tool you can carry. Bring them to me. Now!'

She scurried to obey, staggering slightly in the unaccustomed gravity, righting her balance by leaning against the cold metal pumps.

She went to the toolbox they had already opened and lifted out an assortment of wrenches, pliers and screwdrivers. By the time she got back to Greg he had already twisted off two of the four bolts holding down the domed top of one of the pumps.

'It all gets down to plumbing,' Greg mumbled as he worked furiously. 'All the high technology of this base depends on pipes that carry either air or water.'

'You're going to break the pumps?'

Greg looked up at her, a grease stain already smeared across his forehead. 'I'm going to cut off their air supply. Let them choke to death on their own fumes.'

'Us too?' she asked.

He laughed. 'Of course, us too. We'll die together, Melissa. You'll like that, won't you?'

'I was in love with you,' she said.

'No greater love has any man,' Greg babbled as he yanked at the bolts of the pump, 'than he lays down his life for his ex-lover.'

She dropped to her knees next to him. 'Kill them all,' she whispered urgently. 'But be sure to kill us, too.'

'We'll die,' Greg said triumphantly. 'We'll all die!'

CONTROL CENTER

Doug flew down the tunnel, his feet barely touching the ground, leaping the distance between one closed airtight hatch and the next in a few long, loping lunar strides.

Jinny Anson was already in the control center when Doug got there. So was his mother and Lev Brudnoy.

'They're in the EVC, all right,' Anson was saying, pointing at the big electronic wall map of the base. 'Sonofabitch blew out the garage and now the oxygen partial pressure in tunnel four is below safe level.'

'How could he do that?' Joanna asked, wide-eyed.

Still scowling at the wall map, Anson replied, 'He just opened the main airlock. All the air in the garage got sucked out into the vacuum.'

'But how—'

'There's an emergency procedure in the computer controls,' Anson answered impatiently, 'so we can clear the garage of toxins or radioactives or any other crap in a hurry.'

'Was anyone in the garage?'

'Of course! We're counting heads now, making sure everybody got out okay.'

'What about tunnel four?' Doug asked. 'That's the tunnel that leads into the EVC, isn't it?'

'Yeah, right. He must've shut down the pumps, I guess. Or maybe turned off the air-circulating fans. It doesn't take much.'

'What is he trying to do?' Brudnoy asked.

'Commit suicide,' Joanna replied without an instant's hesitation.

'And take all of us with him?' Anson almost snarled the words.

Joanna nodded silently.

Doug asked, 'Has anybody been able to make contact with him?'

Anson shook her head. 'He doesn't answer, not even the paging system. And he must've knocked out the surveillance cameras somehow, we can't get a picture from inside the EVC.'

'Damn!'

Doug saw that the consoles were fully manned; tight-lipped technicians sat at the monitor screens, headsets clamped to their ears, fingers running over their keyboards as they checked every system in Moonbase.

In the control center's air of quiet frenzy, Anson had naturally, automatically taken charge.

'He's trying to knock out the whole base,' she said, thinking aloud. 'Already blown out the garage and tunnel four's down below safe minimums. It's only a matter of time before he gets the rest of us.'

'What can we do to stop him?' Joanna asked, sounding a bit frantic.

'First things first,' said Anson. Turning, she marched to one of the consoles and spoke to the technician seated there. 'Activate all the emergency air filtration systems. And get a squad of safety people to manually check them.'

Doug saw the question in his mother's eyes. 'Backup systems,' he explained, 'to filter the carbon dioxide out of the air. Even if Greg shuts down the main recycling equipment, the backups will keep our air breathable.'

'For how long?' Joanna asked.

Brudnoy looked at her with sad eyes. 'A few hours,' he said softly. 'At most, a few hours.'

'Shouldn't we get everyone into spacesuits, then?' Joanna suggested.

'There aren't enough suits for everyone,' Brudnoy countered.

Doug added, 'And it would take an hour of pre-breathing

before you could get into a suit without giving yourself the bends.'

'Besides,' the Russian said, 'if the EVC goes down, the suits will only prolong your misery for a few hours more.'

'Very encouraging,' Zimmerman said loudly as he stepped through the control center's entrance. 'I don't suppose you have suits my size anyway.'

They all turned to see the fat old professor walking toward them as carefully as a man negotiating a minefield. Zimmerman's gray three-piece suit looked rumpled, but there was no sign of fear in his fleshy face. He looked more annoyed than afraid.

'I told you to stay in your quarters,' Doug said. 'How did—'

'You expect me to sit in that coffin of a cell, all alone? Never! If I am to die, it will be in company.'

'But the hatches.'

'Bah! Obviously I learned how to open them.'

'You shut them behind you, I hope.'

Anson said, 'They close automatically, don't worry about it.'

'So what is the problem?' Zimmerman asked.

Doug swiftly explained. The old man's face went gray.

'Cut off our air? He must be a madman!'

Without looking at his mother's reaction, Doug said, 'We've got to get in there and stop him before he knocks out all the pumps and kills us all.'

Brudnoy said, 'The security team said the hatch to the EVC was sealed shut. They started to force it open manually but the air pressure kept on dropping in the tunnel and they had to get out.'

'He's got himself barricaded in there,' said Doug.

Anson said, 'At least we got everybody out of the garage and tunnel four. No casualties.'

'Yet,' Brudnoy muttered.

'But even if he stops the pumps,' Joanna asked, 'won't the air recycling equipment keep going?'

'Won't do us a rat's ass worth of good if the pumps shut

down,' Anson replied, brows knitted. 'If he shuts down all the freakin' pumps, we'll all be asphyxiated within a couple of hours.'

'But you said we had backups . . .'

'They'll scrub out the CO_2 for a few hours,' Anson said flatly. 'They were only meant for short-term emergencies, not to replace the main system indefinitely.'

'What can we do?' Joanna pleaded.

'I've got to get in there and stop him,' said Doug.

'You?' Zimmerman asked.

'Me.'

'But how?'

Turning to Anson, Doug asked, 'Is there any other way into the EVC besides the hatch from the tunnel?'

She shook her head gloomily.

Doug asked, 'What about the air ducts?' He turned back to the big electronic map. 'All the air ducts in the base lead into the EVC, sooner or later. Maybe I can crawl through one—'

'Only if you are the size of a little mouse,' Brudnoy said morosely. 'The ducts are too small for you.'

'There must be some way to get in there.'

Brudnoy scratched at his beard, staring at the big wall map. Then he reached up and traced a finger along a ghostly gray line that reached from the EVC to the edge of the base, at the face of the ringwall mountain. It branched four times, once into each of the base's main tunnels.

'The plasma torch vents,' he murmured.

'What?'

'When we started excavating these tunnels,' Brudnoy explained, 'we vaporized the rock with plasma torches.'

'Everyone knows that,' Joanna snapped.

'Yes, dear lady. But everyone forgets that we vented the vaporized rock outside through large ducts.'

'Big enough for a man to crawl through?' Doug asked eagerly.

Brudnoy nodded. 'We made them big so the vapors could get out quickly and dissipate into the vacuum outside.'

'Terrific!'

'But those vents have been sealed off for years,' Anson pointed out.

'The seals were very simple, very primitive, if I recall correctly,' said Brudnoy, furrowing his brow. 'Nothing more than a series of airtight partitions every hundred meters or so. And they can be opened and closed from here in the control center, once you call up the proper program.'

'That program must be ancient,' Anson snapped.

'As old as I am, do you think?' countered Brudnoy, with a smile.

Doug whirled to the nearest empty console and began working its keyboard even before he pulled up a chair to sit in.

'Come on, Lev,' he called. 'Help me find it.'

Brudnoy leaned over Doug's shoulder as the screen scrolled through several menus. Finally, a schematic of the vent system came up.

'Okay!' Doug said, nearly shouting. 'I can crawl through the vent that runs along the tunnel here, work my way into the central vent, and then come down into the EVC.'

'Is there air in the vents?' Joanna asked.

'Yep,' said Anson. 'Same pressure as the rest of the base, too.'

'Then I can work my way through without a problem,' Doug said.

'You'll have to get through the partitions,' said Brudnoy.

'Those partitions haven't been opened in nearly twenty years,' Anson said.

'They're controlled from here, though, aren't they?' Doug asked.

She nodded, but warned, 'Some of 'em might be sealed shut. Dust gets into everything, y'know.'

'I'll need some power tools, then.'

Nodding, Brudnoy said, 'The two of us should be able to pry the hatches open, even if they don't respond to the controls.'

Doug did not reply to the Russian. Turning to Anson, he said, 'Get a repair team suited up and working on the hatch that Greg sealed. Start them prebreathing now. We're going to need every second we can squeeze out. Come on, we don't have any time to waste!'

'Wait a minute,' Anson said. 'If we pry that hatch open, the whole EVC's gonna lose its air. It'll go down to the pressure in tunnel four,' she snapped her fingers, 'like *that*.'

'Can't be helped,' said Doug.

'Yeah, but what if you're in the EVC when they break through?'

With a shrug, Doug repeated, 'Can't be helped. We have to do everything we can, as quick as we can.'

'But the risk—'

'Tell the crew working on the hatch to bring some breathing masks from the infirmary. If they can get them on us fast enough we'll be okay.'

'You're taking a helluva chance,' Anson said.

'What's the alternative?' Doug challenged. 'Let my brother kill all of us? Let Moonbase die?'

Joanna stepped up to her son. 'Doug, I can't let you do this. It's too dangerous.'

'You can't stop me, Mom.'

'Douglas—'

'I'm not going to let him destroy Moonbase,' Doug said firmly. 'He tried to once before, remember? I'm not going to let him get away with it.'

'Your life is worth more than Moonbase,' Joanna said.

He locked his gray-green eyes with hers. 'No, it isn't,' Doug said flatly. 'Moonbase is more important than any of us.'

'Not to me.'

'It is to me,' Doug said. Then he added, 'He's trying to kill you, too, you know.'

Joanna's mouth opened, but no sound came out.

Doug started for the door.

'Aren't you going to at least put on a spacesuit?' Joanna called after him.

'No time, Mom! I've got to get to Greg as fast as I can.'

The bends, Bianca Rhee thought, trying to fight down the panic surging through her. Breathing the low-pressure air in the suit tank means that the nitrogen in my cells will bubble out and cause all kinds of trouble.

How long do I have? she asked herself as she hurried across the emptied garage toward the nearest hatch to a tunnel. Minutes? Seconds?

She reached the hatch to tunnel four, fumbled with the electronic keypad in her eagerness to get it open, and finally managed to get her gloved finger on the proper button. The hatch slid open and she stepped into the little chamber between the outer and inner hatches that served as an airlock.

Okay, she told herself shakily. So far so good.

She got the inner hatch open and, with a sigh of relief, slid up the visor of her helmet.

And choked. She couldn't catch her breath. No air! she screamed silently as she slammed her visor down again. They've pumped the air out of this tunnel! What if they've pumped the air out of all of them?

A sharp needle of pain seared her chest. Got to try the next tunnel. She stumbled through the airlock again, back out into the garage, and headed for the hatch to tunnel three.

Her legs gave way before she reached it. Agonizing pain flared through her. She felt as if she was being electrocuted. Or burned at the stake.

Jesus, Mary and Joseph, she cried to herself. It hurts! Christ! Oh Christ, Christ, Christ it hurts!

Greg got to his feet slowly and admired his handiwork. What had been a set of air pumps was now a shambles of disconnected parts scattered across the cold rock floor of the EVC.

'That's one,' he said, puffing slightly.

Melissa stood beside him, her cool gray jacket smeared with grime, her hands greasy, knuckles skinned from banging them as she tried to help Greg.

'Let's get the next one,' she urged.

'Give me a minute,' Greg said, stretching his arms over his head. He was unaccustomed to so much intense physical exertion.

'They'll be trying to get in here again,' she warned.

Greg gave her a knowing smile. 'Not yet. I pumped down the air pressure out in the tunnel before taking the pump apart. They can't breathe the thin stuff out there now.'

'But they have spacesuits, don't they?'

'Sure. But it takes an hour of prebreathing before you can get into a suit. Unless you want to die of the bends.'

'Prebreathing?' Melissa asked. 'Bends?'

'Never mind,' Greg snapped. 'Let's get to work on the next set of pumps.'

'Good!'

'Four tunnels,' Greg said as he stooped to gather his tools. 'Each one has its own set of air pumps, including backups. Triple and quadruple redundancy.' He laughed, a brittle sound that rang off the stone walls. 'A lot of good it's going to do them!'

'Will we have time to do them all?' Melissa asked.

Walking leisurely to the second set of pumps, Greg replied, 'Plenty of time. And then we'll do the recycling system, just to make certain.' He laughed again. 'That'll be our own little bit of redundancy.'

He slapped the big wrench on one of the nuts holding down the main pump's domed top. It made a beautiful, echoing clang.

'We won't pass out before the job's finished, will we?' Melissa asked. She worried that Greg would screw up, one way or another. They were so close to the final ending, she didn't want to go through this and then find that they had failed.

'No,' Greg assured her. 'This chamber is sealed off from all the others. There's enough air in here for the two of us for days on end.'

'But how will we . . . ?'

'Finish it?' Greg's smile beamed at her. He moved closer to her, whispering like a little boy, 'When all the pumps are done, when I've knocked out the recycling system, I'll open the hatch out into the tunnel. Our air will blow out and we'll be dead in a couple of minutes.'

'You're sure?'

'As certain as death can be,' Greg said.

Melissa kissed him on the lips. 'Then let's make love while the air goes out. Let's die in each other's arms.'

Greg cocked his head slightly. 'Sure. Why not?'

She sighed. It would all be over soon. What was it Shakespeare said? All the heartache and the thousand natural shocks flesh is heir to. It's all going to end, and Moonbase and nanotechnology with it. She felt a peace and contentment that she had not known since childhood.

'Stop daydreaming and help me with this,' Greg snapped.

Startled, she looked at the man she hated, the man she loved, and went to help him.

A dull booming sound reverberated through the shadowy, high-ceilinged cave.

'What was that?' Melissa asked.

Greg peered up into the shadows. 'I don't know.'

Another, like the growl of distant thunder.

'They're trying to get in again!'

'No,' said Greg. 'It's not the hatch. It's too far away, whatever it is.'

Melissa thought wildly. 'Maybe they're launching a ship, getting away!'

Greg shook his head angrily. 'There's only one LTV on the pads and it can only hold a half-dozen passengers, max.'

'Your mother—'

'My mother wouldn't even think of trying to get away,' Greg said. 'It wouldn't even enter her mind. Or Doug's. No, they'll try to figure out some way to save everybody, the whole base.'

'You're sure?'

'Positive. Especially Doug. He'll want to be a hero. He'd rather die than let Moonbase be destroyed. Even if he was safe in bed in Savannah, once we wipe out Moonbase he'll die too.'

'You're sure?' Melissa repeated.

Greg laughed bitterly. 'That noise is probably Doug battering his thick skull against the airlock hatch, trying to ram his way in here.'

VACUUM VENT NO. 3A

'When all else fails,' grunted Brudnoy, 'use the precision adjuster.'

He and Doug gripped the long metal rod they had scavenged from the construction spares supply and rammed it again into the square metal ceiling panel that was the access to the vacuum vent that ran the length of tunnel three. The booming thud reverberated hollowly down the length of the tunnel.

'Well,' Doug panted, 'I don't think we're going to surprise them.'

Brudnoy peered up at the access panel. It had barely budged. 'I don't know about that,' he said, wiping sweat from his eyes with the back of his sleeve. 'They may hear the noise we're making, but will they know what's causing it?'

'Maybe not,' Doug agreed half-heartedly. He gripped the rod again in both hands. 'Come on, let's get it done.'

We're not moving fast enough, Doug told himself. Greg's in there taking the EVC apart and we're stuck here as if we're glued to the floor.

For one of the rare times in his young life Doug felt real anger. He wants to kill us all, kill himself and me and Mom and everybody. He wants to kill Moonbase. He wants to kill my father all over again.

Never! he snarled inwardly. I won't let him get away with it. He rammed the rod with all his strength against the unyielding ceiling panel.

Four more bangs and the panel gave way with a groan. Doug could see it lift away slightly from the lip of the square in the rock ceiling.

'I think that did it,' he said, puffing from the exertion.

'Yes.' Brudnoy was panting, too. Wheezing.

'Okay,' said Doug. 'You'd better get back to the control center and tell them I'm on my way.'

'But I'm going with you,' said Brudnoy.

'No,' Doug said, placing a hand on the Russian's bony shoulder. 'This is something I have to do alone. Besides, I need you to take care of my mother.'

Brudnoy gave him an odd look. Then he shrugged submissively. 'I understand. I'm too old for heroics.'

Doug smiled at him sadly. 'You're out of shape, you know.'

Shrugging, Brudnoy replied, 'Too much soft living. Here, at least I can help you up.'

'I can jump it. Get on back before he starts pumping the air out of this tunnel, too.'

'They can't,' Brudnoy countered, 'now that the hatches have all been closed.'

Doug nodded. 'Yeah, all he can do is knock out the pumps or the recycling system and let us strangle slowly.'

'It's always best to look on the bright side,' said Brudnoy.

With a rueful grin, Doug backed up a few steps, then lunged forward and leaped, arms outstretched. His fingertips caught the open space where the panel had been pushed ajar. Hanging there with one hand, he shoved at the panel with the other. It hardly moved.

'No leverage,' Doug gasped.

'Stand on my shoulders,' said Brudnoy, ducking under Doug's flailing feet. 'Then you can use both hands.'

'You knew this would happen all along, didn't you?' Doug asked, as Brudnoy straightened up under him. He pushed the panel aside; it screeched like a rusty hinge.

'Simple physics,' Brudnoy said.

Doug hauled himself up into the vent. 'Thanks,' he said, looking down at the Russian.

'There you are!' It was Zimmerman, hurrying along the tunnel. He reminded Doug of a big sea lion waddling across a beach.

'You should be in your quarters,' Doug called down to him.

'So? I will be safer there?'

Brudnoy turned slightly to hide the smile that the professor's sarcasm triggered.

'We can't have people just wandering around the base,' Doug said.

'I am not wandering. I came looking for you.'

'Oh? Why?'

'To warn you.'

Brudnoy's smile vanished. 'Of what?'

Waggling a stumpy finger up toward Doug, Zimmerman said, 'You think you are superman, maybe, because you have the nanomachines in you?'

Doug blinked down at the professor. 'I hadn't even thought about that.'

'Good. Forget about them. They will not make you into a hero. They cannot protect you from *all* harm.'

'I didn't think they could,' Doug said.

'They are medical, metabolic,' Zimmerman went on. 'They can heal injuries quickly. But that is all they can do for you.'

'Okay,' said Doug.

'Do not think you can perform superhuman feats. You cannot.'

'Okay,' Doug repeated, feeling slightly exasperated. 'Thanks for the warning. I've got to get going now.'

'Yah. I know.' Zimmerman stood there fidgeting for a moment, then said in the softest voice Doug had ever heard out of him, 'Good luck, my boy.'

Grinning, Doug replied, 'Thanks.'

Brudnoy handed him the power drill they had brought with them. Doug grasped it, then started to worm around for his trek down the vent.

'Turn on the transponder,' Brudnoy reminded.

'Yeah, right.' Doug reached for the little black box clipped to his chest pocket and pressed its stud. Now they could track his progress back at the control center. *If I get killed,* he thought sardonically, *at least they'll know where to find the body.*

'One more thing,' Brudnoy called.

'What?' Doug asked, getting irritated at the delay.

'I want you to remember something your father often said. Every time he had a difficult job to do, he said it.'

'My father?' Doug asked, more gently.

'If it is to be, it's up to me,' Brudnoy said. 'That was your father's motto.'

'If it is to be, it's up to me,' Doug repeated.

'Yes,' said Brudnoy.

'Thanks, Lev. That's good to know.'

'Good luck.'

'Right.'

Brudnoy and Zimmerman watched the young man disappear into the darkness of the overhead vent.

'Come on,' said Brudnoy to the professor. 'Time for us old men to go wait with the women.'

Zimmerman shook his head, glanced up at the ceiling, then let Brudnoy lead him back toward the control center.

Doug tucked the hand drill into the thigh pocket of his coveralls and unclipped the penlight from his chest pocket. The pencil beam seemed feeble as he swung it back and forth. The vent was barely wider than his shoulders, and caked with dust. Should've brought a breathing mask, he said to himself. At least there won't be any rats or bugs. Shouldn't be. All the inbound cargoes are checked Earthside and on arrival here. There won't be anything in this vent to surprise me. Couldn't be.

But he knew he was trying to convince himself of something he was really unsure of.

Joanna almost threw herself at Brudnoy when he and Zimmerman came back into the control center.

'He's in the vent?' she asked, her voice high with tension.

Brudnoy said as soothingly as he knew how to, 'He's on his way. He'll be at the EVC in half an hour, at most.'

Anson muttered, tight-lipped, 'They can do a lotta damage in half an hour, I betcha.'

Brudnoy shrugged. 'As long as they don't damage the recycling equipment too badly . . .'

'Good thing they don't have any explosives in there,' Anson said, turning back to the wall screen.

'It's a question of time now,' Brudnoy said to Joanna. 'Can Doug get there soon enough to stop them from doing too much damage.'

Joanna fought to keep back her tears. Doug was going to have to fight Greg. At best, only one of her sons would come out of this alive, she knew.

'We're picking up his transponder signal,' called one of the technicians from his monitoring station.

'Put it on the big screen,' Anson commanded.

A blinking red dot showed up on the wall screen, half-way down the gray line marking the vent running atop tunnel three.

Zimmerman, sitting on one of the little wheeled console chairs like a walrus perched on a beach ball, pointed and asked, 'That is him?'

'That's him,' Anson replied.

'Can we speak with him?'

'He's got a pocket phone,' she said. 'He'll call in when he hits the first partition.'

Joanna stared at the blinking red dot as it moved slowly along the gray line. Brudnoy stood beside her and put an arm around her shoulders. She leaned against him, grateful for the support.

Roger Deems unconsciously gnawed on a fingernail as the eight others – three women among them – filed into the security office. Just my luck, Deems thought, to be tapped for the security job this month. The others looked equally unhappy.

The security assignment was rotated among the long-time Lunatics. Usually the job required nothing more than keeping the base's surveillance cameras working. Drugs were a minor problem, but the long-timers usually policed themselves pretty well and kept the short-timers under control. The still that produced rocket juice was an open secret and seldom made problems for anyone. The toughest moment Deems could remember had been when two short-timers got into a fistfight in The Cave over a woman they both coveted. By the time that month's security chief had arrived on the scene, like the sheriff in an old west barroom brawl, the other Lunatics had already ended the fight simply by dousing the combatants with all the fruit juice they could grab from the dispensers. Wet and sticky, the two young men felt foolish and embarrassed. Wyatt Earp was not really needed.

Deems had been at his desk, performing a routine check of the surveillance cameras, when the automatic emergency announcement blared from the overhead speakers. The sound of the airtight hatches slamming shut all along the tunnel startled him, but he didn't get too worried until Jinny Anson's voice came on the speakers and ordered everyone to stay put, then ended with an ominous, 'THIS IS NOT A DRILL.'

Before Deems could get out of his desk chair Anson was on the phone, telling him tightly what had happened and what she expected him to accomplish. Deems swallowed twice to keep down the bitter bile that was suddenly burning its way up his throat, nodded once to Anson, and got busy. He punched into the loudspeaker system, startled to hear his own voice booming out in the tunnel as he said:

'THIS IS THE SECURITY CHIEF. WE NEED VOL-UNTEERS TO HELP CLEAR UP THIS EMERGENCY. ANYBODY IN TUNNEL TWO WHO ISN'T INVOLVED IN LIFE SUPPORT WORK AND DOESN'T HAVE TO GET PAST ONE OF THE CLOSED HATCHES, REPORT TO THE SECURITY OFFICE RIGHT AWAY.'

Volunteers. Deems almost laughed. Anybody who could reach the security office without going through one of the closed hatches was a volunteer. By definition.

Now the three women and five men stood crowded, worried and uncertain before his desk.

'The base director's locked himself in the EVC and is threatening to cut off our air,' Deems said to the assembled 'volunteers,' without preamble.

They gasped, shocked.

'We need to open the EVC's hatch,' he went on, running a hand through his thinning hair, 'and we don't have time for prebreathing.'

'Whaddaya mean, "we?" Why do we hafta do it?'

'Yeah, aren't there specialists for a problem like this?'

'Like who?' Deems asked, trying hard to scowl at them.

No one had an answer.

'Listen,' he said, leaning back in his chair and folding his arms over his chest, 'we can sit here on our rumps and let the cuckoo sonofabitch choke off our air or we can try to *do* something about it. Which is it gonna be?'

'You mean we need to get into suits?'

'It's that bad?'

'Air pressure in tunnel four is 'way down, unbreathable,' said Deems, actually beginning to enjoy the feeling of authority, 'and the pressure's dropping in tunnel three.'

'Christ! My wife's in three!'

Deems raised a chubby hand. 'Don't panic. We've already got safety people evacuating three. She'll be okay.'

'But we have to get into suits?' one of the women asked, not certain she had heard him correctly.

'That's right. No time for prebreathing, either.'

'Isn't that dangerous?'

'Not if we do it right,' said Deems. 'We're going to the suit rack at the end of this tunnel and purge a half-dozen backpack tanks. Get rid of the low-pressure mix that's in 'em and refill them with regular base air. Then you won't need prebreathing and there's no danger of the bends.'

'But if you pump up the suits to room-normal pressure they'll get so stiff we won't be able to move in them,' said one of the men. Deems recognized him as an engineer from the mining group.

'You won't have to do any delicate work,' he countered. 'Just set up a laser torch to burn through the hatch.'

The engineer looked dubious and muttered something too low for Deems to catch.

'But we've gotta move fast,' Deems said, starting to feel

ike a real leader. 'No time to waste. We've gotta get into the
EVC before he knocks out all the pumps and recyclers.'

'Isn't there any other way to get to the EVC?'

They don't like this, Deems could tell by looking at their
aces. Not any of it. Can't say I blame them.

'Doug Stavenger is working his way through the old plasma
vents,' he said, 'but we don't know if he can make it all the
way to the EVC or not. In the meantime, we gotta get that
ocked hatch open.'

'Wait a minute,' said one of the engineers. 'If the pressure's
lown in tunnel four and we burn through the hatch, won't that
slow the air out of the EVC?'

'Right.'

'And anybody in there gets killed.'

'Most likely.'

'Then what about Stavenger? What if he's in there when
we blow the hatch?'

Deems shrugged. 'We'll carry extra suits and try to get
them on all three of the people in there before decompression
get them.'

'Fat chance,' grumbled the engineer.

Deems knew he was right.

Shouldn't we be taking the recyclers apart?' Melissa asked.
Her arms hurt from exertion and she could feel blisters welling
up painfully on the palms of her hands.

Greg snorted impatiently, kneeling over one of the pumps.
What good's the recycling equipment if the pumps aren't
moving fresh air? Kill the pumps and you kill the people.'

He seemed calmer now. Methodical. When they had first
ourst into the EVC Greg was frenzied, wild-eyed. Now he
worked with the deliberate, meticulous care of a man who was
otally dedicated to his task. He's really going to do it, Melissa
aid to herself for the hundredth time. He's going to kill them
all. He's going to kill himself. He's going to kill me.

For the first time, she realized that there was no way to stop
Greg. If she tried to interfere with his dismantling of the pumps,
ae would calmly brain her with one of the wrenches.

She shuddered.

'Haven't heard that booming noise again,' Greg said absently as he worked, head bent over the inner works of the pump.

'No,' said Melissa. 'It's stopped.'

'What do you think they're doing, outside?'

'I don't know,' she said. 'Getting into spacesuits, maybe?'

Greg laughed. 'Fat lot of good it'll do them. There aren't enough to go around. Oh, I suppose my mother and her little circle of sycophants are in suits. But the others – no.'

'Maybe they're calling for help.'

Greg looked up at her. His face was smeared with grime, but he smiled brightly at Melissa. 'I'm sure they are. They must be screaming for help. But the quickest any help can come from Earth is six hours or more, and that's only if they have an LTV all ready to go and it's programmed for a high-energy boost.'

'They could be calling to the other bases here on the Moon, couldn't they?'

'My mother, ask Yamagata or the Europeans for help? She'd sooner die.'

'You don't really believe that.'

His dark eyes snapped at her. 'Don't tell me what I believe! If she asked Yamagata or the Europeans for help, they'd end up owning Moonbase. She'd *never* do that. She wouldn't even think of it.'

'But that's better than dying, isn't it?'

Greg pulled a section of pipe away from the dismantled pump and let it drop to the rock floor with a clang. 'Besides, what could anybody do to help her? Before anybody can break through the hatch to get to us, everybody out there'll be dead.'

Melissa paced back and forth along the narrow walkway between pumps, arms folded across her chest, massaging her aching muscles.

'They must be doing something,' she said.

Greg snorted disdainfully. 'If I know my mother, she's spending her last moments writing me out of her will.'

*   *   *

Doug's sneeze rang along the length of the metal-walled vent like a raucous gong. The dust was filling his nose, choking his throat whenever he inadvertently opened his mouth. The vent was big enough for him to crawl on his hands and knees, but still the dust floated languidly up to his face with every step he took.

How on Earth could dust get into these closed vents? With a shake of his head he reminded himself that he wasn't on Earth and lunar dust got into everything, its burnt-gunpowder smell was as common in Moonbase as the odor of frying oil in a hamburger joint back Earthside.

I wonder what the nanomachines are doing with the dust particles that get down to my lungs, he asked himself. Despite the sneezing and coughing, he seemed to be breathing well enough.

He had passed three partitions. Two of them had opened up on the electrical signal from the control center, when Doug had phoned Anson. The third refused to budge, and Doug had to drill off its hinges, which were caked solid with lunar dust.

The partitions had been set up like valves in the blood stream, to flip open in one direction only, letting fumes flow outward toward the vacuum outside the base, but sealing firmly shut once the outward-pushing pressure dropped.

As long as the last seal holds, the one at the end of the vent, where it opens out at the face of the mountain, as long as that one holds the vent will hold air for me to breathe, Doug told himself.

Then a sudden thought struck him. Is there a backup set of controls in the EVC? Could Greg pop the outside hatch open and blow all the air out? And me with it?

No, he told himself. Greg doesn't know I'm coming along the vent, so even if there are backup controls he won't know to use them. It's not possible.

He hoped he was right.

In the thin beam of his penlight he saw that the vent ended in a T-shaped intersection up ahead. That's the junction with the main trunk, he knew. I'm at the end of tunnel four; the EVC is only a few dozen yards away.

He fished the phone out of his pocket again, flicked it on, and said softly, 'I'm at the juncture with the main trunk.'

The comm tech's voice said, 'Hold one.'

Then Anson came on. 'Okay. We've got an emergency team in suits ready to start burning open the hatch.'

'In suits?' Doug blurted, startled. 'But they haven't had enough time—'

'They're breathing regular air at base pressure.'

'Oh. Okay.'

'Are you ready to pry open the access cover in the EVC?' Anson demanded.

'Yes,' Doug said. 'In about two minutes.'

'Okay. I'll start the team working on the hatch. That oughtta draw their full attention.'

'Right.'

'They've got a spare suit with them, for you.'

'Only one?'

'They've got two more, but I told them to be sure they slap one on you before they do anything else.'

'Okay. Thanks.'

Doug stuffed the phone back in his pocket, thinking, Once they blow that hatch all the air's going to rush out of the EVC. Explosive decompression. A spacesuit won't help unless they can get it on before your blood boils and your eyes pop out of your head.

He inched his way to the final access panel. I've got to stop Greg before they blow that hatch, he told himself.

MAIN GARAGE

'There's a body here!'

Deems had to bend over to see the spacesuited figure slumped on the main garage's rock floor halfway between the hatches to tunnel four and tunnel three.

Several of the team gathered around the fallen figure, bending stiffly in their overpressured suits.

'He's unconscious.'

'I think it's a woman.'

'If whoever it is got into that suit without prebreathing, he's got the bends. Or she.'

Just what we need! Deems growled to himself. Some stupid shit who didn't get in to safety in time.

Pointing to the man closest to him, he said, 'Drag him inside tunnel two and call the medics. Then get your butt back out here right away. We're gonna need every pair of hands we've got.'

It felt spooky as his eight men and women waddled cumbersomely through the main garage to the closed hatch that was the entrance to tunnel four. The garage was usually bustling and noisy with tractors being repaired, technicians yelling back and forth, music from individual disk players wailing over the clang and clamor.

Now the garage was deathly silent and still. It seemed to have taken hours to purge the spacesuit tanks of their low-pressure mix and refill them with room air. Then getting into the damned suits took even longer. The metal shell of the torso and leggings were unaffected by the additional air pressure, but the gloves ballooned so badly they looked like boxers' mitts, and all the suit joints were painfully stiff. It's like we've all got arthritis real bad, Deems thought.

He watched four members of his team checking out the cutting laser, clumsy and slow in the overpressured suits. The laser looked heavy and sinister, mounted on a tripod like some kind of gun. Clusters of power condensers and cooling blades lined its length. Another pair from their group sat on the rock floor awkwardly connecting power cables together.

Who the hell got himself caught in a suit out here? he wondered. Personnel claimed they checked out everybody working in the garage, they all got into tunnels one and two okay. And the only guy on the surface made it to the rocket port, so he's accounted for. Somebody's miscounted or screwed up someplace.

Tunnel four was two hundred yards long, Deems knew. Twice the length of a football field. They were going to lug the laser down to the sealed EVC hatch at the end of the tunnel, dragging the cable along, and start cutting the hatch open.

And when we do, he said to himself, we'll be killing anybody inside the EVC. He glanced at the three empty suits on the floor by the hatch. Shaking his head inside his helmet, Deems thought that the suits would be about as much good as an umbrella in a typhoon.

The Stavenger kid's gonna die, he thought. We'll get the two who're trying to wipe us out, but we're going to kill the Stavenger kid in the process.

'Did you hear that?' Melissa asked, looking up toward the rock ceiling of the EVC, lost in the shadows beyond the strips of overhead fluorescent lamps.

Greg was hunched over the display screens at the front of the chamber. Tunnel four was almost a vacuum, and although somebody had shut all the airtight hatches in the other tunnels, the oxygen level in tunnel three was sinking nicely.

'Hear what?' he called to Melissa.

'It sounded like—'

'Wait!' Greg snapped, silencing her. 'Listen!'

Melissa walked to his side. She felt utterly weary. Her

knuckles were skinned, her hands greasy, her clothes a mess. She had stripped off her jacket, and now she felt chilled in nothing but the light sleeveless blouse she had worn beneath it.

Greg tapped on the keyboard and the display screen showed the tunnel outside. Four people in spacesuits were aiming a heavy cutting laser at the EVC hatch.

'They're trying to get through the hatch,' he whispered.

Melissa stood by him and glanced again up toward the shadowy ceiling. She thought she had heard something from up above, but in this echoing cavern, maybe it was a noise from the tunnel outside that had caught her ear.

Greg laughed, shakily. 'It'll take them hours to burn through the hatch,' he said. 'I know the kinds of lasers they use for cutting metals.'

It sounded less than reassuring to Melissa. 'I thought you said they couldn't get through the tunnel at all.'

'They must have set up a death squad,' he said. 'They're just killing themselves faster, that's all.'

Doug clamped his penlight in his gritted teeth and tried to work the edge of the power drill into the dust-caked rim of the access panel. Things don't rust up here, he thought, but the dust packs as solid as concrete after a few years.

He had carefully removed the hinges from the access panel, trying to do it as quietly as he could. Surprise is still a weapon, he told himself. As long as they don't know I'm here I've got an advantage over them.

Perspiration stung his eyes but he kept levering the power drill with both hands, using the drill like a miniature crowbar, trying to pry the damned panel loose. Does Greg have any weapons with him? he suddenly wondered. As far as Doug knew there wasn't a gun anywhere on the Moon. The worst Greg might have would be a steak knife from The Cave. Or a wrench that he could use as a club.

The panel creaked a little. Doug saw light seeping into the vent from below. Worming the point of the drill deeper into the crack he had created, he struggled to his knees – head bent to keep from banging the top of the vent – and leaned all his weight on the tool, wishing for once that they were on Earth where his weight counted for more.

Groaning, the panel edged up an inch or so. Doug grabbed its edge with both hands and pushed, straining so hard he felt pain across his shoulders and down his back.

With a final shriek of protest the panel opened all the way. Doug pushed it clattering aside and looked down into the environmental control center. A pump's disassembled parts lay scattered on the stone floor twenty feet below him. He could see another pump, apparently still working, on the side of the narrow walkway. No sign of Greg or Melissa, though.

The walkway down there looked very tight. If I don't hit it just right I'll land on the pump or the pieces Greg's strewn across the floor. I could break an ankle. Or my neck.

But there was no time to hesitate. Twenty feet down. You're on the Moon; you can drop twenty feet with no sweat. Still, Doug grabbed the edge of the open access hatch and lowered himself slowly, hanging by both hands for a moment.

Then he saw Greg, only ten yards away, by the front hatch. And Greg, turning suddenly, saw him.

Doug let go and started to drop with the dreamlike slowness of lunar gravity to the walkway below. Greg howled madly, grabbed a heavy wrench and threw it at his brother.

Doug felt his left arm shatter with pain as he hit the floor, slipped on a loose piece of junk, and went down flat on his back. As he fell he saw Greg grab for another weapon.

ENVIRONMENTAL
CONTROL CENTER

It was Doug!

Greg turned at the blood-freezing screeching noise of metal grinding against metal and saw his half-brother hanging like an ape from the ceiling. Then Doug let go and dropped slowly, like a monster in a nightmare, toward the floor. Howling, Greg reached for a wrench and threw it at Doug, then leaped to the workbench and grabbed the first tool his hand could reach, a screwdriver, smaller, but comfortably heavy.

Melissa stood frozen against the workbench, screaming, 'Get him! Get him!'

Greg saw that Doug had sprawled on his back. Got to put him out before he can get to his feet, Greg told himself. He leaped toward his fallen brother.

Through pain-hazed eyes, Doug saw Greg springing at him. There was no room on the confined walkway to do more than turn on his side, no place to hide or even dodge.

Greg landed on Doug's side with a thump that drove the air from Doug's lungs. He tried to shield himself, but his left arm wouldn't work. He could hardly move it.

Greg held the screwdriver like a knife up above his head and stared down into his half-brother's pain-widened eyes. For an instant he hesitated. Melissa was screaming something. Greg saw not Doug, but Paul Stavenger looking up at him accusingly. Murderer! he heard Paul call him. You murdered me once and now you're going to do it again.

Through pain-hazed eyes Doug saw his half-brother hesitate,

the screwdriver held over his head like a dagger. Pushing
Greg's weight off him, Doug reached up with his good arm
and grabbed Greg's wrist.

It was a nearly equal contest. Doug's left forearm was
broken, but he was stronger, more muscular than Greg.
Gripping Greg's wrist, Doug pulled himself up to a sitting
position, forcing Greg backwards. Then he began bending
Greg's wrist back slowly, slowly, until Greg grunted and
dropped the screwdriver.

The two brothers sat on the cold stone floor, gasping, glaring
at each other.

'How'd you get in here?' Greg growled.

'Vents,' Doug panted. 'Plasma torch exhaust vents.'

'What do you think . . . you're going to . . . accomplish?'

Doug pointed with his good hand toward the hatch up at
the front of the EVC. 'They'll be breaking through,' he said,
breathing raggedly. 'When they do . . . we're all dead. The
tunnel's . . . almost down to vacuum.'

Suddenly Doug's world exploded. Flashes of light burst
before his eyes and then it all went utterly black.

He slumped over, the back of his head oozing blood. Greg
looked up and saw Melissa standing triumphantly over them,
a heavy wrench grasped tightly in both her gaunt hands. The
wrench was stained with Doug's blood.

'That takes care of *him*,' she snarled.

Greg climbed slowly to his feet.

'You heard what he said,' Melissa urged. 'They're going to
kill us when they get the hatch open.'

'We're trapped in here,' Greg said, looking around wildly.
'There's no way out.'

'Then let's finish what we came here for.'

'We won't have time!'

'We've got to!'

Another thumping sound from the hatch.

'They're going to burn through it,' Greg said, his voice
shaking. He looked down at Doug again; his half-brother
seemed dead.

'Do something!' Melissa shouted.

Greg tried to clear his thoughts. 'He came through the old plasma vents . . .' Straightening up, Greg went to the computer by the workbench. 'Those vents open to vacuum! If I can open them all, it'll suck all the air out of the base in a few minutes.'

Melissa's eyes glowed. 'That'll do it!'

Greg began scrolling through the computer programs, searching for the controls to the plasma vents.

Doug couldn't focus his eyes. Everything was a blur, a red smear. Blinking, coughing, he pushed himself up to a sitting position and slumped against one of the pumps. He wiped at his eyes with his good hand and they came away sticky with blood.

Far, far away he saw a slim figure bent over a glowing computer display screen. Greg. Someone was standing beside him but his vision was too blurred to make out who it might be.

'Hurry!' she was saying, her voice pitched high and shrill. 'Hurry! I can hear them outside the hatch!'

'I've got it,' Greg said, his voice as calm and implacable as death.

'Greg . . .' Doug croaked, his throat raw. 'Don't . . .'

Greg turned and his eyed flashed wide. 'I thought she'd killed you.'

'Don't do it,' Doug said again. 'You'll be killing Mom.'

He saw his brother's eyes widen slightly. But then Greg said, 'What of it?'

Doug pushed himself to his feet, feeling slightly dizzy. He reached out a hand to steady himself against the gutted shell of a pump.

'Stay away,' Greg warned, growling. Yet his fingers hesitated over the keyboard.

Melissa tried to push him away. 'If you won't do it, I will,' she snarled.

Strength was returning to Doug's legs. The pain in his left arm was bearable, a sullen throb. His vision had cleared and he felt stronger with each step he took toward the pair of them.

'Stop it, Greg. Stop it now while you can. Put an end to the killing.'

'I'll put an end to *everything!*' Greg snapped. But he stared at his brother without touching the keys that would open the plasma vents.

'No, you don't want to do that, Greg. You can't destroy Moonbase. It means too much to everyone on Earth. It means the future of the human race.'

'The human race!' Melissa laughed bitterly. 'The world would be better off if the human race were wiped out to the last pitiful one.'

Doug was almost within arm's reach now. The nano-machines had stopped the bleeding from his scalp wound, repaired the blood vessels in his brain that Melissa's blow had ruptured. They were even beginning to knit together the fracture in his forearm.

'I'm warning you!' Greg screeched. 'Stay away from me!'

'Just back off from the computer, Greg,' Doug said as softly as he dared. 'Go to the hatch and tell them you're coming out peacefully.'

'No!'

'You've got to, Greg. This isn't just between you and me. There's more than our lives involved here, much more.'

Greg took an uncertain, lurching step backwards, like a drunk too addled to understand what he was doing.

'Coward,' Melissa hissed. She stabbed a finger toward the keyboard.

Doug lunged forward blurringly fast and caught her frail wrist. 'No,' he said. 'You're not going to destroy us.'

'Leave her alone!' Greg threw himself at Doug, clawing at his throat. Melissa scratched at Doug's face with her free hand.

He staggered back under their assault, flung Melissa aside like a rag doll and grasped one of Greg's strangling hands. His brother was trying to choke him. Beyond his insanely twisted face, Doug could see Melissa reaching for the keyboard again.

Doug jabbed a thumb in Greg's eye. He howled an